# The Merge Series

## FIRST GENERATION BOXSET, BOOKS 1-3

### KYLIE KENT

MCCARTNEY INDUSTRIES PTY LTD.

ISBN 13:
978-1-922816-08-5 (paperback)

Cover Illustration by –
Kate Farlow - Y'all That Graphic

Editing services provided by Editor Shannan Saunders
–https://www.lovebooksediting.com

Re-edited July 2021 by - Kat Pagan - https://www.
facebook.com/PaganProofreading

*To my husband, who was my very own insta-love. The one who has supported me in everything I do for twenty years. Without his support and encouragement, this story would never have been told.*

*Merged*
*"combine or cause to combine to form a single entity"*

# One

## ALYSSA

"SARAH, I CAN'T WEAR THAT!" I exclaim to my best friend, who is holding up the tiniest black dress I have ever seen. "That dress looks like something you took off a doll; no way is all of *this* going to fit into that bit of fabric." I emphasize my curves by waving my hands down my body.

"Don't be dramatic, Lyssa. You want to look hot for this date with Ethan, right?"

I have absolutely no idea who the heck Ethan is, other than some guy that my best friend so helpfully set me up with. I'm not sure if I want to make the impression of a sexy kitten, or the girl you immediately friend zone and never try to hit on again.

"I want to look somewhere between Sex on the Beach and a Dirty Margarita," I try to explain in my friend's true language of cocktails.

"Okay. Okay, I get it. You want to look more like a piña colada. Fifty percent girl you take home to mother, and fifty percent hit it and quit it," Sarah animatedly calls out as she continues to dig through her wardrobe. We shared the townhouse together, and I couldn't want for a better flatmate than my best friend. However, she was delusional if she thought I was squeezing my body into one of her barely-there dresses.

Where Sarah was tall and slim with a runner's body, I was on more of the curvier side with the body of a person who would rather sit at home reading the latest romance on my Kindle, than endure any form of the hell they call exercise. Sarah, though, was a health guru to the core, right down to the god-awful green stuff she drank every morning.

I guess her efforts were paying off; she was beautiful both inside and out. Sarah had those tanned, dark features that every girl would kill for or pay exuberant amounts of money to fake. With long, silky black hair and thick, pouty lips, she was stunning. Where she is tanned and toned, in comparison, I'm pale and curvy.

"*Ah-ha*, I found it!" she exclaims, walking out of the wardrobe triumphantly, holding up a strapless red dress.

Admittedly, the dress was gorgeous and would look so good on someone like Sarah. On someone like me? Let's just say I have a motto for clothes: just because you can squeeze into it, doesn't mean you should.

"I am not squeezing all of *this* into *that*," I plead, giving my best *don't make me pout* look.

"Lyssa, you have a killer bod. You know it. I know it. God knows it. And Ethan is about to know it. Just put the damn dress on already." She shoves the dress at me, waiting with a raised eyebrow.

"Fine." Stomping on the spot, I strip down to squeeze all my curves into the scrap of material that she claims to be a dress.

"Wow!" Sarah lets out a whistle as she grabs my shoulders, spinning me around to face the full-length mirror that stands in the corner of her room. I stand, staring back at my reflection and not believing what I'm seeing. First, the dress fit. It was not ripping at the seams to hold my curves in; instead, it looked like it was made for me, hugging me in all the right places.

My D-sized breasts were popping with the square-cut, strapless top—the fabric hugging at my hips before swaying out in a mermaid-shape that ended just before my knees. I was speechless as I looked at my reflection.

"Well, what do you think?" Sarah asks quietly from behind me.

"I think I love it! I think I love you. How do you always know how to dress me better than I can dress myself?" Turning, I hug her, squeezing tight.

"That's because I know the rocking body you possess underneath your baggy hoodies and jeans. Tonight, the rest of Sydney will know it too. Ethan won't know what to do with himself when he gets a look at you."

I finished the outfit off with a pair of black strappy Guess heels I scored in the clearance bin a few weeks ago and a shimmery black clutch. Sarah, being the makeup artist she is, beautifies my face and hair. Transforming my pale face into something that belonged on a magazine cover, she gave me just the right amount of smoky eye, paired with bright red shiny lips.

"The Uber will be here in ten!" Sarah yells from the living room.

Doing one last-minute check in the mirror, I make my way out to the living room. Nerves are eating at me; I'm not much of a people person. "Are you sure you don't want to tag along with me?" I plead with my best friend.

"Um, definitely not. I did not go to the effort of stalking that smoking hot groomsmen from the wedding I worked last weekend for myself. I did that all for you, sweet pea."

"Thanks?" It comes out as more of a question than a statement.

Grabbing onto my shoulders, she says, "I know you're nervous; you have every right to be after what that prick did to you, but this is different, okay?" I nod, trying to bury the memories that are creeping their way into my mind. Sarah hugs me and whispers, "You will thank me to the moon and back when you see him. Where did you say he was taking you again?"

I didn't give her any details because, knowing Sarah, she would turn up and spy on just how well I was not doing at this blind date thing, just to give me pointers for the next time.

"I didn't say." Smiling, I make my way to the door. "Don't wait up." As I say this, I know I'll be in early as I have a shift tomorrow. Sarah reads my face all too well, knowing I was thinking of having to go into work tomorrow.

"You can always call in sick if you stay out. You don't even like your job. Why not use all your personal leave for getting down and *personal* with a member of the opposite sex?" She wags her eyebrows up and down at me. Shaking my head, because there is no way to respond to all of that, I walk out the door.

Sitting in the back of the Uber, I rest my head against the headrest and contemplate cancelling this date and finding an open coffee shop, getting a vanilla latte and finishing the latest romance I was halfway through. Surely, my current book boyfriend could bring me more pleasure than a blind date with some guy named Ethan, no matter how hot Sarah claimed he was.

I hate meeting new people. I'm not a people person. I keep my close circle of friends small. That circle included Sarah and my other two BFFs, Holly and her identical twin Reilly; they were enough for me.

I process the list of pros and cons for cancelling the date. Pro: I can have a peaceful night with Ken, the current hot alpha book hero I'm crushing on. Con: I will undeniably have to endure Sarah's lecture when she eventually learns of my deceit. I decide to just meet this Ethan and avoid the day's long lecture on my lack of love life from my best friend.

The Uber pulls to a stop on the side of the street. Looking out the window, I double check the name of the restaurant that Ethan told me to meet him at—yes, *told me*. Not asked, not requested, just a simple message stating: *I'll meet you at Red Door Restaurant at 8 p.m.* That should have been my first red flag with this guy.

I can see the red door with a sign above proclaiming it to be the Red Door Restaurant, also taking note that next to the restaurant lays a carpeted walkway with ropes along the edges, leading to a door with flashing lights highlighting the name of the building as The Merge. I've heard about this club. Gary at work talks about his epic nights out every Monday; his anecdotes always mention The Merge. Apparently, it's the place to be, that is, if you're into that scene.

I make my way to the red door, pushing open the heavy door. I give my name to the gorgeous blonde at the front counter, and she informs me I'm the first to arrive and leads me to a table set for four. Thanking her, I sit down, pulling out my phone to send a quick text to Sarah letting her know I made it to the right place.

**Me: I made it to the meeting rendezvous spot. Waiting to see if my night will get more interesting, if I get stood up,**

**or if he shows and I'm required to endure the awkwardness of a blind date.**

***Sarah: You're welcome. Enjoy and try to let loose a little, yolo.***

Laughing a little at her outdated *yolo*, I put my phone back in my clutch and wait. I'm not left to wait long as a tall, blonde-haired man approaches me. Giving him a once-over, I note that he's attractive in the boy-you-dated-in-college kind of way. He has a big, solid frame (like one you would find on an athlete) and strong, wide shoulders with a trim waist. He spends time in the gym. Scraggy blonde hair with dull blue eyes, his face is handsome, with a chiselled jawline and high cheekbones. He smirks as he gets closer, knowing full well that I was giving him the once-over.

Standing, I reach my hand across the table to shake his. "Ethan?" I ask. "I'm Alyssa."

"Yes, you are." He smirks, running his eyes down my body, all the while grasping my hand too long to be an appropriate timeframe for a friendly handshake. His eyes come back up, lingering on my breasts for a beat before finally reaching my eyes and letting go of my hand.

Yep, that does it. My creeper alert is on full blast and, in my head, I am blasting my best friend. Outwardly, I smile politely and sit back down. Ethan takes the seat right next to me. Weird, most people would take the one across the table.

"Thanks for meeting me here," he says. "I hope I didn't keep you waiting long?"

*Mmm*, polite, some manners—there's his first plus. "Not at all. I just arrived."

"You look beautiful, although I'm sure you already know

that and don't need me to tell you. You must hear it a billion times a day," he says, talking to my breasts.

Yep, that first plus point's now stricken from the record. "Thank you," I say, picking up my menu. "Tell me a little about yourself," I add, thinking he might give me some positives to like.

What I did not expect was to spend the next hour hearing all about his accolades in life, right down to his junior rugby league games as a ten-year-old. Turns out, Ethan is in construction, and if you were to ask him, he is the best builder in all of Sydney; he'd probably even go as far as saying the whole of Australia. Bloody hell, I never knew someone could be so fixated on themselves. All throughout, I smile and *uh-huh* here and there. Not once has he asked anything about me.

I excuse myself to the ladies' room. Shutting the stall door, I pull out my phone, sending an SOS to Sarah.

**Me: SOS. Send help now. I am about to die of boredom!!**

*Sarah: Don't be dramatic. Open your mind and try to live a little. How boring can he be? Just stare at his pretty face! That should make up for the boredom.*

**Me: I have sat here for the last hour, listening to him tell me everything great about himself. And let me tell you, the list is small, but he sure drags it out.**

*Sarah: Just imagine him naked while he is talking. Always works for me!*

Realising I'm on my own and have probably spent way longer in the bathroom than what's considered a normal pee break, I shove my phone back in my clutch, wash my hands, and reapply my lipstick before walking back out.

As I'm getting back to the table, the waiter arrives with the bill. Ethan looks up at me expectantly. "Split it?" I offer reluctantly, considering he ordered the $40 steak, and I only ordered a $15 salad.

"I knew you would be one of those equal rights kinds of gals. Sure, I'll be happy to split the bill with you."

"Of course you will," I mumble under my breath.

"So, how about we slip next door for a quick drink?" he queries with a hopeful gleam in his eyes.

I pick up my glass of water, downing the contents as all of my self-preservation senses are screaming at me to say no, to make up some excuse and get out of there. I have to work in the morning so I can use that without telling a lie. Then I think back to my text with Sarah. Maybe I am being too judgmental and should give him another thirty minutes of my time.

"Okay, but just one. I have to work in the morning." I force a smile as I stand.

"Oh, great." He stands and waits for me to walk ahead of him. That is his response: oh great. Not *oh what do you do?* No *wow, you work on a Saturday. What is it you said you did again?* Just *oh great.* I was seriously rethinking the reasons I said yes to a drink now.

Ethan leads me out of the restaurant with his hand resting on my lower back, and it sends shivers up my spine. Not the good kind that make you weak in the knees. No, these are the creepy shivers that make you want to run and hide under the covers. Heading out

onto the street, I step to the side, attempting *unsuccessfully* to step out of his reach. He leads me up to the carpeted walkway of the club. Being only nine o'clock, there isn't much of a line-up to get in. However, while waiting, I attempt and fail to sidestep Ethan's reach a few more times. Flashing my ID to the bouncer, I get let through the doors a moment before Ethan, which not only provides me with a moment to shake the heebie-jeebies feeling out of me, but also to stop and admire the beauty before me.

The club, if you can call it that, is opulence on another level. From where I stand, stunned in the doorway, I look up to see three different levels. People are already filling out the balconies that wrap around three walls of the building and over-look the huge main dance floor in the centre of the bottom floor. Even in the dimmed lighting, I can see the rich colours of the deep red curtains hanging along the walls. There are sectioned-off areas on the bottom floor with various shapes of black lounges and wingback chairs surrounding glass-topped tables.

The tables have gold frames that look like they're sculpted out of two bodies moulded together. As I look around further, I can see that that is exactly what the tables are: some table frames are of a man and a woman, some of two men and others of two women. With each sculpture, the bodies look to be in various forms of intimate embraces, almost as though they are merging as one.

As I'm standing here admiring the beauty that surrounds me, I feel a hand skim down my lower back to grab my arse. Spinning around with a raised hand about to slap the culprit, I stop midway when I realise it's Ethan. On a scale of 1-10, how much would slapping the guy you're on a date with ruin the actual date? As I stand here debating the pros and cons of slap-ping him, Ethan takes my silence as a win and grabs my hand, tugging me towards the bar. I untangle my hand from his, slightly wiping my hand along the fabric of my dress—anything to get the feeling of him off me.

We find two seats at the bar. I order a vodka and lime soda and look around more, while I wait for my drink and contemplate how I will get out of here after this drink, *alone.*

There is so much beauty to take in. My eyes scan up and down the room, and that's when I see him. I lock eyes with possibly the most handsome man I've ever seen. His eyes pin me in place. I wish he were closer so I could see the colour. Leaning against the end of the bar, he lifts his glass to his lips—lips that look full and soft. I watch as he sips his drink, his throat as he swallows... Goddamn, even his throat is sexy. His beauty far outshines the opulence of this club. Inky hair that looks like it has a slight curl to it on top, tanned skin, a chiselled jaw with a little more than a five o'clock shadow. He's wearing a white dress shirt with the sleeves rolled up. *Mmm,* arm porn anyone? The top few buttons of his shirt are left undone, showing off just enough of a smooth chest. Paired with dark blue dress pants, he looks like he has just come from the cover shoot for GQ. As I'm contemplating this, a shadow falls across his face and his features become hard, almost like he's angry all of a sudden, like he wants to rip someone's head off.

I don't have time to dwell on his sudden change as a hand creeps up my leg. I turn to find Ethan with one hand on my leg and the other holding up my drink. Removing his hand from my leg, I smile as I go to take my drink from him, and my head spins. I lose my balance and fall into him. What the heck? I haven't even had the damn drink yet. I stumble as I try to find my way back onto my seat. His arms go around me like a vice and I push him back with both hands against his chest. Suddenly, he goes flying. Man, I'm stronger than I thought I was. I barely catch myself on the bar before I look up and into a pair of green eyes, emerald green eyes. Eyes that belong to the GQ model and he looks mad.

I try to focus on his eyes, but the world is spinning.

Reaching up, I touch his face, thinking, "GQ, you are so pretty." Then I hear it, a rumble? A laugh?

A deep, husky voice mumbles, "Thanks," before his arms reach out and grab my waist. Thanks? Why is he thanking me? Why is the world spinning so fast? I think I just need to close my eyes for a bit. I close my eyes and then feel my body falling.

## ZACHARY

*Two hours earlier*

FOUR HOURS, I've been sitting in this chair for four straight fucking hours. Stretching out the kink in my neck, I rub my thumbs over my temples to relieve some built-up pressure thumping through my head. I've been reading spreadsheet after spreadsheet, dealing with invoices and stock orders. I should hire someone to manage all of this day-to-day shit for me. The problem is I don't trust any fuckers with my accounts.

I'm reading through the latest revenue report—we've doubled our profit margin this month, compared to what it was this time last month. It seems the events and PR manager I hired two months ago has been doing her job this last month. I was close to firing her during her first month here. Her constant attempts at flirting and eye-fucking me were getting on my fucking nerves.

She must have finally got it through that plastic head of hers. It would never happen for her. I make it a rule to not fuck the employees on my payroll; it never ends well for me... *or them*.

The way the club is making legal money this month will make it a hell of a lot easier for the accountant to clean the money from the other business I run here. While owning one of the best nightclubs in Sydney is a very lucrative business, running the underground fight club, Club M, adds a lot more cash to the ever-growing pot.

Looking back through the extensive list of emails I have yet to reply to, I skim through to see which ones can wait, and which ones I will have to find the fucking time to get to before the night's through. I'm just about to click one open from my lawyer, as my office door flies open and my baby brother, all 6 ft 3inches of him, barges through. Obviously, he hasn't learnt the skill of fucking knocking.

"Bray, I see you still haven't mastered the art of knocking." I slide the Glock I was about to point his way back into the slot on the underside of my desk.

"Why waste precious time knocking when I can just turn the fucking handle and *boom*, here I am," he replies loudly as he slumps his big form onto the couch, pouring himself a glass of Glenfiddich 50-year-old whisky. Leaning back, he pops his feet up on the table.

"Help yourself, why don't you, and while you're at it, get your dirty fucking boots off my table." He grumbles as he removes his feet, placing them back on the floor. I give up on staring at the computer screen and join Bray at the couch, pouring myself a glass. "We have ten fully stocked bars in this building. Why are you in my office drinking my whisky?"

The bastard just smirks at me. "You've got the good stuff. Why wouldn't I be here?" I'm not buying that he just stormed into my office for whisky, however, I know my brother and I know when to pick my battles. This is one I don't need to pick right now.

Deciding to change tactics, I ask, "You ready for the fight tonight? Think maybe you should save your celebratory drink for after you win, winning me the thousands I'm betting on you?"

Bray shakes his head, smirking. "Please, I was born ready for this fight. Smith will wish he never challenged *the* Brayden fucking Johnson to an actual fight in the cage."

He's always been so damn cocky; the fact that he's undefeated does not help. I've placed a hundred grand on the line, so he better be fucking winning tonight. "You better be ready. I have a lot riding on this fight, Bray." I try to hit home with him just how much is at stake if he loses.

"I know, bro. Relax, I got this." He sips his drink before adding, "Also, I need you to be present on the floor tonight."

*Ah*, I knew there was a reason he was in my office, and there it is. "And why, exactly, would you need me to be on the floor tonight?" I question.

I do my best not to be seen out on the floor. I would rather be in the basement watching over my fights, than watching over drunks and pushing off girls who have no sense of self-preservation.

They always come across like they're good for the one-night deal I offer, but then here they'll be, hanging around the following weekend with claws out and looking to stake a claim they have no right to stake. I don't do relationships, ever. No woman has ever kept my interest longer than a weekend to even make it seem worth considering putting myself through the hell of a monogamous relationship.

"I have it on good authority that Ella will be here tonight." And there it is, the one reason that would have my ass out on the fucking floor; our baby sister, and when I say baby, I mean fucking eighteen years old.

"Why the fuck would she come here? This is no place for Ella."

"You think I want her here? I have one fight tonight. I don't need to be fighting every other fucking arsehole in this joint who looks at her, on top of the one I have to win."

When I say nothing else, Bray sighs. "She's eighteen, Zac. We can't exactly lock her away, and better that she comes to our club where we can keep an eye on her, than she goes somewhere else where anything could fucking happen." I have to agree with that, not the locking away idea, because that's still a viable option to me.

"What am I supposed to do when she gets here? Just sit back and watch our baby sister get shit-faced and hit on by fucking drunks? Not happening."

He thinks on this for a moment before responding, "When she gets here, have one of your boys take her and her friends to the VIP floor. I've reserved a section for them."

"Fine, but I'm having two of my guys stay in her section all night, and when, not if but *when*, I'm getting locked up for murdering the arseholes who try to hit on her, you better fucking bail me out."

Brayden smirks before getting up and walking to the door. Looking back, he says, "I'll do better than bail you out, bro. I'll bury the fucking bodies so that no one ever finds them. You can't have a murder without a body, right?"

With that, he walks out the door. It wouldn't be the first time he's buried a body or two either.

~

After replying to about a billion emails, I look at the clock. I can hear the house music of the club pump. It's ten to nine, still early in club time, however, I have no idea what time Ella is planning on arriving. Shrugging out of my jacket, I remove my tie and fold the sleeves of my shirt up as I'm walking out of my office.

Dean, my best friend since high school and head of security, falls into step next to me. "What's on the agenda for tonight, boss?" he asks.

Grunting, I relay what little info I know, "Ella and some of her friends are planning to come in tonight. I need you to find two of your best guys to escort her straight to the VIP floor— make sure they stay in her section the whole night. I'm sure I don't need to tell you, but no one touches her."

He looks at me for a moment with a look I can't quite decipher, somewhat furious and confused. "What the fuck is she doing coming to a place like this? Isn't she only seventeen?"

"She just turned eighteen two weeks ago; you were there at her fucking party, you moron. Until now, I've kept her out of here. Fuck, I'm gonna have to kill some motherfuckers tonight, aren't I?"

Dean shakes his head, pulling out his phone. Ready to send off the orders to his men, he adds, "Don't worry, you won't be the only one doing the killing." With that, he turns the opposite way, walking up to the VIP floor, while I make my way down to the first floor.

I find a spot at the end of the main bar that extends the length of the building. From this vantage point, I can see the entrance to the club and every fucker who enters. As I look around, I see people are already filling the top floor balconies that overlook the dance floor. There are groups of people sitting around the sectioned areas that line the red walls of this floor. The tables that people sit around show the vision of The

Merge: bodies entwined in a sexual embrace, when two or more souls become merged to unite as one.

Over the years, I've built The Merge up from the bottom. It's now the place to come for a good night out. What most don't know is the real action happens in the basement, below this very floor, where my underground fight events are held, and where I should be now, instead of sitting at this damn bar waiting for my sister to arrive.

James comes over with my drink before I even have to signal for him. "This is why you're my number one barman, James," I say in way of greeting, taking the drink.

"I'm your number one because my hot bod brings all the girls to the bar's more like it," he exclaims.

I have to admit he makes a killing in tips from the ladies here, even though tipping in Australia is not common. When he first started, James demanded we place a gold tip jar on the bar with his photo on it. According to him, the jar matched the décor (or some shit) so it shouldn't bother me.

The only time I've noticed it is when I see ladies strip their panties off right in front of it and place them in the jar. I keep my face turned towards the door, waiting for Ella.

"If only they knew you would never make use of those numbers or panties they slip in that jar of yours." James laughs. "Nope, but I'd sure as shit make use of your number if you slipped it in." I shake my head at him. He has been trying to get me to swing to his team since he started working here four years ago.

"Waiting on someone?" James asks as he wipes the bar down—nosey bastard that he is.

"Ella," I say, not looking at him. That has him coughing and splattering all over the place. I wait for him to compose himself.

When he finally gets himself under control, his eyebrows

raise in question. "What is she doing coming to a place like this?"

"Apparently, she is eighteen now, and this is what eighteen-year-olds fucking do on a Friday night."

"Well, eighteen or not, she's not likely to have any fun here with you and Bray around supervising."

That thought makes me smile. Looking at him, I say, "You know what? You're right. With any luck, she'll hate it and not want to go clubbing again." I raise my glass in cheers as he walks back down the other end of the bar to serve some early customers.

I turn back to keep watch on the door again and almost choke on the drink I was attempting to swallow. Standing in the doorway is a fucking angel. Long,

blonde, wavy hair, curves in all the right places and those breasts... Holy mother of god, what I wouldn't do to get a taste of them. Even in the dark, she looks like a ray of fucking sunshine.

She stands there in a red dress, looking every bit a fifty's pinup model. Why is she just standing there? She seems to look around, taking it all in. Just as I'm about to get up and offer her a privately guided tour, particularly to my office, some pencil-dicked douche comes up behind her and squeezes her ass.

I'm ready to rip the douches hand right off his arm. She spins so quickly with her arm raised and I wait for the slap that doesn't come. She hesitates before lowering her arm.

The douche grabs her hand and starts tugging her towards the bar. I'm ready to put him in his place for her, before she tugs her hand free and takes up a seat right next to him. Maybe he's her boyfriend? The thought makes me irrationally mad. I don't know this woman. I don't have any kind of claim on her... yet. I watch as she orders a drink from James before spinning around in her chair and watching the room.

Her gaze finally makes it to my side of the bar and as soon as our eyes lock on each other, I'm hypnotised, caught in a trance and soaking in all that she is. She isn't looking away either. I don't know what it is, but this woman has cast a spell. I know I need to look away, but I can't seem to make my eyes move.

Just behind her, I see James place their drinks on the bar top before turning away to serve another customer, and that's when I see the same pencil-dicked douche empty some kind of white powder into her drink.

This has me seeing red. Just as I'm getting up to go over, the douche slides his hand up her leg and she turns around, about to accept the drink, but she stumbles. When he grabs her, I know I'm about to cash in on Bray's offer to bury bodies.

The angel attempts to push him off, but it's useless—he's twice her size. Walking up behind him, I throw him across the room before turning back to my sunshine. Huh, *my* sunshine? I give a hand signal to the security grabbing him, so they know to take him down to the basement and wait for my orders on what to do with him.

I turn just in time to catch the angel as she falls again, steadying her with my hands on her waist. I know she can't be drunk. I watched her walk into the club less than five minutes ago. She was stable, not a wobble to her. Now she can barely stand.

She reaches up and touches my face. "GQ, you are so pretty." I laugh, but before I know it, she's falling into me.

"Shit." Scooping her up into my arms, I instruct James to have her drink, the one I know was roofied, sent downstairs and to tell the boys to wait for me.

I pick up her purse off the bar, carry her up to my office and lay her on the couch. Just as I'm doing this, Dean comes through the door. He looks at me, then at the couch, then at me again.

Yeah, mate, I know. It's strange to see a woman on my couch in her clothes. Although, now that I think about it, that dress doesn't do a damn thing to cover her body from roaming eyes. Before I think about what I'm doing, I walk over to my chair and grab my jacket, placing it over the top half of her body.

As I look back up, Dean is staring at me, mouth gaping like a damn fish. "What?" I demand, getting more and more frustrated at the situation. I need to get my hands on the fucker who did this to her.

He shakes his head and smirks. "*Umm*, nothing, boss. What do you want me to do with the prick the boys brought downstairs?"

"Ella here yet?" I ask.

"Just got here. She's in VIP with her friends—got Steve and Jonno with them."

I nod. "Tell them to bring her up here. Make sure Steve and Jonno come too."

He pulls out his phone, firing off text messages as I empty the woman's purse contents onto my desk. Picking up her ID, I discover she is twenty-three years old. Alyssa Summers. Nice name—it feels like it just rolls off the tongue.

Ella comes stumbling into my office giggling with one of her friends, who suddenly stops and stares at me. Ella is oblivious until I call her out. "Ella, how much have you had to drink?"

She looks up and smiles at me, knowing she can usually get away with murder with that damn smile. This time, I'm not smiling back. She takes a minute, but she sobers and looks around. Noticing the woman passed out on the couch, she looks back to me.

"I've only had one drink, Zac. Why?"

"I need you to stay here and watch over her for a bit," I say, pointing at the passed out and oblivious woman.

"Who is she? And why am I babysitting one of your floozies?"

"She," I say, pointing at the woman, "is Alyssa, and was roofied by some asshole who I need to teach a lesson to. She is not one of my *floozies* as you call them."

Ella takes a moment to digest what I've said before taking a seat on the opposite couch, her silent friend following suit. "Wow, I can't believe someone was stupid enough to drug a girl in your club, Zac."

I don't reply to the comment; the motherfucker won't be doing it again once I'm finished with him.

"I need you to stay outside the door. No one gets in; no one touches her," I demand, pointing at Steve and Jonno, both of whom nod their heads before turning to stand out front of the door.

Turning to Ella, I instruct, "Do not let anyone touch her."

She stares at me, mouth open, before composing herself and replying, "Sure thing, big brother. No one touches her."

I kiss Ella on the head as I walk out of the office. "Don't leave until I get back." I don't bother waiting for her reply. I know she won't leave Alyssa alone.

Standing in a corner of the dark room, I know he doesn't realise I'm here yet. He doesn't know that I relish the sound of his cries and pleas for help... help that's never going to come.

Down here, there is nobody to hear him scream. I wait a few more minutes for the fight that's about to happen in the cage between Bray and Smith to start. The noise of the crowd will drown out this fucker's screams. When I hear the roar of the crowd, I take a breath in, inhaling the smells of the basement—dampness mixed with blood. Counting down in my head, I know that I am going to get my hands on the douche any time now.

I wait until I hear the ref's whistle before I make myself known to the arsehole tied to my chair. "Smell that?" I ask, watching as he jumps, turning his head left and right and attempting to see where I am. It's useless though; he's blindfolded and can't see for shit.

"Who are you? Why am I here? Let me go," he pleads, already begging before the fun begins. *Figures.*

"I'm the guy about to give you a lesson on what happens to fuckers who drug innocent women in my fucking club." I get right up to his face before whispering in his ear, "And I will enjoy every damn minute of this lesson."

He pisses himself, literally just fucking pisses himself, the wet patch growing on the front of his jeans. Not surprising, as any guy who needs to resort to drugging a woman is a weak piece of shit.

Landing a punch to his stomach, then another to his face, I relish the blood splatters that come from his mouth. Now I'm smiling. It's a shame he can't see how damn much I'm enjoying this.

The sight of his blood, and the fact that I caused it, releases something in me.

His cries get louder. "Please... please let me go, man. I did nothing."

Pathetic is what he is. "Scream all you want, mate. No one can hear you down here. And even if they could hear, they wouldn't save you."

He struggles against the ropes on his arms. Holding his

head still, I land another punch to his ribs then one to his face. I let go and he falls backwards, chair and all.

"Fuck you! Untie me and fight me like a real man." Now, he tries to be brave—the fucker probably thinks I won't fight him if he's not tied down. Think again, motherfucker. Bending down, I remove the blindfold and nod to Dean, giving him the signal to cut the ties loose.

"Wha... what... what are you doing?" he sputters as Dean approaches, flicking the knife between his fingers.

"Making your wish come true, fucker. I'm cutting those ties, so you can fight the boss *like a real man.*"

Dean laughs and kicks him in his stomach before leaning down and cutting the ties loose. The douche scoots backwards on his arse until he hits the wall.

"Stand up!" I command.

"N... n... no, please. You don't have to do this. Just let me go. I won't say nothing to nobody." He's shaking his head back and forth violently.

"I thought you wanted to fight me like a real man? Now get the fuck off the floor!" I approach him, and he still doesn't stand up to fight. I kick him in his ribs and he goes into the foetal position, crying like the motherfucking pansy arse he is.

I go at him, landing punches to his face and torso, before I turn back to Dean, who's watching with a huge-arse grin on his face—sadistic bastard that he is.

"Got that drink I had James send down here?" I ask.

"Yep," he says as he walks over to the table, picking up the drink.

"Good, make sure he drinks the whole thing before you throw his ass out to the back alley." I walk out, hearing the asshole screaming and begging. I don't need to be there for the rest. I have an angel who needs taking care of back in my office.

# Three

## ALYSSA

MY HEAD FEELS like a hundred little men with big hammers are pounding away on my brain. *Pound. Thump. Pound. Thump. Argh,* I slowly try to open my eyes to the world. "Bright," I mumble out to nobody but myself.

My angel fairy must be listening today because I hear the shifting of fabric and the room becomes darker. Much better. I try to open my eyes again, slowly coming back to reality.

Why is my bed so damn hard? *Wait.* I open my eyes. That's when I see him. That's when I realise I am most definitely not in my bedroom. Because, one thing I know for sure, the god sitting in the chair across from me would not be following a girl like me to my bedroom, or any room.

"Morning, sunshine." Oh god, he talks. His voice.

A husky rumble that goes straight through to my core. He's looking straight at me with a smirk on his face and one raised eyebrow, like he's waiting for something.

"*Ah... umm.*" I stumble over my words.

"Usually, the response would be good morning. I'd even

accept: Morning, handsome. Morning, sexy. Your choice really. I'm not picky." Picky, maybe. Cocky, definitely.

"Morning?" My greeting comes out as more of a question than an actual greeting. "Where am I? Do I know you? Oh god, we didn't, did we?"

I freak out as I look underneath the jacket that lies on top of my dress—my dress, which is still in place, thank god. I mentally run an internal category of my body: my head hurts for sure, my stomach is seedy, but other parts (the important parts) nothing. Surely if we did anything, I would feel something, right?

Looking at him, I don't see how I wouldn't have jumped at the chance to get him naked. He's wearing a pair of faded jeans, a black V-neck shirt that stretches across his chest and broad shoulders, and black boots. Did he just come from a photoshoot? His biceps are on show from the short sleeves of the shirt.

He's not disgustingly huge like a bodybuilder. Just the right amount of muscle, enough to know he takes care of himself and spends time in a gym. His shirt is tucked in slightly to the waist of his jeans, which hang low on his hips.

His hair is damp like he's just stepped out of the shower —*mmm,* now *that* I would like to see, him in a shower, water running down his body. I'm pulled from my thoughts as I hear his laugh; it's deep and rough, almost like his voice is not used to the concept of laughing.

He's laughing at my obvious distress. "Trust me, sunshine, if we did," he says, raising his eyebrows, "you would most certainly remember, and not to mention, feel it for the next few days."

Yep, most definitely a cocky-ass, probably has girls falling at his feet left and right. Why does that thought make me want to throw up even more?

He hands me a bottle of water and some aspirin that were sitting on the table. "Take these and drink this; you can thank me later."

I swallow the pills and drink half the bottle of water before looking back at him. "Thank you, but you didn't answer my question. Where am I, and how did I get here?" I wave my arm around the office I woke up in, then take a moment to look around the space. It's obvious no money was spared fitting out this office. A huge mahogany desk sits centred in front of wall-to-ceiling windows that overlook the view of the Sydney Harbour. Dark timber shelving lines the walls; some stacked with bottles and glasses, and others with photographs, books and ornaments.

"You're in my office. I carried you up here after you collapsed on me down at the bar."

Bits of the night start coming back. I remember sitting at the bar, I remember staring at the man who now sits in front of me (GQ), and then I remember Ethan.

"Ethan?" I question, unsure what happened to my date, and unsure if I exactly care what happened to him either.

At the mention of the name, Mr. GQ looks away from me, face hard as stone while clenching his jaw. "He your boyfriend or something?" he asks through clenched teeth.

"Or something," I answer, shrugging. He doesn't seem happy with my answer, just stares blankly at me like he's waiting for more. Well, he can keep waiting. I'm not one to discuss my ins and outs with strangers. "Have you got a bathroom I can use?" I ask as I stand up on wobbly legs, looking up at him as I regain my balance.

"Through there." He nods to a door. I pick up my clutch from the table and make my way into the bathroom, shutting and locking the door behind me.

"Shit, shit, shit," I say out loud as I try not to panic over my current situation. I pull my phone out to see a million missed calls and texts from Sarah, Reilly and Holly. Sarah must've told them I didn't come home. I read through Sarah's texts first.

**Sarah: Where are you? I thought you'd be home by now.**

*Sarah: Seriously, Lyssa, text me back so I know you're still alive.*

**Sarah: Okay, if you don't call me back, I will come and hunt you down.**

*Sarah: You left me no choice. I had to call Holly and Reilly. Now you have three pissed off friends. Seriously, call me back so I know you're not dead in a ditch somewhere!!!*

**Sarah: Wait, you're not dead in a ditch, are you? Shit, because if you are, I will revive you just to KILL you myself for making me develop stress wrinkles.**

*Holly: Lyssa, there's no shame in getting your freak on. There is shame in making your friends worry. Text me back so we know you're still breathing.*

**Reilly: Is he hot?**

At this, I laugh a little and then stop myself as I realise I'm probably sounding like a crazy person to Mr. GQ on the other side of the door. I quickly send out a group text to the three of them.

**Me: Not dead, not in a ditch. Be home soon!**

· · ·

Not even three seconds later, my phone vibrates in my hand. I don't bother opening their messages. Looking in the mirror, I audibly shriek at the reflection staring back at me. Racoon eyes much?

"Jeez, no wonder he was staring," I mumble to myself. I make quick work of doing my business, washing my hands and face before picking my phone back up and opening the Uber app.

I walk back out of the bathroom to find Mr. GQ standing at his desk—at least I think it's his desk. He looks like he belongs here. Realising I'm staring at him again, I look back down at my phone.

"I'm just going to call for an Uber and be on my way. Thanks for whatever it is you did for me last night."

"No," he says, staring straight at me. I swear he can see right into my soul; his stare is penetrating... *mmm*, penetrating. Damn it, now I'm thinking of him penetrating in other ways.

Shaking my head, I question him, "No? What do you mean, no?"

"Exactly that. No, you won't be getting an Uber home. I'll drive you." I must look like a confused nut job around this guy; he never seems to make sense to me.

"Well, that's nice of you, but I don't even know you. I'll just take an Uber."

"Do you know every Uber driver in Sydney?" he asks.

"What? Of course I don't know every Uber driver in Sydney," I respond, shaking my head at him.

"So, it's safe to get in a car with a complete stranger, but not safe to get a lift home with the guy who saved you from being date raped last night?" He's so matter of fact.

"What do you mean date raped? I wasn't..."

"No, you weren't, but you would have been had I not

stepped in. That guy you were at the bar with, Ethan…" He clenches his jaw as he grinds out the name.

"I watched him put Rohypnol in your drink at the bar. Although he must have already given you something before you came in here, because you passed out without even touching the drink you ordered."

Holy shit, someone drugged me. No wonder my head feels like shit. I'm stunned. I don't know what to say to GQ, so instead, I stand, awkwardly staring at him.

I finally decide that I have manners. Reaching my hand out, I say, "Hi, I'm Alyssa, and thanks for helping me out last night. It's all a bit foggy for me. I remember being at the restaurant and then coming in here for a drink. I remember seeing you at the bar. I mean, how could I forget seeing you. That's not a face anyone would forget in a hurry, and… oh god, now I'm rambling. I'm just going to shut up now and go home."

Before I can even turn around, he grabs my hand and I'm stunned again at the zap of electricity going through my body. I wonder if he feels it too because he says nothing for a beat, just looks at me, confused.

He gives his head a subtle shake before speaking. "I'm Zac. Zachary Williams, but you can call me Zac, and I'm still driving you home."

With that, he picks up a pair of keys from his desk. He walks over to the couch to pick up his jacket before turning back to me and placing it over my shoulders, wrapping me up in his scent. It seems like such an odd and intimate gesture, something someone I don't know shouldn't be doing. It feels right though.

The fabric is soft. I gather the top of the jacket in my hands and bring it to my nose and sniff. It smells like him, woodsy with a mix of citrus. If he thinks it's strange that I literally sniffed his jacket, he doesn't say anything. He just smirks at me, showing me a dimple I can see myself licking. Before I can lose myself in my head again, he places his hand on my lower back as he leads me out of the office.

"Come."

I shiver at the demand—wild thoughts of him demanding me to come while spread out naked on his desk run through my mind. I contemplate how his hand feels warm, the complete opposite to how Ethan's hand felt when he touched me last night.

The thought of Ethan makes me furious. How dare he drug me. I don't have time to stew on my anger now. As Zac, aka GQ, leads me through the building, I'm focused on trying not to trip over myself with all the people around openly gawking at me? *At him?*

Zac leads me out through a back door that opens to a carpark. Grabbing my hand, he takes me over to the passenger side of the closest car to the door—well, at least I think it's a car. It's shiny, black and has wheels, so it must be a car, right? Zac presses a button on the door, which has the door automatically opening out and then up. Okay, so definitely not an ordinary car.

"Get in," he grumbles.

I tentatively duck into the car, turning to him. "You know, you really don't need to drive me. I can find my way home."

He silently presses a button on the door, and suddenly I'm closed inside what is no doubt the fanciest car I've ever seen. I'm too frightened to move, on the off chance I dirty or break some-thing. Sitting there frozen, I watch as Zac makes his way around the front of the car before climbing into the driver's side.

He shuts his door, turns the car on and then turns and looks at me like he's waiting for something. He doesn't say anything for a minute, and I squirm under his stare, not knowing what he's waiting for.

Unable to handle the intensity of his silent quest, I hesitantly try to break the silence. *"Umm, so..."* That's about as intelligent of a sentence I can put together right now.

"Buckle up, sunshine. It's a fast ride," he says as he reaches over, putting my seat belt on for me. I can feel the heat rise up my neck and reach my face as he plugs the seat belt in.

Zac takes off out of the carpark and into the easy Saturday morning city traffic. *Saturday morning.*

"Oh, shit," I mumble under my breath as I dig through my clutch for my phone to find out what the time is and how late I will be for my shift today. "Dammit!" My phone would choose this moment to be dead flat.

"What's wrong?" Zac questions with a deeply concerned look on his face.

"What time is it?" I attempt in the calmest voice I can muster, externally hoping to appear cool, calm, and collected. Internally, I'm a freaking mess, considering the worst possible scenarios. I'm late. I'm getting fired. I'm going to be jobless and homeless within the month. Maybe I'm being the glass is half empty kind of girl, but when you had the childhood I had, the glass is never half full.

Zac looks at the gold watch on his wrist, before looking back across at me. "It's 9:15."

9:15 a.m. Not so bad... I'm mentally calculating the amount of time I need to get home, shower, and hike to the station. If I hurry, I can probably make the 10:15 train, which will get me to work at around 11:30.

"Fudge it, can this Batmobile of yours go any faster?" I plead.

"Batmobile?" he repeats, laughing a little. "This beauty..."

He taps the steering wheel with pride. "...is a McLaren 570S. Yes, it goes faster."

"Well, do you think you can make *this beauty* go faster and get me home as quickly as you can?" I'm trying hard not to come across as panicked, but, by the look on his face, I don't think it's working.

"Look, if I'm going to go about breaking every road rule in the book, I need to know why you're in such a rush to get home?" He makes a scene of sniffing himself. "I showered while you were passed out on my couch, so I know it's not because I stink that you're in such a rush to get home, so what is it?"

Wow, just wow. *Well, here it goes. Try not to sound desperate in front of the hot guy, Lyssa.* I give myself a mental pep talk before admitting just how desperate I am. "You don't stink. I'm late. I have to be at work at 11:00. I need to get home. I need to shower, then I need to make the trek to the station—it's at least a forty-minute train ride to work. I can't be late... Oh god, I cannot be late!" Well, I think I totally came across as every bit as cool and collected as I was aiming for, right? *Yeah, probably not.*

"Sunshine, breathe. It's okay. I gotcha. I'll get you home in no time. Hold on." Zac cruises through the streets, weaving in and out of traffic a little faster. He reaches over and gives my hand a little squeeze before turning his gaze back to the road.

I'm momentarily stunned by the electricity I feel run up my arm from his touch. I look at him, his muscles stretching out the black V-neck, his forearms tensing as he grips the steering wheel... damn. Unintentionally, I squeeze my legs together and supress the moan that wants to escape. *What the hell is wrong with me?* This handsome stranger is nice enough to give me a lift home and all I can think about is jumping his bones.

I hear him curse under his breath. "Where do you work?" he asks, obviously trying to distract me with small talk. Could this moment get any more embarrassing? It's obvious he knows

I was checking him out. "I work at RNS. I'm a nurse in emergency," I say with pride. Zac looks over and smiles briefly, before masking his face again.

"You should take the day off. You were drugged last night, remember?" he almost grunts out.

"I'm fine. I'm not taking the day off." We're turning onto my street when I realise I never gave him my address. "*Umm*, how did you know where I lived?" Zac looks over at me, supplying me with that GQ smile of his, and says, "I saw your address on your licence last night." As we turn into my street, he looks at the block of townhouses. "Which one is yours?"

I point out my townhouse. "That one, but you can just stop here and I'll jump out. Thanks for the ride, and everything else."

Zac looks at me and shakes his head before pulling into a carpark and turning the car off. He gets out of the car and is around at my door before I can even comprehend what's happening. Zac opens my door, holding his hand out to help me out of the car.

I take his hand and the moment I do, I feel it again, that zap of electricity. Once I'm out of the car and have collected myself, I remove my hand.

"Thank you," I whisper as I walk towards my door. It's not until I get to the top step that I notice that Zac followed me to the door. Turning around, I squint at him. "*Umm*, what are you doing?"

He takes a moment, looking me over before answering. "First, I'm walking you to your door. Second, I'm waiting for you to shower and get ready for work so I can drop you off at the hospital."

I'm not really sure what is happening. Did I wake up in an alternative universe today? I pinch my arm. Okay, so I'm not dreaming, but I sure do look a little unstable to Mr. GQ in front of me.

"Why would you want to drive me to work?" I question. It's been my experience that people don't do anything expecting nothing in return.

"You're running late. You said you were planning on catching a train. Trains are not safe, and you would still be late. I can get you there in half the time, but you might want to get moving on that shower if you want to make it to work on time."

He's right—I know he's right—but it doesn't mean I have to be happy about it. Grumbling, I turn and open the door, before adding, "I'm only letting you give me a lift in the Batmobile because I really, really don't want to be late. You can wait on the couch."

He smirks and laughs as he follows me inside.

I point to the sofa. "You can wait here. I'm just going to run upstairs and shower real quick."

Zac follows my gaze to look up at the narrow staircase before looking back to me. "Sure thing." He heads towards the sofa.

That's when I hear it... I thought just maybe something might go my way today and Sarah would be out already. She always leaves early on Saturdays, claiming she wants to make the most of the weekends by starting them early.

Sarah comes bounding down the stairs in a pair of cut-off shorts and bikini top, looking every bit the drop-dead gorgeous creature she is. She stops dead in her tracks when she sees me and Zac standing in our living room.

Sarah turns towards me and raises her eyebrows as she

states, "*That* is not Ethan." Turning her head, she gives Zac the once-over. "Yep, definitely not Ethan. It is absolutely an improvement though."

I don't know why—I can't explain the feeling exactly—but something happens deep inside me when I see the way she's looking at Zac. Like he was a porterhouse steak she couldn't wait to sink her teeth into. I didn't like it, not one bit.

She must have noticed something flicker across my face because she comes up to me. "Are you okay? You don't look so hot." Concern is written on her face. "Did he do something to you? Because even serial killers can be beautiful, Lyssa." She turns towards Zac like she wants to bury him alive. Sarah is nothing if not the most loyal friend.

Unsure how to handle the situation, I turn to Zac, expecting him to be looking his fill at my beautiful friend, like every other man does in her presence. I'm stunned to silence when I see he isn't looking at her at all; his eyes are fixed on me. He looks pissed off again, jaw clenched tight.

Ignoring his pissed off look, I turn back to Sarah. "This is Zac; he helped me out last night, drove me home this morning, and has kindly offered to wait for me to shower and then drive me to work. Sorry, don't have time to chitchat. I'm late."

I'm just about to the first step when Sarah stops me. "Lyssa, stop right there!" She's using her *don't fuck with me* voice. I look over at Zac, who is now giving Sarah a death glare. I really don't have time to figure this guy out right now, or ever. "Why, and how exactly, did *Zac* have to help you last night?" Her voice rises in pitch as she shrieks and uses air quotes when she says his name.

"Oh, it was nothing. I'll fill you in later. In the meantime, make sure you lose Ethan's details and block him on all of your social media."

I turn to start back up the stairs when someone clears their throat. It's a deep, husky noise, one that sends shivers down my spine; a throat noise that most certainly does not belong to Sarah.

"I wouldn't say that getting roofied by your date and passing out in a packed nightclub is nothing, Alyssa. Your night could have gone a lot differently if I wasn't there," Zac so helpfully points out.

Sarah gasps. "You were roofied?" She doesn't give me time to answer before she starts on her tirade. "By Ethan, the hot groomsman? What the fuck? I'm going to kill him—no, I'm going to torture him. I'll start at his toes and make my way up his legs. I'll skip his manhood, make him think I'm sparing him, and move to his fingers. It can't be too hard to rip fingernails off, right? Then I think I'll chop the fuckers off. Just when he thinks I'm done, that's when I'll strike him where it really hurts. Tie a string around his balls tight, then tie the other end to the door and slam it—you know, like kids do for teeth. I'll keep slamming that door until his balls rip off."

Sarah paces as she continues mumbling to herself. I'm stunned into silence. I mean, I knew she was loyal as shit. What shocks me the most was how much I liked the picture she just painted in my head. I don't recall a time I've ever been this pissed off with someone, and that's saying something, because I've been in some shitty situations over the years.

When I come to this realisation, I tell her, "I'll help, and when were done, I'll help bury the body. We'll burn it in the grave before we shovel all the dirt back in too." Sarah smiles and nods, like it's a forgone plan.

Zac looks back and forward between us both. Fixing his gaze on me with a slight smirk, he says, "No need to get all Jekyll and Hyde, sunshine. I've already taken care of the fucker; he won't be bothering you again." He looks at his watch before looking back up. "Not that I'm not enjoying this episode of

*Murder, She Wrote*, but you might want to get a move on with that shower if you want to make it to work on time. My car's fast, but it's no time machine, sweetheart."

That has me screeching my way upstairs and into the shower. I have the quickest shower in the history of showers, find a pair of scrubs, and pile my hair up into a messy top bun. Just before I'm about to turn to head downstairs, I stop and add a layer of nude lip gloss to my lips.

# Four

ZAC

I LOOK over to Alyssa sitting in the seat next to me. It feels right to have her there. She's only wearing scrubs, but I swear when she came down the stairs after rushing through a shower, I had to tell myself not to be the creeper and to stop visibly drooling. She is gorgeous. Up close, I can see that her blue eyes sometimes flicker with shades of green. Her blonde hair is all piled up on top of her head, with loose strands already breaking free around her face.

"I just have a quick stop to make—be one minute; stay here. I'm locking the doors to prevent people getting in, not you getting out," I say as I pull into a carpark right out front of the café I called while she was in the shower. She looks at me like I need a shrink but smiles and agrees to stay put.

I'm in and out of the café within two minutes and back in the car. "I'm not sure how you take your coffee yet. I went for the safe bet and ordered you a flat white." I hand her the coffee cup, which she takes hesitantly.

"Thank you. You really didn't need to do this, but I appreciate it. I love flat whites; also, vanilla lattes are a regular for me."

I hand her the bag with the two muffins. "One's blueberry; the other's chocolate chip. Eat."

She looks at me like I've lost my head now, her face scrunched up and brows furrowed. "What?" I ask.

"I can't eat this in your car. I'll make a mess. You'll end up with crumbs all over the place; you will need to get a detail. I don't know how much a car like this cost to get detailed, but I know I can't afford that. So, thank you for the muffin, but I can't possibly eat in the Batmobile." She's trying to hand the paper bag back to me, and all I can think is: wow, she is cute when she gets nervous and worked up.

"Sunshine, you are eating the muffin; you will eat in this car. I don't care if you get crumbs everywhere—that's nothing a vacuum can't fix. What I care about is the fact that you were planning on going to work for god knows how many hours without even eating breakfast. You know breakfast is the most important meal of the day, right?" She's still holding the bag out to me. I ignore her and pull back out onto the road.

It takes a moment, and she's quiet when she speaks again. "Thank you." She's not looking at me

when she says it, head down while looking at the paper bag like she can will it away.

Eventually she opens the bag and takes a small chunk of the chocolate chip muffin, popping it into her mouth. Almost as soon as it hits her tongue, she lets out a pleasurable moan. I look over. Her eyes are closed and her head's leaning back; it's a good look on her, a damn good look. I have to will myself to look back at the road and subtly adjust my jeans to allow for my growing cock.

Fuck me, I don't know what it is about this girl, but she ticks every one of my ideal woman list items—a list I didn't know I even had until I saw her. I don't even care that I can see crumbs dropping in my car. I've never let anyone so much as have a coffee in this car before, let alone eat a savoury. Bray would not let me hear the end of it if he found out I let a girl eat in this beast. But the thought of her not eating just pissed me off.

We're almost at the hospital. I don't want to drop her off and not know when I will see her again. My brain is scrambling for ideas on how I'm going to make that happen. I need to see her again. Attempting to not look like the arse I have probably been portraying, I try to make small talk, covertly trying to find out more about this woman who has consumed my mind from the moment she walked through the doors of my club last night.

"Do you work all weekend?" I try to sound casual, like it doesn't matter to me either way, but it does. I don't want her working tomorrow. If she works tomorrow, that's another day I'll have to wait to see her.

She turns and looks at me, inspecting my profile. She must be happy with what she finds because there is a smile to her voice when she replies, "No. I work today and then have two days off. How about you? Do you work all weekend?" She smiles as she asks me the question, like she's already predicted the answer.

"I work every day, sunshine." I send her a wink. She smiles big now, and I swear I would do anything to keep seeing that smile. It makes me feel something good. I can't put a label on the feeling, but I just know it's good. It's not a feeling I've ever had before.

"Okay, well, not all of us are... whatever it is you are." She waves her hand up and down at me. "Some of us, namely me, have normal jobs, average jobs, stable jobs. Jobs that mean I know I will have enough money to eat every week. If I turn up to work on time and don't get myself fired..."

The way she talks about knowing she will have enough

money to eat every week bothers me. Was there a time she didn't have enough food, money, or stability? The way she talks about her job is kind of sad. She doesn't sound like she likes her job, but turns up every week for the paycheck—which is fine. It's what most of the population does to survive.

"Well, I for one think you have an outstanding job. What other job could you have where you get to wear those scrubs, looking cute as hell all day anyway?"

She spins her head so quickly towards me, mouth hanging open. She hides her shock just as quickly as she showed it. "There is nothing cute about these scrubs. They're blue... blue." She repeats the colour like I don't know what the colour blue is.

"It doesn't matter if they're blue, green, or orange; they are cute on *you*." I add emphasis to the you because I've been in hospitals. I know that not everyone can pull off a pair of scrubs. But Alyssa? Damn, can she pull that shit off.

"Blue is not cute; blue is literally the colour for depression. Blue is the colour people use to represent being sad. Wearing blue scrubs is not cute." She really doesn't seem to like the colour blue.

"We can agree to disagree. Why did you choose nursing?" I surprise myself with the fact that I honestly want to know the answer.

"That's a conversation for another time. We're here. You can just stop anywhere near that door and I'll jump out. Thank you so much for the ride. You don't know how much I appreciate it, really, and the coffee and the muffin. Sorry for the mess, but I told you so." Alyssa rushes out her thanks like it will get her out of the car quicker.

It's ten minutes to eleven—she's not late, *yet*. I park the car and I'm around at her door before she can figure out how the door opens from the inside. I reach a hand in and pull her out, almost pulling her flush against me. Every bone in my body wants to pull her in and kiss her like my life depends on it. Shit, maybe my life does depend on it? No, I don't want to scare her off, especially with what happened to her last night fresh in her head.

I show a lot of fucking restraint when I take a step back. "What time do you finish?"

She squints at me. I'm not sure if it's the sun that's shining in her eyes, or if she's trying to figure out if she wants to tell me. "I finish at eleven tonight. I'm doing a twelve-hour shift today. Why?"

She's smart; she seems to know I don't ask questions for the fun of it. "I'll pick you up from this same spot at eleven tonight."

Before she has time to argue with me, I walk back around the car and jump in, leaving her standing there gaping at me as I pull away.

Walking into my penthouse, the first thing I notice is Bray, Dean and Ella sitting in the living room. All at once, they lift their heads, looking at me expectantly.

"What the fuck are you all doing here?" I ask, annoyed that they're in my fucking house. All I want to do is strip off and get into bed and sleep. Well, there is one other thing I wouldn't mind doing, and that's jerking one out to the image of sweet, beautiful Alyssa.

Alyssa, who has had my cock straining within the confines of my jeans ever since she moaned around that first bite of the muffin this morning. Okay, if I'm being honest, it's been fucking hard since she walked through the doors of my club.

Bray seems to be the only brave one out of the group. Well,

it's either bravery or stupidity. I haven't decided which one yet. "Where the fuck have you been?" he shouts.

Raising my eyebrows at him, I don't bother answering his question. I repeat mine first. "What the fuck are you all doing here?"

This time, it's Ella who pipes up, "Last I checked, I live here, but I'll leave you two with the grouch."

I watch as she walks down the hall, not even a minute later hearing the tell-tale sound of the door being slammed, and I cringe at the damage she's doing to the doors. Ella has never been able to shut a door quietly.

I turn back towards Bray and Dean, who are still lounging on my damn sofa and looking like they don't have a care in the world. "She's right; she lives here. You two fuckers, however, do not." I reach into my pocket and pull out the keys for the McLaren, throwing them in Bray's direction. He catches them with ease. "Make yourself useful and take the McLaren to the detailers. I'm going to get a few hours' sleep. I'll see the both of you at the club around seven tonight." I start towards my bedroom, thinking I can make a quick escape.

"Wait, you had it detailed two days ago. Why do you need it cleaned again so soon?" Bray and his nosey bastard questions... I turn back around to see him waiting for an explanation with raised eyebrows.

"Because I ate a muffin in it this morning and made a fucking mess of it. Besides, it's my fucking car. If I want to get the damn thing detailed every other day, I bloody well will." I can't help the frustrated tone; after sitting up all night watching Alyssa as she slept on the couch in my office, I'm too damn tired to care.

"You don't even like muffins," Dean unhelpfully adds.

"Remind me again why you're here?" I give him a death glare that would make most men shit themselves. Not him though. Dean has been one of my best mates since the beginning of high school. I may employ him as my head of security, but he's more than that—he's family.

"I'm here, arsehole, because someone had to give Ella a ride home from the club last night when I realised you weren't coming home. Bray wasn't here either, so I stayed the night so she wouldn't be left here by herself." At my raised eyebrows, he quickly adds, "On the couch, I slept on the fucking couch." He points towards the pillow and blankets that are still spilled out on the couch.

"Thanks for that, but that doesn't explain why you're still here?" I run my hands through my hair, not even sure I care why they're here. "That's easy," he says with a huge-ass smile on his face. "Bray here rocked up this morning. When we noticed you didn't come home last night and still weren't home this morning, we got busy figuring out where someone would have buried your sorry ass, so we could go dig it up and give you the burial we thought you deserved. Seeing as though we couldn't for the life of us think of any other reason you wouldn't have come home, or answered any of our thousand calls or texts."

He's right. I have ignored their calls and texts all morning. Not wanting to explain myself, I just grunt out, "Last I checked, I'm a grown-ass twenty-eight-year-old man, and I sure as hell don't have a fucking curfew. I'll see both you fuckers after I've had some damn sleep." Without looking back, I make my way to my room before locking my door behind me.

I strip off and climb into bed. I almost moan at the thought of getting a few hours' sleep and close my eyes. After lying there for fifteen minutes with thoughts of Alyssa stuck in my head, I realise that sleep is the last thing on the mind of my cock. I reach into the bedside table and pull out a tub of lube. Squeezing some onto my hand, I reach down and give my cock a tight, slow pull. Just this simple touch sends shivers down my spine.

With thoughts of Alyssa, I pull a few more times, thinking of her on her knees, those blue eyes looking up at me as she slowly takes my cock all the way into her mouth, right to the back of her throat, sucking as she shallows her cheeks on her way back up. At this, I moan out loud. With a few more tugs and her name on my lips, I come hard, all over the fucking place.

Shaking my head at the thought of how quickly I just came to the thought of Alyssa, like I'm fucking fifteen years old again, I get up and have a quick shower before climbing back into bed and crashing.

Looking at my watch, I see it's nine thirty. I've been sitting here, stuck in my office with Dean and Bray, since seven o'clock. Let's just say the fact that the muffin crumbs in the McLaren were all over the passenger's side did not escape Bray's notice. For at least thirty minutes, I had to listen to both him and Dean give me shit about letting some chick, as they called her, eat in my car. I let it slide and refused to give them any more ammunition against me.

Now we're going over tonight's plans. We have a new, up-and-coming band called Cyrus coming in to play live for the first time tonight. I've given them a thirty-minute time slot. On a Saturday night, one of the busiest nights at my club, that's a fucking generous amount of time.

Dean and Bray are arguing over how many bouncers we will need to surround the stage to prevent chaos tonight, when a knock at the door stops their argument. "Come in," I call out.

Caitlyn, my PR manager, struts in and looks me up and

down before pasting a smile across her fake-ass lips. "Zac, it will be a great night. We've had a lot of positive feedback from the Cyrus promotions. We're expecting a packed house by ten thirty tonight." She looks at me expectantly.

Does she expect a fucking gold sticker for doing her job? Ignoring her, I turn to Dean. "Have you briefed the security team on the band? I don't want any issues tonight. If we have a full house by ten thirty, security needs to be on point. I want the boys at the door double checking IDs. We had a group of three underage girls make it through last Saturday night. That shit does not happen again."

Dean stands up, ready to head out. "Sure thing, boss. They've all been briefed—no one makes it close to the band."

Before he makes it to the door, I stop him. "I have an errand to run; I'm leaving at 10:30, and should be about an hour give or take. I want you to double check everything. Bray will help," I provide, pointing at Bray.

All three look at me like I've lost my head, probably because I have. I've never left the club to run any errands on a busy Saturday night before. Caitlyn walks over to me, running her hand down my arm as she tries to purr.

"I've set the band up with a table on the VIP floor before and after the show." Looking down at her hand on my arm, I back away from her reach. It has always irked me whenever she tries to touch me, but tonight it just feels wrong.

I shake the feeling off before I dismiss her to get her out of my fucking office. "That's great. I want you out there to greet and meet, mingle for a bit, and make sure they're comfortable but not too bloody comfortable. They're here to do a job, not have a free party." I walk over to the door, holding it open for her. Looking pointedly at her, I clear my throat.

She eventually gets the hint before attempting to recover. "Sure thing, boss. I'll see you out on the floor later," she says as she passes through the open door. I don't reply before shutting it right behind her.

Bray and Dean are both still standing there with shocked expressions stuck on their faces. "What?" I demand, looking from one to the other.

Bray responds first. "What the fuck kind of errand you got to run on a Saturday night, bro?" He raises his eyebrows in question.

"Not that it's any of your fucking business, but I'm picking Alyssa up from work and giving her a lift home."

They both physically gasp before pissing themselves laughing. Once they've recovered, Dean inquires, "What kinda job does this chick have that she's working till eleven o'clock at night? Don't tell me you fell in love with a stripper, man."

I know he's joking, but that doesn't prevent the pissed off feeling boiling up inside me. "First," I say pointing at him, "her name is Alyssa ... Alyssa." I repeat her name for emphasis; sometimes these dicks can be daft. "She is not just some chick. She has a name—next time, fucking use it. Second, she's a goddamn nurse. You know, a professional—smart and uses her brains, not her banging body, to make a buck. And third, I sure as fuck have not fallen in love with anyone." I almost gag at the word. I've never been in love and don't think I ever want to be. Fuck that, I've seen that shit and it never ends well for folk like me.

Bray looks at me, shaking his head like he can't believe what he's hearing. "Okay, bro, whatever you say, but just answer me this one thing." He pauses, thinking he can add dramatic suspense. I wait him out, not giving him the response he's seeking; he eventually asks anyway, "Why are you picking up *Alyssa* and driving her home?" He adds a lot of emphasis to her name and I can't help but smile when I hear it.

I pick up my wallet and keys from my desk, pocketing them before turning back around and making my way to the door.

Just before I open the door, I reply, "Because if I don't pick her up, she will catch a bloody train home, and I don't want her catching a fucking train at eleven o'clock at night." I hold the door open for them to follow me out and lock the door behind me.

Just as I'm thinking they're both going to drop the topic and get on with their jobs, Dean smirks at me. "And why do you think it is that you don't want some girl—sorry, Alyssa—you don't want Alyssa catching a train at eleven o'clock at night?" he questions as he notices the pissed off look I'm sending his way.

Shaking my head, I don't answer him as I walk away, yelling at both of them, "I'll be back. Try not to burn the place down while I'm gone, will ya?"

With that, I make my way out the back to the carpark. I want to make sure I have enough time to pick Alyssa up something to eat. I have a feeling she hasn't eaten much, if anything, since that muffin this morning.

# Five

## ALYSSA

I AUDIBLY SIGH as I take a seat at the nurses' station. I feel like I've been on my feet for ten hours straight, probably because I have been. Saturday shifts are always the busiest in our ER; it seems everyone saves their injuries and illnesses for Saturdays. Today, the ER has been packed with a range of cases, easy and boring cases, but busy all the same.

I've seen at least twenty kids ranging from babies to seven-year-olds with a series of really superficial boo-boos, alongside mothers who don't seem to know how to work a Band-Aid. It seems I studied for four years to apply ointment and bandages to kids' boo-boos while ensuring their mothers that their child does not have a broken bone and does not require stitching.

In a way, I guess it's sweet and nice to know that there are mothers out there who care a lot about their child's wellbeing. But a child having a scraped knee, bruised arm, or small scratches from falling over does not mean you need to rush them to emergency because their life is in danger or their bones are broken. Yeah, they should go to their regular doctor and stop running down to the hospital's emergency room.

On top of the kids with boo-boos, there were five kids who

came in with actual broken bones. Those I liked, not because their bones were broken, but because the parents were usually thankful once their child was doped up enough to stop crying out in pain. These cases were straightforward—keep the patient comfortable until the doctor can see them. Send them for x-rays, send them to the orthopaedist to get a cast put on, and send them home. See? *Simple*. Boring, but still simple.

Finally, having five minutes to sit down, my mind drifts to Zac. Hot, sexy, all male Zac, otherwise known as Mr. GQ—well, in my head that is. What I wouldn't do to get him on a bed. I mentally curse myself for where I've let my thoughts go. It will never happen I tell myself; men like Zac do not go for girls like me, your everyday, girl-next-door type.

I've never had a man take such good care of me. No one has ever walked around the car to open the door for me before—not that I could figure out how to open the contraption he calls a car, anyway. I think about the way he leaned over to put my seat belt on for me, the way he stopped to buy me breakfast... Men like Zac did not exist in the real world. There has to be a flaw; no man can be that perfect. As hard as I try to identify any flaws in Zac, I'm coming up blank. There is nothing, literally nothing, I would want to change about him.

I wonder what he got up to today... I wonder who he's with... *No, Lyssa, stop it*, I scold myself. No good will come from daydreaming of the "never going to happen" Zac.

Trying to clear my mind, I take a deep breath and take stock of my surroundings. The smell of antiseptic and sanitizer assaults my nose. The sound of machines beeping, kids crying, the synchronised sounds of coughing, the elevator doors opening and closing, feet shuffling. I can see the rows of beds separated by blue curtains, colleagues putting on and taking off gloves as they enter and leave each patient's section. Yep, I'm at work. No time to dwell on hot AF Zac.

Needing a distraction, I pull my phone to check for any missed calls or messages. It's the first time I've looked at it all day. I open my text message thread from Sarah—she's sent me five messages today.

**Sarah: I can't believe you're stuck in the hospital. The sun is out and the water is awesome today.**

She attached a photo of the beach. It looks inviting, however, keeping my job and eating is more appealing at the moment. Scrolling down, I read the next text.

**Sarah: It's hot out here today, and I don't *mean the temperature. Although, I may need some urgent medical attention as I'm about to suffer from heat stroke. You can suffer heat stroke from being surrounded by hot, and I mean fire hot, men, right?***

This one makes me laugh out loud a little. Picking my head up, I see that no one is paying me any attention. I scroll through the few photos she attached of the scenery—topless men of all colours and sizes. The only thought that comes to mind when I see these men is: *they don't hold a candle to Zac.*

I really need to get my mind off this guy. I mean, I can't even enjoy the pictures of topless, hot guys at the beach. I should be able to appreciate that view, even if I am living through Sarah. Giving up on trying to see anything else in the photos, I scroll to her next message.

. . .

**Sarah: As hot as the view is here, the view in our living room this morning was ten times better.**

She adds a winky face emoji. I could have gone without the reminder of just how unattainable Mr. GQ was. Choosing not to dwell on that message, I go to her last message, sent about thirty minutes ago.

**Sarah: I won't be home tonight. I'm picking up some cucumber.**

Picking up a cucumber is Sarah's not-so-subtle code that she's getting laid tonight. Having the townhouse to myself doesn't seem so bad. I could use the quiet. I won't make it home until at least midnight anyway, and that's if the trains are running on time. I send Sarah a quick text back. I should get back to the charts I was doing.

**Me: Enjoy, be safe and save the deets for brunch tomorrow.**

Knowing I probably won't hear from her until I see her at our regular Sunday brunch meet with Holly and Reilly, I put my phone away and look back at the charts I have to get done before I can leave in an hour.

I'm halfway through the pile of charts, with forty minutes left of my shift, when I see a cup landing on the desk in front of me. Dr. Mark Allen leans on the counter, smiling at me. "Thought you could use a pick me up. Skinny cap, right?"

Nope, not right, but how many times can you correct someone. "How did you know? Thank you, doctor. I appreciate it." Picking the cup up, I take a huge gulp. It may not be a vanilla latte, but coffee is coffee.

"You know you can call me Mark, right? You don't have to call me doctor all the time." Dr. Allen winks at me.

I can't find it in myself to even contemplate putting up with his flirting today. Dr. Allen is known as a serial dater around the ER, always looking for a new nurse to sink his teeth into. Well, this nurse is not on the menu—well, not on Dr. Allen's menu. Zac's menu, however, that's a menu I could handle being on.

I smile up at Dr. Allen and do my best to get us back into the professional territory. "I think I'd prefer to stick with doctor—we are in a workplace after all. Thanks for the coffee but I really need to get these charts done." I point at the pile of folders in front of me.

His smile drops before he says, "Sure thing, Alyssa, see you around." He turns and walks away, hopefully getting the clue that this nurse is most certainly off his menu.

After finishing my charts, I shower quickly before changing out of my scrubs. It's almost eleven fifteen as I make my way out of the building. Just as I'm about to walk out the door, Dr. Allen catches up to me, placing a hand on my arm.

"Do you need a ride home?" He looks hopeful.

I keep walking, making my way out the exit as I say, "*Umm*, no, it's okay. Thanks, I've got a ride." I lie. I'm planning on catching the train but I'm not about to tell him that. Attempting to change the topic, I thank him again for the coffee and then look around, searching for a way to get away from him without being outright rude.

That's when I spot him, Mr. GQ, leaning up against a black

Range Rover and wearing a suit, a freaking suit—dark blue with a white button-up shirt and no tie. The first few buttons on his shirt are undone, giving me just a glimpse of his chest. How is it he always looks this good? It shouldn't be legal for men to walk around looking like this. I mean, this is how accidents are caused, women stunned by the beauty and all that. It's just plain dangerous. Dangerously beautiful is what he is.

His eyes zone in on the spot of my arm where Dr. Allen still seems to have his hand. He looks up at my face before staring straight at Dr. Allen. GQ does not look happy. I'm stuck, literally stuck in place, stunned. He's here... I know he said he would be back to pick me up, but why on earth would he do that? Not for one second did I entertain the idea that he would actually be here when I finished work.

Zac must realise that I'm in a state of shock. He pushes off the car and stalks towards us, stopping in front of me, removing my gym bag off my shoulder and hiking it up onto his own. He holds his hand out and smirks at me. "Sunshine, your chariot awaits." He's waiting for me to slide my hand into his. I smile, taking the offering, momentarily shocked by the electric heat that comes with the contact. When I meet his eyes, I can see he felt it too.

It's clear he doesn't care to be introduced to Dr. Allen; he is totally ignoring the doctor's presence. I introduce them anyway, because I'm polite like that. "Zac, thanks for coming. This is Dr. Allen. Dr. Allen, Zac." I wave my free arm between the two, making the introduction quick.

Dr. Allen looks between our joined hands, and asks, "Zac, how do you know Alyssa?"

Before Zac can answer, I respond, "We're friends." Looking up at Zac, I can tell he doesn't look like he likes my response. He looks me up and down before giving his own, "Good friends." Zac then turns to me. "Are you ready to get out of here? The night is young, sunshine," he hints, raising his eyebrows suggestively. I laugh a little and nod my head. Zac leads me towards his car as I glance over my shoulder and give a brief goodbye to Dr. Allen; I do have to work with him.

Zac opens my door for me again. He either thinks I don't know how to open my own doors, or he's the last true gentlemen on this place called Earth. Once I'm sitting in the seat, I expect him to close my door, but he shocks me once again when he pulls the seat belt over me and buckles me in.

Smirking, he says, "Need to make sure you're securely in place." I'm assaulted with his mix of woodsy citrus scent that seems to be unique to him alone; his scent travels through my nose and straight to my core. I'm still wondering if it's normal to be so turned on from the way someone smells when Zac jumps into the driver's side.

He reaches over the back of my seat, pulling out a take-away bag from my favourite Thai restaurant. He looks at me a moment then, placing the bag on my lap, says, "I figured you probably haven't eaten properly today, so I picked you up something. It's chicken Pad Thai. There's a fork in the bag; you can eat while we drive."

I'm stunned speechless and left wondering if maybe he has some weird food fetish. "That's twice today you've brought me food. I don't know if you have some kind of weird food fetish or not, but right now I'm starving so I don't really care." Taking the take-away container out and pulling the lid off, I inhale the smell of the Thai dish.

"Thank you, this is my favourite Thai food," I add before digging in, not even caring if I'm making a mess of myself.

"I know it is." He smirks at me.

"Wait, how do you know this is my favourite? You don't even know me." I turn to look at him, secretly praying that he's not some secret, crazy, murdery stalker I didn't know I had.

He laughs at my obvious distress. "Relax, I swear I'm not a stalker. I sent Sarah a message before I picked you up and asked her what you would eat. She told me the restaurant and meal to order, so really all credit should be pointed at her."

He sent Sarah a message. This is what my brain focuses on from his response. "How do you know Sarah? And how do you have her number?" It comes out sounding much harsher than I intended, but something irrational happened when I heard: *I sent Sarah a message.* I got jealous—well, at least I think it's jealousy. I've never been jealous before so it's hard to tell.

Zac stops at a red light, and turns to look at me. I don't know what he sees on my face because he doesn't say anything for a good minute. Suddenly, he smiles, picks up my hand and kisses me on the inside of my wrist before resting our joined hands on his thigh. Well, okay then, if that hasn't put the green-eyed monster to bed a little, I don't know what would. I'm so focused on trying to breathe, and not show just how much that simple gesture has affected me, I startle a little when he talks again.

"Sunshine, you can put the claws away. I have Sarah's number, because I asked her for it this morning when you were in the shower." At this, I try to tug my hand away from him. It doesn't work; he just holds on tighter. "I asked her for her number, because I knew your phone was dead this morning and I didn't know if you would have had the chance to charge it while at work. I didn't have your number, and I wanted a way of reaching you, so I asked for Sarah's."

I can still feel the green-eyed monster wanting to come out a little. "Okay, well, thank you for the ride and the meal," I lamely get out. I use my free hand to pick the fork back up and start eating. I let out a little moan around a mouthful of noodles, and the hand that Zac is holding gets a little tighter. I look over at him to see his jaw tensed and his eyes hyper-focused on the road.

I have no idea whatever storm has rolled up within him again. I really can't keep up with this man's intense moods. I try for some light conversation.

"So, no Batmobile tonight?" I question.

He looks over and smiles slightly, his eyes lighting

up. "No, it's at the detailers; someone left muffin crumbs all through it."

I audibly gasp and drop my fork. The fork drops to the floor of the car with a pile of noodles on it. "Oh my gosh, I'm so sorry. I can pay for the detailing of the Batmobile and this one, but to be fair, I did prewarn you I'm a messy eater. Oh god, who's car is this? Now I've messed someone else's car too. That has to be a record, two cars ruined in one day."

He's full on laughing by the time I finish my little freak-out. I turn and glare at him. "It's not funny. That Batmobile obviously isn't a cheap car and I ruined it."

"Sunshine, I was joking about the muffin crumbs.

It's fine. You didn't ruin any car, and this car is one of mine, so don't worry about putting noodles everywhere." He raises my hand back to his lips and kisses the inside of my wrist again. It's confusing how much this move both calms me and makes me hot and bothered at the same time.

Placing the lid on the Pad Thai and leaning down to pick up the fork, I put it all back in the plastic bag. Zac looks over; he's not impressed. "You need to eat, Alyssa, so eat."

"I'll eat it when I get home. Besides, it's not easy eating noodles in a car." I place the bag on the floor beside my feet and lean my head back on the headrest. "This is a really nice car. I think I like this one better than the Batmobile." I close my eyes a little. I'm so damn tired.

"You look exhausted. I knew I should have made you take the day off today."

My eyes pop back open, glaring at him. "I'm sorry if I look exhausted and am not up to your level of expectations of how one should look, but I just finished a twelve-hour shift in the emergency department. I didn't even get a proper lunch break. And just so you know, there is nothing you could have done to make me take a day off. You don't own me, and I certainly don't answer to anyone!"

Zac looks over and smirks at me. Dammit, I'm mad at him, and it's really hard to stay mad at him when he looks at me like that. "Yet," he mumbles under his breath, almost like he's telling himself something. "Sunshine, I wouldn't have to *force* you to take a day off. I can be very persuasive when I want something, and sunshine, I will stop at nothing to get what I want, even if that's you taking a day off to rest when you need it." I'm gobsmacked, my mouth hanging open. I don't even know how to respond to that and before I can even contemplate a half intelligent thought, he adds, "And as for how you look, you could wear a hessian sack and still be the most beautiful woman I've ever seen."

I just stare at him. Who is this man? And where the hell has he been all my life? I pinch my leg. Yep, definitely awake, and *this* Zac far surpasses anything I could dream up. I'm racking my brain for something to say to him when his phone rings over the speaker system in the car.

The screen reads: Bray calling. Zac looks over at me and says, "Sorry," before answering the call. "Be careful with your words." That's how he answers the call. As I'm contemplating why not a simple hello, a rough voice fills the car.

"Zac, man, you gotta get to the club, NOW!" The guy on the other end sounds like he's yelling.

"Bray, for the love of god, tell me you haven't burnt down my club in the hour I've been gone?" Zac demands.

"No, it's Ella."

Zac's entire body tenses. Who is Ella? Whoever she is, she must be important to both men, as I can see the worry overtake Zac's features and can hear it in the man's voice on the phone.

"What happened? Where is she, Bray?" Zac's voice is strained as he grits out the demands.

"Bro, you have to fucking get back here now. She was in the VIP section, went to go to the bathroom and the drummer from the band fucking attacked her—the about to be dead fucking drummer."

Zac's body vibrates as he listens. He spins the car around going faster than what is probably safe. I stay quiet, not sure what's going on. Whatever it is, whoever this Ella is, he cares about her.

"I'm ten minutes away, Bray. What do you mean he fucking attacked her? What the fuck did he do?"

I can vaguely hear the sounds of someone crying in the background when Bray speaks again. "She's okay, Zac. I'm with her in your office. Dean has the fucker downstairs; he's only keeping him on ice until you get here. I had to make him promise not to go lethal until you got here, man. I've never seen Dean like this. He's a caged lion at the moment, bro. But Ella, she's banged up, cut on her head, black eye. From what I can see, bruises on her arms and legs. She's not speaking, won't talk to anyone. When Dean found her in the bathroom, she clung to him. She wouldn't even let me fucking take her from him and carry her up here. I don't know what to do, Zac. Tell me I can finish this. I don't think I can wait for you to get here."

"Bray, stay with Ella. Don't let anyone in the office who isn't Dean until I get there. I'm going as fast as I can. Just stay with Ella, okay?" Zac sounds like he's trying to calm Bray with his words—whatever he says must do something because Bray agrees.

"Okay, I'll wait for you to get here, but then the gloves come off. I'm going to fucking kill him." With that, the phone disconnects.

Zac turns to look at me; he looks torn. "I'm sorry, sunshine. I have to make a detour. I promise I will get you home. I can have one of the security guys drive you once we get to the club if you want."

I don't really know what's going on back at the club, but I know right now, Zac is struggling and I don't want to add any stress to his night. "Whatever you want me to do, I'll do. If you want me to wait for you, I'll wait. If you'd rather I go home and let you deal with whatever it is you have to do, I'll do that too," I say, giving his hand a squeeze.

"What I want right now is to get my hands on the fucker who thought he could touch my baby sister!" Looking across at me as we pull into a carpark, he says, "I want you to stay. Wait for me. I want to take you home tonight. I *will* take you home tonight."

# Six

## ZAC

PULLING into the carpark at the club, I look over at Alyssa and take a deep breath, attempting to calm my rage. I should get someone to take her home. I shouldn't want her to be here when I may just kill someone in the underground cellar of my club. I shouldn't want her to see the other side of me, the side that will hunt and kill to protect those close to me.

I know I should let her go now, try to forget her and not bring her down with my level of shit. I know I should, but I don't. I don't want to let her go. I don't care if I have to spend the next month grovelling and apologising for whatever she is about to witness tonight, because right now, I need her. I can't explain it or put a label on what it is, but having her next to me feels right.

"Wait there," I instruct her as I jump out of the car and go around to her side. Opening her door, I reach in for her hand to help her out. Although every bone in my body is screaming at me to run up to my office to make sure Ella is okay, I don't. I take another deep breath and silently count to ten in my head.

Gripping Alyssa's hand, I walk as calmly as I can muster. When I notice that Alyssa is struggling to keep up with my pace, I slow a little. We stop at the elevator; stabbing at the button over and over does not make it open any quicker. Alyssa gives my hand a squeeze and looks up at me with those grey-blue eyes of hers. The doors open and I pull her in. As soon as the doors close, my arms go around her. I hold her tight, probably too tight.

"I'm sorry for whatever you're about to see, for whatever I have to do tonight. Know that no matter how much I may want you here, how much I need you here, if at any time you want to leave and go home, you tell me and I will have someone take you."

She rests her head against my chest, wrapping her arms around me. She hugs me back but it's what she says that has me holding her tight and not wanting to let her go. "I want to be wherever you are, but I also don't want to be in the way. So, you need to tell me if I am."

Damn, I think I could be losing my mind. I can't ever recall wanting... no, *needing...* a woman as much as I need Alyssa right now. "Sunshine, you could never be in the way. You are right where you belong." As the doors open, I grab her hand and pull her along the hall to my office.

Nothing could have prepared me for the sight that greeted me as I walked into my office. Ella is curled up on the corner of the couch. She's rocking slightly, crying silent tears that I can see run down her cheeks. She's bleeding from a gash on her forehead, an enormous bruise is forming on her right eye, and her arms are covered in marks. My world is tumbling; the anger I thought I had controlled comes barrelling back full force.

Bray is pacing back and forward throughout the office. He stops as soon as he notices me. "Zac, thank god you're here. She won't let me touch her. She keeps asking for fucking Dean. Where the fuck is Dean?" He looks like he's about to lose it.

Alyssa squeezes my hand before walking slowly over to Ella. She takes a seat on the couch next to her, not touching her and speaking softly. "Ella, my name's Alyssa, but you can call me Lyssa—all my friends call me Lyssa. I'm a nurse. I can help you. Would you like me to help get you cleaned up a bit?"

Bray and I both watch in shock as Ella picks her head up and gives a slight nod. I let out a breath I didn't know I was holding before going over to Ella and crouching in front of her.

"Ella, sweetheart, I need to know..." Swallowing, I try again. "I need you to tell me what happened, please."

Ella looks at me. "Zac?" she questions like she doesn't believe it's actually me.

"Yeah, honey, it's me Zac. Can you tell me what happened?"

"I... I was so scared, Zac. I didn't know what to do. I screamed for help. I kicked, scratched and hit wherever I could, just like you told me to, but he was too big." Her sobs get louder. This is killing me. I can feel my body vibrate with rage.

Alyssa must sense something in me; she touches my shoulder. "Zac, I'm going to take her through there." She points to the bathroom. "I need you to get me a first aid kit. I can help her. The cut on her head is not bad; it looks it because head wounds bleed a lot. It doesn't look too deep." She turns to Ella. "Ella, honey, I'm going to take you to the shower and help you get cleaned." I watch as Alyssa grabs Ella's hand to help her up. Ella follows Alyssa blindly through to the bathroom attached to my office.

Bray watches them go through, then he looks at me. "I'm going downstairs. I can't stand this, Zac. I feel helpless. I should have been there. This shouldn't have happened to her. This won't happen again. I will make sure every asshole out there knows what will happen to them if they even think about touching her," he says, pointing towards the bathroom door.

"Give me five minutes. I'll get the first aid kit for Alyssa and meet you down there. Don't finish without me," I demand. I need this... I need this fucker's blood on my hands. I need to watch the life drain out of him. I dig a first aid kit out of the cabinet and knock on the bathroom door.

Alyssa cracks the door open slightly, not enough for me to see in. "Is she okay?" I ask, almost pleading that she is.

"She will be." She takes the first aid kit before stopping me from entering. "Zac, I'll take care of her. You can trust me to do this for you, for her."

Nodding in agreement, I let out a breath. "I know... I just need to know how bad it is."

She reads between the lines and nods her head. "I'll find out."

"Thank you. I'm going downstairs for a bit. I won't be too long, but I'm locking the office door. Don't open it for anyone. Everyone that needs to be in here has a key, okay?"

She gives a small smile and says, "Okay, I'll be here when you get back." I place a kiss on her forehead. Turning, I walk out the door, looking forward to getting all my rage out on this fucker.

Walking into the basement, I can hear the tell-tale signs of skin meeting skin. I can hear Bray telling the fucker the mistakes he made tonight.

"You think you can come into our club, touch our sister and get away with it? You just signed your own death certificate, fucker."

I walk through the room they're in and see they have the drummer hooked up to chains; his face is already unrecognisable. Turning to Dean, who is pacing the back wall, I ask, "Did you have to start without me? You know how much I enjoy the start of the show."

Dean looks up but doesn't greet me with his usual devious smirk—the one he usually saves for these situations. He's hanging on by a thread.

"Zac, just let me take him out. I need to take him out." I look at him, really look at him, for a moment.

"This isn't just some random fucker who wronged me, Dean. He thought he could touch my sister, my fucking sister!" I yell. Dean bends his head, running his hands through his hair. He lets out an anguished grunt and continues pacing the back wall.

Looking back over, I see Bray hasn't given up on this fucker. I walk over and tap him out. He looks at me, nods his head, and goes to stand in front of the door. Leaning his back against the door, he focuses his eyes on the drummer as he says, "You think Dean was bad? You think I was hard on you? Well, now you're about to wish for death to greet you." Bray laughs a little.

I take my time rolling the sleeves of my shirt up. I look the drummer in the face, although I suspect he's having a hard time seeing me, seeing as though both of his eyes are pretty much swollen shut already. I stand in front of him.

"So, I hear you thought you could put your grubby little hands on my little sister. You know you shouldn't touch things that don't belong to you, don't you? Especially when those things don't want to be touched," I say, oddly calm.

Now that I'm in this space, I can feel my rage simmering. I'm always calm once I get into this zone. It's like a drug—a rush of endorphins runs through me. What can I say? I fucking enjoy teaching fuckers like this a lesson. It's sick... I'm sure I'm a perfect candidate for the nuthouse, but I don't fucking care. What I care about right now is that this fucker put his hands on my sister, hurt my sister.

I look over to Dean. "Pass me the sheers," I say, holding my hand out.

Dean picks up the sheers and walks over to hand them to me, giving me his trademark devious smirk. He knows what I have planned and is one hundred percent on board with it. I make a show of opening and closing the sheers a few times before lining them up with a pinkie.

The fucker must realise what I have planned because he attempts to back up and move his hand away. He can't though; those chains have no give in them.

As I cut through his pinkie, I say, "This little piggy..." and revel in the scream he lets out. I continue until all of his fingers have gone, and the drummer is about to lose consciousness.

Grabbing him by the throat, I say, "I would love to stay and play, but I have more pressing matters." I don't let go until I know he's no longer breathing. Turning to Dean and Bray, I growl, "Deal with this. I need to get back upstairs to Ella."

They don't say anything, knowing better than to question me right now. I walk out of the room, feeling only slightly better than when I walked in.

I stop at a bathroom to get cleaned up a bit. Looking at my reflection, I can see blood splattered over my white dress shirt, up my arms and even on my face. I strip the shirt off and scrub my arms and face the best I can in a fucking sink with hand soap. Deciding it's an improvement, I make my way up to my office.

I find Ella curled up on the couch, asleep. She looks better, her face cleaned and not covered in blood; some butterfly stitches have been placed along the cut on her forehead. Alyssa is sitting on the chair opposite Ella, looking down at her phone. She looks up and turns her head towards me, gasping a little when she sees me. She looks back to Ella before standing and walking over to me. She doesn't say anything as she grabs my hand and leads me into the bathroom.

Alyssa slightly closes the door but leaves it ajar enough so she can still see into the office. She's quiet as she turns the water on in the shower, testing its warmth. Once she seems satisfied, she turns to me. "I'm not going to ask, and you don't have to say anything. What you do need to do is shower, get cleaned. Ella does not need to see you like this."

I'm speechless. How have I stumbled across what is the absolute most perfect woman? I must have done something right in my life, because Alyssa seems like a gift—one I will gladly accept without ever giving back. I take too long staring at her in amazement because she reaches for my belt, undoing it before undoing my pants and letting them drop.

Just as I'm about to tell her I can do this myself, that I'm okay, she lowers herself to the ground to untie my shoes, slipping one off at a time. Seeing her on her knees before me is a sight I want to burn into my memory—one I can recall over and over again. Once my shoes, socks and pants are removed, she stands back up, looking at me. She smiles, like she knows what I'm thinking. And judging by the erection currently residing in my boxers, I'm sure she knows just what seeing her down there did to me.

"Do you need help with the rest?" she asks, pointing to my boxers.

"More than you know right now," I say as I pull my boxers down myself and step into the shower. I expect her to walk out and leave me to it. She doesn't; she hikes herself up onto the basin and sits there watching me shower. Her sitting there, openly ogling me and not even trying to hide the fact that she's watching… let's just say it's not helping the hard situation I have going on.

As I'm washing my hair out, she says, "You know, I see naked bodies all the time. It's part of the job, but I can't say I've ever seen one as spectacularly built as yours." I think I actually fucking blush a little at her compliment.

"You've never looked in the mirror then," I reply, to which she scoffs. I will have to work on her self- esteem at a later time; right now, I'm tired. I need to get Ella home and I need to get into bed, preferably with Alyssa next to me.

Stepping out of the shower, Alyssa holds a towel out to me. "Thanks," I get out gruffly as I make quick work of drying myself so I can wrap the towel around my waist.

"I would say you're welcome, but really, the pleasure's been all mine," she says, blushing a little.

I step up closer to her, grabbing her knees so I can open her legs and step between them. "Trust me, sunshine, I plan to give you the kind of pleasure you haven't even dreamt about yet, over and over again. But right now, I'm going to do something completely selfish, something that is going to give me an unbelievable amount of pleasure." I tuck a strand of hair behind her ear and twirl the end around my finger.

"What's that?" She's breathless. It's good to know I have the same effect on her that she's having on me.

"This." I lean in and kiss her lips, softly at first, seeking, giving her plenty of time to pull back. When she doesn't pull back, that's all the signal I need to go full steam ahead. Grabbing the back of her head, I tilt it to just the right angle before using my tongue, seeking entrance into the haven that is her mouth. Alyssa doesn't disappoint; she opens for me and greedily matches me stroke for stroke. I'm so lost in this kiss… I could kiss her forever and not get enough of this mouth.

Alyssa pulls back. I outright groan in disappointment. "As much as I would love to sit here and do this all night, I think you should get your sister home. She's had a rough night."

Shit, she's right. I can't believe I was so caught up in all that is Alyssa that I briefly forgot why we were even in my office in the first place. "You're right. I need to take her home, but I'm also taking you home with me, with us. Let me get changed and we can head out."

I reach into the small wardrobe, where I keep spare sets of clothes, and pull out a pair of jeans and a t-shirt. Turning, I see Alyssa hasn't moved. She's chewing on her bottom lip, lost in her own thoughts.

"Don't overthink it, Alyssa. I'm taking you home to sleep. Nothing will happen that you don't want to happen. But I really fucking want you in my bed tonight, please." Well shit, that's a first for me. I've never taken a woman home to my actual apartment before, and I've never wanted to sleep next to any woman all fucking night, let alone practically begged one to sleep in my bed.

"I get the feeling that you don't say please often," she says, looking straight into my eyes. "Okay, I'll come home with you, but just to sleep and only because I'm really freaking tired." I feel like I just won the lottery.

"Thank you."

Just before I'm about to walk out of the bathroom, I stop, turn back around to Alyssa and ask the one question that's been nagging at me ever since Bray called me back to the club.

"How... Did..." Taking a breath, I try again. "How hurt is she?" I ask, pointing my thumb back in the direction of the office.

Alyssa grabs my hand and squeezes. "She wasn't raped. He didn't get the chance to get that far before some guy named Dean found her."

"Thank fuck for that. Remind me to give Dean a fucking pay raise." I lead her out to the office.

Crouching down in front of Ella, I reach out and stroke her hair. She doesn't flinch at my touch and I take this as a good sign. "Ella, sweetheart, we're going to take you home."

She nods and lets me pick her up. With that, I walk out of my office with the two most important women in my life.

Stepping out of the elevator into my apartment, I've got Ella in my arms and Alyssa right beside me. I'm greeted by a very antsy Dean and Bray waiting in my living room. Dean is up and moving—probably the quickest I've ever seen the man move.

"Here, let me take her to her room." Dean holds his hands out to take Ella. I don't move for a moment, shocked by my friend's actions. I'm about to say that I'll do it myself when I look over to Bray, who subtly shakes his head no at me. I relent and hand Ella over to Dean; he doesn't say anything as he walks down the hall to her room.

Looking over at Bray, I ask, "Do I even want to know?" I gesture down the hall to where Dean just disappeared into Ella's bedroom.

"No, you really don't, not tonight anyway." Bray stands up from the lounge he was sprawled across and walks towards me. Knowing he probably has some smart-ass shit to say about the fact that I've got a woman here, I attempt to escape his shit.

Grabbing Alyssa's hand, I say, "I'll catch you tomorrow. I'm going to bed." I walk towards the hall, pulling Alyssa behind me.

Bray moves lightning quick, like the fighter he is. I don't even see him move before he's standing in front of me. He holds a hand out for Alyssa. "Since my brother has the manners of a goat, I'll do the introductions myself. I'm Bray, obviously the good-looking brother." Alyssa smiles and takes his hand. I'm quick to pull her hand out of Bray's grasp and get a raised eyebrow from him in return.

Alyssa looks up at me before turning to Bray. "I'm Alyssa. It's nice to meet you. We will have to agree to disagree on who's the more handsome brother though."

Bray laughs. "I think I like you, Alyssa, if he..." He points a finger at my chest. "...messes up, you know where to find me." The bastard smirks at her.

I don't give Alyssa a chance to respond. I shoulder barge past Bray and lead her towards my bedroom, calling behind me, "Don't be a dick. This one's sticking."

He laughs and then I hear the front door open and close. Closing my bedroom door behind me, I walk over to the dresser and pull out a t-shirt for Alyssa to sleep in, before holding it out to her. "You can sleep in this. The bathroom's through that door." I point to the en suite.

"Thank you," she says ever so quietly as she takes the shirt, shutting the en suite door behind her.

I make quick work of stripping down to my boxers and climb into bed, pulling the covers back on her side and waiting for her to return while mentally repeating to myself: *Don't stuff this up. Don't stuff this up.*

All thoughts come to a halt when Alyssa walks out of the bathroom wearing my shirt. Holy shit, I did not think this through. I thought I could keep my hands to myself, but fuck... After seeing her look like this, it's taking every ounce of my self-control to not sink my cock into her and claim her, mark her as mine.

I'm lost for words—whatever game I thought I had just

went out the window. I'm sitting here staring at her as she makes her way to the bed. She looks a little unsure, and I know I need to put her at ease, but how?

"Do I have something on my face?" she asks. All I can do is shake my head no. "Then why are you looking at me like that?"

I don't know how honest to be. I don't want to scare her away, but I also want to let her know exactly what my intentions are. I'm momentarily speechless.

"I don't think I've ever seen anyone look as fucking hot as you do right now, wearing my shirt. Fuck, I can't even think straight right now, sunshine. All I can think about is getting a taste of you, how you're going to feel when I finally sink my cock into your pussy and have your walls tighten around me." I shake my head, attempting to clear those thoughts.

Alyssa is blushing hard and is frozen at the side of the bed. Maybe I was a little too honest. "Don't worry, sunshine. I gave you my word; it's not happening tonight. All I'm going to do tonight is hold on to you, so I know you'll still be here when I wake in the morning."

She nods. "Okay, but since we're being honest and all here, I've seen what you're packing and if you think that..." She waves her hand in the general direction of my cock. "...is ever going to fit into me, you are surely mistaken."

I laugh a little, tugging her closer to me. Wrapping my arm around her body, I hold her tight. Kissing her forehead, I speak into her ear, "Baby, it'll fit. You might not know this yet, but you were made for me." I settle onto the pillow behind her, breathing in her scent. *Huh*, I never thought I would be one for spooning and cuddling. Right now, I can't think of a better feeling than how it feels to hold her close to me.

"I can hear you thinking, sunshine. Go to sleep. There is always tomorrow," I tell her as she squirms around a little more before settling into me, into my arms.

"Goodnight, Zac. I really hope we always have a tomorrow," she whispers.

Her words have slayed me. I can't even respond, so I just hold her, and that's how I fall asleep, having the best fucking sleep I've ever had.

*Seven*

❧

ALYSSA

"**A**RGH," I groan and slap my hand out to reach the buzzing sound that's coming from next to my head somewhere. "Shut up," I say, slapping aimlessly.

A mix of a moan and a laugh comes from behind me and I freeze, my body tensing as I abruptly become aware of the body that's right up against my back, the heavy arm draped over my waist. I breathe in through my nose and inhale that scent, that woodsy and citrus mixture —the scent I know belongs to Zac. With this knowledge, my body relaxes and I sink back into his embrace.

"I'm taking it you're not a morning person, sunshine?" His deep voice vibrates behind me.

The buzzing next to my head starts up and I groan again, turning over and burying my face into his chest. "Make it stop," I plead as I snuggle into his chest, and what a chest it is. If I wasn't trying to fall back asleep, I would have the energy to give this chest the attention it so deserves. It's smooth, wide, solid and smells of him. I inhale deep, not even caring if he can tell I'm sniffing him.

I feel his arm reach across me before he settles back down.

"That buzzing you're so intent on stopping is your phone. I don't think it's going to stop until you answer it." He kisses the top of my head. I've never had anyone kiss the top of my head before. I've seen it in movies, read about it in books a lot, but never experienced it, until now. The simple act brings out a feeling of being cherished, a feeling I'm coming to really, really like having.

"Just turn it off. I'm sleeping. Can't they tell I'm sleeping?" I mumble.

Zac laughs and the damn phone starts up again; he's holding it in his hand. "It's Sarah," he says. "Do you want me to answer it for you?"

Peeking my head up with one eye open, I grab the phone and hit the power button. Handing it back to him, I proudly proclaim, "That's how you answer a phone while you're sleeping." With that, I snuggle back into his chest; his arms wrap around me tight as he pulls me closer.

"For future reference, sunshine, if you ever turn your phone off when I'm calling, I will show up on your doorstep, no matter what time it is."

Shrugging, I look up at him. "All I heard just then was: sunshine, if you ever want to see me in person and not just have a phone convo, switch your phone and I'll be there." I give the most serene smile I can muster this early in the morning. "I'm okay with that."

Zac smiles and leans down. He kisses my forehead, then the tip of my nose, before landing on my lips. His kisses start off soft. I tilt my head up, seeking more of him. Raising my arm, I reach up to his neck and pull him closer. He doesn't let me have control for long. He takes over, swiping his tongue out and seeking entrance. I don't deny him. I moan into his kiss. I need more. Trailing my hand down his chest, I feel the ridges and grooves of well-defined muscles. This has me moaning into his mouth even louder. Just then, a horrible high-pitched ringtone blares. I jump at the sound, pulling away from him.

Zac has an indescribable look on his face. I can't tell what he's thinking, but I don't have to guess for long before he offers his thoughts. "Damn, sunshine, I could get used to waking up like this." He smirks.

"Me too, but definitely without the blaring noise coming from what must be your phone, because I did the responsible thing and turned mine off." I'm sure I sound a little pissed off, because frankly, that phone interrupted a really freaking good moment for me.

Rolling over, Zac picks up his phone, which starts blaring again. His face scrunches up as he looks at the screen. "It's Sarah. Maybe you should answer it. She kinda scares me a little —plus, she's not going to stop calling."

Taking the phone from him to press the green answer button, I give him the best death glare I can, while he just shakes his head and laughs. I need to work on that glare.

"Sarah, why are you calling my—" I stop mid- sentence, avoiding a colossal clingy girl mistake as I was about to say *boyfriend* without even thinking twice about it. Instead, I correct myself. "Zac. Why are you calling Zac's phone at some ungodly hour in the morning? Are you dead or close to being dead?" Sarah knows I'm not keen on being woken up, so she deserves my wrath right now.

"Soooo, he's your Zac now, is he?" Her singsong voice carries through the phone. "Do tell. When in the last twenty-four hours did this development happen?" She's laughing now.

"Shut up. You're obviously not dead or close to being dead, so I'm hanging up now. Have a nice life." I wait, rather than hanging up, because I know she will only call back if I do.

"Wait, I called your Zac," she says with fake sweetness to her voice, "because you switched your phone off, and now I know why you're ignoring me. But you need to get up. I don't care if you're in the middle of purchasing a cucumber, get up and get dressed. We have brunch in forty-five minutes and if you're not there, I will enjoy telling the twins all about your Zac without you."

I look up at Zac, who can hear every damn word Sarah has said. She has a habit of yelling down the bloody phone. He looks puzzled and mouths the word *cucumber?* in question to me. I just shake my head no, in a kind of *don't ask* motion.

"Okay, don't do anything drastic, and just so you know, the cucumber is still at the store. I'll meet you there." Hanging up, I hand the phone back to Zac.

Turning my phone back on, I wait for it to start up. "Shit, I have to go. Sorry, but it's Sunday and Sunday is girls' brunch day. I have to get to the café. Wait, where exactly are we? I need to figure out how to get to the station." I'm rushing around the room, looking for my things, before remembering I left my clothes in the bathroom. I head in there and don't bother shutting the door before I strip Zac's shirt off and put my jeans back on. As I'm doing up my bra, I look up into the mirror. I can see Zac's reflection. He's still sitting on the bed and staring straight at me—well, at my breasts that is.

He slowly lifts his head and meets my gaze in the mirror. Clearing his throat, he says, "I'll drive you. You're not catching the damn train." He gets out of bed and saunters (yes, saunters) into the bathroom. Wrapping his arms around my waist, he whispers into my ear, "Although if you'd rather stay here in bed, I can make sure Sarah won't be able to find you."

I place my hands on his chest as I turn into him—on his rock-hard chest that has me running those same hands up and down the plains of his abs, exploring all the dips and curves that I just want to run my tongue across. "As much as I want to stay here and jump back into bed with you..." I pause for a second when he moans. "I'm not the kind of friend that bails on plans, especially the longstanding traditional plans."

Looking down at my breasts, he moans again. "Okay, but you need to cover these beauties up before I devour them. Once I start, there will be no stopping."

He steps back and walks out of the bathroom. Watching him walk away from me in nothing but his black boxer briefs is a sight I won't be forgetting in a hurry. I stare at his tanned, sculpted back with muscles so defined that anyone would think this man was carved from stone. Then there's his ass. Once my eyes make their way to that perfection, I finally understand the saying *an ass you can bounce a quarter off,* because damn... I'm still staring at his retreating form when he walks into what must be a wardrobe. He looks back over his shoulder at me and smirks. The bastard knew I was checking him out. I feel the blush creep up from my neck.

After putting my top back on, I dig a hairbrush out of my bag and go to work on attacking the bird's nest that has taken over my hair. Zac stands at the doorway and I think I have drool dripping down my open mouth. Wearing a pair of faded denim jeans, a black long sleeve Henley, and black boots, he is sex on a stick.

"How is it you spend two minutes getting dressed and look like the GQ cover model for January through to December?" I ask, not expecting an answer as I go back to detangling the bird's nest.

"Good to know you like what you see." He smirks. His eyes follow my body down my back, stopping on my ass. "Are you sure this brunch has to be a girls only thing?"

I nod my head yes. "You'd be bored to death. All we do is eat, drink mimosas and talk about boys, clothes and shoes."

He narrows his eyes at me. "You talk about boys? And just how many boys will you have to discuss at this week's brunch, sunshine?" I look at his clenched face in the mirror. Is he jealous? It's ludicrous if he is.

Deciding to play on this a bit, I scrunch my face up. "I don't have any boys to talk about." I pause, thinking for a moment. "Oh wait, there was that one guy. Oh, and then that lawyer I met on the train a few days ago." I continue to put on my thinking face.

Zac's jaw tightens even more. "I think we need to get something straight, sunshine. You haven't known me for long so I'll give you that concession. But one thing you need to know is I don't share." He annunciates the three words *I don't share* slowly.

I blink up at him. "Okay, well, I won't ask to have a sip of your coffee this morning." I know full well that that's not what he was referring to.

"Maybe I wasn't very clear, so let me try again." Turning me around so I'm facing him, Zac tilts my chin until our eyes meet before he says, "I will share anything with you; what I will not share, under any circumstances, is you." His stare is so intense, sincere. I think he actually means what he is saying—well, he has me believing, anyway.

"Okay, look, I don't know what this is," I say, pointing between the both of us, "but if you won't share, then I won't be sharing either. So, wherever your little black book of women is, Mr. GQ..." I turn my voice sugary sweet before adding, "...do us both a favour and lose it now, otherwise you might just have more bodies to bury."

"Where the hell have you been all my life, sunshine? You might not know what this is, me and you, and that's okay, because I know. This is us always having a tomorrow, together." He kisses my lips ever so lightly before stepping back. "Finish getting ready. I'm going to check on Ella before we head out."

Zac pulls up into a carpark out front of the café. I go to open the door and he grabs my hand. "Wait here," he says before jumping out and walking around the front of the car. He opens my door, but before he lets me out, he says, "You should always wait for me to open your door, sunshine."

Does he think we're living in the 1930s? "Zac, that's sweet, it really is, but I know how to open doors and I don't need anyone to do things for me. I've been looking after myself since I was five years old, even opening my own doors."

His face tenses up as he holds his hand out for me. Once my hand is in his, he helps me out. "We will come back to that statement when we have more time."

It doesn't register with me that Zac is still holding my hand and walking me into the café until I see the table with Sarah, Holly, and Reilly, all of whom have bugged out eyes pointed towards me and Zac. Stopping, I tug on Zac's hand to pull him back, so he turns and looks at me.

"Zac, you can't crash girls' brunch. I've seen you naked and you're definitely missing the parts that make you a girl. Also, I'm certain you are not gay, although you sure are pretty enough to pull that off if you wanted to."

Zac laughs. "I assure you I'm not gay, and if you want me to, I'm more than happy to prove it to you anywhere, anytime. I don't plan on staying. I just wanted to walk you to your table to make sure you got there. I'll be back to pick you up though. I programmed my number in your phone. Make sure you call me when you're ready to leave, please."

Well, that does it... I think I will do anything he wants when he adds that *please* on the end of a request. "I'll call you. I prom-ise. Thank you." He kisses me like no one is watching, and to be honest, I get so lost the moment those lips of his meet mine, I couldn't even tell you where we were at that very moment. My only care when he's kissing me is how I can keep him kissing me longer.

Before I know it, Zac pulls away from the kiss. "See you soon, sunshine. Have fun with your friends." He gives me that panty-melting smirk and walks out. I'm left standing in the middle of the café, watching him and trying to figure out why I feel like a part of me went with him.

If I thought my friends would be kind enough not to bring up the fact that they just watched what was one of the best kisses I've received in my life, I was sorely mistaken. The moment I sat down, I put myself in the firing line. All three of my best friends are speaking, mostly at me rather than to me, at the same time.

I have answered none of their questions, choosing to sit here quietly, observing the three of them and basking in the feeling of Zac still lingering on my kiss- swollen lips.

Looking at Holly and Reilly, most people wouldn't be able to tell them apart; only those who are close enough to know the very subtle differences know which twin is which. They share the same tall, thin stature, long, wavy, fiery-red hair, pale skin and green eyes.

The differences: Holly has a tiny freckle under her left eye; she also almost always wears her hair up, and has a more reserved personality than Reilly. Holly is a kindergarten teacher. She loves kids, she loves love, and she dreams of her fairytale happily ever after.

Reilly is the more outgoing twin, absolutely no filter and no awareness of social appropriateness. She has confidence busting out of her in spades. Although, if I looked like that, I probably would too. She flaunts her body and would tell you it's her best asset, but it's not. Reilly doesn't like to show her pure, genuine and loyal heart, but she has one of the kindest hearts I know. She will go above and beyond for the people she cares about.

She's also hopeless when it comes to men. She falls in love quicker than a one-click purchase on Amazon. However, as soon as she starts to feel something for someone, she leaves them in the dust, never staying with one person long enough to get too attached.

This thought stops me in my tracks. Is that what I've done with Zac? Not that I'm in love with him… I don't think so. I mean, how can you love someone you only met the day before? I'm not a believer in insta-love; I don't subscribe to the whole idea everyone has a soul mate and when you meet them, you'll just know. But there is something different with Zac. He brings out feelings I've never felt before. Maybe it's insta-lust—that definitely has to be it.

"I'm in lust with Zac." I realise I said that out loud too late; it does however stop the three of them. They're all staring at me with their mouths hanging open. "What? I said lust, not love. Close your mouths before the flies get in."

Reilly is the first to speak. "Well, *duh*. You'd have to be blind to not be in lust with that fine piece of ass. I mean, damn, girl, I'm gonna need deets: how big, length, and thickness." She stops talking once she notices the fact that I'm not smiling. I am, however, about to jump over the table and claw her eyes out. I shake my head to clear the jealous rage that seems to take over my body and soul when she started describing Zac as another random guy we'd see in passing.

"I'm not giving you deets, and you should keep your thoughts about him to yourself from now on—for your own wellbeing, that is."

I can see the shocked faces of my friends. I've never spoken to any of them like this. I don't recall ever being this mad at any of them. I know I'm being irrational, but I just can't seem to help myself.

Reilly looks at me and smiles. "I think you've finally been hit with the love bug, Lyssa. I've been waiting for this day to happen. We need to celebrate. I'll get the first round of mimosas and then you can tell us all about this Zac that we," she says, pointing to the three of them, "apparently may not appreciate in any way, form, or manner that's not pure and platonic." She gets up and heads to the counter.

"I'm not in love with him!" I declare to Holly and Sarah, both of whom just look at me with disbelieving grins.

"Of course, you're not in love. Despite what my sister thinks, it takes longer than twenty-four hours or a night of good sex to fall in love." Holly doesn't sound like she believes her own words.

"You both know Reilly can't tell the difference between being in love with someone and being in love with someone's cucumber. You," Sarah says, pointing at me to drive her point further, "are most definitely in love with the man. I can tell."

"I like him, maybe even like him a lot, but it's not love!" I defend myself.

Reilly comes back with eight mimosa glasses. "You know there are only four of us, right? And it's only like 10:30 a.m. not p.m." I raise my eyebrow at her.

"Well, we are celebrating the fact that you're in love, sorry lust, for the very first time. This is only the first round." She hands everyone a drink and then, holding hers up, she toasts, "To being in lust and not love!"

Taking a sip, I savour the flavours that hit my tongue. Just as I put my glass on the table, my phone plays the chorus of "Stuck Like Glue." I just stare at it. It stops and then plays the chorus again and the girls all start laughing and singing along at a *not so quiet* level. I can feel the redness creep up my neck as I slowly die of embarrassment.

Before my phone makes any more noise, I pick up. There are two missed messages from *my own GQ*. Instantly, I know who it is. I can't believe he programmed his name into my phone as *my own GQ* and personalised the tone. I open the messages to read what could be so important that it couldn't possibly wait a few hours. I mean, he hasn't been gone that long.

**My own GQ: Sunshine, don't forget to order food to go with those mimosas. You cannot survive on liquid diets.**

Holy shit, looking up, I look around the café. Is he hiding out and spying on me somewhere? I can't see him anywhere, but how else would he know I'm drinking mimosas? Looking down, I read the next message.

**My own GQ: I've stopped in at the club. Got shit to do, but I will be available to pick you up whenever you're ready. Please eat something. You didn't get to eat dinner last night. xx**

Okay, so he's not here. He's at the club, but boy is the man obsessed with food. I message him back.

• • •

**Me: "Stuck Like Glue," really? Also, I'm 90% sure now that you have a food fetish. Is it your desire to feed me, sir?**

I don't get the chance to silence my phone before it plays the song again. Dammit, I'm going to have to remember to change his tone back to a normal *beep beep* for a message, like a normal person would have. I open his message. If I thought I was red with embarrassment before, reading his message has me ten times redder, and wet in places I won't admit to in public.

**My own GQ: Yes, it is my desire to feed you, but what I desire to put into your mouth is not food. And now you have me walking around the club with a fucking hard-on. Did I mention I have employees here? I'm sure they don't need to see their boss with a hard-on!**

"Whatever the guy just sent you is good. Let me see!" Reilly holds her hand out.

"Not a freaking chance in hell," I tell her. "And the guy has a name—it's Zac."

"So, now's a good time to tell us all about this Zac of yours, Lyssa. You've kept us waiting long enough." Holly rests her chin on her hands, like she's getting ready to hear a juicy story.

I tell them all about how I went on the blind date, how I got roofied and how Zac looked after me. Sarah then fills in. "He drove her home the next morning, and waited for her in our living room while she had a shower, just so he could drive her to work. The boy sure is smitten." She smiles.

"One, he's not a boy. I can assure you he is all man. Two, he was just helping me get to work on time, considering I was so late. Not smitten, just a kind person."

"So, tell us, how did it go from him dropping you at the hospital to him dropping you here and playing hockey with your tonsils?" Reilly asks.

I decide not to tell them about going to the club to help his sister. Or making Zac shower when he came back into the office covered in blood—the only thought I had on *that* was: *thank god it wasn't his blood.*

Thinking logically, I know I should care about whatever it is he did that had him coming back covered in blood. But for the life of me, I can't bother to care. All I care about is that he's okay, and his sister can sleep at night knowing whoever attacked her did not get away with it, whatever happened to him.

Instead, I tell the girls how Zac was waiting for me outside the hospital when I finished my shift and saved me from the awkwardness of Dr. Mark. They've all heard about Dr. Mark before, so that bit of information is not new to them.

"So, he picked you up, took you home and fed you cucumber?" Sarah asks.

I shake my head. "No, I have not had the cucumber... yet. We slept. That's it. He held me all night."

"Sure he's not gay? Because if I had you in my bed all night, we would not just sleep—that's for sure. Although, that kiss was way too convincing for him to be gay." Reilly likes to say she's an alcohol-fuelled lesbian. Meaning if she's drunk enough, she'd be into it.

"Thanks, I think?" I hold my glass up in her direction before drinking the last of it.

It's one o'clock when we finish the last drink, and it's not until I'm dialling Zac's number that I notice how tipsy I am. "Who are you calling?" Sarah asks.

"Zac. He wants to pick me up," I say with a huge smile.

"I bet that's not all he wants to do," Reilly shouts out. At the same time, I can hear laughing on the other side of the phone.

"Sunshine, I assure you... picking you up is not all I want to do. Are you ready to head out? I'll be there in fifteen."

I sigh. I actually sigh into the phone out loud. Oh god, maybe it's not a good idea to see Zac while I'm tipsy on mimosas.

"Zac, I can just get an Uber home. You don't have to come back here to get me."

"Sunshine, do not get in a fucking Uber. I swear..." He takes a breath. "I'm already on my way. Just wait for me." He pauses and then adds, "Please."

"Okay, I'll wait for you. You'd be a much better view than any Uber driver anyway. Oh god, I said that out loud, didn't I?" I can hear Zac laughing. "I'm hanging up. I'll see you soon."

I don't give him a chance to respond before I hang up the phone. Looking back at my friends, I watch as they all let out the laughter they were unsuccessfully attempting to hold in. It must be contagious because I join them, laughing until my eyes water.

# Eight

ZAC

WALKING INTO THE CAFÉ, I can hear the four women before I see them. I approach their table slowly, even though every bone in my body wants to run and grab Alyssa so I can pull her back into my arms. I stop at the table, sitting in the empty seat next to Alyssa.

Putting my arm around the back of her chair, I ask, "Sunshine, did you have a good time?"

I already know the answer to my question. I can tell by the rosy colour to her cheeks that she's had a few mimosas. She doesn't answer my question. Instead, she turns and smiles at me before practically jumping into my lap. She reaches up, pulling my head down to hers, and plants her lips against mine.

It feels like heaven, her soft, full lips on mine. Swiping my tongue out, I lick her lips, seeking entrance. She doesn't keep me waiting, and I swirl my tongue, tasting her mouth. She tastes sweet, a mixture of orange juice and what I think is chocolate. Whatever it is, she's intoxicating and I'm not talking about the obvious alcohol I can taste on her lips.

I hate to do it, but I have to pull back. If I don't, I'll have her spread across this table before I know it. She groans as I pull away, and I can't help but laugh at how damn cute she is.

"Why... why can't you just keep kissing me? I like your kisses, Zac, like really, *really* like them." She purrs a little, which has my cock harder than it was a minute ago, and it was already fucking hard.

Leaning in, I whisper in her ear so she's the only one that can hear, "Sunshine, I want nothing more right now than to keep kissing you. I want to strip you naked and kiss every part of your body from your head to your toes. I want to worship you the way you deserve to be worshiped, but that can't happen in a café full of people. I already told you *I don't share*."

Alyssa looks at me, mouth open. She eventually says, "Let's go. I'm ready."

I laugh at her eagerness. I don't remember a time I've laughed so frequently, but Alyssa seems to bring it out of me with ease. "Baby, you might want to at least say goodbye to your friends first."

I wave at the three women who are all sitting at the table and staring at us like we're an alien lifeform. Alyssa looks across at them. Before she can say anything, one of her friends speaks up, "*Uhh,* no, you don't, Mister Tall-dark-and-handsome. It's Sunday! Sunday means girls' day. You don't get to take her away from us on girls' day. We have partying to do, we have celebrating to do, and we have cucumbers to pick up."

All four women laugh when Alyssa says, "Well, I don't need to pick up any cucumbers. I have one that's just perfect already."

I have no idea what their fascination with cucumbers is and can't help with that, but the first two points I can address, and still keep Alyssa with me. "Well, it just so happens partying and celebrating are something I can help with. How about I reserve a VIP table for you at The Merge tonight? You all go home, rest, sober up and meet Alyssa at the club at ten tonight?"

The four women look from one another. It's like they're having a conversation without speaking—kind of creepy if you ask me. Sarah speaks up this time. "Will there be bottle service included with the VIP table? If so, we're in. Also, you're giving me a ride home with Alyssa."

"It wouldn't be VIP without table service. I can drop you off at your place, but I'll be taking Alyssa home with me." I leave no room for arguments.

Lucky for me, Alyssa seems onboard with my plan. "Okay, I will see you twinnies later tonight. And *you*, get up. We're going. I don't have all day."

Standing up, Alyssa grabs my hand and pulls, but she stops suddenly. "Oh wait!" She picks her purse up from the table. "I just need to go pay then we can go."

As she's trying to pull away from me, I stop her and pull her back to my side. "I already paid for the table. Let's go."

If I thought she would be grateful for having her and her friends' meals and drinks paid for, I was wrong. She pulls away from me, crossing her arms over her chest, which only makes her breasts look like a fucking offering. I'm finding it hard to look her in her eyes and not stare at them like a creep. Again, I'm struck with the thought, *Damn, she's cute*, which makes me smile. Wrong move again.

"What the hell are you smiling for, GQ? This isn't funny. I don't need you to pay for my meals. I have a job you know. I can pay for my own things. Holly? She has a job; she's a kindergarten teacher. She can pay for her own things too. And Sarah? She's a makeup artist. She makes money. Funnily, she can pay for her own meals. Reilly..." She pauses and takes a breath. "Well, she's between jobs right now, but she's about to get one.

I know it's happening for her soon. But okay, maybe you can pay for hers."

I wait to make sure she's finished with her little tirade. "Are you finished, or is there more?" I unfold her arms and pull her back into me. "I know you have a job, a stable one with stable pay if I remember correctly." She nods her head. "I didn't pay for your meal and drinks because I don't think you can. I paid because I wanted to do something nice for you. As for paying for your friends? They just happen to benefit from me doing something nice for you."

Alyssa doesn't say anything, but leans her body into mine. I take this as a win. Reilly (I'm pretty sure it's Reilly) says, "Well, I for one am all for anyone paying for me! Until I get that next job, that is."

Looking over to Sarah, I say, "If you need a ride, let's go." I take Alyssa's hand and lead her out to the car.

Settling Alyssa into the passenger seat, I walk around and jump in the car. Looking back, I make sure Sarah has put her own seat belt on before I pull out. "Here, drink this, sunshine." She takes the water I hand over but sits it on her lap instead of opening it.

"You're so pretty, Zac. Why are you so damn pretty? I'm gonna go to jail, aren't I?" she asks so seriously.

Picking up her hand and joining it with mine, I bring her wrist to my mouth and kiss it before resting our joined hands on my thigh. I like touching her. If I had it my way, I would always be touching some part of her. I haven't even had her yet, and I'm craving her touch this badly. How is it going to be once I finally get her in my bed and naked?

I'm pulled from my thoughts when Alyssa speaks again. "I really like when you do that. It sends shivers straight through me, but the good kind, not the creepy kind."

Looking into the back seat, she says to Sarah, "I'm definitely going to jail in the near future. You'll come visit, right?"

Sarah laughs and adds, "I'll probably be your damn cell-mate. We'll have to turn lesbian; they don't serve cucumbers in jail, you know."

I have to shake my head to clear my thoughts. All I heard was: *We'll have to turn lesbian.* Usually, the thought of two women would be a major turn on for me, but the thought of Alyssa being with anyone else, even a woman, sends rage through my entire body.

"Sunshine, you are not going to jail. Whatever you did, I'll fix it for you. All you have to do is tell me. I can fix it. And Sarah, you can keep your filthy hands off my woman. Under no circumstances will you be turning her lesbian, jail or no jail. You got me?"

Both Alyssa and Sarah crack up, and laughter fills the car. I could listen to the sound of Alyssa's laugh forever; it's like the best played song I've ever heard.

Sarah mumbles, "Your woman," and then bursts out in laughter again.

This, I don't find funny. "Yes, my woman, my Alyssa, and I don't share."

"*Aw*, you called her my Alyssa, and this morning she called you her Zac." Tapping Alyssa on the shoulder, she says seriously, "Jail is most certainly in your future, my friend."

"Alyssa, baby, what the hell have you done that you think you're going to end up in jail?" Both women laugh again. I'm not impressed. All this talk of jail, after what I just did last night... Fuck me, does

she know what I did? Does she think whatever I do will come back on her? The thought that she would be worried about that has me feeling nauseous.

Alyssa must notice a change in me. Squeezing my hand, she

says, "It's not what I've done yet. It's what I'm likely to do to all the girls who think they can get to you. Well, they will have to go through me now, because I don't share and I happen to be a very scrappy fighter. I learnt young."

It does not escape my attention that she made a comment about learning how to fight young, nor does this morning's comment about taking care of herself since she was five. Now is not the time to bring it up though, and I'm feeling relief that she isn't concerned about my actions coming back to her, not that I would ever fucking let that happen.

Pulling into the carpark out front of Alyssa's townhouse, I open her door for her. "Run in and pack an overnight bag. Or better yet, pack enough for a few days so you won't have to come back. I'll wait out here. I've got a call I need to make."

Alyssa reaches up on her tiptoes and lays a kiss onto my cheek. "Sure thing, stud-muffin." I watch in shock as she grabs Sarah's arm and they walk into their townhouse together.

"I'm just going to freshen up real quick," Alyssa says as she goes into the bathroom and shuts the door. I finally have her back in my bedroom, where I've wanted her to be since she left it this morning. Sitting on the edge of the bed, I toe my boots and socks off. I take my shirt off and start undoing my belt when the bathroom door opens. I look up and all the breath I had leaves me.

Thank you God, Jesus, Buddha and whatever other godly divinity sent this angel my way. Standing in the bathroom doorway, Alyssa is wearing matching black lace panties and a bra. I can see her nipples through the sheer lace of the bra, her hair cascading down over her shoulder.

"Holy shit, sunshine, I don't even know what to say right now."

She's a little shy. She sobered up between leaving the café and arriving here. Looking down, she says, "Well, you could either say you like what you see, or you don't like what you see. I will survive either option."

Is she fucking kidding me? "Baby, I love what I'm seeing right now. You are goddamn perfect. I couldn't even dream you up if I tried." Walking over to her, I grab the back of her head and smash my mouth to hers, devouring and getting high off the taste of her. I think she may just be my new addiction.

She wraps her arms around my neck, pulling my head down further into hers. Groaning, I pick her up from under her legs and push her against the wall. Alyssa arches and grinds against my cock. I think I might be at risk of coming in my fucking pants if she keeps that up. I kiss down her throat.

"I want to kiss and lick every inch of your body," I whisper, nipping at her ear. Her moans are getting louder. I need to get her spread out on my bed before this ends too soon. "Bed, I need you on the bed for me, baby." Still holding her, I carry her to the bed and lay her down, falling on top of her and settling between her legs.

"Zac, I need you inside me. I don't think I've ever needed anything more in my life," she purrs. *Fuck me*. How am I meant to perform when I'm ready to come just from hearing her moans and pleas?

"I plan on burying myself so far inside of you. I plan on ruining you for all time." Kissing my way down her throat, I sit her up and unclasp her bra, letting her breasts fall free. Filling both of my hands with a breast each, I squeeze her nipples. "Sunshine, you have the most perfect tits." Dipping down, I pop one into my mouth and suck, while attending to the other one with my fingers.

Alyssa arches her back up, moaning and pleading, "Zac, oh god, please."

I know what she needs, but I want to hear her ask for it. "Please what, baby? What do you need?" I move on to her other breast, sucking, licking, savouring.

"I need you in me, now, damn it." I laugh at how demanding she is.

Trailing a hand down her flat stomach, I reach my hand into her panties, stopping just above her clit. "What part of me do you need inside you, baby? Do you want my fingers, my tongue, my cock?"

I continue to lick and suck on her nipples. My fingers find their way to her clit—she's wet. I moan at how wet and responsive she is to me. "You're so fucking wet, sunshine," I growl, dipping a finger inside her before pulling it back out and swirling around her clit.

Her moans are getting louder. She's arching her back up, trying to harden the light friction I'm providing with my fingers. "Please, Zac, I need... I need... your fingers. No, your cock. *Mmm,* no, your tongue. Dammit, I want it all."

"All you had to do was ask, sunshine." I leave her breasts and trail my tongue down her stomach. Sitting up, I pull her panties down her legs. Spreading her legs wide, I settle my shoulders between them. I lay my hands on her thighs holding them open.

"I have been dreaming about tasting you since I first saw you. I bet you're sweet like sugar. Do you taste sweet, sunshine?" I ask as I kiss up and down the inside of her thighs. I can see her arousal, I can smell her arousal, and soon enough, I will taste her arousal. I growl at the thought.

"Well, how about you stop talking about it and find out for yourself," she demands breathlessly.

Laughing, I do just that. I swipe my tongue from the bottom of her slit up to the top, slowly.

"Oh god, that's so good." I can tell she's on the brink. I want to ride this out for as long as I can, but I also just really want to see her fucking come.

I go in hard, licking and sucking like my life depends on it. She's squirming underneath me, moaning out my name. I feel like I'm drunk on the smell and taste of her.

"Goddammit, you're so fucking tight. I can't wait to feel your pussy choking my cock as you come." I feel her tighten around my fingers; it seems she likes the dirty talk. *Good.* Pumping my fingers in and out, I curve them inside her until I find the spot I know will send her wild. Circling my tongue around her engorged clit, I lick and suck.

I feel her whole body tense, her pussy squeezing the fuck out of my fingers, as she screams out, "Oh god! Zac! Oh my god!"

I continue pumping my fingers and licking until she comes down. "That was the most beautiful thing I've seen," I tell her as I stand up and remove my jeans, finally giving my cock the freedom he's been seeking. Reaching into the bedside table, I find a

condom and rip it open. I don't waste time getting it on before I settle between her legs. She's barely come down from the orgasm she just had as I push the tip inside her.

I can't think of a better feeling, slowly pushing inside. "I think this is what heaven must feel like," I say, kissing her as I slowly glide my cock further into her.

Once I'm buried to the hilt, I feel her tense. I stop moving, gritting my teeth. It takes everything in me not to fuck the fuck out of her right now. "You're so fucking tight. This pussy was made for me."

Once I feel her muscles loosen, I start to move in and out.

She feels so fucking good. I don't think I'm going to last long. Reaching down between our bodies, I circle a finger around her clit. "I need you to come again. You feel so fucking good on my cock, sunshine."

I pump in and out of her faster and harder, and she matches my movements thrust for thrust. "Zac, don't stop. Oh god, don't fucking stop," she screams out.

Leaning down, I whisper in her ear, "I'm never going to stop fucking you. There will always be tomorrow for us."

Her pussy walls tighten and strangle my cock. She tips her head back, screaming my name. This moment, as she comes on my cock for the first time, will be burned in my memory as the best fucking day of my life.

I can feel the tingling sensation up my spine; my balls tighten as I pump into her roughly until I come undone. I come hard as I continue to pump, claiming her as mine.

"Alyssa. You. Are. Fucking. Mine." Catching my weight as I fall on top of her, I roll to the side, landing next to her. We both lie there breathing heavily, basking in the orgasm afterglow, and catching our breath.

"That was... oh god, I don't even know what that was. What the hell was that, Zac?" Alyssa rolls her head, meeting my eyes.

"That, sunshine, was fucking perfection. You are perfection." She chews on her bottom lip. I've noticed she does this when she's thinking. "Hold that thought. Don't move." I go into the bathroom and dispose of the condom, wetting a washcloth before I go back out to find Alyssa right where I left her. Standing above her, I spread her legs open and use the cloth to clean between her legs.

She stares at me. "What the hell are you doing?" She looks mortified, but I don't fucking care.

"I'm wiping your pussy. Correction, I'm wiping my fucking pussy." My face is deadpan.

"I can take care of that myself. Just give me a few minutes for my legs to not feel like Jell-O," she says, trying to shut her legs on me.

Not going to fucking happen, *ever.* "I take care of what's mine, and sunshine, this pussy..." I cup my hand over her pussy. "...is mine."

Throwing the washcloth in the laundry basket, I climb back into bed and pull Alyssa into me.

As I pull the blankets up, covering us, she looks up at me. "When I have more energy, we will revisit this concept of you thinking you have a proprietorship of my anatomy."

I don't bother arguing that I intend to own every inch of her; instead, I kiss her forehead. "Go to sleep. We can discuss who owns what after we wake up."

Just as I think she's asleep, she whispers, "Zac?" "Yeah?" My voice is just as quiet.

Alyssa keeps her head down. "I'm scared of what this is." She's quiet, and as I'm thinking of what to say to reassure her, she continues, "Of what's happening between you and me."

Well fuck me, I never would have believed you if you told me I'd feel like this for one woman, that I would give anything and everything for just one more tomorrow with her, if that's all I could have.

"Sunshine, I'm scared too. But not of what's happening between you and me, because whatever it is, it's already happened. There's no use fighting it." Pausing, I lay kisses on the top of her head before confessing my real fear to her. "What I'm scared of is what will happen if I don't have a tomorrow with you. If something happens or if I fuck this up and make you realise you could do one hundred times better. Not having you, that's what I'm scared of."

Alyssa picks her head up and kisses my chest, right where my heart lays. "I'll be here for as many tomorrows as you want me to be," she says before laying her head back down. That's how we drift off to sleep.

## Nine

## ALYSSA

I WAKE to the feel of kisses being run down my face, down my neck and back up again. Smiling, I can tell who is responsible for those kisses by his scent alone. Breathing in deeply, I inhale that woodsy and citrus scent. Wait, inhaling through my nose again, I note there is another scent that registers to my brain, *coffee.*

"I smell coffee," I mumble with my eyes still closed. "Please tell me I'm not dreaming and there is coffee in my near future."

I can feel the vibration of Zac's chuckle. "Time to wake up, sunshine. Yes, I have a vanilla latte ready and waiting." Well, that does it.

My eyes pop open and I'm greeted by a vision that has me believing I must still be dreaming. Zac, shirtless, all those tanned muscles on display right in front of me, all within reaching distance. Even better—okay, maybe not better but definitely equal to—he's holding out a coffee cup.

"I honestly don't know what I want to reach for more, you or the coffee." I smile, taking the coffee cup and bringing it straight to my mouth. At the perfect taste of the vanilla coffee concoction, I moan, "*Mmm,* this is worth being woken up for."

"So, I lose out to coffee? Well, if that isn't a blow to the ego, I don't know what is." Zac is pouting. It's cute.

Taking my time, I take a huge gulp of coffee, slowly put the cup down onto the bedside table, and then I'm on him. Reaching up, I grab his head, pulling it closer to meet mine. He doesn't put up any struggle. Smashing my lips to his, I kiss him like it's the first and last kiss, like his lips provide the elements I need to continue breathing. I try to pour everything I'm feeling into the kiss. He doesn't let me down, returning my fever with a frantic version of his own, taking control as he tilts my head and caresses my mouth with his tongue. By the time we pull apart, I'm breathless and I can feel my lips are kiss swollen.

"It was a really, really hard choice. You came a very close second to the coffee, but it's a vanilla latte." Picking up the coffee cup, I inhale the aroma before sipping at it.

Zac shakes his head, trailing his hand up and down my leg. "I'll just have to work on it a bit more. There are things I could do that would give you a much better wake up than that sugary syrup you like to call coffee."

I highly doubt it, but I'm not about to stop him from trying. "Well, hot stuff, why don't you give it your best shot and I'll let you know how you rate." I slowly pull the blanket down to reveal the top of my breasts, stopping just before my nipples are uncovered.

"As much as it kills me right now to say this, we don't have time. You have plans with your friends, and honestly, I'm a little scared of what those women will do to my club if I don't get you there." The whole time he's speaking to my breasts, his eyes fixated on the mounds.

Trying to entice him to forget the plans, I let the blanket drop completely to my waist and with as much innocence as I can put into my voice, I say, "Well, if you're sure there's no time..." I leave the sentence hanging.

Zac licks his lips, bringing his eyes up to meet mine with a hardened stare. "That's not fair. How am I meant to walk away from an offering like that?"

He reaches his hands out and grabs hold of my breasts, one in each hand, squeezing a few times. I arch my back up towards him, moaning a little. How can his touch affect me so easily? Pulling away and standing up, he smirks that panty-melting smirk.

"You know what? I think I will wait to ravish this body when we get home. I didn't do it enough justice this afternoon, but tonight, I plan on rectifying that. Get ready. We need to leave in an hour," he demands, walking out the bedroom door.

Taking one last look in the mirror, I decide it will have to do. I'm wearing a gold sequin mini dress; thin spaghetti straps cross over at the back down to my waist, leaving the top half of my back exposed. The dress is loose fitting. The fabric dips down between my breasts, making them look like they're being hugged. It's short, much shorter than anything I would normally wear.

Sarah threw the dress at me as I was packing a bag earlier today and said, "If you don't wear it, I will comment on your lover boy's endearing qualities all night long."

So, instead of being tempted to kill my best friend with pure, unjustified, jealousy-fuelled rage, I'm wearing the damn dress, paired with a pair of gold strappy heels. I've left my hair down in waves and attempted to give myself a subtle smoky eye, paired with bright red lips. Being best friends with a makeup artist has its perks; you pick up a thing or two over the years.

Coming to terms with the fact that I can't hide out in Zac's bathroom anymore, I take a deep breath in an attempt to calm my nerves. Why I'm nervous, I have absolutely no freaking idea. Well, it could be anxiety about what Zac's reaction to the dress will be; he's either going to hate it or love it. I remind myself on the walk down the hallway out to the living room that it doesn't matter either way. I dress for me, not for the approval of any man.

Stepping into the living room, I search for Zac. He's nowhere to be seen. Dean and Bray, however, are both lounging on the sofas with a drink in their hands. My heels click on the floor as I step further into the room, and their heads snap up and around in my direction.

"Holy fucking shit," Bray says, shaking his head at me. Well, okay then, not really sure what to make of that statement. Before I conjure up a response, Dean speaks up, "I'm guessing Zac hasn't seen her yet. This is going to be fun." He rubs his hands together and smiles wide.

"I don't recall burying bodies ever being fun, Dean, but I guess it might be worth it to see Zac lose a bit of that always calm and in control demeanour."

Having no idea what the hell they're talking about, I walk over to the floor-to-ceiling windows I didn't notice when I was in this room yesterday. The view here is breathtaking. I can see the Sydney Harbour Bridge, the city lights twinkling like fairy lights.

"This view is breathtaking," I say, still mesmerised by the city lights.

I hear a throat clear. "I agree; the view is breathtaking."

Spinning around, I see Zac. His eyes travel up my body from my feet and by the time his eyes meet mine, they are wide open, a mixture of shock and arousal crossing his face.

"Holy fucking shit," Zac grunts out.

"Yep, that's what I said." Bray smirks at me. I can feel the shades of red creeping up my neck.

Tilting my head, I inspect Bray closer. He's good looking for sure, big with obvious muscle on top of muscle. He's wearing black jeans and a grey t-shirt. I can see tattoos covering both of his arms. He has bad boy heartbreaker written all over him. No matter how good looking he is, he just doesn't do it for me. Nothing. Zilch. Not even a flicker of an ember.

When I look at Zac though, who is wearing a very well-fitted navy suit with a white dress shirt—he has a dark navy striped tie hanging loosely around his neck—forget about an ember. Getting my fill of Zac starts a bonfire within me, my panties instantly wet.

Zac walks up to Bray and slaps him across the head. "Get your greedy fucking eyes off her."

Dean and Bray both laugh as Zac continues to move until he stops directly in front of me, effectively blocking their view of me.

"Sunshine, please tell me there is more of this dress you left back in the bedroom." His fingers trail along the hem of the dress on my upper thigh.

Squinting my eyes at him, I take a step back, crossing my arms and asking, "What's wrong with my dress, Zac?"

"Nothing, I love the dress. You look stunning, baby. What I don't like is that every other asshole in a ten- mile radius will have their eyes glued to you, and I'm probably going to have to get dumbo one and dumbo two over there to bury a few bodies before the end of the night."

"I said that too." Bray laughs.

I angle my head around Zac's body and glare at him, raising my eyebrows. He holds his hands up in a surrender motion. Taking the win, I set my glare back to Zac.

"You have two choices and I strongly recommend you choose wisely. One." I hold up a finger. "You can step into the year 2020. You know, where men don't actually get to tell women what they can and can't wear out in public? And when you've come to your senses, you can take me to your club to meet my friends. I might even let you stick around, even though it's girls' night." I pause and Zac grits his teeth, jaw locked. Oh boy, he is not happy with that option.

Continuing, I hold up a second finger. "Two, you can go and do whatever it is you would normally do on a Sunday night. I will call an Uber and make my own way to your club and have a great time with my friends, without you."

"Damn, bro, didn't see that one coming. I thought she was a quiet little timid thing, but kitten's got claws." Bray laughs, coming up to me to wrap an arm around my shoulder. I look up at Zac and see him fuming. Imagine a cartoon character with smoke coming out of its ears, that's Zac right now, only no actual smoke.

"I approve by the way, Lyssa, and if this douche chooses option two, I will be more than happy to give you a ride to the club." Bray smirks down at me in what I'm guessing is a smirk that would melt the panties right off a lot of girls.

Zac actually growls, full on, out loud growls, like a bloody grizzly bear. "Because you're my brother, and you happen to make me a shitload of money with that arm, I'm going to give you five seconds to remove it from my woman before I fucking break it," he grits out.

Bray immediately removes his arm and steps a whole two steps away from me. *Huh,* maybe he thinks Zac would really break his arm. I doubt he would, but it's not worth testing the theory right now.

Thinking back on what Zac said, I question the both of them, "What do you mean he makes you a lot of money with that arm?" I have no idea what Bray does, other than live to get a rise out of his brother.

Zac looks at Bray before giving a nonanswer. "I'll tell you later."

Bray raises his eyebrows in shock, shaking his head. He picks up keys from the coffee table, throwing them at Zac. As Zac catches them, Bray smiles and says, "The McLaren's back from the detailers. You know, I never could figure out how you managed to get chocolate muffin crumbs all over the car when you've never so much as had water in the car, and you don't even like chocolate." He looks directly in my direction before adding, "I think I get it now."

My mouth hangs open and I look at Zac questioningly. I thought he was joking about the car being at the cleaners. Instead of answering, he grabs my hand and starts pulling me towards the door.

Just as we're all about to get in the elevator, I ask, "Is Ella coming tonight?"

All three men, all at the same time, say, "Not a fucking chance."

"*Huh*, you know, it's cute how you all can finish each other's sentences like that." I smile innocently, stepping inside. Turning around, I'm greeted with three very intimidating scowls; but for some reason, I've never felt safer.

Sitting in the passenger seat of the Batmobile, the guilt of making such a mess that Zac had to have his car detailed plays on my mind. "You know, I can pay you for whatever cost you had to pay to clean the car."

I look over to Zac; he's looking back at me with his brows creased. "What are you talking about?"

Rolling my eyes at him, I respond, "It was me that put chocolate muffin crumbs everywhere. If it's true you don't eat in your car, why the hell would you give me, probably the messiest eater on the continent, a bloody muffin to eat in here?"

Bringing my hand up to his mouth, he kisses the inside of my wrist. I can't help but melt a little at the action and he knows it.

"Sunshine, I eat in the car. I just don't let Bray or anyone else eat in the car. I happen to love this car way more than him."

Zac looks across to me, his eyes drifting down to my legs, where my dress has ridden up high on my thighs, before looking back at the road. "Please, tell me you are wearing underwear under that shirt you're wearing as a dress," he groans.

"So, you let me eat in the fancy-ass Batmobile but not your brother. You know, that's crazy. What if I stained the carpet or got crumbs stuck in crevices you'll never get them out of?" Staring at him expectantly, I wait for an actual answer.

"It just so happens I like you way more than I like this car, so you eating is more important to me than having a clean car." Squeezing my hand, he looks over at me. "Now answer my question. You are wearing underwear under that dress, right?"

All I heard out of that was: *I like you more than I like this car.* And I swoon. This is a really freaking nice car. Wondering how much information to give him about the underwear that I'm wearing, I give the best innocent smile I can muster.

"*Umm*, underwear?" I question.

"I swear to everything holy, sunshine, if you tell me you're not wearing underwear, I'm turning the damn car around and taking you home and handcuffing you to the fucking bed."

Well, okay then, I was not expecting that reaction. The mention of handcuffs, and what little underwear I'm wearing is becoming very wet.

"Of course I'm wearing underwear, Zac." Smiling at him, I decide to tell him exactly what kind of underwear. "I happen to be wearing a lacy white thong under this dress."

The car swerves to the side of the road, skidding to a stop. I don't even have time to think about what's happening before Zac's tormented gaze is searing into me.

"Are you fucking kidding me right now? Your ass is uncovered? You bend over and every fucker around is going to see your ass."

"Well, I don't plan on bending over, Zac, and just so you know, I've been wearing dresses for a while now. You know, considering I am a girl, and a girl who likes dresses, I know how not to show my ass to everyone when wearing one. It's a skill really, a talent some might say."

Just as he's about to say something, his phone rings over the Bluetooth of the car, announcing that the caller is Bray. "What?" Zac grunts out.

"What the fuck did you stop for? I've got plans; some of us actually want to get to the club before it fucking closes," Bray yells back. Looking in the rear-view mirror, I see the Range Rover behind us; Dean's driving and Bray's in the passenger seat.

"Oh, I can answer this one, sweetie." I turn on my sugary sweet voice and smile at Zac, who, by the way, is now frowning at me.

"Oh, this is gonna be good," I hear Dean mumble.

"Bray, it's my fault. Obviously, I should have waited until we got to the club before describing what kind of underwear I'm wearing." Laughing a little to myself, I stop when I notice that no one else is laughing.

Zac looks like he's about to burst a blood vessel in his forehead, and Dean and Bray are so damn quiet I thought they were disconnected until I hear Bray's voice again. "Lyssa, don't take this the wrong way, because I like you, like really fucking like you. But could you maybe wait until you provide me with a nephew before you give my brother a heart attack? Because I'm really fucking great uncle material. Uncle Bray has a ring to it, don't you think?"

At the mention of kids, I can feel the panic overtake me. My skin feels clammy. I'm nauseous. I need air. I need... oh god, I can't breathe in here. I need to get out of this fucking car. Searching around the car, I look for a way out, a way to wind the damn window down, something. Zac notices my distress and grabs my arms, stopping me in my place.

"Bray, we'll meet you at the club." Disconnecting the call, he doesn't wait for a response.

"Sunshine, breathe. You're okay." Although his voice is soft, I can hear the worry in it. "Alyssa, baby, breathe with me, okay? In... out... in... out."

He brings his face right up close to mine, his lips just shy of touching mine. I can feel his breath on my lips, breathing in deep as I inhale his scent.

"That's it, baby, just keep breathing with me. You're okay. I've got you. I'm never going to let anything happen to you." His voice is soothing, and he's rubbing his hands up and down my arms. I can feel myself relax, and with that, comes the embarrassment. I can't believe I just had a panic attack in front of Zac, surely now he will see just how broken I am.

Attempting to turn my head so he can't see my shame, I'm stopped as his hands cup my face. "Sunshine, you never need to be embarrassed in front of me, ever."

He's so sincere. I can't take it. My eyes well up and before I can stop it, I feel a tear drop down my cheeks. Zac uses his thumb to swipe it away.

"I'm gonna fucking kill him," he mumbles.

Confused and wanting the focus off me, I ask, "Who?"

"My fucking idiot brother. Whatever he said made you panic and cry."

Shit, I don't want to cause issues with his family.

"It's not Bray's fault, and I'm sorry. Sometimes I have panic attacks. I can't predict when they're going to happen. They don't happen often though. This is the first one in over a year."

Shaking his head, he leans in and kisses my lips ever so lightly. "I'm still going to rip him apart." He pauses and then asks, "What did he say that caused the panic? And don't try to tell me it wasn't him. I know it's something he said."

Not really having any other option, I go for the truth and if it makes him want to run far, far away from me, well, I will survive, I think.

"He wants to be an uncle," I say, looking down at my fingers.

"Why would Bray wanting to be an uncle make you panic?" he asks. He's patient and waits for me to answer.

"Because, well, because I don't think I can give you that. I don't think I want to have kids and if I can't give you that, you'll want to find someone else who will. I can't... I can't..." Shaking my head, I feel another tear escape. Zac swipes it away and kisses my lips again in an ever so light touch of his lips.

"Alyssa, Bray's a fucking idiot. That's all there is to it. He was joking, okay? But it doesn't matter anyway.

Do you know why?" he asks. I shake my head no in answer. "It doesn't matter, because I couldn't give two fucks if Bray wants to be a fucking uncle. I have raised Ella and Bray since our parents died when she was only thirteen. I'd do anything for them. But I don't need to have kids of my own. If we have kids, that's up to us to decide, not anyone else. I don't want kids if it means not having you. There is nothing you can say that is going to make me want to look for anyone else, okay?"

"Okay," I agree, not sure if I believe myself.

"Do you still want to go to the club? I can and will take you home if you want, or anywhere else you want to go."

Reaching up and kissing his lips, I say, "I don't know how I got so lucky to have you, but I'm not giving you back, so I hope you realise you're stuck now. Yes, I want to go to the club. Let's go."

Zac pulls the car back out onto the road. Picking my hand up and kissing my wrist, he says, "There's no one else I'd want to be stuck to."

# Ten

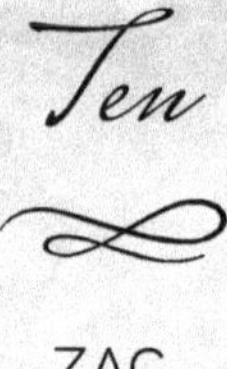

## ZAC

S ITTING in my office, attempting to get an hour's worth of work done while Alyssa is on the VIP floor of the club, wearing that fucking dress—a dress I plan on fucking burning as soon as it hits my bedroom floor tonight—is pure torture. I don't know what I was thinking. I don't think I've done anything productive since I came in here forty-five minutes ago.

My eyes drift to the flat screen on the wall, where I am viewing the security footage of the very floor Alyssa is on. I can't help but watch her; she's mesmerising. Not that she realises how goddamn beautiful she is. I've watched many men attempt to get close to her in the short time I've been up here, each time being intercepted by either Dean or James.

Before leaving Alyssa with her friends, I made sure James was the only bartender serving her table. I may have threatened his job if anything happened to her, or if any motherfucker got too close to her. It appears his job is safe with how well he runs interference on all the motherfuckers with a goddamn death wish, wanting to get closer to my woman.

I was prepared to break my own brother's bloody arm when

I saw him with that arm around her. I don't know what's happening to me. I've never been so irrational before, never been so infatuated with a woman before that it feels like I can't breathe properly unless I'm with her.

When she had that panic attack in the car tonight, my heart felt like it was being ripped to shreds. I've never wanted to hold anybody together so badly; I would have done anything to take her fear away. It would be so easy for me to have Dean run a background check on her, find out all the secrets she holds and what the fuck happened to her to cause such fear.

I don't want to find out about her that way though. I want her to trust me. If I go digging around in her past and she found out, well, I don't think she'd take that very well. I just have to be patient and wait for her to open up to me, to let me in.

Patience is not something I've been known to have, but for Alyssa, I'm willing to give it a go. As I watch her on the screen, I don't think there is anything I wouldn't do for her, or die trying to do. She's laughing, dancing with Reilly or Holly—I really can't tell which is which with those two. Sarah is dancing with some random guy. Bray and Dean are sitting, nursing drinks and watching Alyssa and Reilly.

The fact that they're getting a front-row seat, watching my woman dance like that, in that fucking dress, makes me see red. It should be me getting that front-row seat, not any other fucker... even if I tasked them both with the job of watching her.

Groaning, I turn back to my computer screen. I've been trying to read over the events planned for the next few weeks. I don't know what the fuck Caitlyn was thinking when she booked the same band for two weekends in a row. The same fucking band that was now missing a drummer.

Picking up my phone, I dial Caitlyn. The call goes straight to voicemail. "Where the fuck are you? We've got a problem with Cyrus. You should know better than to book the same band two weeks in a fucking row. Fix it. Get them off next week's schedule and find a replacement act."

Hanging up the phone, I look back at the flat screen. I'm on my feet as soon as I see what's happening. Moving closer, I scan every monitor for Alyssa. I can't fucking see her anywhere. What I can see has me running out of my office and down to the VIP floor.

Down on the VIP floor, I push my way through security. Not that I have to try hard; as soon as they realise who's pushing through, they fucking move out of my way. Stopping at the section that Alyssa should be, I turn in a 360, seeking her out.

Turning back, my gaze lands on Sarah. "Where the fuck is she?" I yell at her. She flinches but shakes her head, tears running down her cheeks.

"Fuck," I growl, turning back around.

I should be concerned with who the fucker is that Bray has pinned under him. He throws punches like his life depends on it, although whoever the fuck he's laying into is all but lifeless under him. Dean steps up and pulls him back. I still can't see her.

Charging up to Dean and Bray, I demand, "Someone needs to tell me where the fuck she is, *now.*" I'm on the verge of a fucking nervous breakdown. Why the fuck can't I see her? She should be here. I'm running my hands through my hair when Dean finally speaks up, "James took her up to your office when shit hit the fan. She should be in your office, man."

"Fuck!" I'm yelling at no one in particular. I look over at Dean and quickly bite out, "Bring them up to the office. Alyssa will probably shoot me if anything happens to her friends in my club." I point back to the three women huddled together.

Throwing my office door open, I find Alyssa on the couch,

holding an ice pack to her face. I feel my blood go cold. I am seething; someone fucking hurt her. As I walk towards her, I can feel my body vibrate with rage at the thought of some fucker laying hands on her.

James gets up from where he was sitting next to her. Just before I reach her, I hear Caitlyn from the other side of the office.

"Zac, thank god you're here! I tried to tell them they couldn't be in here. I told them to leave and they wouldn't listen. James should know better than to bring some floozy up to your office."

Alyssa sticks her head up. She looks back and forward from me to Caitlyn—whatever she is thinking, it's not good. "James, get her fucking out of my office," I tell him, motioning to Caitlyn. He nods and moves towards her, pulling her out by her arm.

If I thought she'd go quietly, I was mistaken. "Zac, you called me, remember? Told me you needed me? I came straight away."

I'm still staring at Alyssa; she's dropped the ice pack and I can see a large bruise forming on the side of her face. I can also see the doubt clouding over her eyes as she stares at Caitlyn, who is not so willingly being shoved out of the room. I need to fix this and set things straight. I can't have Alyssa doubting me.

"James, wait."

James turns around and halts his steps, still holding onto a now smiling Caitlyn. She won't be smiling for long. Smirking at her, I slowly articulate every word so that they are not misinterpreted.

"Caitlyn, I called you because I pay you to do a job. A job I fucking expect you to do, but since you seem more concerned with placing yourself where you don't belong, you're fired for inappropriate conduct. Don't bother coming back."

Nodding at James, I watch as he escorts her out of my office before shutting the door and leaving me alone with Alyssa. Squatting down in front of her, I grab her face in my hands. She flinches as my hands go up to her face. I hate myself instantly. I hate that she would fear my hands. Sliding my hands as gently as I can along her cheeks, I try my darndest to reassure her.

"Sunshine, I would never hurt you. I don't want you to ever be afraid of that. I would cut my own hands off before I used them to cause harm to you. Please tell me you know this, please." She looks at me and nods her head, but that's not going to work for me. "I need the words, sunshine. I need to hear the words."

In an ever so quiet voice, she says, "I know, Zac. I don't know how I know, because I hardly know you, but deep down in my bones, I know you won't hurt me."

I sit up on the couch next to her and pull her onto my lap. "Baby, I need you to tell me who hurt you. I will make sure they can never lay a hand on you again," I say, kissing her forehead.

"I don't know what happened. I was dancing with Reilly when someone came up behind me and grabbed me. I knew instantly it wasn't you, so I turned around and kneed him in the balls."

I'm so fucking proud that she stood up for herself. I can't help but smile. "Sunshine, I'm glad you kneed the fucker in the balls. I think I need to give you a gun. That way, on the very near impossible chance that any fucker ever gets close enough to touch you again, you just shoot them." I lay kisses over her hairline.

She tucks her head into my chest. "It would be dangerous to give me a gun, Zac. I was kicked out of at least ten foster homes for what the department liked to call physical misconduct."

Again, she has brought up her childhood and it sounds like

a fucking nightmare, but we don't have time to hash that out right now.

"We will come back to that topic later. What happened after you kicked the fucker in the balls?" I need to know how she got that bruise on her face, so I know how painful to make this fucker's death.

"He backhanded me," she says so matter-of-factly. I feel like this is not the first time this has happened to her.

Well, never fucking again. I will not let anyone hurt her again, even if I have to be her personal fucking shield twenty-four seven.

She continues, "Then before I knew it, James was picking me up off the ground and Bray was on top of the guy laying into him. Did you know Bray can really pack a punch?" I laugh a little at her question, and she looks up at me, waiting for an explanation.

"Sunshine, Bray is a cage fighter. Underground fighting and currently undefeated. Yeah, I know he can pack a fucking punch. That right hook of his earns me a lot of fucking money."

I watch her face to try to gauge her reaction to this news. She surprises me when she laughs. "Of course he is. Do me a favour, and let's not tell Reilly that bit of information, please."

At that moment, the door swings open and the woman in question asks, "Don't tell Reilly what?" She looks at us and before either of us has a chance to reply, she's answering her own question... sort of.

"Oh, wait, let me guess... Don't tell Reilly that you're going to run off and elope and live HEA?" she questions.

"What the hell is HEA?" This comes from a very rough-voiced Bray.

Reilly spins around, facing him. "Something you're probably going to deny yourself of ever having," she says.

I can tell he still has no idea what she's referring to, but he drops it. Reilly spins back around and at my head nod, she continues her guessing game.

"I know! You've finally quit nursing and you're signing up to work the pole. I've told you, you would make a killing with those boobs."

I growl out, "Over my dead fucking body."

"So no to the stripper career? Oh, I've got it, you discovered Zac's too much man for one woman, and you want me to be your sister wife." She raises her eyebrows suggestively at Alyssa. "Just so you know, Lyssa, if there was anyone in the world I would be sister wives with, it would be you."

I can feel Alyssa's body tense. She's fucking hot when she gets her green-eyed monster on. Before she can say anything, Bray cuts in, "You're not going to be her sister wife. My brother doesn't share well. Besides, a girl like you needs more than sharing a man. You need one all for yourself. It's going to be a tough job, but I'm up for the challenge." Bray turns his full smirk on to Reilly. *Huh*, interesting. But right now, I don't care about my brother trying to get laid. I care about where I can get my hands on the fucker who hurt Alyssa.

Whispering in her ear so only she can hear, I say, "Baby, I'm going to step out the door, just for a minute. I will be right outside the door. Will you be okay here with your girls for a moment?"

Snuggling into my neck, I feel her breathe me in. I love when she does this, although I'm smart enough to not let on that I know that's what she's doing. I love that she takes comfort in me, in my body, in my hold, and even in my fucking smell.

"I'll be fine. Stop worrying so much. It's going to take more than a little slap to keep me down, Zac. I'm not some damsel in distress you have to babysit. If you have work to do, I can just go home with the girls and see you tomorrow, or whenever."

Lifting her chin so her eyes are on me, I say, "You're not going anywhere but my fucking bed tonight, sunshine. I will be right outside that fucking door."

I kiss her, claiming her lips. I pull away far too soon for my liking, but the sooner I deal with this, the sooner I can take my woman home to bed.

Standing, I grunt out to Bray and Dean, "Out." Pointing to the door, I lead the way out.

As soon as the door closes, I am on them. "What the fuck happened? How could you let some fucker get close enough to lay a fucking hand on her, let alone fucking hit her?"

I can feel my body fuming, vibrating with rage again. Now that I don't have Alyssa in my arms, I am an inferno of pure rage. It's almost like she's a balm to my soul, calming me like nothing else can. For a few minutes, in that office while I was holding her, I had forgotten how fucking angry I was.

"Bro, it was the fucking singer for Cyrus. Caitlyn gave the band fucking VIP passes again. We didn't want to draw any attention, so we let them be."

Bray looks pointedly at me. I know he's right; we can't draw unwanted attention from that band. There can't be a link between their missing drummer and our club. I know they'll never find his body, but we still don't need that headache.

"That doesn't answer how he got close to her," I say, pointing to the door.

"He was dancing with Sarah. She was into it, so we left it alone. One of the other guys at the band's table started talking shit about how their drummer was last seen here in the club and never left, started questioning where he was. Bray and I went over to dig out what they knew." Dean shakes his head and runs a hand through his hair. He's frustrated—well, good, because

I'm still fucking fuming. "Look, man, I'm sorry. I shouldn't have left her. I didn't think. I shouldn't have left her."

"No, you fucking shouldn't have. She should not be sitting in there with a fucking shiner. Where the fuck is this fucker now? I can't wait to get my fucking hands on him."

Bray looks at me with concern. "Zac, you can't kill him. You killed his brother last night. You think the band won't start asking louder questions if their lead fucking singer went missing from this club right after their drummer?" He paces, running his hands through the ends of his hair. Stopping in front of me, he looks me square in the eye. "Look, man, the guy had to be taken off in a fucking ambulance. The beating I just gave him... he'd have to be fucking stupid to show his face around here again."

"I know you're right, but it doesn't do anything to help the fact that I feel like I need to kill the fucker. Fuck. Okay, you're right. We don't need anyone questioning the club in relation to missing fucking bodies." I pause and take a calming breath before I go back into the office to Alyssa. I don't want her to see me so worked up. I need to be in control. I need her to see me as someone in control. Walking in, I'm stunned at the scene that greets me: Alyssa and Reilly, drinks in hand, dancing around what I'm assuming is an imaginary pole.

Fuck me, this friend of hers is a dangerous influence. "If my girlfriend ever ends up on a real pole,

I will hunt you down, Reilly, and I won't be kind just because you're a girl."

All four women gasp and stare at me with mouths wide open. I raise an eyebrow in question at them, but they say nothing. Turning my head to the guys for help on this one, I see Dean over in the far corner, texting someone. Who the fuck he's texting, god only knows. Bray is staring at Reilly. I don't know what's going on with him there, but I'm not touching that one with a ten-foot pole. Bray will break the girl's heart if he goes near her, then Alyssa will be pissed at me, and I don't want to have to choose sides between my brother and her. It scares me to think Bray wouldn't come out on the winning side.

"Okay, I give. What'd I say?" I ask the four women but staring directly at mine, at Alyssa.

She doesn't say anything but runs towards me, jumping up into my arms. I brace myself at the very last moment, only stumbling back one step before she's plastered herself to my body, slamming her lips down onto mine. It doesn't take me long to take control of the kiss. I swipe my tongue along her lips, and she opens wide for me. I take everything she willingly gives. This kiss is one of ownership, of me owning her, of her owning me. In this kiss, we tell each other exactly what we don't say with words.

Pulling back from the kiss, I smirk at Alyssa. "Sunshine, if that's the kind of greeting I'm going to get every time I leave for five minutes, I might have to

find reasons to stand on the other side of the door more often."

She smiles and leans her mouth down to my ear, so that only I can hear her reply. Although, looking at the smiles on her friends' faces, I get the feeling they don't need to hear for them to know exactly what's gotten into their friend.

"That kiss isn't because you left and came back, although if it means you're always going to come back, I will gladly give you that kind of greeting kiss every time." She pauses and kisses just behind my ear briefly before continuing, "Sorry I get distracted by your... well, your everything. That kiss, that was because you just called me your girlfriend. Well, at least I think you did, you did, right? Oh god, if it was a slip of the tongue, we can totally just forget—" I cut her off, slamming my lips back onto hers.

A throat clears. "As hot as fuck as Lyssa is, it's not so hot when she's playing tonsil hockey with my fucking brother, my *older* brother, might I add. I'm out." Turning, Bray pulls his trademark smirk on Alyssa's friends. "Any of you lovely ladies need a ride? Home, that is?"

Not giving any of them a chance, I answer for them. "They all need a ride home, bro. I'm taking my girlfriend home to bed." I take extra care to annunciate the word girlfriend, letting them all, especially Alyssa, fucking know that it was not a fucking slip of the tongue. She is mine.

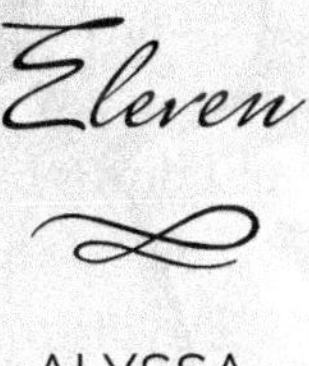

# Eleven

## ALYSSA

STANDING in Zac's bathroom, looking at my reflection in the mirror, I inspect the bruise forming on my face. It's not that bad. I expected it to be a lot worse from the way Zac reacted when he saw my face. This is nothing a bit of foundation won't cover; besides, I've had worse bruises left on my face before.

Shaking my head to clear thoughts from the past, I run the water and wash my face and then strip out of my clothes. Taking one last look in the mirror, I pull my hair out of the hair tie and run my hands through it, letting the waves fall over my shoulders.

Opening the door and stepping back into the bedroom, I freeze, the breath taken out of me. I don't know how he does it, how he affects me so easily. It's almost like as soon as I lay eyes on him, I'm instantly wet and needy.

Zac is standing by the side of the bed, shirtless. He's removed his shoes and socks and has the button and fly undone on his dress pants. I can see the top of his black Calvin Kleins. He just stands there with all those tanned muscles on display.

His torso is strong, with a wide chest and broad shoulders.

A narrow waist with goddamn washboard abs... I always thought the term "washboard abs" was just an exaggerated saying, but I get it now... boy, do I get it now. What I wouldn't do to run my tongue over all of those ridges of his body.

Smirking at me like he knows just how much his body affects me, he asks, "See something you like, sunshine?"

As my eyes roam up and down his body again, for like the zillionth time since stepping out of the bathroom, I can see the outline of his now hard cock trying to escape the confines of his pants. Smiling up at him and fluttering my lashes, I aim for coy.

"Meh, it's not bad, but it sure looks like you're really liking what you see right now." I point to his very obvious and very impressive erection.

"I'm about ten seconds away from throwing you down on this fucking bed, tying you up, and showing you exactly just how much I fucking love what I see right now," he growls out, literally growls.

As he goes to take a step forward, I hold my hand in a stop motion. To my surprise, he stops in his spot, a concerned look crossing his features.

"Stop right there, GQ. Don't you dare move a muscle." Turning, I dig through my clutch for my phone. Finding it, I hold it up excitedly. "I need to capture all this perfectness." At his shocked look, it crosses my mind that he might not actually want me to take photos of him in a state of undress. "You don't mind, do you?"

"Baby, you can take as many pictures of me as you want. In fact, your camera roll should be filled of pictures of just me."

Smiling, I snap away. It's a perfect shot. Looking at the picture, I say, "This is fucking amazing, really." Throwing the phone back down on the dresser, I look up at Zac. "At least now, whenever I'm in my bed by myself, I can look at this picture and scream your name when I make myself come." I smile as sweetly as I can manage.

Zac's eyebrows raise and within five seconds, he has me over his shoulder and storming back towards the bed. Landing in the middle of the bed, I haven't even had time to get my bearings before he's on top of me and his lips are slammed onto mine.

Zac's hands hold my head in place, tilting it slightly, allowing him the access to my mouth he hungrily seeks. I can feel this kiss all the way down to my toes, tingles running through my body. I arch my hips up, seeking the friction that my core is desperate for. My hips meet nothing but air. I groan out loud at the disappointment and frustration of not being able to get the friction I'm desperate for.

Zac laughs into the kiss. Pulling away, he looks at me with those emerald green eyes. Mesmerising, that's what they are, his eyes. They draw you in and hold you captured. I'm lost, so lost to this man.

"Patience, sunshine. I plan on taking my time with you tonight. I rushed too much earlier, but now, now I'm going to savour you." He runs wet kisses down my neck and back up, nibbling on my ear. "I will treasure your body like it was made to be treasured."

I can feel how wet I am. I can feel the moisture dampen my centre. Wrapping my legs around his waist, I arch my hips up again, my core just grazing Zac's hardened cock. But it's not enough. Letting out a moan, I try again to arch my hips up, only to have Zac pull back. Into my ear, he whispers, "This greedy pussy of yours is going to get you into trouble, sunshine. What am I going to do with you?"

"You could start by giving me what I want, now, Zac. I need you inside me now, dammit." I moan as his cock barely grazes my pussy. "Please." I'm at the point that I don't even care that

I'm begging. I mean, I don't recall ever being so wanton that I was reduced to begging.

Zac laughs. He sits up and runs his hands down the sides of my ribs and back up; my body arches up towards him. "I fucking love how responsive your body is to my touch, sunshine."

I reach my hands up to touch him, and run my hands over his pecs. He catches them before I get to those lickable fucking abs.

"*Tsk, tsk, tsk.*" Shaking his head, he puts my arms up over my head. "Leave 'em there, or I will tie them down."

I can't help the moan that escapes me as I think about being tied down and at his mercy. I've never even considered letting any man tie me down before, but the thought of Zac tying me down, that sends tingles straight to my core.

"So, it seems my sunshine likes the thought of being tied up, served up on a platter for me to devour, to worship this body as I see fit." His stare pierces through me. I moan, raising my hips, only to groan out when they meet nothing but air. Zac stands from the bed. Staring down at me, he orders (yes, orders), "Don't fucking move."

He walks into his walk-in wardrobe, coming back out holding a long piece of thin black rope. My eyes are drawn to the rope as he gets closer, kneeling over the top of me as he watches my expression for what seems like forever.

"Do you trust me?" he asks.

Without hesitating, I look him straight in the eyes, hold my arms out towards him with my wrists together, palms facing up, and say, "Yes, without a doubt."

I feel Zac shiver at my answer. He leans down and kisses my lips softly before whispering, "Thank you."

Zac coils the black rope around both my wrists, pulling at the knot. Picking me up like I weigh nothing at all, he positions me in the centre of the bed before raising my arms and tying the rope to the head of the bed. Kneeling between my legs, he spreads my thighs as wide as they will open, staring down at my still covered pussy.

"I actually don't know where to start, what to devour first. Should I start up here?" he says, palming my breasts and tweaking my nipples. "Or..." Moving one hand down my stomach, he cups my now quivering centre. "Should I start at the promise land, and give my pussy the attention she is so greedily seeking."

"*Argh, mmm.*" I don't know whether I moan or groan, but whatever noise I make has Zac sending me his trademark panty-melting smirk. Leaning down, he takes one of my nipples into his mouth, sucking right through the lace of my bra, his other hand paying attention to my other nipple.

"Oh god, Zac, please." I'm not sure what I'm begging for... for him to stop, or for him to keep delivering this sweet torture.

Releasing my nipple, he moves to the other side. As he puts it in his mouth, he asks, "Please what, baby? All you have to do is ask, and I will happily deliver." He sucks harder, flicking his tongue.

When he finally releases my nipple and raises up, he stares down at me. "I fucking love these tits. I could drown in these tits."

"Please don't stop." I'm begging again, going out of my mind with need.

"You don't even have to ask, because I'm never going to fucking stop worshiping your body, sunshine." He unclasps my bra from my back and raises the straps up to where my wrists are tied. My breasts falling free, my nipples are hard and wanting his mouth back on them. Unconsciously, I raise my body up towards him as much as I can.

Zac grabs both of my breasts, squeezing and tweaking my

nipples. Moaning out loud, I question, "Is it possible to come with you only touching my breasts, because right now, I think it's a high possibility... oh god."

He chuckles. "That's something we will have to test out one day, but not today. I'm hungry and haven't eaten dinner yet."

This both confuses me and riles me up. How dare he tease me to the brink, only to leave to eat? "You want to stop and eat food now? Are you kidding me?" I'm sure if my eyes could send daggers his way, they would be.

He looks at me, shaking his head, amused. Reaching down, he grabs the fabric of my panties in both hands and pulls. I hear the tear, the ripping sound. Why this has me turned on, I don't know, but I also don't care. Zac brings my panties up to his nose and inhales.

"I fucking love the smell of you." He throws the panties over his shoulder and onto the floor as he says, "*Mmm*, I'm not hungry for food, sunshine. I'm fucking starved for the taste of you on my lips."

That's a meal I can be down for—well, technically he would be the one that would be down. "Well, what are you waiting for?"

Trying to get him to get on with it, I remember how good he was with his tongue earlier, and I can't wait to get that tongue on me again. Zac starts kissing his way down my stomach. He skips my pussy, lifts my left leg and lays wet kisses from my knee up my inner thighs, stopping just short of where my pussy is begging for his attention. Putting that leg down, he repeats the action on the opposite leg.

By the time he rests his shoulder between my legs, I am crazy with lust, need. I can feel my body quivering. I can feel the moisture seep down my thighs. Just as I think Zac is finally going to put his mouth on my most needy parts, he leans down to my very inner thigh and bites.

"Oh god!" I scream out. The pain of the bite is quickly eased as he licks over the spot. Then he bites again, just higher than the previous bite.

"*Argh.*"

There's pain, but then there is a pleasure, a kind of pleasure I've never felt before. It's intense and I want more. As Zac is licking the bite mark, I'm relishing this mixture of pain and pleasure. He turns his head and bites my other thigh. Again, I squirm and moan, yell out loud. I expect to feel his tongue on my thigh where he bit me, but instead he licks me, from the bottom of my pussy to the top. He licks slowly and by the time he reaches my clit, it only takes one circle of his tongue to send me over the edge.

Screaming out his name, I buck as I squeeze his head between my thighs, keeping him in place. Zac continues to lick me, swirling his tongue around and around my clit, riding the wave. I think I see stars. Zac lays soft kisses on the lips of my pussy as my body relaxes into the bed.

When he raises his head to look at me, he says, "That is the sexiest fucking thing I've ever seen. Your face when you come, I could watch it over and over again."

I'm breathing heavily, still catching my breath from the orgasm of all orgasms, my chest rising and falling in fast motions. "If you're trying to kill me by orgasm, mission accomplished. I think I just died and went to heaven."

Moving up my body, he kisses my lips and I can taste myself. "I don't want to kill you by orgasm, baby, just ruin you for all other men." At the mention of other men, his face becomes hard. I'm realising he has a very strong jealous streak, but apparently so do I, so I guess we're even there.

"You ruined me for all other men from the moment our eyes connected from across the bar," I tell him honestly, and he groans. He stands up and drops his pants and briefs to the floor in one go, freeing one hell of an impressive erection. I didn't know there were such things as beautiful cocks before, but his is a freaking work of art. I'm staring. I know I am staring at it; he knows I'm staring at it.

He picks a condom up off the side table, and I have the sudden thought that I'd rather he doesn't use one. I don't dare voice this opinion, though. I watch, as he slides the condom down his shaft before he tugs a few times as he makes his way back to my bed, wishing I had a camera to capture that material.

Smirking, he settles between my legs. "I can't wait to feel your pussy choke my cock. I've been dying to get back inside you from the moment I slipped out of you today." I raise my hips, trying to reach him. He chuckles and slaps my pussy lightly. "Such a hungry, greedy pussy. What am I going to do with it?"

I don't think he's actually asking me the question, but I answer anyway. "You're going to fuck it, and you're going to fuck it hard," I demand.

I watch as his body shivers before he lines the tip of his cock up to my entrance. "That dirty mouth of yours is trouble, sunshine." He pushes into me in one hard thrust. Buried to the hilt, he steadies himself. Leaning down, he whispers into my ear, "I fucking love your dirty mouth." And with that, he pumps in and out, slowly at first and then faster.

Lifting one leg and resting my calf on his shoulder, the angle allows him to go deeper, every thrust hitting that sweet spot inside. My arms are straining. I can feel the rope burns forming on my wrists, but the pain is adding to the immense pleasure.

"Oh god, Zac, it's so good. Don't stop."

Grunting, he slows his pace as he says, "There's nothing in the world that could get me to stop fucking you, Alyssa. I'm going to be fucking you for the rest of my life." Hearing him use my name, Alyssa, instead of sunshine or baby, I know he truly believes what he says.

Zac pulls out, and I growl at him. He just laughs and spins my body over so I'm on my hands and knees. Looking over my shoulder, I see him lining himself up with my entrance. He looks up and smirks. I can feel my pussy tighten at the sight, a smirk downright dangerous to womankind. Zac groans and slaps my ass. I let out a screech, but the pain quickly becomes pleasure and I hear myself asking for more.

"Again," I say, looking back at him.

"Gladly," he replies, laying a slap on my other cheek before rubbing his hands over the sting. He's pumping so hard into me, if it weren't for his current hold on my hips, I'm pretty sure I would not be able to hold myself up right now.

He lays two more slaps on my ass before leaning over and biting my shoulder. The bite does it. I come, screaming his name. I feel Zac jerk inside me. I feel his come spurting out, filling the condom. He roars my name out so loud I wouldn't be surprised if the whole building heard it.

My lifeless body collapses on the bed. I couldn't move if I wanted to. I barely register Zac untying the rope and rubbing my wrists before pulling the blankets back up over me. I'm so tired, that I don't fight it when I hear Zac whisper into my ear, "Go to sleep, baby. We always have tomorrow."

I look up at him. "Promise?"

"I fucking swear it," he says, kissing me on the forehead, then my nose, then my lips.

I'm woken by the soundtrack of Rocky, which I've come to know as Bray's ringtone. Grumbling, I make half-conscious demands. "Turn it off or I'll break it." Slapping my hand across the bed, in an attempt to make the sound stop, my hand meets a solid wall of muscle. I hear Zac's groan as he rolls over.

"What? There better be a good fucking reason for you to be calling this fucking early." There's a short silence as he listens to Bray on the other end of the phone, and then Zac's getting up out of bed. "Fuck, okay, I'll be there as soon as I can."

Rolling onto my back, I open one eye to see Zac throw his phone down on the bed he just got out of. He walks around to my side. Leaning down, he kisses my forehead and whispers, "I have to go handle something. Go back to sleep. I'll be back before you know it." Nodding my head, I close my eyes, letting sleep take me over.

The next time I wake, it's to my own phone blasting out. I really need to remember to turn these phones off when I'm sleeping. Seeing that it's my boss calling, I answer, trying not to sound like I'm asleep.

"Hello, this is Alyssa," I say in the most professional tone I can muster while also covering a yawn.

"Hello, Alyssa. It's Nicki. Thank goodness. You're the first nurse to answer my call this morning; we're short staffed. Five nurses have called in sick. If you can make it here within the next hour and a half, there is a twelve-hour overtime shift with your name on it." Nicki doesn't take a single breath as she rushes out the request.

I'm tempted to say no, to choose to stay in this bed, this comfy, warm bed that smells like Zac, over going to work in the cold and depressing hospital. Then I remember how much extra money I could make with twelve hours at overtime rates and my decision is made.

"I'll be there, Nicki."

"Thanks, see you soon." She doesn't give me the chance to say goodbye as she disconnects the call. Jumping out of bed, I order an Uber and rush through getting dressed. I'll shower once I'm home and can get into my scrubs. It's not until I'm sitting in the Uber that I get a chance to send Zac a message to let him know I'm going into work.

*ALYSSA: HI, I JUST WANTED TO LET YOU KNOW I'VE BEEN CALLED INTO WORK, SO HAD TO LEAVE YOUR COMFY BED, AS MUCH AS I'D RATHER STAY IN IT ALL DAY. XOXO*

I debate the *xoxo* added to the end of the text but decide to just send it. If he doesn't like it, too bad. I don't have long to dwell on how he will take the *xoxo* because my phone blares out "Stuck Like Glue." Groaning at the song, albeit with an enormous smile on my face, I peek up to see the Uber driver looking at me through the rear-view mirror. I silently apologise before answering the call.

"Hel—"

I don't even get the full hello out before Zac is interrupting my greeting. "Sunshine, where are you?"

"Well, hello to you too, babe. You know most people start a conversation with a greeting like *hello, howdy*... I'd even take a *g'day, mate*," I say in a saccharine sweet voice.

"Hello, beautiful, now tell me, where are you?"

He sounds annoyed but I have no clue what I've done to annoy him. Even an annoyed Zac is a hot Zac. Seeing how far I can push him, I say, "Well, at this very second, I'm in an Uber on my way back to my apartment."

"Take this turn, John. It's quicker," I say to the driver, pointing to my left. He swerves the car left at the last minute, resulting in the car behind us blaring their horn.

This does not go unnoticed by Zac. "Why can I hear tires screeching and horns blaring? Please tell me you're okay, sunshine. Actually, just send me this Uber driver's details. I might need to have a word with him about how he should drive with such precious cargo."

He sounds so serious I have to laugh, which doesn't ease his distress. "You might think I'm joking, but I assure you I am not."

"Oh, I have no doubt you're not joking, but I also know I have no intentions of doing what you just requested either. I'm fine, and John here is getting me home as quickly as he safely can. I have one hour and fifteen minutes to get to work, so as much as I'd love to sit around and chat all day, I really have to go. I'm just pulling into my townhouse now. Bye, Zac. I'll talk to you later."

I hang up without letting him add anything else. Giving John a thanks and a wave, I'm out the door and running towards my townhouse.

# Twelve

## ZAC

STUCK in the police station for two hours, waiting for my brother to be bailed out, is not how I thought I'd be spending my morning today. The mother-fucking asshole from the club last night tried to press assault charges against him. The charges were dropped as soon as Dean delivered the CCTV footage—the video showing that fucker hits Alyssa across the face before Bray pounces on him.

I get a text message from Alyssa on my way back to the penthouse, on my way back to my bed, where I left her. "Fuck!" Hitting her name, I call her rather than text her back. She's in a fucking Uber on her way back to her place. Alyssa hangs up on me though, before I can talk her into turning around and going straight back to bed.

"Dammit!" I hit the steering wheel and turn to look at Bray. "Stop fucking laughing. This is all your fault, you know."

Bray raises one eyebrow at me. "Tell me, brother, how is it my fault that your *girlfriend* is going to work, instead of waiting for you in your bed?" He uses hand quotation marks around girlfriend—that just pisses me off more.

"Because, if I didn't have to get up at the arse-crack of dawn to bail your ass out of jail, I would have been in bed still with my girlfriend. I would have been able to get up to drive her home and to work, and she wouldn't have had to get into an Uber with some fucker named John, driving like he's in *Grand Theft Auto*."

My hands are gripping the steering wheel tight, as I drive towards Alyssa's townhouse. "There is just way too much wrong with that statement. I'm not gonna touch it with a ten-foot pole. You know you're going the wrong way, right? The penthouse is back that way." Bray smirks as he points his thumb over his shoulder.

Shaking my head, I tell him, "We're going to Alyssa's."

I see him scrunching his eyebrows together. "Why are we going to Alyssa's? You heard that she's going to work, right?"

"We're going there, because I plan on driving her to work, so she doesn't have to catch a fucking train or take an Uber." I take a deep breath, in an attempt to clear away thoughts of just what could go wrong if she caught a train.

Bray is quiet. Looking over at him, I see him staring back at me. "You're really hung up on this girl, aren't you?" he asks earnestly.

Thinking on his question a moment, I answer honestly, "I know it's fast, but I've never felt like this. Like I don't breathe properly unless she's in the same room, like every time I have to leave her, part of me stays with her. I can't shake these feelings, but honestly, I don't want to shake them either."

I'm expecting some smart-arse response about being pussy whipped, but instead, I get the very rare, serious Bray. "Good, you deserve some good in your life, but you might have to actually tell her why you don't like her getting public transport. Otherwise, you're going to come across like even more of a controlling bastard than you already are." I know he's right, but how do I bring up a conversation I've refused to have for the last five years?

"I'll try," is all I commit to.

"You do that. I think she will be more agreeable to not using public transport if you tell her. Also, if you're in love with this girl, you should probably lock her down before she comes to her senses and realises she's with the wrong brother." He smirks.

I reach out and punch his arm, not that it affects him any. "Brother or not, I will kill you if you lay a hand on her."

"Oh, I know you would." He laughs.

I knock on Alyssa's front door with Bray standing right behind me. Turning my head back towards him, I say, "You know, you can wait in the car?"

He laughs at me. "And miss this shit show you're about to get in? Never."

Just as I'm about to tell him to get the fuck back in the car, the door swings open to a dripping wet Alyssa, standing there in a fucking towel. I'm instantly hard at the sight, that is, until Bray opens his fucking mouth.

"Damn, I can see why my brother has given up his balls to you, Lyssa."

Stepping into the open doorway, I grab Alyssa's waist and walk her backwards a few steps before slamming the door in Bray's face. Alyssa stands there, staring at me like I've lost my head. I probably have. I can't believe she'd answer the door in a fucking towel. "I'll just wait in the car, kids," Bray yells through the door.

"*Umm*, hi?" Alyssa questions, holding the towel tighter around her body.

"Hi? Hi?" I question back. "Why the fuck are you answering the door with no clothes on?"

Walking her backwards, I've got her backed against the wall before she answers, "Because I just got out of the shower, and then some ass was trying to bang my bloody door down. So, I thought: *huh*, maybe if I opened it to see what the ass wanted, the door would stay intact." She's smiling up at me like butter wouldn't melt in her mouth.

"Some ass, *huh*? What if it wasn't me at the door? Do you let any random ass see you in a state of undress?" Trailing my fingertips down her arm, I watch as her skin pebbles under my touch.

"I, *ah...*" Shaking her head, she pushes me back. "I don't have time for this, Zac. I need to get dressed and get to work." She marches back up the stairs. I follow her like the lost fucking puppy I am whenever I'm around her.

Standing in her doorway, I take in her room. It suits her, matches her. She has a queen-size bed with a large cream fabric bedhead, with white covers and pink pillows in varying shades and sizes. Hearing the slamming of a drawer pulls my attention back to her. She's standing at a white dresser, holding her scrubs.

She glares at me. "Are you planning on watching me get dressed for work? Why are you here, Zac?"

"I'd much rather watch you undress."

Smirking, I roam my eyes up and down her body. Then she does the unthinkable. She drops her fucking towel and stands there, just feet away from me, naked. She smiles like she's just won an argument.

"If you want to actually make it to work in time, sunshine, I suggest you cover that delectable body of yours up, now," I grunt out.

Alyssa tilts her head, her eyes roaming up and down my

body. I can't help the erection that is painfully trying to escape the confines of my jeans. It seems I just have to be in the same room as her, and I'm instantly fucking hard; but being in a room with her naked takes it to next-level fucking hard. As her eyes linger on my straining erection, I groan and readjust myself. I remind her of what she should be doing. "Sunshine, if you want him to come out and play, he's more than willing. But if I get my hands on you, we won't be leaving this bedroom for the rest of the day. Your choice."

She dresses quickly. I watch every move, every curve of her body being covered up by those damn scrubs. When she turns her back to me, I adjust my cock again. He's not getting the message that it's not playtime. Alyssa turns back around and I'm stunned. She looks like a fucking wet dream. I never got the whole nurse roleplay thing before, but fuck me, she can give me a sponge bath any fucking day.

My eyes roam over her. It's like they can't decide which part of her body they want to take in; it's all just that damn good. She stands there in blue scrubs. Her hair is piled up on top of her head and a stethoscope hangs around her neck. Rubbing a hand over my jaw, I try not to let out the moan that wants to escape.

"Dammit, I thought covering your body would give my cock the message it's not playtime. But damn, sunshine, you look like a fucking wet dream in those scrubs." Shaking my head, my eyes continue to roam up and down her body.

She saunters up to me. Laying a hand on my chest, she looks up and asks, "Did you bring the Batmobile?" Confused at her question and with the blood currently all being directed to my cock, I grunt out, "*Uh-huh.*"

Then she does something that blows my mind. Her hand slides down my chest. She has my belt and jeans undone before my brain can catch up with what she's doing. Reaching into my boxers, she frees my cock, stroking up and down softly.

My cock is already fucking hard, pre-cum leaking from my tip. Alyssa drops to her knees and looks up at me. I swear I could fucking come just from seeing her in front of me on her knees. She swipes her tongue, licking my shaft from my balls up to the tip before swirling her tongue around the tip. She repeats this action two more times before she takes me into her mouth fully.

It takes everything in me not to come as soon as I hit the back of her throat. Alyssa moans around my cock, sending vibrations right down to my balls, before swallowing.

"Fuck me."

She looks up and smiles around my cock before sliding her mouth right up to the tip and back down again. I'm not going to last long. The wet, warm feel of her mouth, her eyes peering up at me, it's too much. I can feel my balls start to tighten, tingling sensations running down my spine. Grabbing the sides of her face, I hold her still as I pump my cock in and out of her.

"I'm gonna come," I warn her, giving her the chance to pull back.

She grabs my ass and pulls me into her mouth, sucking harder. I come in long, hot spurts down her throat and she swallows every last drop. She licks my cock clean before I lift her up, holding her chin as I claim her mouth with my own. I can taste myself on her, but I couldn't fucking care.

"That was the best damn blowjob I've ever had," I praise her, using my thumb to rub her now swollen bottom lip.

She pulls away, creasing her eyebrows. "If you ever want to receive another of those, from me..." She pauses to point to herself dramatically. "...you'd be best not to mention previous blowjobs from other women."

I can't help but smile. I love that she gets jealous. It goes both ways.

"Sunshine, you did know I wasn't a virgin, right?" I ask her just to tease.

The question backfires on me when she answers, "Oh, I know you weren't, but guess what? Neither was I."

She smirks and pushes past me through the doorway, making her way downstairs. It takes me a while to clear my head of the rage I encounter at thoughts of her with another man.

Walking out to the car, after making sure Alyssa's front door was locked, I'm stopped in my tracks when I see Alyssa hugging Bray, who notices my approach and smirks as he wraps his arms around her waist.

"What the fuck?" I yell as I approach, ripping her away from him and holding her against my chest.

As Bray laughs and dodges my right hook, Alyssa turns in my arms and smiles as she says, "Relax, Zac. I was just thanking him for last night. You know, for saving me from getting more than just a light bruise on my face."

At the mention of the bruise on her face, my eyes zone into her cheek and my rage only heightens. "You couldn't do that, without having his arms wrapped around you?" I sulk. I know I'm sulking, but I can't seem to help it.

Alyssa wraps her arms around me. Standing on her tiptoes, she whispers in my ear, "It was your cock that was literally in my mouth not five minutes ago. I don't think you need to be jealous of your own brother." She smiles and turns to Bray. "Wipe the smile off your face, before I let him unleash on you. Now, are you driving me to work, or do I need to call an Uber? Because I'm too late for the train now."

The thought of her getting on the train sends my blood cold, I grunt out, "You're not catching a fucking train."

Bray goes to climb into the passenger seat.

"Not a fucking chance. Get in the back." Pushing him out of the way, I hold the door open for Alyssa to climb in. Pulling out of the driveway, I grab her hand and bring her wrist to my mouth before resting our joined hands on my thigh. The first time I did this, I noticed how much she melted and relaxed into her seat, just like she does now.

Nearing the hospital, I ask her, "What time do you finish? I'll pick you up."

She looks over at me. "I finish at midnight, but you don't have to pick me up. I can get a train or an Uber. It's fine, really."

I can't help the rage that comes over me. "Like fuck you will get a fucking train at midnight. Are you crazy? It doesn't matter. I'll be here to take you home."

I hear Bray clear his throat in the back seat as he pretends to be busy on his phone. Alyssa doesn't miss it either.

"You're either a control freak, or have serious issues with people catching trains. I'm good with either option right now, because I really freaking like your cars and appreciate the ride."

Bray clears his throat again, unsuccessfully disguising a laugh. Alyssa turns around in her seat, facing him.

"Care to share why you got arrested this morning, and had to drag Zac out of bed to bail you out?"

The fact that she knew why I had to go and help Bray both surprises and confuses me. How the hell did she know that he got arrested? As I'm racking my brain trying to figure out how she knew, Bray slaps the back of my head.

"You told her? What happened to the bro code, man? Bros before—"

I cut in, not letting him finish his sentence. "I swear to god,

Bray, if you finish that sentence, you'll find yourself walking home." He wisely shuts his mouth.

"He didn't have to tell me. Reilly sent me a message this morning, worried about you and the fact you got taken away in handcuffs." Turning back to face the front, Alyssa continues, "So why did you get arrested, Bray?"

"It's on a need-to-know basis, and you, dearie, do not need to worry your pretty little head about it," Bray says so matter-of-factly.

Alyssa turns back and shoots daggers at him. "That's fine. I don't need to know, but there is something you need to know." She waits for him to acknowledge her.

"And what's that?" he asks.

"Oh, you know, just that if you hurt my friend, I will rip your balls off, cook them in spaghetti and feed them to you. I'd hate to have to tell Zac that I deformed his one and only brother." She thinks about this for a second before looking at me. "Wait, there aren't any more of you, right?"

"Nope, just me, Bray, and Ella," I say.

Deciding it's best to change the subject before she questions any further into the family, I ask Bray, "I need you to put feelers out for a new PR manager."

He grumbles that he's on it, but Alyssa suddenly gets excited. "Wait, you're looking for a new PR manager? For the club?"

Her excitement is contagious, and I can't help but smile at her. "If you want the job, sunshine, it's yours." Bray coughs in the back seat, and I shoot him a glare that he catches through the rear-view mirror. Alyssa's laugh fills the car. It's a laugh that I could listen to all day, a laugh I want to hear a lot more of.

"I don't think I'm qualified to be your PR manager, Zac, but I do happen to be very good friends with someone who does have a degree in public relations and is currently between jobs."

I would have given her the job whether she could do it or not, just because it would mean I would see more of her. Curious to know which friend she is referring to, I ask, "Who's your friend?"

Alyssa looks at me a moment before she rushes out, "Reilly." Noticing my screwed-up face, she adds,

"I know what you're thinking, but she really is good at what she does."

"Not a fucking chance," Bray grunts from the back seat.

It's a good thing it's not his club, and just to rub that fact home, I tell Alyssa, "Tell Reilly she's got the job and to meet me at the club in two hours." I wait for her squeal and happy dance to stop before I finish my thought, "On a one-month trial basis, but no promises, sunshine."

Bray curses to himself in the back seat. Alyssa looks back at him but decides not to say anything.

"I'm going to text her now. I promise you won't be disappointed." Alyssa texts back and forward with who I assume is Reilly for the rest of the trip.

Pulling up in front of the hospital, I hop out and walk around to the passenger door. Reaching a hand in, I help her out and pull her straight into me. Stepping back and away from the car, I slam my lips down on hers, claiming her, not caring if anyone is watching.

Pulling back, I brush her swollen lip with my thumb. "I love these lips. I don't think I've ever enjoyed kissing someone so much before."

Raising an eyebrow at me, she says, "Really? You're going to ruin this moment by comparing me to past conquests?"

"Sunshine, you are anything but a conquest. You're my tomorrow." Pulling her in and hugging her tight, I bury my head into her neck, inhaling the strawberry-vanilla scent I can't seem to get enough of.

"*Mmm*, and you're a charmer, GQ, but I really do need to get in there."

I reluctantly let her go. "Make sure you're free tomorrow. I'm taking you on a date. No friends, no annoying siblings. Just you and me, sunshine."

"Sounds like a plan," she says as she walks away. "I'll see you at twelve," I call out to remind her I'll be picking her up.

I have gone through all the tasks I need Reilly to get done before the weekend. I'm a little surprised at the difference I'm seeing in Reilly today. She's the utmost professional and nothing like the drunk girl I saw last night—the one attempting to teach my girlfriend how to fucking pole dance. I'm about to show her to her office when my phone pings with the song "My Girl" by The Temptations.

Smiling, because I know it's Alyssa, I answer her call. "Sunshine, I assure you, your friend is gainfully employed."

Hearing her laugh brightens my smile even further. I don't recall a time when I've smiled so damn much before, but I think I like it.

"That's good to know, but it's not the reason I called." She giggles.

"Not that I don't love hearing your voice, but do you care to share with me why you called?"

I notice Reilly looking down at her phone, busying herself and attempting to hide the fact that her eyebrows just shot up to her hairline.

I'm making my way out of the office before what Alyssa says

next stops me in my tracks. "I called to thank you for the roses, of course. They are beautiful, Zac. Thank you."

Hearing the joy in her voice makes me wish I did send her flowers.

"Sunshine, as much as I would like to say those roses are from me, they're not," I grunt out. Whoever the fuck is sending my woman roses is a fucking dead man walking.

"Well, if you didn't send them, who did?" she asks quietly. I don't miss the shake in her voice. Is she scared? She has no reason to be scared.

"Is there a card with the flowers, Alyssa?" I ask, desperate to know who just made it to my hit list.

Reilly's eyes go wide as she shakes her head no. My eyebrows draw together, confusion over her reaction taking over.

Alyssa replies in a shaky voice, "Y... yes, there is. I didn't open it because I thought you sent them, Zac."

Her reaction to receiving flowers from an unknown sender sends chills down my spine. Why is she so fucking scared? Attempting to calm her, I tell her, "Sunshine, it's okay. Read the card to me. What does it say?"

Now, Reilly is getting up, rushing towards me. She snatches the phone right out of my hand, puts the call on speaker and pushes me out of the office and towards the elevator.

"Lyssa, it's Reilly. You are okay. You are safe. You're in the hospital. Nothing can happen to you in the hospital." Reilly speaks calmly into the phone while pushing me into the lift and pressing the button for the ground floor. "Lyssa, listen to me. Do not open that card. Don't touch it. We are on our way to you, okay? Zac and I, we're coming to get you, okay?"

Alyssa's voice is so quiet as she agrees with Reilly. "I want you to stay on the phone with me until we get there. Go and tell whoever you need to tell that you're sick and you need to go home, okay?"

Reilly's calm tone is doing nothing to calm my racing heart. What the fuck is going on? Reilly continues to talk to Lyssa, while I stare at the phone like it can give me the answers I fucking need right now.

"Lyssa, don't hang up just put the phone in your pocket while you talk to your boss," she instructs and, looking briefly at me, she says quietly, "Lyssa, it's not him, okay. It can't be. He's still in jail. It's not him."

"It's not him," Alyssa repeats quietly. "I'm going to put the phone in my pocket and tell the registrar I have to go." All I can hear on the line is the shuffling of fabric.

Following Reilly out to the back carpark, I'm quiet when I voice all the questions currently storming through my head. "What the fuck is going on, Reilly? Why is she so fucking freaked out, and who the fuck is *he*?"

Reilly puts her finger to her lips as she whispers, "You need to drive. If you care about Alyssa at all, you need to get to the hospital now. Just know that she needs us. I can't tell you why. It's not my story to tell."

Cursing, I jump into the car. Reilly barely has the passenger door shut before I have the car screaming out of the carpark in the direction of the hospital.

# Thirteen

## ALYSSA

I CAN'T BELIEVE this is happening right now, just when I thought my life was heading in the right direction. I finally met a guy who I actually like, like really freaking like. If I could admit it to myself, I might actually even love him.

This cannot be happening again. I barely survived the last time. I don't think I could survive this. Not to mention the fact that Zac would run at the first sight of just how much crazy I come packaged with. I mean, why would he stick around with a freaked-out nutcase, who can't even get a bunch of flowers without having a full-blown panic attack?

Well, that's not entirely true. I got excited and swooned when I thought the roses came from Zac. I was so excited I called him to thank him without checking the card first. As soon as he said they weren't from him, the panic kicked in, the flashbacks started, and I was back to that place from two years ago.

I'm now sitting in a locked bathroom stall, the roses tossed on the ground, staring at me, taunting me. It can't be him again. I know he's still in jail, at least I thought he was still in jail.

*Oh god, what if he got out? What if he's not in jail anymore?*

I spent six months of my life being tortured by him, all the while not even knowing who it was that was torturing me.

I can't stop the shaking. I know I'm in the midst of a panic attack, but I can't seem to do anything to stop it. How did Zac manage to calm me so easily during my panic attack in his car? This situation is much worse, with the possibility that I will have to spend my time locked in my apartment again because I fear what's waiting for me on the outside. It took me two months after he was sentenced to go outside again, and that was with Sarah, Reilly and Holly all holding my hand the whole time.

Remembering Reilly was still on the phone, I pull my phone out of my pocket.

"Reilly, I can't survive this again. I just can't. Make it stop... please make it stop," I plead with one of my best friends.

"Lyssa, it's not happening again, okay? Listen to me. This is just a misunderstanding. Zac and I are on our way. We're almost there, just hold on." Her voice is calm, the total opposite of how I'm feeling.

Just then, the thought of Zac seeing me like this, this mess of a person, hits me. He's going to run. I will lose him before I even really got a chance to have him.

"Reilly, he can't see me like this. I can't let him see me like this." My breathing is heavy and uneven.

"Who?" Reilly asks.

"Zac, he can't see me like this, Reilly. He's going to get one look at me and run. I'm going to lose him, aren't I?"

There's a loud bang and a growl that comes through the phone before Reilly clears her throat.

"Lyssa, *umm*, you most certainly are not going to lose him. And if he leaves you just because you had a little panic attack,

I'm going to find him and feed him his own balls," she says in her ever-sweet voice.

"I really like this one, Reilly, like really, *really* like. I don't want to lose him. Oh god, why is this happening again? Just when I thought I could be happy, that I found my happy."

"We're just pulling into the hospital now. Where are you, Lyssa? I'll come get you," Reilly asks.

"I... I've locked myself in the ladies, just inside the emergency entrance. I didn't know what to do," I confess.

"Fuck!" I hear him loud and clear on the phone, in that deep and gravelly voice.

Then I hear Reilly yelling out, "Zac, wait up. It's the ladies. You can't just waltz in there, you know."

Reilly sounds like she's running. Before I can contemplate what's happening, the door to the ladies bangs against the wall. The first thing I think is *they're going to be too late. He's found me already*. I see a pair of dress shoes stop at the stall door I'm locked behind.

"Sunshine, I need you to open the door, please." It's Zac's voice. Is it really him, or have I somehow conjured his voice in my mind?

"Zac?" I ask so quietly I didn't think he would even hear me.

"Yeah, sunshine. It's me. Please open the door." His voice sounds strained.

Timidly reaching up for the lock, I slide the latch across and step back to pull the door open. There he stands, on the other side of the door. I don't even have the door open all the way before he's pulling me into his arms. I can feel my body shaking. I can feel the tears running down my face.

Clinging to him as tight as I can, I beg, "Please don't leave me. I'm sorry. So sorry. I'm not always like this, I swear, just... please don't leave."

Zac picks me up, walking to the far side of the bathroom. He sits on the floor with me and I crawl into his lap. I bury my face into his chest; my fingers hurt from how tightly they are clinging to the fabric of his shirt, but I can't loosen them. Zac strokes my hair while planting gentle kisses on the top of my head.

"Alyssa, there is nothing in this world that will make me leave you. We will always have tomorrow, remember?" he says so soothingly.

"Promise?" I ask.

"Promise," he says while he continues to stroke my hair.

Just then, Reilly bursts through the door. "Jesus Christ, Zac, how the hell can you run so freaking fast?"

She's kneeling down beside me, rubbing my arm. "Lyssa, honey, I'm here. It's going to be okay." Nodding my head, I don't attempt to lift it off Zac's chest. "We need to get you out of here. Come on, honey. Let's go home."

I lift my head to look at her. "Okay," I get out.

Zac shoos away Reilly's hand as he lifts my chin so our eyes meet. "Sunshine, let's go home." He stands up, guiding me to my feet, my hands still clinging so tightly to his shirt. "It's okay. I've got you," he says before lifting me into his arms and carrying me out of the hospital.

Stopping at the passenger side of his door, he looks down at me, still in his arms, still clinging to his shirt. Shaking his head, he mumbles, "Fuck it," before reaching into his pocket with one hand and handing a key fob to Reilly. "You drive," he demands before climbing into the back seat and settling me on his lap.

Moments later, I hear Reilly climb into the driver's side of the car. A few minutes later, she turns and looks back at Zac.

"You're sure you want me to drive this car, this very, very expensive car?"

"Reilly, for the love of god, just press *home* on the GPS and follow the fucking directions. It's not rocket science. It's a bloody car."

Reilly starts the car and then turns to face the back again, this time to me. "Lyssa, do you want to go to Zac's, or your place? You tell me where you want to go?" she asks.

Zac growls and answers before I can put together a sentence. "Reilly, I'm your fucking boss and gave you a direction. It's your job to fucking follow it. Drive to my place, now."

"You've been my boss for two minutes, Zac. She's been my best friend for five years. My loyalty is to her, not you. You'd be best to remember that. Lyssa, tell me where you want to go before your beast here rips my head off."

Looking between the two of them, I'm confused. Are they really arguing over me?

Staring into Zac's eyes, I tell Reilly, "I want to go to Zac's. Please take me to Zac's."

Maintaining eye contact like he can see into my soul, Zac whispers, "Home, we're going home, sunshine."

The drive to Zac's was a blur. I buried my head in his chest the whole way, and when we got there, he picked me up and carried me. He held me tight as the elevator lifted to the top floor. When the doors opened, he walked me straight into his room with Reilly following suit.

Standing at the door to his room, he turns and looks at her. "Call Bray. Tell him I want him and Dean here now," he orders, before shutting the door.

～

Zac walks with me into the en suite bathroom, turns the shower on and sits me on the vanity. My fingers curl around his shirt as he steps back. I'm not ready to let go yet. When I'm in his arms, it's like nothing can touch me. I feel the safest I've ever felt when wrapped up in him. Putting his hands over the top of mine, he holds them there. We stay like that for minutes, the room filling up with steam before he says, "Sunshine, I'm not going anywhere. I will wait for as long as you need to feel comfortable to let go, but I'm not going anywhere."

After a minute, I slowly unfurl my fingers from his shirt. Zac pulls my top up and over my head before reaching around and unclasping my bra. Bending to his knees, he undoes my laces, removing my shoes and socks. Pulling me to a standing position, he pulls down my pants and panties in one go. The whole time, I stand as close as I can to him.

Zac's eyes travel up and down my body slowly, before he strips his own clothing off. Grabbing my hand, he leads me into the shower and under the spray of the water. I stand still. I can feel my body begin to relax. Zac reaches behind me and picks up a loofah and squirts some bodywash onto it. He slowly works the loofah over my shoulders; his movements are slow. He moves the loofah down my right arm and back up again, across my collarbone and down my left arm.

The scents of vanilla and raspberry fill the shower as Zac works the loofah over my body. He pays extra attention to my breasts, and I can't help but squirm with the sensations currently running through my body. He works the soap down my stomach then kneels, running the soapy loofah down each leg. When he reaches the apex of my thighs, I can't help the moan that escapes my mouth as I feel the scratchy, soapy fabric rub against the lips of my pussy.

Zac looks up at me as though he is about to say something; instead, he shakes his head and stands. I audibly grunt, at which he fails to hide a chuckle.

I tilt my head back as he runs his fingers through my hair. Zac reaches behind me, squirting shampoo onto his hands before rubbing his fingers through my hair. Massaging my scalp, he watches as I lean my head into him, the fruity smell of the shampoo filling the air.

I have never had anyone wash my hair before, other than at the salon. I don't recall a time since my mother died that I have felt so cherished and loved. I wouldn't say that Zac loves me. I mean, how can he? We've only known each other a few days, but the feelings I have for him are deep and unlike anything I've ever felt before.

I tilt my head back again, and he rinses out the shampoo before repeating the process with conditioner. Zac reaches around and turns off the shower. I have completely submitted my body to his will by now.

Grabbing some fluffy white towels off the shelf, he wraps one around himself, and I can't help but notice the impressive erection he is currently sporting. Drying me just as thoroughly as he washed me, he bends down and lifts one foot, resting it on his thigh. He drags the soft fabric of the towel from my ankle to my thigh, stopping right before the spot that I'm now aching for him to touch.

Smirking up at me, he puts my foot down and brings my other leg up, repeating the process. This time, he does rub the towel between my thighs. As I let out a moan, he pulls the towel away and stands up. He knows what he's doing to me. He knows I'm aching for his touch there. His fingers, his mouth, his cock... right now, I'd take any of them. I'm not picky.

Picking up a clean towel, he wraps my hair up before guiding me out of the bathroom and straight into his walk-in wardrobe. I can't help but let out a frustrated groan. Zac looks back at me and chuckles.

*Chuckles.* The asshole chuckles at me. As I'm standing there, slightly fuming, yet still very turned on, he hands me a shirt and a pair of sweats.

Looking me straight in the eye, he says, "Get dressed. We need to talk."

*Arghh*, what the hell? He expects me to get dressed and talk? I'm so worked up I'm surprised I'm not combusting. Holding the clothes out to the side, I look up at him.

"Either you are going to get me off right now, or I will march my naked self out to your bed and use my own fingers to finish what you started in there," I huff, pointing in the direction of the shower.

Zac's eyebrows raise towards his hairline. He tilts his head, slowly perusing my body from my feet to my head. Before I know it, he comes towards me, bends at the waist, and has me draped over his shoulder, storming towards what I can only hope is his bed. He slaps my ass, the sting registering the same time I'm floating and landing on the cloud-like mattress of his bed.

Yes, this I can work with. Just as the thought crosses my mind, Zac is hovering over me. He has one hand around my neck, squeezing, but not tight enough that I struggle to breathe. His other hand is cupping my pussy.

Bending down, he growls into my ear, "This pussy is mine. It's mine to play with. It's mine to pleasure." He dips a finger in and out of me slowly and nibbles on my neck. "Sunshine, the only way this pussy is getting off is from my hands, my cock, or my mouth. Do you understand?"

I can't help but shiver at his words, my core clenching around his finger.

"Oh, god." Moaning, I attempt to lift my hips, anything to get that extra friction my core is desperate for. Zac continues to tease me, slowly inserting just the one finger.

"Please." I'm reduced to begging.

"You need more, sunshine?" Lifting his head, he looks directly into my eyes.

"Yes, more. Please, Zac," I beg, attempting to lift my hips again.

"I'll get you there, but first you have to tell me..." Bending, he sucks a nipple into his mouth.

"*Ah*, god. Tell you what?"

Letting go of my nipple with an audible pop, he lifts his head up, smirking at me. "That this pussy belongs to me and only me."

I'm just about to tell him anything to reach the orgasm that's floating on the horizon. "It's yours, all yours. Now please, let me come."

My body feels like there are thousands of live wires circuiting throughout, goosebumps coating my skin and a light sweat covering the surface. Zac withdraws his finger and begins circling it around my clit.

Leaning down to whisper in my ear, he says, "I can't wait to watch you come, to watch you fall apart from my fingers. There's just one more thing I need from you before I can let that happen."

"Oh my god, Zac, I don't care. Whatever you need, it's yours, just please." I don't even care what I'm agreeing to.

"After I give you the pleasure you need, you and I, we are going to talk," he demands. "Tell me you understand that is what's going to happen, sunshine."

"Okay... Yes, god... Okay... Talk... we will talk after." I'm reduced to a babbling mess I'm so worked up.

Chuckling, Zac lowers his head to my nipple again. Licking it once, he says, "Glad we can agree on things so easily," then proceeds to suck on my nipple, while roughly inserting two fingers inside me with increasing speed.

My back arches off the bed. "Yes! Oh god. Yes! Please don't stop."

Zac circles his thumb around my clit while thrusting his

fingers inside me. He moves his mouth to my other breast, squeezing tighter around my throat, and I see stars. My body starts to involuntarily shake, my core clenching around his fingers, as I scream out his name through my release.

Zac draws every inch of pleasure from me as I slowly come down from my orgasmic high. He lifts his head to meet my eyes, raising one eyebrow.

"Better?" he questions with the cockiest grin plastered on his face—like he doesn't know how good he is at that.

"*Mmhmm,*" I mumble, feeling completely relaxed. Zac raises off the bed and walks back into his wardrobe, only to reappear moments later wearing a pair of dark denim jeans and a black shirt. He must notice the disappointment on my face at him being clothed, as he laughs.

Roaming his eyes up and down my sprawled-out body, he says, "Babe, we can either have this talk with you dressed, or as naked and spread out as you are now. I don't mind either way."

"Or you could strip those jeans off and let me return the favour," I suggest.

"Oh, you will definitely get a chance to return the favour, but first, we are having that talk." He smirks.

Realising I'm not going to get out of this, I grunt as I get off the bed. "Fine, but I'm getting dressed first."

ZAC

SITTING on the bed with Alyssa across from me, I wait for her to speak. This is uncharted territory for me. I'm not the one who usually digs and pries into a girl's life, but Alyssa is different. I want to know everything, but right now, the one thing I want to know is why she had a fucking panic attack after receiving flowers. I also want to know who the *he* is that she seemed so fucking scared of.

When I got to her in that bathroom, I felt like my world was tipped on its axis. She looked so fucking broken and scared; all I wanted to do was hold her and put her back together. When she clung to me and wouldn't let go, it destroyed me to see her so frightened. I never want to see that again.

"Sunshine, I need to know why you had a panic attack about the flowers."

Keeping my voice soft, I try to reassure her that she's safe here, that I would never let anything happen to her. As she looks me in the eye, I can see the tears starting to form. Her entire body shakes as she takes a deep breath in. It's fucking killing me, seeing her like this.

Reaching forward, I lift her by her hips, placing her on my

lap so she is straddling me. Cupping her face, I wipe away the tears that are freely falling and wait for her to speak.

Taking a few deep breaths, she looks me in the eye, pleading, "I can't lose you. What if I tell you and you decide it's too much, that I'm too damaged?"

I don't know how to reassure her I'm not going anywhere. I try to show in my actions just how much she means to me. I kiss her under each eye, kissing away her tears before lightly pressing my lips to hers.

"Alyssa, I'm not going anywhere, and you are not fucking damaged. Understand?" My voice is getting gruffer as I continue to rein in my anger at whatever the fuck made her think she was damaged.

Nodding her head, she says, "Okay." She takes another big breath in before she finally lets me in. "I grew up in foster care, many foster care homes actually. My mum died when I was five. She didn't have any family; it was always just my mum and me. I don't remember much about her, but I do remember that she was sick, like all the time. I found out later that she died from breast cancer."

Alyssa pauses, looking for something on my face. She must not find the reaction that she expects, as she continues. "It's why I don't want kids; breast cancer can be hereditary and I can't think of anything worse than leaving a child behind with no one to love them, like I was."

I understand her reasons for not wanting children, however, I don't agree with her that her kids would be left alone, or that she is destined to have the same fate as her mother.

"Sunshine, if you had kids, they sure as fuck wouldn't be left with no one. They would have me. Because, if you decided you wanted kids, I'm the only person you're going to have them with." She opens her mouth to argue but I'm not finished yet. Placing my finger over her mouth, I add, "Also, you don't know that you will have the same fate as your mother. I'm sure I don't have to tell you that the medical industry has advanced a lot since you were five."

"I know. I haven't even had the gene test done yet to see if I have the inherited gene mutation linked to breast cancer." She looks down at her lap, twisting her fingers together. "I figured if I don't know, then I won't stress about it as much. Five to ten percent of breast cancers are thought to be hereditary. What if I'm in that five to ten percent?"

"Sunshine, you can't live with that fear. You should get the test, and we will deal with whatever comes our way, together."

I rub my hands up and down her legs, not sure if it's reassuring her or me at this point.

"Promise?" she asks, looking so insecure.

"I swear we will always have a tomorrow together." Leaning in, I meet her lips ever so lightly then sit back and wait for her to continue.

Shaking her head, she says, "Anyway. One foster home I lived in when I was fifteen, they had five other kids living there too. There was one guy—he was seventeen—always gave me the creepy kind of vibe, you know? His name was Steven. I did everything I could to stay clear of him, but he was always there, always staring at me. I knew I had to get out of that house, so I..." She trails off, looking away.

"You what?"

"I slapped the foster mum across the face, wasn't my finest moment, but I knew it would be my ticket out. I was moved to a different home the next day, but not before her husband returned the favour and slapped me around a bit."

I'm doing everything I can to not show the rage rolling through my body at the thought of a grown-ass man slapping around a fifteen-year-old Alyssa. I know my face must tell my anger as I clench my jaw. Alyssa takes in my face, placing her hands on my shoulders.

"I swear I'm not that child anymore, Zac. I don't go around hitting people, really. I became a nurse because I wanted to help people."

Shaking my head, I consider what she must have been like at fifteen. "Sunshine, I couldn't care less if you went around slaughtering people. I'd have Dean and Bray bury the bodies for you. I'd only ask that you don't slaughter me in my sleep." I smirk at her, in an attempt to lighten the mood, even if what I say is one hundred percent truth.

The thought scares the crap out of me. I don't think there is anything this girl could do that would sway my opinion of her. She doesn't even realise the amount of control she has over me.

Smiling, she says, "Of course I would spare you. Have you seen you? I mean, if I slaughtered you, I might as well turn it into a murder-suicide, because life would not be worth living if I don't get a daily dose of the orgasms you dish out."

I'm laughing again. When was the last time I laughed so damn much?

"I will give you as many orgasms as you like," I promise as I lean in and kiss her lightly. "As soon as we're done with this talk, that is."

"*Argh.* Okay. Well, I ran into Steven again at college, two and a half years ago. He asked me out, I declined, and I thought that was that." And the rage is back. I'm grinding my teeth in an attempt to hold it in. "Anyway, he stalked me for six months before the police could catch who it was. It was Steven, my stalker was Steven."

"What do you mean stalked you? What the fuck did he do?" I don't think I can hold in this rage much longer; I want to find the motherfucker and bury him. "It started with roses. He would send roses. At first, without cards. No messages, just bunches of roses."

Shit, her eyes are tearing up again, but I need to hear this. I need the rest. Squeezing her thighs, I encourage her to continue. "Then it was the messages. H... he would send me text messages from random numbers, but always describing what I was wearing and where I was at that time. Like he wanted me to know I was being watched. I never knew who it was. I guess he got bored with that, because the roses started coming with the same message each time."

"What did the message say?" I ask, unsure if I want to know.

"It always said *SLUT* in bold letters. Then the text messages described what he was planning on doing to me in very detailed descriptions, right down to how he would choke the life out of me because, according to him, sluts like me were not worth the air they breathe."

I take a shaky breath in, waiting for her to continue.

"One time, he broke into my house, stole every pair of underwear I had, and left a note on my bed." She shivers, her fingers gripping the fabric of my shirt.

"It got to the point that I couldn't leave the house. I locked myself in the house for two months before he was caught. The girls took turns staying with me, so I was never alone. Then it came time for my practical placement at the hospital. I had to go in. I knew I had to do my placement. I had worked too damn hard to get

to that point in my degree; I decided I would not lose everything I worked for because some psycho had a hard-on for me."

"And then what happened?" I ask.

"Hospital security caught him when he had me cornered in the hallway of emergency, his hands around my throat... attempting to do just what he said he would."

*Shit.*

"Sunshine, I didn't know. You should tell me if anything I do is a trigger for you. I just had my hand around your throat and you didn't say anything. Shit, baby, I'm so sorry."

"Zac, stop. That was not the same. Maybe it should have triggered me somehow, but it didn't. Quite the opposite, I freaking loved it. I can't explain why some things trigger a panic attack and others don't. You are the first guy I've been with since Steven was arrested. Even though that date Sarah pushed me to go on didn't pan out, it did lead me to you."

Taking my hands into her own, she takes a breath, bringing her gaze to meet mine. "I can't explain what it is, but I feel safe with you. I feel like nothing can get to me when I'm with you. I'm sorry, and I will understand if it's too much too soon for you. I've never been this clingy type before. I don't know what's come over me."

I can tell she's nervous because she's rambling. "Sunshine, cling away, because I'm not letting go. In

fact, you should stay with me for a while. We can go pack some of your stuff, and I'll clear out some space in the wardrobe, or I can just order you new stuff."

Alyssa laughs like I'm joking, but she stops when she notices I'm not laughing with her.

"Wait, oh god, you're serious, aren't you?" she asks.

"Deadly serious, babe."

She shakes her head. "I'm not moving in with you. We just met like two days ago."

Her argument is weak if you ask me. "So? And it's not moving in, if it's just a few things and called staying with me." I smirk as I place my hands under her shirt, rubbing my fingers up and down the sides of her stomach. "Besides, think of how many more orgasms we could create together if you stayed here, in this bed, with me."

"*Mmm*, that has merit. But, no, I'm not staying here." Just then her stomach rumbles.

"Hungry?" I ask.

"A little," she says, shyly.

How is it she can be as daring as they come when it's about sex and then shy because she's hungry? It's fucking cute. Lifting her off my lap, I settle her on the bed.

"I'll go fetch you something to eat," I tell her. Just as I'm getting off the bed, she reaches out, gripping my shirt, fear written all over her face. "Sunshine, I'm just going to the kitchen. I'm not leaving the apartment."

I don't make a move to remove her hands. I'll wait as long as she needs me.

"O-Okay, sorry. I just..." She casts her eyes down. I lift her chin with my finger, so I can see those beautiful blue eyes.

"Babe, it's fine. You don't need to apologise to me."

Settling back down, I reach for her and pull her into my arms, kissing the top of her head. I reach over and pick up my phone, dialling Reilly's number.

"Hello, Zac? What's wrong? How is she? I swear I will—" I don't let her finish her tirade.

"Reilly, she's fine. I need you to bring in some food, something that she likes. Check the fridge." I don't wait for her response before I hang up the phone.

"Oh my god, I'm being ridiculous, aren't I?" Alyssa looks up at me, insecurity written all over her face.

"No, you're not. I don't want you to ever be embarrassed to feel how you feel, not with me. I've got you, always." I kiss the top of her head and rub my hands down her back.

"Thank you," she says, wrapping her arms around my waist.

We stay like that for a few minutes, soaking up each other in peace, until the door bursts open and three females push at each other to get in.

"What the fuck, Reilly. I said for you to bring food, not people," I grunt at the redhead in front holding a plate of food.

"How did you all get up here anyway?" I ask, looking at Holly and Sarah.

I feel Alyssa's body tense. Looking down at her, I silently ask her what's wrong with my eyes.

"I'm sorry, Zac. I can leave. I'll take them with me. I swear I didn't ask them to come here."

Leave? Like fuck, she can leave. "Sunshine, I don't care that your friends are here; you need them. I am, however, curious how they got up here, considering you need a key pass to reach the penthouse."

At this, Reilly pipes up triumphantly, "Oh, I went down and rode back up with them. I used your card thingy." I'm speechless. Reilly, however, is not. "I also called your brother. He's currently sulking in the living room. Dean was already here, so there's that. I also introduced myself to Ella. She was a little stunned to see a random redhead in your apartment because, according to her, and I quote: *If you're one of Zac's floozies, you're too late. He's found his forever girl.* I think I might love her already. Here, Ella made you food," she says as she places the plate on the bed next to Alyssa.

Reilly takes it upon herself to sit on the bed next to Alyssa. Raising my eyebrows at her, I say, "Please, have a seat."

At this, Holly and Sarah both stalk forward and sit on the bed. Jesus Christ, what the fuck is going on in here? I look over to see Alyssa smiling. Damn, she's fucking smiling and it's like the sunshine is back within her. I decide her friends can sit wherever the fuck they want if it makes her smile.

"Babe, I'm gonna go see Bray and Dean for a few. Will you be all right in here with your girls, or do you want to come with?" I ask, hoping like fuck she wants to stay with the girls, because she does not need to hear what I have to say.

"*Umm*, I'll be okay in here, if you're sure you don't mind us all being in your room."

Leaning down, I kiss her gently. "I don't mind." I lean further into her, so only she can hear me whisper, "Besides, soon enough, you'll be calling it *our* room." Standing up, I look pointedly at Reilly, who is eyeing the open walk-in wardrobe. "Stay out of the fucking wardrobe, Reilly, unless you want to get fired on your first day."

"*Pfft*, please, as if I would want to see your designer wardrobe," she says while shaking her head.

The other three laugh as they all say in unison, "You so would." Picking up my phone, I send Reilly a text. I don't want Alyssa to know what I have to ask her friend.

## ME: MEET ME IN THE KITCHEN NOW!

I wait for Reilly's phone to beep before I shut the door. Walking through the living room, I see Bray and Dean both look up at me expectantly.

"Wait there a sec," I say as I continue to the kitchen.

Putting a mug under the expresso machine, I touch the icon labelled: *sunshine*. I may have already stored her preferred coffee method into the machine. I grab the bottle of vanilla flavouring and pour a good dose of it into the cup.

"You summoned me, boss?" Reilly says as she strolls into the kitchen.

Stirring the coffee, I hand it to her. "Give this to Alyssa for me."

"You made her a vanilla latte?" she questions, scrunching her eyebrows together. Why the fuck she's questioning this, I don't know.

"It's her favourite," I say as a way of explanation. "Oh, I

know that, but how do you know that already?" She looks at me scrutinizingly.

"I pay attention when she tells me things," I say. As she reaches for the cup, I don't release it straight away. Looking her dead in the eye, I say, "I'm going to need a last name for Steven and what facility he was locked up in."

"Why? He's still in jail. I just called and checked. He isn't the one who sent those flowers. Besides, it wasn't his calling card. This one is different," she says.

"Humour me and text me through those details. What do you mean this one is different?" I question.

"The card, it said: *Dear Alyssa, Condolences on your future loss.* I don't get it, but it freaks me out, Zac. Alyssa can't go through this again. It took her two months before she would even leave the house by herself, and that was after Steven was locked away."

"Nobody will be getting to her. I won't let it happen," I say as I make my way out of the kitchen.

By the time I reach Bray and Dean in the living room, I have a text message with the details I requested from Reilly.

## REILLY: STEVEN JOHNSON, SENTENCED TO FIVE YEARS AT SILVERWATER CORRECTIONAL FACILITY.

"Who do we know on the inside at Silverwater?" I ask Bray and Dean as Reilly walks by us back towards the bedroom.

I don't miss the smile that appears when she pretends not to overhear. I look at Bray, who is currently staring at Reilly's retreating form.

Slapping him across the back of the head, I say, "No, she's an employee and a friend of Alyssa's. For the love of god, just don't."

"You're a bit late with your warning." He smirks at me.

"Why, for the love of god, can't you just keep your dick in your fucking pants for once in your life?"

"What can I say? I'm doing the female breed a kindness by letting them on my dick. The thing is a masterpiece, after all." He laughs. Dean and I both shake our heads at him.

"Do not let this affect the club, or Alyssa. I won't save you from her if you hurt her friend."

At this, Dean laughs. "I don't think Reilly's heart is the one breaking," he says, looking pointedly at Bray.

"Shut up, my heart's not broken. If she doesn't want a go on the Bray train again, well, that's her bad luck. There are plenty of other hot redheads out there more than willing to take her spot."

"Whatever you say, man," Dean says while shaking his head. Well, that's an interesting development I will delve into at a later date. Bray being turned down? I don't think I've ever seen that happen. "Anyway, Silverwater, who do we know?" I ask again.

"A few, why?" Bray says. I tell them about Alyssa being stalked, about what that motherfucker did to her, how scared she was. "Get the few we know a message for me. I will make weekly deposits into their funds account for the rest of their time if they make the fucker bleed."

"On it," Dean says, tapping away at his phone.

I look over at Bray, noticing him deep in thought. "You good, man?" I ask.

"Yeah." Shaking his head, he then says, "I don't know. How can you have one of the best experiences of your life, and then nothing? I mean, I get it might have freaked her out with me getting arrested the next morning and all. But that was for a fucking good cause if you ask me."

"I can't thank you enough for what you did for Alyssa at

the club when that asshole slapped her. Have you told Reilly that they arrested you because the jerk pressed charges?"

He shakes his head, pulling at his hair. "If I tell her, she will tell Alyssa, and I don't want Alyssa to feel responsible or some shit."

"I get you not wanting to tell her, but if she asks me flat out, I can't lie to her, man," I declare.

"I know. I don't expect you to. What do you think all that's about?" Bray asks, pointing at the squashed bunch of roses on the coffee table. I pick up the card lying next to it.


*DEAR ALYSSA,*


*CONDOLENCES ON YOUR FUTURE LOSS.*

*xxx*


"Fuck, I don't know, man, but I intend to find out. God help the fucker who thinks he can fuck with what's mine." I throw the card down, running my hands through my hair. "You should have seen her... She was so fucking scared. I felt like a part of my soul was breaking as she clung to me."

"Well, considering you let Reilly drive the fucking McLaren, I thought you must have lost your damn mind."

Hearing footsteps come down the hall, I look up to see Ella. Her face, bruised and battered, makes me want to murder the fucker who hurt her again. Standing, I walk to her and wrap her in my arms, kissing her temple.

"How are you feeling, sweetheart? Do you need anything?"

Wrapping her arms around me, she looks up. "I'm good,

Zac, really. I just want to forget everything and get ready to leave for Uni in a few months."

"Don't remind me you're growing up, dammit." I let her go, and then her words repeat in my head: *Leave for Uni.* "Wait, what the hell do you mean leave for Uni? I thought you chose to go to ACU here in Sydney?" I ask.

"I am, but I thought it would be good to live on campus, get the total experience," she says with a hitch to her voice.

Bray and Dean both speak up. "No."

Ella stomps her foot, staring them down. "What do you mean no? Don't answer that, because it's not up to you two baboons. I can make my own damn decisions."

"Ella, honey, wouldn't you be more comfortable living here, in your home, while you study?" I plead. I'm not ready for her to leave. I've been raising her since she was thirteen. Even if I was only twenty at the time, I had to step up and go from brother to guardian.

"Please, Zac, I've thought about this a lot. I really, really want to live on campus. You can come check the place out; it's an all-girls dorm, with high security and everything. I'll come back on weekends and semester breaks. You won't even notice I'm gone. Please don't take this away from me."

Dammit, she's pleading with teary eyes. She knows I can't say no to her when she looks at me like that.

"Don't cave, man. Don't look at that angelic face and give in. You're stronger than that, bro," Bray says. I can't do it. Pulling Ella back into my arms gently, I answer, "Okay, I'll check out the dorm building, and you will come home every weekend and semester break. I know things are changing around here, but this is your home, Ella. You will always belong here."

"Thank you, Zac," she whispers. "Whipped," Dean and Bray say.

The fuckers would not have been able to say no either. I've seen Ella work her magic on both of them before. I flip them off. "Shut the fuck up. If she wants the full experience, she will get it."

"How's Alyssa?" Ella changes the subject so well. "She'll be okay. Thank you for making her food. I know she appreciates it. *I* appreciate it."

She looks up to me. "You know, she's a lucky girl to have you. I hope I find a guy as great as you one day."

"I'm the lucky one, Ella, and there is no guy out there good enough for you. I pity any fool who thinks he is."

Ella flinches in my arms and Dean gets up, mumbling something about things to do, and leaves.

I raise my eyebrows at Bray and ask, "What the fuck is that about?"

He raises his shoulders up and down. "No idea, man, but I gotta run also. You good?" he asks.

"Yeah, I'm not going to make it into the club tonight. Can you take over for me?" I ask, eliciting surprised looks from both Ella and Bray.

"Are you sure you're okay?" Bray says as he places his hand to my forehead.

I swipe his hand away. "I'm fine. I just can't leave Alyssa tonight. It's one night, Bray. I'm sure the club will survive."

With that, I walk back to my bedroom, ready to kick three feisty females out of it.

# Fifteen

## ALYSSA

"YOU REALLY THINK they're going to be able to pull it off?" I ask Sarah, pointing to the bathroom door where Holly and Reilly have just switched clothes with each other.

Reilly says she needs a quick escape from the building to avoid, in her words, *all that is Bray*. She wouldn't elaborate on why she was avoiding him, just that it was for the greater good.

"It works on everyone but us—it will work. Not sure why she wants to avoid that piece of delicious cucumber though. I mean, are they just breeding them tall, dark and handsome in this family? If so, please tell me there is another brother hiding somewhere." Sarah looks hopefully towards me.

Laughing, I give her the bad news. "Nope, only two brothers. Sorry you were too late to the party."

We're both laughing as the door opens and Zac strolls in, eyes locked straight to mine. The intense look in his eyes has both Sarah and I suddenly quiet, waiting in anticipation for his next move. He walks straight up to me. Bending down, he cups my face in both of his hands before bringing his lips to mine. I can't help the moan that escapes my lips. Just as I wrap my arms around his neck, pulling him closer to get more of him, Holly and Reilly step out of the bathroom door, not so quietly.

Zac immediately sits up, looking behind him towards the bathroom. Squinting back and forth between Reilly and Holly, he asks, "Why have you switched clothes?"

I watch as both of their jaws drop. No one has ever been able to tell when they pretend to be each other. Sarah is gobsmacked, pointing at Zac as she questions, "Wait, how the hell can you tell they switched? It took me three months of knowing them before I could tell when they did that."

Zac shrugs his shoulders. "I'm observant. They also have very different mannerisms."

Holly looks petrified. Pointing a finger at Reilly, she says, "It's not going to work. Oh god, why did I let you talk me into this?"

Reilly grabs Holly's hand, tugging her towards the door. "It will work; it always works. Let's just go."

On her way out, Reilly says, "Lyssa, call me if you need anything."

I nod my head and thank her.

Once Holly and Reilly are gone, Sarah looks between Zac and me. "Well, I know when I'm the third wheel. I'm out too. Will you be okay?"

I look over at Zac. He tenses, holding my hand a little tighter. Nodding my head, I tell Sarah, "I'll be fine here. I'll head home a bit later when Zac goes to work."

Zac then declares, "She'll be staying here. I've taken the night off. I'll be here all night."

Sarah raises an eyebrow at me in question. I just shake my head. "I'll be fine. Thanks for coming. I will call you tomorrow."

"Okay, but if there's anything else—"

I cut her off before she can finish the sentence. "Sarah, go. I'll be fine."

With a nod, she walks out the door. Before the door even closes, Zac has me wrapped up in his arms. This feels like the safest place on earth.

"*Mmm*, I could get used to this," I say as I snuggle into his chest further.

He chuckles. "I sure hope you do, sunshine, because there ain't no way I'm letting go."

Why does he always know what to say to reassure my racing thoughts? Breathing in his scent, I bury my nose closer and sniff. Yep, all Zac, woodsy with a mix of citrus.

"You always smell so damn good, GQ."

I feel the vibration of his silent laugh. Kissing the top of my forehead, he says, "I'm sure you'd think otherwise if you got a whiff just after I did a gym workout."

Of course he works out. How else would one get a body like this? "You really took the night off work. Can you do that? You know I can always just go home if you need to be there?" As much as I would hate to leave this spot right now, I also don't want to be a nuisance to him.

"Sunshine, I own the place. I can do whatever the fuck I want. And you are staying put. We're going to play a game."

"A game, like a board game, cards?" I look up at him with questions. He shakes his head no.

"I was thinking a getting to know each other game. Let's start with twenty questions, shall we?"

Oh, that actually sounds fun. I'm hungry for all things that are Zac. I can't wait to know more about him.

That's how we spend the night and the whole of the next day and night. In his bed, in his bathtub, in his kitchen. Getting to know each other, both inside and out.

Our game of twenty questions turned into twenty positions. I, for one, did not know I could contort my body in so many ways. Zac ended up taking another night off work to stay in with me. If it wasn't for me insisting that I was, in fact, going into work and he should do the same, we would still be tangled up with each other in his bed.

It's been two weeks since I received the roses. As much as he didn't want to, Zac finally told me the cryptic message that was written on the card. Neither of us could figure out what it meant. I've tried hard to put it out of my mind, but the whole thing freaks me out. What future loss could I possibly be facing, and who would be planning this loss?

I have that feeling of being watched again and I don't like it. I was doing so much better... I *am* doing much better. I stopped looking over my shoulder a while ago; to be reduced back to the skittish scared woman I was two years ago is nerve-wracking. So far, I've held it together. I have Zac to thank for that. He has been there for me in ways I could never have imagined.

Whenever I needed to go into work, he would drive me, then he would pick me up and take me back to his place. The one night I put my foot down and said I was sleeping in my own bedroom, he relented.

He then showed up on my doorstep at two a.m., begging me to let him stay with me. Because, according to Zac, he *wouldn't get a wink of sleep if I wasn't beside him*. I had to admit I was tossing and turning in my bed alone, until he turned up. Once I had his arms wrapped around me, I slept like a log.

I can't think of anything better than climbing into bed and sleeping for a solid ten hours. I've just finished a twelve-hour shift and am waiting out front of the hospital for Zac. It's the first time that he hasn't been there before I walk out. I pull my phone out of my bag and double check that I haven't had any missed calls from him.

Just as I unlock my phone, I hear his car pull in. A huge grin plastered to my face, I start towards the car, only for my smile and steps to falter when it's Bray who steps out of the driver's side and walks around to the passenger door. Immediately, I think of all the worst-case scenarios: Zac was in an accident. He was hurt. Where the hell was he? I needed to get to him.

"What's wrong? Where is he?" My voice comes out panicky as I try to slow my racing heart. Bray squints his eyes at me before coming up and wrapping an arm around me.

"He's fine, Lyssa, just stuck at the club. I am under strict orders to deliver you to him, without a scratch or hair on this pretty little head out of place. His words, not mine." He opens the door and does a sweeping motion with his arm. "Your chariot awaits."

"He's okay, really?" I ask, still not moving.

"Yes, you can call him if you want. I'm sure no matter how busy he is, he will always answer your call."

Shaking my head, I hop into the car. "No, it's fine. I just... I don't know what came over me. I'm sorry."

Bray shuts my door and walks around to the driver's side. Looking over at me, he says, "Lyssa, you don't need to apologise to me for being worried about my brother. It's endearing, really. I'm glad he has you. Just wish I had seen you first."

I laugh. Bray has that effect on people, always able to get a laugh. "No, you don't," I tell him.

Starting the car, he pulls away from the hospital. "You're right. I just wish every woman was as willing to own their damn feelings like you do."

I suspect he's referring to Reilly. I know he likes her and has been trying to get her to agree to a date. Reilly, however, is not having it, which means she likes him a lot more than she's letting on. I haven't managed to get Bray to talk about her with me though. Anytime I try to bring it up, he changes the topic.

"Anyone I know?" I pry.

"Yep," he says, looking out at the road. "Care to share who she is?"

"Nope."

"Want to talk about it?" I give it one last try before I drop it.

Bray shakes his head and says, "Nope."

Well, okay then, subject dropped. I spend the rest of the trip zoned out and eager to see Zac. I know I only worked twelve hours, but twelve hours is a long damn time without his arms around me. We get to the club at 1:30 a.m. It's a Friday night, so I'm assuming it will be crowded.

"Is it busy in there?" I ask Bray as he opens my door, a little nervous about having to walk through the crowd and a night-club in my damn scrubs.

"A little, but don't stress, sweetheart. You're walking through with me. You're about to make every woman in there wish they could be you." He winks.

I raise my hand to knock on Zac's office door. Bray laughs, grabbing my hand away from the door, before he opens the door and lets us in.

"You don't need to bloody knock, Lyssa." He laughs.

I swat him in the arm. "Well, it's polite to knock on a closed door," I say, defending my actions.

Bray rubs his arm like my swat actually hurt him. "Ouch, I thought we were friends, sweetheart. You know I need to fight with this arm. In about thirty minutes, actually. I might have to forfeit the fight now," he pouts at me.

I'm about to respond when I hear that deep rumbly voice wash over me. "Are you done being a moron?" Zac asks Bray as he walks up to me, engulfing me in his arms before planting his lips against mine. I vaguely notice Bray say something before I hear the door close.

Zac breaks the kiss. "Hi, sunshine."

"Hi," I respond breathlessly. But that's what he does to me. He literally takes my breath away with each kiss.

Zac leads me over to the couch. Sitting down, he pulls me onto his lap so I'm straddling him. "I'm so sorry I couldn't pick you up, baby. I had issues to sort out with tonight's fight."

I'm lost in the feel of his hands rubbing up and down my thighs. Damn, that feels good.

"It's okay. I understand you are not my personal Uber. You really don't need to send Bray to get me either. I can get an actual Uber home if you're busy."

The look I've come to learn as Zac's *don't argue with me* look crosses his face. "You are not getting a fucking Uber, Lyssa. If I can't personally pick you up, I will send Bray or Dean to get you." He must realise that his tone is harsh as he quickly follows up with, "Sorry, sunshine, just please let me have this. I need to know that you have a safe way of getting back to me."

"Okay, but you need to tell me why you are so against public transportation, Zac."

Every time I've broached the topic, he has either distracted me with sex or very effectively changed the subject. Looking off in the distance for a while, his body tense, he appears as though he's not going to answer. And then he looks me in the eye. I can see emotions reflected in his gaze.

"My parents were killed at a train station, waiting for a train. It was a mugging gone wrong. Some bastard tried to do a run and grab of my mother's purse. She ended up tripping and falling onto the track.

My father climbed down to help her get back up, but it was too late. The train couldn't stop in time." His voice cracks at the end.

"Oh, my god, Zac, I'm so sorry." I pull him tightly into my arms.

"I was twenty. I had to all of a sudden grieve the loss of both my parents, and take on the custodial role of a thirteen and a seventeen-year-old. But I sure as fuck was not letting my siblings end up in care." He winces. "Sorry, sunshine."

Why is he apologising to me? "No, I'm sorry that you had to endure that. But I'm also proud of how you overcame such adversities and became the man you are today. One, I'm proud I get to call mine."

Leaning in, I gently kiss his lips. My heart is breaking for this beautiful man, who has had to endure so much pain and take on so much responsibility at such a young age.

Knowing it took a lot for him to share that with me, I say, "Thank you for sharing that with me."

We haven't exchanged the L word with each other yet, but I know I feel it—it's on the tip of my tongue to tell him just how much I think I love him. Fearing what his reaction would be to me saying those words, I change the subject instead.

"Who is Bray fighting tonight? Can we watch? I haven't even seen inside this Batcave you guys keep locked up tight."

Zac groans. "Why would you want to see that? I mean, I have to make an appearance now and then.

This is the last fight before we break for the holidays. But you don't need to be there, sunshine. It's dirty down there, and the cage—well, it can get really rough. There are times I even have to look away when Bray is in there."

Leaning in, I let my lips swipe across his before pulling back. "Well, if you're going to be there tonight, then I'll just tag along behind you. You won't even notice I'm there. I promise not to get in your way while you're doing your thing. Please, Zac. Please let me come and watch."

Pleading my case, I pout my bottom lip out and give my

best version of puppy-dog eyes. Running his hands through his hair, he appears as though he is going to relent and take me down to the cage fight.

"First, you could never be in my way, sunshine. No matter where and what I am doing, you will always be my priority. Second, you just have to be in the same vicinity as me for me to notice you're there, and when you're not around, I notice your absence. Third, you can come, but you do not, under any circumstances, leave my side, okay?"

Nodding my head enthusiastically, I say, "Yes, okay, I won't leave your side. And just so you know, whenever I'm not with you, your absence does not go unnoticed by me."

That makes him smile. He has the most beautiful smile and I've noticed he reserves it for moments like these, when it's just us in our little cocoon. Just as I'm about to lean in and kiss him again, the door opens.

"Jesus, does nobody knock around this joint?" Zac mumbles as he turns to see who just walked into his office.

"*Umm,* I knock," I say.

Zac turns back to face me. "You are the only one not expected to, babe." That makes me smile.

"What do you want, Reilly? It better be fucking good," Zac growls.

It's not until that moment that I look over and notice that Reilly has come into the office. Squealing with delight, I jump off Zac and run over to her. I haven't seen much of my friends these last few weeks. I pull her into a deep hug.

"Oh my god, it's so good to see you, girl." Leaning into whisper in her ear, I add, "Your little avoidance method is not working. That boy is so wound up with thoughts of you, it's comical."

She just grunts. "It's good to see you too, Lyssa. How've you been?"

I don't miss that she doesn't acknowledge my little dig about Bray. "I'm good, really good actually."

I feel Zac's presence behind me as he pulls me back against his chest, wrapping an arm around my waist. "Do you have a reason to be here?"

"Yes, I do actually have a reason to be here. I work here, remember?" she sasses back. "Also, here." Reilly holds out a garment bag and shoebox I didn't even notice she was holding. "I got the dress and shoes you wanted for Lyssa, but just for future reference, you hired me as your PR manager, not your personal shopper. If you wanted me to pick up clothing for anyone other than Lyssa, I'd quit." Reilly finishes her tirade with a sweet smile.

"You work for me. That means you do whatever the fuck I need you to do if you want to continue working for me. And who the fuck else do you think I'd buy clothes for anyway?" Zac shakes his head as he walks towards the bathroom with the garment bag and shoebox.

I watch the back and forth between my boyfriend and my best friend. *Sigh.* I can't help but get butterflies whenever I think of Zac as my boyfriend. Anyway, as I watch how Zac and Reilly interact, I realise that they seem to have a love-hate thing going on.

I know from conversations with both of them, they do actually like the other. Neither would admit that in front of the other, though.

Reilly's voice snaps me out of my thoughts. "You have ten minutes to get changed. I'll see you downstairs," she says as she walks out of the office.

Spinning around, I cock a hand on my hip and tilt my head, staring down Zac. He smirks like he sees something amusing.

"You bought me a dress to wear tonight?" I question with a raised eyebrow.

Zac doesn't move, just nods his head. "And shoes, I bought you a dress and shoes. As sexy as those scrubs are on you, I thought you might want to change before we go downstairs." His eyes roam up and down my body.

"So, you knew all along that you were going to be taking me downstairs to watch the fight tonight?"

"Well, I sure as fuck wasn't leaving you up here alone, now was I, sunshine?"

"You just made me beg you to take me to the fight, when you were already planning on taking me." I try to brush past him to enter the bathroom, but the man has reflexes like a freaking cat. Before I know it, he has his arms wrapped around me, pulling me into him. He leans down to my ear, nibbling, before he says, "What can I say? I like hearing you beg."

My whole body heats and shivers at his words. Zac pulls away and playfully taps my butt. "Get changed, babe."

I close the door behind me and then make quick work of undressing. Staring at my reflection in the mirror, I note that the dress is gorgeous and a perfect fit. I'm not convinced that Zac had anything to do with picking it, though.

It's made of thin, black, shimmery material. The dress has a halter neck with a very spacious gap in the front, going from my belly button up. My whole back is exposed. The skirt of the dress frills out and lands halfway down my thighs. It's most definitely not a dress I would ever choose for myself, but now that it's on and I'm thinking of the reaction Zac will have, I think I'm loving it.

Being short on time, I leave my hair up in a high ponytail. Stepping out of the bathroom door, I see Zac has his back to me, putting his suit jacket on. I hold my breath as he turns; his eyes bulge as they travel up and down my body.

"She's fucking fired," he says. I laugh, knowing full well he's not going to fire Reilly.

"So, not the dress you picked, I'm gathering?" Walking towards him, I paste on the sweetest smile.

"Not even fucking close. You can't go down there in that, sunshine. Not that you don't look good, it's just that, well, you look too fucking good. Every damn guy down there is going to be drooling at the sight of you."

He hasn't even seen the back of the dress yet. "Well, it's a good thing you've already snagged me then, huh? You have nothing to worry about, Zac. Trust me, I'm all yours and only yours." Grabbing his hand, I continue, "Let's go. I don't want to be late."

As I drag him behind me out of the office, he gets a look at the back of the dress. I hear him groan and mutter under his breath.

*Sixteen*

ZAC

STANDING in the front row, near the cage, I hold Alyssa in front of me. Partly to cover her exposed back from prying eyes and partly to cover the erection straining in my pants. I glide my hands up and down the exposed areas on her stomach, which again is a fucking lot of exposed skin.

I've lost count of how many daggers I've shot at fuckers who think they can look at her. I'm on edge, ready to rip the heads off anyone who even thinks to look her way. Dean senses my edginess and has planted himself right beside me, constantly looking my way to see if I will explode while aiding in blocking people's view of Alyssa.

Reilly, fucking Reilly. If she wasn't so good at her job... There's also the little thing with Bray being bloody obsessed with her and her being one of Alyssa's best friends. If it wasn't for all of those things, I would fire her ass for buying this dress for Alyssa. She knows too. Standing next to Alyssa, she looks over her shoulder and smirks at my unease. I glare back at her, but she just laughs it off.

I won't admit it to anyone—well, anyone other than my

sunshine—but I think I like Reilly. I like that she can give as good as she gets. The fact that she gets her job done, and done well, without trying to find ways to flirt or touch me, like the last fucking PR manager, was a bonus.

We've watched three fights; Bray's is always the last. He is yet to be defeated. When our parents died, he had so much pent-up anger. Being a hormonal seventeen-year-old didn't help. He started getting into fights at school constantly. I didn't know what to do with him, so I ended up putting him in MMA classes. I figured if he was going to fight, he might as well do it properly and in a contained environment.

He hasn't stopped fighting since. Although we both make a lot of money off his fights, I know he's not doing it for the money. It's almost like he needs it, needs the adrenaline of being in the cage. The six-week break over the holidays that's coming up will make him crazy if he doesn't find another outlet for his energy, or a really good sparring partner.

My phone vibrates in my pocket, pulling me out of my thoughts. As I reach for it, I realise it's not my phone that vibrates; it's Alyssa's. She holds her phone out in front of her to see she has messages.

Alyssa's body tenses and freezes as she reads the text message. She drops the phone and starts looking around the underground basement wildly, like she's looking for someone. Dean bends down and picks up her phone, stepping in closer to her. Reilly turns towards Alyssa, asking her what's wrong but Alyssa doesn't say anything, just holds onto my arm that's around her waist and looks around the crowd.

She's trembling. I turn her around in my arms and bury her head in my chest. Whispering in her ear, I say, "Babe, you're okay. I've got you."

I look up at Dean. I can tell whatever he read on that phone has him raging. His jaw is tensed, and he is now looking across the cage to the crowd on the other side. He hands me the phone, before speaking to his security team through his earpiece. All I hear him say is, "Nobody gets out of this fucking basement without me knowing. Lock the entrances, single file out. I want to see every fucking face that exits this room."

I'm gripping the phone in my hand, surprised it's not breaking under my grasp. The text has my blood boiling. There is a grainy picture of Alyssa with my arms wrapped around her, standing exactly where we are now. The picture was taken from the other side of the cage. The message reads:

**Unknown: You shouldn't touch things that don't belong to you! He was mine first. I saw him first! I won't warn you again, bitch. He is *MINE. He will be with me again, even if I have to take you out myself. xxx***

I'm holding onto Alyssa so damn tight now that she winces.

"Shit." I loosen my grip slightly. "Sorry, sunshine, you are okay. I'm never going to let anyone get to you."

Reilly is almost in hysterics beside me, demanding to know what's going on. I hand her the phone and see her face go white as a ghost as she reads the message. Her hands tremble. I need to get both Alyssa and Reilly out of this damn basement now.

I look up to the cage and hear the announcer call the start of Bray's fight. He's standing in the cage, looking over at us while staring intently at Reilly. He squints his eyes, mouthing the words, "What's wrong?"

I shake my head and hold up one finger. It's our signal for me needing him to finish the fight in one round. He looks back to Reilly, and I swear I see something pass over him as his face hardens. Bray nods his head and turns as the announcer starts the countdown. As soon as he yells out *one*, Bray lands a solid punch to his opponent's jaw, knocking him out cold.

Jumping from the cage, he storms over to us and pulls Reilly into his arms, rubbing his hands up and down her back and whispering something in her ear. For once, she doesn't fight off his touch. She hands him Alyssa's phone, and I watch as his face hardens before we all walk out of the basement together. Dean leading the way with Alyssa and Reilly between Bray and me.

I'm standing in the bathroom of my office, Alyssa sitting on the vanity and clinging to me. My heart is racing, blood boiling. Someone's head is going to roll for putting her through this. Dean and Bray are in the office. I can hear them shuffling around. I'm sure, by now, they are scanning through the security footage, trying to find the fucker who was stupid enough to mess with what's mine.

Rubbing my hands up and down Alyssa's back, I instruct her to breathe, attempting to calm both her and myself. "Babe, breathe, just take big breaths with me, okay? Count them with me: one, in... out; two, in... out." By the time we get to number ten, she has calmed. She lets go of her grip on my shirt and is wiping at her face.

"I'm sorry, Zac. I'm so sorry I'm bringing so much drama into your world. I don't know why this is happening again."

The tears keep rolling down her face. I wipe them off with the pad of my thumb.

"Sunshine, this is not your fault. We will find whoever sent you that message, and they will pay for putting you through this. I promise nothing will hurt you."

Shaking her head, she pushes me back and jumps down. Turning towards the sink, I watch as she runs her hands under the water and then splashes the water over her face. I hand her a hand towel and she dries her face. Looking up into the mirror, she straightens her back and squares her shoulders back.

Turning around, she says, "You know what? You're right. I will not let someone do this to me again."

I'm so fucking proud of how strong she is, how much she can endure. What she says next floors me.

"Plus, I don't care what anyone says or thinks. You are mine, Zac. I love you too damn much to let anyone take you from me. So, if some psycho-bitch thinks she will get you, well, she will have one hell of a fight on her hands."

I'm stuck on the words *I love you* that she just threw at me. I can't wipe the huge-ass grin from my face.

"What?" she says with scrunched up eyebrows.

"You love me, *huh*?" I say with a smirk while grabbing her around the waist.

"I... *umm*... well..." she grunts and then relents, "Yes, okay. I love you, and you're just going to have to deal with that. I don't care if you're not ready to hear those words or if you don't feel the same way about—"

Placing my finger over her lips, I stop her right there. "Sunshine, I think I've been in love with you from the moment you stepped through the doors of my club." She doesn't say anything, just stares at me, so I continue, "I love you so damn much it scares the shit out of me sometimes." This brings a smile to her face.

"You love me too?" she asks.

"So much," I say as I lean in and kiss her. Breaking the kiss, she looks up and says, "Good, because you are so stuck with me now." Stepping back, she looks up and continues, "Let's go figure out who thinks they can take my man." I can't help but smile. I'm so fucking proud of how determined she is. Just before she opens the door, I get another look at her dress.

"Wait," I say as I take off my jacket, "put this on." I don't wait for her to accept or argue before I have her draped in my jacket. She brings the collar of the jacket up to her nose and inhales.

"*Mmm*, god, you smell good," she mumbles as we make our way out of the bathroom.

Dean has the flat screen monitors that line one wall of my office on, playing the video feed from the basement and scanning through each section from the time I entered with Alyssa. Bray is pacing up and down the office with a drink in one hand and an ice pack wrapped around the other. Reilly is sitting on the couch, texting furiously on her phone. They all stop what they're doing and turn to look at us. Reilly is the first to speak.

"Sarah and Holly are on the way. We're having a slumber party tonight." She pauses and looks at me. "Girls only."

I just smirk. If she thinks she is going to get me away from Alyssa, she has another thing coming.

I'm about to say as much to her when Alyssa speaks up excitedly, "Yes, that is exactly what I need right now," as she walks over and sits with Reilly on the couch.

I know I'm pouting, but I don't care. Reilly looks over to me and laughs. "I'm sure you will survive one night without her, Romeo."

I don't think I actually would, but we're not about to find out either. Ignoring Reilly, I walk over to the screens where Dean has a shot paused, zooming in on someone.

"Have you found anything yet?"

Just as my eyes focus on the person he has zoomed in on, Bray stands behind us. "What the fuck? I always knew that chick was a bloody psychopath."

My body vibrates with rage, pure, hot rage directed at the person in that image. I always felt a weird vibe from her, but I didn't think she would be this level of crazy. I knew she had a crush on me, but damn, this, I did not fucking expect. I don't know how far she's willing to go, but I do know there is no hole deep enough for her to hide in from me. I will hunt her down, and when I find her, I'll make sure she fucking regrets the day she thought she could threaten what's mine.

"Who is it?" Reilly and Alyssa ask at the same time.

Running my hands through my hair, my frustration showing, I look at Alyssa apologetically. "Caitlyn, the PR manager I had working here just a few weeks ago."

Alyssa comes up, wraps her arms around me and buries her head into my chest. Just her touch, and being able to touch her in return, calms the raging beast within me.

Looking back over to Dean, I command, "Pull her employee records and send someone over to her house. I want to be certain it's her before we do anything."

Nodding his head, he walks towards the door. "On it. I'll check back in with you in a few hours. You guys going home?" he asks.

"We'll be back at the penthouse in about thirty," I tell him.

I feel Alyssa tense as I say the words. I already know she is going to argue about coming back to the penthouse.

"*Umm*, Zac, I need you to help me in the bathroom for a minute," she says, waltzing back into the bathroom.

I smirk at her. "Sunshine, lead the way."

Once we are locked into the bathroom with the door shut, she doesn't waste any time. "Zac, I can't come back to the penthouse tonight. I haven't seen the girls in a while and I really like the sound of lounging out with my friends right now. I'm tired, I've worked all day, and all I want to do is go home and veg for a few hours, and then sleep. And have all my girls with me for breakfast when I wake up."

I kiss her to get her to stop talking. "Sunshine, if you want to have your girls' night, you can have them all come to the penthouse and make use of the theatre room. I can have whatever you want set up there."

Her eyes well up. "Really? You would let me bring my crazy friends to your place all night? You know they will be there when you wake up, right? They won't leave until you kick them out."

Nodding, I know this. "Babe, if you want them there, I'm okay with it. Besides, I want you to start thinking of it as *our* place, not just my place."

Reaching up, she gently kisses me. "Thank you, I don't know what I did in life to deserve someone as sweet as you, but I'm not about to look a gift horse in the mouth." She kisses me again. "I'm still not moving in though." Laughing, she walks out the door.

"Yet," I tell her; she just shakes her head.

I've spent the last couple of hours listening to the shrills and laughter coming out of my theatre room. If it wasn't making Alyssa so happy, that much noise at four in the morning would annoy the shit out of me. Ella woke up from the commotion at one point. I was about to go and tell them all to get out of my fucking house for waking up my baby sister—well, all of them bar Alyssa—until Ella joined them.

I'm sitting in the living room, looking through the printed images that Dean took at Caitlyn's house. Bray is sitting opposite me, nursing a glass of whisky. Every few minutes, his lingering eyes pass down the hall towards the theatre room.

Pointing at the coffee table that has the printed photographs sprawled across it, he says, "Maybe you should put those away before one of those girls sees them."

He's right. I don't want any of them to see these images. They are disturbing and it's making me sick to my stomach, just looking at them. Caitlyn had an entire wall covered in pictures of me. Some were recent pictures of me with Alyssa, all with a big red X drawn across Alyssa's face. The thought of whisking Alyssa away to some deserted island has crossed my mind.

When I voiced this to Bray, he laughed and said, "Good luck getting her on board with that plan."

After packing the images away, I look over at Bray. "I'm assuming you'll still be here in the morning? I'm going to bed. I'm fucking tired."

Rising, I don't wait for his response. He still has a bedroom here. I will always make sure Bray and Ella have a place they can think of as home. This is that place for them.

I walk into the theatre and, without a word, pick Alyssa up and throw her over my shoulder. She squeals as I walk out with her, her friends calling out random things and Ella groaning while throwing in a, "Gross! That's my brother, girls." I laugh, heading towards my bedroom at the end of the hall.

Putting Alyssa down on the bed, I'm quick to lay my body over top of hers. She's still wearing that fucking dress. "*Mmm*, I've been waiting all night to rip this dress off your body, sunshine."

I trail kisses up and down her throat. Her body shutters, and a few quiet moans escape her.

"Have you now? Well, what are you waiting for? You have me here in your room at your mercy. Whatever are you going to do with me?"

Alyssa unbuttons my shirt, her actions painstakingly slow. "That depends. Are you tired, baby? Because if you want to curl up and sleep, then that's what we'll do. If you want to play, then I'm more than ready to play this body of yours." Grinding my hard cock into her core, I show her just how ready I am.

"*Mmm*, I pick play," she moans.

Sitting up slightly, I smirk down at her and rake my eyes slowly up and down her body. "Stay right here. Do not move an inch," I instruct her as I make my way into the walk-in wardrobe.

After finding the toys I want for tonight, I walk back into the room to see she is still in the same position I left her. She tilts her head up, her eyes going wide when she sees what I have in store for tonight. I watch as she licks her lips and her breathing becomes shallow. She's excited. *Good.*

Placing everything on the bed next to her, I pick up the pair of scissors and cut from the bottom of her dress up to her waist. Alyssa just stares, mouth open, when I cut away the fabric at the back of her neck and push the material off her body.

I smile down at her, taking in all of her beautiful, creamy, white skin. Mouth-watering breasts with the most perfect nipples—nipples I can't wait any longer to have in my mouth. I suck on one nipple while rolling the other between my fingers.

"*Mmm*, I love the taste of you. I could suck on these all day, baby, and still not have enough."

Alyssa holds my head against her chest, like I would willingly leave this spot.

"Oh my god, Zac, that feels so good," she moans. I know she has sensitive nipples. I remember making her come just from sucking and playing with them the other night.

Releasing her nipple with a plop, I sit up to reposition her to the middle of the bed, just where I want her. We have had a lot of sex the last few weeks, but we haven't played like this, the way I intend to play with her tonight. I know she gets off on a little pain. I know she's experimental and submissive in the bedroom.

"Sunshine, if you need me to stop at all, just tell me, okay? I'll stop at any time you want."

She looks up at me. "Okay."

"I need you to know that I won't ever do anything to hurt

you. All I want to do is bring you to extreme pleasure. You know that, right?"

She nods her head. "Zac, I trust you wholeheartedly. Now fuck me already, would you?"

Well shit, since she put it like that. "With pleasure, sunshine."

Picking up two sets of handcuffs, I place one on each of her wrists before securing them to the bedhead. I smirk when I see her pull at them, testing their strength. I trail my fingertips down her arms, slowly down the side of her breasts, right down to her hips and back up again. I can feel her legs tense as she attempts to close them. Too bad, I happen to be sitting between them, keeping them spread.

"You are so fucking sexy, all spread out for me like this. It's like I'm at an all you can eat buffet and I don't know which dish I want to start in on."

Picking up a set of nipple clamps, I hold them up to show her.

"Wh... what are they for?" she asks. "Nervous, baby?" I smirk.

She shakes her head and licks her lips. "No, not nervous, excited."

"Damn, you are the perfect woman, sunshine. These," I say as I place one on her nipple, "are nipple clamps."

I watch her reaction the whole time, the way her breath hitches, her body arching off the bed. The way her face flushes...

"*Mmm*, I think someone may be a fan of the nipple clamps." I chuckle as I lean down to lick and suck at each nipple now that they have been clamped. "Oh god, Zac," Alyssa is screaming. "I will come if you keep doing that. Oh gosh, don't stop."

I keep nipping and sucking while kneading her breasts, moving from one breast to the other. Alyssa is thrashing beneath me, trying with all her might to close her legs, lift her core, seeking friction between her legs that she so desperately wants.

"I love how your body responds to me," I murmur as I trail a hand up and down her thigh, stopping each time just before I reach her centre.

"Zac, please, please, please make me come. I need... need..." She trails off.

Lifting my head, I respond, "I know what you need, sunshine, and I'm about to give it to you. You need to learn to be patient. I think this pussy of ours is a little greedy, wouldn't you say?"

I trail kisses down her body. Licking, sucking and biting on all of her creamy skin. I know she will be left with my marks all over her for the days to come. Inhaling her scent when I reach her centre, I look up to see her watching me.

"You smell fucking delicious, sunshine. I can't wait to feast on this hungry pussy."

She throws her head back, moaning. I know she gets turned on by my dirty mouth; she's admitted that to me before. I grab onto the inside of her thigh and bite down. I can taste her leaking juices covering her thighs. Turning my head, I give her other thigh the same treatment.

"*Ah*, oh god, Zac," Alyssa is moaning incoherently, loudly. I wouldn't be surprised if the whole building hears her screaming my name. Reaching my hands up to her breasts, I release the clamps at the same time my mouth sucks on her clit. She loses it, bucking wildly beneath me, screaming out a mixture of obscenities and my name. I continue to drink from her until she comes down, bringing her back to me with slow, languid licks.

Lifting up, I crawl back over her body and kiss her greedily, her tongue meeting mine hungrily, stroke for stroke. Slowing the kiss, I rise up, looking her in the eye.

"You okay, sunshine?"

She smiles up at me and I swear I see my future in that smile.

"Never been better."

"You want to stop or keep going?" I ask her, giving her full control, even though she's the one currently in handcuffs.

"*Mmm*, don't you dare stop now, Zac," she demands, attempting to look stern. All it does is make her look cute as hell.

"Wouldn't dream of it," I say as I place a blindfold over her eyes. Picking up the riding crop, I lightly trail the tip from her lips, down her throat all the way down to her core, where I lightly tap it against her clit. I watch as her body arches, and listen to the moans she makes. Trailing the tip of the crop back up, I tap each breast slightly harder.

"Your creamy skin looks good with my markings all over it, baby. Want more?" I ask her.

"*Mmm*, more, Zac. Give me all you got," she demands.

I chuckle, knowing damn well I would never whip her with all my strength. I'm not a fucking sadist. I get off from seeing her pleasure, not seeing her in pain.

I tap the crop against her stomach, then along each thigh a few times. By the time I throw the crop to the floor and climb between her legs, she is a squirming mess. Lifting the blindfold, I want to be able to see those blue eyes as I thrust into her. I lower my head and kiss her slowly, which is the total opposite of how much my cock is aching to be buried inside of her right now.

"I need to be inside you," I say as I trail kisses down the side of her neck.

"Yes, Zac. I want you in me, now!"

Guiding my cock to her entrance, I slam into her. Alyssa

brings her legs up and wraps them around me. Her hips meet me thrust for thrust.

"You feel fucking amazing, Alyssa. I don't know how much longer I can last." Reaching between our bodies, I slide my thumb around her clit.

"*Ah*, yes! Zac! I'm coming!"

Alyssa's body convulses, her pussy clenching around my cock. I feel my balls tighten, the tingling in my spine, and then I'm coming hard, spilling into her. Calling out her name...

It takes a few minutes for us to come down from our high. I fall next to her so I don't squash her, our breathing heavy. I get up and walk to the bathroom; it's only then that I realise my mistake. I didn't use a condom and I came inside her. Fuck, wetting a washer, I walk back out to see she hasn't moved.

Using the washer, I wipe between her legs. I love how she doesn't stop me from doing this anymore. But I'm about to ruin her blissful moment when I tell her what I just did.

"Sunshine, I, *umm*, I have to tell you something, but you have to promise not to get mad or hate me," I plead with her.

"Zac, I could never possibly hate you."

Taking a deep breath in, I let it out. "I forgot to use a condom," I spit out really quickly, "and I came inside you."

I hold my breath, watching her reaction. She's looking at me, her expression frozen in place.

"I'm clean, I swear. I can show you my test results from just last month." Great, now I'm blubbering.

The next thing I know, Alyssa is laughing—she's laughing so damn hard there are tears in her eyes. I think I might have broken her. I wait for her to stop laughing.

"Something funny?" I ask.

"Yes, do you really think I couldn't tell the difference?"

Thinking this over, I just shrug.

"Zac, it's fine. You don't need to worry. I'm on birth control and I'm as clean as you can get."

Lying down, I pull her into my arms, the place where she belongs. She sighs as she settles into the nook of my shoulder.

Kissing the top of her head, I muse, "Sunshine, I'm not worried about you getting knocked up. I was worried you would hate me if you did, though. And I sure as shit was not thinking you weren't clean."

"I'm not saying I'd be stoked if I got pregnant, but I wouldn't hate you for it, Zac. I don't hate kids. I'm just petrified at the thought of leaving a child in this world like I was." She's so quiet as she tells me this.

I squeeze her a little tighter. "Alyssa, you are not alone anymore. You have a family now. And whether or not you want us, Bray and Ella, even Dean, we are your family now. I love you. I know Ella adores you and Bray and Dean, well, I feel a little sorry for you, getting lopped in with those two morons. But we love you, and when we make children together, all of our family will love them unconditionally."

Looking up at me, she says, "I love you too. And Bray and Dean are not morons, Zac." She thinks on this a bit before adding, "Well, Bray might be a little, but I'll deny it till I'm blue in the face if you tell him I said that."

Chuckling, I reach over to turn out the light. "You need to get some sleep, baby."

"Good night, Zac. I love you so damn much." "Goodnight, sunshine. I love you too. Now go to sleep. I've kept you awake long enough."

# Seventeen

## ALYSSA

I WAKE up alone in Zac's bed. Reaching over, I feel his side of the bed is cold. He must have been up a while. I debate just closing my eyes for a few more minutes, but mother nature is calling.

After going to the bathroom, I find Zac's discarded shirt from yesterday on the floor. I put it on and roll the sleeves up a little. I decide that it covers enough of me. I mean, the shirt stops mid-thigh; it could almost be a dress. I walk out in search of Zac.

I find everyone in the living room, everyone being: Zac, Bray, Dean, Reilly, Sarah, Holly and Ella. All eyes swing my way when they hear me walking in.

Bray wolf whistles, smirking at me. "Damn, Lyssa, are you sure you picked the right brother?"

Zac slaps him across the head as he stalks towards me. He says nothing, just turns me around and leads me back to the bedroom.

"*Umm,* Zac, as much as I'd love to play around again. I think you need to give my vagina some recovery time," I say.

"Sunshine, there are two hot-blooded males out in our

living room. You need to put clothes on before you walk out." I watch as he walks into his wardrobe and comes out with a pair of my yoga pants I've left here, a sports bra and a shirt. He lays the clothes on the bed.

Roaming his eyes up and down my body, he says, "Maybe I should just kick them all out and leave you in that shirt all day. You look fucking good in that shirt, Alyssa."

Laughing, I grab the yoga pants and pull them on. "Zac, you're not kicking them out. You know Bray only says those things to get a rise out of you, right? I'm pretty sure he is hung up on Reilly."

Groaning, he says, "I know he does, and it works every damn time."

Zac watches intently as I strip his shirt off and put on the bra he pulled out for me. "It's such a shame to cover those breasts up. It's like covering up the Mona Lisa or the David. They are a bloody work of art."

I have no response to that. I just laugh and pull on the shirt —another one of his shirts—which falls down to my thighs. I tie the shirt up so it sits just above my waist line.

Zac groans. Running his hands through his hair, he says, "Really, sunshine, is there anything you don't look like every man's wet dream in?"

Looking down at myself then back up at him, I respond, "I'm literally in yoga pants and a shirt, Zac. Hardly the stuff dreams are made of."

Wrapping me up in his arms, he whispers in my ear, "You are more than what I ever could have dreamed up. You don't even know the effect you have on men."

I step back and towards the door, because, coffee, I need coffee. I look back over my shoulder to see Zac now staring at my ass.

Winking at him, I say, "It's a good thing the only person I care to affect is you then, *huh*?"

Walking into the living room, I notice Dean scrambling to pick up papers from the coffee table; everyone stops talking at once.

I smile sweetly at Dean and, with the sternest voice I can muster right now, I say, "I'm going to go make a coffee, then I'm coming back in here and you will tell me everything that you found out about this psychopath."

Dean's face falls; his mouth opens and closes. He looks behind me to Zac, as if searching for what he should do. I don't give either of them the chance to come up with anything to prevent me from finding out what they are all hiding. Turning around, I grab Zac's hand and start pulling him into the kitchen.

"Babe, can you help me figure out how to use that fancy coffee machine of yours?"

The minute we step into the kitchen, Zac picks me up, sitting me on the countertop before walking over to the coffee machine. He presses a few buttons and returns to me with a steaming cup of vanilla latte. Could this man get any dreamier?

He steps between my legs, rubbing his hands up and down my thighs, as I sip at the deliciousness that is my vanilla latte. Closing my eyes, I let out a little moan as I savour the flavours in my mouth.

"Sunshine, if you keep that up, I will not be held responsible when I fuck you right here."

He pulls me flush against him so I can feel how aroused he is when my core meets the hard length of his cock.

"As fun as that sounds, you have a house full of people just in the other room. And I have a conversation to be had with Dean."

As I try to push him back, so I can jump down off the bench, he grabs my waist and says, "We."

Confused, I scrunch my face and look up at him. "*Huh*?"

"*We* have a houseful of people," he explains.

I just roll my eyes and walk back into the living room, where once again, everyone stops talking at once.

"Okay, out with it. Someone had better tell me what is so bad that you all stop talking the minute I step into the room."

I look from person to person, all of whom are looking behind me to Zac, who in turn is glaring at each and every one of them.

"Seriously, somebody better start talking!"

It's Sarah that breaks. I knew she wouldn't be able to keep anything from me. "*Ah,* Lyssa," she says and then looks at Zac. "Either you tell her, or I will. You aren't scaring me with the scowl that's pretty much permanently planted on your face."

Zac pulls me over to the couch, pulling me down onto his lap as he sits down. Sarah's wrong about the scowl; it's never on his face when he looks at me. All I ever see written on his face are love, adoration and lust—okay, lots of lust.

"Sunshine, you know I'm not going to let anything happen to you, right?"

I nod my head but don't say anything.

"Okay, well, Dean went and helped himself into Caitlyn's apartment last night. He took some photos of something she had attached to one of the walls in her living room."

He watches my face. I'm not sure if he's waiting for me to break, or if he just wants to buy time before actually getting to the point.

"Okay, so show me the pictures. What was on the wall?"

Zac shakes his head no. "You don't need to see the pictures, babe. They were disturbing as shit for me to see."

Pretending to think this over and agree with him, I nod my

head before I stand up to place my empty cup on the coffee table. That's when I move fast, picking up the big yellow envelope I saw Dean

shoving papers into. Tipping the envelope upside down, I empty the contents onto the coffee table before anyone can stop me. I stare down at the images. Lots of images of Zac. Some of Zac and me together. In all of those, a big red cross is drawn across my face.

"Fuck," Zac grunts and curses as he turns me around. "Sunshine, I really didn't want you to have to see that."

I don't move or say anything for a while; a lone tear drops down my cheek. Zac is quick to wipe it away. I don't want to think about this anymore. I want to bury my head in the sand and pretend like everything is perfect. Then I remember the plans the girls and I made with Ella last night to go shopping together today.

"I'm going shopping with Ella and the girls today," I say to Zac, who has shock written all over his face.

Turning, I say to the girls, "Give me ten minutes to get changed and I'll be ready."

Then a fun idea comes to me. Turning back to Zac, I give him my biggest smile. "Can I borrow your car today, babe?"

If I thought Zac's face showed shock before, it has nothing on the look he has now. I hear Bray coughing and spluttering in the background.

Zac stands there, stumbling over his words. "*Uhh*, babe... *umm*... well... you know..."

He's looking for a way to say no. I'm not going to help him. I just stand there and smile sweetly.

Ella is laughing so hard she's rolled over, holding her stomach. "What's the matter, Zac, cat got your tongue?" she teases.

Dean laughs a little before adding, "Stay strong, bro. Don't do it."

Zac seems to recover from his shock. I watch as his face morphs into that cocky smirk that would drop any girl's panties. "Sunshine, I can drive you to the mall, and then come back and get you when you're done." He smiles like he just solved all of his problems.

Leaning up, I kiss him on his cheek, letting my lips just brush the corner of his mouth while pressing my breasts a little harder than necessary into his chest.

"That's sweet, babe. But really, I want to drive. Besides, it will be good for Ella and me to have some girl bonding time, don't you think?"

He groans, running his hands through his hair. I've learnt he does this when frustrated. "Sunshine, it's just that... well, I don't..." He doesn't finish his sentence.

Bray calls out, "Way to tell her no, bro."

Zac flips him off, then smiles at me, a light in his eyes. "How about we go shopping and I buy you your own car?"

Okay, well, now *I* drop my mouth open in shock. Reilly spits out the mouthful of water she was drinking.

Bray continues mocking Zac, "Damn, the boy is whipped!"

Zac ignores them all, smirking at my silenced face. Shaking off the shock, I say, "*Umm,* no, you are not buying me a bloody car, Zac. If you don't want me to drive your car, all you have to do is say so. I'll try not to be too offended, you know, considering you let Reilly drive it that one time. But it's okay. If you don't trust me enough to drive it, I'll survive."

Patting him on the chest, I'm about to turn and walk into the bedroom when Zac grabs onto my wrist, stopping me.

"Baby, I trust you completely. If you really want to drive, then you can take the car." He leans in, bringing his lips to meet mine.

Ella walks past and says, "Damn, that was quick."

I smile up at Zac. I can't help but laugh a little. "Thanks, babe, but actually, could you drive us? There's a new wine bar that I want to show Ella." I feel a little bad for putting him through that stress. I have to confess, "I never wanted to drive the Batmobile, you know, just curious if you'd let me."

"Damn, babe, that's harsh," Bray laughs.

Zac turns his attention to his brother, glaring him down. "Her name's Alyssa. She's not *babe* to you, asshole."

Then turning back to me, he very sincerely states, "You know, I'd give you anything you want, right? And I think the whole car shopping idea has merit. While you girls are shopping for whatever girly shit you shop for, Dean and I are going to buy you a car. You should probably go get ready, babe." He accentuates the *babe* at the end.

Walking down the hallway, back to the bedroom, I call out, "You're not buying me a damn car, Zac."

I hear him laughing just before I shut the door. *He is joking, right?* There's no way he is actually going to go shopping for a car. That's crazy... of course he's joking. Clearing my head, I get changed into a pair of cut-off denim shorts and a tank top. I'm sitting on the edge of the bed, lacing up my Chucks, as Zac walks in.

His eyes travel up and down my bare legs. "*Uhh*, sunshine, I think you're missing some material on those shorts of yours."

Standing, I walk over to him, ignoring his remark about my shorts. It's December in Sydney—it's bloody hot out.

"Thank you for driving us. I really appreciate everything you do for me. You know that, right?"

He tilts his head. "Yeah, babe, it's my pleasure to do things for you. Are you okay?"

"Well, I feel a little bad about making you think I wanted to drive your car. You looked really stressed out there."

He wraps his arms around my waist. "Sunshine, I love you, so damn much. I wasn't stressed about you driving the car, and

I know this will sound irrational, but I was worried about you being out without me. Especially right now, when we have no idea what Caitlyn is capable of."

I get he would be worried about my safety, but that stress was definitely more about his car. I raise an eyebrow at him silently. After a minute, he relents.

"Okay, maybe I was a little worried about my car too. But there is not a shadow of a doubt that I love you way more than I love that car, Alyssa."

Laughing, I reach up and kiss him. "I believe you. Now, let's get going. There's only two weeks until Christmas and I haven't bought a single present yet. Also, you know you *can* say no to me. I'm not a princess, Zac. I'm not going to have a tantrum if something doesn't go my way."

Zac walks over to his dresser and, as he pulls something out, he says, "I know, but I have the means to give you whatever you want, and the desire to see you happy. Here, I had this ordered for you."

He walks out the door, leaving me standing in his room holding a black credit card with my name on it.

I follow him out of the room while waving the card around like a looney and screeching at him, "*Umm*, Zac, this is a credit card. Why would you give me a credit card?"

He laughs. "I know what it is, sunshine. It's linked to my personal account—there is no limit." He looks at me like I'm the crazy one here, like he just hands out credit cards to everyone he meets. What is he, Oprah?

Bray swipes the card out of my hand. "Damn, you gave her the black card? Bro, you wouldn't even give *me* a black card." Bray whistles then looks at me.

"If you don't want this thing, Lyssa, I'll be more than happy to take care of it for you."

Zac snatches the card out of Bray's grasp. "Shut up, idiot."

He places the card back in my hand. "Sunshine, it's for you. Use it... don't use it. But I want you to have it, please."

"Okay, I'll hold on to this, but I'm not using it, Zac. I don't need your fancy money. I work too, you know. I have my own money. Well, maybe not like your money kind of money, but I have money." I'm rambling because the fact that he just gave me an unlimited credit card makes me nervous.

Does he think I'm with him for his money? That I need him to buy me pretty, shiny things to be happy? Oh god, is he going to expect me to become a kept woman? To stop working, stay home and go to brunch with the ladies? I look around at everyone, and they're all staring at me. Oh god, I'm hyperventilating. I don't think I can live up to those kinds of expectations. I went my whole life having to work and fight for everything I needed to survive.

"Sunshine, breathe in... out. It's okay. I've got you." I feel Zac's arms brace me.

"Zac, I don't think I'm the kind of girl you want. I will never be okay with being a kept woman. I can't become fully dependent on someone."

He rubs his hands up and down my back, then brings them up to my face.

Holding my face still so I'm looking into his eyes, he responds quietly, "Alyssa, you are the only girl I want, however you come. I don't need you to be anything but who you are, okay?"

I nod, not able to form words right now. Zac leans down, kissing me until my body feels like it's melting into him.

He pulls back and questions, "You good?"

"I'm good. Sorry, I kind of had a tiny freak-out moment."

"I don't mind—just gives me an excuse to hold you longer before you disappear on your shopping trip." He smirks.

"*Uh-huh*, let's go." I turn around to see the living room

empty. "Wait, where did everyone go?" I ask, looking around the now empty room.

"I told them we would meet them in the garage." Zac picks his keys up off the hall table and throws them at me. "Come on, sunshine, you're driving."

*Ah, wait, what?* Running out the door, I catch up with him at the lift.

"Zac, I can't drive that thing. No way. I can't. I mean, what if I scratch it? Or crash, or worse?"

Zac scrunches his eyebrows at me. "Babe, what could be worse than crashing it?" Laughing, he pulls me into the lift.

"I don't know, Zac. Stop laughing at me." I try to give my best glare, but he shrugs it off.

"Let's get you to the mall. I'm looking forward to seeing the look on Bray's face when I tell him he's going with you girls shopping."

"Why are you making Bray go on our girls' shopping trip, Zac? We will be at the mall. It's a really public place. Nothing will happen." I try to reason with his overprotective nature.

"You won't even know he's there, babe."

I look at him like he has lost his mind, because if he thinks Bray could be anywhere and not be noticed, then he for sure has lost the plot.

"Doubtful," I say as we exit the lift into the parking garage.

～

We've been in the mall for two hours and I still have absolutely no idea what I can get Zac for Christmas. I mean, what do you get the guy who has everything?

"What about socks?" Sarah asks, unable to keep a straight face.

"Socks? You want me to get the hottest man on earth socks for Christmas?"

"I object to that statement. He may be in line for number two, but I definitely have the number one spot, sweetheart." Bray smugly smiles while draping an arm over my shoulder.

I look at the arm he has on me then raise an eyebrow at him. "You know your brother will probably lose his mind when he smells your scent all over me."

Bray immediately drops the arm. "Harsh, Lyssa, harsh."

"What about Victoria's Secret? I mean, the thing Zac seems to want most in the world at the moment is you, so why not get something a little sexy that he can unwrap off you?" Reilly suggests.

"You know, I'd be all for unwrapping you on Christmas morning, princess." Bray waggles his brows at Reilly, who is too busy examining her nails to acknowledge him.

"Hey, maybe I could do that for my boyfriend this year, since you think it's such a great idea and all, Bray," Ella so sweetly drops while winking at me.

Bray stops walking, turning around to Ella and pointing. "No, Ella, just no. Wait, you don't have a boyfriend, right? No, you're not allowed to have boyfriends yet, and you sure as shit are not allowed to wear anything from Victoria's Secret *ever*. Fuck."

"Okay, Bray." Ella shrugs her shoulders as she walks around him.

Ignoring Bray's little meltdown, Reilly links her arm with mine. "What do you think, Lyssa?"

"I think it's a great idea actually. Sarah, do you think you could get your photographer friend to meet us at our place tonight?"

"Yeah, I'll text him now. Wait, are you doing what I think you're doing?" she asks.

Nodding my head, I respond, "Yep, I'm going to do a boudoir photoshoot. It's a good thing my best friend is a makeup artist. Think you can fit me in today?"

"It'll be tough, but I think I can manage." She smiles as we walk into Victoria's Secret.

Okay, I'll need wine, lots of wine, to have the courage to go through with this. I can't believe this is what I came up with. I mean, get me alone in a bedroom with Zac and I can be brazen. Posing in lingerie in front of a photographer, I'm not so sure. But I want to do this. I want to give him something that will blow his mind.

My phone blares "Stuck Like Glue" from my pocket. I still haven't gotten around to changing it yet. I quickly turn my phone to silent. Pulling it out, I see a text message from Zac and a smile automatically grazes my lips.

**My own GQ: Sunshine, hope you're having fun. Quick question, if you had a choice between white or red, which colour would you go for?**

Laughing, because I was literally just thinking the same thing standing in front of the red lingerie. I take a selfie in front of the rack and send it to him.

**Me: Funny, I was just thinking the same thing. I'm leaning towards the red. What do you think?**

Immediately, the little dots on the screen start bubbling, showing that he is replying.

**My own GQ: I think you just gave me a damn hard-on. RED!!!**

**My own GQ: Please tell me you are not in a lingerie shop with my brother right now. Dammit, I knew I should have come with you.**

I knew that wouldn't pass his attention. I take a snap of Bray and Ella arguing with each other at the front of the store and send it to him.

Me: Don't worry, Bray is too busy arguing with Ella. Apparently, she is not allowed to wear Victoria's Secret. His words, not mine. Ella says she's been wearing Victoria's Secret since she was fifteen, and that she's had one of your fancy little black cards for a while and you're not very good at checking the receipts.

My own GQ: Please tell me you are joking!

Lyssa: Nope, sorry.

My own GQ: You have just ruined Victoria's Secret for me, thank you!!

Lyssa: So, you don't want me to buy anything?

My own GQ: Babe, you don't need fancy lingerie. You know I'm just going to rip it off anyway. But yes, buy red, lots and lots of red! Please.

Me: Mmm, since you asked nicely and all, I'll see what I can manage. Got to go, I'm heading into the changeroom now.

My own GQ: Cruel, you are being cruel!!! FaceTime???

Me: Not a chance. Have fun doing whatever it is you're doing... love you.

My own GQ: Right now, I'm trying not to let it be obvious that I have a fucking hard-on in the middle of Mercedes, because apparently all I have to do is think about my gorgeous girlfriend in lingerie for him to be at attention. Love you too, babe.

Putting my phone away, I pick up random pieces of red lingerie.

"*Ah*, Lyssa, not to burst your bubble or anything, but do you really think Zac is going to let some guy take photos of you in lingerie?" Bray grumbles behind us.

"Well, he won't know about it if you don't tell him, right, Brayden?" I glare at him.

"Sweetheart, if you think he won't find out, you're out of your damn mind." Ignoring him, I head for the changing room.

I've just sent Sarah out to get a size larger for the last lacy red teddy I want to try on. I hear footsteps outside of the dressing room and someone comes to a stop in front of the door. Thinking it's Sarah back with the teddy for me to try on, I'm about to open the door when I look down and see the shoes under the bottom of the door and freeze.

Whoever is standing on the other side of the door is not Sarah. I can hear heavy breathing of someone who sounds as though they have been running. I watch as the combat boots shuffle against the floor. I'm reaching for my phone, about to call Bray, when a piece of paper floats under the door, landing at my feet. I watch the boots disappear as fast as they appeared.

I'm frozen in place, standing in a Victoria's Secret dressing room in my bra and panties. I don't know whether to bend down and pick up the paper, or ignore it and leave it there. Curiosity gets the better of me. Picking up the sheet of paper, I turn it over, a blood-curdling scream escaping my throat.

I'm huddled in the corner of the dressing room on the floor. I can hear Sarah and Reilly banging on the door, attempting to open it while simultaneously attempting to coax me into opening the door for them. But I'm frozen. I can't seem to move. I stare at the photograph in my hands, a photo of my mother's headstone, only next to her headstone in the photo stands another headstone, a new one. One with my name and birthdate on it. Underneath the birthday, the tombstone reads:

*Died too young, because she touched what didn't belong to her.*

Why, why is she doing this to me, to us? What have I done in my life to warrant this kind of treatment? How does one person attract two psychopathic stalkers in one lifetime? Not even a lifetime, in the span of just three years? Is the relationship I have with Zac worth putting up with this kind of torment? Am I prepared to face the devil with the possibility she may just be crazy enough to find a way to end my life?

I mean, she got past all of my friends and Bray without being noticed. Bray... With my breathing coming back under control, I can hear him arguing with Sarah and Reilly on the other side of the door.

He knocks lightly and coaxes, "Sweetheart, I need you to open the door for me, okay? Can you do that, Lyssa? Please open the door for me. I can call Zac for you; he will be here before you know it. But I need you to open the door."

It's at his mention of Zac that I'm able to answer my own questions. *Yes*. Yes, I am prepared to endure whatever kind of torment this bitch throws my way, because he is mine. And in this life, you fight for what's yours; you don't cower on the floor of a dressing room. With that resolve, I stand up and unlock the door. Bray takes one look at me before barging into the small dressing room, shutting the door behind him.

Sarah and Reilly are both on the other side of the door, arguing with him to let them in. He ignores them as he picks up my tank top from the bench,

silently putting it over my head and threading my arms through. He then bends and pulls my shorts up my legs. There is nothing but genuine care in his eyes.

Once I'm clothed again, Bray pulls me into his arms. "What happened?" he asks.

Still unable to find words, I show him the piece of paper. "Fuck." He scrunches the paper in his hands, "I'm going to fucking kill her, I swear. Shit, I have to call Zac." Just as Bray is pulling his phone out of his pocket, I stop him.

"Bray, wait, don't call him yet. I'll call him and have him meet us at the wine bar." Taking in a shaky breath, I can do this.

Bray shakes his head no at me. "Lyssa, we have to tell him; he will want to know. Fuck, it's possible he will kill me if I don't tell him."

"I'm going to call him. I don't want him to worry or rush back to get here. I'm not letting this bitch ruin our day again, Bray." Then I smirk at him, needing to lighten the mood. "If you think he'll kill you for not calling him, what do ya think he'll do when he finds out you were in a dressing room with me while I was in a state of undress?"

The look on his face is hysterical—he looks tortured. I can't help but laugh out loud at his torture. "Don't worry, Bray, I'll make sure he doesn't kill you."

He shakes his head. "And how exactly do you plan to do that?"

Smiling, I say, "Simple, I'll just ask him really nicely to spare you."

Bray opens the door to all the girls on the other side. "How the fuck did I get lumped with you all. This is bullshit. Hurry up and check out, Lyssa. We need to get out of here."He storms off to the front of the store.

# Eighteen

ZAC

AFTER DROPPING Alyssa and Ella at the mall to meet up with the other girls and Bray, I made my way to the Mercedes-Benz dealership. I smile as I remember the look of horror he had on his face when I told him he would be joining in on the girls' shopping. The horror faded quickly, turning into more of a scowl when he looked Reilly's way.

I'm sure I'm likely to get pushback from Alyssa about this purchase, but I don't care how much of a fight she puts up. She needs a car and I have the means to get her one. It's a no-brainer, really. We've been here for around two hours, and I've finally decided on the car. I'm waiting for the paperwork to be finalised.

Dean stopped asking if I was sure I knew what I was doing purchasing this car, and if maybe I should look at something smaller—a little coupe like I just got Ella for her eighteenth. I had to tell him to shut up and get onboard. He hasn't questioned me since, although I don't miss the inquisitive looks he sends my way. I've been ignoring them mostly, occasionally answering them with raised eyebrows, daring him to say whatever the fuck he's thinking.

We're sitting in an office, waiting on the salesman to come back in with the final paperwork. I'm working on getting my hard-on to go down after texting with Alyssa. Why the hell couldn't I be in the Victoria's Secret with her right now? I know she's in the dressing room trying on lingerie, and I can't stop picturing her creamy skin in red lace. Groaning, I shake the thoughts from my head.

Dean looks over at me. "What's up with you?"

"Alyssa is at Victoria's Secret, trying on lingerie right now," I say, needing no more explanation.

Dean laughs. "Man, you have it so bad. You know, I think she's good for you, keeps you on your toes."

Yes, she does.

"I know it's quick, but I'm one hundred percent certain that she's the one."

Dean processes this—that's what he does, always quietly processing and analysing everything.

"Then why the fuck are we shopping for a car and not a ring? Because you really should lock that shit down before she wakes up and realises what she's been lumped with."

Looking over at him, I think about it. "Do you think she'd accept a ring yet? We could go hit up Tiffany and Co. next," I ask in all seriousness. Dean laughs as the salesman enters the office.

"All right, Mr. Williams, it's all ready. One red Mercedes-Benz G-Class G63 AMG, in the name of Alyssa Summers. The car will be ready for delivery on the twenty-second of the month."

At first, I was told I'd have to wait until February for the car —it's the middle of December now. When I not so kindly informed them that I'd be paying cash and I expected to have a car delivered prior to Christmas day, the salesman almost shit himself. He came through though. They always do when they realise you have money. I figured I'd put a big-ass bow on it and call it a Christmas present. She can't reject a Christmas gift, can she?

"I just need you to sign here, and here," the salesman says, pointing out where I need to sign. "You'll need to leave a twenty percent deposit today and the rest will be due two days prior to delivery." Pulling out my wallet, I hand over the black card and say, "Put it on this."

He takes the card, and standing, he goes out to the front, returning a moment later before handing over the card and paperwork.

I hand the paperwork over to Dean. "Hold on to this for me, will you?"

He looks at me confused. "*Ah*, why?" he asks. "Because I don't want there to be any chance that Alyssa finds out about this purchase before Christmas Day," I reply as though that should explain it.

Thanking the salesman, we make our way back out of the building. I'm about to get in the car when my phone plays "My Girl." I smile, knowing immediately that Alyssa is calling, with the hope she changed her mind on the FaceTime request while in the Victoria's Secret dressing room.

I throw the keys to Dean. "You drive," I say as I answer the call and walk around to the passenger side. "Sunshine, change your mind about a dressing room FaceTime call?" I ask, hopeful.

"Zac, hi. *Umm*, no... no FaceTime call, sorry." There's a slight hitch in her voice.

"What's wrong?" I ask, knowing something's made her upset.

"*Ah*, nothing's wrong. I'm fine... just, *umm*... wondering if you can meet us at the wine bar. We're heading there now. But if you're busy, that's okay. I'll just… just see you later."

Shit, she's rambling. There is definitely something wrong. "I'm never too busy for you, babe. We'll be there in about fifteen minutes, okay?"

I know she's not okay, but I also know she's not about to tell me that right now.

"Sure, I'll see you soon." Shit, she sounds fucking sad but before I can add anything, she quietly says, "I love you, Zac."

"Love you too, sunshine. I'll be there before you know it."

I'm trying to stay calm, to not let on that I know she's not okay. I don't want her to be any more upset than she already is. I can tell how much she is trying to keep it together.

"Okay," she says before hanging up.

"Fuck, get to the mall as quickly as you can, Dean."

In my head, I'm running through all the possibilities of what could have happened at the damn mall to make her so upset.

"What's wrong?" Dean asks.

"I don't know, man. I could just tell something was off. She wouldn't say, but I just know. Fuck. I should have gone with her. I should have had Bray go pick out the car."

Before I know what I'm doing, I'm dialling Bray's number. He's been with her… Why the fuck didn't he call me himself if something happened?

"Hey, bro, what's up?" he answers the phone in a way too cheery voice—that's his giveaway that something happened.

"What the fuck happened to Alyssa, Bray? And don't lie to me right now. I know something happened."

I hear the intake of breath, and the tell of a hand covering the phone, before he not so quietly says, "You didn't tell him? Damn, Lyssa," in the background.

"Bro, she's fine, okay? Not a hair out of place." Great, now he's trying to placate me. The longer they are not telling me, the more pissed off I'm getting.

"Bray, tell me *what-the-fuck-happened*," I demand. I know I'm yelling, and if Alyssa is anywhere near Bray, she will be able to hear me. Taking a calming breath, I try again, voice quieter, "Please, Bray, I need to know."

"Okay, while she was in the dressing room at Victoria's Secret, someone slipped a piece of paper under the door. None of us saw anything. We were all in the store and we didn't see the person."

Closing my eyes, I'm doing everything I can to not yell right now. "What was on the paper?" I ask in a much calmer voice than what I am feeling.

"*Ah*, it was a photo of a tombstone," he says hesitantly.

A tombstone, someone slid a picture of a fucking tombstone under the door. What the fuck.

"Whose tombstone was in the picture, Bray?" I ask, needing more information.

"Look, she's okay, Zac. I've got her right next to me. Actually, she's so close to me it would probably give you a coronary if you saw."

He's probably right, but I also know he's trying to distract me.

"Bray, do me a favour and send me through a picture of the piece of paper. Keep her fucking close. I swear... if anything happens to her..." I let my sentence drown off, because the thought of anything happening to her is inconceivable.

"Okay, I'll send a picture. See you when you get here, bro." He hangs up before I can reply.

Bray sends the picture through straight away. The moment I've zoomed in on the image, my blood goes cold. There are two tombstones, one older looking one. I can barely make out the name on it to be Sophia Summers. The other tombstone, a newer looking tombstone, has Alyssa's name on it. Her name and date of birth.

"Zac, we're here, man." Dean shakes me out of my frozen state.

Looking around, I see that we're in the mall's carpark. I don't recall any of the drive here. How long have I been staring at this image? I'm going to fucking kill her. I've never killed a woman before, never even thought I'd have it in me to do it. But the woman who is threatening Alyssa's life? I would enjoy watching the life fade out of her as I cut off her air supply.

"Zac, snap the fuck out of it. You can't go in there like this. You'll scare your girl more than she already is."

Dean's right. I know he's right, but he hasn't seen the picture. He doesn't know the inferno that was just set inside me. I will burn down this whole damn town until I find the bitch.

"Dean, I need you to get copies of all the cameras inside the Victoria's Secret store here. Find out what cemetery Alyssa's birth mother is buried in and send someone out there. I want to know if this picture has

just been cleverly edited, or if that psychopath put a tombstone there."

Dean scrunches his eyebrows. "Tombstone? What tombstone?"

"Someone slid a piece of paper under the dressing room door while Alyssa was changing. It was a picture of a tombstone. A tombstone with Alyssa's fucking name on it." I hold up my phone to show him the picture.

Dean nods his head. "Send me a copy of that. I'll get on it."

"Thanks, man. Take the car. We'll get a ride back with Bray. Meet me at mine in a few hours?" I ask.

"Yeah, sure. Do you want to look at hiring personal security for Alyssa? It might be a good idea; we don't know how far Caitlyn's prepared to go."

I'm not sure how Alyssa will take having bodyguards.

"I'll think about it. I don't plan to let her out of my sight again in a hurry anyway."

Walking into the Barrel, the new wine bar that Alyssa wanted to take Ella and the girls to, I notice

her table straight away. I hear her laugh; it registers deep within my soul. I stand there for a while, taking in the room. It's rustic, old wine barrels randomly placed around the middle of the room stand as bar tables. The edges of the room are sectioned off with brown Chesterfield lounges and wingback chairs.

Alyssa is sitting in a lounge next to Bray—the fucker is way too close to my girl. I continue to watch her for a moment. As much as I want to run up to her and wrap her in my arms, I enjoy watching her in moments like these. She's unguarded, a flush stains her cheeks. She's laughing at something Reilly says at the same time Bray is scowling towards the fiery redhead. I watch as she brings a wine glass to her lips and sips, running her tongue along her bottom lip when she pulls the cup away. Fuck, now is not the time for a hard-on. Just as she's about to raise the glass to her mouth again, she looks directly at me. It's almost like she can sense when I'm in the same room as her. I can never stay hidden for long.

A huge smile grazes her face; her eyes light up. Nudging my head, I indicate for her to come to me. I need a moment alone with her, away from the prying ears of our family and friends.

Putting her glass on the low centre table, she says something to Bray before standing. He looks over, nodding his head in acknowledgement. I glare back at him, because frankly, he looked way too comfortable that close to my girl. Bray smirks back at me. *Fucker.*

I watch as Alyssa saunters towards me in those little fucking shorts, her long legs on full display for everybody to get a look at—which, right now, I can clock at least five men who let their gazes linger a little too long on her. I give them all a glare, at which point they advert their gazes.

As soon as she's in arm's reach, I pull her into me, slamming my lips against hers. She instantly melts into me. The taste of sweet white wine lingers on her tongue, as she meets me stroke for stroke. I get so lost in the moment that I forget where we are. I forget about the picture that had my blood run cold. I forget it all as I try to communicate with her just how much I fucking love her with this kiss.

Pulling back, she smiles up at me. "*Mmm*, hi."

"Hi, sunshine. How are you feeling?" I ask, not wanting to ruin this moment but also needing to know if she really is okay. I pin her with my eyes as I wait for her answer.

"I'm better, now that you're here," she responds, batting her eyelashes at me. I laugh and damn, it feels good to laugh.

"How are you really feeling? I saw the picture. Alyssa. You don't need to pretend, or to hide your feelings from me. You know that, right?"

I feel like I need to reassure her that, no matter what, I'm not going anywhere. I know she hasn't had that much in her life, always moving from one foster home to the next and constantly being let down by the people who were meant to care for her.

"I had a little freak-out when I saw it. But I made a decision not to let this crazy psychopath ruin my day, or your day. And I'm not about to let anybody scare me away from you, Zac. You are mine, not hers. I don't care what anyone says—you are mine." She stops to take a breath.

"I like being yours, sunshine. And we will not let anyone ruin what we have. This..." I say, pointing between the two of us. "This is a once in a lifetime kind of love. I'm not about to let that go." She blinks up at me a few times then smirks.

"You know? I get it," she says.

"You get what?" I hope that she gets just how much she means to me.

"How someone can become so crazily obsessed with you. I mean, you're kind of a catch, the complete package. I'm surprised there's only one crazy ex on the loose."

She thinks I'm the complete package. Maybe I should book in that trip to Tiffany and Co. for a diamond after all. I smile with this thought, then the rest of her speech registers. Crazy ex on the loose? Wait, does she think I had some kind of relationship with Caitlyn? Just the thought of that makes me shiver in disgust.

"Sunshine, we will come back to the part where you think I'm the complete package at a later date. But let me be very clear, so there is no misunderstanding. I did not, at any point in time, have any kind of relationship with this woman other than a professional one. She was my employee—that's it. Did I constantly turn down her advances and flirtation? Yes. Was there ever a time where I thought I'd want to fuck her? Absolutely not, not ever."

The only thing I want to do with Caitlyn is strangle the goddamn life out of her for threatening Alyssa.

"Okay, I believe you, Zac. Now let's enjoy our afternoon with your family and my crazy-ass friends," she says, pulling on my arm.

I stop her, pulling her back into me. "Our," I say, correcting her mistake.

"Our what?" she questions.

Smiling, I tell her, "*Our* family and *our* friends. There's no *mine* or *yours* anymore, sunshine. There is only *ours*."

Leaning up, she kisses my lips before ever so quietly saying, "There'll always be a tomorrow together for us." She says it so reverently and quietly, it's almost like a prayer falling from her lips. I don't even think she meant for me to hear it, but I did.

Leaning down into her ear, I tell her the same promise we tell each other every night before we go to sleep, "There will always be a tomorrow together for us, sunshine. I promise."

We've been sitting here in this wine bar for an hour and a half. I can't say I've ever been to a wine bar before, but I'm enjoying myself. I'm enjoying seeing Alyssa relax and have fun. Everyone has gotten louder with each empty bottle of wine that's been left on the table. I have learnt that Alyssa loves any kind of sweet white wine, and I make a mental note to get a supply sent to my office and the penthouse.

"Oh, Lyssa! We need to go. We have to get home!" Sarah exclaims.

My body tenses. Like fuck is she taking Alyssa home. I look to Alyssa, to her mischievous smile as she gazes up at me.

"Oh, babe, I have to do something at my townhouse. I forgot until just now," she says like that's all the explanation I need.

"What is it you have to do?" I ask. I know she's very tipsy, and if she thinks I'm letting her go anywhere without me, she's bloody nuts.

"*Umm...* I, *umm...* I have to... you know..." She's looking to all the girls to help her. Help her what? What could she possibly have to do that she can't tell me?

"Told you he'd find out. You're a fucking hopeless liar, Lyssa." Bray laughs at her.

"Find out what?" I ask very pointedly to Alyssa, who is squirming in her seat.

"*Argh*, it's a surprise and I'm not telling you because it's a surprise for you. But you can't see it because it's a Christmas sort of surprise." She whacks Bray in the arm, then immediately shakes her hand out. "Man, do you have bricks lining your shirt? Damn you, Bray. I told you not to tell."

Bringing her fingers up to my mouth, I kiss each one better. "I didn't tell him, Lyssa. I just knew that he would find out, and I can't wait to see his face when he does." Bray smirks at her.

Now, I'm really intrigued as to what the surprise is, but I'm not going to ruin any surprise she wants to give me. I decide to let it drop. I'll drive her to her house, and even if I have to sit in the car the whole time, I will be there... just enough to not ruin the surprise for her.

Alyssa turns to Bray, a triumphant smile on her face. "Yeah, well, I can't wait to see the look on his face when he finds out you were in the dressing room with me when I was only wearing my bra and panties—" Her mouth stops, and it registers with her what she just said. Everyone at the table goes quiet and watches me.

My body has gone stiff, shoulders tense. *I can't kill my brother. I can't kill my brother.* I keep replaying the mantra in my head as I breathe in and out. Alyssa looks back and forward between Bray and me before trying to fix what she just said.

"*Ah*, babe, it's not how that sounded!"

"Are you sure, sunshine? Because I just heard you say that my brother was in a dressing room with you while you were naked?" I ask her, my voice strained.

"Oh, for fuck's sake. She had just screamed the whole damn store down with a blood-curdling scream. Of course, I would barge in to see what the hell was wrong. And for your information...” Bray points to me. “I dressed her before anyone else saw her.” He nods his head like: *That's that... I should be thankful that he was the only one who saw my girlfriend naked.*

“Plus, I wasn't naked. I had underwear on,” Alyssa adds.

*So not helping like she thinks she is.* I don't know what to think, other than my brother saw my girl naked. I'm so fucking mad at myself for not being there. For not being the one who was there to help her when she needed help.

Blood-curdling scream? Bray said she let out a blood-curdling scream. That's a little more than a *tiny freak-out,* as Alyssa had told me she experienced when she picked up that picture. Fuck, I'm grateful for the foresight to send Bray along with the girls today. I'm grateful that he was there to help her, and I know, without a doubt, he would have been nothing but respectful towards Alyssa. I know my brother, and as much as he clowns around, deep down, he is a fucking decent guy—one of the best I know.

“I think you broke him,” Reilly says, a slight concern to her voice.

Before I can respond, Alyssa slams her lips down on mine, swiping her tongue along my lips until I open for her, granting her the access she is seeking. *As if I'd ever deny her.* I can feel the tension leave my body with each stroke of her tongue against mine. I've never loved kissing anyone as much as I love kissing her. I think I could sit here and kiss her all day and not get bored.

Pulling back from the kiss, she looks at me. “I'm sorry, really sorry. Please don't hate me,” she pleads.

*Hate her?* What the fuck? As if I could fucking hate her...

“Sunshine, I could never hate you. I slightly hate my brother right now, but I'll survive. I'll get over it... maybe.”

Leaning into me, she whispers in my ear, “He was a true

gentleman; he put my shirt on and shorts on without even saying a word. He didn't touch me at all, I promise. But if you tell him I said he's a gentleman, I'll deny it."

I laugh at that. He would hate being referred to as a *gentleman*.

Leaning in, I whisper in her ear, "Babe, I know he would be respectful. I know my brother. I never doubted his intentions. It's just a little fun to watch him squirm for a bit. But I'm glad he was there to help you.

I just wish that it was me. I should have been there."

"You can't be with me all the time, Zac. It's not how life works. Now, I need you to drive Sarah and me to our town-house, because I have someone meeting me there."

Who does she have meeting her at her place? I want to question it, but when I remember how happy she was when she talked about how she has a surprise for me, I can't bring myself to question her. Like I just told her, I trust her completely.

# Nineteen

## ALYSSA

ZAC PULLS UP to the front of my townhouse. The drive here has given me time to sober up, which has returned the nervousness of what I'm about to do. *Think of Zac. Think of Zac.* Repeating that over and over in my head, I can see him on Christmas Day, opening a photo book filled with pictures of me in a range of red lingerie.

I've never felt more desired than when I'm with Zac. He has unintentionally given me a self-confidence boost I didn't know I needed. It's not like I hated my body image before he came along. I knew I was attractive enough, more like a girl next door kind of attractive. But Zac, he makes me feel like I'm more than that. He has no shame in letting anyone and everyone know how much he wants me all the time.

I can see the outline of a growing erection in his pants. The way he moves and tries to not so subtly rearrange his crown jewels also gives away that he's a little turned on right now. I'm actually not sure that he has an off switch. It seems like he's in a constant state of arousal. I didn't know it was possible for a guy to be so ready all the time.

Shit, these thoughts are just getting me all hot and bothered now. I look over to Zac, and he gives me that trademark smirk. His emerald eyes darken as he rakes his eyes up and down me, lingering on my heaving chest—which I'm sure anyone who cares to look can see the outline of my hardened nipples through the thin material of my tank top. Dammit, get it together, Lyssa. You've got a job to do. You can *do* Zac later tonight, many times over, no doubt.

"Okay, thanks for the lift, babe." Leaning over, I quickly peck his cheek. My attempts at a quick escape are halted as he grabs my wrist, stopping my hasty exit from the car.

"Sunshine, if you think for one minute, I'm just leaving you here, then you've lost your goddamn mind!" he exclaims.

Turning the car off, he opens his door and as I'm conjuring up ways to get him to leave, he makes his way over to my side of the car, holding his hand out to help me out. *Ever the gentleman.* I sigh, accepting his hand as I jump down from the car. Bray has a big SUV Mercedes-Benz. I like it a lot; the seats are air- conditioned. I mean, I didn't even know you could get air-conditioned seats, but apparently, they exist.

"I think I'm in love with your car, Bray," I say, turning to see Sarah, Ella and Bray all just staring at me, all three of them making the motions of eating popcorn, invisible popcorn. Rolling my eyes at them, I turn back to Zac. He has a weird, satisfied grin plastered on his face—I have no idea what that's about. But I know I need to get him out of here.

"Babe, you know I would usually invite you in and all, but you can't stay. I just need two hours, tops."

I turn to Sarah to see if my time estimate is right. She gives me a silent nod and a thumbs up, before returning to her imaginary popcorn. Dammit, okay, I'm gonna need to pull out the big guns to win this battle.

Facing Zac, I tilt my head up to look at him. Blinking my eyes, I stick out my bottom lip and ever so quietly plead with the most sugary-sweet voice I can muster, "Please, Zac, don't ruin your surprise. I really want to be able to give this to you. I promise I'm not leaving. I'll wait for you to come back and take me home to your place. And then I'm all yours for the rest of the night, to do with as you please." My voice morphs from sweet to sultry by the end of my plea.

"Fuck. Dammit, sunshine. You know it's bloody impossible to say no to you, right?" He pulls at the ends of his hair. I know he's torn between giving me what I want, and the need to protect me. Finally, he relents. "Okay, I won't come in. But Bray's staying with you."

Just as I'm about to open my mouth to argue that Bray is not staying, he says, "Not negotiable, babe. If I'm not able to be with you, then Bray will be."

I look over my shoulder to Bray for help, but the bastard just grins. Zac tilts my head up towards his. "Sunshine, please don't ask me to leave you unprotected. I can't do it."

Great, it seems I'm not the only one who has mastered the puppy-dog pout.

"Okay, thanks, babe. Love you. See you soon." "Ella, sweetheart, do you want to stay here or come back with me?" Zac asks.

It amazes me how this man, who I know can be ruthless as all hell, is such a big softy with his little sister. I envy how strong the relationships are with these three siblings. I wish I had that.

As a child, I spent many nights lying awake, dreaming of how different my life would have been if my mum didn't die. If I had siblings I could count on to be there in hard times… When I have kids, I definitely want at least three, so they all have each other to lean on.

*Hold the front door.* Where the hell did that thought just come from? *When* I have children?

What the hell happened to the girl who would literally have

a panic attack at the thought of having kids? Zac happened—that's what happened.

I can see how much of a great dad he will be. He stepped up and took over raising a thirteen-year-old girl and a seventeen-year-old teenage boy. That could not have been easy by any standard. But he has never made it out to seem like a chore; he's never complained about having to grow up before his time. He loves his siblings, unconditionally. I know, without a shadow of a doubt, he will love our kids the same.

I'm brought out of my thoughts as I zone in to Bray and Zac arguing. "Zac, take her home. She does not need this level of influence—trust me on this," Bray is saying. Oh crap, he will let the cat out of the bag if he doesn't shut up.

Looking over to Ella, I plead silently with her. She gets it immediately.

"Don't worry, Bray. I'm going with Zac. I'd be bored out of my mind waiting around here anyway. It's not like I haven't seen or done these things with my friends before."

I can tell she is just trying to rile her brother up. There is no way sweet, innocent, little Ella has done this, *right?*

"Take that back, Ella. You can't say shit like that to me. Don't think I won't lock you up in that tower you live in and take away your keys." Bray is fuming. I'm sure a whole lot of unhelpful thoughts of his little sister are going through his mind right now.

"Okay, I'm out. Got things to do. Leave your sister alone, Brayden. Let's go."

I know I'm a little demanding, but I need to get out of this situation before Zac questions what it is I'm really doing here. Walking towards my front door, I don't look back. I'm doing this. I'm really, really doing this.

Okay, I can totally do this.

Sitting in Sarah's room, I'm staring at my reflection in the mirror. She has transformed me from your average, sandy blonde girl next door to a 1950's pin-up model. My hair is made up of big barrel curls, pinned back with diamante hair pins. How she gives my hair this kind of shine, I will never understand. No matter how many times I watch her and attempt to retrace the steps on my own, I just can't seem to figure it out.

My eyes are smoky. She put on glue-on eyelashes, so my lashes are long, thick and dark—with dark eyeliner running along the bottom of my eyes before turning up into a wing on the tops of my eyelids. She has contoured my face, giving me much more defined features than I would normally have. My cheeks have a shiny, golden hue to them and my lips are painted in a bright red, wet-look lipstick.

"Wow." Turning to Sarah, I say, "I think you have really outdone yourself this time."

"Please, it's easy when what you're starting with is already a masterpiece," she says.

I hug her tight. "I know I haven't seen you as much these last few weeks, but I love you. You know that, right?"

"I love you too, and don't beat yourself up. I have been plenty busy myself over the last few weeks." A dreamy look briefly crosses her face before she continues. "I'm so happy that you are finally getting your happily ever after, Lyssa. If anyone deserves it, it's you. That it just so happens to come wrapped in that fine piece of ass is a total bonus," she says with a wink.

I laugh. "It really is one fine ass. I bet I could bounce a coin off it." I make a mental note to enquire about what or who her *busy* is later. "Okay, I can do this. We're doing the pictures in here, right?" I ask Sarah's very gay photographer friend Tom. I smile as I recall Bray's internal struggle with letting the photographer in the room with me.

"Yes, hon. Ready when you are, beautiful," Tom says.

I turn my face back to Sarah, partly so he doesn't see the blush working its way up my neck and face, while also trying to steal some of my friend's courage from her. Sarah would do this without even batting an eye. Me? I have to give myself internal pep talks and think about Zac, think about what his reaction will be.

Picking up the Victoria's Secret bag, I head for the bedroom door. "Okay, I'm going to change in my room. I'll be back in a sec."

"I'll help and also make sure you don't chicken out and make a break for it." Sarah's laugh follows me down the hall.

Our rooms are separated by a shared bathroom. Opening my bedroom door, my steps halt, Sarah running into the back of me.

"What the..." She doesn't finish the sentence. Or, at least, I don't hear her finish the sentence as I take in the scene in front of me.

No, no, no, no. This is not happening. Closing my eyes and reopening them, I attempt to change what they see. It doesn't work. This cannot be real; I must be dreaming. I'm frozen as I observe what used to be a somewhat orderly bedroom.

Everything has been thrown around, drawers opened... My clothes are shredded everywhere. I mean, literally, they are in shreds like someone has taken a pair of scissors and just hacked right through them. There is paint everywhere, red paint splashed all over the room, on the floor, on the walls—it's even on the ceiling.

The message that's written above what used to be my bedhead is what breaks my frozen stance and has me screaming at the top of my lungs. The message painted in what I'm hoping is red paint says:

## I'm coming for you.
## We will meet soon. xxx

OH MY GOD, all of my things, everything I have worked so hard to get, has been destroyed. Running to my wardrobe, I'm scrambling to the mess. No, she cannot have ruined it. I'm crying, rummaging, trying to find it. I can't find it. Why can't I find it?

Strong arms wrap around me and pull me back, stopping me from looking.

"No, I have to find it. It has to be here," I say as I fight my way out of his hold.

"*Shh*, sunshine, I've got you. I've got you. It's going to be okay."

It's not going to be okay; it's never going to be okay. Why doesn't he know? This is what my life is, one fucked-up situation after another. He would have been better off never having met me. But I can't think about that right now. I need to find that picture.

"I need to find it. It's here, somewhere. Please, just help me find it," I'm begging for anyone to help me.

Sarah gets down on her hands and knees and starts digging through the mess. She doesn't need to ask what she's looking for; she already knows.

Zac is still trying to hold me still. "Alyssa, I'll buy you another one. It's okay. Please stop." I hear his voice crack.

I turn to look at him, tears running down my face. "It's the only picture of my mother I have, Zac! You can't buy me another one!"

I feel defeated. Slumping to the ground, I curl into myself and let myself break.

Sarah wraps herself around me, whispering in my ear, "Lyssa, honey, you need to let Zac take you home. I'll stay here. I'll keep looking. I will find the picture for you and bring it to you. Please, just let Zac take you home, Lyssa."

I can't tell if it's Sarah's cries I hear, or my own. I'm only vaguely aware as I'm lifted into Zac's arms, and he carries me out of the house.

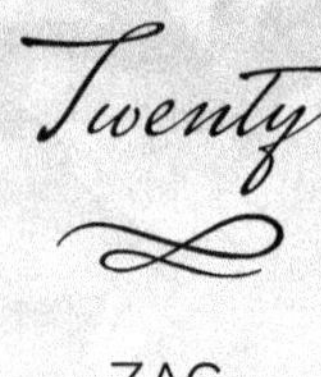

# Twenty

## ZAC

I'VE BEEN STANDING out front of Alyssa's townhouse for an hour. I was never planning to leave her here. Ella made sure I knew how much she did not like the fact I had called Dean to take her home.

Pulling my phone out, I give him a call to make sure Ella didn't put him through too much hell on the drive home. The phone only rings twice before he answers.

"Yeah?"

"I'm judging by the fact that you answered, you're still alive and my sister didn't manage to find a way to kill you yet?" I laugh.

I don't know what's going on with those two; Dean and Ella used to be really close. Lately, it's like they can't stand being in the same room together.

"I wouldn't put it past her to be plotting my demise as we speak. She is your sister, after all," he says.

"Don't I know it."

I'm about to ask him what's up with the two of them when I hear someone scream. No, not someone, Alyssa. I hear Alyssa scream.

"Fuck!"

I'm holding the phone in my hand as I run towards Alyssa's front door, my heart pounding as I take the stairs two at a time. Barging my way past Bray and some other fucker in the doorway of Alyssa's bedroom, my heart feels like it's just been ripped out of my chest.

The room is a fucking mess. Where is she? Turning around, I spot her on the floor at her wardrobe, rummaging through shit while mumbling about needing to find something. *Fuck*. Grabbing her, I pull her back into my arms. She fights herself out of my hold, begging me to help her find whatever it is she's looking for.

Trying to reassure her that I can replace anything she needs, I freeze as her next words to me just break my fucking heart.

"It's the only picture of my mother I have, Zac! You can't buy me another one!"

That's not something I can replace. I watch as her body crumbles to the floor; she bends over herself and cries. I can feel the tears running down my own face. I haven't cried since my parents' funeral five years ago.

But the sight of Alyssa on the floor, looking so fucking broken, I can't take it.

I'm about to pull myself together, scoop her up, and put her back together. I can fix this. I have to fix this. Sarah leans over her, whispering in her ear. She's also fucking crying. She looks up at me.

"You need to take her home, Zac. Get her out of here. Please," she pleads with me.

I can see that she's looking to me to put her best friend back together right now. I'm not sure how I will do it, but I make a promise to anyone who will listen that I will do just that. I will do anything to take away Alyssa's pain.

I pick her up and walk down the stairs with her in my arms. Bray follows me down.

"I'll drive," he says just as Dean comes running through the door.

He takes one look at us and asks, "What happened?" looking at Alyssa's limp form in my arms.

It's just registering with me that she's not clinging to me like she usually would when experiencing a panic attack. This is different. I don't like how limp and unresponsive she's being. I know she's conscious to some extent; she's still crying and mumbling about finding that damn picture.

"Can you stay and help Sarah upstairs? Don't leave her alone. Bring her to the penthouse when she's finished here."

I can't even tell him what happened. I can't bring myself to find the words, confirming that Caitlyn has finally managed to break down Alyssa.

Getting her home, I take her straight into the shower. She's stopped crying; she's just silently staring into space. She won't answer anything I ask her other than nodding or shaking her head. I honestly don't know how to help her. Should I call a doctor in? A trauma specialist, maybe? Fuck, I just need to figure out how to help her.

"Baby, please tell me how I can help you? What can I do?"

I keep my voice quiet, calm, or at least, I try to. But I'm breaking on the inside too. I'm breaking from seeing her like this. This is not Alyssa, not my sunshine, so full of life and promise. The girl standing in front of me, with her once beautiful blue eyes that are now dull, seems to look through me.

She doesn't answer me, so I continue to remove her clothes so I can get her in the shower. Just as I've pulled her tank top over her head, she says, "You can't help me, Zac. No one can."

Like fuck, I can't help her. I know that right now, she believes that, but she will see. We will get through this.

After washing her hair for her, I dry her and bundle her up in one of my shirts. I watch as she brings the material up to her face and inhales. That one little gesture shows me she is still my Alyssa. Mine, and fuck anyone who thinks they can take her from me. I lie down in bed with her and hold her.

Whispering to her, I promise to fix this. I promise her that, no matter what, our tomorrows will always be together.

It's been two weeks since I carried Alyssa out of her bedroom in her townhouse and brought her back here. Two weeks and I still have no fucking clue where the fuck Caitlyn is holed up. I've had teams of private investigators looking for the bitch. I can't find a single fucking trace, and it's doing my head in.

It's been two weeks since Alyssa has left the penthouse. She puts on a brave front to everyone. She didn't fight me when I told her she should put in for a couple of weeks leave at work, which tells me she's not as good as she keeps insisting she is.

She can pretend to be fine, but it's the way she jumps at loud sounds, the way her hands shake a little, the way she clings to me when she becomes overwhelmed... All these little things tell me she is not okay at all. She is spooked, she's angry, and she's anxious about what's next.

Alyssa didn't get out of bed for two days. She barely ate. She spoke only in answer to a direct question and, even then, would only give two-word answers. On the third day after I brought her home, Sarah turned up, having found the photograph of Alyssa's mother. Fortunately, the picture was not damaged, and now lives locked inside the safe in my home office. After she received the picture back, Alyssa's spirits lifted again, and slowly, I saw my sunshine coming back to life.

Still, her laugh is not as full as it was, her smile not as bright.

I didn't know my heart could hurt so fucking much, but the last two weeks, watching Alyssa struggle and fight with her fear, has fucking wrecked me. I feel useless right now. The only time she seems at total peace and relaxed are the times when it's just her and me in the bedroom. Every night, we have been up for hours, me wringing orgasm after orgasm out of her until I wear her out enough that I know she will get some sleep.

You won't hear me complaining about that task though. I will happily give my girl whatever release she needs, anywhere, anytime.

One thing I know for sure is that she is it. She is the girl I see my future with, the one I want to wake up next to every morning. And I will take her any way I can have her. If that means I spend the rest of my life fighting to bring life back, to restore the sunshine and happiness to her eyes, I will. If I have to spend every day proving to her that she is safe with me, that I'm not about to let any motherfucker get their hands on her, then that's what I'm going to do.

I'm lying in bed with Alyssa in my arms and I couldn't think of waking up any other way. It's Christmas Eve. I have her car in the garage with a huge fucking bow on it. I just have to figure out a way to get her to accept it. I've been lying awake for hours, conjuring up ways to get her to accept the car and accept the question I'm planning to ask her tomorrow morning. But first, today, the car.

Alyssa stirs, slowly opening her eyes. She is the definition of *not a morning person*. Grumbling, she smiles up at me.

"Morning, babe." She leans in and kisses me gently before settling her head on my chest.

"Morning, sunshine. Sleep well?" I ask, kissing the top of her head.

"*Mmhmm,* I always sleep well next to you," she mumbles back.

*Huh*, she's in a great mood today. Rolling her over to her back, I pin her down and kiss her. She responds immediately, opening for me. I pull away before I take things any further. A look of disappointment crosses her face as I get up.

Chuckling, I say, "Stay here. I'm going to get your coffee. I'll be back."

Not waiting for her to reply, I make my way out to the kitchen and set up the machine to make her coffee. As I'm walking out of the kitchen, Bray walks through the living room.

"Morning, how is she?" He asks the same thing every morning. He's been sleeping here for the last two weeks, around to help with whatever I needed, without question.

"She's good," I tell him and can't help the smile that appears on my face. Because for the first time in two weeks, I actually feel like it's the truth.

"That's good, bro. I'm taking Ella last-minute shopping today. Apparently, there is more shit she needs to get. Call if you need anything," he says as he walks into the kitchen.

"Thanks, man," I call after him.

Walking back into the bedroom, I'm greeted with the sight of Alyssa sitting up in my bed, smiling at me. Maybe it's the coffee she's smiling at, but I'll take it.

Holding her hands out, she says, "Give me, give me, give me."

Laughing, I hand over her vanilla latte. I watch as she takes a sip and her face morphs into an expression of pure bliss as a moan escapes her. Dammit, I want to be the reason for those moans. I want to hear her screaming out my name in ecstasy. Reaching down and readjusting myself not so subtly, I see her smirk over at my discomfort.

Tilting her head, she says, "So that does still work, I take it?" pointing at my crotch region.

Oh, she did not just say that. Hell no. Does she think it

wasn't working?

"Sunshine, my cock has never not worked. Why the fuck would you think it was broken?" I ask her, mortified that she's questioning my manhood.

"For the last fourteen days, I've woken up to that being buried deep inside me. I thought maybe you had a little problem or something this morning?" She shrugs.

Is she fucking kidding me right now? I look around the room in search of the hidden cameras, not seeing any.

"Babe, I tore myself away from you this morning because I didn't want to get caught up in bed all day. It's Christmas Eve and we have shit to do today. It has absolutely nothing to do with my manhood not working."

"Oh, okay," she says like that's the end of this conversation.

Ah, hell no. Crawling up the bed, I straddle her legs.

"I'm more than happy to show you just how not broken he is. Name the place and time and I'm there," I tell her, leaving the ball in her court.

She looks from me to her cup of coffee, back and forth, like she's trying to decide. Please god, do not let me lose out to a fucking cup of coffee right now. Finally, she sets the cup down on the table, reaches up and pulls my face down to hers, slamming our lips together.

*Home.* That's what this kiss feels like; it feels like returning home after a long absence.

"How about right now?" she asks, raising her eyebrow. Well, she doesn't have to ask me twice. I do, however, look carefully at her face, reading her expression.

"Are you sure?" I ask.

"I've never been more sure of anything in my life," she says.

I make quick work of removing her shirt—well, my shirt that she's been sleeping in. Cupping her breast in my hands, I lean down. Taking a nipple in my mouth, I audibly groan.

"*Mmm*, I missed these beauties," I say as I show the other breast just how much I missed it by sucking, nibbling and biting at it.

Alyssa laughs. "It's only been four hours since you last saw them."

Looking up at her, I respond, "Babe, ten minutes without seeing these beauties is ten minutes too fucking long."

Tilting my head back down, I get back to work, worshiping the fuck out of her breasts.

Alyssa is making the most beautiful sounds, moaning, shivering and squirming beneath me.

"I'd love to take this slow, babe, but I can't hold out. I need to be inside you now—it will be rough and quick. But I swear I'll make it up to you later."

Holding the sides of her lace panties between my hands, I rip, tearing them from her body. She gasps and arches her body while I trail my finger between the lips of her pussy, making sure she is ready for me. I'm pleased as fuck to find her pussy wet and weeping for me.

"Look how wet you are, sunshine. Is this pussy starving for my cock? Has she missed him?"

I feel a gush of wetness escape her as she takes in my dirty words. I settle between her legs, lining my cock up to her entrance.

"Ready?" I ask her.

"Oh god, Zac. Hurry up already and put that in me!" she exclaims.

Slamming into her, I still. Fuck. I'm really not going to last long. This feels too fucking good. I move slowly, thrusting in and out in careful, precise, slow motions. It's not helping. I can feel my orgasm building. Reaching between our bodies, I rub my finger in circles around her clit

"I need you to come for me, sunshine. Come now!" I demand.

She doesn't disappoint. She comes hard, screaming out my name. Her pussy clamps down around my cock, milking me for all that I have to give. Falling onto the bed next to her, I pull her into my arms. We're both a sweaty mess, both breathing heavily, sucking in air, attempting to catch our breaths.

Alyssa's breathing slows, her body relaxing into mine. "You okay?" I ask her.

"*Mhmm*, never been better. God, I love when we do that."

"Yep, you and me both, babe, but what I love most is this, just lying here, holding onto my girl with a feeling of bliss."

"Zac." Alyssa's voice is quiet. She tilts her head up so she looks at me.

"Yeah, babe?"

She's pensive for a while before speaking again. "I know I haven't been the easiest person to live with these past few weeks. But I want you to know that I'm really trying."

Her voice breaks a little. I'm about to say something when she continues, "I am trying. But the images, they keep playing in my mind. I'm not scared of her, you know, Caitlyn. I'm scared that she will succeed. That you are going to finally have had enough and leave me. I don't know if I can survive that kind of loss, you know?"

"Sunshine, there is nothing anybody, and I mean fucking anybody, can do to make me leave you. I will stay in this apartment for as long as you need me to be with you. Until you're ready to go back out to the world. Until then, I'm happy staying here with you." Kissing the top of her head, I continue, "Always have tomorrow together, right?"

I don't know how else to reassure her I'm not going anywhere. Hopefully, tomorrow she will get the picture that I'm in this forever.

"Always," she whispers. "It's not just the Caitlyn stuff. It's the holidays."

"What about the holidays?" I ask her.

"Well, I've never really had a good relationship with Christmas before. I've never had a family to celebrate with, to exchange gifts with. I mean, ever since I met Sarah in college, she has taken me home to her family every Christmas. But it's not the same. I've always just felt like an outsider."

Shit, why did I not think of this before? Of course she hasn't had a real fucking Christmas. "Well, you have a family now. And you just might question the sanity of the family you've joined when tomorrow morning you're woken to the screams of Bray carrying on like a child. Because I can promise you that is exactly what's going to happen."

She lets a small giggle escape. Good, if Bray being his usual idiot self will get a laugh out of her, then I'll make sure he amps it up more than usual tomorrow.

"Thank you. For everything, for being you. For not leaving me alone the last few weeks." She leans up and kisses me. I need to get her back to a better mood, back to happier thoughts.

"So, it's Christmas Eve, babe. I've got an early Christmas present for you."

She sits up, eyes wide, and then they turn watery.

Shit, I fucked up. What the fuck did I say? "What's wrong?" I ask as I rub her arms.

"Your present, I didn't get to make your present the way I wanted to. I mean, I got part of it done that day you went into the club and Sarah and her friend came over. But it's not very good, and it's not what I wanted to give you," she says with tears running down her face. "I... I don't have anything else to give you."

That's what she's upset about? *Jesus.*

"Babe, the only thing I need from you is *you*. If you want to gift me something, I have an idea of what you can give me." An idea starts to build in my head.

"What is it? Anything, I will do my best to get it today," she says eagerly.

I laugh and get up before she can reach out and slap me. "Your gift to me will be your acceptance of any and all gifts I give you over the next two days, without argument." I raise my eyebrows at her, waiting for her to respond.

She stands up, completely naked, as she saunters over to me. Leaning up, she kisses me on the lips. "Okay, but—"

Before she can add a *but*, I place a finger over her lips, stopping her sentence. "No *buts*. All I want to hear is: *thanks Zac, or yes*. Now get dressed. I need to take you downstairs to give you your first gift."

I head into the walk-in wardrobe, of which I have now designated half the space for Alyssa's things. Not that she has a whole lot yet, but that's about to change tomorrow when she wakes up to see it full.

I had Reilly sworn to secrecy and handed over my credit card to her to replace all of Alyssa's clothing, shoes, and bags that were destroyed. Not that Reilly complained one bit about doing that shopping. I've seen the bank statements from her shopping trips. I know she hasn't skimped out. She's going to be in here tonight to set it all up with Holly and Sarah. I just have to keep Alyssa occupied in the home gym.

Alyssa comes out of the bathroom, and I swear every time I see her, she takes my breath away. Even now, she's wearing yoga pants and one of my shirts, but she still steals my breath with how beautiful she is.

Smiling, I hold out my hand. "Ready?"

Taking my hand, she smiles, a little sceptical at what I'm about to give her. "As I'll ever be," she says, following me out to the elevator.

*Twenty-one*

ALYSSA

I'M STARING at a huge, freaking shiny red car with a huge, shiny white bow on it. *Merry Christmas, Sunshine* is written across the windscreen. What the actual fudge?

"*Ah*, Zac, that's a car!"

Turning to face him, I can see an enormous smile on his face. I'm taken aback. I haven't seen him this happy for a while. I know he's been hovering over me and trying to make sure I'm okay. It has taken a toll on him.

"Well, it has four wheels and what looks like a steering wheel inside it. So, yeah, it possibly is a car." He laughs.

I'm stunned, not sure what to do or say. No one has ever given me a gift like a car before. I mean, what do you say to a gift like this? *Oh, thanks, I love it!* just doesn't seem enough.

I've been standing in the same spot, just staring at this huge, bright red car for too long. I can feel Zac's gaze burning into me. Finally, he takes my hand, leading me to the driver's side door. Opening it, he picks me up and places me on the seat before walking around and climbing into the passenger seat.

"I don't even know what to say," I tell him, shaking my head as I look around the car.

"I believe the words we agreed on were: *thanks, Zac.*" He laughs.

Looking around, it dawns on me that this car is exactly the same as another car I've been in recently.

"Wait, is this the same car as Bray's?" I ask.

Smiling, he says, "You said you loved Bray's car, so I figured you could only love the model higher up from his even more."

Not sure what to say to that, I lean over to him and kiss him, hoping that this kiss shows my appreciation of him, of his thoughtfulness, of the care and devotion he constantly provides me.

Pulling apart, I look him in the eye. "Zac, I freaking love this car," I shriek, "but you really do not need to be buying me these kinds of gifts. It's really too much."

He stops me, placing a finger to my lips before I can tell him he should take it back.

"Sunshine, the car is yours. It's in your name. You can do whatever you want with it, but I am not, under any circumstances, returning the damn car. So, before you even think about it, it would mean the absolute world to me if you accept this gift—not to mention the peace of mind it will give me, knowing you can drive yourself around in a safe car for those rare occasions I can't drive you myself."

"Okay." Kissing him lightly on his lips, I whisper, "Thank you, Zac. I freaking love it."

He laughs before grabbing my face in his hands, tilting my head and deepening the kiss. Climbing over the centre console, I settle on top of Zac's lap, grinding against him as he continues to assault my mouth with his tongue.

Groaning, he finally slows down his kiss before pulling back. "As much as I would love to christen this car, I don't think a garage where our neighbours can walk by is the place to do it."

Looking back over my shoulder, I peer through the windscreen to see an older couple waiting at the lift.

"You know when you kiss me like that, I lose all common sense. I wouldn't notice who was watching."

Zac grabs my ass in both hands. Squeezing, he says, "I don't share, sunshine, and that includes letting any other fuckers see this ass that belongs to me."

I grind my centre along the hardness of his cock. Holding my hips still, he says, "Do you want me to show you all the features of the car, or should we move on to your next gift already?"

"If the next gift is your cock in my pussy, then yes, let's move on already!" I exclaim.

Opening the door, he pulls me out of the car with him before placing me on my feet.

"That's not your next gift, but you never know it could be something even better."

Shaking my head, I follow him back to the lift—not that I have any choice, considering my hand is tightly clasped in his. His grip is so firm, it's almost like he thinks I'm going to run.

"Not sure anything could be better than that," I mumble behind him. By the little chuckle that escapes his lips, I know he heard.

I'm sitting cross-legged on the floor in the gym, in a pair of running shorts and a sports bra, waiting for Zac. He told me to meet him in the gym, to be ready to work out with him. Secretly, I'm hoping that the workout he has in mind involves the clothes I'm wearing being removed. All day, he has been surprising me with little gifts, randomly coming up with a box or gift bag in his hands when I'm least expecting it. No one has ever wanted to give me gifts like this before, not to mention the freaking car, which I still can't believe.

Everything from a beautiful silk scarf to a pair of diamond studs, which I can tell are real and probably of some carat I didn't even know existed. The smile on Zac's face when I open each gift is what has kept me accepting them all day with something like a *thanks, Zac, I love it!* response. He seems genuinely excited to see me open gifts. I haven't been able to wipe the smile off my face all day.

Hearing the click of the door opening, I look up, only for my smile to falter when I see Bray sauntering in and not Zac.

Making a dramatic scene of sniffing under his armpits, he says, "Nope, I don't smell. I don't know why you're looking so disappointed to see me walk through the door, Lyssa. Do you realise how many ladies would swap places with you just to sit and watch me get all hot and sweaty?" He waggles his eyebrows up and down at me.

I can't help but laugh a little. "I was waiting for Zac. Have you seen him?"

Bray heads over to the weight bench, pulling his shirt over his head before lying down on it.

"Who?" he asks as he lifts the weight bar over his head.

How he is lifting that thing is beyond me. The weights on it look like they weigh a ton.

"Funny," I say, getting up from my spot, walking over to him and glaring down at him.

"Where's your brother, Bray? He told me to meet him in here. I've been waiting for fifteen minutes already."

Bray continues to lift the weights up and down from his chest. "I saw him just a minute ago with Ella. She needed his help to wrap some shit. I'm sure he won't be long. But feel free to stand there and enjoy your view for as long as you want," he finishes with a wink.

"Oh, okay, I'll just wait then. And *eww*, not even if you were the last man on earth, Braydon." With that, I turn and head back to sit on the floor.

"You hurt my feelings, Lyssa. You know I have fragile self-esteem issues, and you go and say mean things like that to me. I thought we were friends." Bray puts the bar back in its holder before sitting up and pouting at me.

"Oh my god, self-esteem issues? Yeah right. If your ego was any bigger, your head wouldn't fit out the door. And stop pouting. It's not a good look on you," I say with a little giggle.

Just then, an idea comes to me, something I have been thinking about for a while now.

"Bray, since we are both in here and it seems I have some time to kill, how about you make yourself useful to me and teach me a few fighting moves?"

Putting on my brightest smile and fluttering my eyelashes does nothing to wipe the look of shock and despair crossing over Bray's face.

"Do you really hate me that much?" he asks in all seriousness.

Confused, my eyebrows pull together. "What? Why would you think I hate you? Of course I don't hate you."

Bray just stands there, glaring at me. "You're trying to get me killed, aren't you?" he asks.

I shake my head no. I have no idea what his problem is.

"You're asking me," he says, pointing to his own chest, "to teach you," he emphasises as he points to me, "to fight?"

"Well, yeah. Last I knew, you were a professional fighter. So, I figured, who else's better to teach me to knock someone on their ass than you?" I shrug, really not understanding what the big deal is.

"Lyssa, sweetheart. If I taught you to fight, it would be the last thing I ever did," he declares.

I think he actually believes that. However, I still don't understand why he has such a problem with it.

"Why on earth would it be the last thing you did? Do you have some kind of medical issue I don't know about? Like if I accidently punch you in the head, are you going to have an aneurysm or something?" I ask.

"Or something," Bray says. "If I teach you to fight, you're likely to get hurt in the process, not bad but probably a bruise here or there. If you get hurt because of me, I'm a dead man, because that crazy as fuck boyfriend of yours will kill me."

At this, I laugh. I laugh so long and so hard at him I have to wipe tears from my eyes.

Noticing the tears, he adds, "Well shit, now I've made you cry, so I might as well go and dig my own grave."

Shaking my head, I pull myself together. "Bray, Zac won't kill you for teaching me how to protect myself. And if he wants to kill you for it, well, I'll just tell him not to."

Standing up, feeling energised suddenly, I bounce on the spot.

"Okay, so what's the first thing I need to know?" I ask as I punch him in the arm then shake my hand out because, damn, hitting his arm was like hitting a brick wall.

"If I get killed, I'm coming back to haunt your ass until you're in hell with me."

He walks over to a shelf and retrieves a pair of gloves. After securing my fists into pink and purple gloves that look like they must belong to Ella, I bounce around, feeling the excitement building.

"First, you need to stop jumping around like a damn lunatic on speed. Hold your fist up like this." He models holding his fist in the air in front of his face. "Hold your left arm up, protect your face, and jab with your right, like this." He jabs out stopping just before he makes contact with my face. His hand comes at me so fast I don't even notice it until it's stopped just an inch away from my face. "You would have just been knocked out cold. You didn't even try to block."

"That's because I didn't even see it coming, jerk."

Bray bounces around me in a circle, throwing out pretend jabs my way, each time calling out, "KO!"

It's starting to annoy me. I can feel myself getting worked up. He notices the change in my mood.

Stopping in front of me suddenly, he says, "Good. Now that you really want to hit me, give me all you got."

That's what I do. I punch, or at least I try to land punch after punch to his face, his torso. Each and every time, he blocks with what seems like little effort. It's pissing me off more that I can't actually land a punch on him.

I don't give up though. I keep trying to punch him for what seems like hours, my arms burning. I can feel the sweat rolling down my back. But as I continue punching, I feel like a weight is being lifted off me. Who would have thought this would be so cathartic?

I don't notice as the door opens, and I don't stop trying to land a punch as Zac's voice booms across the room.

"What the fuck do you think you're doing?"

Bray stops blocking and slightly turns towards Zac. That's when I see my opportunity and I swing my right arm out, landing a punch on his face. Where? I could not tell you, but I definitely felt the contact.

You can't miss the dramatic yell from Bray, "*Ah*, goddammit, Lyssa! You fucking punched me!" He holds his hand up to his face, covering his left eye.

Oh god, I stop in place. The high feeling of making contact and landing a punch turns into a feeling of dread. I think I hurt him. I can't believe I actually punched him. Sure, I really wanted to land a hit on him, but I didn't want to hurt him.

"I'm so sorry, Bray. I... I didn't mean to. I just got carried away." I try to explain myself. At the same time, I try to not let the tears fall that are threatening to come loose.

Zac wraps me in his arms. "Sunshine, he's fine.

He's being dramatic. Don't worry about him."

Wiggling out of his arms, I don't miss Zac's scowl as I reach up and pull Bray's hand away from his face, a gasp leaving my mouth. Holy shit, the skin around his left eye is red. Zac stands behind me, wrapping an arm around my waist before he starts laughing.

"It's not funny, Zac. I hurt him. I hit your brother. Oh god, I'm so, so sorry, Bray. Let me get you some ice."

Zac tightens his grip around me as I try to move away.

"Babe, he's fine. You probably bruised his ego more than anything else."

Bray tilts his head, examining Zac. "You know, there was a time you would have stuck up for me if I got sucker-punched," he says, pointing at him.

Meanwhile, Zac continues to laugh as he pulls me out of the room, calling out, "Be thankful it was her that landed that punch, because if she didn't, I was already planning to. Don't teach my girl how to fight, dammit. What the hell were you thinking? She could have gotten hurt." I can feel Zac getting worked up as he stops and turns back to Bray.

"She asked me to. What was I meant to do?" "Say no," Zac says.

"Yeah, how's that work out for you? Saying no to her?" Bray asks and then adds, "When you figure out how to do that, let me in on the fucking secret. It might just save my life one of these days."

I pull on Zac's hand, tugging him towards the door. "Come on, I need a shower. And he needs to ice his face."

I'm slowly pulled from my sleep and my hot AF dream I was having about a sex god, a sex god who is currently peppering my neck with kisses.

"*Mmm.*" Rolling over, I face him and open my eyes. "I was having the best dream," I tell him. "I was naked, you were naked, and it was good."

I can feel his body shake as he laughs. "How about I make that dream a reality?" he asks as his hand slowly makes its way up my shirt to cup my right breast.

Lifting my hand up, I cup his face. "I'm all for..." My words die off as something shiny reflects off my left hand. Something freaking big and shiny! Sitting up suddenly, I look around the room frantically, realising I am, in fact, in Zac's bed in his penthouse and not in a hotel in Vegas somewhere. I hold up my left hand. Yep, it's still there. Sitting on my ring finger is probably the biggest princess-cut diamond I've ever freaking seen. I'm speechless. I don't know how this got here.

Oh my god, did Zac propose and I've forgotten the whole thing? How could that even happen? I remember going to bed last night. I remember having a shower with Zac, a very long and rewarding shower. What I don't remember is getting a ring put on my finger.

"Babe, you okay?" Zac asks, sitting up next to me.

*Am I okay?* Is he freaking serious right now? Does he not see this rock sitting on my finger? Oh shit, maybe I'm hallucinating. I must be. I've finally lost the plot.

"*Umm,* Zac, honey, do you see anything on my hand? Anything at all?" I ask, my voice a little quiet and unsure.

Zac grabs my hand and pulls it close to his face, turning my hand from front to back and inspecting it.

"Well, I can see you've still got five fingers, clear skin, no signs of a rash." Turning my hand back over so the diamond is facing him, he adds, "Other than that three-carat diamond on your finger, I don't see anything else. What am I supposed to be looking for?" Still holding my hand, he looks up at my face.

"*Umm*, Zac, how exactly did that diamond come to be on my finger?" I ask, still staring at the huge rock.

"I put it there of course," he replies. That's it, no other explanation.

"Okay, but I think you forgot the part where you ask me a very big question before you put a rock on my finger?"

Zac raises my hand and kisses just under where the rock sits. "I didn't forget. I was waiting for you to wake up. I thought I'd get a better answer when you're conscious and all."

"*Mmhmm*." I continue to stare at the ring. Zac grabs my face, tilting my chin up so I'm looking at him.

"Sunshine. Alyssa. I was going to do this differently, more romantically, but I couldn't wait. I love that the first thing I see in the morning when I wake up is your beautiful face. I love that that's also the last thing I see before I close my eyes at night. I love how you have brought so much light and joy into my otherwise dark and dim world.

"The word love doesn't even begin to describe what I feel for you. I don't think there is a word to describe it. It's like you are a part of me. When I'm not with you, it's like I'm short of oxygen. I would love nothing more than to wake up with you in my arms every morning for the rest of my life, to spend the rest of my life loving you the way you deserve to be loved. Alyssa Summers, will you marry me?"

The tears are running down my face uncontrollably. No one has ever loved me like Zac loves me. As I'm processing everything he just said to me, I can hear Ella and Bray squealing down the hall.

"Babe, I don't want to rush you to answer or anything. You

can take all the time you need to think about it. But we have about two minutes before that door is busted open."

Laughing, I lean in to kiss him. "I don't need any time, Zac, yes. Yes. Yes. Of course I will marry you!"

I barely get the words out as Zac pins me down to the bed and rolls on top of me, kissing the ever-loving hell out of me.

Our moment is broken when Bray barges through the room and jumps on the bed. Jumping up and down, he screams, "Mum, dad, it's Christmas. Get up, get up, get up!" I don't know how the bed is not giving out with how much he is jumping around.

"*Argh*, make him stop, Zac, please," Ella grumbles from the end of the bed.

Zac rolls off me, pulling me up while kicking at Bray's legs. Bray stops jumping. Landing on the end of the bed, he sits down.

"Come on. Why aren't you up already? It's Christmas!" he yells.

It's then that I really look at him and see the shiner on his face. He has a black eye. I gave him a black eye. *Shit*. Sitting up, I move across the bed and reach my hand up to touch his face.

"Oh my gosh, Bray, I can't believe I gave you a black eye."

Before my hand reaches his face, he snags my wrist, holding my hand still.

"What the fuck? Lyssa, do you know there is a rock on your finger?" he asks.

This makes Ella look up and squeal, "*Ah*, yes, yes! I'm finally getting a sister!" She is jumping around and then suddenly stops. "Wait, you said yes, right?"

Bray and Ella both look at me expectantly.

"Of course she said yes," Zac answers for me before continuing, "Now let go of her fucking hand, Braydon." Zac pulls me back as Bray drops my hand.

"I can't believe you said yes to that, Lyssa!" he says before laughing. "I am thrilled to be able to call you my sister though. Lord knows I needed an upgrade on the one they gave me first. *Ow!*" He rubs his arm where Ella just punched him.

"Thank you, both of you. It means a lot you're okay with this. I know it's quick, but, well, I don't really have an answer for that."

Zac kisses the side of my head. "Babe, this would be happening whether they liked it or not. It's just easier on them that they like it."

Looking over to Bray and Ella, I see them nodding their heads.

Bray stands up off the bed and pulls the blankets off with him. "Now get up. I've got presents to open."

He walks over to the door and bends down to pick up something off the floor, before he walks back, holding out my saving grace, a coffee cup filled with coffee.

"I think I love you right now, Bray. Thank you," I say as I take the cup and sip at the deliciousness, ignoring Zac's grunts behind me.

"Get out. We'll get dressed and meet you out there. Don't start without me," he warns Bray.

Standing up, I head into the walk-in wardrobe, only to stop at the entrance, Zac right behind me.

"Oh, my god, Zac. What? When? How?" I shake my head. I am staring at what Zac calls my side of the huge walk-in, which is now filled to the brim with clothes, everything from dresses, shirts, skirts, pants... There is even a whole section of shoes. A dozen bags are placed in neatly arranged rows on the top shelf.

"I had a little help, sunshine. But I believe the words you're looking for are: *thank you, Zac.*" Kissing my forehead, he says, "Merry Christmas, my beautiful fiancée."

I melt at hearing him call me his fiancée. I mean, who the

hell wouldn't? "Thank you, Zac, you really didn't need to do this," I say as I turn and wrap my hands around his neck.

"You're welcome, and I know I didn't need to... I *wanted* to. I want to give you the world, Alyssa, but I'll start with a closet."

What am I meant to say to that? Pulling away from him, I rush to the drawer where I was hiding his present, thanking the stars it's still there. Whoever put all these clothes in here had the good grace to leave it. Picking it up, I'm nervous now. My gift pales in comparison to everything he's done for me.

"Okay, so, this isn't much, and it's not how I wanted it to look, but Merry Christmas." I hand over the gift box.

"You are a gift—the fact that you said yes is the best thing you could have ever given me, sunshine. I don't need anything else from you, just *you*."

Nodding my head, I motion for him to move on with it and open the box. The moment he lifts the lid, I know what he sees. Me, in lingerie, all variations of red lingerie. I'm nervous as he lifts the first picture and sees that there is another underneath it. Suddenly, he sits on the floor, cross-legged with the box in front of him, lifting picture after picture out.

He still hasn't said anything and it's driving me crazy. Does he hate them that much? "I know they aren't that good, and I was planning on the pictures being printed into a book, but I ran out of time and had to settle."

He looks up at me with an undecipherable look in his eyes. "Sunshine, these look fucking amazing. I'm torn right now between how much I love these pictures and the knowledge that someone had to take them, which means someone was looking at you in this lingerie. But don't for a second doubt how goddamn sexy you are."

He goes back to the box and continues to pull out the pictures in silence. Sitting in front of him, I wait for him to say something. As he gets to the last picture, he looks up at me.

"Do you have all of this lingerie still?" he questions.

"*Umm*, yeah. I took these pictures just last week. Of course I have it all."

He nods his head. "Good, because I counted twenty pictures. That means, for the next twenty nights, I get to have you in each piece of lingerie. In fact, I think we should cancel Christmas and start right now."

Laughing, I say, "We're not cancelling Christmas, but I will wear each and every piece one day at a time."

"Thank you, sunshine. No one has ever given me a gift like this. It's hands down the best gift I've ever received, apart from you."

Yeah right, like he hasn't been given better gifts. "*Uh-huh*. Hopefully, over the course of our lives, I can figure out this gift-giving thing and get as good at it as you are. There's always tomorrow, right?"

"There will always be a tomorrow for us together, sunshine," he declares, just like he does every night before we go to sleep.

"Promise?" I ask.

"I promise. There is nothing in this world that could tear me away from you."

Even as he makes this promise, I have a lingering feeling that some things are out of even his control.

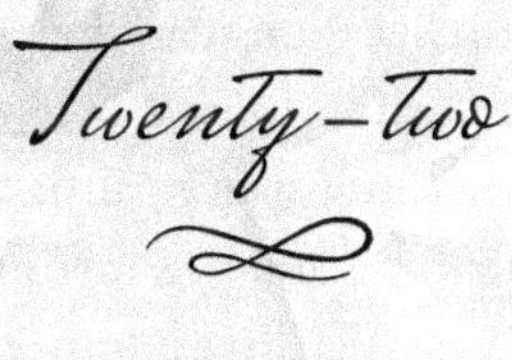

## ZAC

SPRAWLED across the couch, watching some 90s Christmas movie with Alyssa in my arms, I could not be any more content. We've spent the day exchanging gifts and indulging in a gourmet Christmas banquet fit for a king and queen.

I've always attempted to give Bray and Ella a family Christmas and follow on with the traditions that mum and dad had started. Christmas has never felt as complete as it did today though; Alyssa joining our little family has made today more than I could have ever wished for.

I haven't been able to wipe the smile from my face all day, seeing Alyssa enjoy herself so much, knowing that she said yes, without a doubt, to being mine forever. It makes me fucking happy. I can't remember a time I've been happier than I am right now in this moment.

Alyssa yawns as she snuggles into my chest. "Tired, baby?"

Burrowing in deeper to my chest, she says, "*Mmm*, who would have thought Christmas could be so tiring."

Standing, I lift her into my arms. "Come on, let's get you to bed."

"I can walk, you know. You don't need to put your back out carrying me. Put me down."

Laughing, I hold her tighter. "Never, I will never let you go, and please, I could lift ten of you and still not put my damn back out." She gives up her protest and relaxes into me.

Laying her on the bed, I undress her so she can sleep more comfortably, leaving her in just her panties. I make quick work as I undress and climb in behind her, holding her in my arms.

"Sweet dreams, baby. We'll have tomorrow together," I tell her. She's already out of it as she murmurs something in response.

The last few days have been bliss. I've spent almost every waking hour with Alyssa, wanting to get in as much time before we both go back to work today. I tried, very unsuccessfully, to get her to quit and come work at the club with me. If it wasn't New Year's Eve, I think I would camp out at the hospital throughout her entire shift, just waiting for her.

As much as I want to do just that, I can't. New Year's is a big night for the club, and I can't continue to palm my responsibilities off to Bray and Dean. We're also holding the first fight since the holiday break. Bray's been training like crazy the past few days, *shredding the holiday weight* he put on—his words not mine.

I'm also keen to get back to work and expand on the hunt for fucking Caitlyn. It's been nearly three weeks since she trashed Alyssa's room at her townhouse and there hasn't been a sighting of her. No more threats have been delivered either. But I know something is coming. I can feel it in my gut. The sooner we catch the crazy bitch, the sooner I can relax and know my girl is safe.

Alyssa's alarm starts blaring on the bedside table. She reaches out, blindly swatting at her phone. Laughing, I roll over top of her and turn the alarm off.

"Morning, sunshine." I kiss the top of her head. "Don't move. I'll get your coffee."

I hear her mumble something incoherent as I walk out of the bedroom.

Returning with her coffee, it does not surprise me to find her sound asleep again. I take a sip of the sweet crap she calls coffee and then put the cup down. Leaning down, I gently roll my lips over the top of hers, urging her mouth open with my tongue. She doesn't disappoint. Opening for me, she meets my tongue with strokes of her own.

"*Mmm*, you taste divine," she says as she slowly comes to. Laughing, I pull back, pulling her up into a sitting position.

Handing her the coffee cup, I suggest, "Drink up, sunshine. Just think, if you quit your job and come work at our club, you won't ever have to wake up at these ungodly hours again."

"I'll be fine once the caffeine hits my system." She continues drinking, purposefully ignoring my suggestion. I'm not giving up though. I know I'll wear her down, eventually. From what I've seen and heard from her friends, she doesn't even like her job.

"I'm gonna hit the gym for a bit. Do you need anything before I go work out?"

"I'm good. I'm just going to finish this coffee and have a shower."

I kiss her once more. "Okay, but I'm just down the hall if you decide you need me to wash your back, or your front, or your hair."

Laughing, she says, "I think I'll manage, but good to know you'll wash all those hard-to-reach places."

Leaning in, I kiss her again. I don't think I'm ever going to get enough of her kisses. It's like a drug and I'm addicted.

"Anytime, anyplace, babe," I say with a wink and leave her to get ready.

I'm not surprised to find Bray already in the gym as I enter. Jumping on the treadmill, I start my warm-up. Bray eyes me suspiciously.

"What happened? Did Lyssa kick you out already? If so, I want her to get custody of me in the divorce."

"Fuck off. There won't ever be a fucking divorce, idiot."

"Then why the hell are you up at this hour? I haven't seen the likes of you this early for well over a month."

"Alyssa's going back to work at the hospital today."

I shrug, like it doesn't bother me at all that she's going to work and I won't be able to be with her all day.

"Shit, man, is that safe? I mean, we still don't know where the fuck Caitlyn is hiding out," Bray questions.

Like I haven't fucking thought of that already. "I tried to talk her into quitting and coming to work at the club, but she won't have a bar of it."

"Well, at least now I know why you're in such a cheery mood." Bray smirks.

"She also wants to drive herself to work in her car," I grunt as I speed up the treadmill to a slow jog.

"What time is she planning on leaving?" he asks.

"In about an hour, around six. She's doing a twelve-hour shift and is meeting me at the club when she finishes. Why?"

Shrugging, he grabs a towel and wipes his face. "I need to visit a mate at the hospital. She can give me a lift."

I nod, knowing full well he's full of shit. He doesn't have any mates in the hospital, but I'm grateful for the lie if it means she won't be driving by herself.

"Thanks, man," I say as he makes his way out of the room.

After punishing myself for forty-five minutes in the gym, I wander back into the bedroom in search of Alyssa. She should be just about ready to leave. I find her sitting on the edge of the bed, bending over, tying the laces on her joggers. For a moment, I just stand in the doorway, enjoying the view. I forgot how damn good she looks in those scrubs. Then again, Alyssa would be hot as fuck in a burlap sack.

Groaning, I adjust the growing erection forming in my shorts. Alyssa finally looks up, pausing momentarily where my hand is adjusting my cock.

Smirking as her eyes meet mine, she asks, "Good workout?"

Shrugging my shoulders, I make my way to her. Kneeling on the floor in front of her, I trail my hands up her legs from her ankles up to her inner thighs.

"There are much better ways I prefer to get my cardio in these days."

Alyssa laughs while attempting to push me away. As her hands meet my chest, I think my heart literally stops for a minute. There is something huge missing from her left hand. My eyes should be met with a fucking diamond on that hand, a huge fucking diamond that I put there just a week ago. Grabbing her hand, I rub her ring finger, her bare fucking ring finger.

I take a deep breath before gritting out, "Where the fuck is your ring, Alyssa?"

As much as I try to get my voice to remain calm, I don't succeed. I know my words come out harsh.

She looks down at her hand, then back at me before answering, "Zac, I can't wear that ring to work."

I hear her words, but they make absolutely no sense. "Why the fuck not?"

Staring at her hand, I'm racking my brain for reasons she would not want to wear my ring out in public. Has she changed her mind already? I don't think I'd survive if she says she doesn't want me anymore.

Alyssa reaches up, touching my face, and pulls my eyes up to meet hers. "Zac, honey, I'm still marrying you. There is nothing in this world that could stop me from wanting to marry you. I can't wear my ring because it's just too big—it's not practical. I have to put gloves on and off all day. I won't be able to do that with the ring on."

Although I feel like a weight has been lifted, knowing she's not leaving, I still don't like the thought of her walking around without the fucking ring on her finger. I want the world to know she's taken and taken by me. There's also the fact that that particular ring has a GPS tracker in it. I know, not my finest moment putting a tracker on my fiancée, but given the circumstances, I think if I ever had to actually use it, I won't regret putting it there. She of course does not know that her ring has this extra feature. There is no way I'm letting her walk out of this apartment without that ring on her.

Standing up, I ask her, "Where is it?" as I look around the room.

Alyssa walks into the walk-in wardrobe and retrieves the ring from the island bench. I don't tell her that she just left a four-hundred-thousand-dollar ring sitting around like a piece of costume jewellery. I'd never get her to wear it if she knew that stone's value. Instead, I open a drawer and pull out one of my gold chains. It's thin enough and long enough that she can wear it under her shirt.

Threading the ring through the chain, I then place the chain around her neck. Alyssa doesn't move; she doesn't question my actions. Once the chain's clasp is secure, I tuck the ring into the inside of her shirt, letting the stone rest between her breasts.

Damn, for a moment, I'm lost while staring down into her cleavage; that is, until Alyssa clears her throat.

"Thank you. I didn't even think to put it on a chain."

Wrapping her arms around my waist, she buries her head into my chest. I hear her inhale and I smile. I love that she always inhales my scent like it's her favourite scent in the world, even though I'm pretty sure I come second to the scent of coffee.

"It's not too late to change your mind, you know," I whisper my last-ditch attempt at getting her to stay with me rather than go to work.

"As much as I'd love to stay in our little bubble and be with you all day, we need to get back to reality, and reality is *I have a job*. A job that I'm going to be late for if I don't leave now."

"It was worth a try, and you know you don't actually have to work, right? I have enough money that neither of us would have to actually work another day in our lives. We could just move to a deserted island and continue to exist in our little bubble, just the two of us." As the idea runs through my head, I'm liking it more and more.

"Zac, do not buy a bloody island retreat anywhere. We are not leaving our family. Now walk me to the door and kiss me goodbye."

With that, she turns and walks out of the room. I'm left there smiling like a fool. She said *our family*. It's the first time she's referred to my family as her own, as *ours* and not just mine.

"Zac, I'm leaving," I hear Alyssa call from down the hall. I meet her in the living room just as Bray comes running down the hall at the same time.

"Lyssa, sis, thank god you haven't left yet. I need you to give me a ride." His words rush out like he's in a hurry to get somewhere. I work hard to hide the smirk that's trying to form on my lips. He really does go all-in when he's on a roll.

"What's wrong?" Alyssa questions as she pats Bray down with her hands, inspecting for an injury of some sort.

Pulling her back into my chest, I stop her inspection of my brother's body.

"He's not hurt, Alyssa. He's just a fucking idiot," I inform her while sending Bray a death glare.

"Your concern for my wellbeing means everything to me, brother. I'm fine. I just need to visit someone who's laid up in the very same hospital you're driving to. So, can you give me a lift?" Bray asks.

Alyssa looks sceptical, glancing back and forward between Bray and myself. Shit, she is too damn smart for us. She already knows he's full of shit.

"Bray, visiting hours don't start until eight. It's only six now. What are you planning on doing, sitting around the door for two hours to visit a friend?"

I look at Bray pleadingly. I know he'll come up with something; he's always been able to talk his way out of anything.

"Okay, well, I didn't want to tell you this because, well, just because... But you see, there's this nurse I just met, and she wants me to meet her before her shift at the hospital. A before work hook-up, some might call it. It's the next Tinder."

Alyssa shakes her head and screws her face up. "First, gross. Second, I think you're full of shit. You've been moping around for the last four weeks, trying to get Reilly to pay you some attention and now, all of a sudden, you've moved on to someone else? Really, Bray?" she questions him.

Bray looks almost pained when he says, "Reilly won't give me the time of day, so yes, I'm moving on. Let's go. I can't keep a lady waiting—it's not polite." We both watch Bray as he presses the button, opening the doors on the lift.

Alyssa turns to me and whispers, "I can't wait to see what excuse he comes up with tomorrow when he needs a lift to the hospital." Reaching up and laying a quick kiss on my lips, she says into my mouth, "I love you so damn much. I'll see you tonight."

Holding her tighter, I tell her, "I love you more than I thought it was possible to love someone. Text me when you get there. Also, I'll meet you on your lunch break."

Biting onto her bottom lip, she looks at me like she's unsure of what she's about to say. "*Umm,* well... lunch... I kind of already told Sarah I'd meet her in the hospital café. It's just that I haven't seen her since before she went to her parents for Christmas and, well, I've been a shitty friend lately and haven't really spent any time with my friends. The only one I see is Reilly, and that's only because she works for you and is always dropping stuff off here."

I lean down and kiss her. She's rambling; she does that when she's nervous.

"Sunshine, you can see your friends whenever you want, you know that, right? I'm not going to ever stop you from meeting up with your friends. Have fun with Sarah and I'll see you at the club tonight. Also, you are not a shitty friend. Anyone who can call you their friend should thank their lucky stars."

She nods at me. "Thank you. I don't know how I got so lucky to have you."

"Come on, lovebirds, I have somewhere I need to be. I can't hold this button forever, you know," Bray calls out from inside the lift.

Laughing at him, Alyssa pulls away and walks into the lift. As the doors close, an unsettling feeling returns to my gut. I try to shake it off as separation anxiety. That's all it is... I haven't been separated from her for over three weeks now. She's safe at the hospital; there is security everywhere to protect the staff and patients.

Looking at the clock again, I note it's just nearing one o'clock. I've been at the club for the last three hours, going over everything we have on Caitlyn. There's nothing giving any possible whereabouts, or indicating where she could be now, and it's pissing me the fuck off. The foreboding feeling I have in the pit of my stomach hasn't left me all day. Something isn't right; we're missing something. I just don't know what. I've been texting Alyssa all morning, and now and then, she will send a brief response. I have had no response since 11:20 a.m. though. I'm telling myself it's because she's busy, or at lunch with Sarah, and just hasn't checked her phone.

"We will find her, Zac," Dean says from where he sits on the sofa in my office.

"We have to. She had a fucking headstone made up, man. A headstone with Alyssa's fucking name on it."

I know he already knows this. It was him and Bray who smashed that headstone to pieces when they located it at the small cemetery three hours away in the little rural town. Right next to her mother's fucking grave. I haven't told Alyssa that it was actually there, that the photo she received in that dressing room was, in fact, an actual photo and not something edited just to scare her.

"How the fuck have we not found her yet?" I ask.

Dean may be my best friend, but he is also the head of my security, and I want him to do the job I fucking pay him to do and find this bitch.

"I've been working day and night on this, not to mention still ensuring everything in this club gets handled in your absence. I know you're stressed and worried, but Caitlyn is a ghost right now. There's been no activity on any of her bank accounts. She has no traceable family. Nothing... It's like she's vanished off the face of the earth."

"I know, man, sorry. I know the last three weeks haven't been easy around here. But fuck..."

I'm pulling at my hair in frustration when my phone blares from my pocket. It's not the ringtone I want to hear right now though; it's not my sunshine calling. When I look at the screen and read who the caller is, my blood turns to ice, knowing immediately something isn't right.

"What's wrong?" I ask Sarah as I answer the call.

She should be at lunch with Alyssa right now. The only reason she'd be calling me is if something were wrong.

"Where are you hiding her, Zac? You have to learn to share, you know. She was mine first. I've been waiting in this damn café for an hour."

"Fuck!" I yell out, tempted to throw the phone. Sarah's tentative voice comes through the speaker.

"Zac, she's not with you, is she?"

"No, she's not fucking with me. She was meant to be with you right now. Have you tried to call her? Text her?" I ask.

Maybe she's running late, got stuck in the ER. As I think this, I know that's not the reason she didn't show up for lunch.

"I'm heading to the ER now; I'll ask the nurses' station to find her," Sarah says in a huff. "I'm sure she just got held up."

"Don't bother. I'm locating her now."

I place the call on speaker as I open the tracking app on my laptop. It takes only moments before the app loads her exact location on a map, the red dot showing her location is moving.

"What do you mean you're locating her? How the fuck are you locating her, Zac?"

Ignoring Sarah's questions, I stand, grabbing my keys. Dean is already holding the door open. "Sarah, I'm going to get her. I gotta go."

As I hang up, I hear Sarah screaming at me, "Don't you dare hang—"

Putting my phone in my pocket, I tell Dean as I make my way down the hallway, "She's got her; she fucking has my sunshine. Get a team to follow us. We need to go."

"Where? Where did she ping?" he asks while he loads the tracking app on his phone.

As his app loads, he curses, knowing where she's heading.

"She's already got two hours ahead of us." Stating the fucking obvious, Dean follows me into the carpark behind the club. "I'll drive. You keep tracking," Dean says as he climbs into the driver's side.

I don't argue, knowing I'll probably kill us both in the state I'm in if I get behind the wheel.

As we peel away from the club, I pray to a god I don't even believe in that she's still alive. That I can get to her in time. Looking in the side mirror, I see not only Dean's team following behind but also Bray's SUV behind them. I will get there... I will get her back... There is no other alternative.

A half hour passes and the red dot on the tracker has stopped. She's at the cemetery, the one where that fucking psycho had a headstone made. I know she's planning on burying her next to her mother.

"She's stopped at the cemetery," I grit out to Bray as he speeds down the highway.

"Fuck, we're still at least an hour and a half out. Put a call through to the men in Glenvale and get them to the cemetery now. She's there now." Dean speaks into the headset he has on.

"You have guys already in Glenvale?" I ask him.

How did I not know this already?

"I've had two guys there on standby ever since we found the headstone. They're only five minutes away from the cemetery."

"Thank fuck. I want her alive. Caitlyn, I want to be the one to fucking end her," I tell him.

"I know." Dean smirks my way.

# Twenty-three

## ALYSSA

MY HEAD IS POUNDING, I reach up to touch my forehead and find my movements restricted. My hands are tied with rope. *What the hell?* I try to look around, but it's dark. I'm in a small, cramped space. I'm in a goddamn car boot. Closing my eyes, I try to keep my breathing even and recall how I got here.

I remember being at work. I was doing obs on an elderly patient. I remember an orderly entering the room and that's it. I can't remember anything else. I just need to breathe, to stay calm. As much as I want to scream out, I know I need to stay calm. The longer whoever put me here thinks I'm still out of it, the longer Zac has to realise I'm missing and start searching. Oh god, the thought of Zac brings tears to my eyes.

This is meant to be the start of our forever. What if we don't get a forever? What if this morning was the last time I would get to kiss him? Hug him? I should have listened to him. I should have quit my job and just taken any random job he would give me at the club. At least then, I wouldn't be in this predicament now.

Has he realised I'm missing yet? He will be out of his mind

once he notices that I'm missing. I don't know how much time has passed, how long I've been passed out in this car boot. I can hear movement outside and the boot opens, letting in the sunlight. Squinting my eyes, I try to focus on whoever the person is that opened the boot. But I know who this psycho is without even looking. I know it's Caitlyn. I know she wants to follow through with her threats to get rid of me so that she can have Zac to herself.

"Oh good, you're awake. I was hoping you'd be conscious when I make you take your last breath. It would be such a shame to not see the look in your eyes when you realise that I won." She laughs while pulling on the rope that binds my hands. "Get out, bitch. It's time to end this."

I'm roughly yanked from the car, my legs giving out beneath me as I fall to the ground. Whatever drugs she injected into me haven't worn off yet. As I'm trying to find the strength to stand, something hits my head, making me fall onto my back, my vision going blurry. Not something, a foot. She just fucking kicked me in the head. Grunting, I hold in my cries of pain.I will not give her the satisfaction of hearing my anguish.

"Why are you doing this?"

"Why?" she screams into my face, grabbing me by the hair and pulling my face closer to hers. "I gave you the chance to leave him alone. He's mine!"

She lets my hair go, pushing my head back down to the ground.

Pointing to herself, she says, "Mine, I know he loves me. He doesn't love you. He doesn't want you. And once he knows the lengths I'm prepared to go for him, he will know I'm the one he should be with."

As she's pacing up and down in front of me, I look around, trying to identify where I am. When I look to my left, I know exactly where she's brought me. I've only been here once, when

I turned eighteen. I found out where my mother was buried and came here. I haven't been able to bring myself to come back. Dread settles in deep within me. I'm three hours away from the city. There is no way Zac will know to look for me here. This really is it.

I wanted to have it all. I wanted what Zac promised, to always have a tomorrow together. I wanted us to be a family, an actual family. I wanted to have kids with Zac. I haven't admitted that to anyone, too scared of what that means. I've always thought I could never have kids myself because they would grow up on their own, without a mother, just like I did. But I know that Zac and his family, our family, would never let our kids grow up alone, even if I ended up with the same cancer that killed my mother.

I wish I had told him I wanted his babies. I wish I had the chance to tell him how much happiness and love he has brought into my life in the short time I've had him. I've never felt love like the love that Zac so easily and freely offers me. I'm thankful that I got to experience that kind of love. I just wish I could thank Zac for giving it to me. I wish he could know just how much I love him.

Finding the energy, I sit up and push myself over to lean against my mother's headstone. I tell her, "He will never love you." I know I shouldn't taunt her, but she's going to kill me anyway.

Caitlyn pulls a gun out from behind her back, pointing it at my head while screaming at me, "Shut up, shut up, shut up!"

Then I hear the gunshot... I feel a burning, searing pain in my arm. I can't help but yell out in agony. She shot me. Looking down, I see that my arm is now covered with blood, so much blood. My head is dizzy. I can't even cover the wound; my hands are still tied together with rope.

I'm trying to figure out a way to get myself out of this situation, trying to free my hands of the rope that binds them together. My arm is burning, tears run freely down my face, and my wrists are red, raw from the rope burn as I twist and turn them in attempts to free my arm.

Then I hear it, another gunshot. I hold my breath, and close my eyes, waiting to feel the pain of being shot again. Waiting to identify where she has shot me this time. The pain doesn't come. Opening my eyes, I see Caitlyn just before she falls to the ground.

Wait, did she shoot herself? No, she wouldn't have. My head is spinning. I know I need to stay awake. I can't give in to the darkness that calls me to close my eyes right now. A man dressed in black stops and squats down in front of me.

"Alyssa, it's okay. There's an ambulance on the way. Just hold on, okay?" he says as he cuts my wrists free from the rope. I don't know who this man is. I don't know how he knows my name, but right now, I don't care.

"Zac, I... I... I need Zac," I plead with whoever this stranger is.

"He's going to meet you at the hospital. It's okay. You're safe now."

I hear the sirens getting closer and I let go. Closing my eyes, I give in to the darkness and let it take over me.

*Beep, Beep, Beep.* Oh god, someone shut off the damn alarm. The noise continues, my eyes flutter open slowly, and I take in my surroundings. The smell of antiseptic, the beeps of machines, the chill in the air... I know I'm in the hospital. Confusion wraps around my brain. Am I at work? Why is my head pounding? I attempt to lift my arm but a burning pain pauses my movement.

"*Argh*," I groan out loud.

"Sunshine, baby, don't move. Let me call for the doctors."

Zac... Zac's here. He's squeezing my hand like he's afraid I'm going to run off somewhere. He reaches above my head, pressing a button.

"Wh... what happened?" I ask him as I look around the hospital room.

"Alyssa, I am so fucking sorry. This should never have happened to you. I should never have let this happen to you."

Zac bends his head down, leaning his forehead on the hand he has in a death grip. I wriggle my fingers to get him to loosen his grip, which he does, slightly.

"Zac, what happened? Why am I in the hospital?" I ask again.

"You don't remember?" he asks, looking up, concern creeping across his face.

I shake my head no, wincing as pain slices through my head.

"Where the fuck is the doctor?" Zac questions, looking towards the door. "Sunshine, I didn't do my job. I didn't protect you properly."

I have no idea what he's talking about. I close my eyes briefly—the light is really too bright.

"Shit, sunshine. Please open your eyes. Don't go back to sleep yet, please," Zac pleads.

My eyes pop open immediately. "Zac, I'm right here. I'm not going anywhere."

"I was so fucking scared I was going to lose you. When we discovered Caitlyn had taken you, it felt like my world dropped out from under me."

I tighten my grip on his hand in an attempt to reassure him that I'm not about to disappear.

"She took you to the cemetery, the one where your mother

is. Three fucking hours away. By the time we realised she had you, she was two hours in front of us."

"How did you find me?" I ask.

Zac shakes his head. He looks a little nervous. "I *uhh*... well, I..."

I wait for him to decide on what he's about to tell me. His hesitancy is making me nervous.

"Okay, I had a GPS tracker put into your engagement ring. I'm not sorry either. I know it's probably all kinds of wrong, but it's also the only reason you're still alive right now. The only way we knew where you were."

I look down at my left hand, where my engagement ring currently sits. I remember it was around my neck while I was at work, so I'm not sure how it landed back on my finger, but I think I could probably guess. I look back at Zac.

"Okay, let's keep it there," I tell him, honestly not bothered at all that he can track my location through the ring.

Zac sighs like a weight has been lifted. "Yeah? You're not mad? Sarah said you'd be pissed when you woke up and found out I had a tracker on you. You can be pissed at me, sunshine. I can handle it."

"I'm not mad; it's a little disturbing that you did it without telling me. But I'm glad you could locate me easily. I'm glad you got to me before she finished what she started." As I go to move my arm, the pain shoots down again. "What happened to my arm?"

"Caitlyn shot you in the arm," Zac grunts out, "and I didn't get to you in time. Dean had two guys near the cemetery for the last few weeks. They got to you, not me."

I rub my fingers over his hand. "It's because of you that those men were there."

The door to the room opens and a doctor and nurse walk in.

"It's about fucking time," Zac bites out.

"Miss Summers, I'm Dr. Ryan. How are you feeling?" the doctor asks, while holding a light pen to my eyes.

"My head hurts, my arm feels like it's on fire but other than that, I'm okay," I tell him honestly.

The doctor nods. "That's understandable. You had a nasty hit to the head; you had ten stitches placed on your hairline." The doctor picks up my chart, noting something on it before adding, "The bullet grazed your arm, and you lost a fair bit of blood, so you will probably feel weak for a few days."

I take in everything he says. The bullet only grazed my arm. That's good—still hurts like hell.

"What about some pain relief. What are you giving her? She's in pain." Zac's question comes out harsh.

"It's okay," I tell him, trying to keep him calm.

"No, it's not, sunshine. You're hurting. It's not fucking okay."

The doctor looks down at the chart in his hands. "She's on the best pain relief we can safely give her," he says to Zac. Looking down at me, he adds, "You're doing great. We're going to keep you in overnight for observation, but you should be able to go home tomorrow. I've ordered an ultrasound tech to come and check on the foetus, just to be cautious. All your bloods came back good."

I noticed Zac stiffen during the doctor's spiel. He is looking down at me as he watches my face. I run back through what the doctor said; it takes a minute but then it clicks.

"Wait, what?" I question the doctor.

"All your bloods came back good." He places the chart back over the foot of the bed.

"No, go back a bit. Foetus? What foetus?" I ask him.

"You didn't know you were pregnant?" the doctor asks.

I shake my head, unable to speak, and look over at Zac, who

has not said a word. He is still looking down at me, watching for my reaction. It's almost like he's holding his breath, too afraid to move.

The doctor continues, "My guess is it's early; the scan will tell us more."

Pregnant. *Pregnant. I'm pregnant.* How did this happen? Of course I know *how* this happened. I smile at that thought. Then something lingers in the back of my mind.

"Why don't I remember what happened?" I ask the doctor.

"You were injected with propofol. You were asleep for most of your ordeal, I believe."

I nod my head. Well, that explains why I can't remember anything.

"Will that hurt the baby?" I ask the doctor. As I do, Zac looks up to the doctor while squeezing my hand.

The doctor shakes his head. "No, the baby should be fine. Let's get the scan done and find out how far along you are," he says with a reassuring smile.

I'm about to thank him, but before I can, Zac breaks his silence. "*Should be*? Should be fine is not good enough."

He pulls his phone out of his pocket, dialling someone and looking back down at me briefly, before the call connects.

"Dean, find the best OBGYN in Sydney. Get Alyssa an appointment with them tomorrow." He listens for a bit. I can't hear what Dean says but Zac answers, "Yes, I don't care how much," before hanging up the phone.

The doctor looks down at me and smiles. "I'll find out where the ultrasound tech is."

I nod and thank him, unsure what to say right now. With that, he walks out the door. When the door closes, I look back to Zac, who is again staring down at me, like he's waiting for something.

"I'm sorry," I tell him. What if he thinks I got pregnant on purpose? That I'm trying to trap him or something?

"You have nothing to be sorry for, sunshine," he says while absently placing his hand over my abdomen. I don't even think he's consciously doing it.

"I don't know how I got pregnant," I say, to which Zac arches his eyebrow at me. "Well, obviously I know that part, but I didn't once miss a pill, I swear. I didn't lie to you. But I will understand if you don't want this. I can do it. It's okay—"

Zac leans down and kisses me, kisses the hell out of me, cutting off my rambling thoughts. When he leans back, he smiles so wide. "Sunshine, you are crazy if you think I would ever let you do this by yourself. Or that I wouldn't want a child who is made up of us, of our love." Tilting his head, he looks at me, waiting.

"What are you looking for?" I ask him after a few moments.

"I'm wondering where the panic attack has gone. You once had a panic attack on me at the thought of having a child, but you seem so calm right now. It's a little off-putting."

That's why he went stiff and quiet when the doctor mentioned a foetus. He was worried about my reaction.

I smile at him. "I realised that it doesn't matter what happens to me. If I end up having a shorter life like my mother, this baby will still be loved, will still have a family. I won't be leaving this baby alone in a world that can be so cruel."

"I'm not going to let anything happen to you, sunshine. You're never leaving my side again."

He looks serious, like his word is law and nothing will ever happen to me. I'm not as convinced it's that easy.

"I want this life you've given me, Zac. I want a family with you. I want to have this baby." My eyes tear up at the thought of everything I ever wanted coming true. "I want to always have a tomorrow with you," I tell him.

"Sunshine, I want nothing more than to raise a family with you. For all of my tomorrows to be with you. I love you," he says while wiping the tears from my eyes.

The door opens and the ultrasound tech rolls in with a trolley machine. The girl introduces herself before blushing profusely, a reaction that often comes when Zac introduces himself to any woman. Rolling my eyes, I look over at the screen as she places the wand on my abdomen.

This is surreal. I can't believe this is happening right now. After a few swipes of the wand over my stomach, the unmistakable sound of a heartbeat rings out through the room.

"What's that?" Zac asks, like he's ready to go into battle, making the woman jump.

"Relax, you're going to give her a damn heart attack. That sound is the baby's heartbeat. Our baby's heartbeat." I have tears running down my face again.

Zac reaches up, wiping the tears. "What's wrong?" His voice is soft, concerned.

"Nothing, I'm just really thrilled right now."

I stare at the screen, where there is a still picture of my womb. You can't see anything other than a blip on the screen. The ultrasound tech finishes with her measurements, and wiping the gel off of my stomach, she says, "You're about five to six weeks pregnant. Everything looks good. The heartbeat's good, strong. Congratulations."

"Thank you," we both reply as she unplugs her machine and leaves the room.

I look at Zac. "I can't believe this is real; we're having a baby."

"We are, and you should probably get some rest while you can. I've told everyone they can visit you tomorrow, so expect to be inundated with visitors you can't get rid of when you wake up."

I smile, thinking of how hard he must have worked to get my friends to wait until tomorrow to come barging in here. "I don't know how you got the girls to agree to wait until tomorrow."

"I didn't. They're camped outside in the waiting room now, refusing to bloody leave," he grunts.

That sounds more like my friends. "You should probably let them in for a bit. They won't leave otherwise."

"I'm selfish, I know, but I want you to myself. I don't want to share you and this baby with anyone yet." Zac shrugs.

I nod, slightly agreeing that I don't want to share either. "I know, but we always have tomorrow together, right?" I ask him.

"Always," he says.

"Promise?"

"Promise. We will always have a tomorrow together, sunshine."


Want more?
Get the bonus Zac & Alyssa wedding scene here: Zac & Alyssa - The Wedding

# Fused With Him

BOOK TWO

# Dedication

*For my sister, Lynne-Maree, who taught me to always fight for what we want in life and to never stop reaching for our dreams.*

*Fused*
*"to come together to form a single unit"*

# Prologue

GUILTY. The word repeats through my mind as the sound of the judge's gavel bangs heavily, echoing in the courtroom. I can't believe what I'm hearing. *Guilty.* The word keeps repeating. I know the judge is delivering the sentence, but I can't concentrate on anything other than that one word.

I look across to my sister, Holly, my twin, my other half, and see the tears free falling down her face—her hands are trembling slightly. Holly brings her eyes to meet mine. No words are needed. I know exactly what is going through her head right now. What the fuck are we going to do now? How do we survive this?

Holly is sitting on the other side of my mother, both of us grasping one of her hands in ours, knowing if we let go, even for a minute, she would crumble to the floor. My mother's tears are not silent. Her cries I'm sure can be heard across the city.

As I sit here, repeating the word over and over in my head, I have to wonder how much one woman can take before she completely breaks. My mother is strong, probably one of the strongest women I know, but this last year, to say it's been tough is an understatement.

My little brother Dylan was killed in a car accident. My mum was driving home after a footy game when a drunk driver swerved into her lane. She escaped with a broken leg, my brother, my baby brother who was only fifteen, died on impact. Making the sign of the cross, I send a little prayer upwards as I think of my brother. I've never been a very religious person; each prayer I've sent heavenly these past twelve months has gone unanswered and a bit of my faith has diminished alongside them.

There was a court case for the drunk driver, where he got off. He killed my brother and managed to get out of doing any time in a cell, where he bloody belonged. This destroyed my father, to know that the person who killed his son was out walking around free. It did not sit well with him.

My father decided to take matters into his own hands. He followed the drunk home one day and shot him, point blank in the head. A clear kill shot. I don't feel any remorse for the drunk, maybe I should. Maybe I'm a horrible person not caring that my dad took the life of another. But that son of a bitch killed my brother and has led to the events of today. To my family being torn apart even more.

At seventeen years old, I've just finished high school and should be out celebrating and living life to the fullest before I have to start university next year. But as I hold my mother's weeping body up, and attempt to listen as the judge drones on, all I can think is how am I going to survive this? How are my mum and sister going to survive this?

My father has just been sentenced for murder. He's been my rock my whole life, and now I have to figure out how to get by without him, without having his support and guidance, his unyielding love.

My mother's scream startles me out of my thoughts and I watch as she falls to the floor, Holly dragged down with her force. I can see her heart breaking. They were supposed to grow old together. My mum and dad were the definition of soulmates, of true love.

As I watch my mother crumble, I make a promise there and then that I will never let a man have that kind of hold over me. I will never get so attached to a man that my life would fall apart the moment they are no longer in it. And I swear on everything holy that I will never let myself fall in love.

# Chapter One

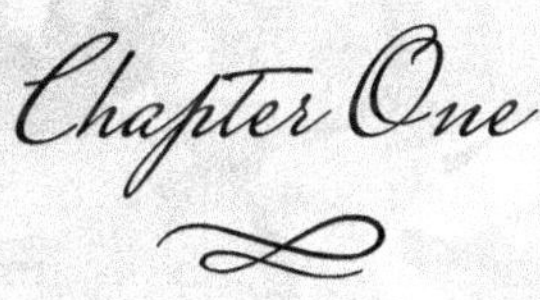

*Reilly*

I FEEL like I'm in a furnace. *Why is it so damn hot in here?* Wait, where is here? As the sleep fog slowly recedes from my brain, and the more alert I become, the more the realisation that I'm not in my own bed sinks in.

My stealthy attempt to roll out from beneath the heavy arm currently draped over my waist is stopped when that arm grips me tighter, pulling my back right up against a chest. I freeze, hoping not to wake whoever that arm belongs to.

Taking a look down at that arm, that very muscular and tattooed arm, a not so silent moan escapes my lips. The events of last night slowly returning to my mind, I know just who that arm belongs to. And the body that goes with that arm, comes in the form of a six-foot something with muscle on top of muscle. Just thinking of what that body can, and did, do to mine has me re-thinking my escape plan.

What can one more round in the hay hurt? One more glorious moment of our bodies fusing together before I make my break and never indulge in this body of sin again. I squirm, rubbing my ass into his crotch. I can feel his hardness as I continue to squirm against him.

The arm around me tightens, somehow pulling my body even tighter against his. His gravelly voice murmurs in my ear, causing goosebumps to rise all over my body.

"You know, babe, if you want junior to come out to play, all you have to do is ask? He'd be willing to be yours anytime."

Rolling over to face him, I grab his junior in my hand and stroke it up and down slowly.

"*Mmm*, I think I'd like to have a playdate with junior just one more time before I have to go," I declare, ducking my head down, not able to make eye contact with him.

I don't know why but the man makes me freaking nervous. He causes butterflies, no, not butterflies, more like a hive of bees buzzing around my stomach. It's unnerving, and usually I'd be out the door before he could blink. But his junior, I know what that thing can do, and I want more of it. *Just one more time*, I tell myself.

"Babe, if you think I'm letting you go after just one more time, think again." His voice is so stern and serious, I look up into eyes that are trained onto my face. Shit, I think he might actually be serious. Just as I'm about to refute his claims that he can keep me, I'm interrupted by the banging of a door. But it's what's yelled through the house that has my body freezing and my mind in a panic.

"Police, open up!"

More banging ensues and more demands to open up. Bray curses under his breath as he jumps out of bed and makes quick work of putting clothes on. Looking back at me, he says, "Whatever you do, stay here. Do not leave this room. I want you here in this bed when I sort this shit out."

Well, fuck that. I'm pulled from my dazed and lust- filled

brain and chuck on the first thing I find discarded on the floor. Which happens to be the shirt he was wearing last night.

My eyes scan the bedroom and land on my phone. Picking it up, I head for the door. Just as my hand lands on the handle, Bray's hand closes around mine, stopping my hasty escape.

"Reilly, you've lost your damn mind if you think for a minute, I'm letting you walk out of here, especially dressed like that."

Pulling my hand out from under his, I turn and shove at his chest, his rock-hard freaking chest. Instead of letting my thoughts wander to what I could do with that chest, I let the anger boil up inside of me, the frustration that I put myself into this position. I can still remember when those knocks and those words were said through the door of my childhood home, only they weren't looking for some guy I just met. No, they were looking for my father.

I can feel the tears threaten to escape my eyes with the memories, which only makes me madder. I am not this vulnerable. I do not let myself be this vulnerable girl. I'm strong, independent, and I plan to keep it that way.

I push him further away from me, which he obviously allows me to do because, let's face it, there's no way I could actually move this hulk of a man. "No, you don't get to tell me what I can and can't do. You and I, we had a great time last night, but that's it. I'm out. I hope you enjoy your time in handcuffs," I say as I step back to the door.

Bray goes to take a step towards me and I hold my hand out to stop him. "If you so much as touch me right now, or try to stop me from leaving this room, I will scream bloody murder, and those cops out there will break your door down, I'm sure."

I watch as he takes a step back, his fists clenching and unclenching as he watches me walk out the door. I can feel him behind me the whole way through the house. I don't turn back to look though.

Pulling the door wide open, I give the officers my brightest smile. "Officers, I believe the man you're looking for is right behind me. You all have a nice day now."

Walking down the path, I don't stop, I don't look back, and I don't let the first tear fall until I'm halfway down the street and out of view.

Swiping the traitorous tears from my face, I straighten my shoulders. I will not let myself go back to that place, back to the memories of my dad being taken away in cuffs. Shit, I have no idea where the hell I even am. How am I going to get home?

"Okay, you can do this, Reilly, just call Holly. She will come and get you." I know I probably look like an escapee from the mental asylum right now. I'm currently wearing a man's t-shirt and nothing else; although said shirt falls down just above my knees. It doesn't matter that I'm more covered than I was last night in the club, yet somehow, I feel so much more exposed. The fact that I'm talking to myself does not make me seem any saner right now.

I call Holly, who, after screeching her way through her holier than thou lecture about yet again having to collect my ass from a strange neighbourhood, agrees to come and pick me up.

So now I'm sitting under a huge shady gum tree, waiting. As I take in my surroundings of a tree-lined street with huge mansions, I'm in awe as well as shock that this is the street Bray lives on. It is not what I would have picked for him. This street screams the family home, wife, husband, 2.5 kids and a dog. Not the hot as sin, tatted-up bad boy I had last night.

*I squeal as I'm swiftly thrown over a shoulder, a big broad shoulder. Clinging to the back of his shirt, I can feel the muscles clenching underneath as he carries me through his house. My head upside down, I can't even get a good look at his home as he makes his way through to what I'm hoping is his bedroom.*

*"Bray, let me down. I can walk. I'm too heavy and you'll probably put your back out or something, and I really like this back. I wouldn't want to hurt it."*

*"Not a chance in hell am I putting you down, pumpkin. Well, not until I'm throwing you down onto my bed, which is happening real soon." He slaps my ass before he adds, "Don't ever fucking try to tell me that you're too heavy again. Your body is the definition of perfection."*

*Mmm, I can't help but squirm at the stinging pain on my ass. As hard as I try not to let the moan escape my mouth, it does. Bray takes note of my reaction, groaning and landing another, firmer slap to my butt.*

*"Like it a little rough, huh? Good news for you, babe, I like to fuck rough and hard. Get ready, because you're in for a night you won't be forgetting anytime soon."*

*All of a sudden, I'm flying through the air, landing on my back, on what can only be described as a cloud. Damn, is this his bed? I don't think I've ever felt anything so bloody soft and comfy. I don't have time to contemplate the quality of Bray's mattress and bedding; my mind is immediately drawn to the hulk of a man currently pulling his shirt over the back of his head, revealing one hell of a body.*

*My eyes travel from his broad shoulders and wide chest down to his—wait, is that an eight pack? My attempts at counting are interrupted by his commanding voice, snapping me out of my daze.*

*"Strip, now, Reilly. I won't ask again."*

*Staring up at him, I'm both at a loss for words and confused at the wetness that just pooled between my legs by his demand. Or is that from the sight in front of me? Because let me tell you, the sight of a shirtless Brayden Williamson is enough to have any girl weeping.*

*The next thing that registers with my brain is the sound of material ripping. Holy shit, I look down to see my dress literally ripped in half. What the hell? Lifting my eyes to meet Bray's, I momentarily get lost in those emerald beauties.*

*"What the fuck, Bray? That was one of my favourite dresses!" "I told you to strip. You were too slow." He lifts an eyebrow at me, just begging for me to argue.*

*"Well, maybe give a girl some bloody warning next time you plan to just strip your shirt off. I can't help it if I was momentarily lost in the Bray-effect. You're replacing this dress, and just so you know, it wasn't cheap."*

*Bray leans down, capturing my lips in his and not so gently parting them to invade my mouth with his tongue. The argument is literally sucked out of me as he kisses the ever-loving shit out of me. Man, I thought I'd been kissed before. But this... this kiss is the one they write movies about. Grabbing the back of his neck, I pull him closer to me, holding as tight as I can.*

*Breaking the kiss, Bray trails his tongue down my neck, kissing, nibbling and biting his way down to my breast. With a groan, he grasps both breasts in his hands before taking my right nipple into his mouth. My body arching off the bed at the contact, I shiver as shots of pleasure shoot straight to my core.*

*It's not long before he's pulling my panties down my legs. I barely register that he's moving before he has my legs spread wide open with his head buried between them. Oh, God, looking down at him was a mistake. The hungry look in his eyes as he licks his lips is almost enough to send my quivering mess of a body over the edge.*

*"Tell me, pumpkin, do you taste as sweet as you look? Because this has to be, hands down, the prettiest goddamn pussy I've ever seen." He growls as he bites into my inner thigh.*

*"Oh, God... Oh, God!" My hips are bucking all on their own, in an attempt to get the friction to my core that it so desperately seeks.*

*"No, I believe, 'oh, Bray' are the words you want to be screaming, babe," Bray states just a moment before he dives his tongue into my centre, licking me from bottom to top. "Mmm, damn, pumpkin, this pussy is dangerous. One lick and I think I'm addicted." Bray makes quick work of diving back in.*

*Moments later, I'm screaming his name as the orgasm of the century rolls through me. Every nerve ending in my body is on fire, exploding with sensation. What the hell is he doing to me?*

*I must have blacked out for a minute because when I open my eyes, Bray is standing in front of the bed. Naked. Completely fucking naked. Thank you to any God who created this masterpiece. My eyes travel hungrily over his body, down his torso eagerly, wanting a glimpse at... wait a hot darn minute. Is that... oh my God, it is.*

*My mouth waters at the sight of his cock, his pierced, beautiful, huge fucking cock. I lick my lips. I can't wait to get a taste of that. Did I mention pierced? Yep, pierced. A Prince Albert, shiny metal sitting on the head of his cock.*

*Beep! Beep!* "Reilly, get up! Come on, I don't have all day!" I'm immediately drawn out of my daydream or memory, whatever you want to call it, by the sound of my sister's voice screaming at me.

Get it together, Reilly. I try my mental pep talk. I'm feeling like a bitch in heat right now. Just the memory of Bray's cock has me wanting to beg for more of it. No, I can't go there. I will not go there.

Getting up off the ground, I'm further reminded of what magic that pierced cock is capable of as my core both burns and tingles with the remnants of last night's events.

I do everything I can to avoid making eye contact with

Holly on the drive home. If I look over at her, she will know the internal struggle I'm doing my darndest to fight off. Just as I thought Holly was actually going to let me sit here in peace for the whole ride home, she decided to break the silence. Reaching over, she picked up my hand and threaded her fingers with mine.

"Okay, enough wallowing. What happened?" she questions while giving my hand a squeeze before letting it go.

Turning my head to give her my best glare, I respond, "I'm not wallowing, nothing happened. I was up late and I'm tired, that's all."

"Nice try, Rye, but I'm not buying it." She shakes her head no, using her teacher voice on me. I hate to admit, it is actually a little scary and firm, almost makes me want to confess everything so I'm not in trouble.

Looking over at Holly, I already know there's no point trying to hide anything from her. We have never been able to hide anything from each other. It's some sort of weird twin thing; we always just know whatever the other is feeling.

As much as I want to confide in her, I just don't think I can right now. She would try to understand, but really, she's never been in this situation. She's never even had a one-night stand. Holly is the relationship or nothing kind of girl. She's looking for her prince charming to share the white picket fence with and 2.5 kids. Meanwhile, I made a promise to myself a long time ago that I would never let myself get attached to a guy.

Holly has always been the good twin, while I prefer to blur the lines and break the rules. Her personality is the complete opposite of mine. She's a kindergarten teacher, loves the kid's she teaches like they were her own, and cries her eyes out at the end of each year when they move up a grade to a new teacher.

Although our personalities may be opposite, our looks are identical. Only those who really know us are able to tell us apart from each other. We share the same tall, thin stature, long red hair with pale skin and green eyes. The only difference being Holly has a tiny freckle under her left eye.

My silence does not get her to back down at all. "Rye, you know I love you most in the world. Please tell me what the hell happened, or I might just turn this car around and hunt down Bray. I'm not afraid to get my hands dirty if I need to, you know. I will emasculate him if he hurt you." Her voice is getting louder. I know she really would turn the car around too.

"You would have a hard time getting to him, Holl, considering the cops banged down his door and arrested him. Hence, why I had to call you to come and get me at this ungodly hour."

Holly looks over at me with sympathy written all over her face. "Rye, I'm sorry. What was he arrested for?"

"I don't know. I chucked on a shirt..." Looking down at said shirt, I then add, "His shirt, grabbed my phone and got the hell out of dodge. I didn't stick around to have a cuppa with the officers, Holly. And frankly, I don't give a shit what he was arrested for. It's his problem not mine."

As I finish my rant, it hits me. I'm wearing his damn shirt, no wonder I can't get him and his magical cucumber out of my bloody head. I can smell him. It's an exotic, earthy scent. It's an odd feeling; I'm torn between being repulsed, because that's how I should be feeling, and a sense of comfort and security in being able to smell him. Okay, it's official. I've gone and lost my damn mind.

As we're pulling into the driveway, Holly locks the car door, stopping my plan of a quick escape.

"Reilly, you know whatever it is, it could have just been a misunderstanding. Not everyone who gets arrested ends up in jail. You like him, I can tell. You like him more than you want to. You should just ask him." With that, Holly unlocks the door, leaving me sitting there contemplating her words.

~

Before getting in the shower and before I can think better of it, I call Alyssa to let her know that Bray was dragged off in handcuffs. Let's just say the conversation was short-lived with me ending it promptly when she started to question how I knew Bray was dragged off in handcuffs. *Arghh,* I shouldn't have called her, of course he would have called his brother for help already. And really, why the hell do I care if he's left rotting in a cell alone or not? I don't, at least that's what I'm telling myself anyway.

I've just had one of the longest showers of my life. Boy, did my body need the hot water streaming down on it. I feel like I've ran a marathon; my muscles are sore in places I didn't know even existed. Not to mention the fact that every time I sit down, I can still feel—nope, not going there again.

As I make my way back to my bedroom, my phone is vibrating on the bedside table where I left it charging. Unplugging the phone, I scroll through what seems to be a million notifications of text messages. Most from an unknown number, a lot from an unknown number. But there is also one from Alyssa.

The curiosity of the unknown number wins out, so I check those first.


**UNKNOWN**: *Where are you?*


**UNKNOWN**: *Hello? I'm giving you thirty minutes, babe. If I don't hear from you, I will come looking.*

· · ·

**UNKNOWN**: *I'm serious. I will hunt you down if I have to!*

**UNKNOWN**: *Reilly, please just tell me you at least made it home safely.*

**UNKNOWN**: *Twenty minutes left, pumpkin.*

**UNKNOWN**: *Fifteen minutes, tell me where you are.*

OKAY, obviously these are from Bray, but if he thinks I'm texting him back, he can think again. I don't even know how he got my number. Without overthinking it, I save his number to my phone before moving onto Alyssa's messages.

**ALYSSA**: *Reilly, how much do you love me? Actually, don't answer that. It doesn't matter because the amount is about to grow tenfold!!*

**ALYSSA**: *I hope you're sitting down. Are you ready? Okay, here it is. I, yes, me, Alyssa, just landed you your dream PR job at only the hottest nightclub in town. The Merge, ever heard of it? Lol. Anyway, Zac fired his PR lady #bitch last night and I suggested he interview you. He skipped the interview and is giving you a trial; you need to be at the club in two hours.*

· · ·

OH MY GOD! *Ahh!* Jumping around and doing a happy dance, I pull myself together enough to text Alyssa back. I cannot believe I have a job at The Merge. It's like winning the damn lottery. I'm starting to like this Zac more and more.

**ME:** *Alyssa, OMG! I freaking love you, girl!!! Thank you! Boy, you must have really screwed that poor boy's brains out last night for him to just give me a job like that. Anyway, whatever you did to that cucumber, keep doing it! Tell him I'll be there.*

**ALYSSA:** *Don't worry, I plan on keeping this cucumber around. I think I really like this one, Rye. And don't think you're off the hook. I know something went on with you and Bray last night. I want deets.*

**ME:** *Sorry, gotta go get ready. I have a job to get to.*

JUST AS I'M walking into my closet, my phone beeps again. Looking down at the screen, my smile falters, as I see the notification from JTPC, the abbreviated version of my warning to myself, that this one I need to stay clear of. Junior the pierced cucumber. No, Reilly, you are not letting him ruin this happy moment for you. I can't help myself; I open the message up.

**JTPC:** *Reilly, I know you're on your phone right now. I can see your messages with Alyssa. Answer me, please. I just need to know that you made it home.*

. . .

BEFORE I HAVE the chance to message him back, telling him where he can shove his concern, another message comes through.

**JTPC:** *Look, I know it was not an ideal situation this morning, but it's been sorted out. I'm sorry you had to wake up to that. Please, for the love of God, tell me you're at home and that you're okay.*

NOT IDEAL, that's laughable. Having the cops banging on the door to arrest the guy you just did all sorts of compromising things with the night before is so far from bloody ideal. My blood is now boiling. I'm mad and I am going to let him have it.

**ME:** *Not Ideal??? You have to be bloody joking, right? You were ARRESTED, Bray. There is nothing ideal about having the cops bang down the door of the guy you were banging the night before! Asshole. Don't message me anymore. I'm fine. Last night was fun and all, but let's leave it at that.*

SWITCHING MY PHONE ONTO SILENT, I throw it over to my bed and hunt for the perfect first day on the job outfit.

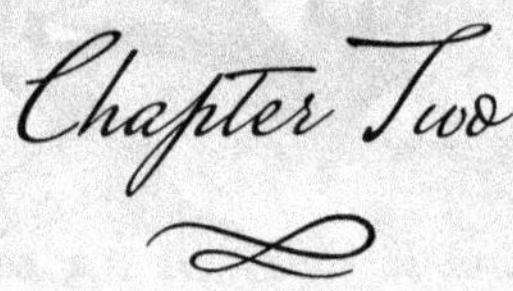

# Chapter Two

*Bray*

AFTER SITTING in the police station for two fucking hours, the last thing I want to do is ride along while my brother plays fucking Uber for his girlfriend. But, as always, whenever my ass has needed bailing out of anything, Zac has always been there, always willing to fight for me.

Ever since our parents died five years ago, Zac has been there; he stepped up, taking guardianship of Ella and me. Let's just say, in no way did I make it easy for him. I was seventeen when my parents were mugged at a train station, my mother falling onto the tracks as the mugger snatched her bag from her shoulder. My father jumped down to help her, but they couldn't get back onto the platform in time.

Zac can't talk about the incident; Ella still cries when she thinks no one is watching or noticing. Me, I just got angry, really fucking angry. I would pick fights with anyone. I was eventually kicked out of school because of it. Fighting helped me though. I needed the pain, the adrenaline, somewhere to focus all of my fucking rage on so it wouldn't consume me.

I joined up in an underground street fighting club—I was good. But it didn't take long for Zac to pull me out. He signed me up for a state-of-the-art MMA gym. Got me in with a great coach and the rest is history. I still fight underground, still have that same great fucking coach. The only difference is now I fight for our own underground club.

Once Zac realised fighting was part of me and what I needed to do, he once again took control and built an underground cage in the basement of his nightclub, The Merge. The Merge Cage is now known as the best in town, our fights get packed audiences, and hundreds of thousands of dollars are bet at our fights. Even more when it's my cage name, Braydon Johnson, on the card.

I'm fucking good at what I do, undefeated, and I will take on any motherfucker who wants to try to beat my ass. The advantage I have? I still have the pool of rage I've carried around with me since I was seventeen; the one place I let myself release that rage is in the cage.

My thoughts are halted as Zac's girlfriend, Alyssa, opens her door in a fucking towel. Damn, I know she's my brother's girl, but fuck, she is hot as hell. Although I can appreciate her hotness, that's where it ends; there is no spark, no chemistry. But there is some kind of weird pull to this girl I can't seem to wrap my mind around. It's like I want to protect her; from what, I don't know.

Maybe it's just that this is the first girl who Zac has actually given two fucks about, and she's good for him. It's early days, but I can see that she's not going anywhere; this one is sticking. That doesn't mean I can't have some fun and piss my brother off a little in the process though. After all, what are little brother's for, if not for being annoying little shits.

Peering around Zac's side, I tease, "Damn, I can see why my brother has given up his balls to you, Lyssa." I raise my eyebrows up and down suggestively.

It doesn't take long for Zac to step inside, blocking my view of Alyssa and slamming the door in my face.

"I'll just wait in the car, kids!" I yell out to the door. Heading back to the car, I lean against it and pull out my phone.

Ever since Reilly stormed out of my fucking house, I haven't been able to get her off my mind. I need to know where the hell she is. Did she get home safely? Fuck's sake, I sound like my fucking brother now.

Rubbing a hand across my chin, I think about whether or not I should text, call or, fuck, just track her down and rock up on her doorstep. Maybe with a bow wrapped around junior, one that she can unwrap with her mouth. Straight away junior stands to attention, on board with the idea as much as I am.

Looking down, I say, "Settle down, mate. It's not gonna happen for us right this second." I'm out here standing in a carpark talking to my fucking cock. Yep, fuck my life.

Deciding that texting is probably the safest bet for both junior and me, considering the state of anger Reilly left in, I pull up her number; the one I had to steal from her phone while she was sleeping, mind you.

When I asked her for her number last night in the club, she laughed right in my fucking face and replied with, "Yeah, that's never going to happen, stud muffin, but what could happen is you getting me a refill." She then proceeded to shove her glass into my chest before reaching up onto her tippy-toes and whispering in my ear, "And, at the end of the night, you can take me home to bed for one hell of a night you won't be forgetting anytime soon."

Needless to say, I did get her that refill. My eyes never

strayed far from her for the rest of the night. Which is also the reason that the fucker who hit Alyssa across the face was able to get so close to her. The rage that overtook my body, mind and soul at seeing some fucker hit Alyssa was off the charts. I barely know the girl, yet I have this weird need to protect her. The same way I want to protect Ella from the whole damn world.

I jumped straight into action without any thought other than killing the guy there and then. My vision went red, zoned in on my target and when I got him, a right hook had him on the ground. But did I stop there? No, I jumped on him, landing punch after punch to his face, then his ribs. The cocksucker didn't stand a chance, and if it wasn't for Dean pulling me back, I would have fucking ended him. Who the fuck hits a bloody woman? A lowlife, that's who. One that should be wiped off the face of the earth and I'm more than happy to be the one to do it.

It's the same fucking cocksucker who thought he could press charges against me, not that those charges stuck. As soon as Zac showed up at the cop shop—with Dean in tow and video footage of the guy hitting Alyssa, which, mind you, up until that point Zac had not seen—I was released. When Zac did see that footage, he lost it and picked up a chair, throwing it across the room and smashing the mirrored window. Needless to say, the cops dropped the charges. But even without that footage, Zac would have just pulled some strings higher up in the department.

Shaking off the thoughts of last night and this morning, I fire off a text to Reilly, asking her where she is. Waiting for her to reply, I think I check my phone a dozen times before Alyssa comes bouncing out by herself, wearing fucking nurses' scrubs. Man, maybe I need to visit the hospital more often if this is how nurses are looking these days.

Thinking she's just going to make her way over to the car

and wait for Zac, I'm taken by surprise when she comes up to me, wrapping her arms around my neck and hugging the shit out of me.

Damn, this girl can hug. It's a bloody good thing junior took my advice and settled down, or she'd be getting more out of this hug than she bargained for. I wrap my arms around her, returning the hug.

"Thank you for helping me last night, Bray. It really means a lot to me that you would stick up for me like that," she whispers in my ear.

"Anytime, sister," I say back to her while smirking over her shoulder at Zac, who is now glaring and storming toward us.

"What the fuck?" Zac yells out, while pulling Alyssa behind him and attempting to land a right hook to my face. One that I easily duck and avoid. I know if he really wanted to land that hook, he would have been able to. I just laugh at him as Alyssa wraps her arms around him and calms his ass down. She has an uncanny way of being able to do that to him. I might have to hit her up for some pointers. Although, I suspect it may have something to do with the anatomy between her legs. Which, obviously, junior does not share any similarities with.

"You know it was bound to happen, right? It didn't take her long at all to come to her senses already and decide I'm the hotter brother after all," I tell him.

"Fuck off, idiot," he says while slapping me across the back of my head. No matter how big I get, that's always the move he goes for to reprimand me for my antics. I'd never tell him this, but when he does that, he reminds me a lot of our dad. Sometimes I say stupid shit on purpose just to get that glimpse of my dad, even if for just a second.

~

Sitting in the back of the car listening to Zac and Alyssa swoon over each other is bloody sickening. I'm half listening as I type out increasingly frustrated texts to Reilly. Why the hell is she not answering me? Where the fuck is she? What if something happened to her when she left my place?

I live in a good neighbourhood, but still, you don't know who is living next door to you, no matter how nice or expensive the house might be. And, damn it, all she was wearing was my fucking t-shirt.

I'm momentarily distracted remembering the sight of her in nothing but my shirt, those long lean legs of hers on display, her fiery red hair a mess down her back. She was definitely sporting the just fucked hair look. The just thoroughly fucked look, if I must say, and yes, I must.

When Alyssa mentions how much she appreciates Zac giving her a ride, I can't help but laugh a little. She turns around in her seat and glares at me. "Care to share why you got arrested this morning and had to drag Zac out of bed to bail you out?"

What the fuck? How the hell does she know about that? Reaching out, I slap Zac across the back of his head.

Yeah, how do you like it, motherfucker? "You told her? What happened to the bro code, man, bros before—"

I don't get to finish the sentence before Zac is once again scolding me.

But what Alyssa admits leaves me with a sickeningly huge smile plastered across my face, one that I can't seem to stop. "He didn't have to tell me. Reilly sent me a message this morning, worried about you and the fact you got taken away in handcuffs," she says while squinting her eyes at me.

If she's waiting for me to confirm that Reilly was there this morning when I got arrested, she will die waiting. I may not be much of a gentleman, but I do not kiss and tell. So, Reilly was worried about me enough to call Alyssa. Hope is not lost after all. Then the question is why the fuck is she not returning my messages?

I try my best to pretend to be busy on my phone. Informing Alyssa about what got me arrested is on a need- to-know basis, and she does not in fact need to know. Normally it wouldn't be such a secret, but because I was arrested for beating the crap out of the guy who hit her, I can't tell her. I have a feeling she would get all guilty and shit. I do not need her feeling bad. If she feels bad, Zac's going to feel bad and when Zac feels bad, we all fucking cop the brunt of it.

Alyssa must realise I'm not going to comment on Reilly, and she starts threatening my manhood if I hurt one of her friends. I feel like asking what she would do if one of her friends hurts me, because let's face it, that's the more likely scenario here. Not that I have the feels or anything for Reilly, but I sure wouldn't mind feeling her underneath me again, the sooner the fucking better.

When Zac starts talking about the need to hire a new PR manager for The Merge, and Alyssa recommends Reilly for the job, I can't help but say no to the suggestion. Being around that body all day or night will be torture if she does not let me touch her again. Of course, Zac, the fucker, likes to bloody torture me. He tells Alyssa to let Reilly know she has the job on a trial basis.

I have mixed feelings; on one hand, I'll know where she is and I'll be able to see her all the time. On the other hand, my balls. My poor, poor balls; the friends to junior are going to be fucking blue. Just thinking about her body is driving me crazy. How the hell am I going to handle being around her?

I can see over Alyssa's shoulder that she is texting with Reilly, and the fact that she's answering her texts and not mine is pissing me off. It's also putting a fire inside me. You can run, pumpkin, but just try to hide from me—I dare you to.

I send her another text, letting her know I know she's currently holding her phone, and I know she can see my messages. I also figure I should apologise for this morning's events. I'm sure it was not what she expected. Having the cops bang down your door at ungodly hours in the morning is not ideal.

Her reply makes me smile. She's mad and I can picture her face now—I can picture her pale skin turning red. It's probably all kinds of messed up, but the image of her mad is fucking turning me on. Deciding to let her text slide and let her think she's won, I don't text back. I know she's going to be at the club in a few hours and my day just cleared up. I might just have to stop by and help my bro out for a bit.

As soon as I get home, I head for a shower. I need to wash away the stress of the morning—it's not every day you get arrested, especially just days after you disposed of a fucking corpse. It's not how I had planned my morning to go.

No, I planned on having Reilly for breakfast, then having breakfast off Reilly, then feeding Reilly breakfast. I'm sure you get my drift; it was meant to be a damn pleasurable morning. I can recall the taste of her on my tongue—it's fucking divine. I've never wanted to eat a pussy out so much in my life. I could spend my life with my head buried between her legs.

Junior's on board with the plan too, currently straining at the thought. Taking some shower gel in my hand, I slowly stroke my cock, sliding up and down, putting just the right amount of pressure on it and twisting my hand around at the knob—right where my Prince Albert sits. It doesn't take long for me to work up the speed. Thoughts of Reilly's taste, her smell, her moans, the feel of her soft pale skin under my fingers consume me. I groan out loud. *Fuck*. Before I know it, I'm coming all over the damn wall of the shower while calling out her name.

~

Walking back into my bedroom, I instantly smell her. Fucking hell, is there anywhere I can go without her entering my fucking head? Because I'm a sucker for pain, I inhale the scent. I pick up her discarded, ripped dress off the floor. Taking a picture of the tag and dress, I send a text to Ella.

**ME:** *Ella, sweetheart, do me a favour. Find this particular dress somewhere and buy two of them for me, in this same size, please.*

BECAUSE SHE'S eighteen and has her phone glued to her hand twenty-four/seven, her reply is immediate.

**ELLA:** *Why do you want to buy a dress, or two dresses? I don't think that size will even fit over one of your arms, Bray.*

**ME:** *Because I ruined someone's dress and need to replace it. So please, just do what you're good at and shop. I need these dresses yesterday. Please?*

. . .

ADDING a please on the end may just persuade her to do it; this is not a task I want to have to do myself. Where the hell do they sell these anyway?

**ELLA***: OKAY, do not need to know how you ruined that dress. Just so you know, that brand is expensive. This is not going to be cheap for you. And while I'm swiping your card, I will be putting a little something extra on it for myself. Call it a personal shopper's fee.*

**ME***: I wasn't about to tell you how. And I don't care what it costs, just get them. Don't go overboard on your shopper's fee. Love you, sissy. You're the best!*

WALKING BACK out to the living room, I notice a sparkling object on the floor. Picking it up, my smile widens as I inspect the little purse thing that Reilly was carrying around last night. Well, looks like someone was in so much of a rush to leave this morning that they forgot to take their purse with them.

Opening it up, I see a range of cards, including her driver's licence, which has her address on it. I snap a picture of it with my phone. I know that I'm bordering on stalker material here, but I don't really give a fuck. She's going to want this purse back, and she's going to have to come and get it. When she does, I might just have to tie her to my bed and show her what she's missing by denying junior and me.

# Chapter Three



*Reilly*

TAKING one last look at myself in the mirror before I head over to The Merge where I am, as of today, gainfully employed, I'm pretty happy with what I've managed to pull off in such a short timeframe.

I'm wearing a black pencil skirt that ends just over my knees and has a split that runs half-way up the front of my left leg. I pulled out my favourite go-to, white, sheer blouse. The neckline is high and hugs around the base of my neck, while the sleeves flow loosely down my arms. I've put on a white crop top underneath; you can see just a hint of skin between where the crop top ends and my skirt begins on my waist. The outfit is finished off with a pair of black pumps, adding a little extra height to my already tall frame.

Not having time to do anything with my hair, I settled for tying it up in a ponytail—one just like Holly usually sports. I'm satisfied that I'm pulling off my professional, badass business bitch look, which let's face it, I need to, considering the only side of me that Zac—aka my new boss and my best girl's new boo—has ever seen of me is the drunk, carefree party girl Reilly. I need to prove that I'm also a professional who is damn good at what I do.

Picking up my black Ted Baker Audrey bag, I start looking around for the clutch I had all my cards in last night. Then it dawns on me. "Fucking Bray," I say out loud to the empty room. I know exactly where I left that clutch last night—right on the floor of his living room where it fell out of my hands, due to being upside down over his damn shoulder.

I'll just text him later and get him to pass it onto Alyssa; that way, I won't need to face him. Yes, that's what I'll do.

Making my way out to my car, I smile when I see it, my beast, my baby, my ride, the one ride I don't mind driving over and over again. Turning the key over, I listen as the engine of my black Mustang GT convertible roars to life. I'm not really sure how he did it, but my dad had cars delivered to both Holly and me on our university graduation day. Holly got her dream yellow VW bug, and me, I got this machine.

Walking up to the back entrance to the club, I approach as the door opens and a wall of muscle clothed in black stands between me and the inside of the club. I have to tilt my head back to meet the wall's face. I reach his face as his eyes not so subtly rake up and down my body. Clearing my throat, I gain his attention.

"Are you lost?" the wall asks with a raised eyebrow.

Tilting my head, I squint my eyes at him. I'm about to get *riled Reilly* on his ass when I remember that this is now my place of business. Taking a deep breath, I gather myself before I respond to him. Holding my hand out, I say, "No, I'm Reilly. Zac's expecting me."

"Yeah, that's what they all say. Sorry, love, but Zac's not interested." The wall steps back, planning to shut the door in my face. I react without thinking and stick my foot out to catch the door, only to have the door slam into the inside of my left foot.

"*Ahh*, motherfucker!" That hurt like a bitch. I'm jumping around on the spot, cursing and rambling for a good three minutes, before I stop and shake my foot a little while inspecting the damage. Yep, that's going to bloody bruise all right.

"You might want to get on that little walkie thing and let Zac know that Reilly, get that name right, Reilly his new PR manager, is here." I can't help but give the brute attitude now. He slammed the goddamn door on my foot.

He steps aside, freeing the doorway. "Okay, sweetheart, settle down, come in and take a seat at the bar. I'll let him know you're here."

"Firstly, I'm Reilly, not your sweetheart or any other demeaning pet name you like to hand out, thinking it will make all of womankind swoon and forget you injured them. Secondly, I'll show myself to the bar, thank you."

I limp my way over to the bar. I'm almost there when the bartender from last night rounds the bar, stopping in front of me. James, I think his name was.

"What on earth happened to you?" he questions. Before I can answer, his hands are reaching out and grabbing me around my waist, effortlessly picking me up and placing me onto the bar. Great, Reilly, first day on the job and you're already sitting on top of the bar.

"The oaf at the door tried to slam said door in my face. I used my foot to stop it." I shrug my shoulders like it's no big deal.

James's eyes widen. "Kid has a bloody death wish," he mumbles, before telling me not to move.

I watch as James digs out a scoop of ice, wrapping it in a towel before making his way back to me. He's gentle as ever, picking up my injured foot and removing my shoe, then holds the ice onto my foot. I audibly moan at how good that ice feels right now.

"You're lucky I'm gay, sweets, or that moan right there would land you in a world of trouble, although..." Pausing, he looks me up and down. "Nope, still gay," he says, shaking his head.

"That's a damn shame to womankind, but if you ever want to really test that theory, hit me up, spunk," I say, waggling my eyebrows at him teasingly.

"I'm not stupid or crazy enough to test that out with you. I like breathing way too much," he responds.

I'm trying to process what he just said. I don't really get how I have anything to do with him breathing. Maybe he's been testing the product a bit under the bar.

"What the fuck is going on?" The deep, rough voice rumbles through me. Oh boy, I know that voice—my body was way too acquainted with that rumble last night. Just don't look up, Reilly. Don't make eye contact. Be strong. You do not need to get mixed up in his mess. Remember the cops rocking up on his doorstep this morning. And that right there does it; my resolve is set.

I look up to James, who looks like he's seen a ghost. He hands the ice over to Bray before saying, "I was just helping her, man. She injured her foot." Then he turns to me. "Sorry, sweets, you're on your own with this one. Like I said, I like breathing." James turns and practically runs out of the bar area.

I'm wiggling my ass closer to the edge, just about to jump down, when Bray puts a stop to my movements. Placing his hands on my knees, he says, "Don't even think about it, pumpkin." He then lifts my foot, inspecting the damage before gently placing the ice back on.

"How'd this happen?" he asks while his thumb rubs up and down the arch of my foot. Jesus, Holy Mother Mary. My body feels like a thousand bolts are currently running through it. Sparks. I can feel them everywhere. Is it hot in here? Oh man, I really need to get him to stop doing that. It's literally frying my brain.

Wait, he asked a question, right? I can do this—I can answer a question. I can jump down and release his hold on my foot. Deciding that's the best plan of action, I place my hands on his chest, on his well-defined muscle on top of muscle chest. Shoving him back slightly, I jump down.

"I tried to tell him that I was here to see Zac. He didn't believe me and went to shut the door in my face. My foot stopped the door. That's all, nothing too interesting. Now, is Zac in his office? Should I just head up there?" Lifting my head to meet his eyes, I can see he doesn't like what he heard. His face is stone and gives nothing away, but his eyes, they are brighter somehow, more intense than they were a minute ago.

"Wait, who the fuck slammed a fucking door on you?" he grunts out.

Okay, so maybe it's not just his eyes that are showing how mad he is. But what does he have to be mad about anyway? It was my bloody foot not his.

"You know, I didn't stop to get his name. Next time I see him around, I'll be sure to tell him Bray would like to know what your name is." Slipping my shoe back on, I walk around him and head to the lift that I remember leads to Zac's office. I can feel Bray's eyes on my back the whole damn way there. At least I'm not limping anymore, my foot feeling numb from the ice.

Sitting in Zac's office, my mind is whirling with possibilities and ideas. I try to rein in my excitement and remain professional though. Zac is thorough, knows what he wants, and has high expectations for his club. I've been given the tour around the building, and shown where my office will be.

Notepad in hand, I'm currently sitting on the couch and taking copious notes of the many tasks he wants me to do. It's almost like he's challenging me, like he expects me to fail. Well, he's in for a rude awakening—Reilly Reynolds does not fail at anything. Well, maybe relationships, but that's mostly always intentional on my part.

"We host new and upcoming indie bands on Tuesdays and Thursdays. You'll notice in the calendar that we're currently booked for the month; you will have to start booking bands for the next month's spots." Zac is pacing his office as he rattles off task after task. Almost without taking a breath.

"We also host live bands on Fridays and Saturdays for limited time slots; the rest of the night is our featured DJs. I expect you to get to know them and work with them. Their contact details will be in your email contacts."

Finally, he takes a breather and pauses. Looking up at me, he squints his eyes, almost like there is something he's unsure of. Like he's trying to figure me out somehow. I sit and wait him out. I will not let his stare intimidate me. Straightening my spine, I arch an eyebrow at him, daring him to say something about me.

Zac just smirks at my silent challenge, asshole. "There are also *other* events we hold here. You won't need to do much for them. They promote themselves and are by invite only."

I didn't miss the way he said *other*. "What kind of other events, Zac?" I ask, my mind now whirling with worst-case scenarios. I can't stop my mouth before I start rambling on to him.

"Because if your *other* events are what I'm thinking, I'm walking out that door and keeping you far, far away from my best friend. Please, for the love of God tell me you are not auctioning off women. Prostitution? Oh boy, you're not selling drugs here, are you? No, you don't seem the type for that. Although, you think you know someone and then, *BOOM*, you really don't."

Zac is staring at me with scrunched up eyebrows. "What the fuck is wrong with you?" he asks before shaking his head. "Actually, don't answer that. No, I'm not running a goddamn woman auction or prostitution ring."

Just as he is about to say more, his phone starts blaring "My Girl" by The Temptations. When Zac answers the phone like his life depends on it, I can't help but laugh a little. Clearly that boy is lovesick.

I'm sitting here, trying not to be the nosy friend listening in on his conversation with Lyssa, but then he mentions roses and a card. He tells her that they are not from him. My blood goes cold and all that goes through my mind is that I need to get to her.

Alyssa is one of my best friends. I know her, and her past, and receiving flowers from an unknown sender is going to draw up unpleasant memories for her. Two years ago, one of Alyssa's old foster brothers started stalking her. She started receiving roses, odd gifts, and then the treats started. This went on for six months before he was finally caught when he attacked her in the hospital while she was doing her practical placement for college.

Reacting on autopilot, I jump out and grab the phone out of Zac's hand. I think he's so shocked by my sudden movements that he freezes for a moment. I have to push on his back to let him know to start moving as I talk to Alyssa. "Lyssa, it's Reilly. You are okay. You are safe. You're in

the hospital; nothing can happen to you in the hospital." I try to keep my voice as calm as I can manage in an attempt to reassure her.

"Lyssa, listen to me. Do not open that card. Don't touch it. We are on our way to you, okay? Zac and I, we're coming to get you, okay?"

Her voice is quiet as she agrees. Shit, this is not good. She's freaking out. I can tell by how quiet and shaky her voice is, her breathing quickening.

"I want you to stay on the phone with me until we get there. Go and tell whoever you need to tell that you're sick and you need to go home, okay?" I do everything I can to reassure her that it's not him. That she is not getting stalked again. I would know if he was released from jail.

Zac halts at the carpark and questions me. I can see he's stressed but I don't have time to deal with him right now. If Alyssa wants to share her past with him, that's up to her, not me.

"You need to drive. If you care about Alyssa at all, you need to get to the hospital now. Just know that she needs us. I can't tell you why, it's not my story to tell." It doesn't take him long to have the car screaming out of the carpark and towards the hospital.

I'm standing in Zac's apartment, correction Zac's penthouse, by myself wondering what the hell I do now. After collecting Alyssa up from the hospital bathroom floor, Zac threw his car keys at me and ordered me to drive. Let me repeat that, he ordered me to drive his Batmobile fancy-pants car because he wouldn't make Alyssa let go of him.

He carried her up to his apartment and then continued down a hallway, with me hot on his trail. He didn't even look behind him as he slammed what I'm assuming is his bedroom door. Deciding that Alyssa is actually in good hands with him, and that she seemed like she needed to be with him, I make my way back out to the living room, staring out of the floor-to-ceiling windows.

"What the hell do I do now?" I ask the city below.

Taking out my phone, I send a group message to Holly and Sarah, letting them know to get here as soon as they can. They both text back immediately that they are on their way. In my haste to get to Lyssa, I left my bag in Zac's office and my car at the club. Before thinking too much about it, I call Bray and he answers on the first ring.

"What's wrong?" he says in lieu of a greeting. "Nothing's wrong. Why does something have to be wrong for a girl to actually call you?"

"Babe, first, you're not a girl; you are all woman. Trust me, I've been up close and personal with your womanhood. I know. Second, women usually don't call me during the day; it's usually late at night. The only girl who ever calls me during the day is my little sister. So, I'll ask again, what's wrong?"

Damn it, why does the mention of other women calling him, clearly for booty calls, make my blood boil? I don't care who calls him for a damn booty call. If I say it enough, it's true, right? Choosing to be the bigger person and ignore his recall of last night's events, I tell him exactly why I'm calling, hoping to God that I can trust him enough to deliver my car to me in one piece.

"Okay, so the thing is, Zac and I had to go pick Lyssa up from work. Something happened and, in the rush out of Zac's office, I left—" I'm cut off by his booming voice on the other end of the phone.

"What the fuck happened to Lyssa? And why didn't you lead with that? Where is she now? I'm on my way!"

"Wait, Bray, Lyssa is fine. We are at Zac's apartment and she's holed up in the bedroom with him. I need you to get my bag from Zac's office—my car keys are in my bag. Can you please drive my car here?"

"No worries, babe, be there before you know it. Are you sure she's okay?" He sounds genuinely worried about her. I'm not entirely sure how to feel about that.

"Yes, she's fine. But you won't be if you even so much as put a scratch on my car. It's the black GT in the carpark."

"You drive a fucking Mustang? Be there soon. Oh, and don't make plans for tonight. You're busy." He hangs up before I can threaten him any further about damaging my car. Or tell him he's out of his mind if he thinks I'm busy with him tonight.

As I'm waiting for the girls, and now Bray, to show up, I come up with a genius plan to escape the building without Bray noticing it was me who was leaving. Well, not really genius since Holly and I have been trading places and fooling people all our lives. Nobody, other than our parents and closest friends, can ever tell when we've switched identities. I will be walking out of this building as Holly and not Reilly. By the time Bray notices, if he notices, I will be long gone.

# Chapter Four



*Bray*

DRIVING REILLY'S car to Zac's apartment is anything but a hardship. This car is a fucking dream. How the hell did Reilly end up with this? I know she's not long out of university, she's had one other job before Zac hired her, and that only just happened today.

The thought crosses my mind that a boyfriend or something bought it for her. That thought has me gripping the steering wheel tighter than necessary. I don't see Reilly as the type to take a gift like this from a bloke though. Maybe she's a trust fund baby—who the fuck knows? I'm damn sure going to find out everything there is to know about the fiery temptress.

Walking into Zac's apartment, it's more like walking into home. This is where we moved to after our parents died. Zac had already moved out of home and was living with Dean in the ultimate bachelor pad. When our parents died, his trust was opened, and he bought the penthouse, moving Ella and me in with him. He also bought the building of The Merge. At just

20 years old, he took on two teenagers and started up what is now the hottest nightclub in Sydney.

I couldn't be prouder that he's my brother; there isn't anything I wouldn't do for him. Knowing him, he would be silently losing his shit over something happening to Alyssa. I don't even know what the fuck happened yet and I'm stressed.

The living area is empty, so I make my way into the kitchen. Stopping at the doorway, I stay out of view, watching Reilly talking to Ella.

Taking Ella's hands in her own, she whispers, "Hunny, if you need help, I can help you. I promise. Who did this to you? Was it Zac? Bray?"

Her questions make me see red, as if Zac or I would ever lay a hand on a woman. Anyone that knows us knows there is nothing we wouldn't do for Ella. The guy who's currently worm food out in the Wollombi Forest would testify to that. If he was actually still breathing and could talk. It's that same guy who left those bruises on my sister's face. Just thinking about her being attacked like that makes me want to bring the asshole back to life just so I can watch the life drain from him again.

"I don't care how big or scary they are; I will hurt whoever did this to you. This is not okay. You do not have to be treated like this! I'm taking you home with me; you don't have to worry about a thing."

Reilly continues to ramble. She's really getting herself worked up, which I find both amusing and something else I can't put my finger on. The fact that she's concerned over the welfare of my little sister and that she's willing to help her without a thought of herself is endearing, to say the least.

The look on Ella's face is fucking priceless. I can tell she doesn't know what to do. Scrunching her eyebrows up, she tries to convince Reilly that she's okay.

"Wait, you think that Zac or Bray would do this to me?

You know they're my brothers, don't you?"

"I don't care who they are; if they're responsible for this, I will have their balls in little glass jars sitting on my mantlepiece." Reilly says this so convincingly I actually believe she would attempt to cut my balls off.

Junior and I are both pretty well attached to said balls, and will not be parting with them anytime soon, ever if I can help it.

Ella looks mortified, so unsure how to handle the fiery siren standing before her. I know one way I'd like to handle her; unfortunately, it's not a viable option in front of my sister. I'm about to make myself known and put Ella out of her misery when she finally speaks up.

"Okay, you obviously don't know my brothers at all if you think they are capable of doing this to me. I was attacked at The Merge. You can ask Lyssa. She's the one who bandaged me up afterwards." Ella's face is blank, like she's telling a story that she is totally detached from.

Not being able to handle seeing her this way, I walk into the kitchen. Not so quietly. Stomping my feet along the wooden floor, I make my way over to Ella and Reilly, stepping between the two so that my back is facing Reilly.

"There you are, sweetheart. I've been looking all over this damn castle for you," I say as I wrap Ella in my arms, placing a gentle kiss to her forehead. She immediately wraps her arms around my waist, settling her head on my chest.

I spin around with Ella still in my arms, my eyes landing on a shock-faced Reilly; although she's quick to recover and replace that shock with a scowl directed straight at me. Raising an eyebrow at her in question, she responds by stomping out of the kitchen. My eyes are immediately drawn to that perfect fucking heart-shaped ass of hers currently hugged by that tight skirt she's wearing.

I thought Reilly was fucking gorgeous in that skimpy club

dress I tore off her last night. But that dress has nothing on work Reilly in her sexy librarian getup. *Mmm*, I wonder if I can get her to wear a pair of glasses with that outfit, while I bend her over a desk.

Stepping back from Ella, I clear my head of thoughts of Reilly as I inspect the bruising on my little sister's face. I can't help the rage that comes over me when I see her like this.

Ella shakes out of my hold. "I'm fine, Bray. It doesn't even hurt that much anymore."

"You're my baby sister. You know I'm always going to worry about you."

Sighing as she begins to clean the already clean bench, Ella looks up at me. "I know and I appreciate that, but you really should worry about yourself. Now that Zac's practically married off to Alyssa, I think it's about time you look for someone stupid enough to put up with you, and lock that down. You don't want to be the eternal bachelor, do you?"

My eyes bug out of my head. Where the fuck is this coming from? Fucking Zac finding his one, that's where; and now it's given Ella ideas that I need the one too. Right on cue, an image of Reilly pops into my head.

"Don't worry your pretty little head about my love life, sis. Trust me, it's not lacking—that's for sure. But what about you? Any boys stupid enough to be hanging around?" I ask, knowing full well there is definitely something odd happening between her and Dean. I'm not sure what, and I trust Dean with her life, but there's an intensity I've seen from him towards Ella lately. I'm not sure if he wouldn't be stupid enough to try to go there with her.

"First, gross. I do not need to know who and how many are warming your bed at night. Second, don't be stupid. You know I'd never tell you if there was a boy I fancied. It's way more fun sneaking around anyway." Ella smirks as she's about to walk out of the kitchen.

"Well, you might want to improve on your sneaking game, sis. It won't be long until Zac notices whatever the fuck is going on with you and Dean."

I watch as her back straightens and she misses a step. She's about to say something when Reilly walks back into the kitchen staring at her phone.

"Miss me already, babe?" I question her.

"Not in this lifetime," she replies as she turns to Ella, who is currently bobbing her head between the two of us.

I see the moment the lightbulb goes off in her head, and a huge-ass grin spreads across her face. "This is gonna be sooooooo good," Ella says excitedly.

"No idea what's going to be good, but Zac asked me to get Lyssa some food. Correction, Zac ordered me to get Lyssa some food," Reilly tells Ella.

Just then the phone she is still clutching starts beeping in her hand. "Shit, the girls are here. I need to run down and let them in."

"Don't worry. I'll get Lyssa a plate of food; you go let them in. You'll have to take a lift card with you to get back up."

I'm watching the dynamic between Ella and Reilly and am in awe how quickly Ella is taking to her. Not that there's much to not like. I mean, damn, just looking at her and I have to adjust junior to give him more room for the growing he's doing right now.

"Wait, you said girls? I'll go let them up for you," I offer, giving her my best smirk.

Reilly looks me up and down, and I can see the fury in those green eyes of hers that she's trying so damn hard to hide. "Not a damn chance, pretty boy," she exclaims as she storms out.

Ella laughs. "Way to get shut down, bro. I think I like her."

"What's not to like?" I ask. Not waiting for a response, I make my way into Zac's office; that's where he hides the good liquor.

After I've slammed back two shots of whisky, I start making my way back out to the living room in search of Dean, only to stop in my tracks at the sound of voices—Reilly's not so quiet whisper to her friends to *shut it*.

I know I probably shouldn't, but I can't help but stop and eavesdrop on the conversation between Reilly and her friends. That is until I hear one of her friends announce, "If you don't want to ride that pierced cucumber again, I'll take it for a spin."

Reilly responds with, "Go for it, see if I care."

That's when I decide to make myself known. "See if you care about what, pumpkin?" I ask, wrapping an arm around her shoulder.

An arm which she's very quick to shrug off. Ignoring her shrug, I turn my full-watt smile onto her sister and her friend.

"Ladies, it's good to see you again."

"Oh no, the pleasure is all mine. I'm Sarah, in case you forgot," Sarah says as she takes a step closer to me.

I look across to Reilly, raising my eyebrows in question. Is her friend seriously trying to hit on me right now? Reilly's oblivious to my question though, currently staring daggers at Sarah. Well, that's an interesting turn of events.

Thinking I could play on her sudden green-eyed monster, I turn and give Sarah the full look over, up and down, then back up and down again. You would have to be blind to say she's not hot as fuck. My mind is telling me she's a ten; however, junior is not budging, not even slightly.

*Huh*, well, there goes that idea. Either Reilly broke junior last night or he just really knows what he wants right now. And I have a feeling what he wants is the fiery redhead standing next to me.

Leaning down into her ear and ensuring her friends can hear, I say, "You can put the claws away, pumpkin. It seems junior has his sights set exclusively on you."

Reilly's mouth gapes open and closed for a few seconds before she straightens her shoulders and replies, "Junior is going to be feeling very lonely if he doesn't find a friend to play with, because I most certainly will not be reacquainting myself with him."

"Sure, we'll have to agree to disagree with that, babe," I say as I walk away, continuing my search to find where the fuck Dean's hiding out.

# Chapter Five



"I CAN'T BELIEVE Zac called us out like that. How on earth could he tell, Rye? No one has ever been able to tell us apart without knowing us before," Holly says as she's stares at her reflection in the lift mirror.

She's in a tizzy because I talked her into changing clothes and pretending to be me so I could walk out of the apartment as Holly, escaping the likes of Bray and his pierced cucumber. It turns out I didn't have to worry about it, because when we walked out of Zac's bedroom, Bray was nowhere to be seen.

"Well, it doesn't matter now anyway. Bray left before us, which means crisis averted."

"Tell me again, if that pierced cucumber of his was so magical, then why are you avoiding it?"

She knows damn well why I need to stay away from that one. She just wants me to admit it, which is never going to happen, ever. Trying to play down the effect that he has over me, I shrug my shoulders at her as we exit the lift. "It wasn't that good."

I'm lying and I know she knows it. It wasn't just good... it was the best damn cucumber I've ever bloody had. And that right there, that is why I can't let myself get attached, that is why I need to stay far, far away from...

My thoughts are interrupted by Holly's gasp. Noticing she's not right next to me anymore, I turn around only to come face to face with a shocked and frozen Holly, currently wrapped in a pair of very muscular tattooed arms. Damn it, Reilly, get your head in the game. You are not Reilly right now you are Holly.

And if Holly can just pull it together long enough for us to get out of here, that'd be great. I'm not liking my chances—by the way she looks like a mouse caught by the bloody cat.

"Trying to run out on me, babe?" Bray says into Holly's neck.

Shit, shit, shit, Holly looks like she's about to pee herself. As I'm racking my brain for a way to get us out of this, Bray curses and spins Holly around to face him.

He looks between the two of us, back and forward a couple of times, before he smirks at me—a smirk that makes my ovaries shiver. Before I know what's happening, Bray storms up to me, grabs my face between both of his hands and lands his lips on mine.

I'm doing my best to resist, to not open my mouth for him. He's damn well persistent though. And those lips, those full soft lips of his just feel so bloody good. I can't help the moan that escapes as he brushes his tongue along the seam of my lips.

For a moment, I give in, returning the kiss just as eagerly as he is giving it. Everything around me fades, and all of my senses are zoned into all that is Bray. His exotic, masculine, earthy scent surrounding me, making me feel like I've been whisked away to the forest. What I wouldn't do to have this man throw me up against a tree trunk right now, the bark scratching at my back as he thrusts into me.

"*Umm*, Rye, I guess I'll just meet you at home."

Holly's voice snaps me out of my Bray-induced insanity. That's what he does to me, makes me insanely freaking horny and forget everything else. Pushing back, I step away from Bray, who is just staring at me with the biggest smirk on his face. Which just adds fuel to my growing fire now.

"What the hell, Bray?" I ask, crossing my arms over my chest. It then occurs to me that I'm Holly right now. Did he think he was kissing Holly?

"Why the fuck are you trying to kiss my sister?" I question.

His eyebrows draw in like he doesn't understand the question. I can tell the minute the lightbulb goes off in his mind, because outcomes that full-watt smile again. Look away from the smile, Reilly. Do not let that delectable mouth draw you in again.

"Babe, I was not trying to kiss your sister." Looking over at Holly, he says, "Not that you're not smoking hot, Holl, because obviously you are."

"*Umm*, thanks?" Holly questions, going beet red. She does not take compliments from men as easily as I do.

"Why'd you switch clothes anyway?" Bray asks me. "That's on a need-to-know basis, and you do not need

to know. Now, if you'll excuse us, we need to get going." I try to step around him, only to have him wrap his arm around my waist, stopping me.

"Not so fast, buttercup. I need a ride home," he says as his thumb trails circles on my waist. Why does his simple touch affect me like this? Just his hand on my waist is creating a storm of tingly sensations that run through me. I'm not even going to mention the effect it's having on my panties. I really need to get away from him.

"Not my problem, call an Uber. You have heard of them,

right?" Internally, I am telling myself to stay strong. *Do not let him affect you, Reilly. This will not end well for you.*

"It became your problem when you asked me to drive your car here, babe. So, stop arguing and let's go."

Bray takes hold of my hand, like he has every right to, like it belongs to him somehow. It feels good to have my hand in his, warm, safe even. But no, I am not falling for that. Pulling my hand away, and shaking out the tingles, I find I'm still walking next to him. I think I may have lost my mind.

Bray stops suddenly, spinning around. "Holly, how are you getting home? Do you need a ride?"

One could be fooled that he is actually concerned about how my sister is getting home. I am not *one*.

"No, I'm fine, thanks. I have my car here," Holly says as she points to her yellow VW out on the street. I watch as Bray looks at the car then back to Holly.

"Wait here a minute, babe," he says as he takes Holly's bag from her and proceeds to walk her out to her car, waiting for her to get in before he turns to make his way back inside.

Okay, well, that was... I don't know what the hell that was. I do know we need to clear up this whole *babe* thing though. I swear my bloody ovaries do a little flip every time they hear him say the word.

"You ready, sweet cheeks?" Bray asks as he takes my hand again, only for me to pull it out of his hold, again.

"Sweet cheeks? No, just no. And while we're on the subject of pet names, I am not now—and I am not ever going to be— your babe, your buttercup or your damn pumpkin. My name's Reilly. Start using it!" I am almost yelling by the end of my rant.

The asshole laughs; that's right, he laughs at me. "Just another thing for us to agree to disagree on. You know you're cute as fuck when you get all worked up?"

"*Argh*, just show me where my car is. And there better not be a scratch on her."

"Sure, *Reilly*, this way. It's in the basement." He puts extra emphasis on my name. I thought him not using pet names would be easier on the ovaries, but I was wrong, very, very wrong.

~

Bray gives me directions to his house and I stop at the gate, waiting for him to get out. He just sits there staring at me. It's making me self-conscious. Do I have something on my face? I'm pretty sure I don't.

"You know, this is usually the part where you say thanks for the ride, Reilly. Catch you around," I tell him, hoping to get him out of my car.

"*Huh*. You know, I'd be happy to give you a ride you'd be thanking me for," he says as he waggles his eyebrows up and down at me. Before I can respond—because yes, it takes a bit for my mind to stop playing images of just what kind of ride he is offering—he snaps me out of my thoughts. "Wind your window down and enter the code, babe. It's 2501."

Like the idiot I am, I do just that: wind my window down, enter the code and drive through the gates as they open. At this point I think it's my ovaries leading me to my doom. Stopping the car at the end of his driveway, I tell him, "Okay, you're home. You can get out now."

Laughing, he shakes his head at me. "I have your purse thingy you left here last night. You wanna come in and grab it?"

I do want to get that clutch; it has my cards in it. But is it worth the risk of entering his house again? I'm not sure. "Can't you just run in and get it and bring it back out to me?" I plead with him.

"Are you afraid that friendly vagina of yours ain't gonna be able to stop wanting to play with junior if you step inside?"

What the... wait, did he really just say that? "My friendly vagina? Really, Bray? Trust me, it's not as friendly as you think. Right now, the right name would be bitchy vagina and the last thing my vagina wants to do is play with junior now or ever!" If I keep saying it, we both might actually start believing it.

"Well, babe, your vagina was plenty friendly to junior last night. I can't help it if he thinks he's found his new playmate. Also, you can't really say he doesn't have good taste, because I can still taste that friendly vagina of yours and I'm starving for another feed."

Holy shit, well, how the hell do I respond to that? God damn it, now my vagina really does want to play, or be played.

"It's not happening, Bray. Please, I really need to go home. I can just get my clutch another time, or you can bring it to the club or something." I can't even make eye contact with him as I practically beg him not to make me go inside.

Bray's silent for a moment as he looks at me, then he shocks me by holding my face, bringing my eyes to meet his. "Reilly, you know I'd never make you do something you don't want to do, right?"

I nod my head because, somehow, I do feel safe with him. I do feel like he would never hurt me. But it's the unpredictable nature of life that will end up hurting me. It's the cops banging on the door at all hours of the morning and taking him off in handcuffs—that's what will hurt me.

"Okay, wait here. I'm going to run in and grab your things." Before getting out of the car, he leans in and kisses my forehead.

Kisses on the forehead are kryptonite. Jesus, why does he have to be so damn perfect? It takes less than two minutes for him to come running back out of the house holding my clutch and some garment bags.

He opens the passenger side door, places the clutch on the seat and then lays the garment bags across the back seat.

"What's with those?" I ask, pointing to the bags.

"I told you I'd replace the dress I ripped, so I did." He shrugs.

"*Uhh,* thanks?" I don't mean it to come out as a question but it does. "You do realise there are two bags there, don't you? You only ripped one dress."

"I know, and I fully intend on ripping this particular dress again, next time I see you wearing it. That's why there's two. Now when I rip the new dress, you already have another one." He ends with a wink.

I actually think he's serious right now. "You're not going to be ripping any dresses off me again, Bray. Sorry, but you wasted your money."

"Agree to disagree, babe, that seems to be becoming a thing for us. Drive safe, and text me or call me when you get home." He doesn't let me respond before shutting the door and walking into his house.

Well, I hope for his sake he is a patient man. Because he's going to be waiting a long time for that text to come.

One week. I have managed to work at The Merge for a whole week without having to run into Bray once. I've dodged corners, and hidden out in bathrooms to achieve this, but achieve it I have.

I've gotten to know a lot of the staff here. The bar staff is great, especially James. He and I are going to be great friends. The security staff on the other hand is hard to read. Other than Dean, they all seem to avoid me like the plague. Whenever I go to talk to any of them or try to ask them something, they mumble under their breaths and make an excuse that they have to go. Dean is always quick to come and find me to see what it is I need. I mean, it's not that I don't like Dean. I do. It's just hella weird. I've never had men avoid me like this; usually it's the other way around, like me avoiding Bray for instance.

"Reilly, are you listening?" Zac asks.

*Oh shit.* Yep, totally zoned out while I was in a meeting with Zac. I should be jotting down all the notes and the endless list he wants me to do.

"Sorry, I must have missed that. What'd you say?" I try for my sweet, butter wouldn't melt voice. It gets me absolutely nowhere with Zac though. He is a man on a mission. He knows what he wants and goes for it. I actually respect the hell out of him, but I will go to my grave before I ever admit that.

I admire the business side of him. The way he has built this business up from the ground and at such a young age is admirable. Again, I'm never admitting that to anyone.

"Well, if you're done daydreaming, and please do refrain from sharing whatever thoughts had you pre-occupied, I need you to go to the store and get a dress," he says.

This has my attention. I don't know whether I should be pissed off, or excited at this point. Pissed off, because I am not his bloody personal shopper, and excited because shopping and Zac's credit card seem like one hell of a good time.

"First, I am not your personal shopper. Second, prepare to lose your balls if that dress you want me to buy is not for Alyssa." I glare at him for extra measure.

He scrunches his eyebrows up. "First, you're my employee, under my employ. If I ask you to run an errand, that's what you'll do. Second, who the hell else do you think I'd be buying a fucking dress for?"

"Good answer, but why do you need to buy Lyssa a dress?"

It seems like an odd request, even from him. Trust me, I've had some odd requests over the week.

"There's a fight tonight after her shift. She's coming, and I'm guessing that she's not going to want to go out into the club or down to the basement in her scrubs."

"You're actually going to take her down to the basement? I haven't even seen this exclusive basement yet. If I buy the dress, I'm coming to the fight."

"I don't have a choice. I have to be there—it's the last fight of the year. And I'm sure as fuck not going to leave Alyssa up here by herself." Standing, he takes a black card from his wallet and hands it over.

"Here, buy something suitable, but make sure it actually covers her. I don't need all the fuckers down there to be staring at what's mine," he says, like I'm going to listen to a word of that.

Inspecting the fancy black card, I ask, "Is there a limit on this bad boy?"

"No, make sure you get her shoes as well, and be back by nine. The fight starts at nine thirty tonight, and I have a feeling that you're not going to want to miss it."

"Are you serious? I've been waiting all week to see what happens down there. I'll be back." As I'm walking out of his office, the pierced cucumber walks in. I mean Bray, Bray walks in. Wearing a pair of sweats, nothing else. And there go the ovaries again. Doing my best not to be obviously checking him out, I hurry out of the office and get the hell out of the building. I think I'll enjoy this little shopping trip.

Just one glance at Bray, and I need to recalibrate my system into the *I don't want Bray Williamson or junior, his pierced cucumber,* mentality. I'm probably the only woman on earth to ever mutter that sentence.

One hell of a shopping trip later, I'm standing next to one very excited Alyssa and one very pissed at me Zac. Let's just say he was not impressed with the dress I picked out for her; but damn, she is owning that dress. Her body is killer and she has curves in all the right places. It's a crime not to show it off.

The crowd down here is pumped. We've watched a few fights already and are apparently waiting for the main event. Although no one will comment on who the fighters are in the main event. The cage has just been cleaned out after the last fighters.

I'm not surprised that even down here, in this underground fight club, Zac has everything running like a fine-tuned machine. All of a sudden, the lights go dark, then a spotlight shines at the fighter's entrance and "T.N.T." by ACDC blasts from the speakers.

I strain my neck to see who this fighter is that's coming out. I really, really shouldn't have looked. Of course, he has to be a fucking cage fighter. Walking out with two women wearing just bikinis, one hanging off each side of him, is no other than Bray fucking Williamson.

He comes out wearing I guess what he is passing off as a pair of black shorts, though they look more like painted on boxer briefs. His whole body is on display for all to see; those two skanky card girls in bikinis sure are getting their fill.

Bray is dancing and playing it up to the crowd. And although those girls try to get up and rub all over him, I do smile a little when I see him shake his head no at them and move them back an inch. *Huh, that's interesting.* The bikini girls look just as shocked as I am at the turn of events. Bray steps into the cage, and I'm ashamed to say that my eyes haven't strayed too far from him the whole time he's been dancing his way out here.

Looking to Lyssa standing next to me, I can tell straight away something is wrong. She's panicked, looking all around the room. Zac is holding her like his life depends on it; his face is as stern and furious as I've ever seen it.

"What's wrong?" I yell over the noise of the crowd.

He doesn't say anything, just hands me Lyssa's phone with a message open on it. My blood goes cold when I see the message. This cannot be happening to her again. I don't know how she can survive living through another stalker coming at her like this.

*You shouldn't touch things that don't belong to you! He was mine first. I saw him first! I won't warn you again, bitch. He is MINE. He will be with me again, even if I have to take you out myself. xxx*

I feel helpless. I don't know what to do right now. I look back to the cage and my eyes land on Bray. He's staring at me, eyes squinted. He looks like he's ready to jump back out of the cage. Then he looks at Zac and nods before indicating to the ref that he's ready.

I watch Bray's movements, unable to take my eyes off him. My heart feels like it stops as the bell rings to begin the fight. It seems like only seconds later Bray's opponent is on the ground, knocked out cold from one hit. Bray leaps out of the cage, ignoring the calls from the crowd and heads straight for us. Straight for me.

He wraps his arm around me, and I let him. I soak up the comfort that he's offering and take everything I can. He says something to Zac and Dean before guiding me along with the rest of our group out of the basement. He doesn't let go and I honestly don't think I want him to right now. That text message even freaked me out, and I don't scare easily.

I'm not scared for myself. I'm scared for my best friend. I'm scared for how this is going to affect her. I know what she needs. What she needs right now is her girls—this calls for a slumber party of the most epic proportions. Lots of alcohol, snacks and more alcohol will be consumed tonight.

# Chapter Six

*Bray*

I'VE JUST CLIMBED into bed, in my old bedroom in Zac's penthouse. I don't really stay here often but he has never changed my room from when I moved out a few years back.

I sat out in the living room for hours listening to the girls laugh and squeal. I'm glad they could help Alyssa relax and try to forget about that fucking psycho Caitlyn sending her those damn messages. I want to fucking strangle that bitch. If she thinks she can hurt my family, she can think again. I will stop at nothing to protect them, and Alyssa is now a part of that.

I know Reilly likes to put on a tough persona, but I've been watching her this past week. I've purposely stayed out of her way, much to the disappointment of junior. The way she looked so broken and stressed in the car when she dropped me off, I know she's struggling with something. As much as I'd like to help her, I also don't want to make things harder for her.

I hear the rattle of my doorknob turning or attempting to turn. I'm about to jump out of bed, ready and alert, when I see those long legs paired with a mop of red hair tumbling into the room. At this moment, I'm really fucking hoping that it's Reilly and not Holly stumbling in here.

It's too hard to tell in the dark. I'd have to touch whoever it is to find out. When I wrapped my arms around Holly a week ago, I knew straight away that something was off. I didn't get that electric sense running through me. My body didn't feel as alive as it does whenever I touch Reilly. That was the first sign that they had switched clothes. The second was the green-eyed monster Reilly, who was dressed as and portraying Holly, was throwing my way.

I watch as this gorgeous redhead stumbles and curses. "Fuck, shit, fuck."

Thank Christ, that is definitely Reilly. I watch as she stumbles her way through the room. There is just enough light coming from the en-suite that I can make out her features. It is also very clear that she's shit-faced right now. A fact that junior is not happy about. I may be a bastard, but I have never and will never take advantage of an intoxicated woman.

I'm silent as I watch her fumble with the zip of her dress. When she finally manages to get the zip down all the way, she just lets the thing fall to the floor. Holy Mother of God, she is standing—okay, she's more swaying—but she is swaying in only a pair of panties. She's been braless all fucking night. Damn it, I need to get junior under control. He's not understanding that it's not time for him to come out and play.

Reilly pulls the sheet back and climbs into the bed, falling half on top of me. It's at this moment she notices she's not alone in the room.

"*Ahh*, what the hell?" She attempts to jump back out of bed, but I don't let her get far. Wrapping an arm around her, I hold her close to me. Reilly does not like this one bit; she tries landing punches on my chest. I really need to get her in a gym and teach her how to actually hit more effectively. I can't help but chuckle at her attempts.

Stopping her fight, she questions, "Bray?"

"Yeah, babe, it's me. Who the fuck else did you think you were getting into bed with naked?" The thought of her getting into bed naked with any other motherfucker pisses me right the fuck off.

"*Umm*, no one, I thought... Ella told me this room would be empty." She sighs, as she snuggles in closer to me. I know, if it wasn't for the alcohol, there is no way she would be snuggling up to me. But am I going to turn away her snuggles? Fuck no, I've never claimed to be a saint and she is a sin I am more than prepared to indulge in.

"Ella sent you in here?" I ask, wondering what my sister is up to, since she knew I was staying the night. Looks like Ella is playing little miss matchmaker. I'll have to send her a huge bloody thank you card for this match.

"*Uh-huh*, I can go. I'm sure there are plenty of surfaces in this castle I can sleep on," she says, making no move to actually move.

"You're not sleeping anywhere else, sweetheart. You're right where you're meant to be."

She looks up at me and fans her fingers down my face, that electric zap very much alive and coursing through my body.

"I really wish I could let myself have you, Bray." I guess a drunk Reilly is an honest Reilly, good to know.

"You already have me, whether you want me or not, babe." I doubt she will remember any of this conversation in the morning, so I may as well lay all my cards out on the table, my balls along with them.

Reilly shakes her head. "No, I can't have you. You see, I made a promise a long, long, longggg time ago," she slurs.

"What promise?"

"That I wouldn't end up like her."

"Like who?" What the fuck happened to her that she can't let herself be happy?

"I can't tell you. But I'm not strong like her. I can't do it. I'm sorry. I really would have liked for you to be mine." She leans up inches from my mouth, about to kiss me. I stop her. It pains me to do so, but I know how wasted she is, and I can't let her do something she will likely regret, well, any more than she already has.

"Go to sleep, babe. I'm not doing anything with you while you're intoxicated. The next time your friendly vagina and junior have a playdate, you're going to be sober and clear-headed."

Reilly scrunches her face up at me. "What? Why? I am clear-headed; I know what you can do with that pierced cucumber of yours and I want you to do it to me. Now, Bray!"

I can't hold the laughter, and when I finally calm myself down, it's evident that she is not impressed by my outburst.

"Pumpkin, you can have this pierced cucumber, anytime, anywhere..." I get down real close to her face, our lips barely millimetres away. "When. You're. Sober."

"*Argh*, you and I both know I'm not going to want your pierced cucumber anywhere near me when I'm sober." Reilly pouts, full on lips sticking out pout. It's fucking adorable. It's taking everything I've got not to lean in and kiss her.

"Agree to disagree, babe. You're going to want to play with junior. You just won't admit it, to me or yourself. There is a difference," I tell her as I position her body so she's snuggled up to my side. My arm is underneath her head, allowing it to rest on my shoulder, her long, red tresses sprawled out behind her. She's so fucking perfect.

I kiss her forehead. "Go to sleep, Reilly. You're likely to feel like shit when you wake up as it is; you don't want to be sleep-deprived as well."

"Thank you, Bray. I know I'll probably regret saying this tomorrow, but you are one of the good ones," she says as she snuggles in.

I doubt I'm going to get a wink of sleep tonight; junior is fucking raging hard, not that I can blame him. I have a practically naked Reilly in my arms. What I need to do is come up with a plan to figure out exactly what Reilly is afraid of. What the fuck happened to make her so jaded? If I can figure that out and know what I'm fighting against, the odds will be in my favour—because one thing I don't do is lose a fucking fight. I have a feeling that the fight for Reilly will be the hardest, but most rewarding one yet.

I'm in the kitchen making coffee, while trying to decide how to make Reilly's coffee. How do I not already know how she takes her coffee? I've been watching her all week. I've seen her drinking it every day as she enters the club.

I'm debating between a cappuccino and that sweet latte shit that Alyssa drinks. Why the fuck am I so stressed about coffee anyway? She either likes it or doesn't like it. I'm just about to make a decision when Holly appears in the kitchen.

"Thank fuck you're up. How the hell does your sister take her coffee?" I ask her.

She seems a little thrown off kilter, as she stares at me with wide eyes. "*Umm, uhh,*" she mumbles before finally telling me, "she just has straight black, nothing fancy."

Straight black, I can do. Turning, I hit the button telling the machine to pour a long black.

"*Umm,* Bray..." Holly's timid voice grabs my attention. It's hard to believe she and Reilly are twins; besides looks, the two couldn't be more different.

"Yeah?" I question with a raised eyebrow.

"How do you always manage to tell Reilly and me apart so easily? I mean, I didn't even say anything when I walked in, and you knew it was me and not Reilly."

"Well, you guys might look the same, but your mannerisms are complete opposites. You also have that little freckle under your left eye where Reilly doesn't." I shrug like it's not a big deal. Then I remember the main thing that helps me know them.

"Oh, also, I don't get the same electric feel from you that I do from Reilly. When I look at you, junior is not aching to come out to play. But when I look at Reilly, he is bursting at the seams to play with her, literally." I wink.

I watch as Holly processes what I just said; it clicks in and her face screws up. "*Eww*, wait, you really call your *you know what* junior? Also, Reilly and I look just the same, so why does junior like Reilly and not me?" she says as she points to my dick, while also silencing the insistent beeping coming from her phone.

I laugh at her unease. I know I shouldn't but she's fucking cute. "Holl, surely you've had boyfriends. All guys have a name for their dicks. And I can't explain why junior jumps for Reilly but not you. I'm not saying you're not hot as fuck, Holly. Obviously you are. I just look at you and see a sister. I look at Reilly and see, well, you get the picture."

She shrugs her shoulders up and down. "I have had a couple of boyfriends, but none of them have had names for their, you know." She gestures to my crotch area.

"Trust me, Holl, they had names. They just didn't tell you."

Holly's phone continues to beep and she continues to silence it.

"You know a good way to get people to stop messaging is to answer them. You and your sister both need to learn how to answer messages." I lean against the bench and wait for her response as she looks down at her phone again, only to silence it once more. Her face screws up a little. I've noticed both twins make this exact same face while thinking.

"I can't answer it until I talk to Reilly. I need her help with something. Speaking of, where is my sister?"

"She's asleep still. What do you need help with? Maybe I can help you?" I offer, because there is no way in hell I'm letting anyone drag Reilly out of my bed this morning.

"Unless you're prepared to find yourself tagging along on a double date with me and this guy, you can't help," she says as she waves her phone in front of her.

"Babe, I don't usually have any issue finding a date. When is this double date?" I ask. It then dawns on me that she was planning on asking Reilly to go on this date, which means Reilly would have taken someone, that same someone not being me.

Before she can answer, I'm jumping on her. "Wait a fucking second, you were going to get Reilly to go on this double date thing with you?"

"Well, yeah, she always comes with me on dates. Not that I date much, but if I do, she tags along. Why?" She smirks at me knowingly.

*Huh*, guess I walked into that one. But I don't fucking care. I smirk back.

"Sign us both up to tag along. Reilly and I are going to be your date buddies. Who's the guy anyway?"

"Oh, he's the physical education teacher from school. He's been asking me out for a while now and I keep saying no. I figured I'd say yes one time and see what happens." She shrugs, then adds, "Good luck telling Reilly she's going to be your date," as she exits the room laughing.

Reilly is still out of it on my bed when I make my way back into the room. Placing the coffees on the dresser, I stand against the wall, debating whether I should wake her or not. I decide on the not; this may be the only chance I get to peacefully look my fill without her giving me a death glare in return. The fact that the sheets have dropped to her waist, displaying all of her glorious breasts, helps this decision.

What I wouldn't do to get my mouth, hands, anything on those breasts. Damn, my junior is roaring to go at them too. Something tells me she would not welcome the ideas I have of just how I could wake her, how I want to wake her every fucking morning.

Shit, where the hell are these thoughts coming from? I really do need to get laid. The only issue is junior; he has not even budged at another woman since meeting Reilly. The bastard is fucking hooked on her, loyal to her.

"Are you going to stand there all day staring like a creeper, Bray? Or are you actually going to hand me that coffee I can smell."

Reilly's sleepy voice draws me out of my own head. "I'll take option one, babe; I could stare at you all day and not tire of the view. I'll let you creep on me as much as you want to because as you know, I'm a giver like that." I raise my eyebrows suggestively at her.

Reilly slowly sits up, pulling the sheet up and covering those breasts I haven't been able to stop staring at. "*Argh*, God, make yourself useful and pass me that coffee, Bray," she says as she rubs her temples.

Like a fucking lost little puppy, I do exactly that. I pick up her coffee and walk it over, holding it out to her. She snaps it up and within seconds is moaning as she sips on the hot brew. Even doing a simple thing like drinking coffee, she takes my breath away; she is fucking gorgeous.

"Okay, your staring is actually starting to creep me out a little here. You might want to tone it down a bit," she says while staring at my crotch. My ever-growing fucking crotch that is on full display in these loose-fitting shorts.

"It's not my fault you're so damn beautiful to look at. You know junior is your number one fan, babe. I can't control what he likes." I make a point of looking down and waving at junior. "You know, if you were a real friend, you'd help a mate out here," I suggest.

Reilly laughs, "We are not friends, Bray, not even close.

Now, turn around so I can get dressed."

"Ouch, that hurts, sweets," I lament, holding my hand over my heart. I walk into the closet and pick up a shirt for her. "Put this on. What are your plans for today?" I ask, making a point of not turning around while she slips the shirt over her head.

"I'm going shopping with Alyssa. Why?" "What about tonight?" I ask.

"Washing my hair." She shrugs.

"How about you come to my place and I'll help you wash your hair," I suggest.

"Not going to happen. Sorry." She stands up and starts looking around the room. "Have you seen my phone?"

I walk over to the dresser and pick up her now fully-charged phone, handing it to her. "I charged it for you."

Reilly tilts her head, mouth open, and seems stunned. She's quick to recover herself as she takes the phone, mumbling out a thanks.

She's staring down at her phone and is just about to the door when she suddenly stops, spinning around and looking straight up at me.

"Why the hell is Holly saying we are double dating

tomorrow night? And by we, I mean you and me?" she says, pointing between me and her.

I smile. I'm finally going to get her out on a date. "Your sister asked me to help her out. She has this date with some PE teacher from her school. She seemed sceptical, almost like she didn't even want to go out with the guy. I didn't like it and I'm not about to let her go alone. I'm a good friend like that. I help my mates out."

Reilly rolls her eyes. "Whatever, I wouldn't have let her go alone anyway." She then walks out the door, slamming it behind her.

# Chapter Seven

*Reilly*

WHY DO I continue to get myself into these situations? I have barely slept all night, trying to wrap my head around just how I'm going to get through a whole date with Bray tonight. Luckily, it's a double date with Holly and that creepy-ass Simon, the PE teacher from her school.

I've met Simon before, a couple of times when I've been out with Holly and she's ran into him. The guy gives me the creeps. I can't point my finger on what it is, but I just get those vibes from him. If Holly's date was with anyone else, I probably would have fought the whole Bray tagging along thing and found myself someone else to go with.

I'll never admit this to anyone, but I do feel a weird sense of peace knowing that Bray will be there. I have no doubt that he would come across as intimidating and protective of Holly while in the company of her creepy date. Why the hell she's even agreed to go out with him, I will never know. But because she's my sister and I love her, and the fact that she dates only once in a blue moon, I will go along with this shamble of a date tonight.

First, I need to find some inner grounding. I need to rebuild the walls back up around my damn heart. Every time I get a glimpse of Bray, another brick comes tumbling down, letting him seep into places he has no business being. I've spent the last five years mortaring and rendering those bricks to ensure they are firmly in place. I'm not about to let Bray bulldoze them down.

I need a plan, a bloody good one to survive a whole night with his torture. Yesterday was bad enough. I spent the day shopping with Alyssa, Sarah, Holly and Ella, and guess who Zac made tag along with us? Yep, you guessed it, Bray fucking Williamson. I had to endure a whole day of his constant charm and good fucking looks.

I don't understand how one person can be as blessed in the looks department as that asshole is. The whole day he was constantly next to me, or close enough that I could smell him. I thought I was going crazy; I was turned on the whole damn day and by the looks he kept giving me, he knew what his close proximity was doing to me.

Then there was the whole dressing room scene. Some bastard slipped through all of us unnoticed, managing to slip a picture under the door of the dressing room Alyssa was in. The soul-piercing scream that came from behind her door is still ringing in my head. I cannot get that sound out of my thoughts. I've never been so scared for one of my friends in all my life.

Sarah and I both tried to get her to open the door for us. Bray came running in from the front of the store and straight away got her to open the door, only to then push himself into the room with Alyssa and shut the door behind them. I felt a strange mixture of jealousy and a calmness at that.

I was jealous that he was in a dressing room with my friend

while she was in her underwear, my bloody hot as sin friend. At the same time, as I listened to him talk to her, I heard him coaxing her into her clothes on the other side of the door and talking her out of her panic. I felt a sense of calmness and relief that my friend had some great people in her corner. She needs this; she needs people like the Williamsons in her life.

We spent the rest of the afternoon in a wine bar. I may have had a little too much to drink, again. I had Holly take me home earlier than everyone else with the excuse that we had a family thing to do. Sarah and Alyssa both knew that we were bullshitting. They know of our shitty family circumstances. They know the only family we have now is our mum. We both still live at home with her, neither of us wanting to leave her alone.

She's strong, probably one of the strongest women I know, to survive the last five years how well she has. She picked herself up off of that courtroom floor five years ago and dusted off her dress, straightened her shoulders and told both Holly and me that we would be fine. That we would get through this together.

And survive we did. We have a great relationship and usually I talk to her about everything. But I've been holding back talking to her about Bray, partly because I know what she's going to say. She'll tell me to open my heart to the possibility. That the best thing that ever happened to her was meeting my dad. Even today, she has stayed loyal to him. He's facing at least another ten years in jail, but my mum is waiting. She won't even contemplate moving on.

She won't visit him in jail. She says that her heart hurts too much to see him locked up like an animal. They write to each other every day and that's how they have managed to stay connected all these years.

～

I'll be seeing my dad today. Maybe he can help talk me out of these stupid feelings I'm catching. I'm the only one who visits my dad. On the first Sunday of each month, I make my trek down to the Silverwater Correctional Facility. I make a day of it, first visiting my dad and then my brother to tell him all about what's been happening.

Deciding this is exactly the day I need in order to re- ground my inner self, I throw the blankets off and get moving. First coffee, then shower, then car. I mentally give myself a list to get on with. I will not think of the pierced cucumber or the body and mind that come with that pierced cucumber today.

Which is a shame. I really would like to be better friends with junior—we could be best friends. Maybe Bray will let me do one of those moulding kits, where you can make a dildo from the mould of your penis. *Huh*, I wonder if you can add piercings to those vibrators? The more I think of it, the more appealing the idea is. There is just no way in hell I am going to ever ask Bray to do a moulding of junior for me.

Coffee, I need coffee. I need to think of coffee and not that damn pierced cucumber!

The guards at the correctional facility all know me by name. I've even become friends with one of them, Dave. He's big, buff and a total meathead, but somehow, we managed to build a little friendship. We text each other stupid cat videos. He makes me send him pictures of my dates before I go out with guys—he says it's a safety thing. I just go along with it, because he doesn't judge the volume of pictures that I've sent him over the years. He also always checks in the next morning, checking if I'm still alive, his words not mine. Dave is yet another person I haven't made mention of Bray to. Not that there is anything to mention.

"Rye Rye, you're early, babe. It's good to see you."

Dave greets me with a hug.

"You too. I have a lot going on today so I needed to come a bit earlier," I say as I start filling in the visitor information forms.

"Give me a sec. I need to organise a few more guys for the visiting room. I wasn't expecting you this early."

"Dave, you don't need any extra guards in there just because I'm here. I come every month and nothing ever happens. What do you think is going to happen?"

He raises his eyebrows at me in question, waiting me out.

"Oh please, it was one time, and that was like three years ago," I tell him defiantly.

"One time? Really, Reilly? One time, where there was a literal riot in the visiting room because one inmate made a comment about you, making the rest of them pounce on him. It took twenty guards to separate that fight. *Twenty*."

"It wasn't that bad—you're exaggerating."

"Doesn't matter. Wait here for a minute, and stay out of trouble. I'll be back to take you through myself." He leaves me waiting at the counter as he swipes himself through the door I know leads to the visiting room. I hate this place, and I hate that my dad is stuck in this place. It's dreary and depressing. My dad needs me though. He won't admit it, but I know he looks forward to my monthly visits. Five minutes later, Dave comes back out, holding the door open and calling my name. He waits for me to enter and then follows behind me. Two steps into the room and I freeze. Something is wrong. I have that weird feeling in the pit of my stomach; one I've been getting lately whenever Bray is around. I thought I was getting sick for a while until I put it down to that pierced cucumber messing my system up.

I look around the room frantically. Dave has his hand on his taser, looking at me with concern written all across his face.

"What's wrong?" he asks as he scans the room.

I look around the room, trying to shake off the feeling, but then my eyes land on the source. I'm caught in an eye lock with Bray. I'm in shock—he is the last person I thought I would run into here. Why the hell is he here? I see he's about to stand up, but I shake my head no at him and continue walking to my dad's table. Just as I'm about to sit, Dave stops me with his hand around my arm, halting me.

"Rye, do you know Bray? And if so, how?" he whispers close to my ear.

"It's fine, Dave. I know him. I work for his brother's club. I told you about my new job."

"You forgot to mention it was at The Merge, Reilly," he accuses.

"Did I?" I shrug like it's no big deal. I totally purposefully forgot to mention I was working at The Merge. Dave has told me over and over again not to go there. Why? I don't know. But I'm guessing it has something to do with Bray being a visitor here.

"We will talk about this later," he says as he moves to the closest wall to where my dad's table is.

I sit down and finally make eye contact with my dad. "Daddy, I've missed you. How have you been?" I use my best daddy's girl voice—the one that could get me out of any trouble when I was younger.

"Don't try and sit there and daddy me, Reilly Lili." He nods his head in the direction behind me, staring daggers at the man sitting behind me. The hairs on the back of my neck are standing up, and I can feel Bray's gaze penetrating through my back.

"Care to explain to me why that guy looks like he wants to pick you up and drag you out of here, while killing every male in the room in the process?" He brings his gaze back to me and smirks, which he only does when he's trying not to laugh. What the hell? Why is he laughing at this?

"He's nobody. My friend Alyssa is dating his brother and I just started working at his brother's club."

"*Mmm*, have you told him he's a nobody?"

I nod my head. "He knows. Anyway, tell me about how you've been?" I attempt to change the subject.

"I've been good. I've missed you. How's your mum and Holly doing?" It looks like we are back to safe conversation territory. This I can handle, even with the flutters currently in my stomach.

I spend the next thirty minutes catching my father up on all the happenings from the last month. I know my time is nearly up. It always breaks my heart to leave him here.

My dad reaches across the table and grabs my hands. "Sweetheart, you can only tell yourself that someone is a nobody for so long. You can only push someone away who is willing to be lost. Do you understand?"

I nod my head, not able to form words. My dad has always been able to read me. It's like he knows my thoughts before I even know them. I don't want him to know the thoughts I've been having about Bray; I don't even want to know those thoughts.

"Reilly, that boy has not taken his eyes off you for longer than a minute the whole time you've been in the room. The only time he's not looking at you is when he's looking at every other guy in here with a direct threat in his eyes."

I shake my head no. I can feel the tears welling up in my eyes. I don't want to cry. Not here, where everyone can see me. My dad reaches up and swipes the lone, loose tear that manages to fall.

His eyes scrunching up, he questions, "Has he done something to hurt you?"

"No, it's not that. He would never hurt me, Daddy. Not intentionally anyway," I confess.

"You're scared. I get it, and I know I'm the reason why you're so afraid to open your heart." He looks down. I hate that he blames himself for my stupid hang ups.

"No, you're not. I just don't need any man in my life. I'm very content with how things are now. Why mess that up?"

He tilts his head at me. "You're content, huh? So, you wouldn't mind if Lucy over there follows that guy of yours out of here then?"

I spin my head around so fast in the direction of the Lucy he refers to that I see the blonde bombshell of a guard standing at the far wall currently eye-fucking my Bray.

Wait, hold up, he is not my anything. I shake my head, turning back to look at my dad, who is now laughing.

"That's what I thought," he says. "You need to let go of what happened to Dylan, and the choices I made after that accident. You need to let a man into your heart, sweetheart, and whoever you choose to do that for will be the luckiest man alive. You are a beautiful person inside and out, Reilly. Any guy would be blessed to have you."

My dad looks behind me then adds, "Even if it is Brayden Johnson."

My head jerks up—Brayden Johnson is the name Bray goes by in the cage. "Wait, you know who he is?"

"Hunny, every inmate knows who he is. They stream the fights from Club M."

"So, you've seen him fight? And you still think I should give him a shot at my heart?" I ask, shocked. Bray is not the kind of guy you take home to meet your father. He's covered in ink up and down his arms. He's big, built and is as cocky as they bloody come. Yet, here my dad is, telling me to give him a fair go.

"Well, obviously he's not the first choice of guy I would

choose for you, but what I see in the way he looks at you, that's why I would be okay with you dating him."

"What do you see?"

My dad thinks for a moment before saying, "I see a man who is so blindsided by love, he's willing to single-handedly take on a room full of guards and inmates for that one person. I see someone who is so besotted, he doesn't even realise it yet. I see someone who is looking at you like you're the reason the earth spins."

My mouth is hanging open; there is no way Bray has those feelings for me. He can't. We barely know each other. I think my dad has nearly lost his mind being locked up in here. "Dad, we barely even know each other. There is no way he likes me like that." Great, now I sound like a teenager.

"Reilly, I know when a man is in love and that man is very much in love with you," he persists.

"We'll have to agree to disagree then," I tell him and the moment I do, I slam my mouth shut. How the hell is that man seeping under my skin so badly that I've now taken on his stupid phrases. *Agree to disagree, my ass.* Just then, the bell rings letting me know my time is up. I stand up and hug my father, squeezing extra tight.

"I love you, Dad. See you next month."

"Love you too, sweetie. Think about what I said, please. Give my love to your mum and sister."

I nod my head. "I will."

I can't bear to see how much it hurts him when he mentions my mum and Holly. Holly comes every now and then to visit with me, but she doesn't like to. It's usually when it's been a few months and I drag her along. She loves our dad. She just hates the jail, which I get—I don't like it either.

As I make my way out, I turn back to look over my shoulder only to be greeted by a pair of green eyes. Bray is right behind me, as he places his hand on my lower back. "Turn around and keep walking, Reilly," he grunts out.

I'm a little stunned at how close he is and by how pissed off he seems. What the hell is wrong with him? I look around the room, seeing all eyes on us. Do I have something on my face? I look over at my dad, who subtly nods his head at me and gives me his *I told you so* look.

I turn back to keep walking towards the door. Dave is standing in the doorway with his arms folded over his chest. He does not look happy either. I don't know what it is with all the men in this place, but I need to get out of here and away from all of their moody asses.

"Dave, it's been a pleasure as always," I say to him as I get to the door. He doesn't answer, and instead he looks over my shoulder at Bray.

"I'm going to have to ask you to remove your hands off the lady," Dave asserts to Bray. I can feel Bray's body vibrating behind me, and I hear him growl. Shit, I have to do something to put this fire out, before he can do something stupid like start a brawl in the lockup with a guard, which for sure would see him in this exact same lock up.

I step forward putting a slight space between Bray and me, only he steps forward with me. Damn him and his macho shit. Fine, another tactic. I step to the side and take hold of his hand. I wait for shock to cross his face at me holding his hand but get nothing. He is stoic. Holding his hand is strangely comforting but I don't have time to deal with those feelings right now.

"Dave, have you met my boyfriend—Bray?" I ask with a huge fake-ass smile plastered across my face.

"Your boyfriend? Really, Reilly? That's what you're going with?" Dave asks me while shaking his head.

"Yes, Dave, boyfriend. Now kindly open the door so I can get on with my day."

"Whatever you say, princess," Dave replies as he opens the door. I feel Bray try to slip his hand free. *Ahh,* no way, mate, not today. I give him my best glare and pull him out behind me. I don't stop to say goodbye to the ladies at the counter, like I usually do. I head straight for the door and wait for them to buzz us out. I don't let go of Bray's hand as I lead him through the carpark right up to my car.

*Chapter Eight*

## BRAY

**I**'M SITTING in the visiting room of Silverwater Correctional Facility visiting my mate Dan. He's been here for five months now for some petty assault; he beat the shit out of someone who fucking deserved it. The government should be thanking him, not putting him behind bars. I visit as much as I can, which some months is not very often, considering we've been mates since grade school. Although my visit now is more business than pleasure.

I'm here to put an end to the fucker who thought they could mess with Alyssa. Even if it was two years ago and she wasn't part of my family then, she is now. Which means the fucktard that stalked and attacked her has to go. I finish telling Dan about what I need done. I talk in code using my fights as a key, because that's something we have in common—Dan has never missed a fight of mine.

"Remember that fight between me and the guy who called himself stalk attack?" I ask him, folding the sleeves of my shirt up.

"Yeah, fucker never saw you coming," he replies.

I nod my head while scratching at my arm, where I just happen to have the inmate number scrawled into the design of a tattoo. "Yeah, good times, can't wait for a replay," I tell him.

I watch as he stares at the numbers that he knows are not permanently there. Dan nods his head and leans back in his chair.

"How's the family?" he asks.

"Good, Zac's practically married up to this chick Alyssa he met a hot minute ago. Ella's getting ready to go off to uni next year."

"Fuck, man, Zac bit the bullet, hey? Never thought I'd see the day."

"Yeah, me either. But he's totally gone. Good girl too, way too good for the likes of that grouchy bastard, but what can you do." I shrug my shoulders.

It's good to talk shit with Dan again. I've missed this, the easiness that has always been between us. I look around and notice a shit ton more guards in the room than normal.

"What's with the extra meat?" I ask.

Dan looks around, spots an older guy sitting at a table and turns back to me. "The guy's daughter comes in once a month. Always the first Sunday of the month. Sometimes there's two of them but mostly just the one. They always put extra guards in the room whenever she visits," he says.

"Are they famous or something? That seems extreme for one chick."

"Not famous, but his daughters are smoking hot, both of them obviously—they look the fucking same."

Just then, the hairs on my arms stand up. Something is not right. I look towards the door where someone has just walked in. "Fuck, what the actual fuck?" I say loud enough for only Dan to hear me. He turns and spots her.

"Yep, that's her. Told you she's fucking smoking hot." He smirks at me.

I give him a death glare. "Watch your fucking mouth, never speak about her like that again."

"*Woah*, mate, what the hell? Hang on, do you know her?"

I don't answer. I can't take my eyes off her. The fact that the guard who walked her in seems way too familiar with her is pissing me the fuck off. Something is wrong—why is she looking around the room like she's searching for something? The moment her eyes connect with mine, she stops, shock showing on her face.

The douche next to her reaches out and touches her arm before asking her something. I'm about to get up out of my chair and drag her back out the door she came through. I stop though, when she subtly shakes her head no at me and continues walking over to what I now know is her dad's table.

Fuck me, this is no place for a girl like her to be visiting. I understand the extra guards in the room now. As I look around, every fucking male has their eyes glued to her. I want to ring the necks of each and every single one of them. I'm making a point to them as best I can when I catch their attention; once they notice I'm giving them the look of the reaper, they avert their eyes.

"Who bit that bullet?" Dan asks me.

"I have fucking bit no bullet, idiot," I deny.

"Are you sure about that? Because you haven't heard a word that I've said for the last ten minutes, and you haven't taken your eyes off that girl for longer than one."

"She's one of Alyssa's best friends. She also works at the club, so I'm just looking out for her, that's all."

"Deny it all you like. I know you better than you know yourself. You, my friend, are head over heels in love with that girl." Dan smirks.

"Fuck. Okay, I like her, junior likes her even more, but she won't give me the time of day. Stop laughing, fucker. We've never had this issue before. You know as well as I do—the ladies have never refused a playdate with junior before." I shrug like it's not a big deal.

"First, stop talking to me about your dick—never talk to me about your fucking dick. Second, stop crying like a little bitch. I never thought I'd see the day Bray Johnson forfeits a fight," Dan laughs. "You're a fighter, Bray. Fight for the girl you're in love with."

He's right. I do need to fight harder to get Reilly to realise that she's mine. "You're right. I'm not giving up, just formulating my fight plan."

"Do me a favour and wait to have the wedding until I'm out of this joint, because that's bound to be one hell of a bachelor party and I want in on that shit," Dan laughs. I ignore him and continue to watch Reilly with her dad, who is occasionally glaring back at me.

"What's he in here for?" I ask Dan.

"Who?" he asks looking around. "Oh, your girl's dad?"

"Yeah."

"Heard his son was killed by a drunk driver. The justice system let the driver off, so the dude went and shot him close range."

What the actual fuck? Reilly had a brother who was killed and her dad landed himself in jail. Well, her resistance to getting too close to men is making sense now. The way she closed herself off that morning the cops showed up on my door, it all makes sense. Fuck, I'm an idiot. Why didn't I just tell her why I got arrested? She probably thinks the worst possible scenarios. How could she not?

I watch as her dad lifts his hand to her; it looks like he's swiping a tear from her face. Why the hell is she crying? It takes everything in me not to get up and go to her. It should be me offering her comfort right now; it should be me wiping the tears away from her face.

I wait until the bell rings and I see her start to stand. "Good chat, mate. Gotta go. See you next time," I say to Dan as I stand and walk towards Reilly.

~

I let Reilly tug me out of the jail, as much as I wanted to pummel the guard who told me not to touch her. Not to touch? He had the nerve to tell me I couldn't touch what's mine. Fuck him. My girl put him straight anyway. Just don't tell her she's my girl, because she'd run a mile.

As soon as we make it to her car, I spin her around, pinning her back to the door. I don't waste time or give her any time for thought as I slam my lips against hers. The moment my lips make contact, I feel like I've just come home, her touch sending bolts of lightning through my whole body.

I've kissed a lot of women, too many to count. But no one has ever made me feel the way kissing Reilly makes me feel. It's at this moment that I consider that Dan might be right. I could actually love this girl. Fuck, now I sound like I've lost my balls.

Pressing into Reilly harder, I make sure she can feel just how happy junior is with this kiss. He's as hard as a fucking rock. Reilly groans into my mouth and pulls on my neck, tugging me even closer if that's possible. We duel for control of the kiss but there's no way I'm giving up control right now. I could fight with our tongues like this forever and not get bored. She growls and I can't help but laugh a little.

Pulling back, I smirk at her as she pushes against my chest. I see the moment that she recognises what she just did. "What the hell, Bray? You can't just kiss me like that whenever you damn well feel like it!" she yells.

"Why not? You didn't seem to be complaining a minute ago, babe." Raising my eyebrows at her, I give her the best panty-melting smirk I can muster.

"Shut up, and stop looking at me like that. It's not fair." She stomps and pouts. Literally pouts, and it's cute as hell.

"Sugar, you told that douche back there that I was your boyfriend. I've never really had a girlfriend before, but I'm pretty sure the title gives me permission to kiss *my girlfriend* whenever and wherever I want. What kind of boyfriend would I be if I left you hanging?"

I watch the redness creep up her pale skin, starting at the top of her breasts and running all the way up her neck and face. She's blushing—I actually managed to get her to blush. Point one for team Bray, zero for team Reilly.

"Well, first, he's not a douche; he happens to be one of my good friends. Second, you and I both know you are most certainly not my damn boyfriend, Bray."

"We'll agree to disagree on that fact until you catch up, because you are mine, Reilly. I'm not about to give up on you. You want to run? That's fine. I'll chase. You want to hide? No worries. I'll hunt. You want to live in denial and tell everyone that you're not mine? I'll buy a fucking skywriter, announcing the fusion of Brielly to the whole of Sydney."

"Has anyone ever told you that you're bloody looney, Bray? And what the hell is the fusion of Brielly?" she asks.

I reach out and pull her body tight against mine, hugging her in a tight hug. At first, she's stiff, but then she softens and leans in, wrapping her arms around my waist. I wait like this for a moment, enjoying the feel of her in my arms. This is what we should be doing, not arguing about me being her boyfriend.

I kiss her forehead and pull back a little to look down at her face, tucking her hair behind her ear so I get an uninterrupted view of the beauty that is Reilly.

"I'm glad you asked. The fusion of Brielly is you and me, babe, Bray and Reilly fused together. Now, there will be hearts broken all over Sydney once all the ladies read that announcement, and all of their broken and shattered dreams will land on my shoulders. But for you, I'm willing to take that burden."

Reilly laughs a little before she catches herself. "If there are so many ladies out there with their sights set on you, what on earth do you want with me?"

"Well, there may be a bunch of other women out there I could have—and you and I both know that's true—let's not try to deny my hotness factor, babe," I say, waving my hand down my body. I don't mind making a fool of myself if it brings a smile to her face, which it does. "There is, however, only one of you. You are the one who I want and I always get what I want. No matter how hard the fight is, I will win."

"Actually, there are two of me!" she exclaims.

"*Uhh,* no, you and Holly may look alike, but you are different people. You are one of a kind, Reilly. I see it—everyone around you sees it. I will make it my mission to make you see it too."

"It doesn't matter. I have things to do, people to see. Thanks for yet again a memorable kiss." She turns and unlocks her car.

"I'll follow you out. I'm just parked across there," I say pointing to my car. I open her door and wait for her to get in before shutting it and walking to my own car.

Why do I have the feeling that she just shut me down? Whatever she tries to tell me and herself, I know she feels something. You don't kiss like that if you don't feel it.

I start my car, pull out, drive around, and pull up behind her car; she hasn't left her spot yet. I wait a moment and then jump out and head to her window. I hear her car try to start over but it's not going. I tap her window and step back and wait for her to get out.

"Need help?" I ask.

"I don't know what happened. This has never happened to her before. I think she's sick or something, Bray." She looks at the car with concern. I laugh a little because it's fucking funny how she talks about her car.

Pulling out my phone, I fire off a text to a guy I know at a garage not too far from here. I get a response immediately, saying he will come and get her car. "I know a guy. He's coming to get your car and tow it back to his shop. I'm sure he'll have it up and running by tomorrow," I reassure her.

"Lock your car, and we'll drop the keys off to the garage for him on the way back."

"Okay, thank you," she agrees as she locks her car and walks to the passenger side of mine. I run to catch up with her, her easy agreement catching me off guard a little. I open her door and wait for her to get in before shutting it and making my way to the driver's side.

# Chapter Nine



## REILLY

SITTING in the passenger side of Bray's car is unnerving. I can smell him everywhere. He's so close I could easily reach over and touch him. Boy, do I want to touch him, all over. I want to slide my hands, my tongue, all over the grooves of his body.

As much as I want to touch him, kiss him and do much more dirtier things to him and with him, I can't. At least not right now. I need to figure out how I am going to get to the cemetery to visit with Dylan. I could get an Uber after I get Bray to drop me home, but that will not leave me with any time to get ready for that stupid double date tonight.

Bray reaches over and grabs hold of my hand. Momentarily, I consider shaking his hold off and removing my hand from his. As I'm staring down at our joined hands, contemplating the mixed feelings I am fighting at the moment, Bray's voice breaks through my fog.

"Babe, I can hear you thinking. What's wrong?" he questions. How is he so intuitive to my mind? I'm leaning more and more towards some kind of witchery shit going on. I've never met a guy who can read me so well, other than my dad.

I debate what to tell him. Can I ask him to drop me at the cemetery? Then I will have to answer all the usual questions and tell him about Dylan. I'm not sure I'm ready for that conversation. The other option is pulling out of this double date with Holly and letting her down, which I just can't do. She hardly ever dates so it's a big deal for her to put herself out there, even if I think the guy is a douchebag. I don't have to like him.

"Do you think you can drop me at the cemetery? I have to do something there. I'll get Holly to come and pick me up from there." I ask him so fast that I don't even know if it's possible to understand the gibberish that just came out of my mouth.

He squeezes my hand; it's so comforting and reassuring and foreign. I should not be comforted by him. I should not want to be comforted by him, yet I do.

"Sure, which cemetery do you need to go to?" he asks. "Uh, the Rockwood one?" Why that came out as a

question, I have no freaking idea. "Are you sure?" he asks.

"Yep, I'm sure. The Rockwood. Thank you." "No problem." He leaves it at that.

I don't get it. Where is the barrage of questions? The *why do you want to go there?* And the *who died?* Or the usual awkward silences and the *I'm sorry* when people find out I had a brother who died way too young.

But Bray didn't even show any kind of emotion or questioning when I asked about going to the cemetery. It's as if I asked him to drive through McDonald's for a Big Mac.

"Why are you not asking questions about why I'm going to the cemetery?" I blurt out. Way to play it cool, Reilly.

Bray looks over and seems to study my face for what feels like forever.

"Do you want me to question you about it?"

"No, I don't. It's just weird. Most people ask me why I visit the cemetery." I try to explain my weirdness.

"Well, I'm not most people, babe. You and I both know I'm better than the rest." He winks at me.

I laugh. I love that he can make me feel that little bit less awkward and self-conscious by just being his usual silly self. I know he does it on purpose—there is a lot more depth to Bray than the pretty face and cocky attitude he lets everyone else see.

"Look, if you want to talk about it, I'm all ears. If not, I'll wait until you do," he tells me, and a heap more bricks tumble to the ground from around my heart. Damn him and his near perfectness.

Bray turns the car off after pulling into the cemetery. He jumps out and walks around to my door, opening it before I even get my bearings together.

"Thanks for the lift. I appreciate it. I guess I'll see you tonight?" I ask.

"Babe, if you think for a second, I'm leaving you here you're crazier than Harley Quinn. You go do what you have to do. I'll wait here," he says as he leans against his car.

"You don't need to do that. Holly will come and get me. It's fine," I argue.

"I know I don't have to, but I want to. I'm not leaving, even if you call Holly. I will be waiting right here for you, Reilly."

Man, he is persistent. I don't even know how to argue with that. "Well, it's just I don't know how long I will be," I tell him honestly; I have a lot to fill Dylan in on from the past month.

"Doesn't matter, take your time. I have some emails and calls to make anyway." He leans in and kisses me gently on the lips, sealing the deal. Okay, I guess he's waiting for me.

I spend a bit of time pulling out weeds that have grown around Dylan's headstone since my last visit. Then I make myself comfortable and sit, leaning up against the headstone, and tell my brother all about what's been happening.

I tell him about Alyssa meeting Zac, I tell him about my new job, about Mum and Holly, and about the visit I just had with Dad. I know I've been sitting here a while but there is one more person I need to tell him about. I lean back and close my eyes; I can see his face when I close my eyes.

*I think I met someone, Dyl. You'd like him, I'm sure. His name's Bray, and he's hot, smoking hot. Not that you want to know that. I don't know how to let him in though. I'm struggling. I want to let him in. I want to say fuck it and let go of all my baggage and issues and give this thing with him a red-hot go. I'm just scared. I'm so fucking scared, Dylan.*

*I'm scared of the possibilities, of him being taken away just like you and Daddy were. I'm scared that I'll end up more invested than he is. I'm scared he will wake up and see how messed up I am and how much better than me he can do. What if I let go and let him into my heart, only for him to crush it? I don't know if I can take that chance of being hurt like that.*

*I'm not strong like Mum and Holly. Dad thinks I should give him a shot. Can you believe that? Dad. Our dad knows Bray is an underground cage fighter and he told me to give the guy a chance. It's very possible Dad's reaching that age we used to joke about, where he starts to lose his mind.*

*I wish you were here to tell me what to do. I could really use your wisdom right now; you always were the smarter and wiser sibling. I haven't told Mum or Holly about how I'm feeling, although Holly probably knows—she always bloody knows.*

*What the hell do I do, Dylan? I need you to give me a sign or something. Is this the person I'm meant to let break down my walls? Because it might be too late if he's not; those walls are crumbling down faster than I can rebuild them.*

I open my eyes and sit up straighter. My eyes land on the man in question. He's still standing, leaning against his car and staring straight at me. Great, he probably thinks I'm fucking looney for sure now. He's just watched me talk to myself for the last thirty minutes. He's still there though, that has to mean something. I look up to the sky. *Please tell me this is your sign, Dylan,* I whisper before standing and dusting off my dress.

I make my way back to the car, back to Bray. He doesn't take his eyes off me. As soon as I reach him, he grabs me and pulls me in tight. His hugs are something else. I can't help but melt into him, returning his hug. I wrap my arms around his waist and bury my head into his chest. I let myself have this moment; I embrace the comfort that he offers me in this hug.

Bray runs his hands through my hair and kisses me on the forehead. Why does that feel so nice? It's odd, almost nurturing. But I'll take it.

"You good?" he asks as he pulls back from our hug.

*Well, I was good when your arms were wrapped around me,* I think to myself. No way in hell I'm telling him that though. Instead, I nod my head, not trusting myself to speak.

"Let's go then. I'm going to stop by my place and shower real quick then take you to yours. I'll wait while you get ready for our hot date tonight." He waggles his eyebrows up and down.

"Not a hot date. I was roped into this, remember. Also, don't let your expectations of how fun it will be tonight run wild. You have not met Holly's date and trust me, double dating with Holl is usually anything but fun," I warn him.

"Well, it'll be fun because I'll be going on my first official date with my new hot as fuck girlfriend." Bray smirks.

"Not a date and still not your girlfriend, Bray," I inform him.

"Sure you are, you just don't want to say it out loud yet." He's so bloody confident, although if I looked like him, I probably would be too. I can't help but smile at him. "You should make it easier on yourself and just admit it already. It's fate, babe. Brielly is happening."

"I'm not sure I believe in fate. I think people make their own paths in life by their own choices." I'm almost one hundred percent certain I don't believe in fate.

"Well, damn, babe, way to be a pessimist. Don't you worry your pretty little head though. I've got enough faith in our *fate* for the both of us."

Why did my heart have to go and get all mushy over this guy? Why not just a quiet guy who didn't challenge me? *Because you'd be bored as hell, Reilly,* that little devil in my head tells me. She's right I would be bored. Also, Bray sure is real pretty to look at.

I look him up and down. The man is fine; it's unfair how bloody good looking those family genes are. His strong chiselled jaw, those green eyes that draw me in and hold me captivated, and don't even get me started on his body.

As perfect as his exterior package is, it's what's on the inside that I'm in trouble of getting attached to. His damn personality is making me want to give in and give this steady relationship thing a go.

He seems genuine—his actions speak louder than any words. As I look at him, I consider everything he has shown me, all the little ways he shows he cares. The way he waited silently at the cemetery, not pushing me for information, that shows me that he wants to give me the time I need to open up to him.

Do I need more time though? I'm certainly not ready to tell him all about Dylan or my dad. I don't need to see the sympathetic look in his eyes. But I could be ready to give him a chance, to give us a chance.

As much as I don't want to admit it, he's already cracked his way through my defences, seeped into my bloodstream. I can't get him out of my head. When I'm with him, I feel comfortable; I feel safe and I feel like I'm at home, where I'm meant to be. All of these feelings scare the shit out of me and make me want to run a mile.

I consider what my dad said to me, how he encouraged me to give love a shot. Maybe it won't end in tragedy. Maybe even if it does, the time we have together now will make it worth it. At least that's what my mum tells me. The years she had with my dad were the best of her life, and the years she will continue to have with him when he gets out of jail will continue to be her best years.

Taking a deep breath in, I quickly confess before I lose my bravery, "Okay, maybe I like you a little bit." The biggest smile spreads across his face.

"But, I don't know how this can work. I work for your brother, Bray. I don't want to lose my job when you decide that I'm not good enough for you. I also don't want to make it awkward for Alyssa and Zac when we don't work out." I tell him all of my fears and reasons we should not be together.

"First, Zac would not fire you because of me. Trust me, he does not make emotional decisions relating to the club. Well, at least he didn't before he met Alyssa. Secondly, you're not good enough for me? You're too damn good for the likes of me and you can most certainly do better, but I don't care. I'm selfish and I'm keeping you anyway." He gives me a look, daring me to challenge him on that.

This is happening all too fast; I don't know how to handle this. I want to take my dad's advice and give this thing a shot. I'm just not sure I'm prepared for the potential loss or hurt that will come from this fusion as Bray calls it. Then I come up with an idea, a trial before you buy kind of thing.

"Maybe we can give this a go and see what happens with us, but it has to stay between us. I don't want any of our friends or family knowing that we are dating yet."

"You want to sneak around like kids—maybe play seven minutes in heaven too?"

"Well, I can always go back to pretending you don't exist?" I tease, like that would ever be possible.

"Harsh, babe! I didn't say I didn't want to sneak around with you. If that's what you want to do, then that's what we'll do. For now." He looks over and smiles at me. "Besides, from what I remember, seven minutes in heaven was a fun game."

"Don't insult junior. You and I both know he's going to need more than seven minutes." Wait, why on earth am I referring to his dick as junior too? I swear this man is rubbing off on me too much.

~

Bray was super quick to shower and get ready. I made sure to stay out in his living room while he was in the shower, otherwise we would probably still be in there. Looking down at my phone, I wonder if we have time to shower together at my house, because the idea of showering with Bray—with his wet and nakedness all on display for me to touch and lick—yeah, that is very appealing.

We pull into my driveway and I groan. Can anything go my way today?

"What's wrong?" Bray asks.

"Okay, listen. I know Holly and I are way too old to be living at home with our mum, but we do, so you just have to deal with that."

He laughs, like full-on belly laughs at me. "It's not funny, Bray. You haven't met my mum. I thought she'd still be at work, but apparently the universe hates me today and she's home. If you want to wait here in the car, I understand. You do not have to come inside and endure the craziness that is my family."

"Babe, if your mum is anywhere near as feisty as you or as sweet as Holly, I will love her. Besides, women love me! I've never had an issue getting one not to." He winks.

Cocky fucking bastard. Well, let's just see how much he loves the attention of Lynne Reynolds, aka my mother. She has not had a male to fuss over in a very long time. Holly and I never bring dates home, so the fact that Bray is here now is a bigger deal than he knows.

"Okay, but don't say I didn't warn you," I tell him as I get out of the car.

I'm just around the hood of the car when I'm met with a sour-faced Bray. "What on earth crawled up your ass in the last five seconds to create that look?" I ask him. I swear the guy is more hormonal than a nine-month pregnant chick.

"You didn't wait for me to open your door." He pouts, like full on bottom lip out pouts. It's so freaking cute it's ridiculous.

"Get used to it, baby. I'm not waiting around for doors to be opened for me. I open them myself. I'm a grown-ass woman like that," I declare as I march towards the house. I need to set him straight from the get-go. I am not a wilting flower who will let his alpha ass come and control everything.

Before I can open the front door, Bray reaches out and grabs me around my waist. He spins me and has my back pinned against the door so fast I lose my balance. The only thing holding me upright is the grip of Bray's arms around my waist. The next second, his lips are on mine, his tongue swiping the seams while seeking entrance.

Entrance that I greedily grant him. I moan into his mouth,

electric shocks raging a war through my body. I need more than just this kiss; I need it all. Grabbing onto his neck, I jump, wrapping my legs around his waist. His hands move to my butt, caressing as he pushes me into the door harder.

Now, this is what I need. I grind my core onto him. I can feel his cock, hard and ready to play. I recall just how good at play it was too.

"You have no idea how much I fucking like you," Bray whispers in my ear as he kisses his way down my neck. "Everything about you is fucking perfect, Reilly. I love that you're strong and independent, loyal and feisty as fuck." He continues kissing and nipping at my ear, while I continue to dry hump him like a dog in heat. "But, no matter how capable you are, I will always open doors for you, Reilly. Not because you can't do it, because I know you can do fucking anything. I'll open them because I want to, because you deserve to be treated like the queen you are and I'd be a pretty shitty boyfriend if I failed at doing that."

More kisses, then he bites down hard on my neck. "*Ahh*, God. That. Yes. Keep doing that," I demand. I'm so close to coming, my core is grinding onto him, and my lace panties are soaked through. Oh God, I'm probably leaving wet marks all over the front of his jeans. I don't care right now though.

Bray chuckles as he continues his torture to my body. "You know, you're the best girlfriend I've ever had, Reilly," he declares.

"I'm the only girlfriend you've ever had, idiot."

"Yeah, but you're still the best," he says as his lips return to mine. I need to move this party inside, preferably to my bed, or shower—either one is fine with me.

Oh God, this kiss is something else. I feel the wall behind me fall away, and the next minute, I'm floating. Bray pulls back, and his hold around my back tightens as he clears his throat.

"*Arghh*, why'd you stop?" I am not impressed with the change of events.

"*Ahh*, that'd probably be for my benefit, Reilly Lili."

Oh shit, my eyes widen at Bray. I've just been caught making out at the front door like a teenager by my mum. "Shit, fuck, shit," I curse my luck as I untangle myself from Bray and get my feet back on the ground.

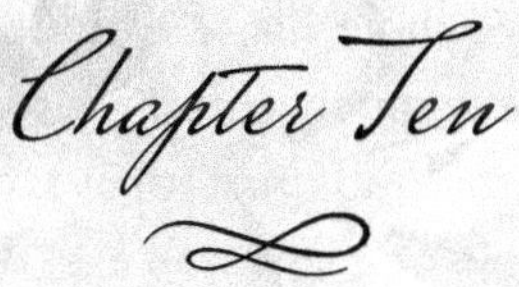

# Chapter Ten

*Bray*

WELL, this is not awkward at all. Reilly climbs down and lands on her feet in front of me. Turning, she goes to step to the side, but I take hold of her hips, keeping her in place. Right in front of me. There are some things that her mother should never see, my hard-on being one of them.

Reilly looks back at me over her shoulder and smirks. She knows exactly why I don't want her to move just yet. We need to get junior under control first. Reaching my hand out around Reilly, I hold it out to her mum.

"Hi, Mrs. Reynolds, I'm Bray. It's nice to meet you." I wait for her to shake my hand. She pushes Reilly aside, squeezing her way between us and hugs me.

"There's no need for such formalities. You can call me Lynne. Welcome," she says as she steps back. "Come in, come in," she continues as she grabs my hand and pulls me through the door. I look at Reilly, who is just staring at me with an *I told you so* face.

At least junior recognised the mum hug and retreated really quickly, saving me from a very embarrassing and uncomfortable moment. It's been a long time since I've had a mum hug, a really fucking long time, and Reilly's mum just hugged me like she's known me my whole life. I wouldn't say no to one of those again—I was very much a mumma's boy growing up.

Zac was always stoic and quiet for as long as I can remember and Ella was the apple of everyone's eye, daddy's little girl, the family princess. Not much has changed there. She's still the family princess.

I let Lynne pull me through the house. It's a nice family home. As I'm dragged through the hallways, I can see tons of pictures on the walls. They are mostly of the twins and who I assume is their brother. I pass pictures where I can't make out which twin is which. We end up in the kitchen where Lynne deposits me at the counter.

"Sit down, love. Now, Reilly didn't tell me she was bringing anyone home, so you will have to excuse the mess and my unpreparedness."

I look around the pristine kitchen, and there is not a thing out of place. It's a large kitchen with oak doors and white bench-tops, and stainless steel appliances. I seek out Reilly because I honestly am at a loss for words. For once in my life, I don't know what to say. Why the fuck am I so nervous? My leg starts jittering under the counter. I get antsy when I get nervous, which is rarely ever. I'd usually just head to the gym and hit something when I feel like this, but that is not a possibility here.

As my gaze connects with Reilly's, something inside me settles. It's odd because I usually need to fight, run, or work out until I collapse when I get jittery like this. For some kind of calmness to come over me just because I've locked eyes with her makes me think I might have had one too many hits to the head, and they are finally catching up with me.

"Mum, we aren't staying. I'm just going to go change and then we're going out with Holly," she explains.

"Oh, nonsense, Reilly. You go get ready. I'll look after your friend here." Her mum waves her off.

"Do not make him food, Mum. We don't want him getting too comfortable here," Reilly says as she turns and walks out of the kitchen, leaving me alone with her mum. That's brave of her. If she thinks I'm not going to pull out all the charm to win her mother over, she clearly does not know me very well.

"What would you like to drink, love? I've got soft drinks, coffee, tea? I don't have any beer, sorry. If I'd known you were coming, I would have catered better for your visit."

"Oh, you don't need to cater for me, Lynne. I'll have a water if it's not too much trouble," I say, giving her my full smile, dimples and all.

"Of course." She busies herself filling a glass with ice and then water from the refrigerator. She places the cup down in front of me and then returns to the fridge, pulling out some sort of cake slice looking deliciousness.

"I don't have much, but I made this fresh this morning, chocolate mint slice. Here, try some," she says as she shoves a huge slice in front of me.

Normally, I would not go for this type of treat; I'm very careful about what I put into my body. But I don't have another fight for a few weeks now—I can afford to let myself go a little.

I take a huge forkful of the slice and moan. "Oh my God, this is good, Lynne. Really fucking good," I say around another mouthful of slice.

I then take note that I just cursed in front of Reilly's mum on the first visit here. "Shit, sorry, I didn't mean to curse. It's just really good slice," I say, hoping she won't hold it against me.

Lynne laughs, "Do not sensor yourself for me, love. I've been around longer than you. There is nothing you can say that will shock me, trust me."

I smile as I take another bite of the slice. I could really get used to this kind of catering. "Can Reilly cook like this? Because if so, I might just have to whisk her off to Vegas tonight and marry her," I confess. The idea sounds appealing—I'd like to see her try to run and hide once I get a ring on her finger.

Where the fuck are these thoughts coming from? I have no idea. Fucking hits to the head, they must be catching up. Or maybe it's sappy Zac rubbing off on me. His happy and in love, nothing can bring him down attitude is enough to rub off on the grinch.

"You might want to hold off that proposal, Romeo.

Reilly doesn't cook or bake." Lynne laughs. "That's a shame," I pout.

"So, you and Reilly. How long has that been happening?" she questions. I'm surprised it took this long for her to bring out the questions.

Driving to the restaurant with Reilly next to me is painful. I have to mentally remind myself to keep my eyes on the road. She's wearing a black dress, or the hankie she is passing off as a fucking dress. It's high up on her chest—there is no cleavage showing whatsoever—but that does not distract from her impressive rack being on full display, the material hugging and caressing her breasts just like my hands are itching to do.

The dress is short—her long, lean legs on display. And then

there's the shoes. I can't wait for dinner to be over so I can take her home and have her in nothing but those fucking stilettos.

My hand rests on her thigh, my fingers absently stroking up and down the smooth skin. Skin I want to lick, suck, and bite all over. Her skin pebbles with goosebumps under my fingers. I don't miss her slight squirm and the way she squeezes her thighs together.

"You cold, babe?" I ask her.

She glares at me. "You know damn well I'm not bloody cold. I'm horny, Bray—so freaking horny that if you don't pull this car over and help a girl out, I am going to excuse myself to the bathroom when we get to this restaurant and help myself."

I don't know if she is serious or not right now, but I'm not taking the chance. I find a side road and turn down it, pulling the car over. I don't say anything.

I unclip my seatbelt then lean across and unclip hers. I'm silent as my hand slides up her legs; she's not shy as she spreads her legs as wide as she can in her seat. My hand slides up under her dress and I'm shocked when I'm met with bare skin.

"Fuck, Reilly, you're not wearing panties," I groan out.

"*Mmm*, I didn't want panty lines in my dress."

That's her answer, she didn't want fucking panty lines.

"How do you expect me to sit through dinner, knowing you're bare under this dress? To know that my dessert is ready and waiting for me?"

I slam two fingers into her warm, wet pussy. My mouth salivates. I can remember the taste of her on my tongue. Reilly arches off the seat, pushing herself against my hand. I use my thumb to circle her clit while pumping in and out of her. Her moans fill the car; her scent surrounds me. My cock is fucking hard; junior wants to come out and join the party.

"I can smell you. I can feel how warm and wet your pussy is

for me. The way it's strangling my fingers, I can't wait to feel this pussy strangle my cock again."

She responds to my words so well, moving her pelvis in time with my fingers pumping. She grinds down on my thumb that continues its slow torturous circles around her clit.

"I'm going to bury my cock so far inside this pussy, you

won't know where I end and you begin; we will be fused together. Do you want that? Do you want my cock inside this hungry little pussy of yours?" I don't expect her to answer but she does.

"Now, I want it now, Bray."

"Demanding little thing when you're horny, aren't you? You can't have my cock now. You're going to come on my hand now, Reilly. Then you will sit through the whole of dinner knowing that by the end of the night, my cock will be buried deep inside your cunt."

"*Argh*, why can't I have it now? I need it," she argues. She's so close to coming though. I can feel her body quaking, trembling all over, the urgency in her movements increasing.

"Be a good girl, Reilly, and come for me now," I demand, my voice husky and filled with need. She does not let me down. She comes all over my fingers, her screams of pleasure music to my fucking ears. I ease up my strokes as she comes down from her orgasmic bliss.

Her cheeks are rosy and her face a picture of pure bliss and relaxation. I ease my fingers out of her, putting them straight to my mouth. Now it's my turn to moan. Her taste is just as fucking sweet and delicious as I remember. I take my time licking all of her juices off my fingers, savouring the taste.

"Thank you," I say to her as I gently kiss her lips. "You're welcome?" she questions.

I can't help but laugh as I pull the seatbelt over her and

buckle her back in. "Let's hope this dinner goes fast so I can get you home and naked in my bed."

As I'm buckling my seatbelt, Reilly halts my movement, grabbing my arm. "Wait, don't you want me to, you know, return the favour?" she asks, waving her hand in the direction of my very obvious cock.

"As much as I would love that, the next time I come is going to be when my cock is buried inside your pussy," I declare.

"*Ahh*, okay then." She lets go of my arm and settles into the seat. "You're really good at that, by the way."

I laugh. "What kind of boyfriend would I be if I wasn't? I can't have my girlfriend left unsatisfied and wanting, now can I? That would not be good for my rep."

"Don't you think you're wearing out that whole boyfriend/girlfriend title thing already?" She smiles.

"Probably, we should go to Vegas and get married by Elvis, then I can move on to calling you my wife already. Also, I look fucking great in a tux." My suggestion is not received well.

"Please tell me you are joking and haven't gone all grade-A crazy on me already. I'm barely accepting that you have the boyfriend label, Bray. There is no way in hell you're getting promoted to husband label after one day of actual dating. Who does that anyway? That's crazy. Like straight jacket kind of crazy. Should I call Zac now and tell him he needs to have you scheduled? Are you sick?" She finishes her rambling with the back of her hand against my forehead.

"Not sick, babe. Relax, it was a joke." I watch as her body begins to relax before I tack on the "mostly" to the end of my sentence. She glares at me. I think I need to remind myself that this one is a flight risk; I need to think before I speak a bit more. It was a joke though; I couldn't actually fly her to Vegas to marry her tonight. I wouldn't be able to get a jet booked until at least tomorrow.

*Chapter Eleven*

## REILLY

THIS DINNER IS the worst double date I have ever been on with Holly. I've been sitting here bored out of my mind, listening to her date drone on and on about being a sports teacher. Newsflash, my twin sister is a freaking teacher. I don't need a play by play on your job, mate.

I'm also waiting for Bray to reach his boiling point. I can tell he's holding back. I've seen the death glare he's been giving the guy each time his eyes spend way too much time on my breasts. Why? I have no idea. Holly's are literally identical—we have the same size and shape breasts.

His leering creeps me out majorly, but I try not to let it show. I'm trying to distract Bray from the fact that he wants to reach across the table and ring this dude's neck. At least that's the vibes I'm getting from him. By the looks Holly keeps shooting me, she is getting the same vibes.

I slide my hand up his thigh. I'm beginning to come around to this whole boyfriend/girlfriend thing more and more. If Bray's my boyfriend, that means I get to touch him as much as I want, wherever I want, and that is very appealing. To have twenty-four hours, seven days a week access to his body, a girl could only be so lucky. Oh, wait! I'm that girl. I'm that lucky, *huh*.

My hand continues to travel up his thigh until I reach the inner most upper part of his thigh. He shifts in his seat. My hand continues its slow pursuit of junior. I finally reach my target and rub my hand over his crotch. I keep my touch light, almost featherlight. I can feel his cock harden under my fingers.

Bray leans in and whispers in my ear, "You're playing with fire, baby."

I smile back at him, challenging him to bring whatever he has. At least my distraction technique has worked. He is not looking like he's ready to jump the table just yet.

I pick up my glass of wine with my free hand and gulp a mouthful. Before I can even swallow, Bray's fingers slam inside me. And the suddenness of the intrusion makes me choke. Wine comes spitting out of my mouth, projecting all the way across the table and landing across the front of the shirt Holly's date is wearing.

I'm still recovering, Bray's fingers still buried in my pussy, when Holly's date pushes his chair back and jumps up. "What the fuck? Are you a fucking idiot?" he yells in my direction.

Just as fast as those fingers were inside me, they were ripped out, as Bray jumps over the table. Like literally freaking ninja jumps over the table. It all happens so fast. I haven't even recovered from my choking episode and Bray has Holly's date by the throat.

I can see his body vibrating from here. Holly moves around the table to my side; she does not do well with confrontation or violence.

"Who the fuck do you think you're talking to like that, fucker?" Bray growls into his face. He doesn't give him time to answer, if he could come up with an answer. The guy's motionless, frozen like a deer caught in headlights.

"I'll tell you who, my fucking girlfriend, my queen, that's who. Nobody talks to her like that and goes unscathed."

Holly's eyes widen as she mouths the words to me. *Girlfriend? Queen?* I shrug in answer because honestly, how does one respond to that? I think this boyfriend label has definitely gone to his ego-induced head.

"*Ahh*, baby, you need to tone it down a notch." I put on my sugary sweet voice and walk around the table. It's nice that Bray was quick to stick up for me, but I've been sticking up for myself for a very long time now and I don't plan on stopping just because I have Bray in my corner.

I push myself between the two men, facing Bray. He looks at my hands on his chest and a confused look crosses his features, then he brings his eyes to meet mine. "Bray, I need you to let go of the douche, please."

He lets go but does not take his eyes off the guy. He hooks his right arm around my waist and turns to lead me away.

"Wait a sec, I just have to do one thing," I say sweetly to him. He lets go of me. I turn and walk up to the douche and without saying a word, I bring my knee up to meet his balls. He drops to the ground, screaming out curses.

"Okay, now I'm ready to go," I tell Bray and walk past him to Holly, who is still standing on the other side of the table with wide eyes. I grab her hand, pick up both of our purses and walk out of the entrance. I expect Bray to be right behind us, except when I get outside, he's not there.

"What on earth was that, Rye?" Holly asks. "Your date was a douche."

"No, not that part. I got that loud and clear. What on earth have you gone and done to Bray?"

"What do you mean? I haven't done anything." I shrug.

"Rye, that guy really *likes* you, like, *like likes* you." She uses air quotes around all the likes.

"I know." I smile. Because he really does like me. I'm a little fonder of him than I'm willing to admit right now too.

"Rye, he thinks you're his girlfriend. You can't play around with this one. He's practically Alyssa's family now." I know where she is coming from. It's my own fault my twin sister thinks I'm so incapable of having a normal relationship. But I am going to give this a good, hot shot.

Just in secret, mostly.

"I'm not playing around, Holl. We agreed to give the whole exclusive dating thing a go. Bray has this thing about being a boyfriend for the first time ever and he's taking it a bit far, that's all. But we are keeping this under wraps. You can't tell anyone yet. I'm not ready for that."

She nods her head. I know I can trust her—she is the one person other than my mum and dad who I trust with anything. "Sure, I won't tell anyone." Then a huge grin spreads across her face.

"What the hell are you so happy about?" I ask.

"Oh, you know, just that you finally have a steady boyfriend. I honestly never thought I'd see the day. Bray, you are dating Bray, Rye. Have you seen the guy?" Holly waggles her eyebrows up and down.

I laugh. "Yes, I have seen him. All of him. And let me tell you, if that's the package my future husband comes with, I'm okay with that," I tell her.

"Wait, your future husband? Oh God, please tell me you are not pregnant, Reilly Lili!" Oh great, the teacher voice has made an appearance.

It's also at this precise moment that Bray decides to catch up to us. Can my luck get any crappier?

"I'm certain my boys are good swimmers, babe. I mean,

how can they not be." He motions his hands up and down his body, my eyes following their movement. "They aren't good enough to swim through rubber though."

He addresses Holly, "She's one hundred percent not knocked up, Holly."

"Wait, what makes you think you're the only guy who's patted my kitty in the last few weeks?" I ask him. He totally is, but he doesn't know that.

Bray's jaw tightens and clenches, his eyes narrow. Oh, he's mad. I have to work really hard to maintain my poker face and not laugh at his reaction. Then as quickly as he got mad, his cocky ass grin emerges.

"I know you haven't been with anyone else. Any other fucker would pale in comparison to me. You and I both know that, babe." He adds a wink on the end for good measure.

I shrug my shoulders. "*Meh*, I've had better." I fake out boredom.

"Challenge accepted," he says then turns to Holly. "Holly, do you need a ride home?"

"No, thank God. I could not think of anything worse than being stuck in a car with you two lovebirds. I'll see you tomorrow, Rye." Holly hugs me. "Bye, Bray, good luck," she says as she walks over to her car.

Bray grabs my hand, leading me to his car. "You and I are in for one hell of a night, babe. You questioned my manhood—junior was very offended. I'm going to spend all night erasing the memory of any other fucker."

Right, I offended his cock, I'm sure. "*Huh*, you might want to stop off for some energy drinks then, hunny."

As he's about to retort, his phone starts blaring out "Hey Brother" by Avicii. "Sorry, it's Zac. I have to take this," he says, as he answers the call at the same time as he opens my door.

"Yeah?" That's how he answers the call, and that's all I hear of it. He hangs up before he makes his way around the car.

"We have to make a quick stop at the club. Zac's not going in tonight, so I have to do a few things. Do you want me to drop you at my place, or do you want to come with?" he asks. It doesn't escape my attention that dropping me home to my own house was not an option.

"*Ahh*, I'll come to the club. I've got some things to do there anyway."

By the time we make it to the club, I have a whole list of text messages with demands from Zac. Apparently, he's not planning on coming in for a few days, and I need to make sure Bray doesn't burn the place down.

"Does Zac often take days off?" I ask Bray.

"I've never known him to take a day off before. Why?" "Lyssa must be in a worse way than she was letting on

if Zac's staying home with her. I should call her."

"I stayed at Zac's last night. Alyssa hasn't come out of their bedroom yet. I think maybe just give them some time. Zac's not about to let anyone near her right now anyway."

"It's funny you think he would be able to stop me from seeing her." I laugh.

"*Shh*, I do not want to be caught in here, Bray," I whisper.

We spent the last few hours at the club, each working on our own things. We ended up back in Bray's room at Zac's place. He said something about needing to stay here so he could be around for when Zac needed him. Down came some more of those damn bricks. He is probably one of the most family-oriented men I've met. There is nothing he wouldn't do for his siblings. All three of the Williamson siblings are like that though; they are a very tight-knit crew. Don't get me wrong, I'd do anything for Holly too—she is my ride or die. I'm just learning that there is so much more to Bray than his cocky attitude and good looks, so much more. I'm not too sure my heart can keep up. The more time I spend with him, the more I'm liking the whole boyfriend label.

"Babe, no one is going to hear us, trust me. And if they do, you really think they're going to barge in here?" he asks as he pulls the zip on the side of my dress down.

"Have you met your brother, Bray? Of course, he would barge in here."

"Yeah, he probably would. So, you're going to have to be quiet. Think you can hold in those screams, baby?"

I'm not so sure I can. My body is already on fire, and all he is doing is stripping my dress off. Bray slowly pulls my dress up my body.

"Lift," he commands. I lift my arms above my head, and the dress follows.

Bray drops the dress to the floor and steps back. His eyes travel up and down my body, slowly, so very slowly. My skin erupts in goosebumps; he's not even touching me and yet my body is reacting to him, for him.

"Damn, babe. You had nothing at all on under that dress? All night? And I'm just learning of this now? Next time, I'm going to have to inspect what's underneath your clothing, before we leave the house." He shakes his head.

"I had a dress on Bray, I wasn't naked all night."

"Babe, I don't care that you weren't wearing underwear—you can wear whatever you like. I pity any fucker who thinks they can benefit from your choice of clothing though. I will not hesitate to make sure everyone knows that you're mine, that I'm the one who gets to take you home to bed. That I'm the one who gets to do unspeakable things with this body of yours."

He slowly steps closer to me, trailing his fingertips up and down the inside of my arm, ever so lightly. He's still fully dressed and I'm completely naked. There is something very erotic in that. But that's not what I want right now; what I want is his body. I place my hands underneath his shirt, close my eyes and immerse myself in the feel of his skin—warm and hard. I run my hands over the grooves of his abs, silently counting each one as my hands make their way up to his chest.

"This shirt needs to disappear now," I tell him as I drag my hands back down to his waist.

"Yes, ma'am," he says as he steps back and pulls his shirt over the back of his head. Why that move is so damn sexy, I have no idea. But it is, his biceps bulging with the movements. *Mmm*, I want to lick him all over. The thought *I licked it so it's mine* comes to mind and I laugh a little.

"Not that I don't love hearing your laugh, babe, because I do. But that's not the reaction I was hoping for when I start stripping in front of you."

"Oh, what reaction would you prefer?"

"A *oh my God, Bray, your body is so defined. I can't wait to jump on it and defile you.* Or *wow, Bray, you are the sexiest man I've ever seen.* Something along those lines would suffice."

"Honestly, my first thought was that I wanted to lick you all over, and then I thought—*I licked it so it's mine.* Holly and I used to fight over the last cookie or lollies or whatever, and whoever licked it first got to keep it. So, I want to lick you first, so I get to keep you." I slam my lips shut; I cannot believe I just told him I wanted to keep him.

Bray grabs me by the back of my neck and brings his lips so close to mine and says, "Well, *I've already licked you, babe, so you're mine.* And I plan on licking you a lot fucking more."

I don't get time to respond before his lips are on mine. His tongue pushes its way into my mouth and I greedily take it. I want it all, all of what he has to give.

I need more. I climb his body, literally jump up and wrap my legs around his waist. He doesn't miss a beat, placing his hands on my ass and holding me to him—the rough feel of the denim on my core sending shivers all through me. I attack his mouth and pull his head as close as I can get. No matter how hard I pull or push myself into him, I just can't get close enough.

"*Argh*," I groan. I want more. I don't know what I want or need at this point. I just know I want more of him.

"Damn, babe, if you keep grinding on me like that, I'm going to come in my pants like a fucking teenager." "I don't care. I need more, Bray," I confess.

The next thing I know I'm flying through the air and landing on the mattress. Bray smirks as he stands at the end of the bed, staring down at me. He unclasps his belt buckle.

"How much more, Reilly? Tell me exactly what you want." He unbuttons his jeans, pulling the zip down. I'm so distracted by what he's doing, and by thinking about what's under those jeans, that I forgot what the question was.

"Tell me, Reilly. What. Do. You. Want?" he demands.

I lick my lips, hungry for a taste of him. "I want you to fulfill every fantasy I've ever had, Bray. I want everything."

Bray tilts his head at me and thinks quietly for a bit before finally speaking. "Do you trust me?" he asks.

"With my body, yes. With my heart, no," I answer honestly.

He nods and smirks. "We'll work on your heart another time, because I will win that. I win everything."

Bray removes the belt from the loop of his jeans and holds it in his right hand, dangling down his side. He is the picture of perfection right now. Shirtless, all those tanned, toned muscles on display. Tattoos running up and down his arms and across his chest. There's script across one side of his chest. I'm not close enough to work out what it says, but I plan to read that writing with my tongue as soon as possible. His denim jeans are undone and hanging loose, black briefs underneath with the tip of his cock peeking out the top—shiny metal sparkling at me and begging me to touch it. His voice breaks through my thoughts.

"Will you do everything I say, Reilly?" His question

throws me; it's not what I was expecting. I must show my confusion and rebuttal to that thought because he quickly adds, "In the bedroom, right here, right now, will you do everything I tell you?"

Immediately, I reply, "Yes," while nodding my head—maybe a little too eagerly.

Bray's smirk comes out, then his features harden. Something flickers in his eyes. "Good, get on the floor. On your knees, now!"

## *Chapter Twelve*

BRAY

"GET ON THE FLOOR. On your knees, now!" I demand. I watch as her body visibly shakes from the command. Then like the good little girl she is she gets up, crawls to the end of the bed and climbs down—sitting on the floor right in front of me on her knees.

I wish I had a fucking camera, because this right here is a Kodak moment if I ever saw one. Goddamn beauty like you've never seen before. Her pale skin is flushed and covered in goosebumps. Her full breasts heaving up and down with her panting. Her red hair a tumbled mess down her back. Her green eyes staring up at me, with a mixture of excitement and need.

"Hands behind your back," I command.

She obeys immediately. I don't think she knows just how much she wants to submit to me. I'm not really one for games in the bedroom. I've dabbled with toys and tie downs, etc., but usually it's just a night to get lost in a beautiful woman and get off. With Reilly, it's different though. I want to consume her. I want to be her whole world. I want to make her out of her mind with need for me.

Walking behind her, I pick up both of her wrists. Leaning down, I whisper into her ear, "Good girl." I wrap my belt around her wrists, giving it a tug to ensure they're secure. She won't be getting out of that anytime soon.

I run my hands up her arms and down over the front of her shoulders, until they finally land on her breasts. Filling my hands with the glorious softness, I give her nipples a pinch. Her back arches as she pushes her breasts into my palms. Little moans escape her mouth.

"You need to be quiet, Reilly. You wouldn't want anyone walking in and finding you in this position, would you now?"

She doesn't speak but shakes her head no. Pushing her hair to one side, I lean into her neck and inhale. I can't get enough of her; she smells like a fucking delicious concoction of fruity flavours. I bite down on her neck, then lick over the bite mark to soothe the spot.

She's so fucking responsive, the way she bends her neck further allowing me more access to her delicate skin. I move my left hand down over the smooth skin of her stomach. I don't stop until I reach my target. Using my middle finger, I glide it through the lips of her pussy. She is wet—beyond wet—she's fucking drenched.

"*Ahh*, oh God," she cries out as I tease light strokes over her and around her clit. Every few strokes, I allow my finger to tease her entrance. As she attempts to move her pelvis out and into my hand, I pull back.

"You're so wet, baby. I fucking love how your body responds to my touch." I continue to pet her pussy for a few more minutes while simultaneously biting down on her neck and tweaking her nipple. I keep my touch light and teasing. I know she's slowly building up to an orgasm. I can feel her body begin to tighten and quake.

"Do you want to come, Reilly?" I ask.

"Oh God, yes, Bray. Don't you dare stop."

"Wasn't planning on it, babe. How bad do you want to come right now?"

"I want it more than you can imagine," she moans out.

I chuckle, I don't need to imagine. I'm getting the show from the front seat. "Beg," I tell her.

"What?" she turns her head looking at me, confused.

"I said beg. You want to come? Beg me to make you come." My tone leaves no room for argument.

"I'm not begging you," she declares. I move my finger off her pussy and instead stroke it up the inside of her thigh.

"If you want to come, beg," I remind her.

She bucks her pelvis out, trying to realign my finger with her centre. It's not going to work. I want to hear her beg me; I want her to need me, then I want to deliver and prove to her that I'm going to be the one giving her everything she needs from now on.

"Oh. God. Please," she spits out.

I chuckle. I knew she wouldn't be able to hold out on me for long. "Please what, baby? What do you need?" I stop my movements with my finger just millimetres to her clit.

"*Ahh*, God, Bray. Make me come now, damn it!" she yells.

So much for being quiet. "Good girl," I whisper into her ear before clamping down on that sweet spot on her neck just behind her ear. I pull and pinch at her nipple as I slam two fingers into her wet, warm pussy.

"*Mmm*, I fucking love the feel of your pussy. I could leave my fingers buried in here twenty-four seven." Using my thumb, I circle her clit, applying just the right amount of pressure I've come to know she responds to.

"I want you to drench my hand in your juices, Reilly. Come, now." Whether it's a coincidence or not, I don't know, but her body obeys. She screams out my name as her body convulses, her pussy strangles my fingers and she pushes her clit down harder into my thumb. It's a sight of beauty, watching her fall apart.

"Fucking perfect," I tell her after her body has recovered. I remove my fingers and bring them to her lips. "Clean them."

I expect her to recoil or hesitate—she does neither. She sucks the digits between her lips, swirling her tongue around them. Fuck me, she's sucking on my fingers like they're my cock. "See how fucking good you taste? I can't wait to lick your pussy clean before I get it all wet and dirty all over again."

Standing up, she shutters as I make sure she has her balance before I walk around to the front of her. She looks up at me, satisfaction written all over her face.

"You good?" I ask, needing to make sure she's good to continue this play of ours.

"*Uh-huh,*" she answers with a smile and a nod. "Want to keep going?"

"Absolutely," she agrees.

The moment I get her agreement, I slip my shoes off and pull my jeans and briefs off in one swoop. Junior comes bouncing up, standing straight and pointing in the direction of the woman who has captured his sole attention.

Stroking my cock a few times, I step closer to her. "Fuck," I murmur as I watch her lick her full, plump lips. I want those lips wrapped around my cock. "I want to shove my cock down your throat. I want to feel the back of your throat as you swallow me."

She nods at me, giving me the go ahead that she's on board with the idea. I'm going to need more than a gesture though; I want to hear the fucking words.

"Tell me, Reilly, do you want my cock in your mouth?" I ask her.

She nods her head up and down.

"I'm gonna need you to use your words, Reilly. Tell me, how bad do you want me to put my cock down your throat?"

"Damn it, Bray. I want your cock in my mouth, now. Please." She adds the please onto the end as a second thought.

I smile. "Thought you'd never ask," I tell her as I place my cock at the seam of her lips. Reilly puts her tongue out, licking the tip and swirling around the piercing. Just the slightest touch of her tongue is sending jolts of pleasure through me. I have to force myself not to slam my cock right down her throat.

Inching my cock into her mouth slowly, inch by fucking inch, I realize this is what heaven is. Reilly's warm, wet, welcoming mouth. My attempts to ease in go out the window when she sucks and slides her own mouth all the way down my shaft.

"Fuck Reilly, shit!" I groan as she swallows with my cock in her throat. What the fuck is that sorcery? I slide back out and slam in again, holding her head to keep her steady while gradually picking up the pace. Fuck, if I keep this up, I'm going to come down her throat, which I don't want to do. Well, not this time anyway.

I slow my movements down and pull out of her mouth. Her lips are swollen and inviting, begging for more of my cock. "Fuck, babe, that mouth of yours is a dangerous weapon," I tell her, picking her up and placing her over the edge of the bed, face down.

She turns her head to look back over her shoulder and smiles at me. "You're welcome."

Stepping between her legs, I nudge them open further with my feet. I kneel down behind her, bringing her pussy in front of my face. I know I should drag this out a bit, but I'm fucking starving for a taste of her. Slowly, my tongue drags from the front of her slit right up to the back.

"*Mmm*, you are the most delicious thing I've ever eaten."

Her body is squirming; I insert a finger just at the entrance of her pussy while pressing my thumb over the bud of her ass. Swirling my tongue around her clit, I keep my fingers still, just applying pressure. Reilly pushes back into my hand, increasing the pressure placed on her two holes, as I continue my torture on her clit.

Her juices run down my hand—she's fucking drenched. "Please, Bray, I need more. Give me more, please." She's begging on her own free will now. I fucking love hearing her beg for me.

Standing up, I pick up my jeans, pull out my wallet and retrieve a condom. "Don't worry, babe. I'm going to give you everything you'll ever need," I tell her while I sheath my cock.

Lining my cock up to her entrance, I wait before pushing in. "Is this friendly vagina of yours going to play nice with junior, Reilly?" I ask with a laugh, not waiting for her answer before I slam into home. I still as my cock bottoms out inside her.

"Fuck me," I grunt. "You're so fucking tight, babe. It's like your pussy is trying to strangle the life out of junior."

I make my movement, sliding out slower and allowing her inner walls time to adjust to the intrusion. Slamming back into her, I grab hold of her hips.

"Hold tight, babe, this is going to be quick and rough," I warn, just before I pick up my pace and slam as hard and fast as I can into her from behind. Her moans are music to my ears, encouraging me to go harder and faster.

"Fuck, I'm going to come. I need you with me, babe," I tell her. Reaching a hand underneath her, I find her clit and press down hard—stroking, pinching and circling.

"Oh God, Bray. I'm..." She doesn't finish her sentence, her

body seizing up and going stiff, tremors shaking through her. Her pussy gets even tighter, if that's possible, pulsing and milking my cock as I come right along with her.

I pump a few more times. "Fuck, Reilly."

I'm lost for any other words. I almost fall onto her before I catch myself and roll onto the bed next to her. Turning to face me, she says, "That was, wow. Just, wow."

"Yeah, it was," I reply while untying the belt from her hands, rubbing both of her wrists, and inspecting for any deep markings. The belt cut into her skin a fair bit, but nothing a bit of arnica cream and some bracelets won't cover.

Picking her up, I lay her under the blankets and climb in next to her before wrapping her up in my arms. Kissing her forehead, I confess, "I really fucking like being your boyfriend, Reilly. I think I've got this gig mastered already."

"I like you being my hidden boyfriend, Bray. What makes you think you've mastered the art of boyfriend in—I don't know, what's it been—five hours?"

I ignore her little *hidden* part, hidden my ass. There is not a soul around who I don't want to scream out at and tell them of my newfound title. "Well, I've got you in my bed completely satisfied from a really fucking good fuck. Now I'm going to spend the night spooning you and holding you as tight as I can, and not just so you can't sneak out on me either. No, I'm going to hold onto you because I actually want to keep hold of you."

"*Mmm*, I wasn't planning on sneaking out," she says around a yawn.

"Go to sleep, babe. I'll still be here holding you when you wake up." I kiss her forehead and settle in next to her, inhaling her sweet, fruity scent.

I have one of the best fucking sleeps I've ever had.

〜

I'm in the gym hitting the weights at five in the morning when Zac walks in and turns the music down. I usually have it blaring while I work out. Zac had the room soundproofed when he got tired of hearing me working out at odd hours. Some nights, when I was younger, I'd spend all night working out just to expel the built-up energy that hit me every now and then.

"Did your house burn down?" he asks. "Nope," I reply and continue my reps.

"Then what the fuck are you doing here at this fucking hour?" He tries to portray that it's shitty I'm here. He's not mad though—I know he'd never say no to having me here.

"I wanted to use your gym, so I stayed here last night," I lie.

"Fuck off, you have a better fucking gym in your own house."

"Yeah, but I was tired after doing your job at your club last night and didn't feel like driving home." I put the bar down.

Zac doesn't say anything, just stares at me, with those creepy know-it-all eyes of his.

"Fine, I stayed because I was worried about you and Alyssa, okay? Are you happy now, fucker? How is she?" My confession turns his creepy look into one of appreciation.

"She's scared. I had her take two weeks leave from work. We're staying in until after the holidays. I think the safest place for her right now is here."

"Good idea. Anything I can do?" I ask.

"Yeah, find me that fucking bitch. Other than that, try not to burn my club down."

"I'll do my best to keep the club as the pristine and well-oiled machine you have it." I salute his back as he retreats to the door. Just before he opens the door, he turns back to me.

"Oh, and Bray?"

"Yeah?"

"Next time you bring Reilly home, you might want to

consider that your bedroom walls are not soundproof, like these ones."

"Oh, I know." I smirk.

Zac shakes his head. "I won't protect you from Alyssa if you hurt her friend, Braydon."

Oh shit, he brought out the full name shit. I'm actually a little scared of how far he'd go to help her castrate me if she asked. He'd probably do it himself, fucker. "I don't plan on hurting her. I just plan on keeping her," I tell him.

"Sure, that's not the same thing. Poor girl, if she's getting stuck with your crazy fucking ass."

"What can I say? The girls all want to be with me and the boys all want to be me." I shrug as I wipe the sweat from my face with the towel.

# Chapter Thirteen

REILLY

I'VE BEEN SNEAKING AROUND with Bray as much as I possibly can in the last three weeks. The fact that he's been filling in for Zac around the club doesn't hurt—we've found all sorts of closets and offices to get to know each other better.

One time, he even picked me up, threw me over his shoulder and dragged me down to the basement. Let's just say, the three rounds I spent in the cage with Bray, we both came out winners. That man has stamina like I've never seen before. I honestly don't know how he does it. I know he spends all morning working out in Zac's gym. Then he comes into the club and works and still finds time to fuck me senseless every day.

I've managed to avoid being caught sneaking in and out of Zac's apartment most nights and mornings as well. I thought for sure Zac was more observant and would have caught me by now, but I guess he's so hyper-focused on Alyssa he doesn't know what's going on around him.

The couple of days over Christmas I didn't stay with Bray, I had at least a dozen messages and calls from him, not to mention the late-night video calls. He even managed to get me off over the phone—okay, it was my hands and vibrator doing all the work—but it was his voice and the dirty things he would say that pushed me over the edge every sweet time.

It's New Year's Eve, the club's busiest night I've seen yet. I'm hyper-alert and anxiety riddles my body. Bray's fighting tonight; this is the first fight I have to watch him in since he's been my boyfriend. I'm torn on how I feel about him fighting. On one hand, it's hot as hell, and on the other, I really don't want to see him get hurt.

His cocky ass has assured me that he's winning this fight. It's not his abilities that I question. On some of those nights I've spent in my own bed, without him, I may have spent way more time than necessary watching YouTube videos of his fights. There's also the illegal, underground cage thing that worries me. How he's managed to stay out of jail this long, I have no idea.

I haven't expressed my fears to him, that one day he will be taken away. I've been trying to push those thoughts down and focus on the present. Like right now, I'm sitting in my office staring at a bloody bouquet of doughnuts.

Who the hell sends someone a bouquet of doughnuts? Bray Williamson, that's who. James, the one and only guy in this club who doesn't run the other way when he sees me. James, the bartender well on his way to earning best friend rights. That James, who is also about to get his ass kicked out of my office, is currently sitting on my desk laughing his ass off as he bites into a huge doughnut covered in pink icing and sprinkles.

He's also holding the card that came with the doughnuts out in front of him, as he mocks me, reading it aloud around mouthfuls of food.

"I hope these taste just a sweet as you do. You can eat your sweets now. I'll be devouring mine tonight," he laughs.

"Shut up, asshole, or I won't share any more with you," I warn.

He looks at the box then back up to me. "You can't possibly eat all of these on your own. You need my help, darl."

He's right. I don't know what Bray was thinking. There is no way one person can eat this many doughnuts. They aren't just your typical cinnamon doughnuts—no, these are extravagant. They're huge and in the shape of hearts and circles; some filled with jam, and others covered in icing of all colours and sprinkles. My mouth salivates just looking at the sweet sugary goodness.

"So, who's the guy who's been licking your kitty lately, *huh*?" James questions. "I can't wait till Bray finds out someone beat him to the cookie jar," he laughs.

I'm not quick enough to hide my smirk at his comment. Bray and I, surprisingly, have done a spectacular job of keeping our little relationship secret. The only people who know are my mum and Holly.

"Shut the front door, Reilly Reynolds!" James screeches.

"What?" My innocent *try to play it cool* attitude does not work on him.

"Don't what me! You're fucking Bray! As in, *the* Bray Williamson. Don't even try to lie to me, girlfriend." It's hard not to laugh as he points his half-eaten doughnut at me.

"I don't know what you're talking about."

*Deny, deny, deny.* I keep repeating the mantra in my head. I'm not sure if I'm ready to leave the little bubble Bray and I have created for ourselves just yet. I like that we get to keep us, just us. No one else sticking their two cents into what's happening in our relationship.

Then again, maybe, just maybe, if my friends knew that

Bray was mine, they'd stop making remarks about how much they want a turn at the pierced cucumber. When I say friends, I'm talking about Sarah—she's the only one who mentions it really. Alyssa is all about everything that is Zac. As she should be; that man treats her like a damn queen.

He even gave me uncontrolled access to that little magical black card of his at Christmas. He wanted to get Lyssa a new wardrobe because hers was destroyed by that psycho Caitlyn who has been stalking and tormenting her. I would really love to get my hands on that girl. I know Dean's had teams out searching high and low, but the bitch is a damn cockroach, hiding in nooks and crannies and unable to be found.

Bray has been stressed, spending way more time in the gym every morning than what I think is normal. He says it's because he's preparing for his fight. I've snuck down to the basement here to watch him train a few times. A sweaty, practically naked Bray is a fucking welcoming sight. I've heard his coach tell him he's overdoing it but Bray shrugs him off and says it's temporary.

He doesn't show it, but Bray worries a lot about his family. That's the reason we've been sneaking around Zac's apartment and not just hanging out at Bray's house. Bray wants to be close, in case he's needed. He doesn't trust that Caitlyn won't try something, even while Alyssa is staying in the penthouse with Zac. Neither of them has left the building for a few weeks.

They are both meant to be going back to work tonight, so I'm expecting to see Zac any minute now. Which means I need to get on with my night and get James and these doughnuts away from me.

"Earth to Reilly!" James waves a new doughnut he's holding—this one coated in chocolate icing and white sprinkles.

"What?"

"You were totally zoned out there. Thinking about lover boy Bray?"

"I'm not sleeping with Bray." I try my darndest to continue denying.

"Yes, you are. I don't know why you're not screaming that shit from the rooftops. If I had that boy, I'd be bragging left, right and centre to everyone and anything that would listen. I mean, look at him. He's what wet dreams are made of. Please, for the love of everything that's holy, tell me he is as good in bed as what I've imagined he would be?"

Okay, I know that Bray is one hundred percent about the vagina, but I can't seem to help the green-eyed monster appearing at James's comment. He's been imagining my boyfriend having sex.

"Stop, you need to stop thinking about my boyfriend that way if we are going to remain friends. Or at the very least, never mention those thoughts to me again," I tell him.

The smile that crosses his face is not the scared and intimidated look I was going for. I really need Holly to teach me her teacher voice tactics.

"I knew it!" James jumps up and down like an over- excited kid on Christmas morning. Then I realise the mistake I made, oh crap.

"Wait, you said boyfriend. This is more than I was thinking. I thought for sure you two have been bumping uglies, but I never imagined you'd actually do the impossible and lock down Braydon Williamson. Bloody hell, your vagina must be lined in gold or some shit."

"Are you done?" I ask, waiting for him to calm the fuck down.

"Oh, hunny, I have so much more."

"Well, it will have to wait. I have work to do, so do you."

"At least tell me one thing; inches, what are we talking

here?" He holds his hands out in front of him, slowly moving them apart further like he's measuring something.

"You want to know how big Bray's dick is? Go ask him yourself, perv."

"Oh, I have, many, many times. The bastard never gives me a straight answer."

I get up and hold the door open for him, waiting for him to get the hint he needs to leave now. It doesn't take too long. He stands, picking up two more doughnuts before walking out the door.

"This conversation is so not over, girl," he says as I shut the door behind him.

After an hour sitting in my office, half dreaming and fantasising about Bray and what I want to do to his body tonight, and half focusing on what I need to do for tonight, I get up and head down to the floor. I have one of the hottest bands in—Dawn. They've topped the Australia top thirty charts for three weeks in a row. I knew they would be big. I saw them on YouTube a few months back and booked them in for the New Year's Eve slot.

They released their single four weeks ago, and it blew up big time. I had to get Dean to arrange extra security, because the expected crowd this band is supposed to bring in is beyond what we can actually cater for here. I held off on releasing the tickets for tonight until just two weeks ago. I'm glad I did, because with Dawn's new status at the top of the charts, I priced the tickets higher and they sold out within an hour of being released.

As I'm heading down to the floor, Zac and Dean both rush past me. They don't stop to talk; they are in a zone. Zac looks furious. I wonder who peed in his Wheaties this time. Then it hits me, Alyssa, something is wrong with Alyssa.

I run to catch up with them. The elevator doors shut before I'm even close. Shit. Pulling out my phone, I try to call Alyssa, but the call rings out. Next, I try Sarah. She picks up on the first ring.

"Reilly, oh God, something's wrong. Alyssa's gone," she cries into the phone. My blood runs cold, my fingers tremble and I struggle not to drop the phone.

"What do you mean gone?"

"We were meant to meet for lunch; she didn't show so I called Zac, thinking he was monopolising her time again. Except she wasn't with him. I was going to go into the ER and ask for her, but Zac started tracking her and said she wasn't there and that he was going to find her."

That's a lot to process. "What do you mean he was tracking her? How's he tracking her?" I'm making my way back to my office to grab my things.

"I don't know; he said something about her ring. Oh God, Reilly, what if Caitlyn actually got to her? I feel so helpless right now."

"Zac will find her. If anyone can find her, it's him." I'm not sure if I'm trying to convince myself or her of this. One thing I do know is that Zac will burn the city down in order to find Alyssa. There is nothing he won't do for her.

"Sarah, I gotta hang up. I need to find someone who can do a semi-decent job of setting up for tonight so I can leave. Find Holly. I'll pick you both up from your place. We are going to find her."

"Okay."

"I'll see you soon," I say before hanging up.

I dial Bray's number. He takes a little longer to answer than Sarah did.

"Babe, is it me or junior who you're missing so soon?" He's overly chirpy for someone who should be going through his pre-fight routine. Which, according to him, is an all-day event, consisting of a deep tissue massage, rub downs and yoga, followed by spending time locked away alone in a room with headphones on and clearing his mind for an hour or two. The whole rub down part did not fly too well with me.

He doesn't sound like he's doing any of that right now though; he sounds like he's in a car.

"Bray, where are you?"

He takes a minute to reply, which tells me he's trying to come up with something. "*Ahh*, I just had to run an errand, babe. I'll be back at the club before you know it."

Run an errand my ass. "What the hell is going on with Alyssa, Bray? Where the fuck is she?" I demand.

He has to know something; he wouldn't have left the club for anything other than an emergency situation. The fact that he doesn't want to tell me just pisses me off more.

"Whoa, babe, calm down. It's going to be okay. I'm following Zac and Dean now. Zac has a tracker on her; he knows exactly where she is. Dean has some guys who will reach her quicker than we can, and they're already on their way to her. As soon as I know anything else, I'll let you know. I promise."

"Bray, where is she? Where are you heading to?" I want to know exactly where I need to get to. I'm walking out of the club and just about to get in the car.

"Babe, I need you to calm down. You're not driving anywhere while you're in this state."

I laugh. *Does the idiot think he can actually stop me?*

"Either you tell me or I'll find out another way," I say as I start my car.

"Fuck, shit. Reilly, please, you can't drive while you're panicked and freaked out. Turn the car off."

It's pretty clear he's not going to tell me where they're headed to, so I hang up on him.

I dial Sarah back.

"Have they found her?" she asks.

"They know where she is and are heading for her. Bray says Dean has some guys who are close and are on their way to her now."

"Fuck, Reilly, that bitch is crazy as fuck... who knows what she's capable of doing."

"I know. Did you get a hold of Holly?"

"Yeah, she should be here in about five minutes." "Good, I'll be there in fifteen. Be out front."

"Okay," she says as I hang up.

Shit, now to figure out how the hell we are going to find where these assholes are heading to. I'm reversing out when someone knocks on the passenger side window, making me jump a mile out of my seat in the process.

"What the fuck, James?" I scream at him as he opens the door and jumps in.

"I've got strict orders to ensure you arrive in Glenvale in one piece, without a hair out of place. Orders directly from Bray. I value my life way too much to not follow those orders."

"Glenvale, what the fuck. That's two hours away, James."

"I'm aware, so let's go. It's only one now, so we'll be able to make it back before the club starts getting busy tonight."

"I have to stop at Sarah's and pick up her and Holly." I reverse out, my hands shaking a little from a mixture of fear and anger. Fear of something happening to my friend and anger that I can't do shit about it right now.

*Chapter Fourteen*

## BRAY

I'VE BEEN SITTING in this plastic hospital chair for three hours. It's uncomfortable as fuck, and if it were not for Reilly cuddled in next to me with her legs draped over mine, I would more than likely be pacing the waiting room. It's real fucking hard to stay still, my body itching to move. Every time my legs start to jitter, bouncing up and down, Reilly squeezes my hand and looks up at me with concern in her eyes.

I force myself to calm down. I do not want to stress her out any more than she already is. She came barrelling into the hospital about thirty minutes after I got here. She would have broken all sorts of road rules to get here that quickly. The way James would not make eye contact with me confirmed that she was fucking reckless. He was meant to make sure she didn't do anything stupid.

Zac's been in there for an hour with Alyssa—the bastard could come out and give us all an update so we aren't just sitting out here stressing the fuck out.

Dean's been staring at his phone texting God knows who

for the last hour. Holly, Sarah and James are sitting opposite Reilly and me, staring at our open show of PDA. Sarah has been switching between questioning—no, not questioning—interrogating us on this sudden development, and pacing the room while cursing out Zac for not coming back out with information.

Holly's been quiet; she's always the quiet observant one of the bunch, but more so now. I want to make sure she's okay, but I know asking her anything in front of the group is not an option—she will pretend everything's fine.

Leaning over and whispering in Reilly's ear, I tell her, "Babe, I'm going to go get coffee. I'm taking Holly with me."

Reilly looks at me confused, then looks across at her sister and nods her head.

"Okay," she says as she untangles herself from me. "Holly, come with me. We're getting coffee." I stand

and shake out the stiffness of my legs. I'm really going to need a good fucking massage to loosen up for tonight's fight, that's if I can make it back in time. I don't plan on leaving this hospital until I know Zac and Alyssa are okay.

Holly stands up and grabs her purse, silently following me out. I can tell something is bothering her and I don't like it. Once we are out of ear shot of the group, I say to her, "Whoever it is, give me a name and I'll sort it out."

"What do you mean?" she asks.

"I know you're worried about Alyssa, but you're not yourself. So, whoever it is who's put you in this mood, tell me."

"You don't even know me, Bray. How do you know I'm not always this quiet?"

"I know you better than you think. You're not yourself.

What's wrong?" She's just as stubborn as her sister, but I'm persistent.

"It's you, actually," she says, which has my head snapping in her direction.

"Me, what the fuck did I do?"

"It's you and Reilly. Bray, she hasn't been in a relationship like what you guys have for over five years. She hasn't let anyone in because she's afraid of getting hurt. What's going to happen when you don't want to be tied down anymore? What's going to happen to her when you break her heart? Or do something stupid and end up in jail or something?"

Well, shit, I was not expecting that. I understand her concerns for Reilly but fuck that. I have no plans of letting go of Reilly. If I could convince her to go to Vegas with me right now, I'd be making her Mrs. Bray Williamson.

"Holly, I promise I have absolutely no plans of letting Reilly go anywhere. I'm all in this with her."

Holly observes me for a moment. "Okay, but if you do break her heart, I will come after you. I may be quiet but fuck with my sister, and I will make your life hell."

I smile at the thought of little Holly coming after me. I have no doubt she would find a way to fuck me up if she wanted to. It's always the quiet ones you need to be wary of.

"You can save the crazy for someone else, sweetheart. I'm not breaking her heart."

"It's about time," Sarah yells out, jumping out of her chair. I look up to see a very exhausted Zac walking into the room while glaring back at her. He's smart enough to hold back whatever he wants to say.

"She's fine; the bullet grazed her shoulder. You can all go back for a minute to see for yourselves, but then you got to go." He leaves no room for argument. Sarah, Holly and James are the first out the door. Zac tells Dean to go with them. "Make sure they don't jump all over her."

Reilly walks up to Zac, wrapping him in her arms. He freezes, unsure what the fuck to do. He looks to me for help, but he's all alone in this one. I just shrug my shoulders at him. I'm close enough to hear what she says, making me fall for her even more. The way she cares for everyone is endearing.

"Thank you for finding her. I'm really glad your overbearing ass put a tracker in her ring. I'm not even mad about it. I don't know what any of us would do without her. She's extremely lucky to have you, and if you tell anyone I said that to you, I'll deny it to the grave."

Zac returns her hug and says, "Thank you," as she releases him.

"I'll catch up with you, babe." I give her the indication to go ahead without me. I want to make sure that Zac is okay.

I wait for Reilly to be out the door before I ask, "You doing okay, man?"

Zac runs his hands through his hair. "I've never been so terrified in my life."

"I know, but she's okay, right? And Caitlyn's been taken care of." I don't really know what to say. He's usually the one giving me the pep talks, not the other way around.

"Yeah, thank fuck. There is something else though." "What?"

"Alyssa's pregnant," he says with a huge fucking smile plastered across his face.

Okay, so obviously this is a good thing. Thank fuck, they could use some good. "Congratulations! That's great. Obviously, you're chuffed about this development but how's Lyssa feel?"

"She's okay. When the doctor told us, my stomach dropped.

She didn't want kids, Bray. The one thing she told me she didn't want and I went and knocked her up anyway."

I raise my eyebrows at this. I didn't know Lyssa didn't want kids. "What do you mean you knocked her up anyway? Did you intentionally get her pregnant?" I ask, appalled.

I would never think that he would do something like that, but he's fucking insane over this girl so who the fuck knows what he's capable of.

"Fuck no, I would never do that. It was an accident. An accident that we are both thrilled about now," he claims.

Yeah, my perfectly calculated, never makes a mistake brother, accidentally knocked up his fiancée. I'm still doubting that it was not intentional.

"Bray, fuck you. I did not knock her up intentionally. I can't help it. I lose my mind and all sense of responsibilities when she's around."

Yeah, that's the more likely story. She does make him go fucking stupid, but in the best way. She's the best thing to happen to him.

"I don't really care how you got her knocked up," I lie —I totally would have kicked his fucking ass if he did that to Lyssa. "I'm going to be an uncle, finally. Jeez, it took you long enough, bro. I thought I'd be sixty before you made me an uncle."

"Shut up, idiot. Let's go see her so I can kick all those fuckers out."

I slap him upside his head. "What the fuck was that for?"

"One of those fuckers happens to be my girlfriend—watch how you talk about her."

He laughs. "Your girlfriend? When did that happen?" "A few weeks back. We've just been keeping it on the

DL. You know, sneaking around like teenagers." I wiggle my eyebrows up and down.

"I wish you fucking snuck around as a teenager with the number of times I had to call cabs for girls you'd leave asleep in your bed. Why the fuck would you start sneaking around now?"

"Please, you only saw a fraction of the girls I brought home, most of them were gone before morning even broke. Besides, it's Reilly who wanted to keep us on the DL, not me. I'd be shouting it from the rooftops, that she was mine."

"Yeah, I can see why she wouldn't want it made public that she's with your ass," the fucker laughs; to which, I slap him up the backside of his head again.

We make it to Lyssa's room. Walking in, I can see all three girls hovering over her, Dean attempting to tell them to move back. Not one of them is listening to a word he says. James, however, is the smart one, standing on the opposite side of the bed, not touching Alyssa at all.

I squeeze my way through the three of them, effectively pushing them out of my way. "Stand clear, I'm coming through," I declare.

"What the fuck, Bray!" Sarah screeches, while both Holly and Reilly give me death glares.

"What makes you think you can just barge your way in?" Reilly questions.

"I'm her favourite brother-in-law. Trust me, babe, she wants to see me. Don't you, Lyssa?" I look down at her. She's laughing, but I can see the torment in her eyes from the hellish day she's had.

"Of course, I want to see you," she laughs.

"Told you so!" I say to Reilly, who just shakes her head at me.

I lean down and kiss Alyssa on the forehead and Zac makes a big deal of clearing his throat. Jealous bastard can't stand anyone touching her.

"You doing okay, sweetheart?" I ask her. "I am now," she smiles.

"Good. Now, do you need anything before your grump of a fiancé kicks us all out?"

"No, I'm good. But you should get going. Don't you have an ass to kick tonight?"

"Yeah, I do." I look down at my watch. The fight is still four hours away; I can make it back in time.

I can hear Reilly groan behind me. She doesn't say anything though. I'm sure whatever it is, I'll hear about it the moment we're alone.

Leaning down, I whisper into Lyssa's ear, "Thank you for making me an uncle. This baby is going to be loved like no other, I promise you." Standing back up, I see tears running down her face. Shit, now I've gone and done it.

"Fuck, Bray. I'm gonna kick your ass for making her cry," Zac growls out. I don't get time to rebut his statement before Reilly and Holly both stand between Zac and me. At the same time, they both say, "Touch him and I'll cut your damn balls off, Zac."

The whole room goes silent. Well, all the men in the room go silent. Sarah and Lyssa are desperately trying not to let their laughter escape. I don't know why they're laughing—that shit's straight out of *Children of the Corn* kind of scary. I'm dumbfounded, looking between the two of them. I can't see their faces as they're facing Zac. But I'm sure I don't need to see them. I know the expression they are both wearing, identically.

Zac looks over their heads at me. "Yeah, good luck with that, mate," he laughs.

I'm still a little shocked. I don't think I've ever had a girl stand up for me like that, other than Ella. Not just one, but both of them. "*Ahh,* babe," I say, pulling Reilly around to look at me. "I appreciate you sticking up for me, but I can handle him all on my own."

She laughs, "Bray, you look like you've seen a ghost." "Well, that shit you two pulled just then is fucking

freaky, okay?" Reilly and Holly look at each other and smile; they both then turn to me and say, "Freaky? Really? Bray the fighter is scared of us two little twins?"

"Okay, stop. Now. That's not fucking funny." I grab Reilly's hand and start pulling her towards the door, as everyone else in the room is laughing. "Reilly we're going." As I get to the door, I dig my keys out of my pocket and throw them to James. "Make sure Holly gets home without a scratch, and Sarah, well, just make sure she makes it home?" I laugh and duck the bottle of water she throws at my head.

Reilly stops, picks up the water bottle, and throws it back at Sarah. "Don't throw shit at him, Sarah," she says before walking out. Everyone in the room looks at me.

Holly laughs and says, "Boy, she has it really bad." At that, I smirk. I like that my girl is feisty and protective.

Reilly has been silent pretty much the whole two hours it took to drive back to the club. Before I let her out of the car, I need to find out what's bothering her.

"Okay, what's wrong?" I ask. "Nothing's wrong."

"Something's wrong. Tell me. I can't fix it if you don't tell me, and we both know I'm not going to stop bugging you until you tell me."

"I'm worried, that's all," she says.

"About Lyssa? She's going to be fine." I try to reassure her.

"Not Alyssa, you."

"Why the fuck are you worried about me?" I ask, dumb-founded.

"You're going to fight tonight, you haven't exactly been prepping all day, and you haven't done your pre-fight routine things. What if you're not ready?"

"Babe, this ain't my first rodeo. Trust me, I know what I'm doing."

"I know you can fight, but what if tonight's the one time that it goes wrong? I just don't want you to get hurt, that's all."

I pull her over the centre console and sit her on my lap so she's straddling me. "I promise I'll be careful. I'll be focused. There is nothing in this world that can take me away from you, okay? I will always fight for us, Reilly. We are worth fighting for."

I gently lay kisses all over her face, and her body relaxes and sinks into me. "I'll fight for us too, Bray. I won't let anyone take you from me," she says before slamming her lips onto mine and claiming more and more of my heart and soul.

*Chapter Fifteen*

REILLY

**I**'M SITTING in the front row of the ring with Dean on one side of me and a hulky beast of a man on the other. I don't know what his name is; he won't talk to me anyway. I'm anxious as hell, waiting for Bray's fight to come on. His is the last one of the night—the main event—as he likes to inform me. He's the fucking star, his words not mine.

I've watched three fights so far. Each one bloody, messy and always ending with someone knocked out on the floor. I send a little prayer up—please, God, don't let that be Bray. I've just found him. I can't lose him now.

The last fight ended about five minutes ago; the basement is full of people. The crowd is loud, people shouting from all directions. I stay seated, glued to the spot and wait.

Dean leans over, trying to calm me. "You know he's literally the best fighter, right? You have nothing to worry about, Reilly."

"No wonder his ego is so big, if you're all going around talking about him like he's some kind of god," I yell back.

"Isn't he?" Dean says with his eyebrows drawn. "Because he's been telling me he is for at least ten years now. He's said it so often I think he brainwashed us all into believing it."

I laugh. Damn, Dean actually cracked a joke. I've only ever seen serious Dean, never this playful side. I think I like the playful side better. This must be what Ella sees.

I know they think no one knows about their little budding friendship, but I know. Bray knows, but doesn't want to know. The only one who doesn't know is Zac; he's too blinded by everything that is Alyssa to notice. I really hope I'm around to watch that shit show unfold.

I'm brought out of my own head from the lights dimming and the music that starts blaring "T.N.T" by ACDC. This is Bray's entrance song. I remember hearing it the first time I saw him fight here.

He comes prancing out, alone this time. There are no card girls hanging off him. They do appear a few steps behind him. They're not touching him though, which is good... for them. I don't share very well.

I watch and can't help but smile as Bray dances and shows off his muscles as he makes his way to the cage. He's just about to the door when he stops, turns and runs the few steps towards me. Grabbing me by the back of my neck, he kisses the ever-loving hell out of me. The noise of the crowd and music fades as I get lost in him. Breaking the kiss, he leans down and whispers in my ear, "I fucking love you, Reilly."

My eyes widen, my mouth hanging open. Bray smirks and makes his way back to the cage. *What the hell just happened?* By the time I recover from shock, Bray is prancing around in the cage, his eyes never leaving me for very long. I smile at him and he winks back.

His opponent is in the cage, although not getting anywhere near the fanfare that Bray is receiving.

The bell goes and before I know it, the fight has started; both men knock gloves with each other. Right away, Bray's opponent takes a swing at his head, which Bray dodges and returns an uppercut to the guy's ribs.

I watch as both men go back and forward at each other, and I try not to squeal as Bray takes hits all over his body. The bell for the first round goes and the fighters take their corners. I can see Bray's coach yelling at him and Bray shaking his head no. There is blood dripping down his face that someone else is wiping off with a towel.

When the second round starts, it's much of the same, each fighter giving and taking blows, kicks, etc. The opponent gets an upper hand, slamming Bray into the cage, pinning him there, and landing blow after blow all over his body. I go to get up—to do what, I don't know—but I see red. I want to strangle this asshole who thinks he can hurt Bray.

Dean's quick to pull me back down. "Settle down, Harley Quinn, your man is more than capable of taking care of himself." As the words come out of Dean's mouth, Bray pushes back, gets his opponent pinned to the ground and slams his fist into the side of his head. The ref leans down and blows his whistle before yelling something out.

The crowd goes wild. Bray stands, leaving the other guy laid out flat on the ground. The medics rush in to help him. Bray's arm is held up and he's walked around the cage. He won. Thank God, he's not the one laid out on that floor.

Bray shakes off the ref and climbs out of the cage. He heads straight for me and lifts me up. I wrap my legs around him and just before I let my lips meet his, I tell him, "I fucking love you too, Braydon Williamson."

I don't know how he manages it, but Bray carries me out of the basement and into his dressing room while delivering the most delicious kisses. He turns on the shower and doesn't put me down. Instead, he slams my back into the wall and grinds his hard cock right onto my clit.

"*Argh*... God... that... keep doing that," I beg. I'm not ashamed to beg him for what I need anymore. I know he'll always deliver and he gets off on hearing me beg him. So, win-win in my eyes.

He breaks the kiss and drops my feet to the floor. I groan, "Really? Now you put me down?"

"I need you fucking naked, now, Reilly. Strip," he commands.

Taking a step back, he watches my every movement. My whole body shivers and my core pulses and weeps at his commanding tone. I don't waste time in getting my dress over my head. I unclasp the black lace bra and let it fall to the ground. Next, I slip out of my pumps and slide my matching panties down my legs before straightening back up and waiting for my next command; because I know there will be one.

"Goddamn, you are fucking gorgeous."

Bray drops his briefs to the ground, releasing his rock-hard cock. My mouth waters at the sight. I don't dare move until he tells me what to do, though.

We've been playing this way long enough that we both know the game. I've never been with anyone that I wanted to dominate me before, or boss me around. But, when Bray does it, damn, that shit is hot as hell.

As I'm raking my eyes up and down his body, my mind is cataloguing the damages he received from the fight. His ribs are bruising on both sides, he has a nasty mark on the outside of his left thigh and his face, well, it's seen better days—that's for sure. I'm about to ask him if maybe he should be seeing a doctor, or medic, when he speaks first and I get distracted by that damn pierced cucumber again.

"Do you want to play, Reilly?" Bray asks while stroking his

hand up and down his cock. That should be my hand. I should be touching, stroking, licking that cock.

"Yes," I answer and nod my head, not able to take my eyes off his cock.

"Good girl, get in the shower under the water, hands on the wall." I follow his instructions, step under the warm water and place my hands on the wall. I turn back to look at him and wait for my next command. I can feel the slickness of my pussy dripping down my thighs already.

Bray silently walks up behind me, and out of nowhere a loud smack lands right on my ass. "*Ahh*, fuck, God." The sting follows the sound; the pleasure follows the sting.

"Did I say you could turn around?" Bray asks as he delivers another delicious slap to the other side of my ass.

"*Ahh*, oh, fuck me. No, you didn't, Bray," I reply between moans.

"That's right, I didn't. Face the wall. Do not move until I tell you to, or I won't let you come."

I smirk at that; we both know that's one thing he can't help, making me come as many times as I possibly can.

Bray reaches around, pinching both of my nipples between his fingers while biting down on my neck. He knows just the spot to bite down on that drives me freaking crazy. My body is on fire, my nerve endings short circuiting, as pleasure rolls through me. My skin is tingling all over and my pussy is pulsing with need while seeking what she needs—Bray's cock filling her up. "Fuck, Bray, don't stop."

"Never going to, babe," he declares. He lets my right breast go as he trails his hand down past my stomach. Just as I think I'm in luck and he's going to go straight for my clit to put me out of this beautiful torture, his hand goes around the back of my thigh. He grabs my leg and pulls on it, effectively spreading my legs further apart.

"I worked up an appetite out there, babe. I'm fucking starving."

"*Uh-huh*." I don't know what he expects me to say. I don't even know if I'm capable of coherent words right now.

"Are you going to be a good girl for me, Reilly, and stay still while I eat?"

"Yes." I nod my head. I'm not really sure what I've just agreed to. Is he going to leave me standing here waiting for him?

"Perfect, you're so fucking perfect," he says as his body slides down behind me. He bites on my right butt cheek.

"Oh, fuck." I push my ass out further against his skin. It freaking hurts but the pleasure that rolls through me at the same time is unlike anything else I've ever felt.

"*Mmm*, I'm going to feast on you until you have nothing left to give, until I've drained you dry."

Bray swipes his tongue from the top of my pussy right up to my ass. He holds me still, his hands spreading my cheeks wide. His tongue delves into my pussy, swirling around, while his fingers flex on my skin. He brings his mouth up to my clit and sucks hard, occasionally twirling his tongue around. I'm not doing a great job at standing still, pushing myself harder into his face.

He inserts two fingers into my core, circling around my G-spot and causing me to cry out. "Oh, fucking, Bray, God. *Ahh*." I see stars and struggle to stay upright.

I can feel an orgasm coming on, my body begins to violently shake, and I'm chasing this bitch like my life depends on it. I can feel it; it's so close. "I'm so close."

One of his fingers starts rubbing around my rear bud, circling and sending all sorts of new sensations through me. That finger then pushes its way in, slowly pushing further and further until it's buried all the way inside my ass.

My core and ass are both clenching onto his fingers, his

mouth still sucking on my clit. He slowly pumps his fingers in and out of both holes. I feel like my whole body is about to explode. I come screaming his name.

The only thing holding me up right now is Bray's arm around my waist. I come back down to earth as one of his hands is caressing my breast, the other still pumping fingers slowly in and out of my pussy.

"Welcome back," Bray's gravelly voice says into my ear.

"*Mmm*, thank you." I can feel the pleasure building again already as his fingers work their way in and out of my pussy.

"I need my cock buried in this pussy of mine, now," Bray says, removing his fingers and lining himself up with my entrance.

I don't give him time to slowly work his way in and torture me in the process. As soon as I feel his cock lined up, I push myself back and slam down onto him.

"Fuck," we both say at once.

"Goddamn, Reilly. Warn a guy next time. I just about came right then. You feel so fucking good, babe."

I laugh. There's no way he's a one pump dump. He's a fucking machine, can last for hours like he's running off Energizer batteries or something. Once he's sure I've had time to adjust to him being buried deep inside me, he starts to move. Slowly at first, building up his speed and thrusts until he is slamming into me from behind.

The metal of his piercing hits my G-spot, over and over again. I freaking love this piercing; it never fails to hit the spot. I have come multiple times because of this piercing. I can feel how wet I am, wetness gushing out and running down my thighs as Bray continues to slam into me.

His thumb starts circling my ass. I feel him slide it down between our bodies, covering it in my juices before going back to my ass and inserting it. He keeps it still and it's fucking torture. I don't know what his obsession with my ass is lately, but I'm not complaining. It's a strange foreign feeling. With his cock in my pussy, and his thumb in my ass, I feel full, with sensations going haywire in my body.

I need him to move that finger though; I pump my hips back and forward, getting little movement of my ass on that finger. Bray is relentless though; he's slamming his cock into me, but won't move that finger.

When he finally starts moving his finger a few minutes later, it causes me to come again—screaming the place down. Again. Bray pulls out and I feel him spurt all over my back.

"Fuck, fuck, fuck, Reilly," he groans out as he comes, milking himself on my back. "I fucking love fucking you," he continues, straightening me up and spinning me around. He wraps a hand around my throat, pushing me against the wall as his lips connect with mine. Our tongues fight for power, and I struggle to overpower him. He wins though—he always wins. I let him take control of the kiss.

His hand around my throat tightens and closes; I moan into his mouth. As he picks me up, my legs wrapping around his waist, he lines his cock up and enters me in one swift motion. I told you—he's a damn Energizer Bunny.

# Chapter Sixteen



*Bray*

THE LAST WEEK has been fucking perfect. I've had Reilly at my house, no more sneaking around, no more staying at Zac's place. Alyssa is doing great; somehow Zac convinced her to quit her job and help him out at the club instead. Although from what I've heard from Reilly, Zac's not letting her actually do much at all, which is driving Lyssa insane.

Reilly's come a long way in accepting our relationship as something that is set in stone and here to stick. Her walls are completely down, finally. I thought I'd have to take a damn sledgehammer to those fuckers.

I've tried to talk her into moving in, but she's staying strong on that refusal. I will wear her down eventually. I get she doesn't want to leave her mum and sister, but everyone has to leave the nest eventually. I offered to buy a house on the same street for her mum; she laughed at me and told me I was crazy and to not even think about doing something stupid like that.

Considering their home holds a lot of sacred memories, I

would never dream of moving her mum out of there. I do however want to move Reilly out, and straight into my house. I didn't buy this big fucking house to live here alone forever.

I bought it, knowing I wanted to settle down one day, to have ten kids running around. I think I'll wait till after she has my name to bring that up though. For the moment, I'm fucking stoked at the thought of being an uncle.

I've just finished working out in my home gym. Reilly went to work a while ago. I don't like when she leaves, but I'm not a clingy fucker like Zac; I know how to let go for a few hours. Besides, I fell in love with exactly who she is, and an independent workaholic is exactly who she is. Why would I change anything about her or try to get her to change? Besides, you can't improve on perfection, and Reilly is fucking perfection in the finest form.

Walking into my kitchen, I find Ella sitting at the counter with a cup of tea in her hands. I'm surprised to see her; she hasn't been around much lately. I walk up and give her a sweaty hug and kiss on her head.

"Hey, princess, I missed you."

"*Eew*, Bray that's gross. Get off me. You stink," she squeals and pushes me off her.

"Well, princess, if you don't want long drawn-out welcomes, don't take so long to visit. Where have you been, anyway?"

"Busy," she replies.

I grab a bottle of water from the fridge and down it while staring her down. Once I finish the water, I lean against the counter near where she is sitting.

"Elaborate, Ella. What does busy entail?"

"Nothing much. Just hanging with friends, you know, getting ready to start uni, that sort of thing," she shrugs.

"*Uh-huh*, so why have you been avoiding me?" I've only

seen her in passing here and there. Normally, she'd spend a couple of nights a week here with me. Even when I stayed at Zac's for those few weeks, I barely saw her around.

"I'm not avoiding you, just giving you space. No one wants their little sister being the third wheel to their new relationship."

Shit, she thinks she has to stay away because of my relationship with Reilly? That's not happening.

"Ella, you'd never be the third wheel, and you're never in the way. You know that, right? You can come here whenever you want. You're my favourite sister so you will always have a place wherever I am." The more I think about it, the more furious I am with myself for not realising she was feeling like she couldn't be around here.

"Bray, I'm your only sister, idiot. And I know I can come here, but honestly, I've just been busy."

"Well, as long as you know that I don't ever want you to stay away because you think you need to." I get the feeling there is more that she isn't telling me. What else is going on with her?

"I know. Thank you."

"Want something to eat? I'm starving and you look like you haven't eaten a cooked meal in forever. Has that idiot brother of ours not been feeding you?"

"Zac's not an idiot, and you know he has a chef cook our meals. God, could you imagine him in a kitchen actually making anything other than coffee?"

I laugh, because it's true. Zac could burn water—he's that useless in the kitchen. "That's true, but if everyone was good at everything, well, then everyone would be me."

"Sure, master of all. Whatever you say." She salutes me.

"Come on, Ella, you and I both know I'm your most talented and favoured brother; the sooner you admit it, the sooner you can put Zac out of his misery and he can stop competing for that spot."

"*Huh*, actually I think Zac has taken the number one spot. After all, he is the one making me an aunty."

"Fuck, do you think Reilly would be on board with the plan of getting knocked up?" I ask her seriously.

"Nope." She annunciates the P sound.

"No, probably not. It is pretty cool that we are getting a niece or nephew soon."

"Yeah."

I dig through the fridge, pulling out sandwich fillings, and end up making chicken and salad rolls for us. As I'm putting it all together, Ella finally spills what's bugging her.

"Bray?"

"Yeah?"

"Why would a guy not want me? I mean, is there something wrong with me that repels men?"

*Let's fucking hope so*, I think to myself. "You own mirrors, right? I know you do. You are fucking beautiful, Ella, inside and out. If some douche is not seeing that, then that's on him not you." It then hits me that she said men, not one particular guy. "Wait, men as in plural, or one man in particular? What are we talking about here?" I ask, needing to clarify just how many men she thinks are repelled by her.

"There's one guy, but he won't even give me a second glance. I thought maybe he felt something, but apparently it's one-sided." She looks fucking heartbroken. I want to go and beat the shit out of the fucker who's making her feel less than worthy.

"Who is it? I need a name, Ella," I demand, handing her a pen and paper.

She shoves the paper back at me. "You will go to your grave waiting on that name, Bray."

She's not going to tell me. "You know I'll find out anyway. You should just make it easier on both of us and fess up, little sister."

Ella stands up. "Nice chat, Bray, but I've got plans. See you later."

Following her out to the door, I wait for her to open it before I say, "Make sure you tell Dean I said hi."

Ella freezes, the door half open, before she turns around with her mouth hanging open. I got the reaction I was looking for, the confirmation that there is something going on between him and Ella.

"I'm going to fucking kill him." My blood is boiling. I suspected that he was fooling around with Ella for a few weeks now. She's just confirmed it for me.

"No, you're not. You are going to shut your mouth and not say a damn word to anyone, Braydon," Ella shouts at me.

I laugh, "You expect me to do nothing while my eighteen-year-old little sister sneaks around with my brother's best friend, who happens to be fucking twenty-eight?" I yell back.

"We're not sneaking around, Bray. Nothing is happening. Like I said, I'm not worthy enough to be noticed." I see the tears forming in her eyes.

"Wait, Dean's the fucker who has you questioning yourself? What did he do, Ella?" I'm doing my best to hold back my temper I can feel bubbling at the surface under my skin.

"Nothing, that's the thing, Bray. He. Won't. Do. Anything! No matter how hard I try, he won't touch me. He's too damn loyal to Zac or some shit like that."

I pull her into my arms. "Ella, you're eighteen. You need to experience life before you settle down. I can't believe I'm saying this, but Dean is a fucking idiot if he doesn't see what a catch you are. About to be a dead fucking idiot, but an idiot all the same."

"Bray, you can't touch him. It's humiliating enough. Plus, I love him and if you hurt him, I will hate you forever." She pulls out of my arms. She can't mean that, can she? By the look in her eyes, it hits me she does.

"Fuck, Ella, okay. I won't touch him, but I want you to promise me one thing."

"What?"

"I want you to go to uni, meet some new friends. Experience everything that life has to offer. Don't waste time or energy on any man who isn't worth it. And any man who would choose their friend over you is not worth it."

"I'll try; it's not like I actually have a choice. I can't force someone to love me back."

She walks out the door, slamming it behind her. Fucking Dean, what the fuck is wrong with him?

Getting out of the shower to Zac blowing up my phone is not how I wanted the rest of my day to go. I don't bother answering, choosing to get dressed first. The second I walk into my closet, his ringtone, that stupid fucking song he programmed into my phone, starts blasting through the room again.

"What do you want?" I answer. "Where are you?"

"At home, why?"

"We have an issue at the club, wanted to make sure you weren't here somewhere."

My blood runs cold... Reilly is at the club right now. "What kind of issue and where the fuck is Reilly?"

I walk into my closet and throw on a pair of grey sweats and a white shirt. I slip my feet into a pair of joggers before grabbing my keys and wallet. I'm out the door in less than two minutes.

"Bray, stay the fuck where you are. Reilly is fine. She's in my office."

Like I'm going to stay here. Does he not know who the fuck he's talking to? "What's going on, Zac? Start fucking talking," I yell.

"I start the car and switch him over to the Bluetooth." "Jesus, Bray, I told you to stay the fuck where you are.

You do not need to be here. We have it handled."

The fucker still has not divulged what is going on and I'm losing my patience. I'm at least a thirty-minute drive away from the club.

"What have you got handled, Zac?"

"Stephen, the lead singer from Cyrus, the one you put in the hospital a few weeks back, turned up with a bunch of guys looking to start problems. Like I said, the last thing I need is to be fetching your ass out of jail right now, so stay where you are."

"I'm not going to sit here like a fucking pussy, Zac. If he's looking for trouble, I'll fucking deliver it."

"Why the fuck do you always have to be so fucking stubborn, asshole? What do you think Reilly will do when she sees your ass being taken away in cuffs again?"

Well shit, I can't let that happen. Not after how far we have come. How hard it's been for her to let down her guard. But fuck if I'm going to sit here while my girl is in that building with a bunch of assholes.

"I won't do anything that will see me in cuffs, Zac. Scout's promise."

"You were never a fucking Boy Scout, Bray. Look, I gotta go. Dean and the boys have this sorted out. Do not just barge in here guns blazing!"

~

I make it to the club in just under twenty minutes, and pull up to the back door. I don't waste any time making my way through the back rooms to the main floor. The scene I'm greeted with has me wanting to choke the life out of someone, whoever the fuck thought they could come into our club and do this.

The club is trashed; it looks like a damn tornado has been through here. Chairs thrown and broken everywhere, tables turned up, all the curtains that line the walls ripped to shreds. Glass litters every inch of surface space. I spot Zac, sitting at the bar, nursing a glass of whisky, and holding an ice pack to the right side of his face.

He's in one piece at least. Looking around, I can't see Reilly anywhere. "Where the fuck is she?" I yell, directing the question at Zac.

He lifts his arm and points behind me. "Over there, in one piece, so calm the fuck down."

Spinning around, I see Reilly at the far end of the bar, broom in hand and sweeping up pieces of broken glass. I stalk my way through the debris of furniture and glass until I reach her. Taking the broom out of her hand, I throw it off to the side before pushing her against the bar and crowding her space. I grab her face in both hands, holding her still as my lips connect with hers.

I pour everything into this kiss, all my pent-up rage, all my fear of something happening to her and my thankfulness that she's unharmed. Reilly gives just as much to this kiss—she's completely open to me now. I succeeded in annihilating her walls, there are no more barriers between her and me, and I fucking love it. I fucking love her.

Pulling back from the kiss, I lean my forehead against hers. "I fucking love you."

"*Mmm*, I love you too," she replies, breathless.

"Are you okay?" I ask as I do a visual inspection of her from head to toe. "I don't know what I'd do if something happened to you, babe. Actually, I do know. I'd burn this town to the ground until I found the fucker I needed to kill."

Her body goes stiff under my touch. Fuck, I should have kept that thought to myself, even if it is the truth. "Babe, I'm sorry. I shouldn't have said that out loud."

"Bray, I don't ever want you to go after anyone because of me. Do not throw your life away because of me, ever."

"I don't have a life without you anymore, Reilly. I will always fight for us, even if I have to find new ways to fight."

"I know." She leans into me.

I look around—this is going to be one hell of a clean-up bill.

"If you two lovebirds are finished, I need Reilly," Zac says as he approaches.

"What for?" I ask. The bastard ignores me, instead talking directly to Reilly.

"We're all going to Hawaii. Book a jet for tomorrow morning. Alyssa and I are getting married."

Reilly lets go of me and faces Zac. I don't like it. With a slight growl, I pull her back against my chest, wrapping my arms around her middle. Zac smirks at me.

"Wait, does Alyssa know about this? You can't just decide you're getting married tomorrow without discussing it with her first. What if she doesn't want to get married in Hawaii? *Huh*? Have you even thought of that?"

Zac holds up his finger, indicating for her to wait, while pulling his phone out and placing it on speaker.

"Zac, this baby is making me bloody horny as hell. Hurry up and get home already please," Alyssa answers the phone.

Reilly bursts out laughing. Zac just looks pained, more pained than he did icing his bruised face.

"Great, I'm on speakerphone, aren't I? Thanks for the warning, Zac."

"Ignore them, sunshine. I'll be there as soon as I can. I just need to handle a few things at the club, but I wanted to run something past you?"

"Sure, hit me."

"Tomorrow morning we're flying to Hawaii, you, me and unfortunately our family and friends. We're getting married. Any objections?"

Alyssa's squeal stings my ears. All the guys around us, who were going about their business, stop and look over at the commotion coming out of Zac's phone.

"Oh my God! Zac, Oh, my gosh. Yes, yes, yes! Let's do this. I can't bloody wait to be Mrs. Zac Williamson," Alyssa continues to squeal through the phone.

"Sunshine, I can't wait either. I'll be home soon." Zac hangs up the phone, raising an eyebrow at Reilly with a huge smile on his face.

"Okay, no need to be so bloody smug about it. Where abouts in Hawaii? Do I need to book a hotel? And why don't you have a PA to handle this sort of shit? This is not in my job description, you know." Reilly is getting fired up. I can feel the energy coming off her.

"Settle down, just book the jet. Everything else will be handled," he says as he starts typing into his phone. No doubt to delegate tasks off to others.

"Okay, I'll be upstairs. Make sure you come and see me before you leave," Reilly says, leaning up to offer a parting kiss.

"I'm not leaving this building without you, babe. I'll come up in a little bit."

I watch as she walks away, the sway of her hips in that tight skirt taunting me the whole way.

"I need you to organise a reschedule for Friday's fight. One, you're not going to be here. Two, I'm shutting the club down for renovations, obviously."

"Sure, I'll get on that, just as soon as you tell me what the fuck happened in here," I demand.

"They came in, about thirty of them with baseball bats, and went ballistic smashing the place up. Dean called in the cavalry and we cleared them out."

"So, how many bodies need to be disposed of?" "None."

"None? You're telling me, some motherfuckers came in here and did this." I wave my arms around. "And you didn't kill any of them?" I don't believe it.

"What can I say? We're turning over a new leaf, Bray. I can't risk not being around for Alyssa and this baby. We need to start handling things in more legit ways."

"I agree, things have been changing. What about Club M?" I ask. I honestly don't know what I'd do without fighting. Could I go professional on the up and up? Probably. Do I want to? Absolutely not. I also don't want to give up fighting.

"I'm not sure yet, but we do need to think about changing that up too. It was okay to take the risks when it was just me who would go down. I can't do that to Alyssa, Bray. She's never had a proper, safe family and I intend to give her that."

"I get that, man, I do. I just don't know what to do with myself when I'm not fighting."

"I know, but even you can't fight forever, Bray. Whatever you need to do, you know I'll be there, no matter what."

"Yeah, thanks, bro. Don't worry about me. I'll figure it out. Besides, have you met me? I'm like the fucking king of all trades, excel at everything I do."

"Whatever helps you sleep at night." Zac gets the hint that I'm not fully ready to discuss me not fighting anymore. Thankfully, he drops the topic.

"So, what are we gonna do about this mess?"

"It's being handled. We are going to Hawaii, and I am getting married to a fucking goddess. By the time we come back, this place will have had a facelift."

"Right, I'll see you on the tarmac tomorrow morning then," I say, walking away and leaving him to it.

"Don't be fucking late, Bray. I will leave without you," he yells out at me.

Turning, I smirk. "No, you won't. Lyssa would never let you get married without her favourite brother-in-law there."

I laugh at his cursing while I walk away.

# Chapter Seventeen

REILLY

"I CAN'T BELIEVE you're actually doing this. You're getting freaking married, Lyssa." I squeeze her into the tightest hug ever, just before we enter the bridal shop.

"That's if I can find a dress. I can't believe I'm getting married tomorrow and I don't even have a dress."

"Please, that man would marry you even if you wore a paper bag." Sarah rolls her eyes.

"*Mmmhmm*. He would, wouldn't he? Let's hope it doesn't come to that," Lyssa says, pushing her way through the door with the rest of us following suit.

"Okay, here's what we are going to do. Each of us pick one dress and Lyssa you pick two that you really love, then you're going to try each dress on." When we all just stare at Sarah like she's lost her mind, she claps at us. "Chop, chop, girls, the day's a wasting."

We all go about finding our version of the perfect dress for Lyssa. I'm going through a rack with Ella beside me.

"So, do you think we'll be doing this again for you soon?" she asks.

I all but choke on thin air. "God, no," I get out, then notice her scrunched up face.

"Not that I don't love Bray, all that is Bray, but marriage is not something I need." I try to explain myself; it's not working too well.

"Does Bray know that? Because I'm pretty certain you are his forever, Reilly."

"I know. Trust me, Ella, he is my forever too. I just don't think you need to get married to be forever."

"Okay, I just don't want to see Bray get hurt. I know he comes across like nothing bothers him, but you have the ability to break him."

Wow, I admire how protective she is of him. I'm wondering if Lyssa got the same speech. Probably not.

"Ella, I promise I won't do anything to hurt your brother. Honestly, I've never loved anyone else as much as I love him. It's different, the feelings I have for Bray. It's consuming, like I can't even breathe properly when he's not around. And when he is around, well, I feel like a damn dog in heat, 'cause all I want to do is jump him. I want to crawl into his skin. It's like I can never get close enough, you know? I don't ever want to wake up without him next to me."

Ella screws her face up. "First, *eew*, I do not need to hear about you and Bray jumping anything. Second, you really do love him. I know that. I just worry more about him than I do Zac. Ever since our parents died, Bray has been a little lost and a lot angry. That's why he fights. Since meeting you, he has a newness about him and I worry what would happen to him if you weren't around anymore, that's all."

I get that, I do. "Never stop looking out for your brothers, Ella. Life is short and can change in the blink of an eye. They're both lucky to have an amazing sister like you. Now, how about we find that dress for Lyssa?" I suggest, changing the topic.

We go about choosing dresses, while I recall the things Holly and I would put the girls through who Dylan used to bring home. The year he died, he had only just started bringing girls around. We didn't get to torture him too much with our overprotectiveness.

"You know, when I get married, I think I'll just fly to Vegas and elope," Ella says as we all sit on the couch waiting for Lyssa to come out of the changing room in her fourth dress. Sarah, Holly and I burst out laughing.

"Ella, hunny, if you ever fly to Vegas to get married, be sure to warn me so I can be around when Zac and Bray find out. Then change your name and go into witness protection with your new husband, because there is no way your brothers won't kill him, whoever he is," I tell her through my laughter.

"Please, the only way you're getting married is by running off to Vegas where those two buffoons can't protest against it," Sarah laughs. To which, I slap her arm, while at the same time Holly slaps her other one.

"*Ow*! What the fuck, Reilly?" she says, rubbing both of her arms.

"One of those buffoons happens to be mine, so you don't get to call him names without getting hurt." I smile at her.

"Well, what'd you slap me for, Holl? He's not your boyfriend." Holly shrugs her shoulders.

"Sorry, Sarah, but I knew Reilly was going to do it the minute the words left your lips, and I had this overwhelming urge to slap you too. It's her fault though, blame her," she says, pointing her finger at me.

"Thanks, Holl. Way to throw me under the bus." I blow her a kiss.

"Okay, this is the one, and I don't care what any of you say, I love it," Lyssa says as she walks out of the dressing room. She looks up and points a finger at Ella. "Don't you ever think about running off to Vegas. No sister of mine is having a Vegas elopement for a wedding."

Ella jumps up and hugs Lyssa. "You look gorgeous, Alyssa. Zac is going to blow a gasket when he sees you tomorrow."

"Thank you. So, what do you all think?" Lyssa asks the rest of us.

She looks absolutely stunning. "I love it," we all say at once.

"Perfect, this is it. Now we can go back and laze by the beach for the rest of the afternoon."

I have a cocktail in hand and I'm lying on a sun lounger on a beach in Hawaii. Can life get any better than this? The sand is white, the water picture perfect and clear blue. It's like heaven, this place. I look over to Alyssa, who is wearing a tiny red bikini, her baby bump just starting to show. She's been drinking mocktails all day and complaining about not being able to drink with us. Meanwhile, Ella has been sneaking sips of my drink all day, because she's not old enough to drink here.

"I can't wait to be an aunt. You know I'll be the favourite; you might as well go and name her Reilly already. Break the news early to the rest, Lyssa; let them down gently," I tell her.

She laughs, "Oh my God, you are spending way too much time with Bray!" She points at me. "That's exactly what he said to me the other day."

I smile thinking about spending even more time with Bray. "He told you to name her Reilly?"

"No, he said I should name him Bray, after his favourite uncle.".

"Well, Bray can take a number. I'm calling dibs. Besides, this baby is going to be a girl," I say around my straw, while eyeing the candy walking up the beach.

Putting my finger between my lips, I let out the loudest wolf whistle I can, gaining the attention of the hunks currently headed in our direction. Although my eyes are zoned in on only one of them.

He's wearing a pair of board shorts and nothing else; *mmm*, I lick my suddenly dry lips. My eyes follow the droplets of water travelling down his smooth, tanned skin, to those abs I want to sink my teeth into. When my eyes finally make it back up to his, he gives me that panty-melting smirk. Yep, my bikini bottoms are now wet, and not just from the water of the ocean.

My favourite parts of Bray though, are those arms. They're strong, can hold me up like I weigh nothing, and are decorated with colourful tattoos. I want those arms wrapped around me. I want those hands all over me. I'm getting more and more heated by the minute. I'm going to need to go back into the water to cool off.

And then the idea hits me, yes. I'm going back out into that ocean, but I'm not going alone. As if he can read my mind, Bray looks back over his shoulder at the water then to me and smiles. He's way too tuned in to the way my mind works now.

Once they meet up with us, Zac heads straight for the towel basket. Picking one up, he places it over top of Alyssa like a bloody blanket, to which she throws it off.

"Sunshine, what if the baby gets sunburnt? You really should cover up." Alyssa glares at him and he eventually backs down, choosing to sit in front of her on her lounger while effectively blocking the view of her to anyone not in our little group.

It dawns on me that Bray has never once cared about what I

wear, or tried to get me to not wear something revealing. It's odd, considering how against revealing clothing Zac is. I've seen how Bray will try to get Ella to change or refuse to let her leave the house until she does. But he's never done this with me.

He squats over top of me, practically straddling me while holding himself up as he leans in to kiss me. I pull back, to which he screws his face up and raises an eyebrow in question at me.

"Why do you never care about what I wear out in public?" I blurt out.

"Babe, you can wear whatever you like. You're fucking gorgeous in anything you wear anyway," he shrugs. "Plus, I can fight." He's so matter of fact.

"What does fighting have to do with how I look?" I ask, confused.

"Any fucker who wants to stare too long or try to touch what's mine will learn very quickly just how good I can fight, babe." Cocky fucking bastard, he is. Problem is it's bloody true, he can fight, and he is good at it.

Deciding I like his answer, I pull his face down to meet mine—his hand quickly going to my throat and holding me still. I try my hardest not to moan out loud, but he knows what it does to me when he grabs me by the throat; shivers wreak havoc through my body.

I push him away with my hands; let's face it, we all know he lets me push him away. "I want to go for a swim, and you're coming with me." I don't give him room to say no, not that he would. Before I know it, I'm tossed over his shoulder and he's jogging towards the water. I have to hold onto my bikini top to make sure my boobs don't jump out of the fabric.

Once he makes it to the water, I think he's going to put me down, but no, he walks until he's waist-deep and throws me in. I come up coughing and spluttering.

"Asshole, I'm going to kill you," I scream at him, once I have my footing and my lung capacity back, that is.

He grabs and pulls me against him. "No, you're not. You love me way too much to do that," he says, so assured of himself.

"*Mmm*, you're right. I need to get a mould of junior made before I can do that. At least that way, junior and I can still have playdates without needing the rest of you." I smirk at him.

"Harsh, babe. That's fucking harsh. Your life would be boring as shit without me, admit it." He starts tickling my sides.

"No, Braydon Williamson, stop!" I scream, but no one is around to help me.

"I'll stop when you admit it," he says, continuing his torture.

"Okay, okay, my life would suck without you, happy?" I give in. Also, it's the bloody truth.

He stops. I jump up and wrap my legs around his waist and his lips meet mine in the softest, most tender kiss he has ever given me. Pulling back, I lose myself in the green orbs of his eyes.

"I want to remember this moment forever, trap it in a jar and keep it on the shelf," I tell him.

"No need, babe, we will have a lifetime of moments like these."

"Promise?"

"I will make sure of it. I'm never giving us up, Reilly." I need him inside me, now, more than ever before. Reaching down between our bodies, I undo his board shorts, just enough to free his cock. I move my bikini bottoms to the side and let his cock slide into my entrance.

"Fuck." He holds me still, buried onto him with my legs wrapped around his waist. To anyone looking, if they could even see through the water, we just look like two people holding each other.

He thrusts in and out, so tenderly and slow. It's the sweetest form of torture. We've never made love like this, each always too hungry for the other and going rough and hard. But this, I like this too.

"I love you more than I thought I could ever love anyone, Bray," I confess while he places gentle kisses all over my face.

"Your heart is safe in my hands, babe. I promise, no matter what life throws our way, you will always have me to lean on. I will always fight for us."

We spend the next thirty minutes making love in the waters of Waikiki Beach. I lock this moment into my memory of the time I knew one hundred percent, without a doubt, that I would spend the rest of my life with this man. The scary thought, if he asked me to run off and elope with him tomorrow, I'd probably say yes. I'll keep that thought to myself though—I do not need to encourage his crazy antics.

# Chapter Eighteen

BRAY

THESE LAST COUPLE of days in this paradise with Reilly have been amazing. I can't even remember the last time I was on any sort of vacation. It was before my parents died. Zac has never taken this much time off work for anything before. He would take time out to attend school events for Ella, or to drag my ass out of whatever trouble it found, but he'd always be straight back to working mode.

During Ella's younger years of high school, Zac never went into the club before Ella was asleep. He made sure he was home during the afternoon and evening with her. And when he went into the club, he had either me or Dean stay in the penthouse while she slept. I didn't mind though; I'd do anything for Ella. Even though I was a shit of a kid when our parents died, I would have done whatever Zac needed me to do to help him and Ella. Family always came first.

Being on this week's wedding getaway has made me take note of how much we need to do this more as a family. Now that our little family of three is growing rapidly, with the baby on his way; and yes, I'm counting on getting a boy. We need to do this; that child needs to experience family holidays like we did as kids. I have no doubt Zac will ensure that he experiences everything life has to offer. He really is going to be a great dad.

"Bray, hurry up, you cannot be late to your own brother's wedding," James yells through the bathroom door. Why the fuck Zac thought he needed to bring the bartender along, I have no idea, something about him being one of Alyssa's people or some bullshit like that.

"James, bang on that door again and I'll bang your fucking head into it!" I yell back.

The fucker laughs. "What would Reilly say if you did that, Bray?"

Fuck, that little shit had to go and make besties with Reilly. Now I can't fucking touch him and he knows it. I can, however, still threaten him.

"She won't know if she never finds the body, and trust me, James, no one will ever find the body."

"Okay, okay, just hurry up. I am not taking on Zac's wrath when we show up late because you need to spend an hour in front of the mirror."

I'm hurrying already, anxious to get back in the same room as Reilly. She left early this morning, claiming they needed the whole day to glam. I tried to tell her she wakes up already full of glam, and she told me where to shove my sweet-talking mouth. I gladly spent the morning following her direction, because only an idiot would say no to getting their mouth on her pussy.

Sitting in the hot sun, on the white sand of Honolulu, I watch my brother stand on the alter waiting for Alyssa, every few seconds checking his watch. She's not late—he's just an impatient bastard. Reilly is sitting to my right, gripping my hand hard, excitement running through her. Ella is on my left; I can see tears already forming in her eyes.

I've never understood why people fucking cry at weddings; it's a happy occasion, or at least it should be. There's no need for tears. I watch as Zac suddenly stops fidgeting and his head snaps up, mouth hanging open. Looking behind me, I see Alyssa standing at the end of the aisle. She looks stunning, a long white dress waving in the wind.

There is just one problem—she's by herself. For some reason, this resonates with me. She should not be walking down the aisle by herself. Call me sappy but every girl should have somebody to walk them down the aisle on their wedding day. I know, I'm a fucking hopeless romantic at heart.

I jump up and everyone looks in my direction. I don't fucking care. Reilly tries to pull me back down, but I wink at her. "I gotta do something. Wait here." I jog down the aisle, stopping in front of Alyssa.

She looks up at me confused. "You look beautiful, Lyssa," I tell her.

"*Ahh*, thanks, Bray," she says, eyebrows drawn.

"I thought you could use my arm to lean on, while you walk down this long-ass aisle. You know, so you don't break an ankle in your heels." I hold my arm out. I can see the tears immediately form in her eyes.

"Don't you dare fucking cry on me, woman. If I make you cry on your wedding day, Zac really will kill me."

She takes a big breath in. "Okay, thank you, Bray. I really appreciate you doing this."

"You're my sister. I'd do anything for you."

Alyssa grabs my arm and we begin our walk back down the aisle. She leans in and whispers, "I know you can see that I'm wearing sandals and not heels, by the way." She holds my arm tighter.

"I know." I smile at her. We get to the end, and I take her hand and place it in Zac's. That fucker is about to bawl his eyes out too. Am I the only one around here who's not about to cry like a fucking baby? Zac gives me a head nod, and I turn and make my way to a sniffling Reilly and Ella. *God, help me.*

The minister starts the ceremony. A lot of it, I tune out until it's time for the vows. They're really the only part that actually matter, right? I think when I convince Reilly to marry me, we will skip all the other shite and get right down to business on those vows. I can hear the emotion in Zac's voice as he reads out his vows.

Zac starts, "Alyssa, you came into my life like a ray of sunshine on a rainy day. You are the most caring, compassionate and kind-hearted person I know. I'm truly humbled that you have chosen me to share your life with. I promise to work every day to be the man that deserves your love. I promise to love you with every fibre of my being. I promise to never let you walk alone, to always be by your side. Sunshine, you are my first, my last, my everything and I promise to be yours for as long as you'll have me. I vow to always be your friend, your lover, and most importantly your family, for now until forever—it's you and me Alyssa, merged as one. I promise we will always have tomorrow together."

Alyssa continues, "Zac, I never dreamed of finding someone like you, ever. I've never known the kind of love and devotion you have given me. I've never had a family to call my own. Because of you, I can say that I am truly loved. Because of you, I can say that I have a family. Because you're by my side, always, I know I can conquer anything. You are the love I thought only existed in books; you are my hero, Zac. You are my home, my safe place and my happy ending. I have seen the best of you and the worst of you, and I choose both. I promise to love and cherish you always. I promise to be your sunshine on the darkest of days. I vow that our love will merge us together throughout all of time. I promise to always be your tomorrow."

"You may kiss the bride," the minister declares, and everyone around me cheers. Reilly looks over at my silent face.

"Bray? Are you crying?" she whispers. I love her even more for not calling me out in front of everyone.

"I'm not crying, just something got caught in my eye." I try to play it off like Zac and Alyssa's vows did not choke me up.

"*Uh-huh*, sure. Don't worry, your secret is safe with me." She leans up and kisses me.

"I think we should get married," I tell her.

"Sure, one day. But today, let's celebrate Zac and Alyssa," she says, standing and pulling me along with her.

It doesn't hit me until hours later that she agreed to get married, that she didn't say no. She said *sure, one day* to me and that's as good as a yes. I plan on asking her properly though, maybe even pay her dad a visit and do this the old fashion way. Not that his disapproval would stop me from marrying her.

The rest of the week flew by—I had Reilly, the beach and an endless supply of food and alcohol. I could not have wanted for anything else. The flight home however was painful as fuck. Alyssa spent half of the flight with her head in the toilet, throwing up. It seems the morning sickness has kicked in for her.

Zac spent the whole flight stressing out and cursing at everyone. He went as far as to demand the pilot have an ambulance on standby the minute we land. Alyssa vetoed that idea quickly. Zac was pissed. I kind of got it. He felt helpless and he couldn't do much to help her. It's also his own damn fault she's in this position, which I gladly reminded him of every chance I got.

We flew in late last night and I ended up staying at Reilly's place. Waking to a cooked breakfast by Reilly's mum is something I would never turn down. I tried to convince Lynne to move in with me, but she laughed it off like I was joking. I'm not fucking joking—I'd build that woman her own wing if she cooked for me like this.

After eating a shit load of pancakes, bacon and eggs, I head to the gym—probably to get blasted by coach for laxing off so much the last week—dropping Reilly off at the club on my way.

Halfway through training, my phone started blaring Reilly's ring tone. Climbing out of the cage, I grab the phone off the bench.

"Hey, babe, what's up?" I ask, breathlessly.

"Bray, I don't know what to do," she whispers down the phone. Something is wrong. I pick my keys up and run out of the gym.

"Reilly, what's wrong?" I'm opening the door to my car, but what she tells me stops me momentarily.

"There's a guy here pointing a gun around. He's on the ground floor."

Fuck. "Reilly, can you get to the lift?"

"Yes, I'm on the top floor. He doesn't know I'm here."

"Good, get in the lift, put the code in for the basement.

Once the basement code is entered, the lift won't stop. Stay in the basement until I come and get you. Do not leave that basement, Reilly. Promise me."

"Okay, I promise, I won't leave the basement."

"Good, stay on the phone until it cuts out. Once you're in the lift, the reception will die. I'm coming for you, babe."

I stay on the line. I hear her enter the code and the elevator start its downward journey, then the line cuts off. Fuck. What the fuck. I dial Zac, no answer. I dial Dean, no answer. I just need to get to the club; once I'm there, I can figure the fuck out what to do about this shit show.

I walk in through the back doors quietly. I have no idea what the fuck I'm walking into. I can hear it before I see it. "Call your fucking pussy-ass brother down here now, before I start dropping cunts," the voice yells. I know I've heard that voice before, I can't place it though.

When I see what's happening, I freeze. Zac has a gun pointed to his fucking head.

"You're going to have to shoot me, motherfucker, because if you think I'm putting my brother in front of your crazy ass, think again."

I'm about to walk out, then the front doors to the club open and my heart sinks. She's meant to be in the fucking basement. Why the fuck would she waltz through the front doors? Then it clicks—it's not Reilly... it's Holly.

Fuck. The guy with the gun, who I now know is that fucking singer from Cyrus, turns and points the gun at Holly.

"Well, well, well. If everyone else here isn't enough to get him out here, maybe his hot little girlfriend here will be."

Holly freezes, dropping everything in her hands. I can see her body shaking. I walk out from the shadows. I will not let anyone else take a bullet that's got my name on it.

"I'm right here, motherfucker. What the fuck are you gonna do about it?" I yell out, getting his attention off Holly, the gun now firmly pointing at me. I can see Dean in the background, creeping up behind him and placing himself in front of Holly, thank fuck. Zac curses.

"You know, I wanted to shoot you. I came here to kill you. I know you assholes had something to do with my brother going missing. I know you did."

"It was me. I choked the life out of him after I cut every one of his fucking fingers off with garden sheers. But if you want to blame someone for your rapist, woman-beating brother being dead, blame him. He attacked my fucking eighteen-year-old sister. He deserved every fucking bit of torture I dished out and then some," Zac growls as he moves closer to me.

"You know what? I have to live without my brother. Now you're going to find out what that's like." The asshole points the gun back at me and pulls the trigger.

I see Dean tackle him to the ground. *A bit fucking late, Dean.* I look at Zac, and his face is ashen. I look him up and down; he's in one piece and I thank God right before I fall to the ground. Zac's screaming. I can't make out the words, but I see his lips moving. He's got his hands over my chest. I can feel a burning, searing pain ripping through me. I go to my happy place and think of Reilly. I smile. Reilly is safe. She's the last thing I think of before I black out.

Chapter Nineteen

## REILLY

KNOW I promised Bray I'd stay in the basement—I should stay in the basement—but something twists in my gut. Something is wrong with Holly. I can feel it. I can't name what it is, but I feel fear like I've never felt before. Bone crunching coldness runs through my veins. My skin is prickling, sweat running down my spine.

Shit, Holly is here; she was bringing me lunch today. There is currently a mad gunman waving a fucking gun around on the ground floor and my sister's going to walk through those doors, or probably already has.

Sorry, Bray, but I can't just sit here. I have to do something.

I punch the code into the lift that will let me out near the back of the ground floor. The trip back up from the basement feels like it takes forever. Just as the doors open, I hear a gunshot. Loud ringing rages through my ears. I know, I'm the idiot in all the horror films that runs towards the bad guy, but instinct takes over and run I do, out towards the middle of the ground floor.

I can hear Zac shouting, and Dean fighting someone on the floor. I see Holly standing at the doorway, intact, thank God. She makes eye contact with me, her eyes filled with an expression I've only ever seen once before, when our brother died. An overwhelming sadness blankets her, tears running down her face.

I can still hear Zac shouting, and when I look in his direction, my whole world falls apart. I feel like the rug has literally been pulled from under my feet. I can't move. I can't breathe. Why can't I breathe? As I struggle for oxygen, I fall to the ground on my hands and knees. A scream retches its way from my throat, but I don't hear it. The room is spinning in silence. Someone touches my arm. James. I look up at him. He is talking but I don't hear a word of what he's saying.

I need to get to him. I have to get to him. I drag myself up and run, stumbling to Bray. Bray, who is laid out on the floor, blood covering the front of his body and spilling out beside him. Falling to my knees next to him, I look up to Zac, who has his hands over the gaping wound in his chest.

"Zac, wh... what do I do? Tell me what to do," I cry,

wanting to do something but not knowing what to do. "Where the fuck is the ambulance? Somebody, get a fucking ambulance here now!" Zac yells out.

"They're two minutes away. Keep pressure on the wound," James says from behind me.

I lean down next to Bray's face and whisper in his ear, "Don't you dare fucking leave me, Braydon Williamson, not when I've just found you." I'm a slobbering mess.

Holly comes and sits next to me; she grabs my hand and holds on tight. My other hand grasps Bray's. Why does he feel so lifeless? Cold? Where the hell is the ambulance? One minute later, I'm being shoved out of the way by ambulance officers. I refuse to let go of Bray's hand; he needs me. I need to help him.

Zac ends up picking me up off the floor and moving me out of the way.

"Reilly, we have to let them help him. They have to help him," he says to me.

I watch as the medics work on the other half of my soul. I watch as they place his lifeless body on the gurney and wheel him out to the ambulance on the street, all the while continuing to work on him. I watch, totally helpless to do anything to save the man I love.

"Let's go," Zac says, dragging me by the hand out of the club. He puts me in the car before running around to the driver's seat and flying out to catch up to the ambulance that just took off. The whole trip Zac manages to stay directly behind the ambulance, not bothering to stop at red lights, screeching around street corners, and ducking in and out of the busy Sydney city traffic.

"I can't lose him. I can't lose him. I only just found him," I repeat over and over.

"We are not losing him, Reilly. It's not a fucking option," Zac yells at me. His hands clench the steering wheel.

As soon as he stops at the emergency room doors, I jump out of the car. The drive has allowed time for some of my shock to wear off. I run through the emergency room, stopping at the counter. I can see Bray being wheeled in by the paramedics through the plexiglass of the triage counter.

There are doctors and nurses rushing in every direction, calling out words I don't understand. Then I spot Alyssa; she's standing there staring at Bray. Her head pops up at something a doctor says and I hear her yell at them, "This is my fucking brother! You do everything you can. Now!"

Another nurse grabs her by the arm and pulls her away from the gurney as they wheel it to another room. By this time, Zac is standing next to me watching the same scene.

"Get your fucking hands off my wife before I cut them off," he growls through the plexiglass window. This makes Alyssa turn and notice us. She runs out the door and straight into Zac's arms, allowing herself only a moment of comfort, before she stands back and looks between us. We are both covered in blood, Bray's blood.

"What happened?" she asks quietly.

I don't even know what to tell her. I go to speak; my mouth opens but no words come out. I can't get the words to work. The panic is creeping up on me. I can feel my skin getting hot, my breathing becoming more and more difficult as I gulp to drag air into my lungs. My hands clutch at my throat, and I bend at the waist, trying to breathe, trying to just count to ten.

Zac grabs my face in his hands. He bends down to my level. "Reilly, fucking breathe. I am not going to be telling my brother that his girlfriend stopped breathing when he comes out of that theatre room." I search his eyes for the lie, that Bray's not coming out of that room. I can't see it, the lie; it's not there. He believes that Bray is coming out of this.

"Reilly, I need you to have more faith in him. Don't you dare fucking give up on him," he tells me.

I nod my head in agreement, but I feel him slipping away already. I feel a loss like no other, like a part of me has died, burnt, and is now ashes blowing in the wind. A part of me that I will never get back.

"I'm going to go back and see if I can find anything out," Alyssa says.

"Wait, why are you even here, sunshine? You told me you quit this job weeks ago," Zac questions.

"I tried to call you to tell you I was coming in. I got called; they were short-staffed and desperate. It's just for the day." She leans up and kisses him.

"I don't care how much money I have to throw at this

fucking hospital, make sure he has the best doctors in that theatre room," Zac tells her. Alyssa nods her head, before walking back through the doors, leaving Zac and me standing in the waiting room—both unsure of what to do now.

Four hours later, I'm seated on the horrible plastic chairs, cuddled into Holly. Ella is clinging onto Dean like a lifeline, silent tears streaming down her face. Alyssa and Sarah are sitting opposite Holly and me, both quiet.

Zac hasn't stopped pacing the room; up and down, he keeps moving. A few times Alyssa has tried to get him to sit down, but he won't. The only times he stops pacing is when she throws herself into his arms and he clings to her, whispering in her ear.

I hate this waiting. Why hasn't someone been out here already? What's taking so bloody long? With each minute that passes, any little hope I have dwindles away. Pretty soon, I'm going to be all out of hope. I'm going to be left with nothing, left to pick up the pieces of a broken heart again. Except this time, it's not just broken, it's shattered into a million pieces.

A doctor walks out and calls out, "Family of Braydon Williamson."

"That's me," Zac and I both say at the same time. I jump out of my chair and rush up to the doctor. Ella comes up and stands quietly next to Zac.

"He looks between the both of us. And you are his..." He leaves the question open.

I look to Zac for an answer. If I say I'm his girlfriend, they are not letting me through. I know the drill.

"I'm his brother; this is his sister." He points to Ella. Then he looks over to me. "This is his wife Reilly." Zac's lie slips out of his mouth effortlessly.

For once in my life, I actually wish it weren't a lie. I wish I was Bray's wife. Why didn't I marry him weeks ago when he wanted to fly to Vegas? The next time he asks if we can fly to Vegas, I'm jumping on that. Please God, let there be a next time.

"Okay, Braydon suffered a gunshot wound to his abdomen. The bullet tore through his small intestine. We had to remove part of the bowel. He also suffered from a dangerous level of blood loss. He's stable for now and is in the ICU. He is in a medically-induced coma for the time being. I can take the two of you back to see him for a few minutes, but you'll have to wait until we move him to a private room for any longer visitations."

All I heard was he is stable. He's okay... he's going to be okay. I haven't lost him yet. My hope wants to climb back up from the ashes, but I need to see him first.

Zac grabs my hands and holds on tight. "Thank you," he says to the doctor. We follow the doctor down long corridors until we finally make it to a ward that reads ICU on top of the doors. Zac squeezes my hand tighter. "He's going to be okay," he whispers. I'm not sure if he's trying to reassure me or himself.

When we make it into the ward, the doctor stops at a curtained-off section. There is a nurse doing something with buttons on machines that persistently beep. I listen to the beeps, taking comfort in the beat of his heart playing out through the machine. Letting go of Zac's hand, I slowly make my way to Bray's side. He looks peaceful, even with all the tubes and cords attached to him everywhere, he looks peaceful.

I gently hold his hand. "Bray, I need you to keep fighting for me. Just hold on that little bit longer and come back to me. Please, don't you dare let go," I whisper to him.

Zac wraps his arm around my shoulder. "He's a fighter,

Reilly, and there's never been a fight he hasn't won. Trust me, he's not giving up." Zac lets go of me, turns to the doctor, and asks, "When is he being moved to a private room? And when will he be woken up?"

"He'll be moved up in a few hours. As for waking him up, we will slowly bring him out of the induced coma starting tomorrow. Sometimes it takes hours, sometimes a day. It all depends on his body. He's not out of the woods yet. The next twenty-four hours are critical to telling us how his recovery will be," the doctor replies.

"Good, I want him in the best room you have. Money is not an object," Zac states like it's a done deal, like money will fix everything.

Money does not fix everything. Money could not save my brother. Money could not keep my dad out of jail. And no amount of money will save Bray. I know that, and deep down, Zac knows that too. Bray's recovery is out of our hands, all we can do is sit back and hope. But hoping has never worked in my favour before.

"It's been two fucking days. Why the fuck is he not waking up?" Zac growls at the doctor, who is currently trying to do his rounds.

"These things take time. The drugs have worked their way out of his system. The only thing keeping him asleep is his own body not being ready to wake up. His brain activity scans are normal, and there is no sign of damage. All we can do is wait," the doctor responds calmly.

"Wait, how long do we have to wait?"

"Zac, hunny. The doctors can't answer that; you know that. We just have to be patient, and let them do their jobs. He will wake up. He has to," Alyssa says, pulling Zac out of the doctor's way.

Zac doesn't reply. He wraps his arms around Alyssa and stares at what the doctors are doing, watching their every move, like he's waiting to pounce on someone.

Me? I'm sitting in the same place I've been for the past two days, in the uncomfortable chair by Bray's bed. Holly has been bringing me changes of clothes. I use the private bathroom Bray has, taking less than five minutes to shower and change. I can't risk him waking up and me not being there. I need to be there when he wakes up. The couple of times I have showered, I made sure Holly took my place. At least then if he woke up, he would still see me, or a very close second.

# Chapter Twenty

*Bray*

I CAN SMELL the fruity scent all around me. I smile—that's Reilly. That's my girl's fucking delicious smell. I don't know where I am. I feel like I'm floating, but I can't see anything around me, surrounded only by a whiteness. I keep getting to this spot. I can hear voices. I can smell, but I can't make anything else out, no matter how much I try.

She's here though. I can feel her presence surrounding me. Reilly is here with me. I just need to find her. I hear her voice like a musical melody calling to me, reaching for me, but I'm trapped in this whiteness.

"Bray, you can wake up now. It's been a week. Stop being a lazy ass and get up. What would your coach say when he hears you've been asleep for a week?"

*Coach would rip me a new one*, I want to reply, except she never hears me.

"Bray, please, you promised me. You promised that you would always fight for us. I'm begging you to fight your way back for us."

Her cries rip through my heart. I want to hold her, to tell her that I'm fucking fighting. I'm fighting to get back to her. I just need to find her. *Where are you, baby?*

I can feel myself slip back to darkness, to nothingness. The sounds around me, the beeping, the talking, it all fades out.

I'm back in the whiteness. I inhale, hoping to get a whiff of that fruity fragrance. It's not there. She's not here. I want to let myself slip back into the darkness, then I hear Ella.

"Bray, I moved into my dorm at the university. You were meant to help me, you know. You were meant to do all the heavy lifting for me. I had to take Zac and Dean—guess how that turned out? Zac decided that the dorm room was unacceptable accommodations. His exact words. I never knew how much of a snob our big brother was. Dean agreed, saying the security was not high enough. It's a bloody girls' dorm room, Bray. What the hell do I need security for there?"

I'm hoping that Zac ended up refusing her move into the dorms. Like I originally did. I knew those dorms would suck. I may not have gone to university, but I spent many days in the girls' dorms when I was younger.

"Do you know what Zac went and did next? No, you don't know because you won't wake up. He went and bought an apartment near the university and said if I had to move out, that was the only option. So, now I have a not so little two-bedroom apartment, five minutes away from the university. No sharing a tiny dorm room with a stranger for me. I gave him hell for it though. I'm not admitting that I love that apartment way more than a dorm room. And if you wake up and tell him I said that, I'll knock you over the head and put you back to sleep."

Thank the Lord she is not in those dorm rooms. I can't

believe Zac had to be showy and buy her an apartment. I would have talked her into moving in with me if she didn't want to continue living with Zac.

~

"Bray, wake the fuck up already. It's been three weeks." It's Zac; he sounds pissed, which is nothing new. I'm used to him being pissed at me.

"Bray, I can't do everything without you. You need to wake up. If not for me, do it for Reilly then. That poor girl has not left this hospital for weeks. She won't leave your room for any longer than five minutes at a time. You can't do this to her. You can't do this to me, fucker. You don't get to just sleep while the rest of us are here suffering and worried."

I'm fucking trying. I want to get back to Reilly. I want to hold her in my arms more than anything. If I can just find the way. How the fuck do I wake up?

~

"Bray, you promised me that you were great uncle material. Being asleep is not being a great uncle. Wake up. Your nephew needs an uncle who can teach him how to fight and how to get all the ladies. That's right. I said nephew; we found out it was a boy. Although, if he takes after his father, he won't need any help. That man is so skilled. The stories I could tell you. And if you don't wake up soon, I might just start spilling my guts and torture you with the horrid details of your brother's and my sex life, amazing bloody sex life. I know you can hear me, Braydon Williamson. Wake the hell up."

Fuck, pregnancy has made Alyssa grouchy. Where the fuck is Reilly? I can't smell her fragrance. All I want is Reilly.

"Bray, I'm falling apart. I don't know what to do." *Mmm*, I can smell that fruity fragrance. Reilly is here. She sounds so fucking lost though. How can I reassure her that I'm still here? No matter what I do, I can't seem to pull myself out of this, whatever the fuck this is.

"You said you would fight. You promised I would never be alone again. Well, I'm feeling pretty bloody lonely right now, Bray. Please wake up. I will do anything. You want to run off to Vegas and get married? Let's do it. Just wake up, please."

Please, God, let me remember that when I eventually make it out of this fog. Let me hold her to that promise of marriage.

"Please," she sobs. I can hear her cries and can't do a damn thing about it. As much as I try to tell my body I'm ready to get this show on the road, nothing happens. The darkness just keeps taking over me again and again.

*Chapter Twenty-One*

*Reilly*

I'M WATCHING the useless bloody doctors do their observations on Bray again. It's been the same thing, day in and day out, for the last fifty-nine days. They can't find anything wrong with his brain; they don't know why he isn't waking up.

Zac has called in the best neurologists he can find. He's flown doctors in from all over the place. All of them unable to give us any answers. As much as my hope has dwindled, I can't give up. He made me a promise to always fight for us, so that is what I have resolved to do. Fight, for me, for him, for us.

I spend my days sitting by his side, researching patients suffering from comas. I have tried every single damn method I can find on the internet aimed at waking up coma patients. I've been playing his favourite songs. I've replayed videos of his own fights. I even made his coach come in and yell at him, ordering him to wake up. As much as he didn't want to do it, I was not going to take no for an answer.

It didn't work though—nothing worked. I'm running out

479

of ideas. I don't want to give up, I can't give up, but I really don't know what to do. Zac and Ella spend hours here every day too. I have been leaving them to have their own time with Bray.

I wanted to make sure I was the person he saw when he woke up. He told me once that the first thing he wanted to see in the mornings was my face; the second my *friendly vagina,* his words, because that was the best way to start the day. I replied that coffee was the best start to the day. I wish I had told him that wasn't true. I should have told him that he was the best start to every day... the best end to every day.

Now, I'm scared that when he wakes up—if he wakes up... no, it's when he wakes up—I'm terrified he's not going to know who I am. I was only in his life for a few months. Maybe it should be Zac or Ella whom he sees first; they're his family. What do I do if he doesn't remember me?

He fell in love with me once, and that was when I was trying to push him away. I can get him to fall in love with me again. I think. Maybe. Hopefully. It's only been a few months, but I don't even know who I am without Bray anymore.

Actually, I do. That's a lie. Without Bray, I will go back to the closed-off, frightened girl I was before. I will go back to being surrounded by people but feeling a bone-deep loneliness. I'll go back to being the fun Reilly, who to outsiders doesn't have a care in the world, while silently dying on the inside.

I can feel myself getting more and more frustrated at the doctors. They walk around looking at this and that, but they can't fix him. I want to yell and throw stuff. I want to stomp my foot and throw a tantrum, to demand they wake him up. I know that won't work though. Zac has already tried. Bray's scans have shown that his brain is responding to hearing our voices. Alyssa says we should keep touching him and keep talking to him, because he can hear everything we say. So, I've been doing just that. I have told him everything, my whole life story, almost.

I haven't told him about Dylan. He knows that I had a brother. He knows that he died obviously; he's been taking me to the jail and cemetery on the first Sunday of the month. He *was* taking me, when he was awake. Twice, he made up an excuse that he needed to visit his friend, who was in the same jail as my dad—his visits always the same time that I would be going there. He would then drive me to the cemetery, without me even asking; he would pull up and then lean against the car for an hour waiting on me, while I spent an hour talking to Dylan.

Bray never complained about waiting so long, and he never asked questions about my visits. Not because he wasn't inter-ested—I knew he wanted to know. He was just waiting for me to be ready to talk about it. But that's the thing, I didn't think I'd ever be ready. There is so much anger, sadness and regret that I have over Dylan's death.

I wait for the doctors and nurses to leave the room, then climb up on the bed and cuddle into Bray. I don't care that I keep getting told off by the nursing staff. He's my boyfriend; if I want to lay in bed with him, I bloody will. One nurse made the mistake of telling me off for doing this while Zac was in the room. Well, let's just say that nurse left in tears.

Zac and I have gotten closer over the last two months. He has been caring and compassionate towards me like never before. It was a little odd at first, since we loved to hate each other, not that we ever actually hated each other. Now, he treats me just the same as he treats Ella and Alyssa. He is constantly asking if I need anything, constantly having food sent to me here at the hospital. Holly even told me he tried to give her that fancy black card of his to go and buy me clothing, toiletries and whatever other *woman crap* I need.

She laughed at him and said we didn't need his fancy money. Which we don't. We both have a nice little trust fund that our dad made sure we received when we turned twenty-one. Alyssa and Sarah know about this, but we don't tend to advertise it. I don't even think Holly has ever touched hers. I went through a phase where I was spending like I was Ariana Grande, then I woke up to myself and stopped.

Zac has also continued to pay me from the club, even though I haven't stepped foot in there since that day. I've told him he doesn't need to, that I don't deserve it. He grunts at me and tells me he's paying it anyway and not to bother arguing with him about it because I won't win.

Once we get out of this hospital, I plan on giving it all back, somehow. Even if I have to withdraw it all and dump a money bag in his mailbox, he is getting that money back. I am not now, nor have I ever been, a charity case. I just haven't had the energy to argue over it yet.

Curling up to Bray's side, I embrace the peace, all but the beeps of the machines. Everyone left a little while ago. These are the times I like the most, being able to curl up next to Bray. To touch him, feel that he is still here. To talk to him and tell him everything I can possibly think of.

The other day, I told him about the time when Holly and I were thirteen. There was a boy, we were playing seven minutes in heaven, and the bottle landed on Holly. She was expected to go into a closet with the boy I had a major crush on. There was no way Holl would kiss a boy I liked. We had completely different tastes in boys. Plus, there's the whole sister girl code thing. We went into the bathroom and changed clothes, came back out and I went into the closet with my crush. That was my first kiss, and it was absolutely horrible.

When I told him that story, I could have sworn I felt his hand move. I called for the nurse and she said it was probably just an involuntary twitch. I don't believe her. I got him to react I know it. I've felt these little twitches more and more lately. They can't be nothing. I won't believe that.

Taking a big breath in, I inhale his cologne. I've been spraying it on the pillows, on him, on the blankets. Just so I can surround myself in his scent. It's oddly comforting.

"Bray, you can wake up now. Everyone's gone home for the night so, you know, if you wanted to get laid, now's your chance, babe."

I grab hold of his hand. I could have sworn it twitched just then. Sometimes I'm convinced that I want it so bad that I'm imagining it.

"You can't leave me here, Bray. I still want you. I need you. I need you to wake up. You can't leave me. My dad left. Dylan left. I will not let you leave me. You know I never told you this, but when Dylan died, I thought I would never feel a pain so deep. I was wrong, because this, this right here, fucking hurts. It hurts that you're not keeping up to your end of the bargain and fighting for us. You're meant to be the undefeated fighter, Bray. Well, guess what, this, whatever this is, it's winning and you're losing. I'm losing."

I swipe the traitorous tears from my cheeks, take big breaths, and count to five before continuing.

"You want to know what I talk to Dylan about on those Sundays I visit him? Lately it's been about you. I tell him about everything that's been happening in my life. I tell him about Holly and my mum and dad. The first time you took me there, I asked him to give me a sign that you were the one I should take a chance on. That you were the one I should open my heart to. That same day, during the visit with my dad, he told me to give you a chance, to give happiness a chance. My dad had never led me wrong before, so I took a leap of faith."

Great, now my eyes are going to be red and blotchy again. I roll over and grab a tissue off the table before settling back in.

"I haven't been to see him, either of them, since you've been asleep. I can't bring myself to leave here, to leave you. If I could talk to Dylan right now, I'd tell him that my heart is shattered… that as much as I want to believe you're going to wake up and come back to me, I'm so freaking scared that you're not. Damn it, Bray, come back to me, please. I can't do this anymore. I'm tired; it's my turn to sleep. You need to wake up. I'm drowning right now and you don't even know. If you don't wake up, Bray, if you don't come back to me, then I'm likely to do something selfish and stupid and follow you. Because living like this, living without you, is not an option for me. I can't do it. I'm not that strong."

Movement of the hand I'm holding makes my whole body freeze. Did I imagine that? I wait and wait. A couple of minutes later that movement is there again. His fingers are curling—that's definitely more than a twitch. I want to look up, to look at his face, to see if his eyes are open. I'd do anything to be able to be entranced by those green eyes.

"*Rrh.*"

My head snaps up at the noise, and I jump off the bed. "Thank you, God. Thank you. Thank you. Thank you." They are there; the eyes, they're open. He's staring up at me, with very open eyes.

"Bray, don't move. Let me get someone."

Shit, what do I do? I don't know what I'm supposed to do. I look around the room in a panic; his curling fingers catch my attention. I'm still holding his hand. The pressure is light, featherlight. It's enough to let me know that he's there though, and that's all that matters.

Okay, think, Reilly. The call button, I press the call button, over and over and over again. It seems to take hours for the nurse to appear in the doorway.

"What on earth..." The nurse stops, mid-sentence, mid-stride. She only takes a minute to recover.

"Mr. Williamson, it's good to see you're awake," she says as she calmly walks over to the bed and presses some buttons on the machines. She then picks up the phone and informs whoever picks up that Bray is awake.

"You've given your wife quite the scare, Mr. Williamson," the nurse says, patting my arm. She moves to the other side of the bed. Bray continues to stare up at me, confusion shining in his eyes.

He doesn't remember me. All I can think right now is he has no idea who I am. He's just woken up in hospital after being in a coma for two months and the first person he sees is practically a stranger. My eyes start welling up. I can feel his fingers applying pressure; they are attempting to curl around mine. I slip my hand out of his, look up to the nurse and excuse myself.

"*Umm*, I'm just going to step out into the hall and call

his brother. He should be here," I say as I leave. The nurse offers me a sympathetic look. I look back at Bray. He's actually awake. He's still staring straight at me.

Closing the door behind me, I lean against it, only to jump out of the way when a heap of doctors come down the hallway and enter the room. I should be in there. I should at least hear what's going on. First, I need to call Zac.

He picks up on the first ring. "Reilly, what's wrong? I'm coming now." I can hear the rustling of keys.

"Zac, he's awake."

"Wh... what did you say?" he whispers.

"Bray... he's awake. He just woke up a couple of minutes ago. You should get here, Zac. He's going to need you."

"I'm on my way. I'll be there in fifteen minutes. Are the doctors in with him?"

"Yes, they just went in." I don't know what to say. I don't know what to do. I've dreamt of this moment for two months, and now that it's here, I just don't know what I'm meant to do.

There's a loud commotion coming from Bray's room. What the hell? The nurse sticks her head out. "Mrs. Williamson, you need to get back in here, now."

Running into the room, I can hear the machine that's hooked up to Bray's heartbeat going haywire. "What's going on?" I ask as I barge my way through doctors to reach the other side of Bray's bed, the one not currently taken up by nurses and doctors.

I grab his hand in mine and watch as he turns his head towards me. His eyes lock onto mine. The machine starts to slow down. The doctors still and look up at me. I can see everyone looking at me, but I don't dare break eye contact with Bray.

"What happened?" I ask, still not looking away from Bray.

"It seems Mr. Williamson had what could be a slight panic attack. It started as soon as you left the room."

I scrunch my eyes up. Bray has never been scared of anything. Why the hell would he have a panic attack now?

## Chapter Twenty-Two

BRAY

SHE'S CRYING. I can feel her body heave with sobs. She's telling me about her brother, begging me to wake up. I'm trying to tell her that I am awake. My eyes are flickering open, adjusting to the brightness of the lights above me. This is the most alert and aware I have ever been. I'm not about to let the darkness pull me back under.

Reilly is telling me how broken she is, how much she needs me to wake up. Why can't I wake up? I'm trying to get my body to move anything. My fingers, I can feel them slightly move. What the fuck is wrong with me? What the fuck happened? And, why the fuck is Reilly sobbing right now?

I should be able to comfort her. I hate that she's upset and I can't do a damn thing to help her. It's my job to help her, to be her shoulder to cry on. I promised her I was going to be the best fucking boyfriend that ever existed and right now, I'm failing her.

I put everything into making my fingers move; they curl the slightest bit and I feel her body stiffen. Just look up, baby, just look up and you will see that I'm here. I'm awake. You told me to wake up and I listened. Just fucking look up already.

My brain is telling my mouth to speak. I can feel the words on the tip of my tongue, yet I'm getting nothing. What the fuck? I want to scream. I want to hit something, anything. Reilly, all I want to say is Reilly. Why the fuck can't I say the one name I fucking love so much?

After a few minutes of trying, I finally make a noise. I wouldn't call it talking, but it's noise and it gets her attention. Like lightening, she jumps off the bed and looks down. Her eyes widen and she starts speaking but I can't actually make out what she says. She's going too fast.

She's panicked. I curl my fingers. I try as hard as I can to squeeze her hand. She looks back down at me and seems to settle. Reaching over, she presses something behind my head. I just stare and watch. She's so fucking beautiful to look at, why wouldn't I stare? She doesn't look as vibrant as I remember; she's thinner, paler. She has black rings under her eyes, red puffy eyes, because she's been crying.

My thoughts are interrupted when someone comes barging into the room.

"What the hell..." Whoever this is, she stops for a second. It takes her no longer than a minute to recompose herself.

"Mr. Williamson, it's good to see you awake." She looks me over from head to toe.

I watch Reilly as she watches what must be a nurse pick up the phone. The nurse hangs up the call then pats Reilly on the arm. "You've given your wife quite the scare, Mr. Williamson," she says to me and looks over at Reilly.

Mrs. Williamson, who the fuck is Mrs. Williamson? Surely if I married Reilly that would not be something I'd forget. I certainly wouldn't be opposed to being married to her. In fact, if we are married, I'd make her marry me again so I can remember that shit. What else am I forgetting if I don't remember an important event like that?

Reilly still looks sad. Why is she still so sad? She excuses herself to the nurse, and says something about calling my brother. Zac, where is he? How long have I been asleep for? Reilly starts walking out of the room. I watch her the whole way. The moment she shuts the door and I can't see her anymore, I start to panic. I need her to come back. I need her to be here. I can't even fucking move. Why'd she walk out? Is she coming back?

The door opens, and I'm about to breathe a sigh of relief that she's back. It's not her; it's a heap of fuckers whom I don't know. Why would she leave me in here with all these people? The beeping starts to get louder and faster. I can feel my heartbeat match the sounds of the machine. I don't want to be here. Get me the fuck out of here.

Reilly comes running back into the room; she pushes her way through the people. People I'm cataloguing to kick their asses for blocking my girl's way. If I could get out of this bed, they would not be standing in her fucking way.

When she makes it to my side, she picks up my hand. I have to turn my head in the other direction, which, by some small miracle, it turns slightly and my eyes are focused back onto hers. I don't dare lose that eye contact. I don't want her to leave again. I can feel my heart start to calm. It's because she's here; she's my calm, my person. I fucking need her to stay here.

I listen as the doctors talk to her about me. They run a heap of tests. One of the fuckers brings a fucking torch to my eyes, and wants me to follow their movements like I'm going to stop looking at Reilly. When I don't move my eyes, Reilly's eyebrows draw down.

"Bray, you have to listen. You need to try, please. Just do what the doctors say. You can do this. Follow the light with your eyes, Bray." Her voice becomes determined, demanding, even. I don't want to take my eyes off her, but I also don't want to let her down any more than I have.

I follow the light. As much as it pains me, as much as it causes my head to thump like the hangover of all mother fucking hangovers, I grit down and do it. Just as the doctor's finishing up with the light, the door bursts open and in comes Zac in true Zac form. Demanding, arrogant and fucking assholish. I wouldn't have it any other way. I smile, or at least I think I do. Reilly gasps.

"He smiled. That's good, right?" she asks the doctors. "That's a very good sign, Mrs. Williamson," the doctor says.

There it is again, Mrs. Williamson. If everyone is calling her that, I must have fucking married her. Now, that thought brings a smile to my head. I look at her, ignoring the ruckus that Zac is causing by firing his million questions off to the doctor.

The excitement I see shining in her eyes when I manage to smile up at her gives me a deeper sense of calmness, that everything is going to be okay. That we are going to be okay. I just need to figure out what the fuck is wrong with me and get my body on board with doing what it's supposed to do.

"Why isn't he fucking talking?" Zac growls at the doctor. I turn to watch, trying to focus on what they are talking about. Maybe someone can tell me what the fuck's going on.

"He just woke up from a two-month coma, Mr. Williamson. These things take time. He has shown positive responses to all the tests so far. We need to take him down for another MRI, but everything so far is looking good." The doctor talks directly to Zac, like I'm not in the fucking room.

Reilly must notice my agitated state, though I'm not sure how because I can't fucking move or say anything at the moment. She squeezes my hand and I flick my eyes back to her.

"Bray, do you... do you remember me? Do you know who I am?" she asks, in the softest almost a whisper of a voice.

I catch the croak of her voice; I can feel the fear coming off her, the shake in her hands. Why the fuck would she think I don't remember her? She's not someone anybody would forget.

"Bray, don't speak, okay? Just blink once for yes, twice for no," she says.

I blink once and stare into her eyes. She breathes a sigh of relief. "Oh, thank God. I thought for a moment maybe you forgot just how freaking awesome I am." She smiles down at me.

I want nothing more than to pull her down and kiss her right now, except I can't. I can't do anything. I want a taste of those lips so fucking bad. I stare at them, so fucking plump and delicious. Reilly laughs; it's probably corny as fuck but it's the most beautiful, welcoming sound right now.

She slowly leans down, places her head next to mine and whispers in my ear, "Even though you just woke up, and you might not be able to talk with words, I can still see what you're thinking right now. Those thoughts should not be thought in a room full of doctors, not to mention your brother." She gently places her lips over mine.

I'm in heaven. I just need her to keep those lips on mine. She doesn't; she pulls back after giving me the gentlest kiss, like she's scared she'll break me or something. I want more. I need more. Reilly laughs and shakes her head. "Rye..." I manage to get out a few sounds. I almost just said her whole name. The whole room goes silent, all eyes on me. I'm only looking at one pair of eyes, the ones that belong to the other half of my soul. Her eyes start glistening. Fuck, I've gone and made her fucking cry again.

"Bray, thank fuck. I knew you'd be back with us. I knew you would wake up," Zac says as he leans down to my ear.

"Don't you ever fucking scare me like that again, fucker," he not so quietly says. As he straightens back up, he grabs my wrist and squeezes. "I think you actually gave me grey hairs for real this time, Braydon. I'm sending all future hair dye expenses to you because I will not be grey before I'm fifty."

I roll my eyes at him. He's been telling me I'll send him grey since I was sixteen. Luckily for us, we were blessed with good hair genes. My dad was in his mid-fifties when he died, and was only just starting to show signs of greys.

"Za..." I try again to speak. I know what I need to say. My brain is working just fucking fine. Why the fuck isn't my mouth? My throat feels dry, like the Sahara Desert. Water, water would be really bloody good right now.

"Bray, don't try to talk yet. It's okay, man. Trust me, we can wait," Zac says.

"Wa... t... r." I think I manage to get the whole damn word out.

"Water, he needs water... of course he needs water. Why didn't I think of that? He can have water, right?" Reilly lets go of my hand, causing my eyes to search her out. Where is she going? I need her to stay here. I follow her movements; she goes over to the table, where a jug and cup are sitting.

"He can have a couple of small sips; too much and it will make him sick. Very small sips," one of the doctors responds.

I keep my eyes on Reilly, watching her pour a cup of water, place a straw in the cup and bring it back to me. She puts the straw to my lips. I try to follow the doctor's directions and only take a small sip. Just that small bit of water feels like fucking heaven. Reilly takes the cup away before I can get any more. She places it down on the table next to the bed.

"Wha..." I want to ask what happened. She grabs my hand again, and I feel myself relax into her touch. I turn my eyes to look at Zac, who is watching Reilly with an odd kind of fondness. How long was I fucking asleep for? Did I wake up in the *Twilight Zone?* Zac does not like anybody other than Alyssa and Ella. He barely tolerates me on most days.

I search his eyes for answers. I'm usually pretty good at reading him, just as he is with me. I try to ask again what the fuck happened. "Wha... t?" I get the one word out, eventually. This shit is frustrating as hell. I can hear the monitors' beeping increasing. I can feel myself getting worked up. I'm used to the feeling. I usually relish it, use it as an outlet when I'm training or fighting. Except I can't do either of those right now. I can't fucking move.

"Bray, you were shot. Do you remember?" Zac asks.

I was fucking shot? What cocksucker fucking shot me? A soon to be dead one, when I can get out of this bed. I don't remember getting shot. I can remember flying home from Hawaii. I can remember sleeping at Reilly's house and waking up to her mum's cooked breakfast. After that, I'm drawing a blank.

"N... n... o," I reply.

"You were shot in the abdomen. Nowhere near your fucking head, mind you. Yet you've been in a coma for fifty-nine days. Fifty-nine days, asshole," Zac growls. Fuck, I was out for fifty-nine days? No wonder Reilly was sobbing when I came to. Has she been waiting here that whole time? Why didn't someone look after her? Help her?

The thought of her sitting by my bed, day in and day out, both pisses me off and makes me happy as fuck that she's mine. She's the most loyal girl you'll ever meet, and she's fucking mine.

# Chapter Twenty-Three

**REILLY**

H E'S COMING HOME TODAY. I actually get to take Bray home today. I feel like I've been waiting for this day to arrive forever. Yet, for Bray, I'd probably wait the rest of my life. If I had to spend my life living in a hospital to be with him, then so be it, I'd do it. I can't be without him. That fact has been made abhorrently clear.

I came so close to losing him. I've never been one to take my loved ones for granted. I already knew they could be taken away in the blink of an eye. It's the very reason I pushed Bray away so much at first, why I didn't want to get involved with him. I knew that if I let myself love him, then I'd really freaking love him. Which also meant I'd be left in pieces when I lost him.

The last six weeks have been gruelling, gut-wrenching, an emotional rollercoaster. Bray has undergone intense physical therapy to be able to relearn everything. It was tough, watching him push himself day after day to do the most basic of tasks like walking, dressing, eating. But it's all paid off. He is now able to walk unassisted; it's still at a slower pace and at times unsteady, but he is walking. His speech came back to normal after two weeks.

The first full sentence he uttered was to tell me he loved me. After I bawled my eyes out, because I honestly never thought I'd hear those words again, I told him just how much I loved his ass and asked him to marry me. I did not get the reaction I would have hoped for.

*"I love you," Bray said—the full sentence—no stops, pauses or breaks. He just told me he loved me in one fell swoop. I can feel the tears well in my eyes. I don't even try to stop them, letting them fall. Bray telling me he loves me is something I thought I'd never hear again.*

*Once I compose myself again, I tell him, "I love you so much, it hurts. I love you more than I thought I could love anyone. You complete me, Bray. I always thought Holly was my other half, but it seems I have another, and that's you. You are the other half of my soul. As soon as we get out of here, I want you to fly me away and marry me." Bray's eyebrows draw in, his eyes shining with unshed tears. "I... already." He points between us both. "Married?" he questions. As I'm trying to decipher, he points to me and says, "Mrs." Then he pauses again before he gets the words out. "Call you Mrs.," he says while pointing to the door.*

*He thinks we are already married because all the doctors and nurses refer to me as Mrs. Williamson. Huh, I never thought to correct any of them. I liked being called Mrs. Williamson, so I let it continue so long that I forgot why it started in the first place.*

*"Wait, you think we're already married? Do you remember getting married, Braydon?" I wait for his answer. To which, he shakes his head no.*

*"No, you know why, because we haven't. Trust me, the day you marry me, you are not going to forget. I'm a damn catch!" I laugh.*

*Bray's eyebrows raise in question. I've gotten really good at reading his gestures and figuring out what he needs or wants over the last two weeks. Right now, he wants more information.*

*"Right. When you were first brought in, the doctor was questioning how I was your family. Zac was there and, without flinching, he told him I was your wife. I just let the little lie continue all this time."*

*I watch as Bray's face lights up; his smile is a welcoming sight that I want to spend the rest of my life receiving.*

Over the next four weeks, as Bray's speech improved, we spent nights planning out our life together. We talked endlessly about what we wanted. Bray wanted eight kids. I vetoed that straight away and said maybe two, definitely no more than three. His reply was, "Babe, junior's boys are champions; they're going to impregnate you quicker than you can blink. They're just going to swim right on up and pop those eggs of yours."

I didn't bother to argue, but in my head, I was reminding myself to make a doctor's appointment for birth control, ASAP. I'd let mine lapse over the last few months. It's not like junior was getting anywhere near my eggs, not that Bray didn't try to persuade me. The number of times he told me to lock the door and *climb on*—yeah, it didn't take long for him to be able to say those words—I denied him. There was no way I was doing anything to jeopardise his recovery. The most he got, because I kind of felt bad for junior, was my hand and mouth. Although, I won't lie, it was different without feeling the metal of his Prince Albert. The doctors removed it the day he got brought in.

I told him how much I was going to miss that thing; he promised he was making an appointment with the piercer to get it back. I silently thanked the gods. Because that tiny bit of metal gives an unbelievable amount of pleasure.

Pleasure like I've never felt before it. Not that Bray's junior isn't impressive without it, because it is.

I'm watching Bray as he dresses. We're waiting on Zac to come and pick us up. Both of us cannot wait to get out of here and go home. I haven't told Bray, I didn't even ask, I just took the liberty and moved myself into his house. I figured he asked me to move in with him enough times before the incident, the offer would still stand.

I had Holly arrange for my things to be moved. My mum cried. She's been amazing throughout this process, spending many hours just sitting in the hospital with us. When Bray woke up, she made sure to visit every other day with baked treats for him. I wasn't allowed to eat any of them.

It pains me to watch how much effort it's taking him to get dressed by himself, to do a simple thing like pull his sweats up and put a shirt over his head. I want to help him, I'm itching to help him, but he's determined to do it all himself. The fact that he's a fighter has never been clearer than it has been watching him through his recovery. He was able to push through pain, frustration and fatigue like I've never seen before.

I admire his grit and determination. I admire how much he fought to be able to achieve the simple things most take for granted. He never gave up; he pushed his body beyond limits that even the doctors were amazed at the speed of his physical recovery. I won't lie, as he stands before me in a pair of grey sweats, no shirt, no shoes, I'm kind of enjoying the slowness of that shirt being pulled on.

My eyes travel up and down his body. He's lost a fair bit of his muscle mass, but he's still toned and defined as hell. The things I want to do to that body. I lick my dry lips recalling the things I have done to, and with, that body. I'm lost in my thoughts until Bray breaks my daydream, my very enjoyable daydream.

"Babe, unless you want me to bend you over this bed and fuck you senseless right now, you need to stop looking at me like you've just seen a tall glass of water in the desert." He finishes his comment with that smirk, the one he knows makes my damn panties wet, just at the sight of it.

I look up at the clock, like I'm actually considering his offer. As much as I want to, there is no way that's happening here. In this hospital room.

"As appealing as that offer is, your brother should be here any minute." I shrug in a too bad kind of motion.

"I'll lock the door and he can fucking wait," Bray offers, just as said brother walks through the door.

"Who can wait? You guys ready to blow this place or what?" he asks.

"I'm ready, so ready," I tell him, as I get up and greet him with a hug. Yep, apparently that happens now. Zac and I, friends? Who would have thought? "Thank you for picking us up."

"I'm doing it for you; that asshole made us wait fifty-nine fucking days. It would only be fair if we made him wait on a ride home."

Zac reminds Bray as often as he can that he slept for fifty-nine days. Tortured us for fifty-nine days. Not that he had any control over it, Zac knows that, but I've learnt that's how they communicate with each other.

"You know, I'm still not sure if I'm on board with this newfound friendship with you two. It's not fair to gang up on the injured. Whatever happened to rooting for the underdog?" Bray says.

"Deal with it. Reilly is my new sister, so if you fuck up again and I have to watch her heart break, again, I'm gonna kick your fucking ass," Zac says, with a very serious tone in his voice.

"I'd let you kick my ass. But, I'm not planning on fucking

up again. We're getting married, we're having eight babies and we are going to grow old and grey together." Bray walks up and wraps his arm around me.

"Two. Two babies," I correct him.

"So I keep hearing." Zac rolls his eyes. It's true, Bray mentions the fact that we're getting married and having babies as often as he can drop it in conversation.

He even has all the nurses swooning over him. Which brings me back to the shirt. There is no way in hell, he's walking out there with only a pair of grey sweats on. I'd end up having to claw some eyes out for sure.

I walk over to the bed where he left his shirt and pick it up. I don't bother handing it to him. I pull it over his head and let him do the rest. Once he has his shirt on, it's no better. He still looks like sex on legs. Damn it, I really need to get laid. Soon. As I'm looking him up and down, I can feel myself getting more and more turned on.

"Reilly," Bray growls, snapping me from my dirty thoughts, again. He really needs to stop interrupting my thought process.

"Okay, if you two are finished eye-fucking each other, let's get out of here." Zac picks up the two bags by the door and leaves the room.

I take hold of Bray's hand and walk out with him. Walk out of this dreary, cold place and into our future. He once made me a promise that he would always fight for us, because we were worth fighting for. He kept that promise. He has fought day in and day out to get back to who he once was, to be able to give us the future we both so desperately want and dream of.

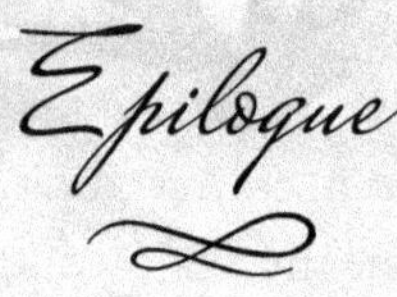

# Epilogue

*Bray*

*Six months later*

I'M speechless when Reilly comes out of the bathroom in a white lace corset, white lace thong and thigh-high stockings. She's fucking perfection standing there, leaning against the door frame while waiting for me to say something, to give her instruction. I'm not finished admiring the view of my wife though, so she can wait a little longer.

My wife, that goddess right there is my fucking wife. I want to run up to the top of this Vegas high-rise and scream it out for all to hear. I, Bray Williamson, put a ring on it and locked it down.

It's been a tough six months. My recovery seems to have taken its time. Although the doctors say I made great progress and recovered quicker than anyone they've seen, I feel like it's taken longer than necessary. The hardest part of this mess is not being able to fight. I tried to get everyone on board with me entering the ring again. I had coach at the house every other day going through routines and training.

Every doctor has advised against it, but they're doctors; they're meant to advise against shit like that. The thing that made me wake up, made me realise that there is much more to life than fighting, was Reilly. The look of utter shock and horror that would cross her face whenever I mentioned going back in the cage.

She was never all for me fighting before, but she never looked like I killed her cat while discussing it before either.

When I asked her about why she looked so terrified her reply was, "I spent two months sitting by your bedside waiting for you to wake up. I spent two months praying to a god I wasn't even sure existed anymore. I spent two months thinking I had lost the best thing to ever happen to me. I don't ever want to experience that kind of pain again. I won't stop you. I won't ask you not to fight, that has to be completely your own decision. Whatever you decide, I'll still be your biggest cheerleader."

I was just as speechless then as I am now. After replaying her words through my head for two weeks, I decided not to go back in the cage. I thought I'd feel a loss at the thought of never fighting again. What I felt was a weight lifted. I still get antsy, my body itching with energy that needs to be moving at times. When this happens, I either seek out Reilly to expel energy together, or I hit the gym and give myself a gruelling workout.

In the last six months, I've managed to regain all the muscle loss that happened after the shooting. It's been a long slow process, but I finally feel like my old self. It was fucking torture those first few months, not being able to get up and walk, do normal mundane everyday things like button up my own fucking clothes. If it wasn't for Reilly and Zac constantly being by my side throughout the recovery, I probably would have gone mad or given up completely.

"*Ahh,* Bray, are you just going to sit there staring all night?" Reilly's voice snaps me out of my own head.

"Well, when the views this good, why the hell not?" I question her.

"For one, it's our wedding night, and you only get one shot at making a memorable wedding night. Two, these shoes, as hot as they look, really are not comfortable and I can't stand here all night." She stomps one of those ridiculously high stilettos on the floor.

I don't make an effort to move. I stay seated on the edge of the bed. I started stripping my clothes off while Reilly was in the bathroom. I got down to just my trousers when she opened the door and I had to sit my ass down before I fell at her feet. She took the breath right out of me.

"Your feet hurt, babe?" I ask, watching as she nods her head.

"What kind of husband would I be if I let my wife get sore feet on our first night of being married? Not a very good one, and I plan to be the best husband who ever existed. Not sure if you noticed, but I'm fucking great husband material. It's like you won the lottery of husbands when you said *I do* tonight."

Reilly laughs. "I want to disagree and bust that ego of yours a little, but we don't lie to each other, so I won't disagree. I did win the lottery of husbands."

As I take her in, I recall the moment she said I do, earlier tonight in a Vegas chapel. We did end up running off to Vegas to get married. We did however let our family tag along. We also switched things up. I wasn't as stupid as Zac. I knew Reilly didn't have her dad to walk her down the aisle. When I questioned her about what she wanted to do, because I was not about to let her walk down that aisle alone, she got teary and told me that nobody could replace her dad's spot.

She then decided that we would walk down together, that it was our wedding and we could make the rules. The idea of walking down the aisle together as equals, as partners, was fucking brilliant. My girl is a fucking genius. So that's what we did—we met at the end of the aisle and walked down hand in hand. After I spent a good five minutes trying to convince her to sneak off to a closet with me first.

She told me to wait, some crap about delayed gratification. So now I'm going to make her wait. First, I need to deal with her aching feet, because there is no way she's removing those shoes until after they've spent hours digging into my back.

"Kneel," I tell her, my voice leaving no room for argument. "Right where you are now, kneel."

Reilly glares at me; this is not what she wanted. Too bad she's not the one running this show. After a minute of glaring, she relents. Following my instruction, she kneels, sitting back on her heels. I don't miss the slight shiver that runs through her body as she does this.

"Put your hands on your knees."

I wait for her to follow the instruction. Silently, she places her hands on her knees, palms down.

"Pull your legs apart, as far as they go. I want to see that pretty pussy I own."

Reilly licks her lips as she slowly spreads her legs apart. She's so responsive to being ordered around in the bedroom. Try to tell her to do something outside of the bedroom and I get a completely different reaction. Her tiny thong does nothing to cover her. It's basically see- through with how wet it is.

Inhaling, I can smell her arousal from here. I can see her pussy dripping for me; it's like a beacon, a siren calling for me to pet it. And pet it, I plan to. Tilting my head to the side, I look her over. I still can't believe that she's mine. I need to keep this scene locked away in my memories. I don't ever want to forget this moment.

"I hope you weren't counting on a night of slow passionate love making, babe, because I plan to fuck you so hard you won't be able to walk straight tomorrow."

"Well, what are you waiting for?"

"Delayed gratification, babe. Good things come to those who wait." I replay her own words back to her.

Reilly growls at me. "Bray, do not make me wait, please."

Fuck, she uses that please like a fucking weapon. She knows I can never deny her anything when she uses that please. Getting up off the bed, I walk over to her slowly, and a small smirk crosses her face. She thinks she's won. Little does she know, I'm planning on toying with her as long as I possibly can. I don't ever want this night to end.

Grabbing her with my hand around her throat, I tip her head back. Bringing my face down to hers, I gently brush my lips along hers as I make my way to her ear. While trailing the fingers of my other hand along the top of her breast, I whisper, "I hope you're comfortable, babe. I'm not planning to rush through my dessert tonight. I'm going to take my time, relish in the sweetness that I know is waiting for me. I'm going to lap up the weeping juices like it's my last meal and savour it."

Reilly moans; she goes to close her legs. I know she's dying to get some friction to her core. Squeezing tighter on her neck, I growl at her, "Don't you dare close those fucking legs, Reilly."

With a grunt, she spreads them back open. With my hand still around her throat, I hold her still as my lips attack her neck before making their way down to the tops of her breasts. This corset is in my fucking way. I can't get to those delicious pink nipples I want so bad. I stand and make my way over to the dining table and pick up a steak knife.

Reilly doesn't even flinch when I bring the knife back,

running the tip of it along the skin of her neck and breast. She really fucking trusts me a lot. Pulling the fabric of the corset away from her skin, so I don't fucking cut her, I slice right down the middle—her breasts bouncing as they're freed from their confines.

I don't waste time getting my mouth and hands on those pink nipples, positioning myself between her legs to prevent her from being able to close them. I take my time sucking and biting on each nipple. Reilly is a writhing mess by the time I come up for air. Her moans fill the room, as she attempts to push me away one minute, only to pull me closer the next, with the hold she has on my head while pulling at my hair.

I kiss my way down her stomach, before twisting and laying my head on the ground between her spread legs. Reaching up, I grab her hips and lift her, positioning her just where I want her, with her pussy right above my face. Ripping the tiny piece of lace that attempts to cover her, I slowly glide my tongue along her slit, from top to bottom.

She falls forward the moment my tongue connects with her clit, her hands landing on the tops of my thighs. It doesn't take her long before those same hands are travelling up and undoing my pants and releasing junior.

As she slowly strokes her hand up and down my cock, I continue my slow attack on her pussy.

The moment her tongue licks the slit in my tip, twirling around my piercing, I almost lose control. Fuck that feels good. I'm not about to lose out in the first round. Sliding my tongue right up to her puckered hole, I lick and twirl around it. This is a move I know drives her insane. She starts bucking against my face, attempting to grind down on me, and I have to hold her hips to keep her still. No doubt, she will be left with my fingerprints all over those hips tomorrow.

I slowly slide two fingers in and out of her pussy while

licking around her back hole. She's so fucking close that she's all but forgotten about junior while her attempts to stay focused on her task are weak. I fucking love seeing her fall apart and to be the one, the only one, making her see the fucking stars.

Picking up the speed, I thrust my fingers in harder and harder, while flattening my tongue out on her hole. She grinds down on me, screaming my name as she comes undone before falling flat on top of me. After a few minutes, Reilly slides off me and onto the floor.

Deciding I've given her enough recovery time, I stand, pick her up, and throw her down on the bed. She squeals as she lands in the middle of the bed. I strip out of my pants before crawling up her body. She looks so fucking perfect, her red hair sprawled out above her like a halo. Her pale skin is glistening with goosebumps. As I look down at her, I send a little prayer up, thanking God that this woman is mine.

"I fucking love you so damn much, Reilly Williamson." I look into her eyes and I can see the pure love she has for me too.

"I love you more than you'll ever know, Bray. More than words can describe." She reaches up, wrapping her hands above my neck and pulling my lips down to connect with hers. I know I wanted to fuck her until she couldn't walk tomorrow. Plans change though, right now all I want to do is love her the way she deserves to be loved.

That's how we spend the rest of our first night of being husband and wife, making sweet, tender love, over and over again. Our bodies and souls fused together as one, and I wouldn't have it any other fucking way.

*Reilly*

*Two years later*

"Aunty Rye Rye!" Ashton, the little chubby two and a half year old runs up to me, arms stretched high. Just as I'm about to attempt to bend down to him, Bray swoops in, lifting him up in his arms.

"Ash, my man. You know Aunty Rye Rye can't pick you up," he says while ruffling Ashton's hair.

"Babies," Ashton says, pointing at my obvious, expanding stomach that is now the size of a house. I guess in a way it is a home.

"Yeah, mate, Aunty Rye Rye has uncle Bray's babies in there," Bray confirms. I roll my eyes at him.

He loves to drop that line as often as he can. He knocked me up, not once, but twice in the one go. Yep, I'm pregnant with twins, and he's taking all the credit for them being twins. Never mind the fact that I am a twin, and that the genetics for twins comes from me, not him.

"Yes, Ash, it is all Uncle Bray's fault that I have babies in my tummy making it so big," I tell him, kissing his cheek.

"Big babies," Ash says, rubbing my belly while I glare at Bray.

"See, even our two-year-old nephew agrees that I'm fat." I'm so grumpy; pregnancy has not been my friend and I still have three months to go.

"Babe, you are not fat. You are fucking gorgeous, glowing even," Bray says as he leans in and kisses me on my forehead. That's his move to calm me, and it works every damn time.

"Ash, mate, clearly your dad has not taught you very well yet. You don't tell the girls they have big tummies; you can tell them they have big boo—" He's cut off by Alyssa's scream.

"Do not think about finishing that sentence, Braydon. I will knock you down. I've done it once. I can do it again," she yells across the room.

Zac walks up and plucks Ash from Bray's arms, then slaps him across the back of the head. "You fucking idiot, do not teach my son your man-whoring ways."

Bray stumbles back, hand over heart. "*Ahh*, bro, that hurts. Besides, who do you think I learnt it from, *huh*? I'll tell you, I learnt it from watching—"

Bray's sentence dies off with the icy glare that Zac throws his way. I swear even after three years, that guy can still scare me with that glare.

"Watching Jersey Shore," Bray finishes, saving himself from another slap to the head.

"You know those two babies you impregnated your wife with?" Zac asks.

"Yep, know them well," Bray answers with a huge smile across his face.

Zac smirks, nods his head towards my belly and says, "They're both girls, bro. Those babies are girls, and with any luck, they're going to look like their mother."

The smile from Bray's face completely vanishes. He goes a bit pale before he recovers. "Shut up, they are going to be nuns. Reilly, we're joining a fucking church tomorrow."

Alyssa, Sarah, Holly and I all burst into laughter standing in the middle of my kitchen. I stop laughing just as quickly as I start. "Sorry, gotta pee," I say, dashing out of the room. Over my shoulder I yell, "But thanks for calling me hot, Zac!"

"Not what I said," he calls back.

I finish in the bathroom, walk back out and see everyone has made their way out to the deck—Zac, Bray and Dean all surrounding the BBQ while the girls sit on the lounge sipping glasses of wine. Man, I miss wine.

I stop and admire the scene. Little Ashton is playing out on the grass. Bray had a play gym installed for him the day after he was born, claiming that it was part of his best uncle duties. It's taken two years, but Ashton is just now big enough to play on it, under the ever-watchful eye of Zac—his eyes constantly wandering between Ashton and Alyssa. I can't believe that this is my family now.

The ringing doorbell pulls me away from the scene. I pull it open to my mum, holding a tray of baked goods. Rolling my eyes at her, I open the door to let her in. It's become her and Bray's thing; whenever she visits, she brings him baked goods, and no one else is ever allowed to eat them.

"Hey, mum." I kiss her cheek.

"How're you feeling, sweetie? How are my grandbabies in there? Is your mummy looking after you?" she talks to my stomach.

"Your grandbabies want one of those chocolate brownies," I say, reaching for the tray, only to have her pull it away.

"Don't even think about it, Reilly. You know these are for Bray."

I give up, nothing works on her. If it was my dad, I'd be able to wrangle those brownies. But not mum, she doesn't fall for any of my tricks.

"Everyone's out back," I say, walking her through the house. I used to think of this house as overly huge with a lot of wasted space, but now that the twins are coming, I'm thankful that we have so much room. Bray said when he bought it, he wanted to fill it with a football team of children; it just took him a while to find his co-coach.

He's dreaming if he thinks I'm letting myself get knocked up again. As much as I'm looking forward to these little girls coming into the world, pregnancy is not for the faint-hearted. I blame Alyssa; she made it look easy.

As soon as my mother is out on the deck, Bray has her

engulfed in a hug. "Lynne, I'm so glad you're here. Maybe you can help me convince your daughter that we should join a church."

I glare at Bray. Holly throws something—I think it's a piece of bread. It hits his head but bounces right off.

"We are not joining a church, Bray," I say, falling into a seat next to Holly.

"Well, I think it's a lovely idea," my mother says—of course she does. Bray just asked an Irish Catholic mother if we should go to church.

"Bray, why don't you tell my mum why it is exactly, that you want to join the church." I smirk at him.

Holly high-fives me. She knows once my mum hears the nonsense, she will switch to our team.

"So our babies, your granddaughters, can become nuns," Bray says so seriously; to which, my mum laughs her ass off.

"Oh, hunny, Bray. I'm sorry, but if those babies turn out anything like their mother, you're going to be chasing boys away from the age of ten." She then scrunches her face up and adds, "Actually, if I recall, the first time Reilly kissed a boy, she was three. It was at a play group and she was adamant that the little boy was her boyfriend. No matter how much her dad told her she wasn't allowed to have boyfriends."

Bray looks over at me in shock. I just shrug at him. I can't help it if I appreciated boys from a young age. He then turns to look out at the yard and calls out to Ash.

"Hey, Ash." He waits for Ash to turn around.

"You and I are going to start training. I'm teaching you how to kick ass, mate," Bray declares, walking up to him and picking him up.

Everyone else is laughing, but the problem is Bray's not kidding. He seriously is going to start teaching Ash how to fight. As he reaches the top of the deck again, Zac is quick to pinch Ash out of Bray's hands.

"*Aw,* come on, man. He needs to learn how to protect his little cousins." Bray then looks at Alyssa.

"You…" He points to her. "You need to start pumping out some more boys. We're gonna need an army." Alyssa looks horrified.

"Me? Why me? You have a perfectly young and fertile sister you know, goes by the name of Ella," Alyssa informs him.

Both Zac and Bray groan and screw up their noses. "No," they say at the same time.

"Fuck no," Bray says again, shaking his head and adding extra emphasis to the no.

I expected their reaction, but what makes me curious is Dean's reaction. He goes still, looking back and forward between the two brothers. They're in front of him so they can't see him, or his reaction.

"You know, she's not a baby anymore. It's bound to happen," he says.

Both brothers turn and glare at him. Bray, who happens to know just how Ella feels about Dean, raises his eyebrows.

"Oh, and just who do you think it's going to happen with?" he asks, then furthers his point, trying to elicit a reaction from Dean. "You think Ella's in her apartment now, busy with some university jock she met last night?"

Dean's face goes blank. Got to give it to the guy, he has one hell of a poker face when he needs it. I notice his hands clench and unclench though. He does not like that thought at all. I can't wait to see how this plays out in the future. That man is in love, stupid for denying it, but in love he is.

"She is studying. I had a call from her earlier. She's alone in her apartment, idiot," Zac says to Bray.

"I know that. I spoke to her an hour ago," Bray confirms. It amazes me how much these two can't let go of their baby sister. It's also endearing to know that my girls are going to experience that same unconditional love.

Bray is going to be the best father. He excelled at being the best boyfriend, he excelled at being the best husband and I know he will be the best father.

"Bray, can you help me up?" I hold out my hands to him.

I can fully get up on my own, sort of; I just want an excuse to touch him and pull him away from everyone else. He walks over and pulls me up, not letting go of my hands until he knows I have even footing. I grab his hand and pull him inside.

"I need you to, *ahh*, help me reach something in the kitchen," I say maybe a bit too loudly.

Once inside, I pull his mouth down to mine. I'm so hungry for him. I thought I was horny a lot before, but that has nothing on these bloody pregnancy hormones. I moan into his mouth as he takes over the kiss.

We eventually pull apart, breathing heavier than we were before. "You good?" he asks while pushing my hair out of my face.

"I'm good. I just really, really love you." This is nothing new to him. I tell him multiple times a day how much I love and appreciate him.

"I really fucking love you too," he replies.

I get lost for a moment in those green orbs of his. I thank God that he was able to bulldoze those walls of mine down. I thank God every day that our souls are fused together as one.

# Entwined With Him

BOOK THREE

Ebook ISBN 13: 978-0-6489981-4-3

Paperback ISBN 13: 978-0-6489981-5-0

Cover Photography by
Simon Xiang - https://simonxiang.myportfolio.com/

Cover Illustration by
Kristine Moran - coverbunnies@gmail.com

Editing services provided by
Kat Pagan - https://www.facebook.com/PaganProofreading

# Dedication

*Dedicated to my friend Catharina. Cat, I couldn't choose a better person to be growing and developing alongside during my writing journey. Throughout the development of Entwined, you have taught me a great deal of knowledge. You have encouraged me to be the best version of myself that I can be; for that, I will be forever grateful to you and for you.*

**Ella**

It's been four years since I picked myself up off the floor and made a plan to escape. Sometimes, the grass is not greener on the other side; it's darker.

University was my fresh start.

A life away from him.

It wasn't enough. I couldn't escape the memories.

My demons are not ones you can see. No, they're well hidden. They stay in the dark, haunting every second of my being. I fight every day to be better, to not give in.

I'm back now.

I'm better now.

I can handle being back here in the club.

I can handle being around him again.

At least, that's what I thought. All my well laid plans go up in flames when my eyes land on him.

Dean, my brother's best friend.

Dean, the one man I've always loved.

**Dean**

Four years ago, I did the hardest thing I've ever had to do.

I walked away from the love of my life.

She was young; she needed to go and live her dreams, without me dragging her into my darkness.

She's also the little sister of my best friend.

Now, Ella is back, and she's not eighteen anymore.

I'm not going to make the same mistake twice.

She is mine. I will make sure everyone knows it, including her.

She claims she's broken. Broken or not, she is my one.

Always has been. Always will be.

# ENTWINED

***ENTWINED***
**W**IND OR TWIST TOGETHER, INTERWEAVE.

## ELLA

Four years earlier

"Oh my god, Ella, there is no way your brothers are letting you in the club wearing that dress," Niki says as we make our way down the street.

"Maybe not, but neither of them will let me walk back out the doors in this dress either, so the way I see it, they have to let me stay in there." I run my hands down my short—very short— black dress. It's skin tight, showing off my tiny waist and sizeable rear end. For a moment, I question my choice of outfit. I don't usually wear dresses this short, but tonight, I wanted to stand out. I wanted him to finally notice me as a woman, and not as his best friend's little sister.

We're heading to my brother's club; Zac owns The Merge. It's currently Sydney's number one club, the place everyone wants to be. The line at the door is already leading down the street. I take Niki's hand and drag her to the front of the line, despite the dirty looks of all the people who have been waiting.

They can hate me all they like, but the one benefit of being the little sister is skipping the queue. As I get to the rope at the front of the entrance, the bouncer's eyes go wide. He immediately says something into his earpiece, more than likely letting Dean, his boss, my brother's best friend and head of security—oh, and also the one guy I want and can't have—know that I arrived.

Good, let him come down here and see what he's missing out on. An evil smile crosses my face; this is the reason for this dress. I want Dean to be out of his mind, to see that I'm not just a little girl anymore.

"So, was it Dean or Zac you were so quick to dob me into?" I ask as I stop in front of the bouncer.

He looks unsettled, unsure what to say or do. He finally says, "Sorry, Ella. I have strict instructions to let Dean know whenever you walk through these doors. You need to go straight up to the VIP section." The bouncer, who seems to know my name yet I have no clue who he is, holds the door open for us.

Walking into The Merge is an experience in and of itself. Although I've been here plenty of times during the day, while Zac was working, I'd either spend my afternoons sitting in his office doing homework or down in the basement watching Bray train.

Zac, my oldest brother, has been my guardian since I was thirteen when our parents died. He has been the best, considering he was only twenty at the time. He always puts my needs first, never missed a school event. I will be forever grateful to Zac for the way he stepped up and took care of Bray and me.

Bray, the middle child in the family, is the typical middle child. He struggled the most when our parents died; he got into a lot of trouble as a teenager, which Zac always managed to drag him out of. Don't get me wrong, he's a great brother; he would do anything for me. Although they can be overbearing most of the time, I wouldn't trade my brothers for anyone. I also would never admit that to them.

The Merge is packed already; it's only ten o'clock and there are people lining the deep red walls of the club. Zac really did a great job building this place. The small intimate sections scattered across the lower floor are all filled with people. Zac had all the tables designed to represent couples in the throes of passion, his vision of bodies merging together.

When I was younger, I was never allowed on this floor; he used to take me in through the back, up the lift and straight to his office. It wasn't until I was sixteen that I finally saw what all the fuss was about. Let's just say, these sculptures made my little sixteen-year-old brain blush the first time I saw them.

Now that I'm eighteen, I don't blush so much anymore; but as I look at the sculptures I'm walking by on the way to the VIP section, I picture what it would feel like to have Dean's body wrapped around mine in these positions.

It's never going to happen though. It's a far-off pipe dream. Dean is loyal to Zac, ten years my senior and only sees me as his best friend's little sister. Hopefully this little black dress tonight is going to change his view of me.

Niki and I are already on our third cosmopolitan. I'm feeling the beginning of a buzz coming on. I'm also feeling the very urgent need to pee. I lean over the table to yell out over the music to tell her that I'm heading to the bathroom.

"I'll be back. Nature's calling." I point in the direction of the bathroom.

"Want me to come with?"

I shake my head; there's no need to take her with me. I have no doubt that there are at least two of Dean's security guys hiding in the shadows somewhere, watching my every move.

As I stand and make my way through the crowd to the bathroom, I stumble slightly—it's the heels. I haven't drunk that much yet. That's what I'm telling myself anyway.

The best thing about the VIP floor: there's no queues at the bathroom. When I enter the ladies' room, it's empty, quiet—the loud noise of the club muted behind these doors. I hear the door open and shut while I'm in the cubicle. Finishing up, I open the cubicle door and head over to the sinks.

Before I make it there, I'm grabbed from behind. A large hand comes around, covering my mouth. I'm momentarily stunned and I freeze. I look up into the mirror and see a large guy with a sneer on his face, his eyes dark and sinister looking.

I remember every move Bray ever taught me and start to fight my way out of his hold. I bring my foot down on his and try to twist and turn, while landing punches anywhere I can.

"Fucking little bitch, you think you can fight me off? Go ahead, give me everything you got. It's just going to make me taking you all the sweeter." His hands start grabbing at my body; he roughly grabs my breast in one of his hands and proceeds to push me up against the wall.

I'm trapped, my front pressed against the wall with this fucker pressed against my back. I can feel his hardness digging into my back. I fight the urge to throw up. I just need to fight back. I will not lose my virginity to rape. But even as I'm thinking this, I know I'm screwed. I can't fight off a guy this big. But I will not go down without a fight either.

I bring my leg up behind him and manage to connect my heel with his balls, not hard enough though. He grunts as he spins me around and punches me in the face. My vision goes blurry. I feel my body slump to the ground.

"Fucking slut, you'll pay for that. I'm going to slam my cock so hard into your little pussy, and when I'm done with that, I'll take your ass too."

One of his meaty hands holds me up by my upper arm as he backhands me across the face. I scream as loud as I can, even though I know it's hopeless. No one is going to hear me. One thing I do know for sure is that when Zac and Bray do find me, this guy won't be left breathing. That brings a smile to my face.

"You like it, you dirty little slut. I knew you would fucking love it." He smiles like he has won.

"You're fucking delusional. The only reason I'm smiling right now is because I know when my brothers find you, you're a dead man."

"Fuck you! Think your brothers scare me, bitch?"

The smile is wiped off my face as he punches me in the stomach. I fall to the floor, the pain radiating through my body. My brain wants to shut down; it wants to black out. I'm fighting to stay alert. I see a boot coming for my head. I brace myself for the hit I know is coming. My eyes squeeze closed and I hunch over, trying to protect my head the best I can.

I freeze in this position, waiting, except the kick never comes. I hear loud shouts and shuffling. When I open my eyes again, Dean is leaning down over me. He's talking but I don't hear what he's saying.

I manage to pick myself up and crawl onto him. I bury my head in his chest and cling to his shirt. This is when I finally let myself cry. I finally feel like I can relax with the knowledge that I'm safe now.

"It's okay, El. I've got you," Dean says as he hugs me back just as tightly, his hand running through my hair, as he holds my head against his chest. I feel my body lift as he picks me up.

"Take the fucker down to the basement. I'm going to fucking kill him," Dean instructs the security guys who are currently picking up the unconscious asshole who attacked me.

Zac carries me from the car up to our apartment. I let him think I'm asleep, because, right now, in my brother's arms, I know nothing can get to me. I know no one can touch me. As safe as Zac makes me feel, it has nothing on the way I felt when I was in Dean's arms.

Dean's energy, the possessive protectiveness he was radiating over me tonight, was like nothing I've ever felt or experienced. The promises he whispered into my ear, the ones no one else could hear, those are the words I'm trying to hold onto right now. Those are the words that bring me comfort.

When Zac carries me into the apartment, and I hear Dean tell him that he'll take me, I want to jump from my brother's arms and into Dean's. I don't though. I let them think that I'm asleep.

When I feel myself being passed over, I know it's Dean who I'm being passed to. His citrus scent assaults my senses. His tight hold of me as he walks down the hall warms me. My fist clenches around his shirt; there is no way I'm letting him let go of me.

Dean walks through my room, placing me on the bed. I hold on tight to his shirt; he's not leaving me here. He can't leave me here. I can't be in here by myself.

"Wait, don't leave me, please. Don't leave me here," I beg. I can feel myself start to panic.

"I'm not leaving you, Ella, just let me turn off the light and shut the door," he whispers.

"No, leave the light on, please."

"Okay, Princess, the light stays on." He untangles my hands from his shirt and makes his way over to the door, shutting it. I watch his every step, ready to jump up and follow him if he walks out.

He doesn't. He walks back over to the bed, takes his shoes off and lies down next to me. I then find myself wrapped in his arms, a place I never want to leave. This is how I cry myself to sleep, in his arms, with him whispering words of comfort in my ear.

## DEAN

Present

I'll never be able to forget the image of her lying on the bathroom floor, bloodied and bruised. Most days, I wish I could bring the fucker who did that to her back to life, just to see the life strangled out of him again. I'd never been so fucking terrified of losing someone as I was when I saw her.

The emotions that ran through me scared the hell out of me. I'd always been protective of her, always wanted to shelter her from the world, from our world—the one her brothers and I were involved with. And ever since she turned sixteen, that need to protect her changed from me wanting to protect a little sister, to me wanting to protect the one whom I loved most in the world.

There was just one problem though, no matter how much I loved her, how much I wanted her, I knew I could never have her. Ella was my best friend's little sister—ten years younger than me.

The moment she turned eighteen, I struggled on a daily basis; she wasn't underage anymore. I didn't feel like such a creep, wanting someone who was underage. She was legal and turning heads in any room she walked into.

She made no secret of how much she wanted me either, made no attempt to hide her feelings from me. The nights after her attack, she would call me in tears, begging me to come and help her. I could never say no. It was risky, spending those nights in her room with her brother, my best friend, just down the hall.

But I couldn't deny her the comfort she was seeking. I couldn't hear her cry and not be the one to wipe those tears away. For two months, I spent those nights in her bed, whispering promises into her ear as she would cry herself to sleep.

I always snuck out in the mornings, before she would wake. I'd go home and jerk off in the shower, relieving the hard-on I'd suffer with all night long having her soft body in my arms—her scent surrounding me, torturing me all fucking night, and reminding me of what I couldn't have.

I knew I had to put a stop to the sleepovers when she started to want more from me than what I could give her. She was young. She needed to experience life, to have the full university experience without me dragging her down with my shit. She needed to be young and carefree, and if I claimed her like she wanted me to, like I fucking wanted to, she wouldn't be able to have that.

I entered her room one night. She was sitting on her bed, knees pulled up to her chest. She looked up at me as I approached the bed.

"Am I that broken that you can't imagine yourself being with me?" she asked, tears running down her face.

My steps faltered momentarily before I climbed on the bed and pulled her into my arms. "There is not a single thing broken about you, Ella. You are fucking perfect," I told her as I swiped at her tears with my thumb.

"Then why don't you want me?"

"We can't do this, Ella. You know I can't do this. I want you more than I've ever wanted anyone. But you're too young; you need to live your life. You need to be young." I wasn't strong enough to keep doing this. I needed to stop coming into her room. This would be the last time.

"I don't need to be young. I need you, Dean. I love you. I want you," she cried.

Fuck, everything in me wanted to give in, every fibre of my

being wanted to claim her and make her mine. I didn't though. I kissed her gently, briefly, way too briefly.

"Ella, don't ever doubt that I fucking love you. I love you enough to let you go and live your life. I love you enough to put your needs above mine. I want you to have the life you're meant to have. I want you to go to university and be free. Be free of any troubles and worries. Not to be dragged down by being with me."

I stood up and walked out of her room. I left her falling apart on her bed. For the first time, since I can remember, I fucking cried. I went down to my car and fucking cried. I promised that one day, when the time was right, I would claim Ella as mine, despite knowing that Zac would want to kill me.


That was four years ago; now she's coming back. She ended up transferring universities to Melbourne. I have only seen her on the rare occasions she has visited her brothers. She wouldn't talk to me; she would go out of her way to avoid being anywhere near me. But she's back now, and she will be mine.

# One

ELLA

Walking into the penthouse, I look around. Everything looks the same as it did when I left four years ago. It's not the same though. I drop my bag on the hall table on my way into the living room.

The same black leather U-shaped lounge, covered in navy and white cushions, fills the room. The view of Sydney Harbour greets me through the floor-to-ceiling windows, the sun shining high over the top of the Harbour Bridge.

It's weird being back here after spending the last four years avoiding the place — avoiding the memories — the good and the bad. The day after what I refer to in my mind as *the incident,* I applied for entry into Melbourne University. I knew I wouldn't be able to stay around here and be okay.

Making my way down the hall, I open my bedroom door. I have not been back in here since the morning after the incident, when I picked myself up off my bedroom floor. I may have been able to pick up my body off the floor, but my heart, my soul, is still left in pieces.

I can see it like it was yesterday, the incident: me begging Dean to stay, not to leave me, then watching him walk out the door without so much as a backward glance. He chose to walk away, taking a piece of me with him, leaving me broken inside.

I haven't slept in this room since that night. I packed a bag and went to stay at Bray's house until it was time for me to make the move to Melbourne. Let's just say that conversation did not go over well with my brother Zac; he attempted to demand that I stay in Sydney.

It was a fight I was not backing down from though, and in the end, I won. It helped that Bray, when he finally woke up from the coma, was on my side. Oh yeah, my brother was shot by some crazy dude at The Merge. He ended up in a coma for two months. I honestly thought he would never wake up. He did though, and when he saw Zac and me arguing about me moving to Melbourne one day in his hospital room, he took pity on me. He told Zac to let me go, that it would be good for me.

He knew; Bray was the only person I ever told about my feelings for Dean. He also knew how heartbroken I was over the whole Dean not wanting me back scenario. Although he fought for me to be able to move to Melbourne, as soon as he was able to, he was on a flight once a month to check up on me.

Zac made fortnightly trips for the first six months. Then Alyssa gave birth to my ever-adorable nephew, Ash. Zac's visits became monthly after that, always bringing Alyssa and Ash with him. The thought of Ash made me smile; the one good thing about being back is I'm going to get to spend so much time being Aunty Ella to him and my twin nieces.

Fate has a funny way of coming back at you. Reilly, Bray's wife gave him two girls, twin girls, who I often remind him are going to be teenagers before he knows it. Lily and Hope are only one and a half now—the cutest little red-headed, green-eyed little girls. Thankfully they take after their mother, Reilly, Bray's wife.

Zac and Bray are both living out the dream, happily married with children and families of their own. As much as they include me in everything they do, and I do mean every little thing, it's not the same. I want the kind of love they have with their wives. I want someone to love me as fiercely as Zac loves Alyssa. I want someone to fight for me, the way Bray fights for Reilly.

I'm not sure that's ever going to be in my future. I'm too broken. I'm tainted by scars both inside and out. You would only see them if you got close enough, and I don't allow anyone that close. The only person who has seen all my scars, really seen them, is Bray. And that's only because he caught me at one of my lowest moments.

Two years ago, Bray came down for one of his surprise visits. Bray, being Bray, let himself in. Me being me, I was totally oblivious that he was there, my bathroom door open, razor in hand, and eyes closed as the razor broke through the skin. Euphoria erupted throughout my body; peace overcame my hectic mind as I was engulfed by the bliss of the pain.

Bray was beside himself. After sitting down—me crying and him holding me in a vice grip as if he was worried that I was going to fly away—he finally calmed down a little. He stayed in my apartment for the next two weeks, researched therapists, and went with me to sessions with five different therapists until I found one whom I was comfortable with.

During those two weeks, Bray also made me join a gym and take up boxing classes. His rationale was some crap about exercise making people happy. I didn't correct him that I wasn't unhappy per se, just broken.

I didn't cut because I was sad. I cut because I needed the pain. The pain not only made me feel alive, it became a distraction to the thoughts inside my head. It was like a drug, and I was addicted to the high that I got from it. I was addicted to the escape it offered.

Bray was right though; exercise did make me feel more balanced. I didn't stop cutting, but I can now go a few months at a time without cutting. I didn't need it as much as I used to. I kept up my weekly therapy sessions. Bray made me promise; he said he wouldn't tell anyone if I kept up with the therapy.

Thinking about cutting now, especially being in this room, is bringing on the urge to do just that. I can feel my skin itching, feel my heart pick up.

Shaking thoughts of the past from my head, I walk out of my room, shut the door behind me and head to Bray's room. I can't be in that bedroom. Dropping my bag on Bray's bed, I dig through until I find my workout clothes. I need to hit the gym before I give in to the urge coursing through me.

I spend the next hour running on the treadmill. I have "Fight Song" by Rachel Platten blasting from the speakers. I jump off the treadmill, my mind set on the punching bag. I really want to hit something right now. I turn around and come to a stop, my hand coming up to my heart.

"Jesus Christ, Bray, give a girl a warning next time you're going to creep up," I yell at him over the music.

Bray laughs, walks over to the wall and turns the music down.

"First, not creeping; you should be more aware of your surroundings, Sis. Second, come here and give your favourite brother a hug."

"I'm all sweaty, Bray. You don't want to hug me right now." I start to walk towards the bag hanging from the rafters — I still want to hit something. Before I reach the bag, I'm picked up and spun around.

"Damn it, Bray, put me down!" I try to get a punch in, but with the way he's holding me, my fists are only greeted by air. By the time he puts me back on my feet, I'm dizzy and stumble back a step.

As soon as I get my bearings, I punch his arm. "Don't mess with me, asshole. I'm not in the mood," my voice growls at him.

"Aww, little Ella wants to take on the champ? Okay, bring it. Give me all you got, little girl."

Bray starts jumping around with his fists up; little does he know I've gotten good at this. Right now, I also have enough built-up anger and frustration that I need to expel somewhere. Why not direct that at the pretty boy's face?

Smiling at him, I laugh a little before swinging and landing a right hook on his jaw. His head swings to the side. I caught him off guard. I wait for him to pounce on me but he doesn't. He just looks at me with a dumbfounded expression on his face.

"Damn, Ella, where the hell did you learn to punch like that?" he asks.

Shrugging my shoulders, I hold my hands up, ready to strike again. "I've been practicing. Come on, there's more where that came from."

"Uh-huh, I'm sure. First though, how long?" he questions.

Every time I talk to him, he will ask me the same question: *how long?* How long has it been since I have cut? I always answer honestly. I can't lie to him; he'd probably be able to tell anyway.

"Six months," I say with a smile, because three months is the longest time I've gone before that.

"Good, let's keep that number growing. Put your arms down before you hurt yourself. I'm not fighting you, Sweetheart."

As he goes to walk away, I stick my foot out, tripping him. I pounce on his back as he's falling to the ground and cling on to him like a monkey.

"Aww, is Brayden Williamson scared of his little sister? What will the fans think?" I tease.

Bray hasn't fought since he got shot. He had to retire from the cage. He now owns and runs a chain of MMA gyms he calls Club M. The original Club M—the fight club they used to run out of the basement of Zac's club, the one they thought I didn't know about—well, the boys closed it down. Everything Zac and Bray do now is way above board.

"Brat, get off me!" Bray turns over, dropping me on the floor and pinning me down. He looks down at me; it's like he can see into my damn soul when he stares like that.

He tilts his head before standing up and reaching his hand down to help me. He doesn't let go after I'm standing. Instead, he wraps his arm around my shoulder and walks us towards the door.

"How are you going to be, seeing him every day again?" Bray squeezes my shoulder.

He's referring to Dean. I'm going to be taking over a lot for Zac at the club. "I don't know," I answer honestly.

"Well, you call me. If you can't handle it, call me."

I nod my head in response. Honestly, I'm scared as hell over how I'm going to cope. Seeing him every day... What if he has a girlfriend? Or if he just has girls all over him all the time? I don't know if I can handle that. It's been four years. I should be over him. I should have moved on years ago. I'm not though, and I never moved on—still secretly wanting him, waiting for him.

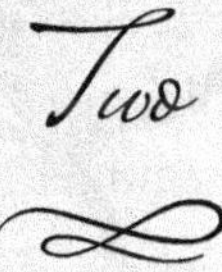

# Two

## DEAN

She's going to be here today. Ella. She won't be able to ignore me anymore. I'm going to make fucking sure of it. I've just sat in Zac's office with him, going over the increased security plans he wants in place now that Ella will be working here. Like I'd let anything fucking happen to her anyway.

Walking into the control room, I notice that every fucker is standing around the wall of screens, their attention on one screen in particular. What the fuck are they looking at?

"A hundred bucks says he closes!" Sam shouts.

"Nah, that chick's way out of even *his* league." Lachlan shakes his head.

Curiosity piqued, I walk over to see what the fuck they're carrying on about. When I see who is on the screen, my blood boils.

"Not a fucking chance. Any of you fuckers even think about touching her, I'll fucking kill you. That's if her brothers don't get to you first," I yell at them as I storm out of the room, heading straight for the first floor.

By the time I get to where she is, that fucker Shawn has his grubby paws on her, touching her arm as he says something in her ear. Ella's eyes go wide as she sees me storming up behind him. I grab his shirt and pull him off her. I don't even think as I uppercut him in the gut. He hunches over, before falling to the ground. *Fucker.* I want to fucking kill him.

I'm about to jump on him, to finish him off, when her voice breaks through my haze of rage.

"What the fuck, Dean?" Ella shoves past me to head towards Shawn, like she's going to help the fucker up.

*Not a fucking chance.* Wrapping an arm around her waist, I pick her up and spin her around. Standing so that I'm blocking her view of the whiny bastard on the floor while leaning in, I growl in her ear, "If you so much as touch him, Princess, I will fucking kill him — *that's a promise.*"

Ella's eyes go wide in shock before she composes herself, crossing her arms over her chest, which only draws my attention to her breasts — her black button-up sheer blouse doing nothing to hide the black bra underneath. Jesus Christ, I can see I'm going to be burying bodies by the end of the fucking day if she's walking around dressed like this.

Raking my eyes down her body, I audibly groan. She's wearing a pencil skirt, a black pencil skirt with white pinstripes; a slit runs all the way up her left thigh. I can see the top of her black thigh-high stockings, my cock instantly hardening as I picture those tanned, toned thighs wrapped around my head.

"Fuck, Ella! Did you leave half of your outfit at home? Because this cannot be all of it," I say, pointing up and down her body. I don't miss her nipples hardening, that poor excuse of a top doing nothing to hide them.

Ella notices where my gaze has stopped. She shivers. "Don't

flatter yourself, Dean. I'm not a naive eighteen-year-old anymore. It's fucking cold in here."

I smirk at her; there is no way she's not turned on right now. I can see the rosy hue come to her cheeks, her pupils dilating. Tilting my head as I inspect her further, I watch her thighs tightening together. I smirk down at her. "Sure, babe, if that's what you need to tell yourself."

I shrug before leaning in and whispering in her ear, "But you and I both know, if I was to stick my hand in your panties right now, you'd be fucking drenched." I straighten.

Ella makes a point to look behind me; she smiles up at me as she says, "Well, I mean, he *is* really hot."

I'm going to kill him. I'm turning around to do just that as Zac shouts out, "What the fuck is going on in here?" My best mate has always had a knack for timing. I turn and smile at Ella. I'm not going to have to kill him now. Zac's here and I'm sure he'll have no issue breaking his whole *do things by the book* code. When it comes to his little sister, there is no fucking book.

"Either of you want to tell me why one of my employees is currently on the floor, whining like a little bitch?" Zac asks as he steps over Shawn without a second glance at him.

"Sure, mate. Shawn here, thought he could touch something that didn't belong to him." I nod my head in Ella's direction, so he knows that something is Ella.

I can see the moment it registers in his brain — his features harden. This is the look he gets right before a kill. Well, used to get; we haven't done things that way for years. I'd happily go back to killing, to burying bodies right now though.

"Don't be an ass, Dean. Zac, that's not what it was. We were just talking, when your goon over here came and knocked him to the ground." Ella pushes past me, walking up to her brother.

Zac's eyebrows go up to his hairline when he gets a full view of her. He looks over to me, catching me staring at her fucking delicious heart-shaped ass, her skirt wrapped around it like a glove. I don't apologise or back down from his stare.

Ella's a grown ass woman now, and she is fucking mine. Nobody will be keeping me from her. I'll always be loyal to Zac, but Ella comes first — she always fucking has — even if I did have to break her heart four years ago.

I did that shit for her, not me. She deserved to have the experiences of university, of being a new adult, without me dragging her down. Now though, I want nothing more than to drag her to my bed and tie her fucking ass to it.

After what feels like an eternity, Zac looks back to his sister. "Ella, where the fuck are the rest of your clothes?" He shakes out of his jacket and attempts to wrap it around her shoulders, which she dodges.

I watch as she straightens her spine, ready to go toe-to-toe with her brother. "Zac, I will walk out of this door and not look back if you think you're going to be treating me like a child. I'm here to work, not to be bossed around by the likes of you two," she asserts, pointing to us both.

I smile as I watch her stand up for herself. I've always admired her spark. Now though, I couldn't be prouder of her. I fucking love her determination, her strength.

"Oh, and Dean?" she smiles.

"Yeah, Princess?" The nickname I gave her — the name I've never actually said out loud in front of anyone other than her — slips freely from my mouth. It catches her off guard. Zac's gaze spears into me, questions and doubt in his eyes.

"Who I choose to let touch me has absolutely nothing to do with you. If I want to let your whole security team touch me, I will." Her voice is sweet as she gives me a glare, dropping the saccharine smile from earlier. "Oh, and drop the fucking 'Princess'. I'm not anyone's Princess, asshole," she says as she storms off.

"Hey, Ella!" Zac shouts.

She turns to look at him, waiting for him to continue. However, Zac doesn't continue his sentence. He walks across the room and over to the DJ equipment. Picking up a microphone and turning some switches on, he looks at her, smirks and then speaks into the microphone.

"Listen up, fuckers." He waits so that everyone in the room, which now includes the whole security team who have come out to be spectators of the show we've been giving, is listening.

"Any of you even think about touching my sister, you're fired. Anyone who lets another man touch her, without putting a stop to that shit, is fired." He points over to Ella. "That woman there is Ella, my little sister. Treat her as if she's your own sister and we won't have any problems. Understand?"

The fucker looks directly at me for that last part. I refuse to acknowledge the question. I won't lie to my best friend. I also won't deny that I plan to do very unsisterly things to Ella. I stand there and fold my arms over my chest, refusing to budge from his stare down.

Ella huffs as she walks out of the room. I'm thankful she's walking towards the lifts, and not the front door, like she threatened to do just minutes before. I want to chase after her and let her know just how wrong she is. She thinks I don't have a say over her body, over who touches her fucking body. It's laughable really. She's going to have to learn real quick that her body is mine. Her heart is mine; her fucking soul is MINE! That lesson is going to have to wait though. I have a mess to clean up here first.

~

It's been a long-ass fucking day. Ella has gone out of her way to avoid me as much as possible, mostly locking herself away in

Zac's office. Zac has purposely had me doing shit on the floor. Every time I make it to his office, he's quick to get me out of there. It's only a matter of time before he confronts me about Ella.

I'm ready for it though. Maybe I should just come clean to him first, beat him to it. I'm currently sitting in his office, whisky in hand. Ella's been hiding out in the bathroom for the last twenty minutes. I'm not sure if she's listening or just waiting to hear me leave before she comes back out. I can hear the shower running, maybe she's just taking a shower.

I'm about to confess to Zac, to tell my best friend that I'm in love with his little sister. Tell him that I plan to keep her and there's not a damn fucking thing he can do about it. As I'm contemplating my words, Bray barges into the office, shocking both Zac and me. Bray hardly ever comes to the club anymore. He's been busy building his own empire these days — not to mention being a dad and husband.

"Good to see you haven't mastered the skill of knocking," I say to him. To which, he just flips me off as he walks to the bathroom door. He doesn't say a word to either Zac or me. Knocking on the door, he calls out, "Ella, it's me. Open the door."

The door opens slightly. Bray pushes himself inside before shutting the door, then I hear the sound of the lock clicking in place. Why the fuck is he locking himself in a bathroom with Ella?

"What the fuck is going on?" I ask Zac.

"No fucking clue," he says as he bangs on the door. "Bray, what the fuck's going on in there?" he yells.

Bray opens the door a crack, sticking his head out. He glares at me before telling Zac, "Ella's sick. She's not working tonight. I'm taking her home. I need you two fuckers to back up and give her some fucking space."

She's been fine all day. What the hell could she be sick with now? Bray's about to close the door when I stick my foot out, stopping it from closing.

"What's wrong with her? She's been fine all day," I ask.

"None of your fucking business. Stay the fuck away from her!" he shouts in my face. Most men would walk away from a confrontation with Bray. I'm not most men though. I push the door open further and walk into the bathroom. What I see, though, has my blood running cold. What the fuck?

# Three

ELLA

I've spent the day following Zac around, being his shadow, and learning everything I can possibly learn about the club, while avoiding Dean as much as I possibly can. I couldn't get away from him quick enough this morning.

The fact that he was right, that I was so turned on just by being so close to him — having him whispering in my ear, his woodsy scent surrounding me, his touch sending jolts of lightning throughout my whole body — I felt like I was burning up from the inside. And he knew it. He knew the effect he had on me.

Then I remembered him walking out on me four years ago, leaving me broken and sobbing on my bed. I remembered the months I spent waiting for him to tell me he made a mistake, waiting for him to come back and claim me, to take me as his own.

That's when I found my inner rage. I let that shit boil to the surface and let him have it. I'm stubborn and there is no way I am going to come back and let him try to control my life, like he didn't leave me a mess of broken pieces.

He used to call me his Princess; now I'm just the broken Princess. Not his, not anyone's, just broken. And I don't know how to fix myself. I thought I had it under control. I thought I was finally beating it — this need to inflict pain on myself. The need to cut, I've fought it successfully for six months.

I'm itching in my own skin at the moment. I know I should tell Zac I need to leave. I should just go home or go to the gym, somewhere other than this place. I can't. I need to suck it up and get on with it. I'm here to do a job. I'm going to prove to Zac that I can handle this, that I can take over for him.

It's hard being back in this club, the place it all started. Images of the night I was attacked play in my head on repeat all day. I've avoided going up to the VIP floor. I know I'll have to face it eventually; there is no way I can avoid that floor forever. Just like I know I can't avoid *him* forever. Although I sure am going to try my best.

"Are you sure you're okay?" Zac questions me for the millionth time today. It's nine p.m. The club is just starting to get busy. I'm not on the floor. I'm just watching the camera feeds from the wall of screens in Zac's office.

"Yes, I'm fine, but if you don't stop asking me, I might not be," I grit out.

Truth is, I'm not okay... I'm far from okay. I'm not about to admit that to Zac, especially not on the first day of the new job. I'm going to suck it up, and get out of here as soon as I can. I plan on hitting the gym as soon as I get home.

Sitting on the couch, with my MacBook on my lap, I'm looking over the spreadsheets of last year's, which Zac sent me. Something is off with them, but he hasn't figured out where they're going wrong. Whatever is wrong with them, I'm making it my mission to figure it out, before Zac does.

I know I'm a little competitive. I also want to prove that I deserve this job. I may have gotten it because I'm family, but family or not, Zac would never keep someone on his payroll if they didn't deserve to be there.

Just as I'm getting comfortable, and sinking into the numbers, *he* walks in. Dean swaggers in like he owns the joint. He looks directly at me, his gaze intense, searing through me, and burning me up from the inside. I try my hardest not to squirm, not to fidget. *Do not let the lion know you're afraid.* That's what he looks like right now, a goddamn lion about to pounce on his prey. His prey being me!

Nope, not going to happen. I will not roll over and be his prey, be the thing he decided is good enough to play with now. Maybe it's all in my head again... I'm reading too much into his looks, into his words. I've probably conjured the whole thing up from my wanton imagination. I wasn't good enough four years ago, I'm certainly not good enough for him now.

I need to get out of here. Throwing my laptop on the couch, I head for the bathroom, locking the door behind me. It's so quiet in here. Too quiet. I pace up and down the small space for a few minutes before the quietness of the room starts to become too much, and the walls start to close in on me.

I turn on the shower, the white noise of the running water somewhat soothing. Also, if Zac hears the shower running, he won't wonder why I'm in here so long.

Sitting on the floor with my knees pulled up to my chest, I'm staring at the tiny razor I'm currently holding between my fingers. I can feel the pain already, just one little slice and I can escape these thoughts in my head. I want to do it so badly, my hands shake. Tears run freely down my face.

I can't take it. If I just do one little cut, that won't be so bad. I can just do a little bit and then everything will feel better. This is what I'm telling myself in my head. There's another voice though, a quieter one. This one is telling me no, don't do it. It's only my first day here. How do I expect to cope in this place if I'm curled up in a ball, and locked in the bathroom, on my first fucking day?

Through my foggy haze, I know what I need to do. I need to call Bray. He will be able to help; he's always able to help me. Taking my phone out, I press the green button next to his name. He answers straight away, like he was waiting for my call.

"Ella, how's it being the big boss lady?" His voice is cheerful, but I can hear the undertone of worry there. It's always there, ever since he first caught me cutting a few years ago.

This time, that worry is warranted. I suck in a deep breath before whispering into the phone, "Bray, I... I need... I need help. I... I can't."

"Where are you? I'm coming now, Sweetheart. Where are you?" I hear the jostle of keys and the shuffling sounds of him moving around.

"I'm... I... in Zac's bathroom. Bray it's bad. I... I really want to right now." I try to explain to him how badly I want to cut right now. Maybe I should just do it. It would be easier to give in to the temptation.

"Ella, I know you want to. But you can do this. How long?" he asks, reminding me just how long it's been.

"Six months," I whisper.

"That's right. You are stronger than this, Sweetheart. I'm almost there. I'll be there in five minutes. Where the fuck is Zac?"

"Please, Bray, you can't tell him. Don't tell him." I'm crying into the phone, begging him to keep this secret.

Bray exhales loudly. I can hear the engine of his car roaring. "Okay, I'm not going to tell. But, Ella, it might be time to talk to him about it soon."

"I know, just... not yet. I'm not ready."

"I'm pulling in now. I'm going to hang up. I'll be up there in a sec. Ella, wait for me in the bathroom. Do not move, okay, Sweetheart? I'm almost there."

"Okay," I agree, not sure where he thinks I'd go.

It feels like an eternity before I hear him knock on the door. Crawling over to the door, I flick the lock and open it slightly, letting him in. I crawl back to the corner I was in, curl my knees back up to my chest, and continue to stare at the damn razor in my hand.

Bray locks the door, squats down in front of me and plucks the razor out of my hand, putting it in his pocket. He tilts my chin up so I'm looking at him.

"You did it, Sweetheart. You fought it. You did it," he whispers as he pulls me into his arms, squeezing the life out of me. I always feel so safe here. My brothers have been my lifeline for as long as I can remember. But Bray, the last few years, he has been everything. Sometimes I worry that I'm taking too much. He has his own family. He should be at home right now with Reilly and the twins, not stuck in this bathroom dealing with my shit.

"I'm sorry." I cry into his chest.

It's not long before Zac is banging the door down. "Please don't tell him," I plead with Bray. Bray kisses my forehead. "I won't say anything. I promise." He stands and goes over to the door. I listen to the arguing between Bray, Zac and Dean. This is my fault; they wouldn't need to argue if it wasn't for me.

I'm still sitting on the floor, my legs still tucked up to my chest, and tears still running down my face. I hear a commotion and as I look up, I stare into a pair of blue eyes. The same blue eyes that haunt my dreams. The same blue eyes that sear deep into my soul.

Dean stops in his tracks. He stares down at me, his mouth open and shock evident on his face. He doesn't say anything. He doesn't need to. I know what he's seeing. He's seeing the broken mess that I am. I can't handle the look in his eyes—that look of pity. The questions running through his mind, I can see them all.

I look past him, somehow finding the strength I need to stand up. "Bray, can you take me home please?"

"What the fuck's going on? Ella, what happened?" Zac questions. I shake my head. I can't answer him.

Bray grabs my hand and pulls me past both Dean and Zac. "Come on, Sweetheart. I have a set of twins who are going to love seeing their favourite aunty when they wake in the morning."

"Bray, I swear to God, you'd better start talking. What. The. Fuck. Is. Wrong?" Zac demands.

"Chat later, Bro. Things to do, people to see, you know how it is." He looks at Zac, like he's communicating messages with his eyes. Zac looks at me, worry all over his face. He gives the slightest nod. I make the mistake of looking behind him at Dean. He hasn't said a word, nothing. He's still just staring at me like he can't figure out what he's seeing.

I wake up to shouting. Zac and Bray are downstairs shouting at each other. "Argh." I pull a pillow over my head. "Make them stop." Nobody is here to hear my protests. What the hell are they arguing about now? As the sleep fog slowly clears from my head, memories of last night hit me all at once. Fuck, they're arguing over me. I should get up and go fix the mess I've created. I probably should have stayed in Melbourne. Maybe it's not too late to go back.

I throw the pillow off my head. I'm going to have to face the music. I might as well get up and get it over with. Sitting up, I slowly open my eyes. I wipe the blur away, a little gasp escaping my mouth, as my eyes focus on the figure sitting on the end of the bed.

A very large figure, with familiar blue eyes staring into my bloody soul. Anger rises up to the surface. What gives him the right to be sitting in here, watching me fucking sleep, like a creeper?

"What the hell, Dean? What the fuck are you doing in here?" I whisper harshly at him, while pulling the blanket up to my chin.

His eyes follow the blanket as I yank it up, a smirk pulling at his lips. That fucking smirk never fails to make me wet. Damn it. Where the hell did my anger go? I have to dig down deep to pull it back to the surface. It doesn't take long, considering he still hasn't answered my damn question.

"What are you doing here, Dean?"

"What happened last night?" he questions me back.

"No," I say, shaking my head.

Dean's eyebrows scrunch. "No, what do you mean no?"

"I mean no. No, you don't get to come in here asking questions. No, you don't need to know what happened last night because it's none of your fucking business, Dean!" Well, that anger sure is back tenfold now. I'm ready to wrap my hands around his throat and choke the life out of him. How dare he come in here thinking he can demand answers.

He smiles at me; the bastard looks like he is holding in a laugh. "That's quite the potty mouth you've got on you there, Princess," he says, smiling like a fool.

"First, not your Princess. Second, what the fuck are you smiling about?" I ask, my hands itching to slap the smile from his face.

"You're really fucking cute when you're mad, Princess. Keep swearing at me all you want. Your filthy mouth only turns me on. I'm currently thinking of the ways I'm going to fill it, before washing it out with my seed and cleansing the filthy with filthy." He shrugs.

My mouth hangs open. Did he really just say that to me? He just said he's going to shove his cock in my mouth. Why the hell is that image in my head turning me on so much? Damn him. Before I can even get my bearings, he starts talking again.

"Oh, and Princess," he says moving forward, grabbing my chin in his hand, and forcing my eyes to meet his. "Whatever concerns you is very much my business. You are my business. Don't think for a second I won't throw you over my shoulder, carry you out of this house, take you home and tie you to my bed until I get the answers I want."

"Mmm." My hands fly up to cover my mouth. Shit! I can't believe I just let that moan escape. So much for my *you don't affect me* attitude. But, boy does the idea of being tied to his bed sound good. No, it's not going to happen. I need to think with my head, not with my heart or that traitorous bitch of a vagina I have. She wants nothing more than for me to spread my legs wide open and offer a warm, wet place for his cock to live.

"Argh!" No, I can't do this. I need to get away from him. Pushing the blanket off, I stand up. I am just about at the door when a big beefy arm wraps around my waist, picking my feet up off the floor. The next thing I know, I'm flying through the air and landing back on the bed that I just climbed out of.

*Four*

## DEAN

I look down at her spread out on the bed, her dark brown hair above her. She's a fucking goddess, her tiny shorts and tank top doing little to cover her golden skin. My mouth waters at the sight of her nipples pebbled under her tank, her mouth open in an O shape from the shock of being thrown down on the bed.

This is a look I could get used to seeing. I wonder if her mouth makes that same shape when she's out of her mind with pleasure — pleasure I plan on giving her daily.

Jumping up on the bed before she recovers from her shock, I straddle her hips, then reach up, grab her wrists and pin them above her head.

"There is no way in hell you're walking out of this room dressed like this, Princess. You might as well be walking around naked."

I nuzzle my face into the side of her neck. She struggles underneath me, trying to free herself from my hold. She's not getting free. I won't be letting her go anytime soon.

"There's no one here other than my brothers, idiot. Pretty sure they're not going to be staring at my ass," she hisses. "Let me go, before you fucking hurt yourself, old man."

I laugh, which only pisses her off more. "I let you go once, Princess. It was the hardest thing I've ever had to do. I won't be doing it again."

The struggle leaves her. Her body goes limp under me as she stares up, her eyes shiny with unshed tears. It fucking breaks my heart, the lost look that glazes over her eyes.

Shaking her head, she whispers, "You didn't let me go. You left me. To let someone go, they have to want to be freed. I did not. No, you left me, broke me, and now, I'm nothing but a broken piece of who I used to be."

I swipe the stray tear that falls down her cheek with my thumb, my other hand grasping both of her wrists together. "There is nothing broken or imperfect about you, Princess. I did the right thing. I did what was right for you. I chose you over myself. You think it didn't fucking shatter me to walk away from you, to give you the freedom to live a little without being tied down to someone like me?" I ask.

Trailing my lips up the side of her neck, I whisper promises into her ear — promises I should have fucking told her four years ago. "I wish I could take it back. I wish I had kept you. But I've got you now, Princess. You are mine, and I'm not letting you go, no matter how much you fight me."

My fingers trail up and down her wrists. My body freezes when I feel them. I look up and see the countless little scars that decorate both sides of her wrists. She tries to pull her hands away, tries to cover up. That's not going to fucking happen.

It all happens so fast; her breathing increases. I can feel the erratic beat of her heart; her body becomes covered in sweat. She's shaking her head no. "I... I can't breathe. Dean, I... I can't."

She's having a fucking panic attack. I sit up, bringing her with me, and cradle her in my arms. "It's okay. You're okay, Ella. Just breathe, in and out." She follows my direction as she breathes in and out, burying her head into my chest. I don't move. I just continue to whisper in her ear, to rub my hand up and down her back. I feel fucking helpless right now. And like an ass, for making her have a fucking panic attack.

Once I feel her body relax, I ask, "You good now?"

She nods her head as she moves off my lap. The only reason I let her go is because I don't want to cause her to panic anymore. I watch her every move, ready to catch her if she falls again.

Ella crawls up to the head of the bed, sitting with her legs drawn up to her chest. This is how she was last night in the bathroom. I should have picked her up and walked out with her then. Seeing her like this shocked me stupid. I don't know what to do. I don't know what is wrong with her. Is this my fault? I can't help but think I actually did fucking break her... *Fuck.*

I sit next to her, grab hold of her hand and intertwine our fingers together. Then I wait. As much as I want fucking answers, I know I can't push her, can't add anymore extra pressure or stress to her already heightened levels.

After ten minutes, yes, ten minutes — I've been watching the fucking minutes on the clock, tick minute by minute — I have to know. "It's my fault, isn't it?"

Ella looks at me, sadness in her eyes. "It's not your fault, Dean. I have panic attacks, that's all. It's nobody's fault. That's what was wrong with me last night. That's why Bray came to get me."

Panic attacks do not explain the scars on her arms. As much as I want to know about them, I can tell she's not ready to answer those questions. "How long have you been having panic attacks, Ella?" I ask, fearing I already know the answer.

"Since the night you left me," she answers honestly. "But they're not that bad anymore. I don't have them as often anymore. It was just being back in the club. I guess I thought I would handle it better."

"I'm so sorry I did this to you. I'm never going to fucking forgive myself." What the fuck have I done? I thought I was doing the right thing by leaving her. She's needed me all this time and has not once reached out.

"Why didn't you call? You know I would have come. I'd do anything for you, Ella. All you have to do is ask."

"I asked you not to leave me, and you did." She tries to pull her hand free of mine. I grip tighter.

"I didn't leave you. I gave you time. I thought I was doing the right thing."

Ella shrugs. "Well, you weren't. And you can't just come in here and think everything is hunky-dory. It's not okay. I'm not okay. Now you know I'm broken."

"I don't think that we're going to pick up where we left off. We have shit to work out, like dealing with your fucking brothers. But you are mine, and I'm not about to let anyone get in the way of us again."

Leaning in, I do what I've wanted to do for four years. I claim her mouth. I lick the seam of her lips and push my way inside, invading her mouth with my tongue. She doesn't return the kiss for a few seconds; then, out of nowhere, her tongue duels with mine. Before I know it, she's climbing on top of me, straddling me.

My hands go straight to her ass. God, I've wanted to get my hands on this ass for so fucking long. I let her take control, let her think she's in control for a little while. She grinds her pussy down on my cock. *Fuck*. "Argh," I groan as I break away from the kiss. "Fuck, Princess, as much as it pains me to say this right now, we need..."

My words are cut off when she slams her mouth back onto mine, aggressively. She's taking what she wants, and I'm prepared to give it all to her. Just not right now, with her fucking brothers still arguing downstairs. I pull back again; she grunts in disapproval.

"Princess, I want to do this. I really fucking do, just not with your brothers right downstairs." I kiss her forehead. I can't read the look that crosses her face. She tries to move off me. Wrapping my arms around her waist, I pull her body tighter against mine. I lift my hips so my rock-hard fucking cock grinds into her clit.

Ella's gasps are music to my ears. Her little moans, like a fucking symphony. "Feel that?" I grit out through clenched teeth. She nods her head.

"That's all for you, because of you. My cock is fucking hard and I'm in danger of coming in my pants right now, because of how much he wants to be buried inside of your cunt. This is happening, Ella. *It will happen.* Just not right now."

I kiss her gently, hoping she gets the message. Just because I'm not an asshole and taking her for the first time in her brother's house, does not fucking mean she is any less mine.

"Okay," she says shyly. "I should probably go downstairs and sort them out anyway." I let her climb off me.

"Do me a favour, Princess. Put some fucking clothes on before you walk out that door." Standing, I make no attempt to hide the fact that I'm adjusting my cock in my pants. Her eyes dart down, the slightest blush creeping up her tanned cheeks.

"Just so you know, I was already planning on having a shower and getting dressed. I'm not changing because you told me to." Stomping her way into the bathroom, she slams the door behind her. God, I've always loved her spark. Now to go deal with the shitstorm that's about to go down when I tell them that Ella is mine.

I make my way downstairs; I don't try to hide the fact that I snuck up there in the first place. Both Zac and Bray are going at it in the living room. "You realise both of you fuckers woke her up with all your fucking yelling, right?" I have to yell to be heard over the top of both of them.

Ever had two grizzly bears turn on you at once? Yeah, me neither, but I imagine this is what it fucking feels like. Both Williamson brothers spin and aim their deathly glares straight at me.

Bray looks up at the staircase, where I just came from, then back to me. Without a word, he walks up and throws a fist right to my jaw. Fuck, he's got a good right hook. As much as it fucking hurt, I'm not about to start throwing down with him. Well, not here anyway. In a gym, far away from Ella, sure. I know he didn't put his all into that punch; he held back. When I look up at him, he smirks at me, before yelling out a bunch of random curse words that would make a sailor blush. This is exactly where Ella gets her filthy mouth from.

He finally stops cursing, then says, "Good to see you finally found your balls, asshole. Is she okay?" He nods his head in the direction of the stairs. I give a slight nod. This fucker knows whatever the fuck Ella is going through and he hasn't said anything. I squint my eyes at him. I'm about to ask him how long he's known for, and what exactly it is that he knows… Does he know she's been self-harming? Because that's the only thing I can think of that would explain all those tiny, thin scars up and down her wrists.

But I'm interrupted by the barrel of a Glock being pointed at my head. I'm not scared. He won't shoot me. At least, I'm pretty sure he won't. I know him as well as I know myself, so I'm ninety percent sure the fucker won't shoot.

"Why the fuck are you still carrying around a Glock?" I ask. Bray goes to stand in front of me.

"Bro, put that thing away," Bray says to Zac as I shove him out of the way.

"Get your ass out of the way. We are not watching you sleep for another two months when you get yourself shot again." I have to put more effort into moving his huge ass.

"Give me one good reason why I shouldn't shoot you right now?" Zac growls at me.

## Five

### ELLA

I make quick work of showering and dressing. I do take my time applying makeup to my wrist, ensuring it's blended well. I still can't believe Dean saw them. I don't let anyone see them, ever. I'm usually so careful with covering these scars up. I held my breath waiting for Dean to ask about them.

He never asked though. He didn't question me about my panic attack. He simply sat with me, held my hand and waited. Dean's always had a way of comforting me and making me feel safe. I wasn't sure I'd ever feel that way again, until he held me in his arms, whispering promises of a future in my ear.

I want to believe him. I want to give in and take that chance. But he broke me once. I will not survive that again. I'm still not recovered from four years ago. I don't think I ever will be. How does someone move on from having their heart ripped from their chest?

I want to let him claim me and see where it goes. I want him just as much as I did four years ago, maybe even more. I've been in love with him since I was fifteen. I tried everything to get him to notice me, to get him to want me. Then I was attacked, and he was my saviour.

He spent the next two months sneaking into my bedroom every night. He held me as I cried myself to sleep on his chest. I know he was feeling something for me, something more than just the platonic feelings. He was seeing me as more than just his best friend's little sister. The asshole just wouldn't act on it. He chose his friendship with Zac over me, at least that's what it felt like at the time.

Now, he's here, claiming that I'm his — whatever that even means? Do I want to be his? Fuck yes, I do. I want it more than anything. I want him more than anything I've ever wanted, especially after that kiss. I felt like I couldn't get enough of him. I literally wanted to crawl into his skin, to invade his nervous system like he was invading mine.

I almost came apart when I felt his hardness underneath me. I know I'm inexperienced at this, at sex. I've been kissed before, back in high school, but I've never let another man touch me. I tried to date a few times at uni, but I just couldn't do it. They weren't *him*. Will he still want me when he finds out just how inexperienced I am? What about when he really discovers how broken I am? He saw a mild panic attack. How's he going to respond when he knows what I do to myself?

Why can't anything in my life ever be easy? I'm torn from my inner torment by the yelling downstairs. I'm going to have to go and face the music eventually. I might as well get it over with. When I say music, I mean Zac. I know I have to face him. I know how he's going to react too. That's exactly why I made Bray promise not to tell him.

I stomp down the stairs, my stomach dropping when I see what all the commotion is about. Zac is currently pointing a gun at Dean. Images of seeing Bray in that hospital bed after being shot run through my mind. No, this is not happening again.

"Give me one good reason why I shouldn't shoot you right now?" Zac directs, unflinching, with his features hard as stone. He looks like he would actually shoot him, without a care in the world. I've never been afraid of my brothers, but right now, Zac is scaring the ever-loving crap out of me.

"Because I fucking love her, man. You can shoot me. It won't change anything though. She will always be mine, no matter what the fuck you fuckers do."

My steps freeze. He loves me. Well, it would have been fucking nice for him to tell me that before he told my brothers. Men are such idiots, clueless fucking idiots.

"How long have you been fucking my sister behind my back? I fucking trusted you, asshole!" Zac yells.

Stomping forward, I go to walk past Dean and Bray. I plan on walking up to Zac and slapping the fuck out of him. How dare he speak about me like that. How dare he point a gun at Dean. Dean's strong arms wrap around my waist, stopping my movements, and attempt to pull me back behind him. I smile.

Bray laughs. "Well, *this*, I can't wait to see." He rubs his hands together. Dean doesn't know that I'm not the helpless little girl I used to be. When he had me pinned to the bed earlier, I pretended to fight. I didn't actually want to get out from under him. I let him think I was weak. I should feel bad for what I'm about to do. I don't though.

Bringing my left foot down, I stomp as hard as I can. I should feel bad, that I'm about to hurt him, but once again I don't. No amount of physical pain will equate to the emotional turmoil I've been suffering from for the last four years. Also, I've spent many hours watching Dean and Bray train together. I know he can handle anything I dish out.

Bending at the waist, I pull down on his arm. Taking him

down with me, I have the power of surprise right now, so I use that to my advantage. He's not expecting this. I use his own weight against him as I flip him over. He lands harshly on his back.

I look down with a smile on my face; his shocked expression brings me way more joy than it should. I don't waste time. I know he will recover and jump back up. Jumping over his body, I go up to Zac and pull the Glock out of his hands. He is in just as much shock as Dean. Meanwhile, Bray is laughing his ass off.

Removing the magazine, I use my thumb to pop out fourteen rounds, each one landing on the floor at Zac's feet. Once the magazine's empty, I cock the slide and eject the round from the chamber. Then I hand both the gun and the magazine back to Zac with a smile on my face.

"Don't ever pull a gun on a family member again, asshole." Turning to face Bray and Dean, who is now on his feet with a huge ass grin on his face, I ask, "So which one of you wants to take me out for breakfast? Because I'm starving."

"Sorry, Sis, no can do. I need to go meet Reilly at the gym. The girls are running wild on her."

Dean screws his face up at Bray and shakes his head. "As if I was going to let you be the one to take her anyway. Princess, let's go." He holds his hand out for me to take. I look from his face to his hand as he waits for my decision.

After a minute, I take his outstretched hand. His fingers entwine with mine. It feels right. It feels natural, like we've been holding hands forever. There's a growl from behind me, then the unmistakable cursing of Zac. "Deal with that, can you, please?" I say to Bray as I walk past. I don't look back as I walk towards the door, hand in hand with Dean.

"Ella. Wait," Bray calls out.

Turning, I look at him and wait. I know what he's going to say.

"How long?"

"Six months." I smile and walk out the door.

The car ride to the café was silent. Dean held my hand the whole way, his thumb rubbing small circles around my wrist. I tried to pull my hand away. I knew he would be able to feel the scars I work so hard to hide. He just gripped my hand tighter, refusing to let go.

Now, sitting here in the café and overlooking the Sydney Harbour, we are in a comfortable silence as we both look over the menu. The sun is shining down on the water. Large white yachts fill the harbour; they have a peaceful look to them. To be out on the water, sailing off into the sunset, seems like a pretty good way to spend the day.

"What are you in the mood to eat?" I ask him. I can't decide. Maybe he will have a good idea.

Dean chuckles. "Princess, what I want to eat is not on the menu."

Okay, so I'm not the quickest today; it took me a good minute to realise what he was referring to. When I do, my eyes widen and my cheeks get hot. Thank god that my olive skin hides the redness that would otherwise be very prominent right now.

"Ah, well. Um..." Shit, I have nothing. I don't know how to reply to that. *At all.* "Have you ever thought about buying a yacht?" I blurt out randomly.

Dean's eyes light up as he laughs. "A yacht? I already have one," he says so casually, like it's not a big fucking deal to have a yacht.

"When did you get a yacht? And are we talking a pimping

kind of yacht, or a little rowboat you call a yacht?" I ask curiously.

"It's not a rowboat. I inherited it from my dad. I'll take you out on it one day."

"Okay, so I'm thinking pancakes," I announce, folding the menu back up and placing it on the table.

The waitress comes up to the table, briefly looking at me, before giving Dean bloody goo-goo eyes. *Um, hello, Malibu Barbie. I'm right here.* I don't like the jealous, possessive feelings I have running through me right now. It's irrational. I pick up my butter knife, gripping it tightly. I'm running through all the ways I can possibly use this knife right now without anyone noticing.

I'm about to slide the knife under the table... I just need to feel a scratch. I need to escape these feelings. I can do a little scratch on my thigh; no one will notice. At least, usually no one would notice. Dean reaches over the table, grabbing hold of the hand that is currently gripping the knife like my life depends on it.

"What was it you said you wanted, babe?" he asks, not breaking eye contact with me.

I loosen the grip I have on the knife, slightly; my eyes water as I stare into his. How does he read me so well? How did he know what I was going to do?

"Uh, pancakes, with cream and strawberries," I whisper. Dean smiles at me.

"Two servings of pancakes with cream and berries. One Mocha and one strong black. Thank you." Dean dismisses the waitress. I wait for the questions to start coming as soon as the waitress walks away. I don't know how to answer them, but I can see the questions in his eyes.

## DEAN

I watch as Ella wraps her hand around the knife, grasping it tightly, her knuckles turning white with the force. Her eyes glaze over, like she's zoned out. I'm not sure what has caused her mood to change so drastically. I'm also not one hundred percent sure if she's planning on using that knife to gut the waitress she's staring daggers at, or on herself.

I have a hunch, a really fucking good hunch, how she came to get all those scars on her arms, and I'm sure if I inspect her body more thoroughly, I will see a lot more. As she slowly begins to drag the knife towards her, it's clear she's attempting to get it off the table without drawing attention to it. *Not gutting the waitress then.*

Fuck, I reach out and grab hold of her hand. Squeezing tight, I stop her from removing the knife from the table. No fucking way will I sit here and let her hurt herself. I need to draw her out of her own mind. I rub circles around her hand with my thumb, in an attempt to soothe her.

"What was it you said you wanted, babe?" I prompt, my

eyes never leaving hers. I try to convey that I know, that I want to help her. She just has to want me to help. She whispers that she wants pancakes.

I tell the waitress what we want, without breaking eye contact with Ella. Once the girl walks away, I feel Ella's hand loosen its grip on the knife. Her whole body relaxes slightly. She's still staring at me with a look of uncertainty, waiting for whatever I'm about to say.

The conversation we need to have is not one that needs to happen at a fucking café. I need to put her more at ease, to change the tone back to the fun first date this should be.

"Tell me about university?" I ask.

Ella looks back in shock, over the fact that that's the question I asked. "What do you want to know?"

"Everything. I never got to go, so I want to know everything. Who were your friends? What did you do for fun? What subjects did you like the most? What did you hate the most? Like I said, everything."

"Everything?" she repeats. "You want me to tell you about the last four years of my life over pancakes?"

"Well, mostly everything. Feel free to leave out any and all information pertaining to boyfriends. I do not want to fucking know that." My jaw tenses as I grit out the words. Thinking about Ella with other men makes me want to punch myself. Because that would be all my own doing. I was the fucking idiot who pushed her away.

"Well, that's easy, because there haven't been any." She shrugs her shoulders. She's unable to make eye contact. I can't help the fucking huge-ass smile that greets my lips. I'm about to tell her how happy that fucking makes me when the waitress comes back, plops the two coffee orders on the table and walks away in a huff.

"Princess, look at me." I wait until her eyes meet mine.

There's really no point beating around the bush. I need to know. I blurt out the question that's burning the tip of my tongue. "Are you a virgin?"

The question takes her by surprise; her mouth opens and closes. I hold my breath waiting for her answer. She looks around the café before looking back at me.

"Dean, you cannot ask me that in a fucking café!" she hisses.

"Why the fuck not? Answer the question, Princess, or I'll ask it again. Only louder." I raise the volume of my voice slightly. I don't give a fuck who hears me.

"Okay, shut up. Yes, I am. Are you happy now? Are there any other invasive questions you feel the need to ask over fucking breakfast?" She crosses her arms over her chest, my eyes following her movements as her breasts push up. Fuck. She's fucking gorgeous when she's mad.

"Yes, I'm fucking ecstatic actually. To know I'm going to be the first and only man to enter your pussy. That makes me a very happy fucking man." To know that she's untouched, that she hasn't been with anyone... I can't describe the feeling, only one word comes to mind. Mine.

"You're pretty sure of yourself. What makes you think I'm going to let you into my panties? Four years ago, I would have jumped at the chance. But I'm not a little kid anymore. I grew up, and trust me when I say this. I have no plans of letting you fuck me anytime soon."

Fucking hell. I have to adjust my cock in my jeans. Hearing those words from her mouth... *fuck me*. Those fucking words made my cock instantly hard.

"Besides, how do you know I don't have my sights set on someone else. This is Sydney. There are a lot of fine fish in this sea." She waves her arms around.

There goes my boner. "Princess, if you let any fucker touch

you, you might as well be signing their death certificates. Because I will fucking kill them. I will tear them limb from fucking limb. I'll gut them like a fish, reach into their chest and rip their fucking heart out with my bare hands."

Ella screws her face up at me. I'm surprised that she's not disgusted with my promises of violence. "Well, that's... graphic and slightly disturbing. You can't actually be serious."

The waitress again interrupts our conversation, when she comes over and places two plates of pancake stacks on the table. I wait for her to disappear before I speak again.

"Are you prepared to test the theory? Because I can assure you, Princess, I am deadly serious."

"Uh, okay." She tilts her head as she thinks. "Does Zac know you have these psychotic thoughts, by any chance?"

"Why?" I am not going to be the one to tell her that her big brother, who she fucking idolises, is crazier than Bray and me put together. That's saying something, because Bray's a fucking crazy bastard with no fear. Even after being shot and left in a coma for two months, the fucker has no fear.Except for his ridiculous fucking fear of flying. Get him on a plane and you'd think the world was fucking ending.

Ella picks up her fork and reaches out on the other side of her plate for her knife. She lifts the plate looking underneath it, as if somehow the knife would be under there.

"Huh, where'd my knife go?" she asks, as she bends down and looks under the table.

"You mean this one?" I hold up her knife, which I swiftly swiped without her noticing.

"Did you...? How? Why? How'd you take that without me even seeing? And why would you take it?"

"I have skills. You'd be surprised what I can do with these fingers." Holding up my hands, I wriggle said fingers in her face.

"Okay. Well, eat up before they get cold." Using her fork,

she points to the pancakes. We both eat in silence for the remainder of breakfast. I finish mine long before she does hers. It's fucking torture sitting here watching her eat, listening to her little fucking moans as she chews the syrupy goodness. I wonder if that's what she'll sound like when I drink her syrupy goodness straight from her pussy.

As she licks her fingers clean, she smirks at me, sucking each finger into her mouth one by one. I want to reach over the table, grab those fingers and suck the syrup off myself. I also want those delicious fucking lips of hers sucking on something much bigger and wider than her fingers.

"Just curious, if I do decide I'm going to let you hang around me, how much backlash will Zac dish out? Obviously he knows you better than anyone, so if he knows you're fucking bonkers, there is no way in hell he's letting you near me. He already pulled a gun on you today. How long do you think until he pulls the trigger?"

"You're wrong, you know."

"About what?"

"Zac's not the one who truly knows me. You are."

Ella shakes her head no. "I've hardly seen you in the last four years. I feel like I barely know you anymore." The lie slips off her tongue with ease. The way she diverts her eyes, the little tick in her jaw... That's her tell. That's how I know she's full of fucking shit.

Standing up, I drop some cash down on the table and reach my hand out to Ella. She doesn't hesitate to take it. I love the warm feel of her hand in mine, the sparks that run up my arm as my fingers entwine with hers. It's like no high I've ever felt. She can try to deny it, but I know she feels it too.

～

Shutting the passenger door, I walk around the front of the car. After I pull out of the carpark, I take Ella's hand in mine and place it on my lap. I'm turning into a fucking girl, but I like holding her fucking hand.

"Where are we going?" Ella asks as she looks around my car. "And why the hell does everyone have a nicer car than me?"

I laugh. She has a one-hundred-and-eighty-thousand-dollar car. I know how much it was because I was there when Zac bought it for her. "Ella, your car is plenty fucking nice, but if you want a new one, I'll buy you one."

"I have a trust fund, you know, and a job now. I'm more than capable of buying my own car."

"Just because you *can*, doesn't mean I *can't* buy one for you."

"Okay, don't take this the wrong way. I'm totally aware that what I'm about to ask is rude and crosses every social rule. But I'm curious. Where do you get your money from? I know this particular car is around three-hundred-and-fifty-thousand dollars. You work in security. It does not add up."

"First, there is no question you can't ask me. Those social rules do not apply to us. Second, I don't take a fucking cent from your brother for the job I do. I do that job because you Williamsons are the family I choose. I'd do anything for any one of you."

"You know that we love you too, right? There is no way Zac would have pulled that trigger," she says with shiny tears.

"You love me, huh?"

"Shut up, idiot. You know I fucking do. I have since I was fifteen."

My face hurts from how hard I'm fucking smiling right now.

"You can wipe the smile off your face. Just because I love you, does not mean I'm letting you into my panties."

"Well, just in case you weren't sure, I fucking love the shit out of you. I know I stuffed up. I know we have work to do to build us up. But there is no other option, Princess. You are mine. We both know it."

"So, where does a volunteer security worker get enough cash to buy a car like this?"

"You really don't know? Zac never mentioned it?" I ask. How have I known this girl since she was eleven, and she does not know who my family is?

"Know what? Wait, are you secretly a mob boss? Are you taking me back to your compound now, to lock me up and never let me out?" she asks, almost as if she wants that to be the truth. I almost wish that it was the truth.

"You read way too many books. But thanks for the idea; it's oddly appealing. No, I'm not a mob boss. I'm a McKinley. I get my money from old family money."

Ella's mouth drops open. I knew as soon as I dropped my last name, she would connect the dots. I fucking hate being a McKinley. I'm definitely the black sheep of the family, my mother's greatest disappointment.

"Holy shit, Dean! How the hell have I never known your last name? How the hell did I not know you're a fucking McKinley? Wait, we are talking about *the* McKinleys, right? As in the ones who own all the shit around Sydney and have all those racehorses and crap?"

I grit my teeth. Don't get me wrong, I love my mother. *In small doses*. She is my mother after all. She's also a fucking stuck-up bitch with a pole up her ass.

"Yep, those McKinleys. Well, there aren't too many of us. My father passed away a few years back. Now it's just my brother, me and my mum."

"I'm sorry about your dad. Why haven't I ever heard you talk about your family?"

"Don't be sorry. I'm not. He was not a good man. And, because when I was young, the moment people found out who I was, they expected shit. The only exception was Zac. When he found out who my family was, he shook his head and said *you poor bastard*. That was that; we were best mates ever since."

"Okay. Well, you know I don't want anything from you, right? I don't even know if I want *you* yet."

"I know." I squeeze her hand. "Also, Princess, stop fucking lying. You're no good at it."

"Where are we going anyway? You never answered me."

I smile. "Home. I'm taking you home."

"Uh, my apartment is in the other direction. This is not the way home, Dean."

"We're not going to the apartment. We're going home, as in my home, which is now going to be your home."

"Ah, I don't even know what to say to that. Did you forget to take your crazy pills this morning? Because I'm pretty sure you just asked — no, not asked — you just declared that I was moving in with you. That's not how this works. You can't just make a decision and decide for both of us."

"Babe, relax. You are my home. Wherever you are is where I am. And wherever you are is my home. Whatever building that may be, I don't fucking care. But there will not be a night, from now on, where you are not in my fucking bed."

## ELLA

"Holy fucking shit, Dean!" I yell as I crane my head out the window. What the fuck is this? He has to be kidding, right? He does not live here. Why would he not invite us over for a dinner party or some shit. Well, I mean, it's Dean, of course he's not hosting dinner parties.

"Is it a hotel? Wait, you don't secretly have a harem of women in there waiting for you, do you? Because you can't possibly live here alone." I'm rambling, I know. But damn. This fucking house.

It's three stories high. There's a large wrap-around veranda on the bottom floor, and balconies on the other two floors.

A row of white pillar columns line the front of the house. Dean pulls the car around at the front house, jumps out and opens my door. I know I can open it myself, but I grew up with Zac and Bray always getting cross at me whenever I did. So, now it's easier to wait.

"Thank you," I say, taking Dean's outstretched hand. No

sooner than he shuts my door, a man appears, like poof, out of thin air. Where the hell did he come from?

"Good morning, Sir," he directs at Dean with a, "Ma'am," to me. Do I look old enough to be a ma'am? As I'm debating this, Dean introduces me.

"Geoffrey, this is Ella. Ella, Geoffrey. Ella's going to be around a lot; whatever she wants see to it that she gets it," Dean says as he pulls me towards the house.

"Ah, no, Geoffrey you do not need to do that. I won't be around that much anyway."

Geoffrey laughs before coughing into his hand. "Of course, Sir, whatever she wants," he affirms before getting into the car. I don't see where he goes in it. The wind gets knocked out of me as Dean bends then throws me over his shoulder.

"What the hell are you doing?" I yell. "Put me down."

"I'm carrying you across the threshold. That's what you're meant to fucking do. Be quiet."

"That's when you get married, idiot. We are not married. Put me down."

"Yet, we are not married yet. But we will be. How's next Tuesday work for you?"

I laugh, because he made a joke. Except, he's not laughing. I can't actually ever remember a time when Dean made a joke. "I'm busy." I finally get out.

"Doing what?" he asks as he opens the front door.

"Washing my fucking hair." A loud smack rings out through the room. Then I feel it, the sting radiating from my ass. The delicious burn, the slight twinge of pain. A small moan escapes my mouth before I can stop it. It's a nice kind of pain. I feel tingly sensations running through me.

As I'm trying to process how I'm feeling about this slight pain, I realise I don't have the brain fog, the haze I usually get when I cut. It's different. Why is it different? Don't get me wrong, I'm loving this feeling, the freeness. I can't describe it. When I feel pain, my brain quiets down, my body tingles in pleasure. But this... although I'm tingling, my mind is clearly not quiet. I don't understand it, and that scares the shit out of me.

I land on my feet, my heels clanking on the floor. Dean holds onto my arms, steadying me. Once I'm satisfied that I'm not about to fall on my ass, I pull myself out of his grasp. Spinning around in a circle, I look up.

My mind is going a million miles per hour, trying to process the pain sensations, as well as what my eyes are seeing right now.

We are standing in what looks like the setting of a Hollywood movie. I'm in the middle of the entryway. To my left, there is a staircase with black metal balustrades, to my right, the exact same thing. He has two staircases. Grand does not even come close to describing this entryway. From above, a large chandelier hangs right down the centre.

Taking a step forward, my heels clank on the floor. Looking down at the white marble flooring, there is a huge fucking family emblem in the centre of the entryway, all fancy in black and standing out against the white.

I come from a wealthy family. Before my parents died, we certainly were not poor by any means. When Zac took custody of me, he had doubled my trust by the time I received it at twenty-one. But this, Dean and his family, this is another level of money. This isn't just money; this is the goddamn bank.

I'm about to walk ahead, to go explore, when Dean pulls on my arm, dragging me behind him and up the stairs. "I'll give you the tour later. Right now, we've got shit to discuss."

"Ah, okay." My voice comes out a little uncertain. What the fuck does he want to discuss? I'm praying it's not my scars, which I know he saw. I also know he feels them as he rubs his thumb up and down my wrist. No matter how much I try to pull away from his touch, his grip just gets firmer.

Dean drags me into a bedroom. He shuts the door behind him as I look around. Clearly, this is more than just a bedroom. This is like an apartment all of its own. It's also got Dean written all over it. I take a few steps further into the room.

There's a huge sitting area with four single sofas facing each other. Why would anyone need four sofas in their bedroom? It's all dark and gloomy in here. Maybe he should try going for some lighter colours. The sofas are black, with dark navy cushions. A glass coffee table sits in the middle of them.

The bed? It's huge. I bet you could easily fit five adults on it and still have room. Dark navy, fluffy-looking bedding covers the bed. The room is meticulously clean. I honestly didn't peg Dean as a neat freak.

Walking past the sofas and bed, I head to the far corner. There's a bar there. Now, that does seem very Dean-like. Walking behind the bar, I pop open a bottle of Jack and pour myself a glass. Some liquid courage could be a good thing right now. Dean stands at the door, just watching me. It's unnerving. He's also blocking the only exit from the room, which has my skin crawling and not in a good way.

I pour another glass and as I bring it to my mouth, it's ripped out of my hands. Dean downs it, before slamming the glass back down on the bar.

"Let's play a game," Dean says as he picks up the bottle, grabs another glass and pours two drinks.

"Okay, what game?"

"Twenty Questions. I'll go first." He hands me the drink. He waits for me to bring the glass to my lips and take a sip, before he asks his question. "When did you start harming yourself?"

I choke on my drink. That was not what I was expecting

his first question to be. I don't even know how to respond to that. How do I tell him that I started before I left for university?

"I, um... a few years." There's no point denying it. He should know the level of instability and broken that I am.

"Why do you do it?" He asks his second question.

"Uh, no, it's my turn. Why didn't you ever have us over here for a dinner party?" Jeez, that's what I ask? Out of all the things I could have asked...

Dean laughs. "I don't do dinner parties. That's more my mother's scene. And trust me when I say, you're not missing out by not going to them."

"Well, I just don't get it. You live in this big house, by yourself. You do live here by yourself, right? Of course you do. Why didn't you ever invite me over?"

"Zac and Bray have both been here. You were barely eighteen when you went to uni. If I had brought you here, did what I wanted to do to you back then, your brothers most certainly would have killed me."

"What did you want to do to me?" I ask.

"Nope, it's my turn. Why do you need to inflict pain on yourself?"

"I'm going to need another drink. Okay. This is not something I've talked about to anyone other than Bray and my therapist."

"Babe, there is nothing you can say that will change this. This, us, it's fate. You can't break fate." I want to believe him, but I don't know if there is such a thing as fate.

"I'm really messed up, Dean. I'm broken. I cut myself to escape the thoughts in my own head. When the noise gets so loud, I can't cope. The memories so vivid... The only way I was able to quiet them was to cut. I don't know why. It was an accident the first time it happened. But when I do, I feel more at ease. I feel more peace than any other time. Almost any other time."

I can feel the tears running down my face. "I understand if you want me to leave. I can call Bray; he'll come get me." I'm giving him an out.

"You're not fucking leaving, Ella. We are going to talk about this. I don't care how broken you think you are. I happen to think your kind of broken is my kind of perfection."

"You don't know how broken I am yet, Dean."

"And you don't understand the extent I'm willing to go for you."

*Eight*

## DEAN

**E**lla tips her head sideways, those deep brown eyes of hers searching for truth behind my words. She can search all she fucking wants. She won't find anything but the truth.

"Why now? Why do you all of a sudden want me now? When four years ago you left me. You fucking left me, asshole! You walked out without even a second glance." Her voice raising, she throws her glass across the room. It shatters as it hits a wall, broken shards falling to the ground.

I don't move. I don't flinch. If she needs a fucking punching bag, I'm more than happy to be it. Besides, I deserve her anger. I deserve her distrust.

I watch her movements as she starts pacing the room, ready to catch her if she attempts to walk out that door. She can be angry; she can curse me out all she wants. What she can't do, what I won't allow her to do, is fucking leave.

"You ripped out my fucking heart and stomped all over it!" she yells as she starts throwing the books from the coffee table at me. She misses every time. One thing Ella has never been any good at is ball sports. She can't aim for shit, never has been able to.

I stay quiet, watching. She's like a caged animal, all of her rage towards me coming to the surface. After years of being stamped down, she can finally let it out. Then hopefully let it the fuck go.

"I would have done anything to be with you back then. Why? Why the fuck did you walk away from me?" She flips the glass coffee table over, letting out a frustrated scream when it doesn't break.

Turning around, she looks at me — stares me straight in the eye — as she whispers, "I fucking needed you. I needed you and you left me." Her words destroy whatever was left of my soul. What the fuck did I do to the one woman I've always loved?

She falls to the ground sobbing. Seeing her like this, seeing what I fucking did to her, it's wrecking me. I walk over to her, bend down and pick her up. Settling her in my lap, I cradle her head to my chest and let her cry.

I don't know how long we sit like this for. My legs are numb, but there is no way I'm moving, no fucking way I am letting go of her. I don't even notice that I, too, am crying until she looks up at me with red-rimmed eyes. She reaches her thumb up to my cheek and wipes away my tears.

This beautiful fucking creature in my arms, crying her heart out because of what I did to her, still wants to comfort me.

"I will never be able to tell you how fucking sorry I am. I promise to do everything in my power, every day, for the rest of our fucking lives to make it up to you. To show you just how much I fucking love you. I love every little thing about you, Ella. Always have. Always will."

Turning her around so she's straddling me, I grab her face and slam my lips down on hers. Her soft, plump lips are even softer from her tears, a salty taste lingering on her lips. Plunging my tongue inside of her mouth, I groan, as our tongues entwine together. I can't seem to get close enough. I need more. I need it all. I try to convey in this kiss just how much I fucking love her, try to show her with my touch how fucking special she is to me.

Standing up, I carry her into the bathroom. I don't stop kissing up and down her face, her neck, anywhere my lips can reach. Reaching into the shower, I turn it on; water falls from the ceiling. I don't wait for the water to warm.

Stepping in, I slam her against the wall of the shower. The water cascades down us both, cleansing us, washing away the past and baptising us with a fresh future.

With her legs wrapped around my waist, and her hands running through my hair, my cock strains in my now soaking-wet jeans, aching to be released. To find its home. Grinding into her pussy, I savour how she moans in my mouth, the cotton of her dress sticking to her skin and showcasing all of her soft curves. I need to get rid of these fucking clothes.

Walking to the seat at the other end of the shower, I sit her down. Squatting down in front of her, I slowly lift her dress. Our eyes connect. Our souls connect, the way they always have been. She doesn't stop me as I lift the dress. As the wet fabric slides up to her chest, her arms lift. I rip the dress over her head and throw it behind me.

Falling to my knees, I'm speechless as I stare at the fucking goddess in front of me. Beautiful, golden skin. Curves in all the right fucking places. She's wearing black lace, and she wears it so fucking well. Her chest heaves up and down with her breathing, her breasts popping out. I can see her nipples through the lace of her bra. They're calling to me, begging me to give them the attention they deserve.

"You are so fucking gorgeous, Princess. Your body is an untouched canvas I want to paint with my goddamn tongue.

You are nothing but perfection." I'm so mesmerised in all that she is. I could sit here and stare at this beauty all fucking day. My tongue waters as my gaze travels down, her pussy on full display through the thin black lace of her panties.

She starts to close her legs. *That's not fucking happening.* That little bit of black lace is doing nothing to cover her pussy. I can't wait to get a taste of that. I want to fucking devour her. I move closer, placing my body between her thighs, preventing them from closing. I'm on my knees in front of my queen, exactly how it should be.

My hands travel up the smooth skin of her legs, up her sides, and around her back. Using one hand, I unclasp her bra and watch as the straps fall down her shoulders. Ella takes a big breath in as she pulls the straps all the way down her arms — her breast free with her hard nipples right in front of my fucking mouth.

I don't waste any time. Moving in, I wrap my mouth around her right breast. My tongue swirls around her nipple, and her body arches, pushing her breast even further into my face. Her hands tentatively go to the back of my head, her fingers twirling in my hair.

I grasp her other breast in my hand, tweaking the hard bud before pulling and twisting slightly. Her moans fill the room, echoing off the walls. It's the best fucking sound ever. My mouth moves, switching between breasts and showing each one just enough attention to get her worked up. I wonder if I can make her come from just nipple play. By the way her body is arching, her legs tensing and trying to close, and her pussy rubbing against my stomach, I don't doubt she would come apart like this.

That's not how I want to give her, her first orgasm. No, I want that to be on my tongue. I want to lick every drop of her juice. Her hands grasp the hem of my shirt, bringing it up.

Pulling away from her breast, I tug the shirt over the back of my head. Her hands travel up and down my chest, and around my back tentatively, her fingers so soft.

Shivers wave through my body at her touch, my skin alight. If she keeps this up, I'm going to embarrass myself and come in my fucking pants, like a thirteen-year-old.

With a slight growl, I rip her panties, pushing them aside. I bend my head down, holding each of her thighs in my hands. I don't give her time to think or to protest what I'm about to do. I just dive in. Dive in and fucking drown.

My tongue swipes from the bottom to the top. Her body arches off the seat. My grip on her thighs tightens, keeping her right where I fucking want her. I swirl my tongue around her clit; she screams out in pleasure.

I pump my tongue in her entrance, fucking her with my mouth. Her hands grip my hair, pulling my head away, and then pushing me closer. Moving back to her clit, I suck it into my mouth and nibble with my teeth. She's so fucking close.

I insert two fingers inside her wet pussy. I know, I'm an asshole. I should use only one. She's untouched, but I can't help it. She's so fucking tight, wet and warm on my fingers. Two pumps of my fingers and she's coming undone. Her body tenses, and her head falls back, hitting the wall.

Her legs quiver as she rides out the high of her orgasm. I lick every last drop of her release. She's the best fucking meal I've ever eaten. I plan on making this a daily requirement. Fuck, I could eat her for breakfast, lunch and dinner and still not get enough.

Once I feel her body relax, I remove my fingers. Bringing them to my mouth, I moan around the taste left on them. She smiles down at me shyly, innocently. Ella Williamson will be my undoing. In fact, I think she already is. Always has been. Always will be.

$$\mathcal{N}\!ine$$

## ELLA

Holy fucking shit! What the hell just happened? What was that? Okay, clearly, I know what it was. It was the best fucking orgasm I've ever had. Considering up until this very moment, every other orgasm I've had has been from my battery-operated friend that lives in my bedside drawer, it's probably not a lot of competition. But Fuck.

My body feels like I'm floating. Opening my eyes, I look down at Dean, who is staring at me with an odd expression. I smile, albeit awkwardly. What does one say after being given the orgasm of all orgasms? It dawns on me that I am completely naked.

Naked! In front of Dean. My brother's best friend. The same guy I've been in love with since forever. How many times have I had this dream? Countless. I pinch myself on the arm. Ouch, yep, I felt that. Dean's eyes follow my movements.

"I'm not dreaming, am I?" I ask.

He laughs, a full-belly kind of laugh. It's the contagious

kind of laugh. "No, Princess, you're not dreaming. You are a fucking dream! My Dream."

"Oh, okay. Well, uh... Thank you?" My gratitude comes out as more of a question than a statement.

"Thank you? What the fuck are you thanking me for?" Dean asks, his eyebrows drawn in confusion.

"For... you know. That thing you just did," I say quietly. I can feel my face heating up. Why do I have to pick now to lose my cool?

"No thanks required, babe. That was my pleasure, a fucking privilege. One I'm going to be taking advantage of as often as possible."

He stands up, the outline of his hard-on evident through his wet jeans. My lips suddenly dry, I swipe my tongue along my bottom lip. Dean growls then lifts me up from under my arms.

"No, do not fucking look at me like that, Ella. I'm holding on by a thread here," he grits out between clenched teeth.

"Like what?"

"Like you want me to shove my cock down your throat. Thrust in and out of your pretty little mouth until you're swallowing my seed."

I don't even know what to say to that except, "Well, it's not an unappealing picture you just painted."

Dean lets out a string of curses, before he steps out of his shoes and pulls his wet socks off his feet. Damn it, why do his feet even have to be attractive? My eyes travel up his body unashamedly. I watch as his hands unbutton his jeans and he pulls them down, stepping out while leaving himself in a pair of black briefs.

My hands itch to pull them down, to free his hard-on, which I can very clearly see. At the same time, it scares the shit out of me. That thing does not look little. As I'm contemplating this, Dean pulls me under the water, running his hands through my hair.

He then places me just out of the water's reach. Picking up a bottle from the shelf, he squirts liquid into his hands. I watch as he brings his hands to my head. He starts massaging the liquid, which I now assume is shampoo, into my hair. I close my eyes, inhaling the scent. He's washing my hair with his shampoo. It's been a long time since anyone, other than a hairdresser, has washed my hair for me. The last person to wash my hair with this much tenderness was my mum. She had her own salon chair set up in our house; she would take me in there and wash my hair as she sang along, albeit badly, to Cher songs.

She used to tell me she loved my hair so much. She always wished she had hair as thick and beautiful. She'd tell me that, one day, I would have a daughter of my own, with dark hair and dark eyes. I got my eyes from my dad, whereas my brothers got their green eyes from our mum, who had lighter features.

A tear slips from my eyes before I can stop it. Dean's quick to notice; he bends and kisses the tear away. Then he moves me back under the water and washes the soap out of my hair.

Dean takes his time as he washes my body with a loofah. It's clearly a richy-rich loofah because I've never felt anything like this. No loofah I've ever had has been this soft. By the time he's finished, my body is alive with electricity. My core is pulsing, seeking... something.

I take the loofah out of his hands. This, I'm going to enjoy. I smile up at him.

"Lose the briefs." My voice leaves no room for argument. It's time to even the playing field.

Dean smirks before pulling his briefs down his legs and kicking them to the side. I can't help my mouth dropping open when I finally see what's been straining to get free. His cock — long and hard — stands, touching his belly button. The head of his cock leaking pre-cum, all I can think — is how badly I want to lick it off.

"Does that hurt?" I'm genuinely curious; his face is scrunched up like he's in pain.

"Like you wouldn't fucking believe. I want nothing more than to bend you over and slam my cock into your pussy. Filling you up, entwining our bodies until we are one." He shakes his head.

"But that's not happening right now. The first time I make love to you is not going to be a quickie in the fucking shower."

"Okay." Squirting soap on the loofah, I start to wash over his shoulders, then his arms. I work my way down his rock-hard abs. He really is moulded out of stone. My free hand follows the path of the loofah. The feel of his skin under my fingertips sends sparks flying up my arms. My stomach fills with butterflies.

I can't believe I finally have Dean in front of me. *Naked.* Mine for the taking. And I don't have the faintest fucking clue what to do with him. How do I pleasure him like he did me? I feel way out of my depth. His chest rises, his breathing getting heavier. His eyes droop as he watches the trail of my hands. He doesn't say anything. He stays perfectly still as my hands explore what they have been itching to touch for years.

I make my way down to his cock. He hisses as I rub the loofah over the top. Gripping him with my free hand, I gently rub up his length. He wraps one of his hands around mine, squeezing tight and stopping my movements.

"You don't have to do that, Ella," he whispers. I can see how turned on he is right now. I want to do this. I want to be able to please him, to pleasure him.

"I know I don't have to. I want to. Do you not want me to touch you?" I ask, looking down at where our hands are joined over his cock, unsure I can handle it if he says no.

He lifts my chin until my eyes meet his. "Of course I want you to touch me. I just want you to know that you don't have to. I don't want you to do anything you think I want. I want you to be comfortable. Shit, I don't know. I don't want to screw this up again, Ella. I want to take this at your pace."

"Well, I want to do this. So, show me how. Show me how to pleasure you, Dean."

"Fuck," he grunts. "Okay, squeeze tighter, like this. Move your hand up and down."

Dean's hand stays over the top of mine, guiding me on the amount of pressure and speed. His head leans back, his eyes closed. "Fuck, Ella, just like that. Keep doing that," he says as he removes his own hand.

His hands start roaming over my body. I continue to explore, gripping firmly and swirling my thumb around the head of his cock, as I pump him up and down. It doesn't take long before he lets out a string of curses. He wraps a hand over mine and points his cock in my direction.

Next thing I know, he's coming all over my stomach, spraying his seed over me. *Marking me.* When he's done, he claims my mouth. His tongue pushes its way into mine. I smile, happy that I could actually make him come apart like that. Seeing him lose himself in pleasure, yeah, I need to see that again. Soon. I wrap my arms around his neck and pull his head closer to mine. I can't seem to get close enough. Jumping up, I wrap my legs around his waist. He catches me, his hands digging into my ass.

I'm pretty sure I'm going to be left with fingerprint bruises from how hard his fingers dig in. I moan into his mouth, pressing my core into his cock. Sparks fly. I continue to rub my clit over his length, which is still rock hard.

I'm chasing that high again; it's so fucking close. Dean pushes me against the wall, my back hitting the cold tile as he grinds into me. One of his hands comes up and pinches my nipple. At the same time, he bites down on my shoulder.

The pain from the bite sets me off. I don't just fly over the edge, I fucking soar. I scream out his name as I come. Once the fog leaves, I realise what just happened. The pain, mixed with pleasure, that just took me to a higher level of any high I've ever felt from cutting. It scares the shit out of me, because I think I may have just found a new addiction.

I look into his eyes. Does he know what just happened? Can he tell how screwed up I am? Is he going to want to throw my ass out the door now? There are so many questions running through my mind.

"I fucking love you, Ella Williamson. Always have. Always will," he finally says, his voice hoarse. He leans in and kisses me so softly on the lips.

"I fucking love you, Dean McKinley. Always have. Always will," I repeat back.

Dean washes me off again. He then wraps me in what has to be the world's softest towel, before carrying me to the bed. We lie together in the middle of his huge-ass fucking bed, a sheet covering our naked bodies.

A girl could definitely get used to these kinds of sheets. They're probably something ridiculous like a million-thread count. Lying here with my head on Dean's chest, my leg draped over his body, this is bliss. The silence surrounding us is comfortable. His fingers run up and down my back. His heartbeat is steady under my ear.

"Do you have cameras in this room?" I ask.

"Uh, no, why?" He's cautious with his answer. I wonder if

that means there are cameras in other rooms. There would have to be.

"No reason." I shrug. Looking up at him, I add, "But if these sheets happen to go missing, it wasn't me."

Dean laughs, his body shaking mine. He probably thinks I'm joking. I'm not. I will find a way to steal these sheets.

"What time is it?" I ask. I have no idea how long we were in that shower for. Or how long we have been lying here like this.

Dean reaches over to his phone, cursing when he swipes the screen on. "It's two o'clock. Shit, Princess, we have to leave the bubble."

I give him my best pout. "But I like the bubble."

Dean leans down and kisses me gently before he rolls me off him. He lands on top of me. Mmm, this is a much better position.

"I love this bubble. But we both have to get to the club. You're going to be late. You know how much your brother loves it when people are late."

At the mention of the club, I jump. Or, at least, I try to jump. It's not an easy task when you have a six-foot something beast of a man on top of you. When I shove at his chest, he gives in and lets me up.

"Fuck, Dean, I have no fucking clothes. My dress is wet." Picking up the towel, I wrap it around my body.

"As much as I love this towel, which also, if it goes missing, it wasn't me, this isn't going to go over too well if this is what I have to wear to the club." I wave one hand over my body.

"It's fucking funny that you think I would let you walk out that door in that towel, Princess. You really should consider becoming a stand-up comedian," Dean deadpans.

"Yeah? It's funny you think you would have a say in what I wear," I challenge back.

Dean just smirks at me, grabs my hand and pulls me

towards a door. When he opens it, he lets me go in first. "I'm sure you'll be able to find something in here."

"What the fuck!" I am standing in a walk-in wardrobe. Although it could very well be another bedroom, it's that fucking huge. But it's what's in the wardrobe that has my blood boiling. It's full of clothes. *Women's clothing.* There's one wall that's full of shoes. Heels in every colour, it's like a rainbow wall of fucking shoes. Rows of handbags line the shelves.

"What the fuck is this, Dean? Why the hell do you have a wardrobe full of women's clothes? Oh fuck, you're not fucking married, are you?" Just my luck, to fall for the guy who's married and cheating on his wife. *With me!*

"What the hell are you talking about? You know damn well I'm not fucking married. This is yours. It's all brand new. I had it purchased for you. As soon as I knew you were coming home." He almost looks uncertain — it's a look that flashes by quickly — before the confident smirk reappears.

"You bought all of this for me?" I ask. "Why?"

"I wanted you to have stuff here. For times like this. You need clothes, Ella. You're not fucking walking out in a goddamn towel. Besides, I had help. So, I'm sure you will find something in here you like."

"You had help? From who?" I cross my arms over my chest. Why does the thought of someone else helping him make me so mad with jealousy?

"Reilly. Who else is going to volunteer to willingly do all this shopping? And she assured me you'd like it."

Reilly. I smile. I know Reilly's taste exactly. And it's good. She has great taste, and it's usually always very revealing. "Okay, I'll get dressed. Go. You need clothes too." I push him out the door, shutting it behind him.

"Why do I feel like you gave in way too fucking easily then, Princess?"

"Because I did. Don't get used to it. It won't happen often."

I run my hands along the racks of dresses. My eyes land on a silver sequined dress. It's shiny, and form fitting. I open drawers until I find what I need, the drawer full of lingerie. Picking out a pair of white lace panties, I'm quick to get dressed.

The dress fits like a glove, leaving absolutely nothing to the imagination. I love it. I send a little thank you to Reilly as I hunt for a light jacket to throw on top. I do not want Dean to see this until we're already in the club. By then, it'll be too late. He can't object. And he might think twice about letting Reilly loose with his credit card again.

I find a beige cotton coat that falls to my knees, I pick up a pair of black Louboutins and slip my feet in. At the end of this ridiculous wardrobe is a vanity table with all sorts of cosmetics laid out.

Rummaging through the various bottles of lotions and potions, I find some leave-in conditioner. I lather it in my hair. I don't have time to do anything else to it. It's unruly and wavy, like I just got out of bed, which is fitting. I did just get out of bed after all.

Settling for some red lipstick and mascara, I take one last look in the mirror at my reflection. I know it's not work attire, but I work in a nightclub, and this is most certainly nightclub attire.

"Okay, I'm ready," I call out as I walk out. My eyes roam up and down Dean's body. He's wearing navy blue dress pants with a white business shirt. He's folded the sleeves of the shirt up to his elbows, showcasing those delicious forearms.

"Are you sure you want to wear that?" I ask. Don't get me wrong, he looks hot as hell. That's the issue. Every girl who enters that club will be eyeing him.

"Why, what's wrong with it?" he asks, looking down at his clothing.

"Nothing! That's the point." I throw my hands up. "Let's just go get this over with."

I don't even make it to the door before Dean grabs my hand. "Whatever your brothers have to say, I will not let you go, Ella. You. Are. Mine."

"Okay. Don't worry, if Zac decides to pull a gun on you, I'll save you. *Again*." I laugh.

"Don't think I've forgotten about that little stunt you pulled. You caught me off guard once. There won't be a second time."

I laugh and follow him out to the car, each step increasing my nerves over having to face Zac. Bray, I'm not so worried about. He already knows how I feel about Dean. He was worried that I would come back and fall apart at seeing Dean, fall back head over heels and not be able to be with him. He doesn't know I never fell out of love with him. In the back of my mind, I was always hoping, always waiting, for our time. This, now, it's our time.

Sitting in the car, holding Dean's hand, I whisper, "Always have. Always will." I didn't mean for him to hear it. But when he repeats the phrase, before kissing my hand, I know that he did.

*Ten*

## DEAN

**I** can feel Ella's nerves radiating off her. I can see her fidgeting with the belt on her coat. I'm not sure why she's wearing a coat in fucking October. Surely she's not cold, unless she's getting sick.

"Are you sick?" I blurt out.

"Uh, no." Shaking her head, she looks at me, confused.

"Just checking," I say, shrugging like it wasn't an odd question to ask right now.

I know that Zac will see us the moment we walk into the club. There's no point in trying to avoid the situation. I might as well get it over with. I lead Ella to the back lifts, my hand firmly on her lower back. As much as I want to push her against the wall in the lift and smudge that red lipstick off her lips, I know at least one of her brothers is watching right now.

I don't need them engraving my name on the bullet. *If they haven't already.* It's got to be the slowest fucking trip up the lift.

"Are you nervous?" Ella asks.

"Not at all. Why would I be?" It's not like I have seen Zac kill men for much less crimes than dating his baby sister. Is that what this is? Dating? I feel like it's so much more than that.

"We should get married." There goes my mouth, blurting out every fucking thought around this girl. Any cool I had, flew out the fucking window a long time ago when it came to Ella.

"Ah, sure. When were you thinking? I think I have an opening on Tuesday at noon. Does that work for you?"

I honestly can't tell if she's joking or not. I was not. "It sure does, Princess. I'll book the courthouse." I make a mental note to do just that: book the courthouse for every Tuesday at noon for the next few months. I'm pretty sure she won't cave by this coming Tuesday. But one of them, she will.

Walking down the hallway, I lean down and whisper in her ear, "I can't fucking wait for you to be Mrs. McKinley."

She doesn't have time to reply before I shove open Zac's office door, only to be greeted by the squeals of women and kids.

Reilly and Lyssa run up to Ella, engulfing her in hugs while pulling her away from me. I scowl at them both. They don't notice.

"Aunty El! Aunty El!" Ash screams as he climbs down off his dad's desk and runs full speed to Ella. She bends down, catching him in her arms, as she picks him up and spins him around.

I'm so mesmerised by her, I don't notice the little red-headed bundle pulling on my leg. I pick her up and look at Reilly. "Is this twin one or twin two?" I ask. I can never tell them apart. I don't know how anybody does; they look exactly the same. It's either Lily or Hope.

"One," Reilly says, before turning back to Ella.

"Well, at least with this baby in my arms, I know Bray's sure as shit not throwing punches." I smirk down at the little drooling redhead, then walk towards the back of the office. I need to face these bastards.

"Sunshine, take Ash and the twins down to the bar. Get them some ice cream from the kitchen for a bit," Zac demands.

Lyssa laughs. She's probably the only one in the world who can get away with laughing at one of Zac's demands. Well, she, Ella and Reilly. He and Reilly developed some weird fucking relationship when Bray was in a coma. They went from hating each other to practically braiding each other's hair.

"Not a chance, babe. You are not running poor Dean over the coals because he finally grew a pair and admitted he was in love with Ella."

"What the fuck, you knew too? Am I the only fucking idiot that didn't know this was going on?" Zac asks, pointing between Ella and me.

"Uh, first of all. Hang on. Ash, can you build Aunty El a castle?" Ella places Ash on the floor and runs to the corner, where there is a big basket of Legos.

"Okay, first of all. This." Ella points between herself and me. "Was not going on until today." She then starts to undo the belt on her coat. She continues talking to Zac as she shakes out of the coat.

"Second, language! There are young children here," she scolds.

Once she has that coat off, she throws it on the couch.

"What the fuck are you wearing?" I growl at the same time Zac and Bray do.

Ella looks towards me, which makes every other pair of eyes look towards me as well. "Don't you like it? I thought you wanted me to wear something out of that ridiculous closet you had put in your house for me?" She even goes as far as flashing those damn eyelashes at me.

"You are never getting near my credit cards again, Reilly.

Take it back. Take it all fucking back. Fuck, donate it to charity. I don't give a shit. This is not a fucking dress, Reilly. It's a — I don't know what the fuck it is." I can't take my eyes off Ella; she's fucking stunning.

Standing there in a shiny silver dress, her hair a mess of waves down her shoulders with bright red kissable lips painted on her face, she's a fucking dream.

"You had a fucking closet put in your house for her. What the fuck, Dean? How long have you been planning this little charade of yours?" Zac yells.

Hope starts crying in Bray's arms. Bray glares at Zac.

"Don't worry, Hope, Uncle Zac is just a cranky old man. Don't listen to him," Bray coos as he bounces Hope up and down in his arms.

Zac walks over and plucks her from him. "Sorry, baby girl, but Uncle Dean has some kind of death wish," he says in a singsong voice, while rubbing circles on her tiny back.

Hope giggles; she has no idea what Zac's saying.

"Truthfully? You really want to know how long I've been in love with your sister?" I ask. The whole room goes quiet. All except Ella.

"Uh, Dean, he really doesn't need to know all the details. Some things are better left between us, you know." She's obviously worried and wary of Zac's reaction.

"Sure, might as well tell me how long my best fucking mate has been stabbing me in the back."

"Okay, stop your fucking sulking, Zac. He has not been stabbing you in the back. He wouldn't even touch me. I practically threw myself at him when I was eighteen and he walked away. So, no! He has been nothing but the most fucking loyal friend to you. Stupid, but loyal. You don't get to sit here and rip him apart." Ella is furious as she points her finger at Zac.

Bray walks over and takes Hope back. "I think I'll take this one back. Have at it, Sis. He's all yours." He walks out of the way with a laugh.

"What do you mean you fucking threw yourself at him when you were eighteen? And why the fuck would you turn down my sister? Is she not good enough for your snooty ass? Not fucking well-bred enough for mummy?"

Okay, this fucker is losing his damn mind. First, he doesn't want me to touch his sister. Now, he's questioning why I didn't.

"She was fucking eighteen, Zac. Of course I wouldn't touch her. She had a great future ahead of her. Had university to go to. She needed to live. So, no, I didn't follow my fucking heart all those years ago. I thought I was doing the right thing by everyone. *Everyone*, but my fucking self. If I had known, I would have gone to Melbourne and dragged her ass back here years ago."

Ella gasps and shakes her head, tears forming in her eyes. "What's wrong?" I ask, reaching for her.

"They don't know. Please don't do this now," she whispers, begging. Looking around the room, I see it's already too late. No one in this room is going to let go what I just said.

"Fuck!" Bray dumps Hope in the stroller. He looks over his shoulder. "Babe, take the girls downstairs for ice cream." He pauses before he adds, "Please."

Reilly looks around the room before agreeing. "Sure, come on, Lyssa. I think Ash needs to teach his cousins how to eat ice cream without making a mess."

"Okay," Alyssa agrees. She engulfs Ella in a hug and whispers something in her ear.

As she's walking out the door, she stops, turns around and says to Zac, "Hunny, I am really attached to Dean. Try not to kill him." She blows him a kiss before walking out the door with Reilly and the kids.

"Fucking hell, now I can't just slit your damn throat like I was planning to." He smirks at me.

The fucker probably *was* planning to, probably had the knife picked out already.

"Uh, I think I'll just go with the girls." Ella tries to leave. Bray steps in her way.

"Not so fast, El."

"Brayden, if you do not move, I will give you a twin to the shiner you got there." She points to the slightly black and blue eye Bray has.

"You got lucky. This conversation is long overdue, El." He pulls her over to the lounge and sits down with her, still holding her hand.

I want to go and rip her away. I want to be the one holding her hand. I should have been the one holding her hand all these fucking years. But it was Bray she relied on... it was Bray she leaned on. I settle for sitting next to her.

I cup her chin and turn her face so she's looking at me. "Princess, Zac should have known about this a long time ago. This is not the sort of shit you keep from your family." I glare in Bray's direction. I'm fucking pissed he knew and didn't say anything.

"Zac, get the whisky and sit your fucking ass down." I know him, which means I also know he is going to blame himself for what Ella has gone through. And he's going to want to fix it for her. She is like a daughter to him. He's raised her from the time she was thirteen.

"Someone better start fucking talking. What's going on?" he growls as he plops down on the couch opposite to where we are seated.

"I—I can't. Bray?" Ella looks pleadingly at Bray.

"Ella, sweetheart. Whatever it is, you can tell me. You know you can tell me anything. I can't help you if you don't tell me." Zac sits forward, his forearms resting on his legs.

Ella shakes her head no. "You can't help me, Zac. No one can."

"Fuck that. Princess, we are going to help you. We will get through this," I assert, my voice raising. I feel fucking helpless right now.

"Ella. Oh fuck. Are you pregnant?" Zac looks like he's ready to jump across the table and wring my neck.

"What? No. I'm not fucking pregnant, Zac. I'm still a goddamn virgin. Because I've been waiting four fucking years for Dean to wake up to himself!" she yells.

I can't help but smile at the fact she's untouched. I know I'm an asshole. I just don't care.

"Wipe that fucking smile off your face, asshole. That's still my sister." Zac points at me, then Ella. "Okay, not pregnant. Good. So, what is it? Are you in trouble? Do you need money? I've got plenty stashed away. How much do you need?"

"She doesn't need your money. She's not going to want money for the rest of her life. She's going to be a fucking McKinley," I growl. As much as I hate dropping my family name, and rarely fucking do, on this occasion, I'm more than happy to remind the asshole of who I am. Of what I have.

Bray spits out his drink. Zac squints his eyes at me. "You're serious about this, aren't you?"

"Deadly."

"Okay. Just how exactly do you plan on making her a McKinley without mummy interfering and vetoing this relationship? Because, let's face it, you and I both know she will."

He's probably right. My mother is going to have a coronary when she finds out I plan on marrying Ella, without a fucking prenup, mind you.

"Easy. We're getting married on a Tuesday at noon. At the courthouse." I smile.

Zac shakes his head. But I see the fucker trying to hide a smile. Maybe I will leave this room with my life intact?

"*She* happens to be right here. *She* is also not getting married anytime soon. So don't go getting any crazy ideas. Any of you," Ella says, pointing her finger at each of us individually.

"Okay, so what is it that these two buffoons seem to know that I don't?" Zac's impatience over not having the information is clear in the way his leg bounces up and down. It's the one and only tell of his frustration. Looking at his face, you'd think he was as cool as a cucumber.

"I... um... well, I have some things I've been working through over the past few years. But I'm better. I'm getting better. I promise. I am getting better, right, Bray?" Ella is so uncertain of herself. I want to pick her up and shield her from the fucking world.

"Yes, you are. How long?" Bray asks.

Ella smiles and says, "Six months."

"Six months since what?" Zac asks.

"Since I last cut myself... on purpose," Ella whispers, rubbing at her wrists. I grab hold of her hand, stopping her movements. She is not alone anymore. She needs to know that I am here, no matter what.

After sitting on that couch for an hour, listening to Ella retell her story to Zac (a lot of it, I was hearing for the first time), I want to fucking slit my own mother fucking throat. She should never have had to feel that alone. I should have been there, helping her.

Bray just took her downstairs to find the kids before they

had to go home for the night. As soon as the door closed behind them, I rushed into the bathroom before emptying the contents of my stomach in the porcelain bowl.

Once I'm satisfied nothing else is coming up, I flush the toilet and sit back, leaning against the cabinet. Zac stands in the doorway. He throws a bottle of water at me.

"You good?" he asks.

"Not really," I answer honestly. He comes and sits down on the bathroom floor next to me.

"How could I not know? How did I not see that she was having trouble?" he asks.

"She didn't want you to see."

"I should have been able to tell. Fuck, she's been in Melbourne for four fucking years by herself. I'm meant to look after her, Dean. It's my job to fucking look after her." His head rests on his knees. I knew he wouldn't take this well. Fuck, I'm not fucking taking it well.

"I shouldn't have walked away from her. If I had stayed with her… If I had admitted to her back then how I felt, she wouldn't have even gone to fucking Melbourne."

"Maybe not, but four years ago, I would have fucking killed you for touching her."

"So, what I'm hearing is: *Dean, I'm not going to kill you for claiming my little sister.*" I smile at him.

"Fuck off. I'm still contemplating it. I just have to work out what accident you're going to have. Because if Alyssa or Ella find out I knocked you off, I'd be meeting you in Hell the next day." He laughs.

"Are we going to get through this?" I ask. "Because I love you, man. You're my best friend. But if you make me choose, I will choose her."

"We're family. Family works through their shit, without killing each other. *Usually,*" he says. And that's good enough for me. "So, can I be there when you take her home to your other family. Because, that, I gotta see." He laughs.

"You know I won't let them anywhere near her, right? Besides, Mum has been strangely different since the old man carked it." I shrug.

"How so?"

"I don't know. It's hard to explain. But way less judgy and all up in my business. My mum almost sounds happy and sober, the few times I've spoken to her."

My mother would be what you'd call a functioning alcoholic. Anyone can function though, when you've got McKinley wealth behind you.

"That's good?" Zac questions.

"Yeah, it is."

"Okay, I gotta ask."

"What?"

"Are your intentions with my little sister pure? Are you certain she's the one? The forever one. Because if you break her heart again, I will not think twice before ripping yours out and dishing it up to her on a plate."

"She is my always. I was serious about marrying her, you know. I asked her in the lift on the way up here. She thought I was joking."

"Okay, Romeo. So, let's figure out how to get her to marry your sorry ass. Because, as much as it pains me to say this, you are a good guy, Dean. I know you'll do right by her."

"That hurt, huh?" I laugh as I roll some of the tension out of my shoulders. I really need to get up off this fucking floor.

"You have no fucking idea how much," Zac grunts out.

*Eleven*

## ELLA

It's been two weeks since I came home. Two weeks, since Dean and I have been able to be us. It's fucking bliss. That is, when Zac isn't hovering over me and treating me like a fragile piece of glass.

I've been putting up with it. Because he needs it. He needs to feel like he's helping me. I appreciate how much I am loved by him and Bray. A girl really could not ask for two better brothers.

It's the end of October. Tomorrow is my birthday. Usually, my brothers make a huge deal out of my birthday. They try to make up for our parents not being there for all my milestone birthdays. But this year, it's dead silent. Nothing. They haven't even mentioned it.

It's possible they've forgotten. They do both have children of their own, wives and businesses to run. It really shouldn't bother me. I'm turning twenty-three for Christ's sake. It's not like it's a big deal. I will be fine. If they all forgot, I'll take myself to the spa, get a massage, get my hair done. Whatever. I don't need to acknowledge another year of getting older anyway.

A pair of strong arms wraps around me from behind as I'm bending down counting bottles of vodka under the bar. I smile. I know who these arms belong to. Me, that's who. Standing up, I spin around and wrap my own arms around Dean's neck. Standing on my tiptoes, I smash my lips on his. He lifts me off the floor, sitting my ass on the bar top. I spread my legs open as far as they will go in this skirt, wrapping them around his waist, as he steps between them and claims my lips again.

"Mmm, have I told you how much I love working here?" I ask him between kisses.

"You're about to be fucking fired. Both of you!" Zac yells from behind me. I laugh, looking up at Dean. It's not the first time Zac has caught us like this. It won't be the last.

"Ella, get your ass off the bar. People eat off that. Dean, don't you have, I don't know, work to do?" Zac says.

"Nothing more important than what I'm doing right now." Dean winks at me. I melt into him.

"Okay, gross. That's still my fucking sister, asshole."

"Well, I actually do have work I have to get back to." I push on Dean's chest, and he steps back, allowing me to jump down. I bend back over and continue counting the bottles of vodka.

I hear Dean curse and groan behind me. "Don't you have staff to do stocktake for you? There is no reason why you need to be fucking bent over like that in that fucking skirt. Well, not at work at least."

"Fucker," Zac says as he throws a cushion at Dean's head. I look up just in time to see the cushion hit him straight between the eyes. "Next one's gonna be a fucking bullet," Zac grunts as he storms off.

Dean looks back at me. "Well, don't you have someone else

to do that? Because if you don't, I can get one of the guys to come do it."

"No, I need to do it myself."

"Okay, well, I'm staying put right here until you're finished. I'll keep you company while you count."

"Suit yourself." I shrug as I bend back down under the bar.

"Fucking hell," Dean growls. I laugh.

As much as we have explored each other's bodies over the last two weeks—and it's been a lot—we still haven't had sex. He says that my first time needs to be special, that he wants to wait to make sure it's as special as what I deserve.

I'm getting tired of waiting. I want him, more than ever. I want to give him something of myself that no one else will ever get. I'm going through the million ways I can continue to torture him like I am now, bending over like this. I could definitely squat down, sit on the floor. But where would be the fun in that? Dean clears his throat.

"We have plans tonight, Princess. You're taking the night off," he then says out of nowhere.

"Uh, no, I'm not. I have work to do, Dean. I can't just take a night off. It doesn't work like that." I stand up and cross my arms over my chest.

"Well, I happen to be really good friends with the boss, and he agreed to give you the night off."

"Dean, you can't do that. You can't just tell me to jump and expect me to say how high."

"It's not like that, Princess. I have a surprise. I want to take you out somewhere nice before I give it to you." I squint at him. It's not that I don't trust him. I just know he's really fucking good with his words, and sometimes, what he says and what I hear are two completely different things.

"Why do I feel like you're hiding something?" I ask.

"Because I am, obviously. I just said I had a surprise for you. But you need to take the night off to get it."

"Okay, I'll take tonight off. But only tonight. Do not make this a regular thing, Dean. I want people to take me seriously at this job. They won't do that if I'm slacking off."

"Anyone that doesn't take you seriously can fuck off and work somewhere else. You were made for this job, Princess." He wraps his arms around me, pulling me in tight. I get lost in his scent, his touch, his everything.

"What do I need to wear to this thing?"

"What you've got on is good. I'll meet you in your office at six. Be ready to leave." He kisses my forehead before walking away. I watch his ass until he's out of sight around the corner. Damn, he's got a fine ass, especially in those grey dress pants.

I shake off the thoughts of stripping him out of those pants and having my way with him. I have work to do. And apparently, I have to do it faster, considering I won't be here tonight.

I'm starting to get anxious about what and where it is Dean's taking me. I've been pacing my office for the last ten minutes, trying to figure out what this surprise could be. I'm really fucking hoping we're finally going to have sex.

I didn't wait four years for him to decide he wants me, only to then be denied and told I have to wait longer. That's bullshit. I don't need some place fancy or candles lit everywhere. I don't need some grand romantic gesture. I just need him. Why can't he see that? Just him is what will make it special to me.

My door opens and Dean swaggers in. Yes, swaggers. He's still wearing those grey dress pants. Although, now he has on a matching jacket and a white business shirt with the top buttons undone, giving me just a peek of that delicious skin he's hiding underneath.

When I look at him like this, I can definitely see the refined McKinley bloodline. I don't know why I never saw it before, probably because I was focused on remembering the times I saw him shirtless, in nothing but a pair of workout shorts or sweatpants.

His muscles on full display, his skin would glisten with sweat as he worked out with Bray. I used to stare at the tattoos on his arms and shoulders. I would doodle drawings of the swirls in my notebooks. I'd pretend to be doing homework, while storing those images in my memory and keeping them for myself.

"If you keep looking at me like that, Princess, we won't make it out of this office." Dean grabs my hand and pulls me out the door.

"Well, that doesn't sound like a bad idea," I suggest. "Where did you say we were going anyway?"

Dean turns his head back to me and smirks. "I didn't."

I follow him out to his car and let him open my door. I sit down and buckle my seat belt. I really don't like surprises. It's unnerving.

Dean jumps in the driver's seat and pulls out of the carpark. He reaches over and grabs my hand. I'm trying really hard not to freak out. I've been trying to be the normal Ella, the one whom everyone needs. But it's getting harder and harder. Like right now, not knowing where I'm going, what I'm going to be doing, it's killing me.

"I can hear you thinking, Princess. Talk to me. What's wrong?"

"Nothing," I lie.

"Don't lie to me, Ella. We are better than that. We are more than that. There is nothing you can't tell me." He brings my hand up to his mouth.

"Okay. Don't take this the wrong way. Because I love that you want to surprise me and all. But I kind of really don't like surprises. It's making me anxious, not knowing where I'm going, what I'll be doing. I can't shake this feeling of doom and gloom when I don't know. It makes my skin itch."

"Fuck. I'm sorry. I should have known. I'm really sorry. You've been stressing about this all day? Why the fuck didn't you come and tell me you needed to know more details? I never want to make you feel anxious," he rambles.

"I was trying not to be," I admit.

"Never try to be anything but yourself with me, Ella. You are the most perfect version of you."

"Okay."

"I mean it. All right, well, I may have planned a little get away. We're heading to the airport. We're getting on a jet. We're going away for two nights."

"What? Two nights? Dean, I can't be gone for two nights. I have work to do!"

"Well, that's not all of the surprise, Princess. I also have our entire family waiting for us on the plane. They're meant to jump out and yell surprise when you walk on. This is your birthday trip, Ella. Happy birthday, Princess."

"You remembered? I thought everyone forgot," I admit.

"I'd never forget the day that God created the most perfect fucking creature. My Princess." Dean looks across and winks at me.

"I'm not perfect, Dean. I'm nothing but a broken Princess. I couldn't even handle letting you surprise me for my birthday. What the fuck is wrong with me?"

"There is nothing wrong with you. Who the fuck cares if you need to know where we are going? That's not being broken, Ella. That's being cautious. And cautious is a character strength, not a weakness. You are not broken. I will keep telling you that until you believe it yourself. I don't care if I have to tell you for the rest of our lives."

"Thank you. This is going to be the best fucking birthday I've ever had. Because on this birthday, I get to wake up next to you. That's all I need. I don't need fancy grand gestures and gifts. Although I'm not saying no to gifts. Just so we're clear, gifts are most certainly welcome. But the best gift of all, I already have." I can't help but smile.

A few minutes pass, and we're almost at the airport. It's killing me not knowing exactly where it is we are going. I don't want to ask. I trust Dean with every fibre of my being. Knowing my brothers are also waiting on the plane, I can breathe a little easier.

I'm just glad I thought to grab my laptop before leaving the club today. If Dean thinks I'm going to stop working for two solid days, he's dreaming. There is no way I can slack off now. I'm so close to figuring out the puzzle around Zac's accounts. I can feel it. I know whatever is happening is right in front of me. I just need to dig a little deeper to get to it.

Dean pulls into a little private airport. I've never been here before. He stops right alongside a small private jet. There's a red carpet that leads up to the stairs of the plane.

"Did you seriously hire a private jet, Dean? You know I'd be more than happy to fly commercial. This is too much."

"Ah, not exactly. I didn't hire it, Princess," he says as he looks out the window at the jet in question.

"Well, who did? Please tell me Zac did not do this. All I sent him for his birthday was a pair of socks." I really need to put more effort into my crappy gift giving.

"It wasn't Zac. I didn't hire the plane because I own it. Well, my family owns it." He's a little uncertain as he tells me this. I know his family's wealth is an issue for him. But a private jet. Damn.

"You've had your own jet this whole time?" I punch him in the arm. "You mean, every time we went on trips, I didn't have to sit in a commercial plane, next to smelly guys and screaming kids. Way to hold out on a girl, Dean!" I smile at him. I don't think I can hold in my excitement. I want to get on this plane already.

"Ella, everywhere you've been, you have flown first class. That's hardly roughing it, Princess. And the only smelly guys you've ever sat next to were your own brothers." He laughs.

"Yeah, but Bray!" I don't need to say anything else, just his name alone is an explanation.

"Don't worry, babe. I'll make sure you won't be sitting anywhere near him. Nobody should be put through the hell of sitting next to him on a flight. Ever."

I lean over, grab his face and kiss him. "In case I forget later, thank you for taking me on this trip. I've had the time of my life."

His face lights up as he smiles. I get lost in those eyes. They are so blue, like the ocean, the prettiest damn eyes I've ever seen.

"The fun's just beginning, Princess." Dean gets out and walks around to my door, opening it for me. I take hold of his hand and climb out of his car.

We walk, hand in hand, up the steps of the plane.

"Remember to act surprised," Dean whispers in my ear, just before we enter the doors.

As if on cue, everyone jumps out and screams, "Surprise!" Within seconds, I'm scooped up off the ground and spun around in circles by Bray. By the time he puts me down, I'm so dizzy I have to hold on to the wall next to me.

"Happy birthday, Lil Sis. How the hell are you twenty-three already? It seems like just yesterday you were in nappies?" Bray ruffles my hair, which lands him a punch to his stomach. To his credit, he at least pretends that my punch hurts.

"Oh fuck, Ella. What was that for?" He leans over, pretending to be winded.

I don't have time to answer him before Zac has me wrapped in his arms. I sink into him, burying my head in his chest. His chin rests on my head. There's something about Zac's hugs. They've always seemed like home to me.

"Happy birthday, Ella," Zac whispers as his hand runs down my hair. He's squeezing a little tighter than usual, and for a little longer. It's almost like he doesn't want to let go. I don't make a move. If he needs a moment, I'll give it to him.

"Thanks, Zac," I whisper back.

"Okay, move aside. Stop hogging her. She's my sister too," Reilly says while shoving Zac. She sends him a wink and a grin while she pries me out of his arms.

Zac clears his throat. I look up at him to see his eyes watering. This happens every birthday. Zac will go over the top on the gift giving, get emotional and clingy towards me. And then the next day, he goes back to the normal, brooding, grouchy Zac. I think occasions like this make him miss our parents more than usual. We all do.

"Happy birthday, Ella. I picked out your gift too, so if Bray tries to take credit, don't believe him," she says while hugging me. She lets go with a huge grin on her face. Looking over my shoulder towards Dean, she adds with a devilish smile, "I also packed for you. I went shopping and got you everything you could possibly need for this trip."

All three men groan at the same time. I laugh. They do not approve of Reilly's fashion choices. Well, Bray approves of them on her, just not on me. I personally love her taste. She has style. I do think she purposely chooses the most revealing outfits she can, just to get a rise out of the guys.

"What the fuck, Reilly? I thought Alyssa was doing the shopping. Princess, forget about leaving the hotel room if you don't have appropriate clothing. Actually, I'll just order you some new stuff," Dean says.

Bray punches Dean in the arm. "Ow, the fuck, Bray?" Dean curses.

"Don't yell at my wife." Bray smirks, then punches him again. "Also, my sister and a hotel room. No, just fucking no!" Bray says as he walks down the aisle of the plane.

"Sorry, Reilly, I shouldn't have yelled. But really? You couldn't let Alyssa shop?" Dean says with a pout.

"Sorry, I got caught up. Don't worry, I'm sure it's fine. Reilly also went shopping for me for this trip. I haven't even looked at what goodies she got me yet." Alyssa comes in to hug me with Ash in her arms.

"No! Fuck no, Sunshine. Whatever she bought you, it can be donated. Probably to the local strippers," Zac growls.

"Aunty El. It's your birthday," Ash says while reaching his arms out for me.

Taking him off Alyssa, I kiss all over his face. "It sure is, little guy."

"Do we get cake?" he asks, all serious.

"I hope so. What kind of birthday would it be without cake?" I ask.

"A yucky one," Ash replies, nodding his head.

"Okay, Ash, come on. We need to get you buckled in." Alyssa takes him back and walks down the aisle.

I look down the aisle, finally getting a chance to take in the room. There are luxury cream leather seats. Two sets of four seats face each other in the middle of the plane, while another set of seats sit behind them.

Bray and Reilly are getting the twins clipped into baby seats in one section, while Alyssa settles Ash into one on the other side. Zac sits, watching them intently with a whisky in his hand.

"Come on, I'll give you a little tour." Dean takes my hand, leading me down the aisle past the seating. He walks through a little doorway. Behind the wall is a small galley kitchen with staff busying around. Two blonde flight attendants look up the moment we walk through.

One plasters on a big fake smile while pushing her tits out. "Mr. McKinley. Welcome. Is there anything I can get you?" Her sickeningly sweet voice runs through me like nails on a chalkboard. Why do I have the sudden urge to claw her eyes out?

"Kristy, this is Ella. My girlfriend. Whatever she wants, make sure she gets it," Dean says, then he continues to pull me through to the other side of the kitchen. I don't miss the scowl "Kristy" sends me.

"Nice staff," I mumble once we're on the other side.

Dean looks down at my face, his eyes scrunched. Without warning, he bends and picks me up, throwing me over his shoulder.

"Ah, Dean. Put me down!" I squeal.

"Not a chance," he says as he opens another door. I can't see where we are, due to the fact that I'm upside down.

He shuts the door behind him and throws me down. I scream as I land on a mattress. I get a brief chance to look around before Dean's on top of me, caging me in.

We're in a bedroom. On a jet, in a bedroom! Seriously, this is another level of traveling.

"It's cute that you're jealous, Princess. But you have absolutely no reason to be," Dean says as he kisses up my neck.

My legs wrap around his waist. I lift my hips to grind my core along his hardening cock. "Mmm, I'm not jealous," I moan.

"Sure you're not. But if you were, you don't need to be.

There is only one you. And you, Princess, are all I've ever needed. You are everything I could ever want, all wrapped up in a fucking beautiful package." He lifts his head to make eye contact with me.

"Always have. Always will," he says.

"Always have. Always will," I repeat our little declaration.

Dean jumps up. "Okay, we need to go get seated. We're taking off in less than five minutes." He holds his hand out for me.

I groan. "I'd much prefer to stay in here," I grumble.

"Yeah. And I prefer to stay alive. You moaning out loud back here, that's one sure way to have Zac pulling the fucking trigger."

Taking his hand, I ask, "What's up with him today? He seems off?"

"Not sure." He shrugs.

"Okay. Let's go sit with the riffraff, shall we?"

Dean laughs. "That riffraff is our family."

# Twelve

## DEAN

"I'm just going to sit with Alyssa for a bit." Ella turns to me just before we make it back out to the main area of the jet.

"Okay. Do you want anything to drink? Eat?" We're back in the galley with the overly friendly stewardess. Ella looks over at the two women, then shakes her head. "No, I'm good," she whispers and walks out the door.

"I need a bottle of Cristal and six glasses," I tell Kristy and Chantel. Before I walk out, I add, "Chantel, I want you to serve us throughout the flight. Kristy, you can keep yourself busy back here, I'm sure."

Chantel nods. "Of course, Sir," she says while busying herself pulling out champagne flutes and placing them on a tray.

When I walk out, I see Zac is sitting on a seat behind the two sets of sofas. Ella is sitting across from Alyssa and Ash, smiling and chatting with Ash.

Looking across, I can see Bray is about to lose it. For

618

someone who can hop in a cage with any opponent without a trace of fear, he's a fucking pussy when it comes to flying. He catches my eye. Great, I knew better than to make eye contact.

"Dean, how many times did you say the pilots did the pre-flight check again?" he asks.

"I didn't."

"But they did more than one check, right? You know what, maybe we should stay behind. You know, take care of shit here." He's about to unbuckle his belt, which is done up hilariously tight around his waist, when Reilly interjects.

"Babe, calm down. If you get off this plane, you're going alone. The girls and I are going on this trip," she says.

"Fuck, Reilly, we can have our own little staycay here. We don't need to be in a death trap millions of miles in the damn air." I can see the sweat run down his face. He really doesn't like flying.

"We're taking off. It's too late to get off the plane, Bro." I smirk at him.

"Bray, it's fine. It's a short flight. You will survive," Reilly says. "Here, make sure Lily drinks this as we're going up." Reilly shoves a pink sippy cup with water in it at him.

I take a seat next to Zac and settle in. I'd much rather be sitting next to my girl. But at least I can try to figure out what's crawled up Zac's ass today.

"What's up?" I ask.

"We're about to be," he says and laughs at his own bad joke.

"You should save the bad dad jokes for Bray; he's better at them," I say.

"Probably."

"Okay, chatty Kathy. No need to talk my fucking ear off," I retort, my voice dripping with sarcasm.

Zac breathes in heavily and sighs. He looks over my head to Alyssa and Ella, both now playing with Ash.

"Not here," he says, then nods his head towards the back of the plane.

"Let's go." I get up and lead him towards the bedroom in the back. Once inside, he takes one look at the ruffled bedding.

"Nope, no. Fucking hell. I'm not sitting in a room where you just had my sister on that bed." He scowls.

"Grow up. We were in here for two minutes, asshole."

"Nope, a lot can happen in two minutes," he says.

I scrunch my nose at him. "For you, maybe."

He just stares at me, his face stone hard.

"I haven't slept with her, you know. Your sister is still very much intact." I tell him. Not really sure why, but hopefully it puts his mind at ease.

He tilts his head at me. "She's still a virgin?" he asks.

I nod. "For now."

"Fucker!" he growls, then breathes out through his teeth. "Okay, have you suddenly found Jesus? Waiting for marriage? Cause I can get on board with that." He smiles.

"I think it's a bit fucking late for Jesus. *For both of us.* Now, tell me what the fuck is going on with you."

Zac sits on the edge of the bed, running his hands through his hair.

"I received an email today," he says.

"Okay, I'm sure you get plenty of emails every day. What was special about this one?" I lean against the wall, crossing my legs out in front of me.

"Here, look for yourself," he says as he hands me his phone. "I got this about ten minutes before you guys got here."

I take his phone and look at the screen. I scroll up and down the email a few times, not believing what I'm seeing, what I'm reading. This has to be some sort of sick joke. It can't be real.

"What? Who? What the fuck is this?" I ask, my shaking hands gripping the phone. I look at the door. I should be out there. I need to be out there. I'm about to go back out when Zac stops me.

"Wait. Dean. You can't go out there like this. They will all know something's wrong."

"Something *is* fucking wrong, Zac. *That* is fucking wrong," I say, pointing to the phone.

"You think I don't know that?" he shouts. "Fuck!"

"I'm not leaving her side. From now on, where she goes, I go. I will not let anyone get to her, Zac. I just got her back." I'm not sure if I'm trying to convince him or myself.

"We all just got her back. We can't tell her about this, Dean. I don't know if she can handle it," he says.

"That's not fair. We can't keep this from her. She shouldn't be expected to be blind to this. And I'm not about to lie to her."

"Okay. But let's wait until after the weekend. I don't want to ruin her birthday."

I agree. I won't let anything ruin her weekend. "Fine. But I'm putting a team on this now," I assert, pulling out my phone. I need to know who the fuck sent that email.

"I've already got external friends working on it. No one from the club can know about this. We don't know who it is, but it is someone from the inside."

"Who's working on it?"

"A hacker friend." Zac's being purposefully evasive with his answer.

"You don't have any friends. Other than me," I counter.

"You're right. But, in this case, this friend, she is doing me a favour."

I can't just sit around and do nothing. And he can't expect me to sit around and do nothing after seeing that email.

"Well, she had better be fucking good. I want to know who

the fuck thinks they can threaten Ella and live to see the next day!"

My mind replays the images of the email, over and over on a loop. There were three photos. All of Ella. One of her in her office. One at the gym. One at her apartment. All times when she's been alone. But the cryptic message that accompanied the pictures, that's what's most disturbing.

**People who look too hard don't see what's coming.**

There is not a doubt in my mind that that message is a direct threat to Ella. I need to get back out to her. I need to have my eyes on her.

The rest of the flight was uneventful, apart from Bray having a major fucking panic attack about the landing. The fucker actually prayed a Hail Mary. It shocked me that he even knew the prayer. Although, I don't think he could say enough of them to save his soul. After the shit we've done in our lives, I know where I'm going, and I'm fine with that.

Ella is craning her neck to see out of the car windows, trying to take in all the scenery. I think it all looks the same. Palm trees and beaches, there's not much more.

We're on our way to the boat terminal, where we will be getting on a ferry to the island resort I've booked. She still doesn't know where we are, or where we are heading. I know it's got to be killing her, the not knowing. Yet, she hasn't asked.

"You still like the beach, right?" I ask.

"What kind of person doesn't like the beach, Dean?" she throws back at me.

"An idiot?" I question. Personally, I'm not a fan. But I

know she loved the beaches in Hawaii. I couldn't make that possible for a two-day trip. So, I picked the next best thing, the tropics of North Queensland.

"Yes, only a fucking idiot would hate the beach." She smirks at me, knowing full well I don't like it.

"Well, it's a good thing you love it. Because we are heading to Green Island. We're going to be stuck on the beach for the next two days, Princess." I try my hardest to hide my disgust. This is for Ella. Her happiness is my happiness.

"Wait, where are we?" she asks excitedly.

"We're in Cairns. The island we're going to is about a forty-five minute boat ride from the mainland. It's small. I booked the whole resort out, so it's just us. And it's on the Great Barrier Reef."

The squeal she lets out is enough to deafen the whole damn country. She's jumping up and down in her seat like a kid on Christmas. I guess I picked the right place.

"Oh my god! Dean! The Great Barrier Reef! Are you serious? Do you know how long I've wanted to come here? Fuck, I can't wait. Oh my god! I fucking love you!" she screams.

Her excitement is contagious. I fucking love it. I can't help but smile and be excited with her. "I fucking love you too, Princess." I smash our lips together, our tongues entwined.

I'm just about to unplug her belt and pull her on top of me when the car comes to a stop. She groans when I pull back, her kiss-swollen lips looking so fucking inviting. I want nothing more than to slide my cock between those lips.

I have to adjust myself before stepping out of the car. I've been waiting to take things further with Ella. Much to her disagreement, I want us to take things slow in the bedroom. We've done plenty, don't get me wrong. I make sure she comes more times a day than she can count. But we haven't had sex.

I told her it's because I want to make it special. It's her first time. She deserves romance, candles, flowers, all that crap. But really, it's because I don't want to hurt her. And I know it's going to hurt. I know she has a strained relationship with pain. How will she react to that kind of pain? Is it going to set her back in her progress? I have no fucking idea what I'm doing.

What I do know is that I need to man up and put us all out of our misery. Her, me, and my fucking blue balls. When I step out of the car, the humidity hits me like a fucking freight train.

Sweat instantly starts to drip from my head. It's six o'clock at night and it's this fucking hot. How am I going to handle the day hours? How do people live in this shit?

I help Ella out of the car and we walk hand in hand to the rest of the bunch, who are already waiting. Bray has both twins in his arms, one on each hip. Reilly looks flustered and is busy doing some shit to her hair. Zac stands there with a scowl on his face, Ash sitting up on his shoulders. Alyssa's holding his hand and arm like she's trying to hold him back.

"What the fuck took you so long?" Bray asks. He looks at Ella then adds, "Actually, don't bloody answer that. I don't want to know."

"Bray, I swear if he starts copying those words of yours, you will pay," Alyssa scolds him while pointing to Ash.

"Uncle Bray said bad words," Ash says.

"Uncle Bray is allowed. When you're big, you'll be allowed to, too, mate," Bray says to Ash.

"I'm nearly four. I am big now," Ash says.

"Huh, four. No way! I thought you were at least twenty," Bray says with his most serious voice.

"Did you really have to pick somewhere so humid? My hair will not cope with this heat, Dean," Reilly complains.

"Yes, I did. Ella likes the beach." I shrug.

"You know what else Ella is going to like?" Reilly asks me with a devious smirk.

I don't want to know what she's going to say. But I can't fucking help myself. I play into her bait. "What?"

"Those little string bikinis I got her." Reilly smiles.

"Burn them," Zac says to me.

I don't get time to reply as we're greeted by the ferry staff.

"McKinley Party?" a young guy in a tank and board shorts asks while staring at Ella.

"That's us," I say while pulling Ella in close and kissing her forehead. The fucker looks away. That's right. She's mine.

"Right, we're ready to board," he says, then turns, leading the way to the ferry.

"Way to mark your territory, Bro," Bray remarks with a laugh.

"Shut up, idiot!" Ella steps up to him and takes one of the twins. Don't ask me which one it is. I still can't fucking tell. Everyone else seems to know though.

"We're going on a boat, Lily," Ella coos. "I can't wait to get there." She smiles at me.

The sight of Ella with a baby on her hip shouldn't look so damn good. But damn, do I want to make her the mother of my children. One day. Right now, I'm happy having her all to myself.

We all follow the douche onto the ferry, and settle in for the forty-five minute boat ride. It's so fucking hot. I take my shirt off, before using it to wipe the sweat from my face. Ella is sitting there playing with Lily and Hope. She looks up at me, and her eyes widen.

"Ah, Reilly?" she asks, not breaking her stare from me.

Reilly laughs. "What's up?"

"Take the girls back. I'm going to go get a drink from the bar. Anyone want anything?" she asks.

She doesn't wait for an answer. "Dean, you can help me." She pulls my hand, dragging me behind her through the boat.

She gets to a bathroom door, looks around, then pulls me through it before shutting and locking it behind us.

Before I know it, she jumps up, wraps her legs around my waist and clings to me like a damn spider monkey. My hands instinctively go to her ass, holding her weight up easily.

Her lips find mine; her tongue pushes through, seeking mine. Her pussy grinds on my cock. Spinning us around, I pin her back against the wall. I groan out loud. I want her so fucking bad. My cock is fucking aching. My hands slide under the fabric of her skirt, landing on her bare ass. My hands squeeze the fleshy globes so hard, I won't be surprised if she ends up with my fingerprints marking her.

Her moans of pleasure echo in the small room. The only thing between us are my shorts and the thin lace of her thong.

"Dean, I need..." Her words trail off.

"What do you need, Princess?" I ask while grinding into her core, dry humping her like a fucking teenager.

"More, I need more!" she moans out.

Picking her up higher, I sit her thighs on my shoulders. Her hands go to my head to help her balance. My face now buried in her sweet pussy, my tongue runs along her lips and over the lace of her already wet panties. I can taste her through the lace. It's intoxicating. I want to drown in her.

Her thighs tighten around my neck, trapping my head. Her fingers pull at the strands of my hair. Then she's screaming my name. Fuck, I love hearing her scream out my name like this.

# Thirteen



"Oh my gosh, Dean, this place is amazing. I can't believe you did all this. *For me.*" I spin around taking in the opulence of the room. There's a four-poster bed. A huge four-poster bed with white netting draped down the sides and white bedding.

There's rose petals over the bed, with the words "Happy birthday, Princess" spelled out. The room is filled with natural wood décor and beachy tones. The blue sofa is covered with white and blue cushions. Shells decorate the coffee table in front of it.

Sheer white curtains hang from the large sliding glass doors that overlook the ocean. We are literally on the beach. The sound of the waves crashing fills the room.

There's a bottle of champagne on the bench with two glasses next to it. *That* needs to be opened sooner rather than later.

"It's so beautiful, Dean. I don't know what to say."

"You don't need to say anything, Princess. I'm glad you like the place." Huh. He seems a little off. I've noticed since he came out of the room with Zac, he's been a little weird. I didn't want to bring it up. But I really can't read him at the moment.

"Are you okay? I know you don't really like the beach. So, you know, if you want to head back to the mainland, we can. I don't mind."

"We're not leaving here, babe. I'm good. I promise. Now, let's pop this bottle and get the celebration started." He heads over to the champagne and pours us each a glass.

"Mmm." I moan at the taste of the sweet bubbly goodness on my tongue.

"Fuck, Ella! If you keep moaning like that, we won't be leaving this room."

"I'm good with that," I say with a shrug as I jump onto the middle of the bed.

"No. We have dinner reservations with everyone. In twenty minutes. Your bags should be in the closet already," he says, looking towards the closet.

When I don't make an effort to leave the bed, he groans, "Come on, Princess. Don't make this harder than it already is for me." His eyes avert down as he adjusts his cock in his pants. I can't help but lick my lips at the sight. His shorts are doing nothing to hide his hardness. "Oh fuck, don't do that! Let's just get dinner done. We'll be back here before you know it," he begs.

I laugh. "Okay. But just so you know, I would have preferred to have you for dinner." I wink as I walk past him towards the closet. I hear him curse under his breath.

Digging through the suitcase Reilly packed me, I'm giddy like a kid on Christmas. God, she's a good shopper. I choose a sheer Camilla halter dress. I pick out a black strapless bikini to wear under it. Taking my goodies, I walk into the bathroom for a quick shower and to get changed.

"I'll be five minutes, then the bathroom is all yours." I kiss Dean on the cheek as I pass.

"You know we can save time, and water, if we shower together."

I consider his offer briefly. "If I get you naked in that shower right now, we most certainly won't make dinner," I say.

"Good point."

I shower in less than five minutes. leaving my hair hanging wet down my back. I'm sure, in this heat, it won't take long to dry anyway. The dress Reilly picked out, is more sheer than I thought. You can clearly see my bikini underneath it. I love it. I throw on the hotel robe. I'll wait until we're walking out the door before I drop this outfit on Dean.

I wait while Dean showers and gets dressed. It's bloody torture, knowing just what his body looks like with water dripping down it. I close my eyes and envision his rock-hard abs, suds running down them and leading to his hard cock. I can almost feel the girth of it in my hands. Mmm, maybe I should have taken him up on that offer to shower together.

"Good thoughts?" Dean's voice makes me jump out of the chair.

"Jesus! Warn a girl next time," I shriek with my hand on my chest.

Dean tilts his head. His eyes rove up and down my body. My cheeks heat at the thought of being caught daydreaming about his cock.

"Sorry, what were you thinking about just now?" He smirks.

"Uh, how great it's going to be to get in the ocean tomorrow."

"Sure you were." He winks. "We should get going." He heads to the door. When his back turns, I take the robe off and throw it on the bed. He doesn't look back up until he's holding the door open for me.

"Oh, hell no!" he growls, the sound momentarily stopping me in my tracks.

"What's wrong?" I ask, trying to use the most innocent voice I can muster.

"What's wrong? What's wrong, she asks! Did you forget something? You know, like the rest of your fucking clothes?" He shakes his head.

I walk out the door before he gets a chance to lock us in.

"No, I didn't forget anything. Why? Do I not look good in this dress?" I ask on the other side of the door, taking small backwards steps while picking at the fabric. His steps follow me.

"That's not the problem. You are fucking gorgeous! The problem is that's a... I don't know what that is. But I do know dresses are meant to cover your body. That does not hide a damn thing."

"Well, I like it. Remind me to thank Reilly when I see her," I say as I turn around.

"I'm going to fucking kill..." His voice trails off. I turn to look over my shoulder at him. He's stopped, his eyes wide, and staring directly at my ass.

"Jesus fucking Christ. Ella, I can see your ass," Dean complains.

"I thought you said and I quote: *Princess, you have the best fucking ass I've ever seen.* What's wrong with it now?"

"Nothing's wrong with it! Your panties are not covering it is what's wrong. Every man and his dog are going to be ogling that fine fucking ass. I'm going to have to bury bodies. My weekend is going to be spent burying fucking bodies. Do you know how hard it is to dig six feet down *in sand*?" he asks, all serious.

"I thought you said we had this resort to ourselves. No one

else is here, Dean. I hardly think Zac and Bray are going to be checking out my ass. Relax. Come on. We're already late."

"Fuck. There is staff here too, Ella," Dean says as he wraps his arm around my shoulder.

"Don't worry, babe. I'm sure Bray will be your muscle if you have to bury anyone." I shrug.

"Do you know how much that fucker complains about digging?" he asks. For a second, I actually think he's serious. He sounds serious. But he has to be joking. I know my brothers have done some shady dealings in the past. But burying bodies seems extreme.

I shake the thoughts off as we enter a gazebo. Fairy lights cover the roof. Our entire family is already sitting at the table chatting. The table is gorgeous. A white linen table cloth covers it with a blue runner down the middle. Candles are scattered around the table.

Dean stands behind me, his hands on my hips keeping me in place.

"You're late," Zac states, glaring at Dean.

"We wouldn't be if Reilly knew what was classified as a dress," Dean says.

"What?" Bray asks, confused.

"Oh, your extremely helpful wife bought this... whatever this is," Dean says, pointing to my dress.

I roll my eyes.

"It looks great! I love it," Reilly says.

"You look beautiful, Ella. Don't listen to the grouch," Alyssa adds.

"Thank you. He's overreacting," I tell Bray and Zac.

"Overreacting? Really. Okay. Princess, can I have this dance?" Dean steps in front of me, holding his hand out.

I'm confused. What's he up to? His eyes spark with mischief. But I'm hardly going to pass up an opportunity to dance. I take his hand, and he twirls me around. I hear him count to three under his breath. Then I hear Zac.

"Ella, what the fuck?! Where are your fucking clothes?" he yells.

Dean pulls me against his chest, whispering in my ear, "Still think I'm overreacting?" He smirks as he leads me over to the chair and pulls it out for me.

"Babe, I love you. You're fucking perfect. But you're never shopping for my sister again!" Bray says to Reilly.

"Leave her alone. I love the stuff she got me. Thank you, Reilly."

"You're welcome." She winks at me. All three of us girls laugh. At the same time, the men at the table groan.

Dinner was great. I'm stuffed. We had a variety of deliciously fresh seafood and salads. Thankfully, Bray and Zac had to get the kids to bed, which means we got out of there early. I'm eager to get back to the room. I want Dean so bad right now. Is tonight the night? I feel like I've been waiting for this night forever.

As soon as we're through the door of our room, I pull the dress up over my head. I turn around and face Dean as I reach behind myself and unclip my bikini top. Walking backwards towards the bed, I pull my bikini bottoms down my legs and kick them off to the side.

"Dean, if I asked for something for my birthday, would you be able to give it to me?" I ask as I climb up on the bed and sit on my knees. I spread my legs, keeping them open. His eyes roam all over my body.

Shivers run up and down my spine, my skin tingling, burning, with his gaze. My own hands begin to travel up and down my thighs.

"Princess. I can get you anything you want. You know that. Money is not an object. What is it that you want?" he asks as he licks his lips. He still hasn't moved. He's standing in front of the closed door.

"What I want won't cost money," I say as my hands travel up the sides of my waist, his eyes following their movement. "I want you to make love to me, Dean. Now. Right here. I don't want to wait anymore."

He's at the side of the bed before I can even blink, his hands in my hair. He tilts my head up. Looking into my eyes, he asks, "Are you sure?"

"Yes. One hundred percent."

"Okay," he says as he pulls his shirt over his head.

I reach up and unbutton his shorts. I've been waiting all day to get my hands on his cock. I need it. *Now.* My hands are shoved away as he pulls his shorts down his legs.

Dean climbs on top of me, pushing me back onto the bed. My legs wrap around his waist. I can feel his hardness at my centre. I rub my clit along his cock.

Dean's hand comes around my throat. He doesn't squeeze, just holds my head still. "I love you so fucking much, Ella Williamson," he says before slamming his lips onto mine. His hand leaves my throat and travels down, between our bodies and right to my clit, where his fingers rub in slow, torturous circles.

I'm going crazy with need. I can feel my vagina pulsing, searching for something. Dean inserts two fingers. I feel so full... I wonder if his cock is even going to fit inside me. The thought does not stay long as pleasure ripples through me.

"I need you inside me now, Dean," I groan. His fingers feel great, but they're not what I want right now.

Dean pulls his fingers out. I can feel him line the head of his cock up with my entrance. He stops kissing me as he stares down at me, his cock slowly creeping into my core. *Inch by inch.* I'm stretched, so fucking full.

It hurts, slightly. But I like it. I want him to stretch me out. He gently pulls back and slides back in, with just the tip. Not all the way. I'm so wet, I can feel my own juices dripping.

"Tell me if it hurts too much. If the pain is too much, I'll stop. Promise me, Ella, that you'll tell me to stop if you need me to?" His voice is so strained. Is that what's been holding him back? He's worried about hurting me. I'm not afraid of the pain.

But that's the problem. He's not afraid of me hurting. He's afraid of me liking the pain too much. I can't guarantee that I won't. But I can give him the promise he needs. "I promise I'll tell you if I need you to stop."

Dean buries his cock all the way, in one thrust, ripping right through the barrier. A searing pain tears through me. It's wrong how good I feel right now. I embrace the pain. I let it wash over me. Dean holds still inside me. My pussy convulses around him. I try to fight the pleasure. It's wrong. I shouldn't feel this good right now. I try to fight the fog that washes over me, but it feels so good. I grind my clit against his pelvis and it sends me over the edge into pure bliss.

An orgasm takes over as I scream his name. My whole body shakes with intense pleasure. Dean stays still, buried inside of me. When I open my eyes, he's staring down at me. "Fuck, Ella! I fucking love watching you fall apart. We're going to talk about what just happened later. Right now, I need to start moving. You good?" he asks, not breaking eye contact.

"Mmhmm, better than good." I smile, probably looking like the lovesick fool I am. The lovesick fool who's no longer a virgin. Dean leans down and kisses up the side of my neck, nibbling on the lobe of my right ear as he begins to slowly thrust in and out of me.

"Fucking hell. You feel so goddamn good, Princess. I want to live inside your pussy. I want to stay cocooned in here forever." He pants as he begins to pick up his pace.

My legs are tightly wrapped around his waist, my hips meeting his thrusts. "Oh Fuck!" I scream. I'm chasing that oblivion again. I'm so close. I need it, like I need my next breath. No matter how close I get, I can't reach it.

Dean sits back on his haunches, lifting both my legs into the air. My ankles rest on his shoulders as his hands dig into my hips, holding me up off the bed. He slams his cock all the way in, hitting an all new spot. What the fuck was that?

"Yes, that. Do that again," I demand.

"As you wish," Dean says as he starts to fuck me harder. Gone is the idea of making love. I want him to fuck me as hard as he can. With each thrust, I can feel euphoria getting closer and closer. I don't know what's wrong with me. Maybe I'm a one and done girl. Fuck that. I know I can get there again.

"Dean, I need..." I trail off not sure how to tell him.

"What do you need, Ella?" he asks, slowing his pace.

I shake my head no. I can't tell him. I can't let him see how messed up I am. "Nothing," I lie. "Keep going."

I can feel his intense stare on me. I can't look him in the eye. I don't want him to see that I can't find my orgasm again. That it's pissing me off. That I want him to hurt me so that I can get there.

Then he starts fucking me hard again. He turns his head and clamps his teeth down onto my left ankle. "Ah fuck. Yes!" *That.* That's what I need. My eyes roll back at the pleasure coursing through my body. I can feel my core quiver and tighten.

Dean bites my ankle again, in a new spot, the pain pushing

me over the edge. My orgasm comes out of its hiding spot and hits me head-on. My body seizes up. I'm screaming, but I don't think any coherent words are coming out.

"Fuck!" Dean growls. I can feel his cock harden even more before I feel spurts of warm liquid inside me. He pumps a few more times with a mixture of curses and my name spilling from his mouth.

He lets my legs drop to the mattress and catches himself as he falls on top of me. I groan as he slides his cock out of me and lies down beside me. He pulls me into his arms, my head resting on his sweaty chest. I can feel the rapid beat of his pulse.

"Is it always like that?" I ask.

"No," he says without further explanation.

Was it bad for him? He came, so it couldn't have been that bad. But what if I did it wrong? Should I have done something else?

"Did you... Did you not like it?" I ask timidly.

Dean picks me up from under my arms, draping my whole body over top of his. My legs straddle his waist. I can feel the mixture of our fluids seeping out of me. I go to move off him. I'm just going to make him messy.

"Don't move," Dean says, holding me tighter. "Look at me, Ella."

I look up, my nerves going haywire.

"I fucking loved every minute of it. Don't ever question if I like fucking you. I don't just like it. I love it. I said no because it's never been like that before. It's never been that good before. It's different with you, because I fucking love you, Ella. Always have. Always will." He brings my face to meet his as he kisses me ever so gently.

"So, can we do that again? Because I'm a fan," I ask.

# Fourteen

## DEAN

The sun shines on my face. I can feel the coolness of the sea breeze sweep over me. I roll over, reaching out for Ella. It's odd that she's not already locked in under my arms. I've gotten used to waking up with her body thrown all over mine.

My arm reaches out and finds nothing but air, my hand slapping down on the empty spot where her body should be. The sheet's cold... She's been gone for a while. Then it hits me. She's gone. She's not there. She should be there.

I jump up and look around the quiet room. "Ella!" I call out. She's probably in the bathroom. Opening the bathroom door, all I see is the remnants of our mess from the night before. After we... well, I'd like to be a gentleman and say we made love, but what we did was fuck. After that, we sat in a bubble bath together until the water went cold. Bubbles and water ended up all over the place.

The realisation that she's not in the room sets in. My pulse quickens as panic takes over. Grabbing my phone, I hit her number. Come on, Princess, pick up the phone. The call rings out. Fuck!

I need to calm down, she's probably with one of her brothers. I dial Zac. *Come on, pick up, fucker.*

"What?" he asks grumbly. Fuck, he's still asleep, which means he's not with Ella.

"Is Ella with you?" I ask, trying my best not to let the panic run through my voice. The last thing I need is Zac tearing the place apart in his search for her.

I hear movement. "No, she's not. I'm up. I'll see you in two. She's probably just gone to the gym. Meet me there." How the fuck has he become the voice of reason?

"Okay, yeah. I'll meet you there," I stumble out.

"Dean. Calm the fuck down. We're on a deserted fucking island. Like I said, she's more than likely at the gym."

"Yeah. I know. It's just..." I let my sentence drift off.

"I know," he says before hanging up.

On my way to the gym — I know I shouldn't but I can't help myself — I call Bray. If Ella is at the gym, she'd likely meet up with him there. She likes to think she can kick his ass. I know for a fact that he lets her win every time she does.

Don't get me wrong, if she catches you off guard, she'll get you down. Fuck, she did it to me, and I'm fucking six foot two. The girl can fight. She shouldn't ever have to, though.

The phone rings once before he picks up. Bray's always been the early riser type. "Yeah?" he answers.

"Is Ella with you?" I say, while running over to the gym.

"No, why? She get sick of your ass already?" he asks.

"I woke up and she wasn't in the room."

"Where are you?" he asks.

"Heading to the gym, to see if she's there." I'm just pushing through the gym doors when I come face to face with Bray.

We hang up the phones.

"She's not here," he says, while staring at me. *Reading me.* I turn around at the sound of Zac opening the door.

"She's not here," I say.

"Yeah, I gathered that," he replies. "Okay, Bray, go check the pool. We'll head down to the beach and look there."

"Ah, what the fuck is going on?" Bray asks. "Why are you all bent out of shape because Ella's not in your shadow?"

"Just find her. I'll explain later," Zac says, as he turns and walks out the door.

"What did you get up to last night?" Zac asks as we walk to the beach.

My eyes widen; my eyebrows go up to my hairline. There is no fucking way I'm telling him what we did last night. I'm not that fucking stupid. I don't have to, though. By the look on my face, he already knows.

"Fucker! Don't you dare fucking say a thing," he says. I don't miss his hands twitching, opening and closing into fists by his sides. He wants to hit me. I'm surprised he's holding back.

"Wasn't planning on it, Bro." I smirk.

Once we're on the beach, we head back towards the portion alongside my and Ella's room.

There's not a soul out here. We're nearing the room when I see her. Everything inside me settles instantly. She's okay. She's walking out of the water.

"There she is." I point to the water. "Ella!" I yell out, getting her attention. She turns and waves at us.

"Fucking Reilly," Zac curses. For a moment, I don't understand what he's talking about. My eyes are too busy taking in the sight of Ella.

Then I get it—Ella, walking up out of the water, her dark hair wet down her back. She's wearing a white string bikini, the white contrasting against her olive complexion. Fuck me. She's fucking gorgeous, all curves in all the right places. Her breasts bounce as she picks up her speed, heading towards us. They look like they're in danger of falling out of the tiny bit of fabric, which is doing a shitty ass job of covering them.

Fuck, I have to adjust myself in my shorts. Zac lifts his shirt over his head and steps in front of me just before Ella reaches us. Before either of us knows what is happening, Zac's got his shirt over the top of Ella's head, covering her body from anyone's view.

Ella immediately pulls the shirt back over her head. "What the fuck, Zac?" she asks him, holding his now wet, scrunched-up shirt in her fisted hands.

"You obviously forgot your clothes when you left your room this morning. I thought I'd give you mine." He shrugs.

Ella slams the shirt into his chest. "You might want to reconsider taking your shirt off in public these days, old man," she says.

Zac's eyebrows draw down as he asks, "Why's that?"

Ella lets go of the shirt; it drops to the sand. She points up and down his body as she says, "Well, you know, that whole dad bod thing you have going on now."

The look on Zac's face is fucking gold. He looks down, rubbing a hand over his chest and abs. The man is as vain as they bloody come. Ella knew exactly how to hit him where it hurts. He's speechless as he picks up his shirt and shakes the sand out of it. Me? I'm busy laughing my ass off at him.

"Okay, well, I'll catch you both later," she says as she turns and starts walking the other way. My laughter dies really fucking quick when I see the view Ella is giving. The full view of her uncovered ass. She's wearing a fucking G-string bikini. I'm going to have Reilly banned from every damn store in Sydney.

I pull my own shirt over my head and throw it to the side.

"Ah, I'll catch you later, man," I mumble to Zac as I run and pick Ella up around the waist from behind. She lets out a mixture of squeals and curses as I run into the waves. Ever tried running with a hard cock? It's not bloody fun. I don't even like the fucking ocean. But it was either run into the ocean, or risk letting my best mate notice the raging hard-on I have for his sister.

Once I'm waist-deep in the water, I let Ella go. Throwing her a little, I watch as she goes under the water. Coming back up, she gasps as she wipes the water from her face and attempts to push her wet hair back.

She looks at me with murder in her eyes. It's a little scary how I've seen that exact expression on her brother, right before he actually killed someone.

"Morning, Princess." I smirk as I wrap my arms around her. Her body floats into mine, her legs wrapping around my waist. She doesn't get time to answer before my lips are connected with hers.

She opens for me instantly, our tongues duelling. The salty taste of the ocean water is strong on her lips. Her legs tighten, and she grinds her pussy against my hard cock. "Mmm, goddamn," I growl as I hold her ass still, cradling her pushed up against me.

Ella lays a trail of kisses up my neck, then stops to nibble on my earlobe. Fuck me! That feels good. "Babe, if you keep that up, I will fuck you right here, in the middle of the beach for everyone to see."

She blows on my ear gently, sending goosebumps along my arms. "That sounds like a great idea. Let's do that after..." Her whispered words trail off.

"After what?" I ask.

"This!" she shrieks, before she spins herself around my body. I don't know how she does it, but she ends up on my fucking shoulders. The unexpected movement causes me to lose balance. I go head first into the water. When I come up, the sight that greets me steals my breath away.

Ella is standing, what she probably thinks is a safe distance, away. Her face is lit up with a huge fucking smile. She's laughing, albeit, at my expense. I'd let her dunk me every day if it meant having her this happy. She cups her hands and starts splashing water in my direction, still laughing. She seems so carefree in this moment.

It dawns on me that this, right here, is the most carefree I've seen her since she's come home. I make a note to make sure she has more experiences where she can just be herself — the beautiful, young woman with a heart of gold.

I'm in awe of her every single day and I don't even think she knows it. Ella stops splashing when she notices I haven't moved. I've been struck still with the breathtaking view of her. She starts floating closer to me.

"What's wrong?" Concern is written all over her features. And I'm the fucking asshole who just stole her happiness. *Again.* I'm starting to think that I'm too toxic for her. I've always known she's too good for me. Unfortunately for her though, I'm a fucking selfish bastard and I have no plans of letting her go. Ever.

"Nothing's wrong." I smile. "I was just caught up in your beauty. It's been a while since I've seen you so happy and carefree." She's within my reach now. I grab her around the waist and pull her so her body is flush with mine. "I like it. I love seeing you smile, hearing you laugh. It's like everything is right in my world when you're happy."

Ella sighs and melts into me. "What's not to be happy about? I have everything I've ever wanted right here in my arms." She smiles up at me.

"Oh yeah? What's that?" I ask.

"Well, there's the ocean. And not just any ocean. We are literally in the Great Barrier Reef, Dean!" She looks up at the sky, letting her head fall back, her dark locks floating on the water. She picks her head up. "I am happy, Dean. With you, I'm happy. Don't ever doubt that. I can't promise that I won't have times of..." She doesn't finish the sentence. She doesn't need to.

"Princess, I need you to promise me something."

"What?"

"If you ever feel the urge to cut... If you ever get to that place, I want you to find me. Just find me. Please." I can't fathom the thought of her being alone and in that mindset. It scares the shit out of me... what could happen... what could go wrong.

"I promise I will try," she says. It's all I can ask, really. It's not like I'll be leaving her side until I find the fucker who sent that email to Zac anyway, which reminds me how I ended up on the beach so damn early in the morning.

"I need one more promise, babe. I need you to not leave the room without waking me again. When I woke up and you weren't there, I panicked. I don't like not knowing if you're safe. I don't ever want to relive those feelings."

"I'm sorry. You looked so peaceful sleeping. I didn't want to disturb you. And in case you've forgotten, there's no one else here. Look around. What could possibly happen to me here?"

"A lot," I grumble.

"Okay, well, I will do my best to wake you up. But if you end up with bags under your eyes because you lose beauty sleep, don't come blaming me."

I laugh. "Nice try. But I'm not as vain as your brothers, babe."

"How quickly do you think Zac ran to the gym?" She grins mischievously.

"He would have made it there in two minutes flat."

"Well, it's a good thing you aren't at risk of having a dad bod any time soon. I'd hate to lose you to the gym." Her hands travel over my chest. "Although, whatever you're doing is most certainly working for you."

"Glad you approve," I say as I start walking out of the water.

"Where are we going? You can put me down you know. I have legs."

"Back to the room. And I don't want to put you down." My hands squeeze the fleshy globes of her ass as I make my way back to the room. I really need to remember to cut this bikini up.

# Fifteen

ELLA

Dean carries me straight through our room and into the shower. He doesn't put me down until we're under the water. And even then, my feet are only on the floor long enough for him to undress me. He curses and mumbles something about buying new swimwear.

Right now, my back is currently shoved up against the cold tile wall. Dean is holding my body up like I weigh nothing, as he sucks and nibbles on my breasts. My back arches off the wall when he bites down on my right nipple, while twisting the other one between his fingers.

Fuck, I don't know what it is about being bitten. The pain of it is almost enough to send me over the edge alone, without anything else. I'm going to have to remember to talk to my therapist about this. I'm not sure it's a healthy thing for me to be wanting.

All thoughts of therapists, and whether this is right or wrong, disappear out the window when Dean moves his mouth to my left breast. Without warning, his teeth are clamped down on my nipple.

"Fuck, that feels so good. Don't stop. No, stop. No, don't stop."

Dean chuckles around my nipple. My hands are pulling or pushing on his head. I can't decide if I want more or less of what he's doing right now. He takes his mouth away from my nipple, the little *plop* sound echoing in the shower.

His tongue licks up the side of my neck. "Mmm, you taste so fucking good, babe."

"Uh-huh." I'm out of my mind with need. All I can think of is being filled and stretched again. "Dean, I need you inside me now."

"Are you sure? You're not too sore from last night?" Dean asks, although he's already lining the head of his cock up with my opening. Tightening my legs around his waist, I bring myself down on him.

"I'm positive. I'm not a fucking wilting flower, Dean." A loud moan escapes me as he bottoms out inside of me. The slight twinge of pain quickly gives way to pleasure as my walls convulse around him.

"Fuck, Ella. Hold on tight, babe. Things are about to get rough," he warns as he pushes my back harder into the wall, my arms and legs clinging on to him as tightly as I can.

Dean starts to fuck me. Literally, it's like a crazed animal has been let loose. He thrusts in and out, quick and hard. My head falls back, hitting the tiles. My eyes roll back into my head. I wouldn't be surprised if the whole island can hear my screams right now.

Dean brings a hand up to my throat, holding my head still as he continues to plunge in and out. I'm so close to coming. "I'm going to... oh fuck!" I yell out as Dean's hand tightens around my throat. I open my eyes; he's staring intently at my face.

My mouth is hanging open and my chest is starting to burn. That's how I find my orgasm. Dean's hand loosens as my walls spasm around him. He grunts as warm spurts of him fill me.

My whole body shakes as I try to find the strength to continue holding onto him. Dean turns around and sits down on the floor of the shower. He doesn't let go of me. He doesn't pull out. I can feel his cock twitching inside of me.

We sit like that, catching our breath while basking in the afterglow of that orgasmic release. We hold onto each other. I want to stay like this forever.

"I wish I had known it felt this good," I say.

"Mmhmm, why is that?" Dean asks as he nuzzles his face in my neck.

"Because I would have tried harder to get you in my bed years ago."

"You would have got me killed is what you would have done. All those years of wanting you and not being able to touch you, it was fucking pure torture."

"Oh, trust me. I know the feeling."

Sitting on the patio drinking a mimosa, I'm mesmerised by the view as the waves roll in and out. I love the ocean. It's always been my dream to have a beach house. There's something about it that's just so peaceful, the smell of the salt in the air, and the relaxing sounds of crashing waves.

Which is the total opposite to watching Dean on the sand, pacing up and down the beach. He's been on the phone for over thirty minutes. I can't hear what he's talking about, but whatever it is, he looks stressed.

Deciding not to wait for him any longer, I dig out my laptop. I can use this time to get some work done. We're not meeting up with everyone else until lunch time. That will give me a few hours of work time. Well, at least until Dean finishes with his call, really.

I log into the remote servers for the club and pull up the spreadsheets I've been working on. I've narrowed down that the accounts for the bars are off. I've managed to track each date that money has been missing. The new cash registers that Zac had installed a couple of years back are connected to Wi-Fi. They upload data to the club's servers after each transaction, giving each night a total figure.

Zac never bothered to tell the staff about this feature. I'm not one hundred percent sure he even realises that the system does this. He still has the bar managers counting the tills and keeping digital ledgers each night. I'm halfway through matching the nights with missing funds to the staff rosters — who was covering those shifts and who was signing off on the nights' earnings.

I've accounted for over one hundred and fifty thousand dollars that's been stolen in the last twelve months. I have a really good hunch who it could be. I just don't want to believe it's this person. I want to prove myself wrong. That's why I'm still digging, looking for any evidence that it's not her. It just can't be her.

How could someone so close to our family betray us like that. If she needed help, she could have just asked. Most people wouldn't know this, but Zac would help out anyone that needs it. He's always trying to find ways to help others. He just usually does it anonymously. He doesn't want recognition for it.

The other day, I saw a transaction for a donation of one million dollars he made out to the breast cancer association.

When I asked him about it, he told me if I wanted to keep my job, I wouldn't tell anyone. I know his threats of firing me are empty. There's no way he would. I mean, I'm almost certain they're empty threats. But I'm not about to push the boundaries to find out either.

Growing up, I was always the good child. I tried my hardest in school. I stayed away from trouble as much as I could. I never stayed out late. I did everything I could to make it easier for Zac. What twenty-year-old wants to be dumped with the job of raising his younger siblings?

Zac never complained though. He always made sure Bray and I had everything we could ever need or want. He was there at all of my school's parent-teacher meetings. Although, thinking back on it, my teachers were all overly friendly with Zac. I wouldn't be surprised if he hooked up with half of them.

As I'm going through the staff roster, checking off who was working on the dates in question, my computer freezes. A message screen pops up. What the hell is happening? Did I open a window somewhere? I'm clicking the escape button, trying to get out of the window, when the text appears.

It's like someone is typing in real time, each letter of each word appearing on the screen. The words are all in caps; the message they convey is loud and clear.

**PEOPLE WHO LOOK FOR MISSING LINKS TEND TO FIND THEMSELVES MISSING!!!! STOP LOOKING!!!!!**

My eyebrows draw down in confusion. Why would someone be sending me this? The lightbulb goes off and I slam my laptop closed. I can feel the panic creeping up under my skin. My breathing increases; my heart beats faster and faster. I need to escape.

I look up and see Dean still on the phone. He's looking back at me. I smile and wave. I can't ruin this weekend for him. He put so much thought into giving me the perfect getaway. I refuse to allow my panic to ruin it.

I'm cold and shivering as I make my way back inside. Whoever's stealing from the club knows that I know. They want to shut me up. I can't go back to living where I'm scared of my own shadow, waiting for the bogeyman to jump out and grab me.

But that bogeyman just became all too real. Someone does want to jump out and grab me. I throw the laptop on the bed and head straight for the bathroom. I'm digging through the cabinets and searching for a razor before I even know what I'm doing.

It's not until I'm holding the blade between my fingers that some part of my subconscious kicks in and tells me to stop, that voice in the back of my head telling me I don't need to do this. I shove it aside though, not listening to a word of what it says.

I know it's the wrong choice. The moment the blade connects with skin, the moment the pain takes over, my mind drifts off into the hazy fog. I know I shouldn't have done it. But why the hell does something so damn wrong, feel so right?

Sitting on the bathroom floor, I drop the razor to the ground. Pulling some toilet paper off the roll, I hold it over my forearm. It's not a big cut. But as the haze wears off, the full reality of what I've just done sinks in. Fuck. I need Bray. I need to call Bray. He will know what to do. He'll be able to help.

I'm about to get up and go search for my phone when Dean bursts through the bathroom door. He takes one look at me on the floor. His eyes scan over my body, stopping on the blade that fell by my feet. He doesn't say anything.

He walks in, picks me up and takes me to the bed. Dean sits with his back against the headboard and holds me, straddled over his lap. His hands run up and down my back, and through my hair. His gentle, comforting caresses break me. The silent tears stream freely down my face.

We sit like this in silence. As I fall apart, yet again, in this man's arms. How many nights did he hold me like this until I fell asleep when I was eighteen? Countless.

He deserves so much better than a broken Princess for a girlfriend. "I'm so sorry," I whisper.

"Ella, you have nothing to be sorry about, babe."

"You're wrong. I'm sorry that I'm so broken. I'm sorry that after six months I caved in at the first sign of trouble. I'm sorry I can't be the girlfriend you deserve. I'm sorry that I broke my promise to come and find you when I felt the urge to cut, just hours after making that promise. I'm sorry."

"Look at me," Dean commands as he places his finger under my chin and straightens my head so that I'm facing him.

"You have nothing to be sorry about. No, you're not the girlfriend I deserve. You are so much more than I will ever be deserving of. You are not broken; there is not a damn thing about you that I would change. You didn't break a promise, Princess. You promised you would try to reach out to me for help, not that you always would. You are my everything, Ella. Always have. Always will. These hurdles that life is throwing us, they will only make us stronger. They will not break us. Nothing can break us. We will get through this together. I promise."

"I love you. I don't know how to put it into words, but you are my everything too. Always have. Always will," I say as I lean up and kiss him.

After sitting on the bed for a while, I climb off and search for my phone. Dean watches me the whole time. Once I find it, I look back at him. I should be able to talk to him about this. I know that I can tell him anything. In theory, I know that anyway. But right now, the one person I want to talk to is my brother.

"Call him, Ella. It's okay," Dean says, already knowing who I want to call. A wave of relief washes over me. I didn't realise I was trying to find a way to tell him I wanted to call Bray.

"Thank you," I whisper.

"Babe, he's your brother. If you need him, call him. Don't ever think that you can't go talk to him whenever you need to." Dean walks over and kisses me on the forehead. "I'll be on the patio if you need me."

I nod, unable to form words right now.

Sitting on the floor, with my back against the bed, I dial Bray. The phone rings and rings. I'm about to hang up, thinking it's going to ring out, when he answers, breathless.

"Ella, what's up?"

Why am I calling him? He's on holiday too. Why am I ruining everyone's weekend? I bring my knees up to my chest.

"Ella?" Bray asks.

When I still don't answer, he asks me the one question I never fail to respond to. "Ella, sweetheart, how long?" His voice is quiet. I can hear the uncertainty in his words.

"A few hours," I whisper.

"Where are you? I'm on my way."

"No, you don't need to come here. I just... I don't know."

"Don't move. I'll be there in a minute," he says.

"Okay." I hang up the phone. I don't hear Dean come back inside and sit down next to me. I feel his arms wrap around me. I hear his promises whispered in my ear.

## Sixteen

*DEAN*

The image of Ella sitting on the bathroom floor... A razor dropped at her feet... Holding tissue paper over her forearm... This image is fucking haunting me. I don't know what I'm doing here. I don't know how to fucking help her.

I wish I could be the one she leans on. The first one she thinks of to call when she needs help with this. It's killing me that I'm not. But I can't let her know that. I'm not that much of a fucking asshole. I know that Bray's been the one to be there through the years. I've got no one to blame for that but myself.

I made the choice that put all of these events into motion. If I hadn't left her, maybe she wouldn't have turned to such drastic measures to escape the pain. To escape the memories that torture her. I hold her in my arms, not knowing what the fuck to say to make it better.

Bray barges through the front door of the villa. He spots us sitting on the floor. He stands there, watching. I know he's pissed. I also know he's blaming me for not stopping her in time. He wouldn't be wrong. It is my fault. I shouldn't have left her side. I knew something was wrong the moment she smiled and waved at me.

"Ella, Princess. Bray's here." I kiss her forehead. She picks her head up and looks at Bray. She doesn't move. I know I've got to let her go. That I need to remove myself from the room so she can talk to Bray. I don't want to. But I will for her.

"I'm going to be on the patio. Will you be okay?" I ask her. She nods her head.

Standing with Ella still in my arms, I sit her on the bed before I walk out to the patio. I shut the door, giving them the privacy they need.

Around thirty minutes later, Bray comes out and sits on the chair opposite me. He's silent for a moment as he looks me over. Letting out a sigh, he tells me, "It's not your fault, you know."

I shrug. "It is. I shouldn't have left her alone. I was down on the beach on a call. I kept looking back up, watching her. I should have come back up sooner when she went inside."

"It's not your fault. As much as I'd love to place the blame on someone, we can't. It's not fair to Ella to walk around blaming people for what's going on inside her own head. She's come so far in the two years she's been getting help. This... this is just a little bump in the road. She will overcome this."

"I know." I shake my head. "What am I meant to do, man? How do I help her with this?"

"You be there to pick her up when she falls. You learn to recognise the signs that she's not coping well. These attacks of hers usually come on fast and can pass just as quickly."

"I know. I've seen her panic attacks. But this... She walked inside looking fine. Smiling. Two minutes later, I find her on the bathroom floor, a razor dropped at her feet. What the fuck happened to make her lose control?"

Bray shakes his head. "It's not about her losing control. She does this to take the control back. She only cuts when she's feeling out of control. I don't know what happened. She wouldn't tell me, which is fucking strange. She always tells me."

I look behind me. Ella is in the kitchenette making coffee. She seems okay.

"What was she doing before she walked inside?" Bray asks.

"She was sitting here on her laptop." Her laptop that's on the floor at the end of the bed. Fuck. Why didn't I think of that earlier?

"Well, whatever it was that set her off, it's more than likely on that laptop. Think you can go distract her while I grab it?" Bray asks.

I'm already picking up my tablet, which I left on the table earlier. "There's no need. I can see everything that happens on the club servers. Whatever she was doing, she would have been on the servers."

Pulling up the feeds from the previous hour, right around the time Ella was sitting out here, I dig through the files until I find the ones with her login on them. "Looks like she was looking at staffing rosters from the past twelve months." I don't mention the name that seems to pop up the most in the data she's collated on her spreadsheet. If she's uncovered that this person is the one stealing from the club, I'm not sure how that fucking betrayal will go down.

What else were you looking at, Ella? Another folder further down has her name next to it. The folder's untitled. Clicking it open, I read the message that pops up on the screen of my tablet.

"What the fuck!" I yell, causing Bray to jump up to look at what I'm reading.

**PEOPLE WHO LOOK FOR MISSING LINKS TEND TO FIND THEMSELVES MISSING!!!! STOP LOOKING!!!!!**

"What is that?" he asks, puzzled.

"Someone is not happy Ella is digging around in the club's accounts."

"Some fucker sent that shit to Ella?" Now he's yelling.

Why wouldn't she tell me about this? I don't get it. She shouldn't be keeping this sort of shit to herself.

I click around in the file for a bit, satisfied that this was sent from Sydney. From inside the club, to be precise. The sender, that fucker is going to wish they never met the Williamson's.

Storming inside, I'm about to ask Ella about the message when she looks over her shoulder and smiles. A genuine happy smile.

"Want a coffee? I just made some."

"Ah, no. I'm good, babe." I look to Bray and he shakes his head. We're in agreement that we won't bring this up right now.

"Okay, nugget. I'll see you at lunch," Bray says to Ella, ruffling her hair as he walks by her.

He stops at the door and asks, "Do either of you know why Zac's been holed up in the gym all morning? Grunting something about a dad bod?"

Ella bursts out laughing before batting her lashes and replying, "No, I wouldn't have a clue."

"You're the worst fucking liar I've ever met, El." With that, Bray walks out the door, leaving Ella and me alone. We have exactly forty minutes before we have to meet the others at lunch. I know what I want to do.

"Princess, put some shoes on. I wanna show you something."

～

"Almost there. It's just up over this hill." I pull on Ella's hand behind me, as she curses and swats flies and mosquitoes away from her.

"Dean, when you said you wanted to show me something, I was kind of hoping it was your cock. Not a bug-infested forest a thousand miles away."

"Princess, we've been walking for two minutes. Literally, two minutes. And look. We're here."

Down the slight hill is a little water hole. Crystal clear calm water. It's surrounded by rainforest. A little hidden bit of paradise. I may hate the beach, but I fucking love being in nature like this. Surrounded by trees, by wildlife, this is peace.

"Want to go for a quick dip before lunch?" I ask. Ella's already throwing her shirt on the ground and undoing her shorts before I even finish the question. Guess that means we're getting in then.

"Last one in's a rotten egg!" Ella shrieks as she runs barefoot towards the edge of the water. She stops just before she touches the water.

"Wait. Dean, how do we know if there's crocs in here or not?" She bites her bottom lip. I laugh. She's worried about getting in this clear water, but has no drama diving headfirst into the ocean? That makes a lot of sense.

"You can't be serious?" I laugh, which does not go over too well with her. I get her famous death glare in return.

"Are you really laughing at me right now?" she grits out between clenched teeth.

One thing about Ella, she's never been a fan of being laughed at. Ever. When she was fourteen, she filled Bray's hair gel tube with super glue. All because he laughed at her when she cried about getting a B on her English test. Bray ended up having to shave his head.

"No! I am not laughing at you, Princess. I would never." As much as I try not to laugh, I can't help it. Her pout, her clenched fists, she's just so fucking adorable.

I take her face in both my hands, and my lips meet hers. "You're so fucking sexy when you're mad. Come on." Entwining our fingers together, I pull her into the water. "Besides, I'm not about to share my meal with any crocs."

Ella's body relaxes as she floats around on top of the water. I really need to start carrying a camera with me. She's so fucking beautiful. Her full breasts barely contained by a black bikini top. Her tanned skin, glistening in the sun. My eyes travel down her body. Her flat stomach. Her long, toned legs. My cock is painfully fucking hard. *Again.*

Grasping one of her ankles, I pull her towards me. She straightens up. Her legs instinctually wrap around my waist. I want nothing more than to sink my cock inside her again. But we have a lunch to get to. And I have some answers she needs to give me.

Picking up her arm, I kiss over the small cut that she's placed a band-aid over. "I need you to tell me what happened? Why did you feel like you had to do this?" I ask. I already know why, but I need to hear it from her. I need her to trust me enough to tell me everything.

"I..." I watch as her mouth opens and closes. She's not sure if she should tell me.

"Babe, you know anything you tell me will stay between us.

It's just you and me. We're in this together now. You don't need to do things alone."

"I know. It's just... I'm so close to finding out who's been stealing from the club. Actually, that's not right. I know who's been doing it. I just want to find evidence to convince me I'm wrong."

"Okay, who do you think it is?"

"What if I'm wrong, Dean? If I come out and accuse this person, it would devastate Alyssa. I can't do that if I could be wrong."

"Do you think you're wrong?"

Ella shakes her head no. "But I could be."

"Ella, you are the smartest person I know. You're not wrong about this." I try to reassure her. As much as I want her to be wrong, I don't think she is.

"But the message... I just don't believe that this person would send such a message to me. Stealing is one thing. Threatening to kill someone is totally different."

"People who feel cornered are dangerous, babe. You'd be surprised what they can be capable of."

She tilts her head at me. "You already know, don't you?"

See, the smartest person I know. Nothing gets past her, ever. I nod my head.

"And you've seen the message I received this morning?"

"I have." My jaw clenches. "I promise that I will not let anything happen to you, Ella. I just got you. I'm not going to lose you to some psycho, greedy fucking thief."

"How am I meant to go to work? They know I know. Maybe I should just tell Zac. Have them arrested," she suggests.

"Do you trust me?"

"More than anyone." She doesn't miss a beat with her response, even if I know it's inflated. The people she trusts the most in the world are her brothers. And that's how it should be. I'm glad she's got those two assholes in her life.

"Let's not tell anyone yet. Let's enjoy the weekend. You're safe here. That message was sent from inside the club. Which means, whoever sent it, they're still in Sydney."

"Okay, let's enjoy the weekend. I really like my present by the way."

"What present?" I ask. I haven't given her anything yet.

"The island getaway weekend. You didn't have to do all this. I would have been happy with a mug or chocolate."

I laugh. There is no way I would have gotten away with giving her a mug. "Yeah, okay, I'll remember to get you a mug for your birthday next year. I'm sure that will go over well. But this isn't your gift. Your gift is back home. You'll have to wait to get it."

"Well, I love it already."

"You don't even know what it is." I laugh. I don't think I've ever laughed so much before. "Come on, we need to get to lunch. Next time, remind me to leave everyone else at home. I don't like sharing you."

"That's the best idea you've ever had."

# Seventeen

## ELLA

We get to the restaurant for lunch. Bray and Reilly are already there waiting. They are seated on opposite sides of the table with the twins sitting in highchairs at the end of the table next to them. Reilly looks drop-dead gorgeous; she's wearing a black sheer coverall with a bright yellow bikini underneath.

To look at her, you would not think she had twins. She's a little curvier than she used to be, but those curves stuck to the right places. I'm envious of her pale complexion. She looks even more pale when she's near Bray, who's more tanned and olive-toned.

Thankfully, the twins get their looks from their mother, just with darker features. They've got big beautiful green eyes, each with a thick head of dark red curls.

"Hey," I say before taking a seat next to Bray, while Dean takes the seat next to Reilly. I'd much rather be sitting next to Dean, but that would have been odd, to leave Bray sitting on one side of the table by himself.

I can't meet Bray's eyes right now. Does he think I've failed again? That we're starting back at day one? Technically, we are. But I feel okay right now. I don't need to keep cutting. I'm going to keep saying that in my head until I believe it.

One thing I noticed today, when I did cut, it felt good. But it didn't feel as good as it used to. I couldn't help but compare it to when Dean hurts me—well, when he dishes out slight pain to get me off. We haven't discussed that yet. But I know that conversation's coming.

Is that going to be my new addiction? Sex with a side of pain? I'm not opposed to lots of sex with Dean, but what if it's not healthy? The way I like sex, I'm sure it's not normal. Maybe I should ask Bray? If anyone's competent to give sex advice, it'd be him. He had a revolving door of women before Reilly.

Bray reaches under the table and takes hold of my hand. I didn't notice I was wringing my hands together on my lap. He gives a little squeeze, but doesn't let go. I look up to see everyone looking at me. Did I say something out loud?

"Where's Zac and Alyssa?" I ask just as they walk through the door. Alyssa looks grumpy, and Zac looks... tired.

"So sorry we're late. How are you?" Alyssa comes to my side of the table, hugging me before sitting next to me.

Her eyes drop to my lap, and to Bray's hand still holding mine. She smiles gently at me but doesn't say anything. I wonder if they all know. Did Bray tell them I relapsed? I look over to him and he gives me a slight head shake no.

I'm starting to think all these assholes are telepathic. How do they keep doing that? Knowing what I'm thinking, without me having to say anything?

"What took you guys so long? Bad traffic?" Bray directs at Zac.

"Something like that," Zac says as he sits down next to Alyssa.

Okay, so apparently, I'm the only one that cares about having even numbers of people on each side of the table. Ash sits next to Dean, playing on an iPad. He's using his finger to draw pictures — well, scribbling, really — on the screen.

"Oh, come on. No, your idiot brother here has been in the gym all morning. Ash and I had to literally drag him out of there fifteen minutes ago."

"You've been in the gym all morning? Why would you do that, Zac? Haven't you heard? We're on a weekend holiday. Now's the time to indulge, not workout," I say sweetly.

"Shut it," Zac replies, pointing a fork at me.

Dean coughs, in an attempt to hold in a laugh. "Really, man, why you gotta be that fucking vain? Just grow old gracefully."

"We're the same fucking age, idiot," Zac grumbles back at Dean. Alyssa slaps him on the chest.

"Language," she scolds at both Zac and Dean.

"Daddy said bad word." Ash sticks his head up to dob in Zac momentarily.

"We really need to have a chat about the bro code, little man," Bray tells Ash.

"You know, Zac, we may be the same age and all. But I happen to have it on good authority that I do not have anything close to resembling a dad bod." Dean sends a wink in my direction.

"Nope, not even close. The things I wanna do with that body..." My thoughts trail off. Bray lets go of my hand, like I've burned him.

"Gross, Ella, never — and I mean fucking *never* — say anything like that around me again."

"But you always tell me I can talk to you about anything, Bray?" I remind him, my voice dripping with sugary innocence.

Bray sighs while rubbing a hand down his face. "Yeah, I know."

"Hang on!" Alyssa shouts, causing us all to look in her direction.

"You spent all bloody morning in the gym because you think you have a dad bod? You idiot!" She laughs at him.

"No, I did not. I just felt like working out." Zac tries to lie. When Alyssa raises her eyebrows at him, giving him that don't fuck with me look, he caves — just like he always does with her.

"Okay, but it's Ella's fault. She's the one that told me I have a dad bod," Zac pouts.

"Oh my god! You are an idiot. Have you looked in the mirror? There's not an ounce of fat on you. Those grooves on your abdomen, that's called a six-pack, hunny. You do not have a dad bod. Ella, tell him he doesn't have a dad bod."

Alyssa looks at me pleadingly. She wants me to put him out of his misery. Yeah, that's not going to happen.

"Lyssa, I know you're Zac's number one fan. So, chances are you're blind to the truth. But he very much has a dad bod." I shrug. In my mind, I'm not even lying. He is a dad, and he has a body: dad bod.

"No, don't listen to her, hunny. You are still GQ worthy. I'm the one that knows your body better than anyone. If you had a dad bod, I'd tell you," Alyssa says. Zac shrugs his shoulders, pouting.

He's such a bloody baby. I should put him out of his misery. But where would the fun be in that?

"Okay, this is stupid. Zac, you don't have a fucking dad bod. I mean, you even give Bray a run for his money and that man is fine with a capital F." Reilly laughs. "Honestly, do you know how many staff I had to warn off when I was working at the club? Pretty much all of them; they were very pathetic, really. I mean, you're cute and all, but that whole brooding attitude is a bore."

I thought she was finished with her spiel. Picking up the glass of champagne that's in front of me, I take a sip. Reilly chooses this time to speak again.

"Besides, Ella's cock blind at the moment. The only body she cares about seeing is grouch number two over here. Give it time, it'll wear off. Maybe." Reilly shrugs her shoulders.

My champagne comes spitting out of my mouth. Did she really just say I was cock blind?

"Cock blind? What does that even mean, Reilly?" I ask

Bray and Zac both groan, very loudly.

"Babe, stop. Don't mention my little sister and cock in the same sentence."

"Okay, Ash, come with mummy, sweetie. We're going to go have a look at that fish tank. And when we come back, all inappropriate language better be finished with." Alyssa uses her expertly honed in mum voice on all of us.

"Okay, cock blind, little El, means you've become so taken by this lover boy over here that you don't see or notice anyone else. You're hungry for what the big guy gives you." Reilly looks Dean up and down, then back at me.

"I mean, I don't blame you. He's a little rough around the edges and could use a shave. But I've seen what's hiding under that shirt and I approve." She winks.

This is one time I'm thankful for my olive complexion. I would otherwise be beet red from embarrassment right now. I would normally feel jealousy when another woman checks out Dean. But when Reilly just did, I didn't feel like that at all. I actually think she's saying that to rile up Bray.

It's clearly worked. He's currently twitching his leg up and down under the table. His fists are clenched. And he's directing his icy cold stare towards Dean.

"Unca Bray. Unca Bray. Look!" Ash yells out from the other side of the restaurant. Bray gets up and walks over to the fish tank to see what he's being summoned for.

The rest of lunch went down very PG. I think we are a little too afraid of Alyssa to go against her no swear order. Dean has us all booked in for a reef tour on a glass bottom boat in forty minutes. I'm so excited to see the reef. I've always wanted to come out here.

Everyone's leaving the restaurant at the same time. I need to steal Bray away so I can ask him about some stuff. I know I can talk to Dean about it, but honestly, I'm so worried that he's going to leave me again. I've tried so hard to be the girlfriend he deserves. And I failed, royally, at that today.

I'm also afraid of hearing the truth. What if he thinks my need for pain during sex is odd? I wish I had girlfriends to talk about this sort of stuff with. I could probably talk to Reilly or Alyssa. I know they would listen and offer advice. But it's awkward.

The only person I've ever been able to talk to, without embarrassment about anything, is Bray. He's always been the one I have heart to hearts with. Don't get me wrong, if I wanted to, Zac would absolutely take the time to talk with me. He would hate every single minute of it, but he would try.

When I was fourteen, I got my first period. Yes, I was a late bloomer. Zac tried to give me the whole birds and bees chat. He tried to explain about how my body was changing, about what I had to do. He tried. And he failed big time. He got so flustered when he tried to tell me I was becoming a woman. He demanded that I just stop growing up, that I stay his little Ella. He didn't want me to become a woman.

That's when Bray walked in on the conversation, took me by the hand and led me into his room. We sat on his bed for hours that night. He told me everything he knew about the female body. He told me that just because I could have sex, didn't mean I should. Clearly, I held on to that piece of advice.

When I was sixteen, Bray took me to the GP and got me on the contraceptive pill. I tried to tell him I wasn't interested in having sex. It was a lie. I totally wanted to bone the hell out of Dean by then. It was never going to happen though.

Bray convinced me that it was better to be safe than sorry. He then took me to a group centre for teen mums. After that day, I have not missed a day of taking that little pill.

I just need to find an excuse to get him away from everyone else. Then it hits me.

"Oh, crap. Bray, you were meant to show me that thing in the gym you told me about." I implore him with my eyes.

Bray laughs before agreeing with me. "Shit, yeah. Sorry, Sis, I forgot all about it. Want to go in there now?"

I nod my head.

"Dean, Bro, you wouldn't mind helping Reilly back to the villa with the girls, would you? Thanks, man. We'll meet you all at the jetty in forty," Bray says as he starts pulling me away by the hand.

We bypass the gym. Bray leads me around the resort until he finds a spot he deems suitable. The garden we stopped in has a gazebo. We head for that and both sit down with our backs against the railings.

"Okay, spill it. What's so important you had to drag me away? You know, I had a seventy percent chance of getting laid while the girls were taking a nap just now."

"Well, shit. Sorry. And I actually mean that." I never used to care about being a cock block to Bray. "I mean, now that I know how good sex actually is, I am sorry for all those times I cock blocked you. Kind of."

"Wait. Shut the front door? Rewind the fuck up. You had sex?" he yells.

"Thanks, Bray. I don't think they heard you in Perth. Do you want to shout it out a bit louder?" Sarcasm drips from my lips. Maybe I should have just kept this to myself. I should just talk to my therapist about it. I look down at my shirt, my hands wringing in the hem.

Bray sighs, then shuffles around to sit cross-legged in front of me. He takes my hands in his and stops them from fidgeting.

"I'm sorry. You just took me by surprise, that's all. You're so young, El. You don't need to be having sex yet," he says so seriously.

"Bray, I'm twenty-three. Losing your V-card at twenty-three is not young by any means."

He shrugs his shoulders and smirks at me. "It was worth a shot. So, who was it? Do I know him?" He has the best bloody poker face, because as he asks this question, he legitimately looks serious, like he doesn't know who it was.

"Seriously, don't be an idiot. You know it was Dean." As much as I tell him not to be an idiot, his jokes do settle my nerves — a lot.

"Okay, did you like it? Do I need to kick his ass? Is he treating you right?" He fires question after question at me.

"Oh, I like it. I like it a lot. You're not allowed to kick his ass, or any part of his body for that matter. And it's Dean. Are you really questioning if he treats me right?"

"I have to ask. Because, frankly, I'd love for you to give me a reason to punch the fucker again."

When I don't respond, he clarifies that he's only joking. I don't know how to broach the subject of what I really need to know.

"Okay, so you had sex. With Dean. What's going on in that pretty little head, El? What's wrong?"

"Do you think I'm too broken to be a good girlfriend? I've never been someone's girlfriend before. What if the things I like are too weird for him?"

"First, you're not broken. Dean is counting his lucky stars that he has you. Trust me — I've seen him counting the stars. What things are we talking about here, El?"

"I like pain, Bray. That can't be normal," I admit.

"That's not a secret. And if Dean can't handle you the way you are, then that's his loss. You had one slip in six months, Ella. That's not weird. We knew that there is no telling when everything's going to get to be too much. We can't predict when you're going to slip up. That doesn't make you weird."

"No, it's not that. During sex, Bray, I like pain. It's almost like I need it to, you know..."

"Oh, well, that's normal. Everyone has kinks. As much as I really don't want to fucking know this... What are we talking about? A light spanking? Whips and chains? Floggers?"

"Ah, no. I don't know. I just know, when he bites into my skin, it's like a thousand bolts of pleasure go through me. The first time he, you know... It hurt, but it hurt so good. That can't be normal, can it?"

"Trust me, it's more than normal. You're getting in your own head, El. I've been with a lot of chicks; most of them liked being bitten somewhere during sex."

"Okay. Thank you."

"Why aren't you talking to Dean about this?" he asks.

My shoulders move up and down. "What if he thinks I'm weird? What if he can't handle my broken pieces and he leaves me again? I don't think I'll get through that again."

"Babe, unfortunately, that boy is not going anywhere. He couldn't be more in love with you if he tried. You're stuck with him now. I really hope you do love his ugly ass, because we might have to bury him to get rid of him if you don't."

"I do. I've never stopped loving him. I'm just so afraid he's going to leave again."

"You need to tell him how you're feeling, El. It's not fair to him to keep him shut out. You know I'll always have time for you. You know that no matter what, you can talk to me about anything. But you also have Dean now. He should be the one you turn to first for everything. He should be your partner in everything."

"Okay, I'll talk to him."

"He loves you, Ella. As much as he knows you need to talk to me, it's clear it's hurting him that you're not talking to him."

"I don't mean to. It's just easy with you. You don't judge me, and I'm not afraid you're going to leave me. No matter how much I might wish you would sometimes."

"Never ever. God, imagine if Zac was your only sibling. You'd be a lost cause, that's for sure."

We both laugh as we stand up and make our way to the jetty.

# Eighteen

## DEAN

I watch as Ella and Bray make their way to the jetty. I'm suddenly nervous and I don't fucking know why. I know she talks to Bray about everything. She always has. But I want to be the one she turns to when she needs someone to talk to.

Why would she not talk to me about things? I don't know what else I can do to reassure her that I'm here for her. Always. I know we will get there soon. I just have to work harder on building her trust back. She might say she trusts me, but she's holding back.

It's almost like she's waiting for something to go wrong with us. Well, fuck that. I won't fucking let it. I've just got to work harder. I need to be patient with her. It's my own damn fault. If I hadn't made that choice to let her go four years ago, she wouldn't be doubting my commitment now.

I wonder how she'd feel about a more permanent commitment. If I whisked her off and made her Mrs. McKinley, would she want that? Would that be enough to prove to her that I'm not going anywhere?

Her smile is bright as she reaches me. Her arm wraps around my waist. I cling to her, probably a little tighter than I should. She doesn't complain. No, she lets out a little sigh, leaning her head on my chest. My chin comes to rest on top of her head.

Bray gives me an odd look as he walks past us and towards Reilly and the twins, who are strapped into a stroller contraption thing. I can't read his expression, but it's a mix between being pissed and not wanting to be pissed. I don't have time, nor do I care to figure him out right now. I have Ella in my arms; everything in my world is right again.

"You ready to go see the reef, Princess?" I ask.

Her head nods against my chest. "So ready." She tilts her head back and smiles up at me. "I love you so damn much."

I lean in and kiss her, gently, slowly. Breaking the kiss off way quicker than I would have liked, I tell her, "I love you too. Always have. Always will."

Letting my arms drop from around her, I take hold of her hand, entwining our fingers together. "Come on, let's go see this reef I've heard so much about."

Ella's excitement is contagious as she jumps up and down on the boat.

"I swear you're going to break the glass bottom. Sit your ass down, El. These princesses, as advanced as they are, can't swim yet. It's their one flaw." Bray sighs. He likes to think his kids are genuine geniuses. I don't see it. All I see is drool and spit up.

"Bray, no baby their age can bloody swim," Ella says in defence of her nieces.

"Ash could." Zac smirks, sticking his chest out like the proud father he is.

"That's because Ash is a fu... genius child," I say, quickly muffling my "inappropriate" language before Alyssa can scold me. Because if any child is a genius, it's that one. He's smart as shit for someone so young.

"Please, you just wait. My girls are going to be the smartest people around. They're probably going to cure world hunger or some shit. The next Mother Teresa in the making!" Bray declares.

He's been claiming that they're going to be nuns since Reilly was pregnant with them. I can't wait for the day they start bringing boys home. That day, I'll make sure to have a fucking camera.

The boat comes to a stop. We're literally in the middle of the ocean; the only land in sight is a small sand dune island not too far from where we've stopped. There are two young guys that are staffing the boat. One of them opens a metal storage trunk sitting along one side.

"There's snorkelling gear in here. It's a great spot. You'll be able to see reef sharks, sea turtles—the coral life is amazing here. You'll also find yourself a few Nemos and Dorys if you go down close up to the coral."

Ella squeals as she rips her shirt over her head before yanking her shorts down. The guy who's trying to give directions stops talking, mouth open wide, while he openly gawks at my girl.

"Mate, you have exactly three seconds to avert your eyes from her before I make sure you end up as shark bait," I snarl.

The guy looks at me with shock, then a challenging smirk comes across his face. He thinks he can take me. The fucker has no idea what I'm capable of. I've killed for much less of a crime than someone ogling my girl. I'd take pleasure in choking that smile off his face right now.

"I wouldn't, mate. I've seen him in action. It's not pretty.

Besides, that is my little sister. If he doesn't slit your throat, you can be certain I will."

Alyssa just put headphones on Ash; she's taken to carrying around a set of headphones with his iPad lately. Probably wise. The kid's going to have a vocabulary worse than a sailor by the time he's five.

"Sit down and shut up. Both of you. You're being ridiculous." Ella points at me and Bray. She then turns to the guy with a sweet smile.

"I want to go snorkelling. I can't wait. Thank you." She picks up a set of flippers, goggles and a snorkel.

"Ah, yeah. Okay. Sam over here can take you over to the sand dune. There's loads of buckets and toys for the kids already there. You can't see it from here, but around the other side of the dune, there is a hut with shade."

"Great, Reilly and I will head over there with the kids. You three morons behave. Have fun snorkelling, Ella," Alyssa directs us all.

While Alyssa and Reilly are settling into a little boat that's attached at the side of this larger one, Zac looks torn. He wants to stay with Ella but also wants to go with Alyssa and Ash.

"Hey, El, I'm gonna give snorkelling a miss. I promised Ash some sandcastle time," he says before kissing her on her forehead.

"Sure. No worries. Take Bray with you. He's just going to dampen my fun anyway," Ella replies.

Zac laughs. "Okay. We'll see you guys over on the sand. If a shark comes, make sure you offer Dean up as a sacrifice and save yourself."

"Oh, I will. Don't worry." Ella winks at me.

～

Ella and I spent most of the afternoon in the water. She loved every minute of it. Her laughter and smiles greeted me the whole time, soothing my soul. I must admit we saw some amazing shit while snorkeling around the reef. I have to remember to bring her back here often.

She really needed this. By the time we make it to the little sand island, the afternoon sun is setting. I have plans for Ella tonight. Those plans do not include the rest of the crew.

We all head back to the boat. The ride back to the resort is quiet. The kids are all asleep by the time we make it to the jetty, each of us parting ways with plans to catch up tomorrow for breakfast before we start our trek back to Sydney.

I've ordered room service for dinner; I'm sitting on the patio waiting for Ella to finish in the shower. It's fucking hard for me not to stay in the bathroom with her. My skin is itching, my heart racing. What if she's not okay in there? I made sure to clear every single sharp object out of there. She can look all she wants; she won't find anything that she could use to cut with. It does not ease my rapid heartbeat as I wait for her to come out.

I'm ready to just head in there. How hard could it be to think of an excuse to go in there? Then again, Ella naked and soapy in the shower is enough of an excuse. My mind's made up. I stand up and am halfway across the room when the bathroom door opens.

Steam billows out of the door, surrounding the goddess who stands in the doorway. She's wearing one of my white shirts. It ends halfway down her thighs. Her olive skin glistening, I can see her nipples harden under the fabric of the shirt. She's so fucking sexy.

"Fuck, Princess!" I run a hand down my face. I really want to pick her up, throw her on the bed and ravish her body. But it's more important that we have this dinner. I want to have a chat with her. I made a call to my lawyer while she was in the shower. I'll have the papers drawn up and ready to be signed by the time we get back to Sydney tomorrow.

I just need to get her to agree to sign them. I don't expect it to be an easy battle. Part of me hates myself for even suggesting that we do it this way. But there really is no time to go down the traditional route. I'll do anything to protect her; there is nothing I won't stop at.

Right now, making her a McKinley is one thing I can do. Nobody's stupid enough to fuck with the McKinley family. If they are, they usually find themselves out of breath. Literally.

My family may not be the mafia or mob, like Ella once asked about, but somehow, they're worse. They hide behind their dirty money. Growing up, the one thing I learnt from my father was that there is nothing money can't buy. And there are no limits to what people are capable of doing to keep hold of their wealth and luxurious lifestyles.

"What's wrong?" Ella's concerned voice drags me out of my own head.

"Apart from the fact that I have a raging hard-on and I want to tie you to that bed and have my filthy way with you? Nothing's wrong," I deadpan.

"Well, that doesn't seem like a problem."

The white shirt sticks to her body. Her nipples are still hard and clearly visible through the damp fabric. No. We are having this dinner and this conversation. Reaching out, I grab hold of her wrist and pull her out to the patio. I purposefully sit on the other side of the small table. I want to be able to see her eyes, her face, when we have this conversation.

She's never been able to hide anything. Even when she tries to lie, or omit the truth even a little, her face twitches. Her eyes tend to roam the whole room. She has other tells too. Too many tells. Let's just say she gave up on learning to play poker only a month into trying to play. She was shit at it. But damn, did she look hot trying; even her fucking frustration at always losing was hot.

"Okay, so that's a no to the whole being tied to the bed thing?" Ella asks.

I swear she is testing my resolve, her eyes begging me to take her back inside and do whatever I want to her body.

"Not a no. Before the night is over, I promise, you will be tied to that bed, Princess." I smirk, as I watch her squirm in her seat.

"Eat. There are some things we need to discuss," I say, pointing to her food with my fork.

Her whole demeanor changes. Almost instantly, her body freezes up. But as quickly as she froze, she shakes it off. With a shaky voice, she asks, "What is it that you want to talk about?"

"Babe, relax. What's wrong?" I grab hold of her hand over the table.

"Well, I may be new at this. But even I know nothing good ever comes from the line *we need to talk*." She looks down, stabbing her food with her fork.

"What are your thoughts on marriage?" I blurt out, needing to test the waters. We've never had this conversation, aside from the comments I have dropped, and she's ignored. I'm hoping we are on the same wavelength here.

"That depends?" She shrugs.

"On what?"

"On who's getting married?"

"What if it was us?" I suggest, pointing between the two of us.

"Dean, are you proposing right now?"

"Babe, I'm not a fucking idiot. When I propose to you, I'll be sure to have a ring fitting of a fucking Queen."

"Okay, well, as long as there's a ring involved, I guess I'd be open to the idea." She laughs.

"You'd be open to the idea, huh?"

"Well, if someone else doesn't come at me with a ring before you get around to it, you're in with a fighting chance." Her smile lights up her face.

"If someone else tried to give you a ring, Ella..." I pause and wait for her to look up at me again. When she does, I deliver a promise I fully intend to carry through with. "I'd cut his fucking hands off, before ripping out his tongue."

She stares blankly at me for a long time, like she's trying to figure something out. "Why do I get the feeling you're not kidding?"

"Because I'm not." I shrug.

"Dean, you realise how crazy you sound, right?" she asks.

"Crazy about you, yeah." I smile, trying to ease some of her shock from my overly graphic proclamations. "Ella, you're not blind. And you sure as fuck are not stupid. You know I've done things that cross over the line of good and bad. I know there's a place in Hell waiting for me. I'm okay with that. But are you going to be?" I hold my breath waiting for her response.

"There isn't a damn thing I would change about you, Dean. I love you just as you are. And you're wrong. You are not going to Hell. We'll just stay right here, in purgatory together. Because, even in death, I will not let you leave me again."

"There is nothing that could possibly make me leave you, El."

Deciding to change the subject, I ask her what's been on my mind all day.

"What was it you had to talk to Bray about earlier today?"

Her cheeks heat up. Although her olive tone does a great job at hiding her blush, I can always tell when she's blushing. Her eyes divert, bouncing around the room. Her face begins to twitch.

"Don't even try to lie to me right now, Princess. I know you want to."

She lets out a huff. "Okay, you really want to know? Sex! I talked to Bray about sex, okay. Are you happy now?" she yells.

I drop my fork. It lands with a clank on my plate. "You spoke to your brother about sex?" I ask in disbelief.

Ella nods her head. "I don't exactly have a surplus of girl-friends lining up who I can talk to about these things. So, I talk to Bray."

"You spoke to your brother about sex? About the sex you have with me?" I ask again.

"Well, I'm not having sex with anyone else. So, yes." She sounds kind of annoyed with me at this point.

"You spoke to Bray about sex with me and I'm still alive? Shit, babe, it's lucky I wasn't fed to the sharks out there today." I point to the ocean in front of us.

Ella laughs. "Are you afraid of my brothers, Dean?"

"Not usually. But when it comes to you, those two assholes are unhinged." I shiver at the thought of the torture Bray is currently putting me through, even if it is only in his head.

"As opposed to you? You just threatened to cut off an imaginary man's hands and tongue." She points at me before scooping more rice onto her fork and shoving it in her mouth.

"I did." I smile. "So, what did you talk about?"

"I already told you."

"In detail, Ella. What specifically did you talk about? And why wouldn't you just come to me? You know, for this to work, you need to start talking to me about things. You used to talk to me about everything."

"That was before you..." Her mouth snaps closed. She doesn't need to finish the sentence. I already know what she was going to say.

"Before I left you." I nod, understanding.

"So, did you tell him how good I am at it at least?" I joke, trying to lighten the mood.

"No, that part must have skipped my memory."

"I'll be happy to refresh your memory, soon. First, I wanna know what exactly it was you talked about."

"You're not going to give up on this are you?" she asks, resigned.

"Nope." It's important I make her talk to me about this, even if she doesn't want to. It's like a band-aid — you just have to rip it off to realise it was way worse in your head. I need to get Ella out of her own head. I know she's scared to open up to me, because she thinks I'm going to leave.

"Okay, I asked him if what I like was normal," she says quietly.

I tilt my head at her. What she likes? "What do you mean? Is there something you like that I'm not doing? Because I'm pretty much open to anything you want to try in the bedroom. I only have a few hard limits." I wink at her.

"No, it's not that. I just... I like pain, Dean. I like it when you bite me, choke me, all of that. That's not normal, right? Bray says it is, but how can it be normal? I understand if you think I'm weird or whatever. But I've come to the conclusion that I don't care."

"First. Bray's right. It's completely normal. Besides, I like doing those things to you too. Second, you don't care about what, exactly?"

"I don't care if you try to leave me again." She shrugs her shoulders before smiling sweetly at me and adding, "I'll find a way to lock you in the basement of that big fancy house of yours. I'd keep you locked there forever if that's the only way I got to keep you."

I laugh so much my stomach starts to hurt. "And I'm unhinged?"

"Are you laughing at me, Dean?" Ella puffs out.

"No! I'd never dare to," I try to say with as straight a face as I can muster.

"I would hate for you to encounter an unfortunate accident," she threatens.

"Babe, you're not going to do anything to harm this body. You like it way too much." I'm pretty confident in that fact.

"Maybe?" She smiles and continues to dig into her food. I don't mind so much that she went to Bray about this stuff. But I sure as fuck want to be the one she comes to in the future.

"Ella?"

"Yeah?"

"I wish you had talked to me about this first," I say quietly.

"I was afraid that you would think I was weird or something..." Ella stares down at her plate.

"Babe, look at me," I command, my voice leaving no room for argument.

When she looks up from her plate, I tell her, "There is nothing weird about you. There is nothing about you that I don't love. Who the fuck cares if you like a little bit of pain with your pleasure? It's more normal and mainstream than you think."

"Yeah, but I don't have a normal relationship with pain, Dean. What if I'm using that as a way to get my fix?"

Shit, I didn't even really think of that connection. No wonder she's so worried about it.

"Does it feel the same? When you experience pain during an orgasm and when you cut?" I ask.

"No. At first I thought it was. But then, when I..." She pauses and a blank look takes over her features.

I stand up and walk around to her. Picking her up, I sit on the chair with her in my arms. "Go on," I encourage her.

"When I... when I cut today, it wasn't the same. It didn't feel the same," she says.

"Okay, that's good. Right?"

"I think so."

"Do you want me to get a therapist on the phone? We could do a consult over the phone right now if you want."

"Dean, it's eight o'clock at night. I can wait until we are back in Sydney. I'll call my therapist from Melbourne. I haven't found one in Sydney yet."

"Okay, but if you want one now, I can do that."

Ella leans into me, her lips connecting with mine. Her tongue pushes past my lips and entwines with mine. The sweet taste of her wine on her tongue makes me hungry for more. More of her. More of us. I pick her up and carry her inside. Laying her on the bed, I break apart the kiss.

"It's your birthday, Princess. Whatever you want, I'll do it. Tell me what you want?"

# Nineteen



"Anything I want, huh?" I tap my finger on my chin, thinking of what I could possibly use this *anything I want* moment for. I must take too long thinking. Dean leans into my neck, kissing his way up to my ear.

"So, what'll it be? My tongue on that delicious pussy of yours. My fingers pumping in and out of that tight cunt I cannot stop fucking thinking about?"

I'm already a squirming, moaning mess. He's barely even touched me yet. But his words, oh, they've touched me. They have lit me up from the inside out.

"Or I could take your ass. That tight virgin ass." A growl leaves his throat. I can feel the vibrations of it on my neck.

I guess he likes the idea of fucking my ass. Me, not so much. I need to put a stop to this before he seduces me into letting him do just that.

"I know what I want," I declare, my voice a breathy sigh.

"Yeah, what'll it be, Princess?"

"I want you to strip for me." My cheeks burn with embarrassment. But I want to see Dean strip.

"Okay, sure." He stands up, eyebrows drawn in confusion, as he starts to pull his shirt over his head.

"Wait, stop!" I hold my hand out in a stop motion.

"What?"

"Not like that. You need music. I want to see you dance while you do it. I want a show, Dean."

"You want a show?" His mouth hanging open, he scrubs a hand down the back of his neck. "Ah, babe. You know when I said you could have anything, I was kind of thinking: position, toy, body parts. Not dancing."

"Oh, well, that's okay," I say in a quiet voice. He immediately looks relieved.

"I mean, Magic Men are performing in Sydney in a few weeks. I'm sure Reilly will go with me." I shrug like it's not a big deal.

"Fuck no! You are out of your goddamn mind if you think you're going to watch a bunch of naked guys dance and gyrate. Not happening." Dean is fuming at the idea, exactly the reaction I knew he would have.

"I wasn't asking permission, Dean. I'm not your child, although you are basically old enough to be my dad. Well, if you can't give me a strip show, I'll go and see the professionals do it. It's not a big deal." I look him dead in the eye. I work hard on evening out my breathing. I'm the worst liar. I have no plans to go see a strip show. But I don't want him to know that.

"First, I'm ten years older than you, babe. I am not old enough to be your father. Although, I could be your *daddy*." He wags his eyebrows up and down.

I laugh at the thought, but some part deep inside me is kind of on board with that idea too. That's something I'll need to explore another time. One battle at a time.

"And second?" I ask.

"Okay, if I do this, you have to promise me you won't go to a fucking strip show."

"I promise." I jump up and down on the bed in excitement.

"I can't believe I'm fucking doing this. Only you could make me do this, Ella," Dean says as he thumbs through his phone. A smirk appears on his face as he hits play.

Ginuwine's "Pony" starts blasting from the phone's speaker. Oh. My. God. My hands are itching to pick up my phone and capture this on camera.

Dean starts to slowly move his hips, as his hands travel up and down his body and his chest, his movements a little awkward. The awkwardness does not last long though.

Grabbing his shirt between his hands, he rips the fabric straight down the middle, as he rolls his body. My mouth hangs open as he begins a full-on choreographed number.

He comes over and picks me up then settles me in a dining chair. I reach my hands up to touch his chest.

Dean swats my hands away. "No touching the talent." He winks and then starts giving me a lap dance. He's so fucking good at this, it's actually starting to piss me off. Has he done this before?

My thoughts are distracted by his abs though, before he flips himself upside down into some sort of handstand maneuver, his pelvis now gyrating near my face. I have to sit on my hands to stop myself from reaching out.

Why didn't I know he could dance? I feel like there is so much I don't know about him.

Dean rights himself and comes to straddle me again. His face goes into my neck, his chest heaving. The song's finished, which means my show is now finished. I've already decided this is so not going to be the last time he dances for me.

Dean slides his body down mine, until he is on his knees in

front of me. He spreads my thighs apart as far as they will go. I don't get any warning before his face is buried between them, his tongue weaving magic over my body.

"Oh god! That, I want that now." I pant as I grab hold of his head, pushing his face harder into my core.

Dean doesn't complain. He lets out a guttural roar as his tongue plunges in and out of my pussy. Dean hooks his arms underneath my thighs, lifting my pelvis off the chair, and giving himself a better angle. His fingers are digging, bruising, into my thighs.

"Oh, fuck me!" I yell out. Dean pops his head up with a smirk.

"Don't worry, babe, I fully intend to."

"What the hell, Dean? Don't stop." I shamelessly shove his face back down into my pussy.

My whole body seizes and I come apart when he uses his fingernails to scratch into the sensitive skin of my upper thighs. I don't know what I'm yelling out, but I do know I'm making some incoherent sounds right now.

I must black out, because when I come to, I'm in the middle of the bed. *Naked.* Dean is straddling my body, naked as well, and smirking down at me. His ocean blue eyes are sparkling.

When I attempt to reach up to his face, my arms are met with restriction. I pull with no luck. Looking up, I see both wrists securely tied together with a silk tie, which is then fastened to the middle of the headboard. What the actual fuck? I thought he was joking about tying me to the bed.

I yank on my wrists again; the tie won't budge. Looking back at Dean, who still has a shit-eating grin on his face, I try to settle my racing heart. This is Dean. I trust Dean. I can handle being tied up and defenceless with Dean.

Dean tilts his head, inspecting my every reaction to my

current predicament. His fingertips lightly graze down my body, from my neck to the middle of my breast. My skin erupts in goosebumps. A hot blaze follows his touch.

He trails his fingertips around both of my nipples, pinching, pulling, and twisting them at the same time. My back arches off the bed, the sensations going straight down to my core. I try to move my pelvis, looking for any kind of friction I can get. I don't get far. My legs are pinned down.

I'm literally held captive, my body at his mercy. And I'm absolutely loving it. In a matter of minutes, I've gone from scared to crazily wanton.

"Dean, please," I beg. Although I don't know what it is I'm begging for.

"Please what? What do you want, Ella?" his raspy voice asks.

"I want you to touch me," I manage to get out.

Dean's fingers leave my breast and start trailing in swirls around the sides of my waist. "I *am* touching you, babe."

My head shakes no. He is not touching me where I need to be touched. As soon as I make the motion, his fingers leave my body.

"No, you want me to stop?" he asks with a chuckle.

If I could send daggers with my eyes, they'd be going straight into him right now. "Don't you dare fucking stop."

"Tsk, tsk, tsk. You know that little potty mouth of yours is going to get you in trouble. I think it needs to be cleansed out."

Dean shuffles up the length of my body, until he's squatting over my chest. He's holding his cock in his hand, stroking it up and down slowly. My mouth waters at the sight. Pre-cum glistens the tip.

My tongue darts out to lick my lips. Dean grunts as he rubs the tip of his cock along the seam of them. "Open," he demands.

I don't hesitate as my mouth opens and he glides his cock in as far as I can manage it. I flick my tongue up and down the underside of his cock, the smooth velvety skin a welcomed texture. The tangy, salty taste of him makes me thirsty for more.

"Suck, little girl. This is what happens to little girls who have potty mouths." He smirks.

I hollow my cheeks out and suck. Dean slowly begins to slide in and out of my mouth with long drawn-out movements.

"Fuck, Ella, your mouth feels so fucking good." He curses as he gradually picks up his speed.

"Mmmm," I moan around him. I'm so turned on and wet right now. My hips move on their own, seeking something. No, not something. My body is a greedy bitch, because it wants Dean's cock filling every hole.

Dean takes his cock out — a plop sound audible in the air — his movements so fast. One minute, he's squatting over my chest with his cock in my mouth. The next, he has my body flipped over. He positions me up on my knees so my ass is in the air and his cock is slamming into my pussy.

I'm so wet he glides in easily. Although it still takes a while for my body to adjust to the intrusion, I love the feel of him stretching me out. I love the slight tinge of pain as he fills me.

"You're so wet, hot, tight. I'm going to fuck you so goddamn hard you'll feel it in every fucking step you take tomorrow." He growls as he starts to do just that.

"Ahh, yes! Fuck! Oh god!" My mind is a mess, my body overcome with sensations. We haven't done this position before, the depths he is hitting inside me all new. Goddamn, what else has he been holding out on me? I know it's not a rational thought. I literally just had sex for the first time yesterday.

I can feel his hands everywhere, all over me. He pulls his cock out. I let out a whimper. Looking back over my shoulder, the best I can in this position, I watch as he gives me a devilish smirk while he inserts two fingers into my pussy. As quickly as he puts them in, he pulls them out.

He holds them up in front of his face, and I can see them glisten with my juices. My head falls back down to the mattress when he slams his cock into me again. He thrusts in and out, slowly. One of his hands comes around underneath me and starts rubbing circles around my clit.

His other hand lands on my ass with a loud smack. "Ah, fuck. God." I let out a mixture of curses and moans as the sting turns to pleasure. I want that again.

"Do that again," I beg.

"Gladly," he says at the same time his hand rains down on my ass. Three times. Each time a little harder than the first, and each time, that delicious sting sending waves of pleasure through my body.

I tense when I feel something moving around that forbidden little hole. No, he can't seriously think he's sticking anything in that.

"Relax, Princess. There is not a single part of this body that's not mine. That I won't treasure. That I won't pleasure." His words send shivers up and down my spine. He curves his body over mine and assaults my spine with feather-light kisses. He then finds a spot on the left side of my body, and bites down on my waist.

Intense pain radiates through me. Just as that pain is morphing into that wonderful bliss, I feel one finger slide into my rear hole. Fuck. His cock pumping in and out slowly, his fingers rubbing slow circles around my clit, and now my rear hole filled with a finger, he is keeping still.

I want more. I feel so full, so full of him. My hips grind back onto him. He gets the hint and picks up his pace. He begins fucking my pussy with his cock and my ass with his finger. It's not long before I'm drifting over the cliff.

I hear him call out my name as he comes, filling me up with his seed. After a minute, he leans over the top of me and loosens the ties around my wrists. We collapse on the bed next to each other, our breathing heavy. Dean has my wrists in his hands, rubbing over the marks left behind from the tie.

"Where on earth did you learn to do that?" I ask with a yawn.

He looks at me like I've grown two heads. "Ah, babe, you really want me to answer that?"

"Yes, I want to know."

"Well, I've been doing it ever since Miss Brighten. She was my year nine English teacher. Let's just say, she added an extra element to after school tutoring." He smirks.

"Your English teacher taught you how to dance?" I ask, confused. The look on his face tells me we are not talking about the same thing.

"Ah, not exactly," he answers as he looks up to the ceiling.

"Oh my god! Dean, you slept with your teacher?" I'm mortified. I mean, who actually does that?

"Well, yeah," he answers with a shrug. "Doesn't everyone?"

"No, Dean, everyone does not sleep with their teachers. I clearly never did."

"Please, your teachers weren't stupid enough to touch you, Ella. Trust me, they wanted to."

"No, they did not." There is no way that any of my teachers wanted to do anything like that with me.

"Babe, there is not a straight man alive that wouldn't want to get into your panties. They'll just never get to. Because. This. Is. Mine." He annunciates his claim slowly, firmly, as he cups his hand over my bare pussy.

"Uh-huh, all yours. Only yours. But I still wanna know. Where did you learn to dance like that?"

"My mother made us take dance lessons all through our childhood. When I was thirteen, I bribed the ballroom dance teacher to cover for us. Instead of the ballroom lessons my mother was paying for, we were learning hip hop."

He says this like it's totally normal for a thirteen-year-old to be bribing grown adults. Then my mind clicks on the *we* and the *us* he mentioned.

"Who's we?" I ask.

"Me and my brother."

"Wait. You have a brother?" I sit up fully now. "How do I not know you have a brother?"

"Josh. He's two years younger than me. Spends most of his time out on the family horse stud. He's also the CEO for McKinley Industries."

"Okay, well, I want to meet him."

"Sure, one day." He doesn't sound too convincing, like he wants me to meet his brother. I would dig into that further, but I'm too damn tired.

Lying back down, I rest my head on his chest. Placing a little kiss over his heart, I say, "I love you, Dean, so much it scares me. Because if I lose you again, I won't just be broken, I'll be fucking shattered into a million pieces."

"Ella, you're not going to lose me. I'm not going anywhere. In fact, when we get back to Sydney, anywhere you go, I go. I'm not leaving your side for a second. It might be a good idea to work from home for a bit too."

"I'm not hiding from her, Dean. If she wants to come at me, let her." I will not be run out of my own club. Well, technically, it's Zac's club, but that's a minor detail.

"It's not hiding. If I don't think it's safe for you to be at the club, you won't be at the fucking club, Ella. I will not take risks when it comes to you."

"We can talk about this later. I'm tired." I yawn.

"Sure, Princess. Go to sleep." He kisses the top of my head, while tightening the arm that's draped around my waist and anchoring my body to his.

*Twenty*

## DEAN

The weekend went by way too fast for my liking. I can't help but shake the feeling of dread in the pit of my stomach. Something isn't right. The fact that we are flying back into Sydney, back to where there is currently a psycho sending threats to my girl... That shit's not sitting well with me.

Every fibre of my being is telling me to direct this plane elsewhere. To take Ella somewhere else. To find a tower and hide her away from anyone who wants to harm her. I can't do that though. If I'm not in Sydney, I can't find the bitch and kill her myself.

Unfortunately for her, I know exactly who she is. Where she lives. Where the fuck she works. There is no rock she can fucking hide under that I will not turn upside down. I'm going to enjoy getting her blood on my hands.

We're all getting settled on the plane when Reilly asks Alyssa, "Hey, Lyssa, did you know Sarah was going away with that new guy of hers?"

"Yeah, she mentioned something to me last night about that," Alyssa answers.

I feel Ella go stiff next to me. I squeeze her hand and guide her to the back of the plane. She sits on the bed. Squatting down in front of her, I grasp both of her hands. "It's going to be okay, Ella. I won't let anyone get to you."

At that moment, Bray barges through the door. That fucker never fucking knocks.

"El, you doin' all right?" he asks her while leaning against the wall and making himself comfortable.

"I will be, Bray. I just... I don't know. It's not that I'm scared for myself. It's just... this is going to destroy Alyssa."

It's that moment that Zac decides to enter the room. What is it with Williamsons and not fucking knocking?

"What the fuck is going to destroy Alyssa?" he growls. He looks ready to murder someone.

Ella looks up to me and then to Bray. She doesn't want to say it. She can't bring herself to actually admit this to him.

"We know who's been taking the money from the club. We know who's been sending the threats to Ella," I tell him.

"Threats? As in there's been more than one?" he asks.

"Someone sent her a message yesterday over the club's servers. Dean was able to trace it. But Ella already knew who it was... The person is not happy that she's discovered their dirty little secret," Bray says between gritted teeth.

"Fuck! Why the fuck didn't you tell me this yesterday?"

"I... I had... I didn't want to ruin your weekend. I don't want this to be true. Why would they steal from you guys? I just don't get it. It doesn't make sense to me. But all the evidence is there."

"Who is it, El? Trust me when I say this. Whoever this fucker is, they will not live long enough to see any of their threats through. I will not let anyone hurt you."

"It's Sarah," Ella whispers with silent tears running down her face.

I watch as realisation dawns on Zac... as he grasps what this means for him and Alyssa. Sarah is his wife's best friend.

"How long has she been working at the club for anyway?" Ella asks him.

"She started a little over a year ago. She needed extra money so we gave her bartending gigs. She worked her way up to managing the bar," I tell her.

"Okay, this is what's going to happen. Not a word of this to Alyssa yet. I'll figure out how to tell her. We don't know where she is right now. She's desperate, which means she's dangerous." Zac paces around the small room.

"Dean, Reilly and I need a place to crash for a few weeks. Think you can spare a few rooms in that little house of yours?" Bray asks.

"What's wrong with your house?" Ella queries. I smile. I know exactly what he's up to.

"Sure thing, man. I'll send a text and have a room set up for the girls too."

"Thanks. My house is getting some work done to it. I don't want the construction work to upset the girls' routine," he replies, answering Ella's question. He then looks directly at me. "Don't go fucking overboard on setting up a room for Hope and Lily. They're babies, Dean. They don't need much."

I just shrug. If I want them to have a room fit for the princesses they are while they are in my house, then that's exactly what they'll have.

"Think we should get them a couple of ponies while they are with us, babe?" I ask Ella.

She laughs while Bray vetoes the idea.

"Oh, shit. I just remembered. You said Alyssa and I could

stay at your house this week while ours was being painted," Zac says.

"Fuck, I forgot about that. It's fine. You can have your usual room, and Ash is already set up there."

"Thanks. He'll be thrilled. He loves staying at your place."

I honestly don't know how Ella did not inherit the lying abilities that her brothers have. They both managed to come up with that shit quick. Even though I know they are both full of shit, Ella is none the wiser.

"Maybe I should just stay at the penthouse this week, Dean. Sounds like you're going to have your house full anyway."

"*We* are going to have our house full, Ella. You're not leaving your home just because your idiot brothers decided to both do home renos in the same week. Besides, our house is big enough that you'll barely notice they are there."

She looks between the two of them, both standing stoic with their arms crossed over their chests. "That's doubtful," she says with a smile when she looks back at me.

"Okay, let's get home. Not a word of this to Alyssa until we figure out how we're going to handle this." Zac points at all three of us.

"Sure," Bray and I say at the same time, while Ella nods her head in agreement.

"Zac, wait up, man," I say, wanting to talk to him alone. I kiss Ella on her forehead. "I'll meet you out there in a sec. Save me a seat."

"Okay."

"Babe, make sure it's far away from Bray," I call out as she's walking out the door. I hear Ella giggle and Bray curse under his breath.

Once they're both out the door, I close it behind them. I turn around and head for the cabinet where I know there's a bottle of whisky. I pour two glasses, handing one to Zac.

He downs it in one go. He's struggling to rein it in right now. I can tell.

"You aren't doing this one, Zac," I tell him as I refill his glass.

"What do you mean I'm not doing this one? That bitch is threatening Ella. Not only am I going to do this, I'm going to fucking do it with a goddamn smile on my face."

"No doubt. But how do you think you're going to face Alyssa afterwards, knowing you killed her best friend?"

That wipes the confidence off his face. "Fuck! This shit is going to fucking hurt her, man. She loves Sarah like a fucking sister. Why wouldn't she just come to me if she needed money?"

"Because your warm, cuddly, welcoming personality just screams at people to come ask you for money. Sure, man."

Zac sits on the bed and runs his hands through his hair. He's probably not going to like what I've got to tell him next either. I just need to do it, rip the band-aid off. It's happening whether he likes it or not anyway.

"I'm going to marry Ella," I blurt out fast. I know I don't need his approval, but I'd still like him to be with me on this, not against it.

He smirks at me. "Does she know about this?" he asks.

"We've talked about it. I haven't exactly asked her yet. She also doesn't know it's happening sooner rather than later," I admit.

"How soon are we talking, Dean?"

"The papers will be waiting when we get home. All we have to do is sign them."

"Fuck no! I get that you want to marry her, but fuck, man. You can't do it like that. She deserves a fucking proper wedding. A white dress and all that shit."

"I know. And she will get that, as soon as this shit is settled. But right now, I need to make her a McKinley. I called Josh."

"Why the fuck would you call him? We don't need his kind of fucking crazy, Dean. We can handle this shit ourselves." He curses as he gets up and starts pacing the room.

"Because this is Ella, Zac. I'm not taking any fucking chances. I will use whatever resource I have in my arsenal to make sure she's safe."

He knows I'm right. He knows that we need to do everything we can to make sure Ella is safe.

"Okay, so what's the plan? I know you got one." Zac raises an eyebrow at me in question.

"I'm taking Ella out to the stud farm. We're going to draw Sarah out there. All you need to do is get Alyssa or Reilly to let it slip that Ella and I are staying at the farm for a few weeks. You won't have to know the details. You don't need to be involved in this, Zac. I will make sure she's never seen again."

"Josh still got the pigs?"

I laugh. My crazy-ass brother makes all of us look like fucking choir boys. "Yeah, that fuckers attached to those things. Treats them like his damn kids."

"Let's hope he never actually breeds and has human kids then."

"Not sure there's a woman alive stupid enough to breed with him. Come on, let's get out there so we can get home."

Walking into the kitchen, I find Ella showing Alyssa how to operate the coffee machine. I'm not really sure why. I don't think I've ever seen Alyssa make her own coffee.

"Princess, you know we have staff for that, right? Alyssa, if you need anything while you're here, just talk to Geoffrey. He'll make sure you get it." Geoffrey has been with the family for longer than I can remember. It still amazes me, the things he is able to get his hands on at short notice.

"Oh, I also asked Beth to check with you on what Ash eats. She's going to need a grocery list and a menu," I tell Alyssa, who looks at me like I have suddenly grown two heads.

"Who's Beth? And seriously, a menu? Dean, we don't need to be catered for. I'm more than capable of cooking and cleaning and all of that. This isn't a vacation. I didn't even know Zac arranged for the house to be painted until today."

"I know you're capable, Lyssa. It's Beth's job to cook for the household. It's her livelihood, Lyssa. She takes great pride in what she does here. Don't take that away from her. Humour her for me and give her a menu fit for a prince."

"Well, shit. When you put it like that, Dean, okay, I'll give her some ideas," Alyssa relents. Thank God, I did not want Alyssa and Reilly messing around in my kitchen.

"Great. Thank you. Ella, I need to show you something." I take her hand and lead her out of the kitchen.

"What is it?" Ella asks.

"You'll see," I reply. Then I remember the whole not great with surprises chat we've already had.

"It's your birthday gift. I bought you a house. But I'm not telling you where. That part you will have to trust me with and let me take you there." I've stopped us in the garage.

"What do you mean you bought me a house? Dean, people don't go around buying their girlfriends houses for their birthday. That's too much," she protests.

"Babe. Do you want to see the house?" I ask.

"Shut up. Of course, I want to see the house! I can't believe you bought me a house. You know, even if it's a Barbie dream house, I'll be thrilled," she says.

"Uh-huh, I think you'll like this one more than a Barbie dream house, babe. Which car?" I ask her.

This makes her take in her surroundings. She hasn't been in the garage yet, hasn't seen the stupid collection of cars that are in here. Most of these cars were obtained by my father; he had a penchant for flaunting his money. I prefer to fly under the radar. But there are a few in here that I've splashed out on.

"Um, Dean, what the hell? This is nuts." Ella waves her hand around the garage. She starts to stroll through, weaving in and out of cars, before stopping at a white Maserati MC20. I smile. That baby is my newest purchase, drives like a fucking dream.

"This one." Ella runs her hand down the side of the car. I inwardly cringe at the idea of her handprints being left behind on the otherwise meticulously clean surface.

I find the key fob on the wall. "Okay, let's go."

As we're driving out of the estate, Ella is examining every little detail of the car. She grew up with Zac, so she knows her cars well.

"Does Zac know you have this?" she asks.

I laugh. Zac's wanted one of these since he heard they were being released. I just happened to have the first one in Australia. He doesn't know yet. Like I said, I don't flaunt my wealth. "No, he hasn't seen it yet."

"Well, that explains why it's still in your garage and not his then."

She adjusts the volume of the music. Some god-awful sounds scream from the speakers. I turn it down slightly. "El, I love you... but your taste in music fucking sucks," I tell her, grabbing hold of her hand.

"Yeah, well, your taste in..." She looks me up and down, trying her hardest to think of a comeback. "I don't know what yet. But whatever it is, it sucks."

The rest of the drive to Palm Beach is spent with us laughing and being carefree. As we pull onto the street the house is on, I tell her to close her eyes. To my surprise, she actually does.

"Don't open them until I tell you to." Jumping out of the car, I jog around to her side and open her door. "Keep them closed," I whisper in her ear as I lean over to unbuckle her seatbelt. Holding onto both of her hands, I help her out of the car and guide her until she is standing in the middle of the driveway.

Standing behind her, with my arms wrapped around her waist, I run my tongue up the side of her neck. "You're such a good girl, Ella, keeping your eyes closed all this time. Good things happen to good girls." I trail my hand under her skirt, heading straight to my promised land. Her body shivers. I didn't miss the way her body sank into mine, the little sigh she let out at being told she was a good girl. I'm going to have to explore that a little more.

Ella moans. I wasn't planning this. But I can't seem to help myself where she's concerned. With each touch, each taste, I crave more. My fingers push aside her panties, rubbing circles around her clit. Her little whimpers and moans sooth my soul. I'll never tire of seeing Ella in the throes of pleasure.

"I'm going to give my good girl a little treat before her surprise," I tell her and watch as her body quakes, her knees buckling beneath me. I nibble lightly on her neck, grazing the skin with my teeth and teasing her with the promise of that bite that she's craving.

"I think you like being my good little girl. Do you, Princess? Do you want to be my good girl?" I ask her.

Ella groans as she pushes her pussy harder down onto my hand. "Yes." She says the single word, confirming my suspicions.

"We are going to have so much fun exploring this new little development, Princess." I thrust two fingers inside of her. My cock is fucking aching in my pants, desperate to replace my fingers and fill her up.

"Right now, I need you to be really good and come for me. I need you to be my good girl and come right now, Princess." I feel her body tense up. Her pussy tightens and clamps down on my fingers. She's trying to be quiet, unsuccessfully. Her juices drip down my hand.

Pulling my fingers out, I bring them to my mouth and lick them clean. Her taste is the sweetest of any treat I've ever had.

"Open your eyes, Ella. Happy Birthday."

*Twenty-One*



## ELLA

I open my eyes; my mind is still fog-induced from the orgasm Dean just sprung on me. Not that I'm complaining — I'll take them as often as he wants to hand them out.

My eyes focus in on what it is I'm standing in front of. It's a house. A large white house with blue trimmings around the awnings and windows. I honestly thought he was kidding about the whole *I bought you a house* thing.

"Uh, Dean, this is a house. Whose is it?" I ask. We are standing in the driveway of a house and he just finger-banged me. Here, out in the open, for anyone to see.

"It's yours. Come on inside and have a look." Dean tugs on my hand, leading me to the front door.

He opens the door and walks straight in. I stop in the foyer. This isn't just a house; this is fucking huge! Stunning. I turn in a circle, trying to take as much in as I can. There's a staircase off to the left-hand side of the foyer. The space is open, a wide hall leading you into other rooms. I can see three doorways along the hall and a larger opening at the end.

"I thought you were kidding, Dean. You can't seriously buy me a house. This is too much."

"Come on, you haven't even seen the best bit yet."

I follow him through the hall. We end up in a large open-space living area. There's a galley style kitchen with timber benchtops and white cabinets to one side. But it's the floor-to-ceiling windows that have captured my attention.

I head straight for them. There's a large sliding door that leads onto a deck. Opening the door, I'm assaulted with the smell and sounds of the ocean. This house is on the beach. Literally. The deck I'm standing on leads to the sand.

I know this beach. Looking up and down the familiar beach, I hardly notice as Dean's arms come and wrap around my shoulders from behind me, pulling me up against his chest.

"Do you like it?" he asks tentatively.

"Ah, this is Palm Beach, Dean," I say.

"Yeah, I know. What do you think of the house?"

"The house is gorgeous, but it's way too much. You can't buy this for a birthday present." I shake my head. Who buys someone a house for their birthday?

"I can and I have. It's yours. It's already done."

I pull out of his arms and turn around to face him. "Did you buy me a house because you want me out of yours?" I question, my stomach doing backflips.

"What? NO!" Dean reaches for me but I step back.

"Ella, no. I bought you a beach house because it's been your dream to have one ever since I've known you. I bought this house so we could spend weekends here, *together*. But I guess if you want to live here full-time, then we can move in here. The closet space isn't as big though."

"You bought a house on Palm Beach as a weekender? Dean, that's crazy expensive."

He just shrugs. "Come on, there's something upstairs I want to show you."

I hope it's a bed. Actually I don't even need a bed. I'll settle for a wall, a bench, the floor. As long as it ends up with his cock inside me. The moan I thought was only in my head must have come out loud, because Dean turns his head back to me and smirks.

He leads me up the stairs and to a doorway. We end up in what must be the master bedroom. There's no bed. The otherwise empty room is, however, decorated with flowers, red roses everywhere and candles. Standing in the middle of the room, I'm lost for words. It's beautiful.

"Ella, I know you deserve so much more than this." Dean gets down on one knee in front of me. He holds both my now shaking hands in his.

"Ella, you are my everything. I want to wake up next to you every day. I want to create a lifetime of memories with you. I will always put you first, above anything and anyone else. Ella, will you marry me?"

Reaching into his pocket, he pulls out a ring and holds it up to my finger. He looks up at me, waiting for my answer. I nod my head.

"Yes," I whisper, before I jump on him. He falls back. I don't care though; my mouth is finding his before he even has time to put that ring on my finger. Our tongues mash together.

Dean pulls on my hair, breaking our kiss apart. "As much as I'm enjoying being mauled by you right now, Princess, I've been waiting a really fucking long time to put this ring on your finger."

I hold my hand up and he slips the rock on my finger. It's a huge princess-cut solitaire diamond. I fucking love it. "It's beautiful, Dean. Thank you."

"Babe, it's me that should be thanking you. You just made me the happiest fucking man around."

Dean sits up, holding me to his body. My legs wrap around his waist. "I can't believe this is happening. This is real, isn't it? It's not a dream?" I ask.

"It's a dream for sure, Princess, but very, very real. This is happening. You are going to be my wife. Actually, about that, I have to run something by you."

"Okay, if this is the part where you tell me you have other wives, and I'm going to be a sister wife, you can forget it. I'll kill them and have Bray help me bury the bodies." I give him my sweetest smile.

"Ah, no. Trust me, El, you are the only girl for me. Always have. Always will."

"Okay, good answer. What is it then?"

"Just know that I plan to make sure you have your dream wedding, with the white dress, the cake, the party, all that jazz. But I have papers sitting on my desk at home. I want us to sign the papers tonight. I want you to marry me tonight. And then we can plan the wedding, the honeymoon. Everything."

He wants to marry me tonight? On paper. "Why?" I ask. Why does he need me to sign papers tonight, to be married tonight?

"I want you to be my wife. I don't want to wait."

"Okay. On one condition."

"Name it. Anything you want, it's already yours," he says while rubbing his hands up and down my thighs.

"I want to drive that fancy car of yours back home." I smile.

Dean groans. "Ah, babe, are you sure that's what you want? You could have anything." He tries to talk me out of wanting to drive.

I laugh. "I'm sure. Now let's go. I want to drive that thing."

"Okay. But, Ella, seriously, I love you and all. But do not hurt my damn car." Dean looks stressed as he says this.

I practically run out to the car.

"Oh my god! We have to do this again. I love this thing!" I scream as we come to a stop out front of Dean's house. Dean looks a little green at the moment.

"Never again! How did you even pass a driver's test, El?"

"What? I'm a perfectly good driver. You're still in one piece, aren't you?" My arms fold over my chest.

"No, I think I left half my insides at that first red light you ran." He opens his door and starts walking around my side of the car. I don't wait for him this time. Before he can get to my door, I'm out of the car and slamming the door, which only makes him cringe.

"It was orange, not red!" I yell.

"I'm not colour-blind, babe. It was red. I'm probably going to have at least ten speeding fines coming in the mail too. How is it I've never actually seen you drive before?"

"Oh, I don't know, probably because I'm surrounded by alpha-holes who always insist on driving me around." I throw my arms up in the air as I stomp towards the house.

The door flies open, Zac standing in the doorway. "What the fuck are you two yelling about out here?"

"Just the fact that your sister almost killed me! Have you seen her drive?" Dean yells back at him.

Zac smiles. "You let her drive?" Then his eyes land on the car. "What the fuck, D! You let her drive that? When the fuck did you even get this?" Zac's making his way to the car. Me? Apparently I'm forgotten about.

"Just last week. I'm lucky she's still in one piece." Dean shakes his head.

Deciding to leave them to it, I head for the door. "This conversation isn't over, Princess," Dean says. To which, I flip him off without even a look back at him.

Walking through the house, I look for Reilly or Alyssa—either of them will do. I just need to show someone this ring. I can't believe I'm actually going to be married. I'm going to marry Dean. The person I thought I'd never get to have, I get to have him forever.

My smile hurts my face, but I can't stop. I'm staring down at my hand as I'm walking. I don't notice my surroundings until it's too late. I walk straight into someone. Hands instantly grab my arms to steady me. I look up, about to apologise. The moment my eyes land on his face, my whole body freezes. I don't know this person. I've never seen him around here before. The emptiness in his eyes, staring back at me, sends chills down my spine.

I react on instinct. My knee comes up, connecting with his nuts. This makes his hands fall from my arms. I take the opportunity of him being crunched over to grab hold of one of his arms and flip him onto his back.

"Fuck me!" he howls out. But instead of the angry expression and fight I'm expecting to receive from him, he stares up at me, a huge smile spread across his face.

"What the fuck are you smiling at?" I cross my arms over my chest.

He laughs as he says, "I take it you're Ella."

"Josh? What are you doing here? And what the fuck are you doing on the floor?" Dean questions, looking from me to this Josh guy.

"I'm here because it's not every day your brother gets married. I'm on the floor because, apparently, you're marrying fucking Harley Quinn," Josh says as he stands up, cupping his junk. "I approve by the way."

"Wasn't looking for your approval, asshole." Dean comes and stands in front of me. "Babe, did he do something to you?" Dean asks me.

"What? No." I shake my head.

"Then why'd you put him on his ass?"

"It was my fault. I wasn't looking where I was going. I walked into him and he grabbed my arms to stop me from falling." I step to the side so I can see Josh. I should apologise. What a way to make a good impression on Dean's family.

"I'm sorry. Do you want some, um... ice... or something?" I ask him, pointing to his junk.

"Don't apologise to him. This is your house. He shouldn't be lurking in the fucking shadows," Dean growls.

"It's okay, sweetheart. It's not the first time my balls have taken a knee. Probably won't be the last either," Josh says, totally ignoring Dean's comment.

"Her name is Ella, Josh. Not sweetheart," Dean grunts.

"I really am sorry. Let me get you a drink at least. Come on, I happen to know where he keeps the good stuff." I step around Dean and start towards the room I know there is a bar in. "Also don't worry about him; he's just grouchy because I'm a way better driver than he is," I add as Josh and I make our way to the bar.

"Okay, so I want all the juicy embarrassing stories — quick before he comes in and puts a stop to this," I say as I pour us both a shot of Dean's top-shelf whisky.

"Yeah, I'm actually a little shocked he let you walk in here with me alone. Although, the fucker probably has the place rigged with cameras everywhere." Josh looks up at the ceilings of the room.

"Oh, he does for sure. But you're his brother. Why wouldn't he let me walk into a room with you? You don't look that scary... and then there's the fact I already put you on your ass once. I can do it again."

"You caught me off guard. Trust me, sweetheart, it won't happen again. Don't be fooled by the good looks. I can be plenty dangerous when I need to be."

"Maybe." I pour us another shot each.

"Here's to new family and making memories," I toast as we click glasses together.

"You know, I think I'm gonna like having you around. Trust me when I say that's a compliment," Josh says. Reaching for the bottle, he pours our next shot. At this rate, I'm going to be smashed before I have a chance to sign those papers of Dean's.

"Well, too bad if you don't. Because I'm not going anywhere," I inform him.

He chuckles as he takes a sip of his whisky. Okay, I guess we're slowing down on the drinking. "So, sweetheart, what is a girl like you doing with a dope like my brother?"

"I happen to love that big dope very much. Plus, he's really, really good with his..." I'm interrupted by Bray's booming voice.

"For the love of God, Ella, do not finish that fucking sentence!"

"Tongue." I finish my sentence anyway. Bray groans as he comes and takes a seat at the bar.

"Family trait, I'm afraid," Josh says.

"I'll take your word for it."

"I have references — you want them?" Josh starts digging out his phone.

"Nope, I'm good. I do not need to see your DLBB, thank you very much."

"DLBB?" Josh raises his eyebrows in question.

"Your digital little black book." I grab the bottle of whisky from him and refill our glasses. I grab another glass out for Bray. Filling it, I hand it over.

"They send you in to babysit?" Josh asks him.

"No, but when I heard you were in here alone with her..." Bray points to me. "I was suddenly thirsty." He sips at his glass.

"Well, you don't need to worry. Ella and I are getting along like a house on fire. She is perfectly safe with me," Josh directs at Bray.

Bray squints his eyes at Josh, then asks me, "How much has he had to drink?"

"Not much. We were just getting started when you came in with your whole buzzkill attitude." I wave my hands around in front of his face.

Bray reaches out and grabs hold of my hand. "What the fuck is that?" he yells, dropping my hand like it's burned him.

Holding my hand up, I can't help but smile at the shiny rock. "Dean asked me to marry him," I squeal.

"And you said yes? Ella you're so young. You shouldn't rush into this." Bray gets up and starts yelling curse words and pacing. I'm about to apologise for Bray's antics. But when I look at Josh, I feel like I'm looking at a whole new person.

That empty icy glare is back in his eyes, his body tense. I watch dumbfounded, as he stands up and positions himself in front of me.

"You might want to stop yelling at her before I make it so you can't yell at all." Something in Josh's voice tells me he's not making empty threats.

"Fucking hell, I forgot just how crazy your ass is. She's my sister. If I want to yell some sense into her, I will." Bray keeps pacing up and down the room, not deterred by Josh's threats at all.

"Yeah, guess what?" Josh asks him in a calm tone. A very eerily calm tone.

"What?"

"She happens to be my sister now. And nobody yells at my sister and lives to tell the story. I don't care who you are." I need to step in here before these two idiots decide to take their pissing fight further.

"Okay, that's it. You're both ruining my buzz now." I jump on top of the bar, sit crossed-legged and pour another drink. This is the exact moment Dean and Zac decide to walk in.

Dean looks at Josh, then at Bray before asking me, "What's going on?"

"Well," I start, then hold up my hand, indicating for him to hold that thought. As I'm tossing my shot back, Josh answers for me.

"He seems to think it's okay to yell at Ella. Either one of you put a stop to it, or I will."

"What? Why the fuck are you yelling at her?" Dean asks Bray at the same time Zac walks over and smacks him upside the head.

"Leave her alone, idiot." Zac uses his *dad* voice on him.

"Are you seriously going to let her get married?" Bray asks Zac.

"She's fucking twenty-three, idiot. I'm not letting her do shit. If she wants to marry the idiot, that's her choice, not ours."

*Twenty-Two*

**DEAN**

What the hell is happening? I walk into the room to find Ella sitting on the bar top with a bottle of whisky in her hands, my fucking psycho brother standing in front of her like he is her self-appointed bodyguard.

Bray's fucking pacing up and down the room not happy about something.

When Josh says Bray's been yelling at Ella, I have a feeling he's not too happy about the ring on her finger. My suspicions are confirmed when he starts yelling at Zac about letting her get married.

Because any of us let Ella *do* anything. That girl does what she wants, despite what anyone else thinks. I'll also be damned if any fucker is going to stop us from signing those papers tonight.

With that thought, I head over to the bar. "How much have you had to drink, Princess?" I need her sober to sign these papers.

Ella holds the bottle up. "Not much?" she answers with a question.

Okay. We need coffee. Reaching over the other side of the bar, I pick up the phone and dial through to the kitchen. When Beth answers, I tell her to bring a pot of coffee in here. I pry the whiskey bottle out of Ella's hands, much to her annoyance.

"Hey, Joshy and I were bonding over that bottle." She pouts.

I glare at my brother. Joshy? Really. What the fuck did I miss?

"Princess, we have very important plans tonight. I need you to be sober for them."

Ella reaches up and wraps her arms around my neck, then brings her legs around my waist. "Do these plans involve your tongue? Because I was just saying how you can do good things with your tongue," she whispers harshly.

"Well, if you drink some coffee and sober up, babe, I can guarantee you that I'll make that happen," I promise her.

"Okay, where's the coffee?" she asks, poking her head around my shoulders.

"Did I miss the party invite?" Reilly heads over to Bray. I watch as his body relaxes the moment she wraps her arms around his neck.

"No," Bray says at the same time Ella holds her hand out and says, "Yes, look what I got!"

The sound that comes out of Reilly's mouth should be illegal. I'm not even sure what it is, but it's fucking high-pitched and goes straight through my bones.

"Babe, calm down. You're going to make us all deaf," Bray groans.

"I don't care! Let me see! Let me see!" Reilly jumps up and down as she pushes me to the side and pulls on Ella's hand.

Josh's features harden as he takes in Reilly tugging on Ella's hand. I give my head a slight shake. This is not something he wants to comment on. Instead, he speaks to Ella.

"Sweetheart, I think you should maybe hop down off the bar before your friend here pulls you down."

"Josh, this is Reilly. Reilly, Josh. She's my sister. For some reason, she married Bray." Ella sticks her tongue out pretending to gag.

"Oh, there's a reason — it's his pierced cucumber. That thing is bloody magic." Reilly laughs. At this, Bray's chest puffs out, and a smirk crosses his features.

Ella screws her face up. "Yuck, I do not need to know about that. Do you want to hear about Bray's cucumber?" she asks Josh.

"Fuck no."

"Well, let's get back to the fact that I'm getting married. Tonight." Ella jumps up and down in her spot. She's still on the bar.

"Either you get her down, or I will," Josh says to me. I'm already grabbing her by the waist and picking her up. I sit her on the barstool in front of her.

Beth walks into the room rolling a coffee cart. Her cart automatically stops when she spots Josh. She makes the sign of the cross with shaky hands as she mumbles a prayer under her breath.

Josh smirks at her, which she does not like one bit. She leaves the cart where she stands in the doorway, turns on her heel and walks away.

"What the hell did you do to that poor woman?" I ask Josh.

He smiles. "I think it's probably more what I did to her granddaughter."

"I think it's more that she knows the devil when she sees him," Bray counters.

"Probably," Josh says, unfazed by the comment as he walks

over and pours Ella a cup of black coffee. He's about to bring the cup over when he looks at her, then adds milk before handing it to her.

"Thanks, Bro," Ella says as she takes the cup.

"Just so you know, you may be her new brother, but I'm her favourite brother," Bray says as he stalks up to Ella.

"El, if you're one hundred percent sure this is what you want to do, then I'm happy for you. But if there is the slightest doubt, let me know and I'll get you out of here."

Even though I don't doubt Ella's love, I still seem to hold my breath at Bray's question, waiting to hear her answer. She keeps me waiting a while too, damn it. As she slowly sips her coffee, she puts the cup down on the bench.

"Bray, I am one hundred percent certain. This is what I want. He is what I want," she says, pointing her thumb over her shoulder at me. I let out the breath I was holding, a huge smile plastered on my face.

"Okay, we'll be back. Let's meet in the ballroom in an hour." I pick Ella up off the barstool and steady her on her feet. She gets her balance pretty quickly. Maybe she's not as drunk as I thought.

"You have a ballroom? Seriously, Dean, who the hell has a ballroom in their house?" She shakes her head in disbelief.

"We do, babe."

As I'm leading her out of the room, I stop at Josh. "Don't kill anyone." I shouldn't have to tell my younger brother not to kill anyone, but it's Josh — you never know when his crazy ass is going to do something stupid.

"Sure thing. I'll be like Mother fucking Teresa." He salutes me.

~

"Holy shit, you really are good with that tongue." Ella pants and puffs as I kiss my way back up her body. I chuckle at the memory of the look on her brothers' faces when she mentioned that little fact to them.

"I'm good at a lot of things, Princess. Things I plan to show you, right after we're married tonight," I promise.

"Uh, Dean, I'm pretty sure it's a bit late for the whole waiting until marriage thing."

"Oh, I know it's too late for that. But we have to get out of this shower. We have somewhere to be."

"I can't wait to be your wife."

"Mmm, I can't wait to do unspeakable things to my wife." I nibble on her earlobe. I don't think I'll ever get tired of hearing her little moans of pleasure.

"I'm going to try, you know. I want to be the best wife you could ever dream of having."

"Ella, you don't have to try. You don't have to be anything that you're not already. I want you just the way you are. I wish you could see yourself through my eyes — you're fucking perfect, babe." It wrecks me that she thinks she's not perfect.

"I just don't want to disappoint you."

"You won't. I am crazily in love with you, Ella. No one else. Just you. You are the one who has my ring on your finger. You are the one who will be the mother to my children — if we decide to have any."

"I know you're getting on and all in age, but I don't know if I want kids just yet. Maybe in a few years." Ella laughs.

"Sure, babe, I can wheel them around in the mobility scooter I'll be getting around in by next year."

The sound of Ella's laughter fills the room as we dry off and head for the closet. I had Alyssa find her a white dress. It's not a wedding dress, but it's at least white. It's draped over the island bench.

"I hope you don't mind, but I had Alyssa find you a white dress. I know this isn't ideal and it's not the way we should do this getting married thing. But it means the world to me that you're doing it this way. We will absolutely be having the wedding of your dreams." I kiss her forehead and pull her body tight against mine.

She wraps her arms around my waist. "Dean, I don't need a big fancy wedding. I don't need all the frills and whistles. I just need you."

"Okay, let's get dressed so I can put a ring on you."

"Let's."

# *Twenty-Three*

## *ELLA*

I cannot believe I'm about to sign a piece of paper and be officially married to Dean. The dress that Alyssa found for me is beautiful. The top is fitted white satin and square cut, which makes my boobs pop up. The rest of the dress is chiffon fabric, which drapes over my curves. It's long, falling down past my feet. I love it. I forgo wearing shoes and opt to be barefoot. We are only walking down the hallway after all.

Leaving my hair out, and letting it fall down my back in thick waves, I put on some mascara and lip gloss and call it a day. As much as I want to make myself look my absolute best for Dean, I'm running out of time. Also, I'm just really anxious to be married to him already.

I know Dean thinks I need to have a big flashy wedding with all the bells, but I don't. The fact that it's simple suits me just fine. I used to daydream about marrying him and what our life would be like together.

The reality of what it's like is so much better than anything

I could have ever dreamt up. I get butterflies every time I see him still. I want to climb him like a tree every other second. I thought I'd be nervous when I got married. People make it out to be such a big deal.

Stepping out of the dressing room, I see that Dean's waiting for me as he leans against the dresser. His eyes slowly roam up and down my body. Not once, but three times. I'm suddenly nervous. Does he not like the dress? Did he expect me to get more done up?

"Fucking hell, you look fucking stunning, Ella." Dean walks over to me. "I can't even put into words how fucking amazing you look right now, Princess. I'm... you are beautiful."

"Thank you. You don't scrub up too bad yourself," I tell him.

Dean's wearing a pair of black slacks, a white shirt underneath his jacket with a grey tie. I know I see him in a suit every day at work. But damn, I can never see him dressed like this enough. Knowing what's underneath the suit makes it all that much better.

As we walk through this museum Dean calls a house, my white dress flows around my legs. But all I feel is peace.

I'm calm. I'm grounded. I feel like I'm finally home. "Thank you," I tell Dean as we walk hand in hand towards the ballroom I didn't even know was here. This house is ridiculous. If it were up to me, we would be spending most of our time in that beach house he bought.

"What are you thanking me for?" Dean asks.

"For marrying me, for choosing me."

There was a long time I didn't think he would choose me. I thought this was completely one-sided. I've been infatuated with Dean for so long... it's hard to remember a time where I wasn't.

"No need to thank me, Princess — you're giving me everything I've always wanted. The one thing I thought I'd never get to have." Dean brings our joined hands up to his mouth and kisses each one of my knuckles.

"Ready?" he asks.

"Like you wouldn't believe." My smile is so big. I'm trying my hardest to contain my excitement. I don't want to be jumping up and down right now like a kid on Christmas, even if that's exactly what I feel like. A kid on Christmas, unwrapping everything that was on her list.

I'm so giddy with excitement that it's not until I'm almost to the middle of the room that I notice my surroundings. I stop on the spot, my mouth hanging open. I've never seen anything more beautiful. There are white flowers everywhere, and candles all around the room. White drapes hang low from the tall ceilings with fairy lights entwined around them.

"Oh my gosh, Dean! This is stunning." My voice chokes with emotion. In the middle of the room is a long dining table. My whole family is sitting around it, all staring at me.

The attention from everyone at once making me somewhat anxious, I withdraw a little and stand behind Dean slightly more. I spin around in a circle, taking in the rest of the room. When I make it back around, everyone is still staring at me.

My hands go to my wrist, trying to cover as much skin as I can. It's like they can all see my scars, even though I know I covered them.

"Princess? You good?" Dean asks.

"Uh, yeah. Of course." I plaster a smile on my face. Although by the squint of Dean's eyes, he can tell it's fake. I look beyond Dean, at everyone sitting at the table. This is my family. I shouldn't feel like this under their gaze. But I can't help it.

My eyes connect with Josh's. He looks pissed off. I don't

know why. Is it me? Maybe he doesn't want Dean and me to get married.

"Okay, fuckers, let's eat. I'm starving," Josh says, breaking everyone's attention away from me. He then winks at me. I send a small smile of thanks to him as Dean leads me over to the table.

Once we're sitting, Dean takes hold of my hand. "Before we start, I just want to thank you all for being here. It means a lot to Ella and me that you're here for this moment."

In front of me is a pen and some papers. A tall, leggy blonde enters the room and Dean nods at her as she approaches the table. The way she smiles and licks her lips at Dean, yeah, I already don't like her — whoever the hell she is.

"Ella, this is Stephanie, our solicitor. She is here to witness the papers being signed." Dean introduces her, although she doesn't take her eyes off him.

"Hi." I smile politely. She still pays me no mind.

"How've you been?" She talks directly to Dean.

"Good, you?" Dean's answer is short, his tone sharp. Please, God, tell me he hasn't slept with his damn solicitor.

Something nudges my foot under the table. Across the table from me, Josh is smirking. I have no idea what he finds amusing right now.

Bray is sitting to my right; he leans down and whispers in my ear, "You doin' all right, El? Want me to wipe the smirk off the bastard's face?"

"I'm fine," I whisper back.

Dean's arm comes around my shoulders. I expect him to rest a hand on my shoulder, except he pulls my chair closer to him. His arm drops around my waist, his hand landing on top of my hand. It's not until he squeezes my hand that I realise I was gripping the knife. I loosen my grip on the knife.

Taking a deep breath in, I relax my body into Dean's.

Holding my head up higher, I will not let some tall blonde solic-itor intimidate me. Dean is marrying me tonight. I have no reason to feel insecure.

"Hey, babe?" I direct to Dean, while staring at Stephanie.

"Yeah, Princess?"

"How inconvenient would it be for us to find a new solic-itor tomorrow?" I ask with a smile on my face.

Bray laughs a little too loudly next to me. I elbow him in the ribs to shut him up.

"Oh, hunny, you're new here. So, I will forgive you for not knowing how things work around here. You don't pay my fees, sweetie. You can't fire me." She picks some imaginary fluff off her dress.

I see that Josh is getting out of his seat across from me. He's seated right next to where she's standing. I kick him under the table, the movement stopping him from getting up.

"Oh, I'm sorry — I didn't know. Who is it, exactly, that pays your fees?" I ask her.

"That would be McKinley Industries." Stephanie smirks.

"Oh, so you'd need to be fired by, I don't know, what do they call that person that runs the big companies? Oh, yeah, the CEO. You can only be fired by the CEO of McKinley Indus-tries?" I ask her, using the ditsiest voice I can muster. Dean chokes on his drink, his grip now firmly around my waist — like he's afraid I'm going to get up and wipe the smile off his solicitor's face.

"That's right, hunny. Now, should we get on with this? I have other meetings to be at tonight. Dean, I know you said you didn't want a prenup, but really, someone in your position needs one. I drew an iron-clad one up today."

"Hold on a sec." I hold my hand up to stop her annoying voice from carrying on. Looking at Josh, it's hard to believe he's the CEO of a billion-dollar company. He's covered in tattoos and piercings—not your average nine-to-five look at all.

"Joshy," I say, giving him my sweetest voice.

"Yes, sweetheart." He smirks. He's smart. I can tell. He knows what I'm about to ask him.

"If your new sister wanted one thing as a wedding present, would you give it to her?"

"Anything you want, El. I'll make sure you get it." He smiles.

Everyone at the table is silent, waiting for my request, barring the kids clattering away at whatever they can get their hands on.

"Would you fire your solicitor and get a new one?" I ask.

Josh looks to Stephanie. She stares at him, mouth opening and closing like she doesn't know what to say.

"Check your phone, Miss Stewart. I believe you'll find a message from Daddy," Josh instructs.

She does just that. She pulls her phone out and taps a few times. Then her face goes beet red with anger.

"Josh, you can't do this to me. You can't be serious. Because of her." She points at me while yelling. She doesn't stop there; no, she keeps yelling. "You will regret this, you stupid skank! You think..." Her words are cut off by the tattooed hand currently wrapped around her throat.

"You know, it appears I don't like it very much when people yell at my sister. Let me walk you out, Stephanie. I think you need some air." Josh lets go of her throat and takes hold of her arm. Stephanie's whole body begins to shake. She's pale.

"No, it... it's okay. I can find my own way out," she stammers.

"I insist." Josh starts dragging her out of the room.

"Joshua, I'm sure her father is expecting her home in one piece," Dean yells out to their retreating backs.

"He's not actually going to do anything to her, is he?" I ask Dean.

"Ella, Josh can be a little unhinged at times. It's best not to encourage him," Dean says.

"A little is an understatement. Ella, that guy makes the Joker look normal," Bray tells me.

"Well, maybe, but he's been nothing but pleasant to me." I shrug. Who am I to judge? I have enough crazy problems of my own.

"Don't you think it's a little odd, how protective he seems of you? Dean, that's odd, right? He's a legit psychopath. He doesn't care about anyone," Zac interjects his thoughts.

"That's not true; he loves his pigs," Dean says seriously. "Plus, what's not to love about Ella? It would be strange if he didn't like her."

"Okay, whatever. How are we going to do this now if we don't have a solicitor?" I ask.

"I can witness it. Go on, sign your lives away." Josh waltzes back into the room.

I pick up the pen. "Where do I sign?" I ask, looking at the paper.

"Here. Oh, wait, I'm meant to ask if anyone objects to this union? But if you do, you might want to reconsider your objection. For your own health and safety." Josh looks around the room.

"Okay, sign here, Ella. Dean, you sign here." Once we've both signed, Josh takes the paper, signs and then hands it to Zac.

"We need one more witness," he says, handing Zac the pen.

Zac signs the paper then hands it back. "Congratulations, you're married. You can kiss the bride etc. etc." Josh waves his hands around.

Dean grabs my face between his hands and slams his lips

onto mine. The kiss is just getting heated, and I'm about to crawl into his lap, when I hear a loud throat clear. That's when I remember we are not alone.

Breaking away from the kiss, I stare into Dean's eyes. So much love and emotion stare back at me. "I can't believe we're actually married. It is real, right?"

"As real as it gets, Princess." Dean picks my hand up, digs into his pocket and pulls out a rose gold ring. It's flat with little pink diamonds all the way around it. It's also very familiar. This is my mother's ring. How the hell did he get my mother's ring? Tears fall down my face as he removes the ring he gave me only hours ago. Once he has the band on, he slides the engagement ring back into place.

"I don't have a ring for you. Fuck, why didn't I think of that?"

"Does she cry like this a lot?" I hear Josh ask Zac.

"Unfortunately," Zac says.

"Does it get any easier? The need to strangle whoever it is that made her cry?"

"Nope."

"Well, we're all fucked then," Josh says.

"Okay, I'm about to remove these headphones, which means you all need to stop the swears," Alyssa scolds.

"Is she serious?" Josh asks me.

"Yep, no swearing around the kid who can talk. Those two can't repeat anything yet, so they don't count," I say, pointing to the twins.

"Aunty El! Aunty El!" Ash starts yelling as soon as his attention is off his iPad.

"What's up, Ash?"

"You bootiful, Aunty El."

"Thanks, Ash. I just got married," I tell him.

"What that?"

"Well, Uncle Dean is now my husband." I have no idea how to explain this to a three and a half year old.

"Oh. Will I get a husband?" Ash asks.

"Only if you want one. You might want a wife," I tell him. He seems happy with that answer and goes back to looking at his iPad.

Dinner was served shortly after we signed the papers. After eating as much as I possibly could of the chicken pesto pasta, I'm now in a food coma. I can't move. I'm so full.

"What's the plan now? When are you heading out to the farm?" Josh asks Dean.

"Tonight. You'll be following, right?"

"Yeah, I got some shit to do. Send me a text and let me know when you're leaving." Josh stands up. "Ella, welcome to the family, Sis." With that, he walks out of the room.

"Ah, Dean, what farm are you going to?" Surely, he's not planning to go away when we just got married. He wouldn't do that.

"*We*, babe. *We're* going out to McKinley Ranch for a few days."

"Dean, we just came back from a few days away. We can't go on another trip. I have to work," I protest. As much as I haven't been looking forward to going into the club, especially now that we don't know where Sarah is, I was still planning on showing up for work tomorrow.

"Ella, you're going to be working remotely for a while. You can do it from the farm." Zac uses his *dad* voice on me.

"There's stuff I need in my office, Zac. How am I meant to have time to get it?"

"Oh, where's the farm at?" Alyssa asks.

"Down in the Hunter Valley. Why?" Dean answers.

"I think Sarah's planning on going through that way on her

way to Tamworth. Isn't that where she said she was heading, Rye?" Alyssa looks at Reilly.

Reilly taps through her phone. "Ah, yeah, she's gallivanting. At the moment, she's in the Blue Mountains, then on Wednesday, they're driving to Tamworth to meet this new boyfriend's parents."

"I'll ask Sarah to bring you whatever files you need, Ella. You should go and enjoy a couple more days away from this slave driver. You just got married." Alyssa's smile is kind.

I don't know how to answer her. How do I tell her I don't want Sarah anywhere near me? Dean beats me to it.

"That'd be great, Alyssa. I've just sent you through the address; send it through to Sarah for us. Come on, babe, we need to pack a few things before we leave."

"Sure." I don't know what else to say. I walk around the table, hugging and kissing everyone goodbye. I thank them all for being here tonight. Regardless of what anyone else thinks, this was my perfect night. I'm married to the man I've always loved.

# Twenty-Four

DEAN

"So, do you want to tell me the real reason why we're going to this farm of yours?" Ella asks.

She's currently sitting in the passenger seat, her legs crossed. We're about an hour into a four-hour drive. My fingers tap on the steering wheel. I can't lie to her, but I really don't want to tell her the truth either.

"I'm hoping Sarah's crazy enough to show up at the farm. Because then we can put a stop to all of this bullshit."

"Do you really think she will? She knows that I know. Why would she show up anywhere I am?"

"At the moment, she thinks you haven't told anyone. The fact that Alyssa and Zac are still talking to her like they don't know anything—that will give her confidence that you're the only one who knows. For her to continue to get away with this, she wants to silence you before you can tell anyone."

My blood boils at the thought of someone wanting to harm Ella. Glancing in the rear-view mirror, I see Josh's car directly behind me, and then his fucking entourage behind him. We're travelling in a convoy. It's over the top. I wasn't going to take any chances with Ella's safety though.

"Why are there so many cars following us, Dean? It's only Sarah, how much can she possibly do?" Ella asks as she looks out of the side mirror.

"The car behind us is Josh. The ones behind him are his security, not ours, babe." It's not really a lie. Those cars *are* Josh's security. Although I know he only has them following tonight because of Ella.

"Why does your brother need all that security?"

I laugh at her question. "Josh is a crazy motherfucker, Princess. He pisses people off on a daily basis. People with endless means. He has enemies worldwide, no doubt."

"Oh, don't you worry about him? I mean, if people are after him, what if something happens to him, Dean?"

I look across and examine her. She's worried about Josh, someone she met only a few hours ago. To say their instant connection is weird would be putting it lightly. "You don't need to worry about him. He can take care of himself."

"Maybe someone ought to worry about him. He is your brother, Dean."

"I know he is, which is why I also know I don't need to worry about him. I know he won't do anything to hurt you, El. I've actually never seen him be protective over anyone or anything other than his damn pigs. Someone could point a gun to my head and he wouldn't bat an eye. But for some reason, he's taken a liking to you. I don't get it."

"You don't get why someone could possibly want to be my friend?" She folds her arms over her chest; my eyes are drawn to her breasts as they get pushed up from her movements.

"That's not at all what I meant, Princess. What I meant was that Josh has never had an actual friend. Ever. Apart from me.

He doesn't really like people very much so he tends to steer clear of them."

"Well, then, that's just more reason why I'm going to be his friend." Her smile lights up her face.

"You are maybe the only person that's ever wanted to be his friend, babe."

"That can't be true. I bet he has women falling at his feet and wanting to be his friend." Ella laughs.

"Well, good genes run in the family." I smirk at her. "There was one girl in high school, who tried to befriend him. She learnt her lesson really quick that Josh was not someone that wanted friends. Poor girl, she never stood a chance."

"What happened to her?" Ella's eyebrows draw down in concern for someone she doesn't even know.

"Babe, as much as I love how kind your heart is and that you want to be friends with my brother, it's our wedding night. I'd prefer not to be talking about Josh."

"I like being married to you," Ella says around a yawn.

"I fucking love being married to you, Princess. Go to sleep. I'll wake you when we get there." Picking her hand up, I kiss each one of her knuckles before resting our entwined hands on my thigh again.

"I'm not that tired. I'd rather keep you company," Ella protests. Five minutes later, she's out of it.

It's dark by the time I pull into the farm. Stopping directly in front of the doors to the house, I jump out of the car at the same time Josh pulls in behind me. Ella is still asleep in the car. I stop at the back of the car, where I can see her through the windows still.

"Is she good?" Josh asks me. I'm thrown a little by his question. I don't think I've ever heard him ask about how anyone else is.

"She's good." I nod. "What are you up to, Josh? What's the deal with Ella?" I ask him

"I'm not up to anything. She's your wife, in case you forgot during the whole five hours you've been married," he grumbles.

"Seven hours. But that's not the point. Why do you seem to care so much? It's fucking weirding me out."

"You and me both, brother. I don't know. It's not like I fucking want to. I don't know what this feeling is. Something in me tells me she needs to be protected. I don't want her to get hurt." His face scrunches up; he looks pained. "You know, it's almost like that with you. You're my brother, so I don't want to see you hurt. And I would rain hell down on anyone who thought they could harm you. I just happen to like her more than I do you." He shrugs.

"Yeah, I get it. That girl is my whole world, Josh. Nothing can happen to her."

"Don't worry, I got this. As soon as that fucking bitch shows up here, I'll make sure she never breathes the same air as Ella again."

"Okay, let's get inside. It's late," I say as I head to the passenger side and pick Ella up out of the car.

She stirs in my arms. "Are we there yet?" Her eyes slowly open.

"Yeah, Princess, we're here." I kiss the top of her forehead.

Ella's head pops up and looks around. She spots Josh standing in front of the door, holding it open.

"Hey, Josh, you and I are having breakfast together. Meet me in the kitchen at seven thirty in the morning," Ella informs Josh of her plans. He's a little unsure how to respond to her. It's amusing really, watching him squirm.

"Why?" he eventually asks her.

"Because you are my only friend here, and I like having breakfast with my friends," she says. I'd like to know why I'm not included on her list of friends. I should be at the fucking top of the list.

"Babe, I'm pretty sure I'm at the top of your friends list." I know I sound like a wounded child. I just don't care.

"Well, yeah, you're my only friend who gets to see me naked. But I am having breakfast with Josh."

I look to Josh, who still doesn't have any idea how to handle the situation. He eventually agrees to meet Ella in the kitchen before stomping inside.

I take Ella straight to the bedroom I've always used whenever I come back here, which is not very often. The last time I was here was over a year ago—for my father's funeral. It was not a sad occasion, and he's certainly not missed by anyone.

Sitting her down on the bed, I walk over and pull a shirt out of the closet for her to sleep in. As much as I'd love to have my way with her right now, I know she's tired.

"Here, you can sleep in this if you want." I hand her the shirt. Ella puts the shirt on the bed as she stands and starts removing her clothes, her eyes never leaving mine.

She tugs her singlet over the top of her head, then slowly unbuttons her jeans and drags them down her legs. When she stands back up, her fingers trail up her smooth stomach before reaching around and unclasping her bra. Letting the white lace fall to the floor, she's now standing in front of me in nothing but a little piece of matching white lace covering her pussy.

Fuck me, she's fucking beautiful. I'm staring, my eyes taking in every inch of her curves. She then removes her panties, the last bit of fabric she had on. Turning around, she pulls back the covers and climbs in the bed.

"Are you coming to bed?" Her voice is husky with need. I don't need to be asked twice. I strip out of my clothes, and by the time I make it around to the other side of the bed, I'm slipping between the sheets naked.

The moment my back hits the mattress, Ella is on top of me. Straddling me, she positions herself above me. Wrapping one hand around my cock, she strokes it up and down a few times before she lines the tip up with her entrance.

My hands go to her hips, fingers digging into her flesh as she slowly, torturously, sinks herself onto my cock. We both moan once she has fully sunk down, her wet, warm pussy wrapped around my cock like a fucking glove.

Ella starts rocking her hips back and forward slowly. "Princess, I don't know how long I can take this kind of torture," I say through gritted teeth.

Ella pauses her movements. She worries her bottom lip between her teeth. "Am I... Is this not good for you?" she asks.

"It feels fucking amazing. You feel fucking amazing, Ella. The sight of you on top of me, your tits bouncing around as you grind your pussy on me... The feel of your tight, wet pussy strangling my cock... It feels too fucking good — that's why I'm about to come after thirty seconds, like a fucking fifteen-year-old."

"Oh, well, do you want me to stop?" She smiles down at me.

"Fuck no, you're not stopping. You started this. Now you gotta finish it, babe." I start to rock her hips back and forward, guiding her movements.

"Oh, fuck, Dean! I think I like this position best." Ella groans as I lift my hips, pushing my cock as far in as I possibly can. I'm not going to last much longer like this. I need to get her off first. I need to feel her come around my cock.

I release my hands from her hips, one landing with a hard sting on her ass. I fucking love how responsive she is, her harsh intake of breath, the way her pussy just got instantly wetter. I snake my other hand up to her throat, squeezing a little, as I bring her face closer to mine, causing her clit to rub against my pubic bone.

Her whole body shakes and convulses as she comes undone, her juices leaking all over me and her screams echoing through the room. Just seconds after her pussy chokes the life out of my cock, I'm filling her up with my seed. Pump after pump, it feels like I come for hours.

Letting go of her throat, I watch as her body slumps down on top of mine. My fingers trail up and down her spine as we catch our breath.

"Dean, I really like sex with you," Ella's sleepy voice whispers.

"That's probably a good thing, considering I'm the only person you're ever going to have sex with." I laugh as I kiss the top of her head. "I love you, Ella. Always have. Always will."

"I love you too. Thank you for marrying me." She yawns.

"Trust me, babe, I'm the one winning out with this marriage of ours. I'm batting way out of my league here."

"No, you're not. But can we talk about this in the morning? I'm really bloody tired."

"Sure, babe. In the morning. Go to sleep."

Twenty-Five

**ELLA**

I wake with the warm sun on my face. I slide out from under Dean's heavy arm. It's a more difficult task than one would think. He wraps that arm around me like a damn vice. It's almost like he's afraid I'm going to disappear.

I write a quick note for him and leave it on my pillow — like I have every day this week.

> *Dean,*
> *Gone to the kitchen for coffee and breakfast with Josh.*
> *Xoxo*
> *Ella.*

Every day, since I've been here, I've met Josh for breakfast. He's slowly warming up to me more and more each day, and slowly letting me see glimpses of himself that I doubt anyone else gets to see. To say Josh is complicated would be putting it lightly.

Dean and Josh have both been hovering over me all week.

It's like they're expecting the boogeyman to show up and jump out of the shadows. Sarah's obviously not going to show up here. She would have done that by now if she was planning to.

Alyssa called a few days ago to apologise. She said Sarah had changed her plans and wasn't able to drop the files off that I wanted from the club. I ended the conversation as quickly as I could. How could I pretend like everything was okay? Like her best friend wasn't stealing from her? The only reason why I'm not telling her is because as long as she doesn't know, she is probably safe.

I'm up earlier than usual today. Josh won't be down in the kitchen until seven thirty. I have half an hour before he gets down here. This is probably my one chance to go and explore outside a little before everyone else gets up. I throw on a pair of wellies and a cardi that I left hanging by the back door and head towards the horse stables.

Over the last week, Dean's been teaching me how to ride. To say I'm a beginner would be an understatement. I do love the animals though, one in particular, Pixie. She's white with brown socks on her feet. Her mane is a beautiful chestnut colour. I could spend hours brushing and talking to her.

I head over to Pixie's stable. I probably should have brought an apple out for her.

"Hey, beautiful girl." I stroke her nose as she sniffs at my chest over the door. There's a commotion a few stalls down. One of the larger horses starts bucking around and making loud noises.

"What's wrong with him? Not a morning horse?" I ask Pixie, laughing at my own joke. Just as I turn to go and check out what's causing him distress, something hard hits my head.

I can feel myself falling; my vision blurs as I hit the ground. I can make out a blurry figure leaning over me before darkness takes over.

"Argh." Why do I hurt so badly? My head feels like a thousand elephants are stomping around in it. Reaching my hand up to the side of my head, I feel wet stickiness. Bringing my hand back down, I see that my fingers are now covered in blood. What the hell happened?

I remember talking to Pixie, then nothing. Looking around, it's obvious I'm not in the stables anymore. The room is dark; a putrid, damp smell fills the air. I'm sitting on an old mattress, in the corner of a room. I can see a sink along one wall. And that's it. The room is barren. There are two windows along one wall with metal bars across them, letting in slithers of sunlight.

Dragging myself across the floor, I pull myself up, using the window ledge to help balance me. I'm dizzy. My head is aching and spinning. I feel nauseous.

Stopping my movements, I take a few deep breaths in with my eyes closed. Focus, Ella. You have to focus and get out of here. Walking slowly along the wall, I find a door; it would have been too easy for it to be unlocked. I spend more time and energy trying to budge the handle than I should have.

Slumping down next to the door, I need to rest for a bit. I just need to close my eyes for a little longer. Then I'll have the energy to get out of here. I'll be able to break the glass... call out for help... something.

I come to again when the door handle jingles, opening and closing quickly.

"Good, you're awake. You and I need to have us a little chat." Sarah sneers at me as she leans down into my face. She's resting a small pistol on her leg.

"I have nothing to say to you."

"Oh, but I have plenty to say to you, little Ella. You've ruined everything for me. It was all working out fine until you had to come home." Sarah stands and starts pacing around the room.

"You stole from your best friend. You stole from my family. Why? You know Alyssa and Zac would have helped you if you needed help."

"You don't get it. No one gets it. That should be me. I should be the one living the life of luxury, not a care in the world. I was the one who pushed Alyssa to go out that night. I should have gone myself. Then Zac would have seen me. He would have saved me."

I watch as Sarah taps the gun repeatedly on her thigh, while she walks up and down the small room. This bitch is crazier than I thought. I don't know how I'm going to get out of this situation. I know I need to keep her talking, but the more shit that comes out of her mouth, the crazier she's sounding. And the angrier I'm getting.

Getting angry right now won't help. I need to focus. I need to calm my rapid heart. I absently scratch at my wrist as I take deep breaths. I want to close my eyes and focus on the pain. The pain in my head. The scratching on my skin. I want to let the pain take over and soothe me.

I can't close my eyes though. I can't take my eyes off her. I need to be prepared. Sarah stops moving and stares at me. She looks directly at my wrist, which is now bleeding from my own nails digging into it.

She lets out a cackle. "I know what you're doing. I've heard all about your little mental health issue." Pulling out a tie from her back pocket, she walks towards me.

"You're not escaping that easy, bitch. Hold your arms up, wrists together." Sarah tucks the gun into the waist of her jeans.

She yanks on my arms, holding them together. I should fight her. I should try to overpower her, but as she pulls me around, the room starts to spin again. I know I don't have the strength to overpower her yet.

"What exactly is your plan here, Sarah?" I ask as she ties my wrists together. I use the trick Bray taught me, the one where I place my wrists in a position that makes it look like the ties are tight. I'll be able to get my hands out of this when I have more strength.

Sarah slaps me across the face. "I don't have to answer to you, cunt. You are nothing. Do you think anyone is going to miss you? They're not. I bet no one even knows you're missing yet. We're going to wait until dark. Then I'll be able to get out of here without detection. I'm smarter than you, Ella."

She drags me across the floor, away from the door. I can see the small bits of sunlight through the window. That's all I can see though. I can't see any buildings, trees, nothing. I have no idea where we are. We must still be on the farm.

"Do you really think you'll make it off this farm without Dean finding you?" I ask. My heart aches when I think about what he must be going through looking for me. Oh god, what if he called my brothers? They'd both be on their way here.

I feel like hours pass. I've tried to keep her talking as much as I can. Sarah sits across from me with the gun pointing directly at me. She's been rambling about how it should have been her with the easy life instead of Alyssa. That she was prettier. That she was more suited to be with someone like Zac.

I have no idea what happened to the Sarah I met four years ago. This clearly isn't her. She needs serious help. A white jacket, meds, a padded room—the whole works.

I see a shadow move outside the window above Sarah's head. I send a prayer up to whoever listens that someone has found me. My heart sinks when I see a girl pressing her face into the window. She sees me. I see the moment she notices me. Her big blue eyes widen in shock. I give a slight shake of my head; she cannot come in here.

From where she's standing, she can't see Sarah. "No!" I yell out. She ducks her head down, under the window.

"Sarah, you can't do this. What do you think Dean and Josh will do when they find you? I can help you. Let me help you!" I yell as loud as I can, trying to relay to the girl to go and find Dean or Josh. To tell them where I am.

I don't know how long I've been in here. My whole body aches. My head is still pounding. My own yelling is making me feel nauseous.

"Nobody is going to know. Did you think they'd be out looking for you? Where was Dean for the four years you were gone? Huh? Did he ever come to visit you? No." She shakes her head at me, then smirks.

"Do you know why? I'll tell you. Because he was too busy fucking every chick who walked into the club. I even warmed his bed more than once. But I won't bore you with the details of how he likes to choke his women while he fucks them."

My blood boils. She's wrong. She's just trying to get in my head. I know that, but it does not stop the tears from forming in my eyes. How does she know about the choking if she doesn't have first-hand knowledge?

I'm being irrational. Dean was not the virgin. *I was.* Of course he's slept with other women. But Sarah. Really? Why did he have to sleep with her? My fists clench. I want to choke her. I want to watch as that smirk is wiped off her face.

As I'm clenching my fists, the huge rock that Dean put on my finger just days ago digs into my hand. "You know, he may have fucked you. But he married me. Did you hear I'm now Mrs. Dean McKinley?" I smile at her.

It's obvious she doesn't know. Her eyes widen in shock before she quickly smooths out her features. "Well, it's going to be a short-lived union. Don't worry, I'll be sure to keep Dean company while he's a grieving widower."

I'm about to tell her to get fucked when the door's kicked in, the action causing us both to jump and scream. Sarah drops the gun in her shock, and the gun, which I thought probably wasn't even loaded, goes off. As it turns out, it was loaded. Very loaded.

## Twenty-Six

DEAN

Eight hours earlier

When I walk into the kitchen, I'm expecting to be greeted by Ella's voice as she chatters away to Josh over breakfast. Every day this week, she has made a point to meet him for breakfast. I'm not sure he does too much talking during these meetups. That hasn't deterred her though — she's made up her mind they are friends, whether he wants to be or not.

Josh is sitting at the counter drinking coffee. *By himself.* Looking around the kitchen, I note that Ella is nowhere in sight.

"Where's Ella?" I ask Josh.

He shrugs his shoulders. "Haven't seen her yet. Thought she was still in bed with you."

It's ten past eight. She should have been here forty minutes ago. "She left her usual note, saying she was coming down here to see you. Where the fuck is she?"

Josh stands up, heading for the doors. "She probably went

out to see the animals or something. Come on. She couldn't have gone too far."

I barge past him and start yelling out her name as soon as I get outside. It's irrational. I know. But something in my gut is telling me something's wrong. Please don't let that be the case.

"Ella!" I scream as loud as I can. The dogs start barking.

"Ella!" Josh joins in on calling out to her. "You go over to the equestrian yard. I'll head to the stables." Josh starts running towards the stables.

Something is wrong. She wouldn't wander off for this long. I run around the other side of the house, calling out her name as I go.

Fuck, she's not anywhere in sight here either. I make my way back around, towards the stables. Josh comes screaming towards me on a dirt bike.

"Go get a bike and start scouring the fucking farm!" he yells at me over the revs of the engine.

"What'd you find in the stables?"

"There was blood on the ground out front of Pixie's door. Drag marks leading out the back of the barn. Dean, we're going to fucking find her. Get your shit together and get on a fucking bike." He takes off towards the far paddocks.

I call Zac on my way to the shed.

"Yeah?" he answers.

"Zac, you gotta get down here. Ella's missing." As much as I'm trying to keep the panic out of my tone, it's not working.

"What do you mean she's fucking missing? Where the fuck is my sister, Dean?" he yells. I can hear Alyssa in the background, telling him to calm down.

"I don't know. She's been getting up early and meeting Josh for breakfast. She didn't show up to meet him this morning. Just get here, man."

"I swear to God, Dean, if your psychotic brother has done something to her, I'm gonna kill him."

"It's not Josh. You haven't seen them together. He's different with her."

"I'm on my way. Fuck. I'll get Bray and we'll be there soon."

The phone cuts out. I jump on a bike and start making my way through the tracks towards the front of the farm.

An hour after hanging up, Zac and Bray are landing on one of the paddocks in a fucking chopper.

"Anything?" Zac asks as he storms towards me. If ever there was a time that I thought my best friend would off me, it was now.

"Nothing."

"She couldn't have just fucking disappeared into thin air. We just have to keep looking. We will find her." When it was that Bray became the voice of reason, I do not fucking know.

"Yeah. Josh has three chopper crews about to start searching from the air. We have every man and his dog out searching through the bushes and tracks, all over the farm. I've put guards on the gates. No one is getting off this farm." I lead them towards the equipment shed.

"Grab a bike and let's go." I have to get back out there and keep looking. I have to fucking find her. She's my everything. Without her, I have nothing.

It's been hours. She's not anywhere. I've scoured every damn inch of this farm. She has to still be here somewhere. There's only one way in and out that leads to a road. No one has gone out that gate all day. I've checked the footage of the cameras all around the buildings.

We saw Ella walk towards the stables around 7 a.m. And

then nothing. It's like she's fucking vanished. We also saw footage of Sarah sneaking around the stables not long before Ella went in.

"How certain are you that she hasn't been taken off the farm?" Bray asks from the deck. He's been staring out at the empty fields, like Ella's just suddenly going to appear there.

"There's only one way a vehicle can get in and out. She's still here somewhere. We just have to find her. We will find her," I grit through my teeth.

I have to find her. Because the alternative is not one I can contemplate. Josh has had three choppers in the air for hours now, searching all the bushland on the outskirts of the farm. They just keep going around and around.

Every member of staff on this fucking farm is scouring the acres of land looking for her. Some on foot, others on horses or quad bikes. Yet, there's still not a fucking clue where she could be. When I do find her, I'm putting a goddamn tracker on her ass.

I once thought Zac was a fucking idiot for putting a tracker on his fiancée. Now, I wish I'd have fucking thought of doing that.

"We know Sarah can't just drag her off the farm without a vehicle," I rationalise, not sure if I'm trying to remind myself, or the others that she is still here somewhere.

"I'm going to fucking kill the bitch. Motherfucker!" Zac throws the glass he was holding.

No one says anything. We are all feeling the exact same way. Whichever one of us finds her first will take pleasure in erasing Sarah from the world.

"I'm going to go watch the footage again. Make sure we haven't missed anything." I slam every door in my path on the way to the office.

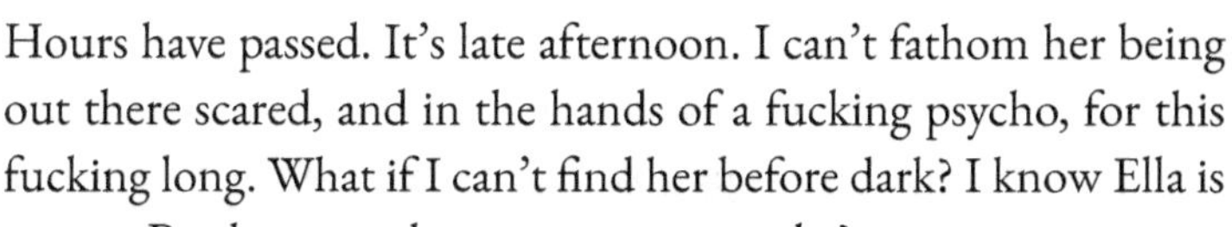

Hours have passed. It's late afternoon. I can't fathom her being out there scared, and in the hands of a fucking psycho, for this fucking long. What if I can't find her before dark? I know Ella is strong. But how much can one woman take?

Josh walks into the office, shutting the door behind him. I've never seen him so rattled before. The fact that he is even the slightest bit worried, *that* is fucking me up. He's never been worried about anything or anyone.

"Why do I feel like I'm a fucking volcano about to erupt and spill blood everywhere?" he asks.

I look him over. His body is tight, his hands opening and closing into fists and his jaw ticking.

"You're angry, Josh. That's what it feels like to feel something for someone else," I tell him.

"I don't fucking like it. I was content not caring. Why the fuck did she have to go and make me fucking care?"

"She's not the first girl to make you care. She's just the first you can't scare away. We will find her."

"The pigs are starving. The sooner we find this Sarah chick, the sooner they'll be able to eat." He smirks. And we're back to my psychopathic brother. This Josh, I can handle. I know what to expect.

The angry Josh, who's unpredictable and frankly, scary as fucking shit. "We're going to find her. I have to. I only just got her back. I can't lose her, man. I just can't." My eyes water with unshed tears.

"I'm going to go back out. Check down near the river again," Josh says. As he turns the handle of the door, his phone rings and his whole body goes stiff.

He pulls his phone out of his pocket, staring at the screen while letting it ring.

"Who is it?" I ask?

"It's Emmy." He doesn't look like he's going to answer. I press the green button and bring the call up on speaker phone. His voice cracks as he answers the call.

"Emmy, what's wrong?" Josh asks after a moment.

"Josh, I... I'm down at the cabin. Um... our cabin. There's a girl in there. She's in trouble, Josh. I saw through the window. I went to help her, but then she started yelling at someone named Sarah. And she... she said your name. I don't know what to do... What do I do?" Emily's voice cracks over the phone.

"Where are you now?" Josh asks as he storms outside and jumps on a quad bike. I'm hot on his trail. I have no idea what cabin Emily's talking about. But I have no doubt my brother knows exactly where it is.

I signal for Zac and Bray to follow. They do so without question.

"Stay hidden, Em. Do not come out of that spot until you hear me or Dean calling for you, okay?"

I don't hear her reply before he cuts the phone off and starts heading towards the scrub behind the stables.

We ride for twenty minutes before we come to a stop behind Josh.

"We need to walk from here. About five minutes away, down that direction, is an old cabin. Sarah has Ella holed up in there. The cabin only has one door and two windows. Let's go," Josh says as he leads the way.

When we come to a small clearing, the cabin comes into sight. Bray starts running towards the door before we can come up with any sort of organised plan. Well, fuck, I guess this is how it's happening.

That fucker is fast; he has the door kicked in before any of us make it there. As soon as he disappears through the door, a gun goes off.

"Ella!" I scream as I barge my way through the door, almost tripping over Bray, who is now squirming around on the fucking ground. Ella's sitting against the wall, dried blood down the side of her face.

I lean down in front of her, gently cupping her face in my hands. "Princess..." There are so many things that I want to say to her right now. I want to yell at her for leaving the house alone. I want to tell her how much I fucking love her. I want to cradle her in my arms and never let go.

"What took you so long?" she asks with tears falling freely down her face.

"You are never leaving my side again! I mean it. I will hand-cuff our wrists together if I have to." I gently lay kisses all over her face.

"Where are you hurt?" I ask as I start to loosen the tie holding her wrists together. She manages to twist her hands around, pulling them free before I get the knot untied.

Her eyes go wide as she looks at something behind me. Then I hear it. That snap. That very unique sound of a neck being snapped. Ella gasps as she covers her mouth with her hands.

A brief look over my shoulder confirms my suspicions. Josh is standing above a lifeless Sarah. With a smirk on his face, he tells Zac, "I'll be back to clean this mess up later. Don't fucking touch it."

He's about to walk out of the cabin, when he turns back and walks over to where Ella is still sitting on the floor in front of me. Josh reaches a hand out, brushing her hair out of her face. I expect Ella to flinch away from his touch after what she just saw. She doesn't even bat an eyelash.

"I'm really fucking glad you're okay, sweetheart," Josh says, kissing her forehead.

"Thank you. I'm really glad you're okay too," she tells him.

Josh steps over Bray as he walks out the door.

"It's okay, fuckers. I'm still alive down here. Don't worry about me. I'll just bleed out quietly."

"I wish you'd fucking bleed out quietly, idiot," Zac says.

"Hey, I don't see your ass on the ground with a bullet in it. Why the fuck am I always the one who has to get shot?"

Zac bends down to inspect the ass that just got shot. "Because you're reckless. You deserved that, barging in without a second thought. Also, the bullet only fucking grazed your ass. Grow a pair and harden the fuck up," Zac grunts out.

"I want to go home," Ella whispers to me.

"Let's go." I pick her up and carry her out of the building. I sit her on the front of the quad bike, just as Josh comes around from the back of the house, carrying a screaming Emily over his shoulder.

"Put me down, you asshole! I can bloody well walk, you know!" she yells at him while hitting on his back. Josh continues on without saying a word. He places her on the dirt bike, jumps on behind her and kicks the bike to start. Within seconds, they're out of sight.

"Who's the blonde?" Ella asks. "Is she going to be okay?"

"She'll be fine. Josh, not so much."

"Who is she?"

"She is Josh's undoing—Emily."

## DEAN

Two years later

I'm sitting on the deck of our beach house, watching Ella float around in the waves. I've been watching for a while now, but she's only just noticed that I'm up.

She still has a habit of getting up early and leaving the fucking bed without waking me. I swear I'm starting to get grey hairs from the stress of waking up and her not being there. Even after two years, my first thought every morning is her. When she's not in the bed, I panic. She doesn't know this of course.

A mixture of thoughts of her being taken by someone, or her hurting herself, runs through my head every fucking morning. I can't shake the feeling that something bad will happen if I take my eyes off her for too long. She is better though. We found a new psychologist in Sydney for her. She has gone sixteen months without cutting.

She tells me the need to cut isn't there anymore. I can tell there are times she thinks about it though, the way she digs her fingers into her palms. She looks around the room searching for something. The way she silently counts to ten taking deep breaths, I know she fights these demons still. I'm right here beside her, fighting them with her.

That panic in the mornings never soothes until my eyes land on her. The beach is the first place I look. Nine times out of ten, she's swimming. I don't know where she keeps finding those pathetic bikinis though. I've destroyed every pair I see on her. Yet, every damn morning, she's sporting new skimpy two-piece swimmers.

This morning is no different. I groan, my cock hardening at the sight of her walking up the beach towards me, her long, dark, wet hair falling over her shoulders. She's wearing a bright pink string bikini, her golden skin shimmering as water drips down all over her.

My eyes roam from her face down, my cock hardening more and more, the further down her body my eyes travel. I can't help the smile that comes at the sight of her little round belly. At four months pregnant, Ella has never been more beautiful.

She's a fucking goddess. One that I thank God for every damn day. Her tits bounce in the tiny bits of fabric as she picks up her pace, climbing up the steps to the deck.

"Morning, you're up early," she says as she bends and twists her hair around, wringing water from the locks.

"You weren't in bed." I shrug in response.

"I felt like a swim. I didn't want to disturb you," Ella says as she comes over and straddles me. Her arms go around my neck, her wet body pressing up against me.

My hands grope at her ass, her full, soft cheeks fill my palms. "Mmm, I like it when you disturb me," I mumble into her neck as I lick the salty water from her skin.

Ella grinds her pussy into my cock. Ever since getting pregnant, she's horny twenty-four seven. I'm not about to ever say no to her. "I can disturb you now."

"Oh yeah? How you gonna do that?" I ask her. Leaning her

body back, I move the fabric of her bikini top away, take one of her nipples into my mouth and bite down on it.

"Argh, Dean, I need you to get your damn cock out and put it in me now!" She groans as I move on to the other nipple. Her impatient hands dig into my boxers, pulling out my cock. Her hand fists around me, stroking up and down.

Pulling on the little strings on the side of her hips, I watch as the material falls away, revealing that pretty fucking pussy I can't get enough of. Ella lifts her hips and sinks herself down on my cock in one go.

"Fuck, I love how your pussy wraps around me, Princess. So. Fucking. Wet. So. Fucking. Tight." I grunt out between thrusts.

Before long, we're both heading over the edge.

"Dean, I'm going to..." She doesn't finish her sentence, her words turning into sounds of pure pleasure, as her orgasm hits her. Her juices soaking my cock while her pussy convulses around me sends me over the edge with her.

I hold her close as we both catch our breath. "I know that you're not a spring chicken anymore, but do you think we can do that again? Or do you need a few hours?" Ella giggles at her own joke.

"Babe, really? I'm about to show you just how young I still fucking am." Carrying her into the bedroom, I lay her out on the bed. "I fucking love you, Ella McKinley. Always have. Always will."

"I love you too, Dean, even if you are getting grey hairs." Her giggles continue to fill the room.

# Epilogue

## ELLA

**S**ix months later

"I fucking hate you!" I scream as I throw the plastic cup, completely missing him.

"Princess, I think you need to calm down," Dean says.

"Calm down? You can't be serious? Calm down? You try having something the size of a watermelon come out of your vagina and see how calm you fucking are!" I continue screaming.

"I should have shot you when I had the chance," Zac mumbles, glaring at Dean.

"Hey, El, want me to hit him good for you? Give him a little pain for you?" Bray asks.

I glare at both of my idiot brothers. "Neither of you are touching him! I'm sorry, Dean. I love you, I really do." I'm now crying, tears streaming down my face.

Dean brushes the sweaty hair off my forehead. "Princess, I love you. If I could do this for you, I would."

I brace myself through another agonising contraction. "Oh really? Well, you should! This is all your fault, Dean. You did this to me!" I'm back to the yelling. The smirk that crosses Dean's face at my words does not help my anger.

"Hey, Zac?" I turn my head to look at my brother. Zac stops pacing up and down the small room.

"Yeah, El?"

"I know I said I didn't want you to... but how do you feel about killing your best friend? Because if you don't, I just might." My whole stomach stiffens, and I scream as another contraction tears through me.

"For you, El, I'd kill just about anyone. How bout you let me know tomorrow? If you still want him gone in the morning, it's a done deal." He smiles at me.

"Thanks, mate. What happened to our twenty years of fucking friendship?" Dean questions him.

Zac shrugs. "You slept with my sister."

It's the same response whenever Dean and Zac argue over anything. Zac always comes back to the "you slept with my sister" remark. They're still very much best friends. If you looked up the definition of a Bromance, I'd be surprised if you didn't see their pictures.

"Yeah, I did. A lot!" Dean laughs.

"Well, maybe if you didn't, we wouldn't be in this predicament right now," Bray grunts out.

"Okay, Mrs. McKinley, let's check how things are doing." The doctor walks into the room. Looking up from the chart, she stares at the three men in the room. Asking me, she says, "Which one of these gentlemen do you want to keep around? Because the other two have to go."

Bray and Zac both start to argue, to which, the doctor holds her hand up stopping them.

I make a point of looking between the three, like I am actually going to choose someone other than Dean.

"Princess, I swear to God, don't even think about it," Dean threatens.

I laugh a little. "Those two are my overbearing brothers. They can wait outside."

"Okay, you heard the woman — *out*." The doctor shoos them out the door and shuts it behind them.

"Okay, let's see how far along you're dilated, shall we?"

As she sits on a stool at the end of the bed, positioning my legs up and spread wide, Dean grunts beside me. He has hated every single physical exam the doctor has performed during this pregnancy.

"It hurts so much, Dean. Make it stop," I beg him, even though I know he can't do a damn thing. It's been hours. I've been in labor for what feels like an eternity.

"Ella, one more push, a really big one. Come on, you can do this," the doctor says from between my legs.

I shake my head no. I can't do this. I just want to go to sleep. I just want it to be over.

"Princess, let's just try one more. Okay, you're doing great. Come on, babe, you're Ella fucking McKinley! You can do anything," Dean whispers into the side of my head.

"Okay." I brace myself.

"Ready? One, two, three and push. That's it. Keep going. We're nearly there," the doctor calls out like a damn cheerleader.

I keep pushing, screaming unsavory things as I grit my

teeth. Then I feel it happen. The moment the baby is out, I hear the sound of a newborn's cry.

"Congratulations, you have a beautiful baby boy!" The doctor places my son on my chest. I can't explain the overwhelming feeling of love that washes over me.